Lovers & Murderers is the third of Czech author **Vladimír Páral**'s twenty-one novels to appear in English. Born in 1932, Páral (pronounced *Paah'-ral*) has been the most popular literary novelist in his home country from the mid-1960s to the present day, loved for his humor, his dark satirical vision, and the way his prose style makes for an unusually exhilarating reading experience. Although he spent almost his entire adult life in Ústí nad Labem, the small industrial city in northwestern Bohemia where *Lovers & Murderers* takes place, Páral now lives in Marianské lázně, a spa town seventy-five miles west of Prague, best known to Americans as Marienbad.

Craig Cravens is the Chair of Czech Studies at the University of Texas at Austin. This is his first book-length translation.

Other Novels by Vladimír Páral
Published by Catbird Press

The Four Sonyas
Catapult

Lovers & Murderers

a novel by
Vladimír Páral

translated from the Czech by
Craig Cravens

Catbird Press
A Garrigue Book

Translation of *Milenci a vrazi* © 1969 Vladimír Páral

First English-language edition

CATBIRD PRESS, 16 Windsor Road, North Haven, CT 06473
800-360-2391; catbird@pipeline.com; www.catbirdpress.com

Our books are distributed to the trade by Independent Publishers Group

Library of Congress Cataloging-in-Publication Data

Páral, Vladimír, 1932-
   [Milenci a vrazi. English]
   Lovers & murderers : a novel / by Vladimír Páral ; translated from
the Czech by Craig Cravens.
     p. cm.
   "A Garrigue book."
   ISBN 0-945774-52-4 (hardcover : alk. paper)
   I. Title: Lovers and murderers. II. Cravens, Craig Stephen, 1965-
. III. Title.
  PG5039.26.A7 M513 2001
  891.8'6354--dc21
               2001005981

Translator's Preface

What initially attracted me to Vladimír Páral's novel was his use of the comic to present a somber vision of the world and of human affairs. But *Lovers & Murderers* is not a comic novel in any traditional sense, nor is it in the absurdist tradition, which also used every comic device in the book to conjure into existence a world that is profoundly unfunny, sad and disturbing. Páral draws the reader in to this world through his own distinct style. He combines all language levels, from the archaic to the colloquial, into sentences that often chatter on to half a page and longer, often involving multiple subordinate clauses and parenthetical narratorial asides. At the same time, his sentences possess a certain trochaic cadence that hurtles the reader forward at a breathless pace and which seems effortlessly maintained.

Trained as a chemist, Páral displays his fascination with science and technology in his concise and meticulous descriptions of characters and events, which are so precise as to be almost overdetermined. Fortunately, this makes the translator's job fairly straightforward. Besides parsing his extremely lengthy sentences and hunting down specialized scientific terminology, the principal difficulty of translating Páral lies in trying to impart the rhythm of the original to the translation.

Another major difficulty for a translator of Paral's works lies in recognizing and consistently translating all the repetitions he makes. Certain phrases recur throughout in both narration and dialogue, and when a repetition occurs, as in poetry, it echoes its previous manifestations and thereby gains resonance. Sometimes phrases are slightly altered when they reappear, making the translator's job that much harder. Characters and events also repeat themselves with slight, but often significant, adjustments and realignments. Yet the fluent lilt of the prose keeps these deviations from drawing too much attention to themselves. Since rhythm and repetition are the forms employed by Paral to produce the book's emotional power and to keep this sprawling novel so surprisingly compact, it is of utmost important that the translator recognize and preserve them wherever possible.

For Paral, form also embodies meaning. The novel's cadence causes its characters and events to be submerged and impelled onward in a rush of words and events beyond their own control. And Páral's iterative method is a reflection of his dark view of humanity. *Lovers & Murderers* is a representation of the eternal battle between the haves and the have-nots, the besieged and the conquerors, who wage war for material goods, better living conditions, and sexual gratification, in which the poor become corrupt as soon as they displace the rich and begin to defend their positions against new sorties from below. To be sure, Páral provides his characters with individual biographies and meticulous character descriptions, but the author's method of precision within repetition creates a grotesque cyclical world based on the deep hopelessness of human relations, in which everyone feels justified in battling for what they want by seeing themselves as victims, even after they attain what they were seeking.

Thanks is owed to several people who assisted me with this translation. I would like to thank, first of all, Hana Pichová, friend and colleague, who spent many a midnight telephone conversation helping me make sense of Páral's quirkiness, colloquialisms, and cultural references. Robert Clarke helped with technical difficulties. Caryl Emerson, as always, provided intellectual stimulation, and Charles Townsend kept me in line. Finally, and most of all, I would like to thank Rob Wechsler, editor extraordinaire, whose infallible instinct and truly heroic editorial labors kept this translation on track, on time, and within the bounds of translation propriety.

Characters, Place Names, and Pronunciation

This page and the next contain the pronunciation of and information about the novel's major characters and locations. If you like to read aloud or be able to say what you read, this will help a lot.

This page can be used as a bookmark, for easier reference. Simply cut along the line, or fold the page each way a couple of times, and rip the bookmark out.

If this book is yours, don't hesitate to mutilate it, no matter what your teachers said. If it's a library's, please leave this page for others to use.

The pronunciations are approximate, as close as possible without lengthy explanation. The order of the characters is roughly that of their appearance in the novel.

TEO *Tay'-oh* (very old building manager; his son is **Iša** *Ee'-shah)*

BOREK TROJAN *Boar'-ehk Troh'-yawn* (the closest thing to a protagonist, moves all the way up the ranks at the chemical company where everyone works, **Cottex** *Kah'-tex)*

MADDA SERAFINOVÁ *Mah'-dah Sare'-ah-feen-oh-vah* (wild young woman)

ALEX SERAFIN *Al'-ex Sare'-ah-feen* (wild electrician, Madda's brother)

JULDA SERAFIN *Yoohl'-dah Sare'-ah-feen* (religious fireman, Madda and Alex's brother)

FRANK SECKÝ and **HELENA SECKÁ** *Frank Sets'-ky and Hell'-eh-nah Sets'-kah* (manager and his research lab wife)

DÁŠA ZÍBRTOVÁ *Dah'-shah Zee'-ber-toh-vah* (doctor and slave to Alex, who calls her **Europa**)

BOGAN TUŠL and **JOLANA TUŠLOVÁ** *Boh'-gan Too'-shell and Yoh'-lah-nah Toosh'-loh-vah* (couple seeking an apartment)

EVŽEN GRÁF and **ZITA GRÁFOVÁ** *Ave'-zhen Graaf and Zee'-tah Graaf'-oh-vah* (Cottex director and his wife; they have a teenage son named **Roman** *Roh'-mahn)*

The Itinerant Workers: **Olda** *Ohl'-dah,* **Dízlák** *Deez'-lahk,* **Valtr** *Vahl'-ter,* **Stěpa** *Steh'-pah,* **Limon** *Lee'-mohn*

JANA RYBAŘOVÁ *Yah'-nah Ree'-barzh-oh-vah* (newcomer to building)

DOMINIK NEUMAN *Dah'-me-neek Noy'-mahn* (young computer programmer)

BŘETISLAV TRAKL and **JITKA TRAKLOVÁ** *Brzhet'-ee-slahv Trahk'-el* and *Yeet'-kah Trahk'-loh-vah* (the Tušls of the next generation)

BROŇA BERKOVÁ *Broh'-nyah Behrk'-oh-vah* (Borek's sexretary and Jitka's roommate)

DEPUTY FRANTIŠEK STŘELÁK *Frahn'-tah-shek Strzh'-el-ahk* (effectively the director of Cottex under Borek; his last name is difficult to pronounce)

ÚSTÍ NAD LABEM *Oo'-stee nad'-lah-behm* (small industrial city in northwestern Czechoslovakia, on the Elbe River (in Czech, the Labe: the last two words mean "on the Elbe"), right near the border with the then East Germany; it is the city where the author lived most of his adult life)

Leopards break into the temple
and drink the sacrificial pitchers dry;
this is repeated over and over;
eventually it is predictable
and becomes part of the ceremony.
Franz Kafka, "Leopards in the Temple"

Six circular mirrors gleam from washbasins placed on a worn, scratched, and furrowed floor like six seas on a mini-map of Earth. The eight white posts of two beds pushed together ascend from the water, so that all eight legs are submerged in the six (four inside legs in the two inside) basins (a defense against ants). A mountain of nine mattresses, three down comforters, and six pillows rises from the bedstead up beyond the window, almost reaching the ceiling. Everything here is quite old (Teo is ancient), and it all merges – the white enamel washbasins, the white lacquer of the beds, and the white comforter covers – to form a tall white cloud in the gloom of the room.

Old Teo lies on the bed, right next to the upper plates of the enormous eight-paned window. On the inside, the glass is painted over with lime, into which Teo has scratched with his fingernails so dense a labyrinth of thousands of hair lines that when he moves his head slightly back and forth, he sees a stroboscopic image (like the image you see when driving quickly past a picket fence) of the sky and the street in front of the building, while Teo himself remains unseen, hidden behind the cloudy window.

Of the eight window panes, which take up the entire wall (at one time the display window of Teo's shop), two upper and one lower can be opened, as well as, of course, the entire window casement, so that Teo is able to reveal sky and street partially or entirely, as he likes. But he almost never does. Why would he – an ancient man in bed?

Nevertheless, Teo, as befits a building manager, is well equipped for direct intervention into outside events. A metal bar two meters long juts out of the upper left window pane, and he can thrust it through the lower right pane like a lance or a barrier. A long whip of coarse leather hangs from its hard wicker handle on the windowsill (Teo once cracked it threateningly at some brawlers outside the door, but this just angered the men all the more, and they moved off into the dark and killed somebody), and on the wall hangs the oval-shaped handle of a rod used in emergencies to lower a metal roller blind over the front door (an expedient only in case of the greatest emergency and as yet unused, since there will always be greater emergencies).

Hanging from a blackened nail is a small fire extinguisher that shoots an ice-cold flurry of carbon dioxide (Teo once used it on his ward Jolana when she wanted to bring a boy upstairs with her at night, but then Jolana got herself impregnated in the afternoon, and the boy made a set of his own keys), and resting on a top shelf near the ceiling is a revolver (Teo used to fire it to protect the tender girls of the dormitory from the lecherous hoodlums from the nearby factories, but then the hoodlums smashed his window and the girls rubbed excrement on his door handle. Then, after profuse copulation, they married the hoodlums). His quiescent arsenal lies covered in a fine beige dust.

Teo lies on the supple cloudy mass of bedding, and his eternally ancient face stares vigilantly at the street and sky. The continuous tremor of Teo's face before the labyrinth of lines on the window creates the impression that Teo is nodding his head YES or shaking it NO, but Teo is simply securing himself a partial or complete image of the street and sky through the hairline scratches in the lime-painted window.

Footsteps rushing upstairs and down, the slamming of doors and windows, water and waste through the pipes, and the day has passed; one comes down with a suitcase, another goes up with a suitcase, a new face and a thousand days go by–

(Teo built this house years ago but surrendered its ownership and for years now has silently looked after its upkeep and continual repair and reconstruction, the first of which was declared to be the last)

– laughter, footsteps, shouts, weeping, even in deepest night you can hear the burbling of passion and the sobbing of sorrow, sounds quite resembling one another, for what is human is damp ... Through the walls perhaps Teo perceives this dampness itself as well as the odors and warmth (humans emit odors, but they are warm), and perhaps he perceives even more subtle information about his building, No. 2000.

CONQUERORS

(An Illustrated Novel in Installments)

> *Born of hate, I organize a hunt for love!*
> Michel de Ghelderrode

Torn from sleep by a blaring alarm clock, a searing erection, and the quick sharp pain of his yanking back the sheet dried fast to his most tender of extremities, Borek ran over to the faucet on the wall, annoyed by the ferocity of his body's longings (which he felt before he had sensed his body itself). He opened the faucet all the way, set his face, shoulders, and chest against the briskly spurting cone of water, and gulped greedily until his hunger had somewhat abated. He hopped around naked (towels are for the rich) in the low June morning sun and nearly choked on an insane, groundless joy, the sort of utter joy that invigorates the body and convulses the muscles.

The blue-gray outline of the factory, tower, concourse, and warehouse, resembling in the morning mist an aircraft carrier at anchor, a magnificent, riveting, and thrilling technical, metallic toy for men, was the work of a young engineer at 1,082 crowns a month and took up a third of Engineer Borek Trojan's time, but consumed only a fraction of his vital energy. The things one could do here –

"Of course, of course..." said Borek's boss, a kindly but listless gentleman who smelled of refined soap and was completely worn out from years of reorganizations, conceptual transformations, and an endless supply of new tacks (whose effectiveness progressed in a steady downward spiral), an enfeebled, sterile chieftain of technology standing perpetually by a window looking out upon a patch of sky beyond the cooling towers, wearily dictating elegant formulations for the conclusion of this or the planning of that, a dotard who collected matchbox labels, whose interest in technology (the ways to make things more quickly) no longer glowed even faintly (except for *Chemical Engineering News*, which Borek smuggled out of the Prague Academy of Sciences beneath his shirt, against his naked body): "Japanese rapid antioxidants? ... Well, cut it out and pin it to the wall."

After lunch (a quarter kilo of the cheapest salami and a free half liter of milk), Borek stole up a metal ladder to the third floor, through a hole in the ceiling to the water tank, and from there up the fire escape to the steel roof. He stripped down and on the soft, blazing asphalt spread out his overalls in the shape of his body and carefully lay down on them. The minute spots breaking out all over his body were causing him serious concern. Since he didn't have any lotion or even coal-tar soap (and also lacked "frequent and ample sexual relations"), Borek mixed up in the laboratory a five percent (doctors prescribe only two percent, to protect the keratin) solution of salicylic acid and conscientiously applied it to his skin three times a day. And as much sun as possible. The high June afternoon sun rained down its heat and energy in unremitting abundance.

When he was covered with sweat, he rose and crept over to the edge of the roof. Down in the courtyard in front of the entrance to the administrative building (the "White House"), two girls in white coats were watering a garden of white gladioluses with tiny watering cans. They collected water from the old black tender in front of the boiler room and (one for 1,460 crowns, the other for 1,530 crowns a month plus a five percent bonus plus an annual participation) stood over the flowers and poured.

Attempts to win over each of them (the first, Erika, ensconced in the personnel department, during the first few minutes of his employment) failed miserably in the face of horrified looks and frigid politeness, behind which Borek could sense their disparagement of him, forever excluding him from their world ... Sweet little daughters of powerful papas, brought up in the stunningly opulent mansions of exterminated Jewish and displaced German business directors, lawyers, and surgeons, with greenhouses large as Borek's family cottage, with balconies, balustrades, and music pavilions in private gardens behind high, ornate walls and heavy, decorative lattices bearing various heraldries. Inside, the heavy chandeliers of the original owners, dark, enormous paintings and sliding glass doors running the entire length of the hall (Borek had peeped in from their treetops with fascination and deadly rancor), little blue princesses nourished on scarce veal and the juice of pampered oranges, accepted to the best schools, where they read Komsomol booklets in the Soviet original while resting on pillows in company limousines, bathing in warm water flowing day and night from nickel-plated faucets, bidets, and showers of a kind rarely seen today. Kept in shape by badminton, tennis, and sailing (the smaller of their sailboats cost twice Borek's monthly salary), skiing in the Tatra Mountains in winter, swimming along Black Sea beaches in summer during those shamelessly long three-month (Borek studied engineering in the evenings, fourteen hours of work a day and fourteen days a year of vacation) vacations, exchange-student camps in France, Sweden, and England, lightly smelling of imported perfumes (which cost the entire monthly salary of an ordinary factory woman, but an ordinary factory woman, even if she won the lottery, would so douse herself with such perfume that she would stink again), well-read, cultivated, smart, fresh, delicate, desirable –

Borek looked down at the two girls, longing for their gentle caresses, longing with a painful, choking hatred that began in his genitals and climbed slowly up his spine.

"Erika ... Hey, girls! ..." he called down to them. Erika glanced up at Borek (the other one didn't even take the trouble), looked at the sky high above his head and, unperturbed, returned to her gladioluses.

"Don't bend over backwards, Mesdames!" Borek roared. The girls glanced at one another, quickly finished watering, and disappeared into the White House.

Seeing red circles on his eyelids, squinting, and holding on to the handrail, Borek descended the stairs in darkness. "Going swimming with us?" the coarse Slávka called to him from the storeroom. He looked disparagingly down at her (he was a step higher than she was) through the narrow slits of his eyelids, *my girl stands on a white pedestal like a gentle statue of the Madonna –*

"No, I'm not!"

Of course he went and of course alone. As always, she was lying on her spot right up against the chain-link fence that separated the river's public swimming area from the private manicured lawn of the Yacht Club reserved for only the few; unapproachable, she lay on a blue air-mattress as on a small rococo cloud, *I will call You, Berenike,* her long, luminous arms embraced the resilient blue rondure under her chin, and with unseeing eyes she looked up past the vulgar, rowdy crowd, *I see what You see, a white port above a blue inlet,* completely absorbed in the soft tones emitted from a small radio pressed against her cheek, *I hear the music with You, like the soft whisper of the lightly rippling sea, and I would like to sing along with it and with You, Berenike –*

A young man in imitation leopard-skin trunks (the smell of the hot oil shining on his chest wafted to Borek through the chain-link fence) raised a hairy leg, placed it on Berenike's back, and pressed down until the girl and her cushion buckled all the way to the ground. Then he took her by the shoulders and pulled her up to him, slender Berenike leaned away from the young man and pounded his hairy chest with her pale fists – Borek jumped up to the fence and grabbed the wire – the leopard man pulled the girl to him and kissed her above her slender collarbone, and as his grip tightened, her resistance grew weak, gentle, and then ceased. She lay her head on his shoulder and began to fondle his cheek. The young man threw her over his shoulder, carried her to a white motorboat, and in a cascade of foam sped off across the river. In the middle of the river, the craft fell silent and swayed and rocked upon the little waves, and the couple disappeared behind the blindingly white side of the boat, and when the waves rotated the boat, all that could be seen was the legs of the couple, from knees to toes, rising up, their intertwining calves divulging the intersection of their bodies on the craft's floor.

Struck hard, Borek slipped his fingers out of the fence, turned around, and trod as if wounded back toward the changing cabin, down the kilometer stretch of beach, stepping over bodies offered up to the brutal sun, and with disgust he stripped off his worn trunks made of coarse nylon (4 crowns from a second-hand store). He was afraid to look in the mirror, he looked in the mirror with hatred for his vulgar, thunderingly ravenous nakedness, mastered himself by force of will, and pressed the damp trunks to his skin until he calmed down, and then he ran from the cabin straight to the shower, onto the bus, and across the burning city with wet hair that soon dried and glistened no more. He tossed his trunks onto his cot and buried his face in them, tasting their saltiness, the salt *of the blue inlet beneath the white port* or of tears – and angrily he heaved himself upright on his cot.

In his ground-floor room (the "guest room" or "itinerants quarters" for the temporary housing of temporary workers, where we've been waiting two years now for something to open up upstairs) were five cots, a table, a single chair, a metal wardrobe, and a sink on the wall. From the half-empty cardboard suitcase containing all of Borek's belongings (four shirts, two of them nylon, a few socks that didn't always have a match, five books, and his most valued possession, acquired for half a month's pay from a smuggler down at the docks, a West German switchblade), he took out a grubby issue of LIFE magazine and looked at his watch. Well, let's learn some English.

On the cover a blue sea, to the left a green isle, in the center in the distance a battleship, and taking up the whole right side of the page a slender yacht with a ladder down which a nearly naked woman is descending into the water. *LUXURY AND LANGUOR OF RIVIERA YACHT-ING. Aboard some of the world's most elegant yachts.* Borek reached into the suitcase for his dictionary (purloined from the company library). *Languor*: inertia, faintness, dejectedness; apathy.

Borek sprang up, picked up yesterday's socks from where he'd tossed them on the wooden floor, stuffed one of them into the drain of the cast-iron sink on the wall (the administration no longer supplied plugs), filled it with water, and added some detergent (pilfered from the lab). Then he carefully submerged one white nylon sock into the cleansing waters.

The burning sun beat against the window. Hot air quivered above the metal windowsill and through the open window wafted swirling beige dust from passing trucks and the sweet tar-tinged fragrance of melting roofs.

In the room it was nearly 30°C. Borek undressed and lay down on his gray blanket to read *LIFE*. A two-page spread of blue sea and sky, a blonde in a bikini diving from the deck: *Yachting in the grand style – really the way to live.* A full-page color photograph of the deck: in the foreground a close-up of a gold bottle of *BLANC DE BLANC* in a silver ice bucket, mountains of fantastic food in crystal bowls, and a young man in white shorts with three beautiful tanned girls in tiny bikinis: *Eva Lau, French pianist Michel Valcourt and Ingeborg Boehm, and another German girl stand by a table set with lunch and the composer's favorite white wine, Blanc de Blanc.*

RAINIER AND GRACE HAVE A 54-FOOTER. Like many yachts-men, Prince Rainier of Monaco has owned a succession of vastly different motor-powered boats. A ten-ton trailer passing beneath his window rattled the glass. *FLEET OWNER ENJOYS THE ELEGANCE OF HIS FLOAT-ING VILLA:* a white suite, blue bathroom, red dining room with two wait-ers in white smoking jackets, a library paneled in natural wood, and a green-carpeted bar, a white swivel chair and two more waiters in white smoking jackets. *"I don't consider my yacht an extravagance,"* insists Sam Spiegel, producer of The African Queen.

Seen from behind, a half-naked man with the arms of a half-naked woman on his shoulder and his hands on the white wheel protruding from the boat's operating panel, its white prow, and a strip of blue sea. *Niarchos, who is 56, and his wife Eugenie maintain homes in Bermuda, St. Moritz, Paris, London and Cap d'Antibes. But they feel most at home aboard the* Creole, *sailing through the Greek islands, or on his private island, Spetsopoula,* a two-page spread of Monte Carlo at night, with thousands of lights glowing from white palaces, the surface of the black sea glowing red, turn the page, RED CHINA'S PREMIER CHOU IN AFRICA, and Borek carefully examined three portraits of a severe-looking gentleman with black, bushy eyebrows.

In the room it was well above 30°C. The blanket underneath Borek was already drenched with sweat, and a soft silver sound, like the patter of rain from a distance, was mixing with the rumbling of the trucks beneath the window ... On the second floor His Lordship was showering. Borek whipped out his white shirt (that is, one of two white shirts he owned), ripped the sock from the drain (which he now considered to be washed, even though it was in tatters), opened the faucet all the way, and leaned his body into the cone of water – but this is a far cry from a shower – more water splashed onto the floor than onto his body, and what if he wanted to wash his back? Borek angrily turned off the water and glared with hatred at the ceiling, where the weak silvery purling had once again grown louder. Of course the water pressure in this building is low – and in revenge Borek turned on the water again, full blast, until it began to shudder, if I can't take a shower, then neither will the second-floor nobility, let all the water run into the sewers! If only they would die from lack of water – and soon – there would be an empty room upstairs. They have to die soon: *languor* is inertia, faintness, dejectedness; apathy.

Borek took his pants out from beneath the straw mattress, which had pressed them so flat they could almost stand by themselves, and he put them on. Water sloshed behind him: the drain was too narrow to accommodate such a deluge, and the water was surging over the edge of the sink and heading straight for Borek's cardboard suitcase. And into the silence that followed the turning off of the water – between Borek's furious broom-blows against the hateful ceiling, at least let them be frightened up there – came the taunting of the victorious silver timbrel.

Her bus passes through around 21:20, and at 21:04 Borek was already crossing over to the bus station, repeatedly glancing at his watch. The gray bus arrived just short of nine-thirty. Borek ran over to the bus, got on, and made his way to the back, there she was in her usual seat and as always she didn't even look up at Borek when he stood there right next to her. Three stops through the darkness of Factory Street, then the light of the main avenue, and then the square, the girl shifted slightly in her seat, and Borek wiped the palm of his damp, trembling hand along the seam of his trousers. The bus slowed, the girl rose and, in the crush of bodies, passed Borek, who stroked her breast; it lasted but a moment, they never looked at each other, the girl stepped off the bus and Borek stayed on until the stop near the bridge over the Elbe.

Above the black river along the railing of the bridge, sixteen shadows were waiting for women who would never arrive. In the windows of the new apartment buildings on Potter's Street, high above, as if from a fortified wall, the little reddish lights of bedroom lamps flickered contentedly. The train station glowed in the darkness like an inviting port.

The Prague train brought carloads of women who were quickly spirited away by their husbands – handshakes, flowers, kisses and laughter, car doors slamming, running to the trams, and then once again emptiness.

The fluttering hum of fluorescent lights wafted down from the ceiling of the train station like falling snow. In the waiting room a girl rested her cheek upon a tabletop. Borek looked her over through the window, went into the waiting room, and sat down across from her. She looked him straight in the eye. Borek smiled, abashed. The girl didn't budge, she stared at him for a long while, then raised her head and placed her other cheek on the table. Sticking up from the back of her head were two delicate little plaits held together by two red clasps.

The trams had almost all stopped running when Borek stepped out into the night on his endless journey home. Chilly stars glared down at him from the black sky, stars that had already borne witness to so many midnight marches, those of Alexander and Caesar, and to so many midnight retreats … And an endless succession of new sorties.

He unlocked the door to his building and walked down the hallway through the back courtyard to the fence. He felt around for the loose board, squeezed through the hole into the neighbor's miserable garden, and searched for eggs beneath the rabbit hutch. They've got a television, so what do they need so many eggs for? On the way back, he harvested a handful of currants and stuffed them right in his mouth.

Back home he cracked the eggs on the edge of the table, sucked them dry, and washed them down with tap water. He took off his trousers and spread them out carefully beneath the straw mattress. He hung his coat on the back of the chair, lovingly fluffed up the shoulders, and patted the lapels. He put his shirt on a hanger and hung it from the window latch. His underwear had already come off with his pants, the elastic had worn out long ago and it was now fastened with a safety pin, he kicked it, along with his socks, into the pile on the floor. He rubbed his body with the burning salicylic acid solution and, naked (pajamas are for fuddy-duddies), buried himself under the coarse gray blanket. He felt around in his suitcase under the bed for his switchblade, stuffed it under his pillow, and gripped it tightly.

Of course it was easy with Madda, but Madda Serafinová isn't … she isn't clean.

"Really, you could?" Borek rejoiced. "Today? Well, that's great, that's fantastic. At five? Of course that's fine with me, it's incredibly fine with me. Where should we meet? Somewhere in town? Just say where and I'll come for you…"

"It's awfully hot in town. I don't want to go there."

"Okay, how about the swimming area…"

"It disgusts me to have a million idiots gawking at me there."

"I know this little pond in the woods. If we took the four-thirty bus–"

"The bus! No way."

"Well, I'd try calling a taxi if … What am I saying, that's piddling, I have loads of cash now…"

"Don't be stupid. I'll come for you. At five."

"Here? ... to the itinerants quarters? ... No way. At first I thought ... Of course, I'd like to, it'll be wonderful, fantastic, fabulous..."

Borek dashed home after work and arrived at two-thirty, remade all five cots, scrubbed the floor, swept the cobwebs from the corners, washed the windows with newsprint, wiped up the stain drying on the floor, ran to the store, covered the table with crepe paper bearing a green apple motif, and on top a kilo of oranges and a chocolate cake, a bottle of white wine called Prague Medley, two wine glasses borrowed from the Corner Pub for a deposit of 20 crowns – and an enormous box of chocolates from the confectioner Royal Bonbonniere for 140 crowns. So you'll like it at my place –

Madda leaned back comfortably on the bed, resting on her elbows, and Borek lit her cigarette. She isn't clean. But she is very young. And beautiful. How do I start?

"It's incredibly broiling in here," Madda said as she flicked her ashes onto the floor.

"Yes, it really is hot ... extremely ... If you want, I could cover the window with a blanket to keep out the sun..."

"Yeah, and then we'd suffocate," said Madda, and she lifted her arms above her head, took off her dress, and lay down once again. "What is it exactly that you do? You're never around."

"Me? I'm always doing something ... you know, always something new ... Right now I'm studying English..."

"Really? Good for you. Hey, what's *dlaendz* mean?"

"Dlaendz? ... That sounds weird..."

It's from an English song. *Dlaendz ev yuuu*," sang Madda. "I know that *ev yuu* is like *your*, but what's *dlaendz?*"

"It's not *hands* or *hearts* or ..."

"I'm telling you, it's *d-l-a-e-n-d-zzz*. Don't you have an English dictionary?"

"I do, but you have to know how to spell it. In English–"

"I know, everything's written differently. I ain't *that* stupid!"

"Sorry, I just ... You're right ... It's even starting to bother the English themselves, and so now they want to simplify and reform the language..."

"*Dlaendz ev yuu, dzi hoorios deyzvizant yuu*..." Madda sang as she ate Royal chocolates by the handful and washed them down with lukewarm wine. "Hey," she said after exhausting her rather long repertoire (some songs she sang two and even three times, all of it completely incomprehensible, except for the all too numerous *dz* and *yuu*), "have you ever had a girl?"

"Me? ... What makes you ask that ... and why right now..."

"So, you haven't. That's too funny. But cute, too. No, really, it's cool. How old are you?"

"Twenty-five ... A quarter century."

"That's nice. Really."

"But I'm not a virgin. In high school in Brno..."

"Forget about it. So how do you study Engish, with a dictionary or what?"

"With books, newspapers, magazines..."

"Do you have any magazines here? Let's see!" Madda leafed through LIFE, Madda in her black chemise, beautiful, like those women on the yachts, and her fingers went from the chocolates to the lines of text, "yachting in grand style ... really the way to live ... not bad, huh? ... Rainier and Grace, that's Grace Kelly, Princess of Monaco, but what's a *floating villa?*"

"A house that floats on water..."

"I wouldn't mind having one of those..."

Borek tenderly placed his hand on her shoulder, and Madda suffered his touch. In fact, she seemed offended when he removed it, but he'd just done it in order to pour the rest of the wine –

"Too–too–too–too–too–" someone honked outside the window. "Five times!" Madda counted, she quickly pulled her dress back over her head and already she was leaning out the window. "I'm coming–" she yelled into the street. In his blue convertible, Engineer Secký was parked conspicuously inconspicuously, the swine –

"I'm not letting you go with him," said Borek, blocking the door with his body, and behind his back he was decisively gripping the handle and the hinge.

"Don't be silly. I can't explain right now ... but I have to go see him, okay?"

"I won't let you."

"But I want to!"

"No!"

"You know, you're really cool and ... We're both incredibly different, Borek, but at the same time kind of similar ... Please, let me go."

"No."

Madda angrily stomped her foot, stomped across the room to Borek, grabbed the doorhandle, and squeezed it till his knuckles whitened – then suddenly she jumped to the side and, pushing off with her hand, somersaulted across the bed, jumped up on the windowsill, kicked her shoes off into the street, and jumped down after them. Laughter, the roar of the car, and silence.

Borek pounded his fists against the metal tubing of the bed, why was I so considerate to a whore, and nobody would have guarded the door or the window, I shouldn't have held the door – I SHOULD HAVE HELD HER!

Please show your mercy at last and descend to me, *I want to gaze up at You standing upon a pedestal*, but YOU don't want me to, NONE OF YOU want me to, you all yearn to be hunted and ravished, a defenseless man banished to the despair of his lonely burrow, the nights are the worst, the burning blanket burns my blazing nakedness, even the iron tubing of the cot is already burning hot, and the damp pillow sticking to my belly is achingly not a woman – Borek felt the rivulets of sweat flowing down his back, sides, and thighs, and he feverishly breathed in his own warm body odor, in the black sky a jungle of stars above the jungle of the earth – on which love is prey to be conquered.

In the afternoon the sky was so blue it turned the river blue as the sea. A blindingly white steamship, the *Elbeschloss*, stood at anchor beside the dock.

The girl smiled, and then again. Dressed in white, with white shoes and ribbons above her ankles, *I would like to kiss Your ankles*, she finally walked from the deck along the gangway and hesitantly stepped off onto the towpath. They faced each other and smiled.

"What's your name? ... I'm Borek. Borek Trojan. And you?"

"Ich? Inge. Ingeborg Boehm." *and Ingeborg Boehm, another German girl ... Blanc de Blanc*

The siren sounded again, and the German tourists hastened back to the boat.

"Where are you sailing, to Prague or back to Germany already? ... And where do you live ... Do you understand?"

The girl didn't understand and emitted a succession of incomprehensible words. Then they simply stood close to one another. The siren sounded once again.

Almost involuntarily, the girl placed her hand on Borek's shoulder. He turned her palm up and brought it to his lips. The girl snatched her hand away and to the sound of the siren ran to the gangway, passed through passport control, and with upraised arms stood behind the railing.

The boat headed upstream and gently turned its prow, *I would go with You to Sweden and beyond, to the clear white ports of the North*, the boat's engines slowed, *sitting with You on the deck, laughing, drinking orange juice through a straw*, the current slowly turned the boat's prow from south to north, *in a white wicker chair beneath Your window until You awaken*, the engines opened wide and the boat moved slowly toward the horizon. Ingeborg, on the top deck with her arms upraised, receded into the distance ...

My girl on a white pedestal – only she went away. SHE'S GONE.

And so it's me up on the pedestal, *languor* is only for blue cretins with yachts, from whom we take water so they'll die sooner rather than later, take the plinth by storm –

Like a wild dog he wanders the town well into the evening and then the night, along the asphalt a herd of antelope, there's one – she's gone already, there's another – she was waiting for that idiot, this one – is entering her building, what about these two – they're waiting for the streetcar, that one – too old, that one – they're all escaping the poised hunter, some tactics, tricks, and subterfuge are necessary … where does the beast pass the night?

The soft whisper of fluorescent lights wafted down into the deserted train station like falling snow, empty stairwells and drowsy waiting rooms. A pair of silhouettes huddled on a platform bench, and near the metal railing … on the gray concrete a woman's shadow.

After her: she's taking the last train (dancing shoes, a small purse), so she's coming from somewhere, no, she's going somewhere (alone), it didn't work out for you, me neither (legs like on the cover of LIFE), twenty at the most – twenty-two years old. She walks to the end of the platform toward a group of dark, empty cars, turns (face like the Virgin Mary).

After her, along the shining rails toward the amusement park of signal lights, her face illumined in red, green, and white, her ankles, *I want to kiss Your ankles,* again to the end of the platform toward the silent, sleeping cars, *I would go with You to Alaska and further,* the red masquerade of lights washed away in the green, *to the white beaches of the Pacific, where naked girls laugh and play with a beach ball,* back off along the concrete, *to sit with You on the terrace, laughing and drinking orange juice through a straw,* already the last night train is rumbling through the grade crossing *in a white wicker chair with a mandolin on the grass beneath Your window, till You awaken,* and Borek caught up with the girl and stood in her path.

"You don't happen to know…" Borek got out weakly, "when exactly our train leaves, do you…"

She took a step back, walked around him, and hurried to the end of the platform. After her, to the group of empty cars – if she were to take another ten steps (Borek pulled a handkerchief from his pocket and clutched it in his damp palm like a weapon), run ahead of her, open the door to the first car, with one hand stuff the handkerchief into her mouth, with the other hand lift her up, throw her in, and close the door, secure it with the latch, and right there on the floor the prey of the conqueror –

The girl ran toward the approaching train, rushed up the steps, and slammed the door behind her. I didn't want to hurt You, but … The doors slammed, and the night train trundled off.

At night it's deserted enough for murder or for love. The more I think about these two acts, the less difference I see between them.

After his noon (large predators sleep at noon) sunbath on the steel roof, Borek prowled around, squinting and seeing red circles on his eyelids, in three hours the great hunt begins, the site for consuming the prey has already been chosen: behind the restaurant Větruše.

"Going swimming with us?" the coarse Slávka called to him from the storeroom. He looked down disparagingly at her (he was a step higher than she was) through the narrow slits of his eyelids, *my girl* – through the slits of his eyelids he could see everything and divulge nothing, this antelope is a fine piece, in the dark you won't see the tough meat or the scabs.

"Okay, let's go together. And then dancing at Větruše. Dress like you're going to a wedding!"

"You're really going? Great!" the antelope exulted. They all long for their own vanquishment.

As the lights from the restaurant's terrace dwindled among the tree trunks, Slávka went less willingly. Borek bit down on his lip to control his breathing, his eyebrows were drenched with sweat (he had the switchblade in his pocket along with the handkerchief to be used as a gag), and he gripped her hand with his moist palm, dragging her behind him from the light in the distance to the site he had chosen.

"We're going to see something out here?" she said, and then she suddenly stopped.

"Just a little farther ... We're almost there..."

Just to the little bridge and then to the path on the other side, up the slope, then just another twenty steps. There's this pit there.

On the other side of the bridge, the girl stopped and jerked her hand away. "I'm not going any farther."

"Don't be silly, it's just..." (His anticipation made his voice falter.)

"No."

"But we just have to get past these trees and then we'll be there already."

"If you could only see how you look..." In her voice the first sound of fear.

"I can't see myself ... Unless you were to lend me your little mirror."

The girl took a step back and handed him the mirror she was already holding in her hand. Borek grabbed her roughly by the wrist and pulled her toward him with a strength that surprised them both, but at least the girl's resistance suddenly abated. Paralyzed, she stepped over the mirror lying on the dark lawn, and like a calf she let herself be led up the final twenty steps. Borek glanced into the pit: thick bushes like in the jungle. He listened to the night air: the band had begun to play again on the distant terrace. Here she could scream her head off – nevertheless, Borek was ready to gag her with the handkerchief.

"You can't see anything here … " she said in a toneless voice, and when Borek embraced her, the girl cold-bloodedly and effectively thrust her hard, square knee into his inguinal region, successfully crippling him. Then with a long loping stride she ran back to the bridge and disappeared down the roadway tiger-striped with the shadows of the tree trunks.

The cooling spittle on the tufts of grass, which in pain Borek had ripped from the ground with his teeth, soothed Borek's hot, throbbing cheeks. Slowly he got to his feet. Out of the dark heavens, the disk of the moon gazed lovingly down at him, *that lazy, fattened, celestial cow   Which we have in an electronic halter and we start milking her without looking   Meanwhile we pull at Venus to try to break her in before the Moon runs out of milk and begins to give blood instead   And we'll start driving her into the herd of the North Star and the big-breasted Cassiopeia   One cow after another   And the Big Dipper will gather together the sextillion buckets of analytically pure iron and nickel   That stud Mars … we'll leave him to his elliptical orbit, he'll be good for semen and school outings   And we'll waylay the Sun and fuck it, and through a magnetic pipe we'll convey the burning phlegm of its plasma to Antarctica   And we'll thrust it into the Milky Way until its guts scream and bulge with passion into the transgalactic, nickel-plated autobahn –*

Fox-trotting his way back, Borek tripped on a root and fell onto the cool grass. Pushing off with his arms and legs, he rolled down the hill laughing, and when he stood up by the bridge, he felt a powerful thirst and a powerful hunger. He was once again fit as a fiddle, and after feeling about, he ascertained that he was fit as a fiddle down there, as well. He went down below the bridge, drank handfuls of water, and washed his face. Then he tore off a few young shoots, stuck them in his mouth, bit the leaves off, threw the stems away, chewed the leaves, then spat them out. He was filled with an intense regret that he hadn't knocked her down before she did him. He lifted his fists to his chest and set off running down to the city with a long loping stride along the silvery-black, tiger-striped asphalt.

The city shone like a birthday cake, waiting in the valley, rumpled and pressed against the arm of the dark river embracing it. With Indian steps – one hundred running, one hundred walking – Borek proceeded toward the city along asphalt, concrete, and paving stone.

WHO'S WHO
Madda Serafinová (19)

A barefoot, dark-haired little girl in a frock, without panties, sitting on the edge of the street, where the wind has created smooth, even drifts of beige dust, uses her hands to shovel the dust over her legs, leans back against the curb, and shovels more of it further up her little body, all the way up to her chin. Like children in Ostend, Biarritz, Yalta, Cannes, and Miami (on the beach in the sand beneath their parents' loving gaze).

"… But you shouldn't say we don't need a mama and papa…" her beautiful golden-haired teacher whispered in alarm (the white edge of her chemise peeped out from under the blue covert-cloth of her skirt). The entire class had roared with laughter when the teacher ripped her skirt and chemise as she tried to rise from the glue spread on her chair. The entire class had told on Madda, they raised their hands, their eyes still damp with laughter.

Madda had no parents. When the children had gone home to supper and darkness had obliterated the streets lined with endless fences, warehouses with boarded-up windows, and thickets of weeds behind rusted wire fences, the streetlights began to flicker like the neon signs spinning on the silver electric marquees of large cities all over the world in movie magazines. It was never so beautiful in the sunshine.

She was the only one in the class who didn't get the name of the Czech president right. In the blank after the question, "What is the most beautiful city in the world?" she wrote, "Luxemburck" (of 34 pupils, 19 answered "Prague," 11 "Moscow," and three didn't know).

Madda had gone to three different schools – all primary schools – and she'd left them all uncompleted. By the age of fourteen she was working six hours a day packaging an anti-inflammatory poultice (it was completely harmless, and some of her co-workers rubbed it on their bellies to protect against fallopian tube inflammation). As the youngest employee, she made a little less than 400 crowns a month. It was beautiful in poultices, all the women wore white coats and took their coffee breaks together beneath the magnificent old chestnut tree (which was later chopped down to accommodate an employee parking lot. Of 512 employees, 4 owned Spartak autos trimmed with gray paint rather than chrome, which was in short supply).

A product development technician, Filip Očko, Doctor of Pharmacology, suggested Madda use his laboratory for sunbathing. She liked going there, even though she preferred her skin to be as white as possible (she was, however, brown year round). They both would don leather eye protection with smoked glass, Madda would strip to the waist, and the pharmacologist would turn on his UV lamp.

Then she was transferred (a certain dapper engineer and a kindhearted researcher explained to her the necessity of signing a statement to the effect that she was leaving of her own volition, which cost her a week's vacation) to the bottling department, where she examined bottles illuminated from behind as they approached on a conveyor belt. There were no collective coffee breaks here. For one thing, export orders followed hard on the heels of priority orders, and people were always rushing off to celebrate some anniversary or other. For another thing, everyone was paid by piecework and therefore wanted to make some money. One day, for reasons unbeknownst to Madda, she was transferred to the slaughterhouse. The stench and blood didn't bother her a bit, and for the first time in her life she actually got enough to eat. She watched with curiosity as they unloaded, killed, and butchered the cattle.

During her defloration at the hands of a young, handsome, married butcher, Madda felt only pain and fear of pregnancy. Immediately after the act, because her sudden paleness had frightened him, the butcher gave her a permission slip to go to the dentist, but she had to promise she wouldn't go to the doctor or she'd face some unpleasantness (it had happened in the morning during business hours), and besides, she'd heal up in a week. Madda took a tram into town, it was raining and she walked for a long time through the streets, stopping at display windows and going into shops, there were so few people around it was wonderful, such luxurious freedom – it was the first time in her life she'd been in town during business hours, and she loved it. At the Grand Café she took a seat near the jukebox, she was the only one there, the rain ran softly down the picture windows and Madda played record after record, ordered a pack of expensive Memphis cigarettes, and smoked two of them. It had been a beautiful half-day, and she did not return to the slaughterhouse until the end of the shift. She went with the butcher a few more times, but he wouldn't give her any more permission slips because the first time she'd stayed in town too long.

To make wine-flavored sausage they brought in a tub of red wine that was to be salted so the employees wouldn't drink it up, but they came to an agreement with the foreman that they could drink some of the wine and salt what was left over. Like everywhere else, stealing was rampant, and when they'd locked up plenty of butchers (hers got nine years for some salami), they sent Madda to the Střekov soap factory across the river.

There she packed up sanitary ceramics, taped up beer cartons, scrubbed potatoes in the factory kitchen ... all in all, it's pretty much the same whatever you do. When she met one of her former co-workers from poultices, she reminisced with her about the coffee breaks under the old chestnut tree. But only briefly, otherwise they had nothing to say to each other.

She learned of the Kennedy assassination when the "Jacqueline" hairstyle came into fashion, but this made no impression on Madda, such things are for people who don't have to get up at five in the morning for work. Only when all the other girls from her section had given money would Madda contribute a crown for Algeria or North Vietnam. During her ten-minute breaks she learned of the Cultural Revolution in China, and for the first and last time she spoke out publicly, proclaiming we should open fire on our own bosses as well. The next day, the company director spoke with her for the first time in her life, he wore a golden signet ring ("We toil for these scoundrels."), she rode in a private car for the first time (often in trucks, and once she'd made love in the cab of a moving five-tonner), and finally got a week-long vacation out of it all, to the spa at Karlovy Vary.

On the very first day (she'd arrived in Karlovy Vary at 16:52), she became intimate with a Berber student and for the first time experienced sexual delight. She never reached orgasm, but she did enjoy it and could do it as long as she wanted. They did it in his room for six whole days, and every evening, just before the ten o'clock curfew, she would run back to the Suvorov Hotel, where she shared a room with three older women from a collective farm in Hungary and didn't understand a word they said.

The final afternoon of the trip, after the Berber had left, was unforgettable: Madda discovered Karlovy Vary. The aristocratic Public Gardens fascinated her, she kept going back and spent the entire evening there, enchanted by the cream-colored metal ornamentation of the colonnades and the artificial pond with colored lights just beneath the surface. On the grass beside a path, nearly within reach, slept two white swans.

The second floor of the Grand Hotel: dim, smoky, hot, noisy, a hundred teenagers, one waiter in a sweat-soaked shirt (he'd put a beer in front of you without asking and then demand immediate payment), and one jukebox – Madda's love.

By three, everyone's here already: Robek, Šmudla, Jaryn, Čára, Citron, Tarzan, Torero, Runda, Sajtka, Fizule, Mikádo, Mrcina, and Panda. "Slide over–" Madda growled at Fizule, she sat down in the corner at the table closest to the jukebox and placed her white beer coaster in front of her, Yveta Simonová and Milan Chladil were singing "Somewhere to Go."

"...and legs like a popsicle stick!" said Čára, and everyone laughed except Mrcina (the legs were hers).

"Well, yours are chunky," said Mrcina.

"If my pooch had legs like that, I'd whack him one and howl myself!" said Čára (who was our jokester, but otherwise a complete moron), and everyone laughed except Mrcina.

"Well, yours are chunky," said Mrcina (last time Čára was working the late shift, Mrcina went into the park behind the chemical factory with Robek, Citron, Tarzan, and Torero all by herself).

"If my bed had legs like that, I'd be afraid to reach for the chamber pot," said Čára, and everyone laughed, including Mrcina (today, apparently, Čára would be going with Mrcina into the park behind the chemical factory).

A beer was placed on the white beer coaster in front of Madda, she counted out 1.40 crowns from her handful of coins. With her other crown, she went to the jukebox and played "Michelle." She placed her hands on the round, plexiglas cover and gently caressed it. Today I'll be with my darling for the first time.

"*I love you   I love you   I love you*"

"Stop spluttering!" bellowed Torero from behind her (once me and Sajtka took him to the park behind the chemical factory, and the guy went completely limp on us, he got incredibly sweaty trying to get it up, and it looked like a pig's tail).

"*I want you   I want you   I want you*"

Frank has beautiful white hands, like a priest   He just whispers and caresses   One more record and then I'll go   Today will be the first time we're completely alone   Frank is my bleu blues   And my first true love.

"*I need you   I need you   I need you*"

"Hey, Madda, you're really grunting it out..."

"She sounds like a stuck pig..."

The record ended. Madda returned to her seat, raised her half-liter glass, and took a long pull. They gaped at her. The girls hate me because I'm the best-looking one here, by far. The boys ... we know each other from the park behind the chemical factory. Šmudla is simply Šmudla. Tarzan's the coarsest member of the group, with a chest like an army blanket, and the lower you go the hairier he gets, like the Tibetan yak in the Děčín Zoo, and he smells like it too, during sex he's like a steam hammer and afterwards he bleats with delight like a freshly milked goat. The best was Robek, a really good-looking, fiery-blooded, dark-skinned boy, and a regular wizard on the guitar – he left me with a wet belly lying in a pile of muddy leaves.

Madda shoved aside her unfinished beer and put some chiclets in her mouth – they make your mouth smell good – and threw another crown in the jukebox, again "Michelle." "I lav yoou, I lav yoou, I laaav yoou" – she crooned as she leaned over the glistening, rotating record. "That sappy song again?" someone interjected behind her. But she was no longer listening, I'm leaving this place, "I vant yoou, I vant yoou, I vaaant yoou" – she chewed her gum assiduously, nodded to the beat, and as soon as she heard the refrain, *"I need you,"* walked out with it.

The overcrowded tram drove through the factory quarter of the city in the valley, where all the walls have the same strange, murky color and none of the tram wheels make that merry sound of metal on metal (trainloads of ash fall from the sky), and it clambered up the hill at a wobble. As the first trees, still beige with dust, began to appear and the first passengers were getting off the tram, a fresh wind blew across the plateau, a sweetish wind, and at the last stop, all the way at the top, it was suddenly really summer, you could see the green crowns of the blooming linden trees, and when Madda stepped off the tram ("Saints alive! There's even grass growing between the rails!") a brisk, fresh blast of air dealt her a stupifying blow.

Building number 26 was an enormous, pastel-blue structure with enormous windows from another century. Two more decent-size apartments could have fit into the entrance hall, and the tenants could have walked three abreast up and down the stairs without getting in each other's way.

On the tall white door of the second-floor apartment were two silver nameplates: Eng. F. Secký and Eng. H. Secká – already twice divorced but for some reason still living together ... who would budge from such a castle?

Madda reached out for the bell but suddenly jerked her hand back. My chiclets! She spit her chiclets on the floor, but the little ball of gum stood out so garishly against the blue-white tiles that she picked it up and stuck it on the inside of her heel. Then the bell sounded somewhere within, and for a long time no one came. Finally the door opened slightly, and Madda slipped through the crack.

"Wait a minute..." said Frank as he dodged Madda's kisses in the dark, "First come in..."

He led Madda into a large room and sat her on the edge of the couch. "How about a gin fizz?"

"All right!"

Frank disappeared, and Madda gazed at the large, white and pale-violet rug. She shed her shoes and carefully crossed the rug in her stocking feet. The stereo played softly. The room was too big. Against the wall stood a nearly life-size wooden statue of a naked negress decidedly larger than poor Mrcina. Go do it with Čára under a bench, you lame-ass.

"Why did you take your shoes off?" asked Frank, who was holding two glasses.

"You wear shoes inside?"

"Sometimes I wear shoes, and sometimes I'm naked head to toe."

I can't look like a silly goose. Madda slipped on her shoes and walked across the rug again, trying to dig deep furrows in the shag with her heels.

"Why don't you sit down?"

"I don't feel like it."

"Cheers."

An amazingly good drink, but this is probably not the place to slam it down. Frank slammed his down.

"Drink up, I'll make another."

"I don't drink like a farmer."

He laughed and brought in a shaker big enough for six glasses. They poured, slammed them down, and laughed at each other.

"So, why exactly do they call you Madda?"

"When I was little I couldn't pronounce my name right."

"How cute."

"But I'd rather be called Maggije."

Frank laughed like a rocking horse. "I've heard that you've got some kind of trouble with your brothers."

"It's horrible. Julda's a prophet, truly a saint, but sometimes he can really be annoying. And Alex ... Alex is simply a devil. An insane devil."

"Insanely interesting, but I mean ... does Alex sometimes ... molest you?"

"Oh yeah, he's wanted to do it with me quite a few times; boy, could I tell you some stories."

"But of course you didn't..."

"Of course not. Look, I'd just have to crook my little finger – but nothing's happened."

"Crook your little finger at me–" Frank grinned like a rocking horse.

"You're grinning like a rocking horse!"

"Now, let's not get in a huff..."

"Then don't make me mad."

"I just wanted to know..."

"Don't worry. Nothing's ever happened with Alex ... and now that I have you..."

"Come here..."

Madda walked over to Frank's chair and closed her eyes. Frank smells wonderful ... *And Frank's beautiful white hands   Slightly cold, like a priest's must be when he works his wonders in church   Frank never kisses me, he just whispers those secret and frightening words of his   And those two delicate, clever animals of his enchant* and destroy –

"Frank, dear ... I don't want it to be like this..."

"Neither do I. Go take a bath. Then put on the red bathrobe."

A red bathrobe had been thrown across the little table next to the bathtub, and Madda pressed her forehead against the cool, black tile, I love him so much, I'm afraid of myself, pull yourself together, girl, for a second at least – but lock the door first. What for?

An enormous, beautiful bathroom – my first real bathroom 'cause at home we just have a faucet on the wall, and the factory washroom is just a communal slaughterhouse steamchamber for pigs. What are all these funny-looking silver doodads for? Water shoots out up, down, and sideways, and in the tub there's a fixed shower head above and a hand-held one down here, both with hot and cold water, three enormous bars of soap in white nets, with a fourth resting on a dish, like a big grapefruit.

Madda dried herself with a small bright-colored towel, then tried a larger cream-colored one, and then an even larger one with orange stripes, just so he doesn't think I don't know how to use a real bathroom, and she yanked a towel as big as a bed sheet off of a chrome bar. Then she scattered the armful of used fabric across the floor, *a bathroom like this should come with a maid.*

It never hurts to see things the way they really are (in a gigantic, irregular mirror): Perfect shoulders. I only need a bra under my bathing suit, for decency's sake, and otherwise only in the winter to keep warm (36 in.). My tummy doesn't need to be pulled in at all for modeling – waist, a fabulous 23 in., and all I can say about my hips is 35 in. – supermeasurements for Hollywood. Legs and all the rest: the perfect cover girl. It's obvious. I know it. And now I know that you didn't drive me into the bathroom out of love, but so that I wouldn't smell. It's healthy to see things the way they really are.

"Do you think maybe I'll see you anytime soon?" Frank laughed his raspy laugh on the other side of the door, let's lock it. "Just a couple more seconds..." and I'll primp a little more to make it an even twenty minutes. Madda rummaged with relish through the crystal and gold perfume bottles under the mirror and sprinkled herself prodigally with Chanels, Revlons, Rubinsteins, and eau-de-colognes, the cyclamen-colored *Pearl Cutex 73 Orchidea* for the nails, and this mascara, or this one, no, this one, for the eyelashes. What do you have for my eyelids? Revlon again? Let's see: *Frosty*

Green, Frosty Blue, Frosty Brown, Frosty White, Frosty Lavender, Frosty Smoke – that's it? No gold? Shocking! There better be some next time! Well, for today I'll throw together some white, a little blue, a touch of lavender, and a little frosty smoke. And now some body spray, I love body sprays no matter what shoots out of them ...

Frank was already pounding on the door. "I'm coming–" Just ten more minutes, darling.

Madda put on the red bathrobe that was meant for her, but there were two more hanging on the door, a blue and a violet, both decidedly better than the red one, which was already a bit worn, so Madda tossed the red robe onto the floor and after trying on the other two, finally decided on the blue one and buttoned herself all the way up to her neck.

"I hope I didn't make you wait too long, dear..." she smiled at Frank.

"You were in there half an hour." Frank grimaced like someone scattering burning coals.

"Now, let's not get in a huff..."

He pretended to be hurt and said nothing. These aristocrats sometimes need to be smacked between the eyes.

"Frank – I have an idea."

He tried to look kind again. He dissimulated.

"Let's have sex."

He swallowed dryly and said after a moment: "Do you want to?"

"Yes."

"Say it louder!" He was almost shouting himself.

"Yes! I do!"

He jumped up, ran to the double doors, and opened them wide to display an even bigger room than this one, which itself was too big.

And what a room it was ... *Blue and white and perfect   And beautiful A wide, magnificently white bed   And flowers on a table beside it*

"Frank, dear ... I was just fooling around before, because I thought..."

"That's okay. My sweet little girl ... Madda..."

"...because I didn't want to tell you that until now I've almost always experienced love lying in a pile of muddy leaves behind a bench, or on stairs, in trucks, tents, in the bushes, or in a freight elevator, and they were always coarse and rude and mean..."

"Take your clothes off ... You're wonderful, Madda. You're ... almost perfect."

"You're splendid ... You're perfect..."

...because you whisper and you caress me and have hands like a priest, the Pope's hands couldn't be more tender   You're my bleu blues   And my first love ...

"Do you want to make love with me now?" Frank was speaking too loudly now.

"I already told you I did…"

"I want you to say it again … But don't whisper! Do you want to have sex with me?" He was almost shouting.

"Yes, I do."

"Say it louder!"

"Yes! YES!"

"Then will you do something for me?"

"Anything."

"Put this on…" His voice suddenly tensed, and he pulled a long, white lace dress out of the closet and handed it to Madda –

"But that's a wedding dress!"

"It's okay, don't worry … You promised me you'd do anything…"

"Anything in the world."

"Then put it on."

"But I won't have anything on underneath…"

"That doesn't matter. Put it on! Please … and don't get angry that I … but I…"

Madda carefully ran her hands over the dress, raised it above her head, and devoutly slipped it on.

"Frank, it's splendid…"

… and you don't have to apologize for anything, my earlier lovers wouldn't even take my clothes off, or even their own, *a white wedding dress to church*, I've made love with the dirty strap of contemptible overalls between our bodies, and with a belt and bloody buckle between our damp waists.

She adjusted her hair and sat on the corner of the bed where the flowers were, but Frank took her hand and made her stand up again.

"Not there – come here!"

He sat down at a small, round table made of white leather.

"Kneel!" he shouted in a completely different voice.

Madda knelt before the table, *I promised You anything in the world, and You shall have it   And I shall never cease to be grateful to You, Frank … My Frank* – She raised her glowing face. Frank was staring somewhere above her head, toward the double doors, staring as if –

Between the open, tall white doors stood Helena Secká wearing the violet bathrobe that had been hanging in the bathroom, and already she was coming toward them.

"Take that off!" Helena said harshly. "Now!"

Still on her knees, trembling with fear, Madda pulled the wedding dress over her head, and Helena Secká helped her roughly. "And now get out! Scram!"

Helena Secká shook as she pulled the dress from Madda's hands, put it on, and walked toward the bed where Frank was already waiting, and even though Madda's humiliation grew into an overwhelmingly murderous jealousy, Madda couldn't tear her eyes from the two of them as they gently approached one another, *both white, slender, perfect*, there's a certain family resemblance between them, something almost racial ... *Two nobly born thoroughbreds from a country estate.*

In front of the house, the linden trees smelled like marijuana, they even fuck up the trees, Madda hurried down the hill along the track set in the grass by those bastards, that's why he never wanted to kiss me and drove the little streetwalker into the bathroom, so she wouldn't soil Her Highness's filthy pajamas like some kind of pig, the scraggly robe for the whore, even the flowers by the bed weren't for you, my poor little tart, not even the bed, the most you're allowed to do is kneel, kneel to that filthy pig – my bleu blues!

Robek, I've given myself to you before, and I'll do it again, you too, Tarzan. Šmudla, Torero, Čára, Jaryn, and Citron can come with us, and the girls, Sajtka, Fizule, Mikádo, Mrcina, and Panda, too, I'll show you an apartment like you've never seen before in your life. Robek, you're the handyman, you'll pick the locks, and you guys can take whatever you want, and believe me, there's plenty to take, and the rest we'll throw into the bathtub, douse it with gasoline, seal the doors, then turn on the gas, their mere existence is an injustice to us all I WANNA SEE THAT BLUE APARTMENT BUILDING FLYING INTO THE SKY –

The second floor of the Grand Hotel: dim, smoky, hot, noisy, and everyone's sitting right where they were before.

"Robek–" Madda waved her arms excitedly, "Tarzan, Šmudla ... come here. I've got something..."

The girls looked on with undisguised anger as Madda dragged the boys away. I'll always drag them away, every last one of them.

"...and there's an incredible amount of stuff, and when we're done we can make a little bonfire..."

"What, what's that?" Jaryn, the rather deaf welder from the boiler factory, was cupping his hand to his ear.

"At the Seckýs' place..."

"Yeah, but Secký's a big cheese at the factory..."

"He'll have the cops, the prosecutors, the ...

"The bonfire thing's ridiculous..."

"Totally ridiculous," Robek concluded, and he went back to his seat.

"At least we could stick a pin in the mortar on the windowsill and stretch a black thread across the street, and make it so there's an awful racket when you yank on it; women pray and men shoot..." said Torero, and when Madda fixed him with an icy glare, he went back to his seat.

"Or cover a live sparrow in soot and mail it to him, and then when he opens it up at home..." said Šmudla, then he lowered his eyes against Madda's glare and went back to his seat.

"Let's forget about it," said Tarzan, "and go for a little walk. It's broiling in here–"

"I'd probably claw you to pieces today," hissed Madda, "so you'd better go back and sit down while you're still in one piece."

The jukebox crooned "A Thousand Miles," and everyone sat at the table just as before.

A perpetual snow-like layer of beige dust covers the streets of the city in the valley, forming a spongy layer of moss on the pavement, which you glide across rather than walk along.

In the formerly men's one-room flat, third floor on the left, Alex was lying naked on his back, snoring beneath his blanket, one black heel protruding like a hoof. Madda sank onto her cot (Julda's cot was also there, all three made of metal tubing with straw mattresses, a metal wardrobe, a table, a single chair, and a cast-iron faucet on the wall), cramped, hot, and smelly, so here we are, home again.

From down below, a gentle, silver murmur mixed with Alex's snoring, like rain from a distance ... water. Madda removed her clothes and turned the faucet on full: a few rusty drops, rattling, then nothing. (The water pressure is low in the building, and only a tiny bit reaches the third floor, and when the nobility takes a shower on the second floor–) Madda tripped over Alex's heavy boots and angrily stomped on the floor, is the water only for the assholes downstairs –

"That's it, stomp on them, the bastards, it's all their fault," Alex grumbled. He coughed up some phlegm and turned toward the wall.

Madda crawled beneath her blanket, closed her eyes, and ran her hands along her damp body, supermeasurements for Hollywood ... No, I want a *pure beautiful boy with the body of a thoroughbred and the gentle, white hands of a priest*, but he can't run his hands across my body because the excitement would *no longer be pure, I would simply hold him by his hand, and we would lead each other somewhere where there's lots of water, to one of those famous spa towns with little ponds and colored lights just beneath the surface, and swans and pavilions made of glass and blue metal, in which eternal, healthful springs shoot up into the air or we'd go to a port and sit on the terrace looking out at the sea, drink iced gin fizzes and listen to the play of water and soft music, something really cool and really slow ... and each of us would have his own enormous bed, a round one just like in that French film, made of white leather, and we would drift off to sleep holding hands* like brother and sister.

"You woke me up, asshole..." Alex said to the silver murmur rising from the floor.

"Go back to sleep, my dear brother."

"I don't want to anymore, asshole. Where were you?"

"I thought it was going to be such a wonderful blue afternoon. But it all turned to shit."

"So fuck it."

"I did already. Alex ... could you do something for me?"

"Anything in the world for my little Madda..." Alex whispered sweetly as he raised himself on his elbows.

"Do you know the Seckýs?"

"You mean that conceited bastard and that pale slut?"

"Yeah, them. It would really make me happy if you could rough them up a little bit."

"It'd be a pleasure for me as well as good for the general welfare of society." Alex grinned, kicked off his blanket, and stood up. "What's in it for me..."

WHO'S WHO
Alex Serafin (36)

In those distant times before the Second World War, the brothers Serafin were the pride of Father Gott's boys choir at the Holiest Trinity Church.

When as a seventh-grade pupil Alex became acquainted with the mysteries of his body, he threw himself into these new delights, perishing from dulcet horror. The director of the classical *gymnasium* noticed the boy sniffing his fingers in Greek class. Alex confessed tearfully in the director's office, promised to give up his sin, and received a chocolate-covered cherry. No one had ever received a piece of chocolate from the director himself. Alex would once again succumb, confess, and promise not to do it again. He soon had enough chocolate to open his own confectionery shop. In his lectures, the director would read some passages over the heads of the other, uninteresting pupils as if to Alex alone.

Young Alex soon discovered that in sin one rises above the chastity of the herd.

From the choir, Alex Serafin thrilled the golden, baroque magnificence of the cathedral with his gently veiled voice, often turning to the cathedral itself and the people below instead of to the choirmaster. And the kind-hearted choirmaster devoted himself more to the prodigal choirboy than to the choir. In triumphant pride, Alex refused to serve mass when his turn came and sometimes had the nerve to do small improvisations in the midst of the choir. At the sound of his voice, the worshipers turned away from the altar. Alex became the star of the choir and of the *gymnasium*. Not until he sang a few notes (in honor of the French teacher's wife) of a toreador song during mass did the choirmaster banish him from the choir, pointing a furious finger toward the dark hole of the spiral staircase. *Ne quid nimis.*

What to do with the rest of that Sunday? *Nulla dies sine linea.* The sun was shining outside, and the cast-out Serafin went swimming at the Knínič Dam. The French teacher's wife had a cottage on the lake shore. She was touched by the boy's bravery and bestowed upon him unusual delights, making him three times a man before the sun had fallen.

"Don't be silly, son, you'll just bring unhappiness upon yourself–" the history teacher said to Alex, who was standing near a window in the *gymnasium* hallway, as he snatched from the boy's hand the slingshot he wanted to fire at a passing car (on 15 March 1939 the German army pulled into Brno. In a black, convertible Mercedes sat a general with red silk lapels, he drove through town below hundreds of roofs and thousands of windows, tens of thousands of people lined the streets, all of them fervently longing to see him dead, and certainly many of them could have arranged it right there and then – as if protected by a strange force, behind glass, as safe as in a tank, he drove through with a ruler's indifference) – "and you'll bring unhappiness upon us all."

"Fine, we'll just be happy then, sir," said Alex, and he stuffed the slingshot into his pocket. *Suae quisque fortunae faber.*

While Himmler's dashing young fellows were having a roaring good time conquering Europe, sipping cognac in the city of Cognac, Samos wine on Samos, Moldavian wine in Moldova, eating Libyan dates in Libya and caviar in Odessa (in which they can even indulge today; they can, moreover, fire away at their countryman von Braun with rockets apparently perfected in Texas and Arizona), the twelfth-grade class of the Brno classical *gymnasium* was drinking its .125 liter portion of separated milk, quacking out "Aurea prima sata est aetas" in the choir, collecting metal for the dashing young fellows of the invincible German nation, and after graduation signing on as assistant factory workers at the electronics company Siemens & Halske. Alex had had enough of the rarified poetic life of the student. *Ne quid nimis.*

With his mind delivered from the versified ingeniousness of P. Ovidius Nosy as well as from all that woefully oft repeated (how many times already?), bankrupt, classical, humanistic hocus-pocus, Alex was discovering the omnipotent regularity of polarity, open circuit–closed circuit, the heavenly, or devilishly, simple mechanics of putting things in motion and stopping them at will. He became the perfect electrical engineer, and after a night course he acquired the right to put Eng. in front of his name and thrash his former classmates. This he did only when the desire arose, thereby earning their devotion and respect. *Quidquid agis prudenter agas et respice finem.*

In June of 1943, after High Mass at the Church of St. Thomas, Alex became engaged to the anemic daughter of the owner of Electrostar, who had fled in time to the U. S. After lunch, Jarmila Goldová refused ("Not till we're married, darling") to give herself to Alex on her father's leather sofa, and Alex – what to do with the rest of that Sunday? *Nulla dies sine linea.* Outside the sun was shining – he went swimming at a private German pool on Lake Svratka. Through the planks between the cabins (light work, swimming, and tennis had developed and firmed up the boyish attractions of the former student's body), a gloomy forty-year-old wearing golden wire-rimmed glasses was watching Alex hungrily. Alex exuberantly demonstrated some of his seventh-grade tricks and by the following Sunday had been transferred, as an electrical engineer of the inspectorate, to a special engineering section, directly subordinate to the chief construction advisor, Maj. Otto Bauch, Professor of Architecture (and homosexual masochist).

From Solund all the way to Kodan, Otto inspected a certain type of equipment, and at his side Alex traveled across vanquished Europe, lasciviously, with the loop of a black riding crop around his wrist. Before bed, the vanquisher of Europe read aloud from Eckermann and happily drifted off to sleep after his flagellation. Alex would then step into the night air on the balconies and terraces of the Astorias, Imperials, and Grand Hotels of the flagellated European elite, and listening to the constant roar from large production plants that worked with ever more refined technology and increased speed on the mutual manufacture of self-destruction, he completed his apprenticeship.

Still not sated by five years of warfare, the defeated demanded their own slaughter, invariably en masse, rather than far more amusing beatings, and the victors' delight in power began to wane in the wearisome striving for mere self-preservation. Both categories began to mingle, extinguishing the élan of war, and in February 1945 it became an outright bore. *Ne quid nimis*. Alex had had enough of the martial way of life.

At the end of March 1945, Otto Bauch passed away in unexplained circumstances, and Alex returned to Brno at the beginning of April with twenty-five thousand marks, or a quarter of a million protectorate crowns, just in time to invest it all in the slowly dying Electrostar, marry Jarmila Goldová, welcome the Red Army on the Germans' main arterial road, and drive along with them victoriously to what used to be called Freedom Square, then Hitler Square, and once again Freedom Square. *Respice finem.*

Papa Gold returned from the U. S. poor as a church mouse but with a head full of plans, and his sturdy son-in-law "came in quite handy." After restitution, they renovated the fourteen-room mansion in Pisárky, started up Electrostar again, sired juniors, and were the first in Brno to go waterskiing at the Knínič Dam. A spirit of "rapidly expanding enterprise" reigned.

With his mind delivered from the diffuse reflections of the aging von Goethe as related by the tedious Eckermann, as well as all that (how many times already?) bankrupt, tough-sounding bluster about the New Order, Alex discovered the system of credits and payments, the convoluted mechanics of putting things in motion and increasing their turnover. They can't be stopped – oh, the pure realm of electrical laws. His riding crop experience served him beautifully.

Alex, however, did not enjoy himself as before. At Gold's you worked ten hours a day and then some more after supper, money flowed from account to account without ever being seen, Papa Gold revealed himself to be a tightwad, and just between us, after Jarmila's second baby ... with relief, Alex left to put the Děčín branch on its feet.

The summer of 1947 turned out to be splendid (of course the sun nearly killed the nation's agriculture), and over the heaps of orders rolling in Alex looked out enviously upon the Děčín docks where half-naked, dark-skinned boatmen lolled blissfully in the sun on tugboats (the dried-up Elbe had ceased to allow boats through) with their delectable Gypsy girls in pink bras who couldn't have been more than fifteen, if that. In the evening the strumming of a guitar and the laughter of girls penetrated the office, and Papa Gold sent urgent and diligent telegrams well into the night. *Amici, diem perdidi.* The "rapidly expanding enterprise" revealed itself to be an enervating tedium. *Ne quid nimis.* Alex had had enough of the business way of life.

In February 1948 Papa Gold tried to abscond to the U. S. with the money, but fortunately he was shot in a snow-covered vineyard in the southern Moravian border district of Satov, and Jarmila, with her two snot-nosed kids and squishy belly, poisoned herself, thank God, and her brats when ordered to leave the Pisárky mansion. *Suae quisque fortunae faber.* Alex quietly assumed the job of waterworks electrical maintenance foreman at the factory in Záluží u Mostu named after Comrade Stalin.

With his mind delivered from the ballyhooed slogans of the overseas god of Productivity, as well as from all that (how many times already?) bankrupt and boring twaddle about freedom and democracy, Alex discovered the comfort of the simple, carefree way of life and the mechanics of accelerated careers, which can be halted overnight – oh, the pure realm of electrical laws!

Exerting a fraction of the effort required by Siemens & Halske or Electrostar, Alex garnered the Best Worker honors of his section, the factory, the company, and the region, he received special prizes, material rewards (9 oil paintings with smelting or foundry themes by a local graphic artist, 6 plastic miners with head lamps, and all 11 volumes of the collected works of that notable writer of working-class novels Marie Majerová), honorary diplomas, distinctions and medals, and dozens of section, division, factory, company, civic, local, city, district, regional, and branch orders. Alex stopped using soap or a title in front of his name, wearing a tie or a hat, and cleaning his shoes; he treated his two lazy assistants like hidalgos, and his frightened neurotic female engineers like vulgar street urchins – his riding crop experience served him beautifully.

However Alex did not enjoy himself as much as before. The endless meetings in poorly ventilated halls smelling of lousy tobacco, the thousands of barely distinguishable versions of the same poorly worded and pitifully presented speech, the monotonous delivery of standardized awards bound in red cloth at raspy podiums from the hands of unkempt secretaries devoid of make-up into the hands of men with poorly cut double-breasted suits made invariably of the same dark-blue covert-cloth of high synthetic content, the same institutional hot dogs and watery coffee at 10:00 and 16:00, at noon the same pork cutlet, tepid beer, and sugar beet-sweetened jelly doughnut, and long, sleepy nocturnal rides home in overcrowded cars with poor suspension over pothole-riddled local highways, or Czech rum straight from the bottle and drudging sex without a hint of fantasy in unheated hotel rooms without bathrooms, alternating with fellow delegates: Alex was disgusted, he'd had enough of the committee way of life.

Ne quid nimis. In the mid-1950s, factories named after Comrade Stalin were renamed, and it was decided that the town of Most be relocated to make more room for mining, and because of Alex, the first, still modest demands for electricians began to emerge.

On the highest platform of the rectifying column, high above the factory and the town, Alex would lie naked in the burning sunshine, in solitude, in meditation. For the first time in fifteen years, he opened the white package of letters from his brother, Julda (he'd been receiving them for fifteen whole years and had always angrily balled them up and tossed them aside unread). "Just come," wrote his seraphic little brother. "We belong with one other."

Alex rose, took delight in stretching his arms above the metal railing as if it were the captain's bridge of an aircraft carrier (from his angle of vision, the rumbling factory lay beneath his feet, and beneath his elbows the town destined for destruction, stretching skyward its mutilated fingers), and in a surge of vital energy he roared inarticulately – his parting words to this foolish, bloody, masochistic, dying continent.

Alex had completed his apprenticeship.

On Sunday morning he got out at the Ústí train station wearing a loose-fitting (lately he'd lost weight) double-breasted suit made of dark-blue covert-cloth of high synthetic content and a black tie he'd received at graduation, a cardboard suitcase in his hand (a gift from the Energy Ministry) containing a few shirts, several pairs of socks, an Electrostar razor, and his black riding crop.

That was a Thursday I'll not soon forget.

That morning I saw eighteen patients at the slaughterhouse, nothing special, a few with chronic bronchitis due to the Ústí air, a few with gall-bladder problems due to chronic overeating, several scratches, splinters, and chips, and a few vouchers for special exams.

On the way to Cottex I stopped for groceries, a half liter of milk and two yogurts, I'm not picky about what I eat anymore. For a year now I've always made do with a nylon net bag. Out of potatoes, I'll get some going home. The sun was beating down like in Egypt.

In the Cottex exam room, Nurse Jandová had pulled out the maintenance worker ID cards for me. We nodded sympathetically to one another: a preventive check-up of the maintenance workers, what a nuisance, there's twenty-five of them.

Here we go: "Strip to the waist – open your mouth – Cough – Turn around – Inhale – Does it hurt anywhere – Next. Strip to the waist – Open your mouth–" There are so many pyknic types here I'd almost enjoy examining an asthenic. Why did you mutilate your chest with this tattoo? ... If only your little nymph had matching breasts. Everyone here's fit as a horse, but almost all of them have afflicted bronchi, which of course we can't do anything about. "Cough – Inhale – Does it hurt anywhere–" Once I wanted to be a neurosurgeon ...

"Doctor, telephone."

"I can't right now."

"It's Monika..."

"She's calling me here again? Give it to me. Hello, this is Dáša, sorry, but right now ... What? An engineer with a sailboat ... well, if he'd lend it to me and then go away ... No. No, I just don't feel like it. What? ... I have to get potatoes ... No, it's over with him ... I don't know if it's for good, but it's definitely going to be for a while. And now if you'll excuse me."

"Next. Strip to the waist – Open your mouth–" Monika's become an absolute tramp. What can the poor thing do when she's got less than seven hundred crowns to deck herself out with ... a third of the little I have? "Cough – Turn around–" This isn't exactly what I had in mind, but since there's nothing else, it's a decent job. And worthwhile. And good. You get used to it. Peace ...

It's gotten hotter in here, as if something from outside were ... "Does it hurt anywhere – Next. To the waist – Open your mouth–" It's going smoothly, as always. But of course sometimes you want a little something else– "Cough – Turn around–" But what can you do? "Inhale – Does it hurt anywhere?" Nearly done. Still have to get potatoes. If they don't have any, I'll make fried bread again. I've got bread. "Next. To the waist – I said to the waist!"

He stood stark naked in the center of the examining room, covered everywhere with thick black hair, smiling right at me.

"What are you doing, a striptease?!" He must have seen the look I gave him, which ... which ... I've seen a few thousand male bodies in my time, but this magnificent specimen – The look I gave him revealed more of me than he had of him.

"I'm sorry, Doctor," he said softly, and he quickly got dressed. Tapered, black corduroy pants, black moccasins, a thin black turtleneck sweater that came all the way up to his chin. Suddenly it was unbearably hot in the exam room. On his card was typed, "SERAFIN, Alex, Group Leader of the TS Electronic Maintenance Department" and next to that Nurse Jandová had written, "Eng.," and crossed it out again, "single." ... An embarrassing silence.

"Serafin ... Serafin ... You don't have a brother here or..."

"Yes, a brother. Unfortunately."

"That fireman, Doctor," said Nurse Jandová.

"We've already done him ... Or haven't we?" I said, just to have something to say. The stethoscope made my neck tingle.

"He'll come traipsing along in here," said Alex Serafin (in a surprisingly pleasant voice). "He always turns up whenever I turn up."

I took the stethoscope and pretended to blow on it. I had to do *something* with my hands. A year ago I stopped smoking, and sometimes you– I suddenly got an incredible craving for a cigarette.

Alex Serafin took out of his pocket a red pack of Pall Malls and a silver lighter. "May I offer you a cigarette?" he whispered. And smiled. How could he have known I wanted a cigarette? You've probably been opening that empty mouth of yours, dear.

"Smoking's not allowed here, Comrade ... Serafin. This is an examining room!" He retreated, smiling an apology. I didn't have to snap at him ... it's embarrassing. I went back to his card. "You're an engineer?" He almost looked like an intellectual. Not with his splendid musculature, though.

"That as well. But after a while it started to bore me."

I realized I was giggling like an idiot. The back of my jacket must have been completely soaked.

"I'll wait outside," he whispered as he slipped out of the examining room.

What happened? I didn't tell him ... but I– "Give me a cigarette, Nurse Jandová!" "But Doctor, it's been a year–" "I feel like one. My head hurts..." "I noticed." "You noticed what?!" "Well, just that you completely forgot to examine Mr. Serafin..."

That's never happened to me before. "To hell with it, give me a cigarette, you witch! And send the next patient in!!"

"In the waiting room there's only..."

"Who, damn it?! If only you could ... Do I have to show them in myself?"

"But Doctor..."

The devil was sitting in the waiting room.

"I'll wait," he chuckled sweetly, and I couldn't think of anything else to do but slam the door.

The guy was flirting with me brazenly ... And I was behaving just like a country bumpkin!

My knees were shaking. If I tremble when he's here in the consulting room ... I've given those things up. I've had enough. No more. I'll soon be thirty. It's better this way. I'm perfectly fine. You get used to it. Peace ...

"Jandová, have a look in the waiting room and see if he's still hanging around."

"Should I call him?"

"No! Are we finished otherwise? I won't leave until he's disappeared. I don't need anyone to..."

"He's gone."

I extinguished Nurse Jandová's repulsive Cuban cigarette. Last time I was smoking Pall Malls, that time at Monika's when ...

"See you!"

"Bye, Doctor. Tomorrow the review commission's coming and ...

"I know. At six a.m."

The waiting room's completely empty. Those stupid posters from Health Services ... have to order new ones. They'll be even stupider. He was sitting in this chair, so he must have been able to see directly in ... Surely he's got flocks of women. So, I still have to get some potatoes.

He was standing right outside the waiting room door. "May I give you a lift home?"

"But I ... right now I'm going to buy potatoes and..."

"Great." He snatched my net bag out of my hand and yelled through the window at the dispatcher: "Frantík, I'm going into town to get some spuds!"

"Want me to have them delivered?" Frantík yawned. (To me, of course, he was forever Comrade Doležal. When I was moving, after our divorce, he explained to me for half an hour why he couldn't set up the delivery. It was a twenty-minute drive to my new place.)

"I'll take the car."

The gentleman in black was walking out through the courtyard carrying my net bag. Outside it was hot as the Palestinian wilderness, and I no longer cared. Two minutes later he drove up in a large black limousine. Well, thanks to the omnipotent Electronic Maintenance Department Group Leader, a little doctoress is getting a lift.

He's obviously used to seducing women with the director's car. But this time it won't be quite so easy, señor, I've already ridden around a bit with men as well as sat through Monika's school of hard knocks. But really, it is extremely nice in here. I'm curious to see how he'll begin. I'll manage the cutting remark and conclusion myself. From here it's only a shout to my place.

He braked in front of the first vegetable shop we passed, the one I stopped at on the way from the slaughterhouse, I know they don't have any potatoes.

"Really?" He laughed and ran into the shop, and soon returned with both arms full: three two-kilo sacks of Egyptian potatoes, a carton of Bulgarian strawberries, some tomatoes, and a bunch of bananas.

"Are you stocking the factory kitchen?"

"No, just you."

"But that's..."

His eyes were sparkling with boyish glee. He turned off onto what used to be a soccer field. The limousine showed off its splendid suspension going through some bushes. I was feeling almost sorry I'd have to sock him in a minute.

"I cannot accept from you such..."

"Instead of flowers."

"Unacceptably expensive flowers."

"Totally free."

"?"

"I installed a refrigeration unit for the boss."

"That surely must have taken a long time..."

"I sent an apprentice."

We drove across the soccer field and stopped before a dive called Lid'ák, probably the worst dive in all of Ústí, a direct supplier of patients for our surgeons. Around the entrance, nettles a meter high, obviously the result of urination. It looks like a bulldozer drove through the large, low-ceilinged main room last night. But on the wooden terrace stood a small partition, an almost white tablecloth on a table, and through a little window a magnificent view of the mountains. It's been a year since I've...

He returned with two glasses and a bottle of St. Raphael. In this dive? "Another refrigeration unit?"

"An electric stove. I supply both cold and heat."

I decided to have one glass. After all, he was quite charming and amusing. I lit one Pall Mall off another. After three glasses he placed his hand on the back of mine, as if unconsciously, underneath the table I readied my other hand for the "grip." I felt sorrier for him than for the unfinished Raphael, which I adore, or for the eggs sitting back in the car. And the yogurt and milk ... The "grip" can be extremely painful. I had to give that kid first aid myself after he drove both Monika and me into a garage and pulled down the door.

He looked at his watch and rose. "You said you were in a hurry."

"Yes, of course. You're very..."

My head was clear, my legs, however, wobbled a little as I stood up. He drove me directly home, placed his "flowers" into a black Lufthansa bag, and shyly asked: "May I carry them upstairs for you?"

I sort of laughed a little. I felt like a silly goose. My former escorts didn't ask a lot of questions.

In my apartment, I placed the Lufthansa bag on the table. I felt his gaze upon my neck. There hasn't been a man in this room for a year. There used to be a lot of them, once Monika and I did two on five ... those days are gone for good. Oh, he brought the Raphael ...

"I don't know how to thank you..."

"You'll think of something."

"Lately, I've gotten used to living alone..."

"Me too. Shouldn't we try to do something about it?"

We were standing right next to the bed. Why hadn't we sat there longer by the window looking at the mountains? Not this, I don't want to start this again ... Really, I don't.

"Would you like to go to Lid'ák sometime again?" he said softly.

"I'd love to! – We could again, sometime."

"Perhaps you'll find a moment for me sometime."

He was really leaving already! I reached my finger toward him in jest, he snatched at it and kissed my wrist in such a way that ... that ...

That would knock you out for a week and then would fling you up to the ceiling. Alex was howling with laughter as he ran down the stairs, jumped into the car, and sped away in a cloud of beige dust. *Quidquid agis prudenter agas et respice finem.*

The car bounded its way across the dried-up puddles and shallow depressions of the undermined earth, Alex tore down the alleyways on the outskirts of town, between woefully cracked facades, out along a sinuous little road between field and forest, he headed up to the Střížovický Hills, joyfully braked until the tires squealed, and then he stopped at a group of trees and went for a blissful swim in a pond of green lizards. He then drove back to the factory and ate a substantial lunch in the cafeteria (a triple portion of meat for our golden Mr. Alex, who can repair it all), he punched out at 16:32 (two-and-a-half hours overtime at time-and-a quarter plus hazard pay), and with his tufts of hair still wet arrived home at building No. 2000.

The enormous eight-paned window (once the display window of Teo's shop) was closed as usual and covered over on the inside with lime paint, Alex grinned into the opaque panes, it's true that ancient Teo had scratched on the glass with his fingernails an entire optical system, but these days all the old man does is snore away in there ...

The window casement opened a little into the quivering heat of the afternoon air. From the mountain of comforters and pillows piled up to the window top, ancient Teo's angry face looked out over the street. Scrunching his head down into his shoulders, Alex went in a wide arc around the window and crept in through the front door.

In the formerly men's one-room flat, third floor on the left, Alex took his clothes off and, scratching the hair on his chest, lay down on his bunk thinking about what he might think about, nothing came to him (Europe's writhing, America's gone insane, Africa's in convulsions, and Asia is in flames), he wondered whether to go to the Corner Pub tonight for beer and pool or to go to the Svět Café on the square for whores, he yawned and licked his lips, what will not be today will be tomorrow, *la dolce vita in northern Bohemia*, he fluffed up his pillow and quietly went beddy-bye with vulgar little thoughts of the succumbing Dr. Dáša Zíbrtová.

Woken by an angry stomping: sister Madda's stomping in heavy boots on the floor and thus on the ceiling of the Gráfs', who live directly below.

"That's it, stomp on 'em, the bastards, it's all their fault," Alex grumbled, and then he spat and turned toward the wall. It was hot under the blanket and hot in the room. Alex turned over and scratched at his wet thatches of hair. Sister Madda looks delicious in the sack. *Nulla dies sine linea.*

"Anything in the world for my little Madda..." Alex whispered sweetly as he raised himself up on his elbows.

She was angry at Eng. Secký and his wife. They did it without you, huh? It's horrible what people indulge in today! The heat increased. Alex kicked off his blanket and got up.

"Just lie back down, dear brother," Madda said with a smirk. "I've already seen one today."

Alex acted ashamed, he covered himself and sat on the edge of Madda's bed. With solicitude, he placed his hand on Madda's forehead. "You don't have a fever, do you?"

"No, I'm angry! I could kill someone. Those conceited, elitist pigs!"

"They're all a bunch of crooks. And when you think that we have to work for those bastards..."

"I'd–"

"...a couple of kicks in the head, while they drive around in fancy cars with all our proletarian money..."

"If you could only see their bathroom ... Why, we can't even get any water here!"

"...while they bathe in champagne and have those tremendous orgies."

"Alex, have you ever been to an orgy?"

"The stories I could tell..."

"Okay, let's hear some..."

"You want to hear about them?"

"Well, why not ... Hey, get your paw away from me, okay?! Now!!"

"But I just wanted to caress you ... like a darling brother..."

"Look, we know each other pretty well, and brothers don't caress their sisters that way."

"How about like this?"

Madda tore herself away from Alex, reached down under the bed, and with his big shoe whacked him in the face. "I've had it up to here with that, okay?! To here!! With all guys, all of them! Revolting's what it is. Our brother Julda's right…"

Alex suddenly stopped rubbing his forehead. "I understand, dear Madda, and I imagine what it's like for you. You know I understand you. You have a perfect right to be a bit hysterical, but look, you're smart, and young, and beautiful, with your entire life before you. The entire world, in fact…"

"Julda's right. What he says is the holy truth…" Madda repeated. She didn't believe it much herself, but knew it would make Alex angry.

"Julda, Julda, Julda…" Alex was angry. "Sure, Julda's holy! Is he holy or simply stupid? Can't you see he's made himself into a flunkey, the way he grovels and demeans himself, the way everyone treats him like just a piece of dirt…"

"Julda's right," Madda stubbornly repeated.

"Really? So then why don't you listen to him, why don't you practice what he preaches? Sit at home and twiddle your thumbs, read pretty little books, take night courses for nice little girls, and greet the director obediently…"

"That might be best. What am I now? Nothing! A whore."

"And what would you be then? In an office you'd make five hundred crowns a month less than you do right now, and you'd be groped by some fatcat head of invoicing."

"I don't have to give in to him."

"Then they'll ship you right back to the bottling department, like they did Zděnka Stolbová and Jiřka Háková."

"They shift me around like that already."

"But at least you don't have to worry about losing your job, like those office sluts. You don't have any deadlines, reviews, inventories to take, stressful situations to handle. If you don't quite feel like working, you can sleep behind some boxes or take off somewhere on the other side of the fence. And no sucking up to some dimwitted clod. What sounds better: Yessir! or Youknowwheretostickitpal? The lower you are, the more freedom you have. And what if tomorrow all of Cottex flew off into the wind?"

"I'd probably burst out laughing."

"And then we'd go to work next door. It's easy on the nerves when you have nothing to lose."

"Julda's still right," said Madda, but she was already smiling.

"Really? But I can do what he does! Hey, my little Madda, get up. How come you're lying in bed in the middle of the day?" Alex was making fun of Julda.

"My feet hurt!" Madda yelled from bed, and already she was laughing.

"Well, be a good girl and get up. Have you cleaned your shoes yet? And give your neck a nice rinsing."

"There isn't any water!"

"There's plenty in the basement."

"I'm not about to drag a bucket up and down the stairs!"

"The devil finds work for idle hands. And what have you been doing this afternoon?"

"I spent the day at the Grand Hotel!"

"Oh, Madda, Madda, it's not good to–"

"And then I was with a married man!"

"But Madda, you unhappy girl, have you really–"

"At his apartment!!"

Alex theatrically clutched his heart and keeled over, Madda roared with laughter, Alex knelt beside her bed and begged her, both of them roared with laughter when Alex moaned wretchedly in Madda's lap, then their laughter softened, and then gradually became nothing but an occasional giggle.

"But just the same, Julda is right." Madda sighed and ran her fingers through the blue-black hair on Alex's back. "But I still have a lot of fun with you ... Like with no other boy in the world..."

Contemplor meliora proboque, deteriora sequor.

"But I'm no boy!"

"You're right. You're the devil."

Of blood, milk, and juice   Of a girl's memories of Christmas carols

Of a woman's lament in damp leaves   And of the mineral springs of devastated land, water, and air   Of a nine-year-old's poems   Of the sirens of revolution   And the wail of electric motors, centrifuges, rock music   All this now is mine, and I can do with it whatever I want   No you can't   Enough   Please don't   I'm serious, that's enough already   Pretty please   Not that   I really want a gentle love   Pavilions of glass and blue metal   And endless fountains spouting healing waters   And soft music, something really cool and really slow   And a little pond with colored lights beneath the surface   And swans ...

And you wouldn't want to recite the poetry of P. Ovidius Nosy   You'd fall asleep, like this you're so fresh, so splendid   With a sheaf of splintered garnets in a glass pavilion   Instead of tepid mineral water, hot oil in the pond ignited with a flame-thrower   That's a different kind of show

*And we'll chop the swan's burnt feathers off with a chisel and eat its flesh
That's what you really like   Just look at what you're doing   Just
look   You're doing it   It's really horrible what we're doing here together
I really didn't want to   It's you   Ow, that hurts: You act like you want
to kill me, not make love   Ow! I resisted so long   Ow! Ow! Ow!*

*How blissfully the wild boar squeals as it's torn apart upon the springy
moss in the eternal shadow of our Quaternary forest where the desiccant
light of Denaturating fails to penetrate   This has been the most intense
experience of his life   Give me another bite   You take a bite too … Meat*

*This is different fare than slimy moss, drowned bugs, and rotting beech
nuts from the bog   Ow!   Now you're biting too hard   Ow! Ow! Ow!*

*I love meat   I've gotten used to it   They sent me to the slaughter-
house when I was fifteen*

*They didn't send me till I was eighteen   The tempo increases   Along
with the consumption of meat   Everyone loves meat   And now how
wonderfully we eat and drink one another*

How splendidly one another

("My God—" Julda Serafin shouted in a high voice from the doorway.)

All that could be seen of the planning department on the second floor was
the green shrubbery of two philodendrons in the window. From his chair
behind the plants, right next to the window, Bogan Tušl looked past the
rattling adding machine and through the leaves of the plants, watching
vigilantly over the entire courtyard, from the porter's lodge to the boiler
room and garage.

As soon as the small figure of Schejbal (chair of the Works Committee)
emerged from the darkening gates of the opposite building, Bogan leapt
from his chair, flew swift as an arrow down the dark, damp hallway of the
administration building (the "White House"), and in the intense heat of the
sun threw himself headlong upon the little man.

"…but one can't live like this, my wife and I are desperate, and Jolana
started crying again and said the best thing would be to jump out the
window–" Bogan spouted several centimeters from the pale face of the
nervously blinking chairman, in an increasingly loud voice (two passersby
had already turned to look at them, and a woman pulling a cart had
stopped and gaped). "I know we're going to have to try to work this out
again…" stuttered the chairman, slowly backing away. "But last year, on
October fifth, you postponed the order till the first of April, and today's the
twelfth of June, I've already given you two doctors' confirmations of
Jolana's pregnancy, and this is totally destroying her. Papoušek, who has no

children, could get an apartment, and Ruml too, who just went out and bought a car–" Bogan's attack was persistent, and Schejbal backed away into the building he had just emerged from.

Coldly keeping watch over the courtyard, Bogan traversed decade after decade on his adding machine and then got back to work on some price calculations for Jolana (who worked in an office on the same hallway, in the pricing department, and in turn helped Bogan with the operating lists – they both were extremely efficient), suddenly he saw, between the leaves, the engineer Papoušek and, still tapping the adding machine with his right hand, he phoned Jolana using both his left hand and his chin. He kept on tapping, and by the time he reached the subtotal, Jolana was already down in the courtyard shoving into Papoušek's hands some tickets to *The Fountain of Bakhchisaray* (we're going to save the ten percent commission on tickets sold to buy some furniture).

Borek Trojan, sojourner from Brno, barged in to complain about the money taken from his foreman's fund, and both young men immediately locked horns. Bogan coldly looked into the boy's burning face, you want to rule with the help of my ten crowns, but I need them for something else, kid. Borek even tried stomping his feet, enough of these warm-ups, I've earned the right to stomp, no you haven't, Bogan Tušl stomped on Borek Trojan and threw the angry young upstart out the door.

Down in the white heat, Valach (secretary of the Housing Committee) sat down on a barrel in the shadow of the cooling tower to have a snack, Bogan jumped up, flew on down the hallway, and blitzed the secretary before he'd even unwrapped his sandwich. Then, as he was walking back down the hallway, he met Jolana carrying a typewriter, took it from her, and sent her forth against Valach. He tossed the typewriter onto Jolana's desk and watched her from his observation post as she pecked at the secretary, who wrapped his sandwich up again and crept away, sweetie's well trained, and what a lamb she was that first time I got her in the sack.

Bogan nimbly sailed down the dark hallway of the White House between the bright rectangles of forty glass-paneled office doors, by the silhouettes behind the glass he could guess who his possible prey was and hook them instantly. From the director's office the lanky, stooping Bělička (chair of Youth) staggered out, still reeling from a five-hour meeting and crushed by the number of tasks he'd been assigned, Bogan pounced on him, grabbed him roughly by the shoulder, dragged him (on the way, he tapped out on Jolana's door the code they'd agreed upon) to his den, where he attacked him with the sword of his apartment tirade. Ere long, Jolana barged in with three perforated pages of tickets to *The Fountain of Bakhchisaray*, and both of them mercilessly tore into the terrified young man until he promised to intervene with the chairman on their behalf and took all thirty of the tickets at fourteen crowns apiece (a profit of 42 crowns).

From his chair Bogan kept watch over the sluggish village green of our workaday world, buzzed along on his adding machine, and kept creeping out into the dark hallway, the offices, and the courtyard. Jolana and he passed each other like two barracudas in a warm, slumberous sea, exchanging words in full stride ("Schejbal's in the cashier's office" or "the director went to the bathroom") as they set out on new sorties.

In their nest in the former women's one-room flat, third floor on the right, they met late in the afternoon (Bogan still had to deliver a two-hour lecture on the class struggle to drowsing daddies for twenty-eight crowns at the factory school, Jolana did two hours on a work brigade in the packaging warehouse) and sat down to smoked mackerel.

"Schejbal didn't want to listen to me anymore, he says we're ruining his nerves," Jolana said, and she used her fingers to pry open the belly of the fish.

"That bastard, he still won't do shit. And what about Valach?" asked Bogan, tearing into the meat with his hands.

"He promised again. Tomorrow Buřina is going to the district. I reminded him."

"I'll jump on him again tomorrow morning. I told the director again."

"Věrka told me. Tomorrow is the Party Committee meeting, I'll do Abrt, Bárta, Caha, Dolejší, and Erben."

"I'll attack Fojt, Gittler, Holec, Chodovský, Invald, and I'd better lean on Abrt, Bárta, Caha..."

"I no longer believe we'll ever escape this room..." Jolana sighed.

"We will, don't worry."

"Everybody has their own apartment already, while we're forced to keep on begging, they're all laughing at us behind our backs, what they're worried about now is taking care of their cars and summer cottages – everybody has their own apartment! Do you hear me, Bogan, nobody gives a damn about us, those with-their-own-apartment types, and we keep bothering them with ours. THEY ALREADY HAVE ONE!"

"We won't have to keep at them much longer, just until–"

"Two kinds of people inhabit this planet: those who have an apartment and those who don't. And between them a barbed-wire fence. And when I think that soon the baby'll make three..."

Jolana broke out in sobs, and Bogan grit his teeth at the sight of her swelling womb and bulbous legs, crushed his thumb in his fist and, like a thousand times before, tried cheering her up with the battle cry of their first

victory: "Jolana ... there, there! Don't cry ... Jolana ... Jolička." He wiped
her eyes with a finger glistening with fish fat and gently shook her by the
neck, "so far we've won at least this room, and now we'll win an apartment! ... Remember when this was still a women's one-room flat, and you
were living with that Jiřka Háková, and I came here and started seeing you
– she wouldn't even let me in, she said she wouldn't let the room become
a brothel. Then remember when she went home on vacation and she
purposely broke the key off in the lock and scattered broken glass beneath
the sheets and went to Valach to file a complaint with the Works
Committee..."

"But we lost that time, and for three months you couldn't even show
your face here..."

"But then? Remember when I slammed the door on her ankle..."

"You could have crippled her. If she hadn't been wearing ski boots..."

"I wouldn't have slammed it quite so hard then. Just a little."

"If we hadn't gotten married, you still wouldn't be able to come here.
Let alone live here."

"We did get married, though ...You're not regretting it, are you?"

"Of course not, but I kind of regret ... Perhaps our wedding was a bit
too hasty..."

"And the Monday after it..."

"I'd rather not remember that."

"In two hours Jiřina's piano was outside in the snow, and I was tacking
my name to the door."

"I was completely beside myself."

"But you threw Jiřina's shoes out the window, right at her head."

"And you chased Valach up and down the stairs with a knife. And then
the business with the police..."

"In the end, they had to give us this room. And now they have to give
us an apartment!"

"They don't have to do anything. And take that shirt off, I'm doing
laundry ... in our laundry room under the faucet..."

*A little white house   A glassed-in veranda   And a large garden beneath
an old tree   A bright green pump   My husband sings to himself half
naked, picking apples   At the window of our house my wife is laughing
Our child runs toward us across the lawn, playing with a little white puppy
He's afraid of those dark clouds   Don't worry, we have a roof over our
heads   And when the first few drops of rain begin to fall, we'll all be sitting
'round the fireplace   Oh, how the birch logs burn*

Jolana turned on the water faucet: a few rusty drops, loud rattling,
then nothing. The Tušls looked at one another, eyes ablaze. And from below

a merry silver humming, like tambourines at a garden carnival. The Gráfs on the second floor are showering.

"Nice job they have – just lounge around all day in the bathtub and send all our water into the sewers!" Jolana shrieked and started beating her fists against the cast-iron plates above the faucet. "One can shower all day and night, while the other doesn't have a drop of water; one lives on the second floor in a three-room apartment with a car and summer cottage that has a glassed-in veranda, and the other is expecting a baby in a miserable cubbyhole beneath the attic; one wallows in his four thousand a month, and the other kills himself for a few coins – and both the one and the other are same!"

"Wait, not like that!" Bogan shouted, and he started beating on the water pipe with his shoe.

"I'll probably have to take the baby to the basement for its baths!"

"Move over!" Bogan yelled, and using a wrench, with heavy, blacksmith blows, he doggedly pounded metal on metal until his arm gave out. He paused for breath, switched hands, and raised his arm.

"Wait–" Jolana whispered. "Something's going on out there…"

A rising din and clamor on the other side of the door, and then a sudden knocking: in the hallway Julda Serafin, from across the hall, a step behind him a barefoot, disheveled, and apparently bitten Madda wearing just an inside-out chemise. Leaning against the door across the hall was Alex Serafin, likewise nearly naked and covered with bloody scratches –

"You have to take in Madda," Julda Serafin implored. "Please…"

"What – what – we have to what–" Jolana blanched and grabbed both sides of the doorjamb.

"Something horrible has happened. Alex and Madda…" Julda softly said. "Please be so kind … Help us…"

"To stay!" Jolana's blood returned immediately to her face, "What are you bleating about? You're crazy–"

"Move!" Bogan hissed from behind, he pushed Jolana aside and from several centimeters away hissed right into Julda's face: "What are you babbling, you stupid moron, you idiot, you–" word after word like knives into his pale, dumbfounded face.

"Why so rude, Tušl, old boy?" Alex intervened. "Don't forget you're living in a women's flat. Are you a woman? Show us!"

"You idiot, tell me again where I live, and I'll – ! – !!"

"A women's one-room flat," Alex obliged him gladly, "into which you moved without authorization, unofficially and illegally."

"You bastard–" Bogan Tušl howled as if kicked below the belt, Jolana meanwhile surveyed Madda's unchaste, sluttish beauty as revealed through her chemise, her nipples erect from passionate massaging in the dark, her firm flat belly on which, she assumed, it all had happened– "That slut of yours should have been shipped to the glue factory long ago!" she shrieked with hatred.

"People, please … people…" Julda dolefully whispered.

"What'd you call me–" Madda screamed and leapt upon Jolana, "you bloated cow, got yourself knocked up to get an apartment, you ugly rat, you office whore–"

The girls went at each other, pulling hair and scratching faces, Julda and Bogan pulled them apart, and Alex stepped out for a cigarette, cheering both sides on. "You'll love it there, my Maddička," he prodded, "you'll have a better view…"

With all his strength, Bogan extricated a scratched-up Jolana, dragged her into their room, and slammed the door. On the other side of the door, the din and clamor resumed, with lots of panting.

"What happened exactly?" Bogan asked while carefully touching a piece of Madda's fingernail embedded in Jolana's temple.

"What didn't you understand? Alex and Madda…" Jolana wet her fingers and carefully dabbed the scratches on her face, all the while hissing with pain.

"You have to move down to the itinerants quarters," Julda said to Alex. "There's only one guy down there now, Borek Trojan, and four empty beds."

"Not a chance," said Alex.

"But you must realize that after what's happened, you can't go on sleeping in the same room with Madda…"

"But with a guy I can? What if I take a shine to him as well, and slide into his bunk?"

"What a pleasant little family–" Jolana was already shaking again.

"Hear that…" Bogan hissed. "Jolana! This could be fantastic … Look: Alex doesn't want to move into the itinerants quarters – wonderful! And Madda can't keep living with him. She can't move into the itinerants quarters either, Borek Trojan's there. And so there's nothing left to do but have Comrade Madda move in here!"

"What are you talking about?! – With us?!?!"

"She really has no other place to go. Come on, Jolana! But there's one condition: we must get an apartment first – So let's go: arrange it so Alex can't get out of it. I'll run downstairs and get Borek."

Borek Trojan lay completely naked on one of the bunks in the itinerants quarters, looking at pictures. "Come quickly!" Bogan shouted, "they're saying Alex Serafin has to move in here with you, that slacker, 'cause he fucked his sister, come on, get up" "But what do I–" "You can't be happy about this, come on, I'll stuff that foreman's fund for you again, just hurry up!" "At least let me put some clothes on–" "Underwear's enough, and hurry up or else we'll meet him on the stairs, suitcase in hand–"

Meanwhile back upstairs, Jolana was yelling: "The itinerants quarters is a room for itinerant workers!"

"Thanks for the support, Jolana dear." Alex grinned and then pulled a long nose at Julda.

"Jolana, you have to recognize that under these conditions…" Julda pleaded.

"And what about *my* condition?" screamed Jolana.

"Go get him, Jolana, don't give up," Alex urged.

"And I want a room to myself!" screamed Madda. "I'm an adult!"

"You're going to get one!" yelled Jolana. "As soon as we get our apartment–"

"My sister Madda is indeed an adult." Alex roared with laughter and with his finger dabbed his bitten neck.

"Comrade Borek Trojan is coming to have his say!" Bogan Tušl howled from the stairs. "He too would like to live like a human being. And in this building there's a men's one-room flat."

"And when we get our apartment, there'll be a women's flat, too!" Jolana yelled.

"Exactly how it's supposed to be, according to regulations! Enough of this crap!" young Bogan blustered.

Roman Gráf was creeping hesitantly up the stairs from down below, obviously sent on reconnaissance by his parents, Bogan grabbed him firmly and shouted over his head so Papa (the company director) could hear it from their second-floor apartment: "Tell your father that the Housing Committee has decided to introduce the rule of law and order: a single apartment for the Tušls would free the women's flat for Madda, a spot for Borek Trojan in the men's flat, and the itinerants quarters for itinerant workers – a single flat for the Tušls satisfies all four petitioners!!"

"We all would like to live like human beings!" shrieked Jolana.

Young Roman Gráf was dumbfounded, he stared at the wild, half-naked group that stood around an almost totally naked Madda, gulped, then pulled himself out of it and ran downstairs.

"So, shall we try it together?" Alex turned to Borek, patting him on his naked back.

"Borek will live in the men's flat! That's what it's for!" asserted Bogan.

"I don't want this guy in my room!" Alex objected. "Hey, look how all you guys are backing away from me! Come on! I don't have anything against poor Madda!"

"He's the one we should throw out!" yelled Borek, hoisting a finger at Alex. "He's the perpetrator, after all!"

"And you wanna live in the itinerants quarters with such a disgusting pig!" Bogan Tušl yelled.

"Pardon me, Mister Tušl," Alex shouted, "I'm helping you get an apartment, and I'm a disgusting pig? I'm being forced to rethink my position!"

"Bogan didn't mean it, he just has a violent temper..." Jolana pacified Alex and even patted his hairy arm, Bogan gave Alex an unctuous smile and kicked Borek's ankle to insist he watch himself.

Mrs. Zita Gráfová came up from their apartment on the second floor, sent by her husband as was her son, she was wearing white sandals, a damp blue bathrobe, and a blue turban – fresh, redolent, beautiful, and smiling: "Has something happened?"

"Nothing much, Mrs. Gráfová. Just that a girl was raped right above your very head. You may go back to your restful bath." It didn't work when I tried being nice, Bogan decided, so nothing left to do but fan the flames.

"What? Who? This girl?"

"It's surprising this is the only thing that's happened in this brothel, which is a result of your husband's negligence. It's surprising no one's been murdered yet. YET–" hissed Bogan.

"Two years I've been waiting for a room–" shouted Borek Trojan, his first request to management.

"We all would like to live like human beings!" Bogan descanted.

"But I don't understand..." Zita Gráfová objected, and she wrung her wet hair in perplexity, two silver drops of water fell through the hot air, but by the time they hit the floor, they were already nitroglycerin.

"She doesn't understand!!" Jolana screeched with hatred.

"It will not perhaps surprise you, Madame, that the building is not inhabited on the second floor alone!!" Borek yelled as if he'd been stabbed.

"You're not the only ones who live here!!" Bogan bellowed.

"I want my own room just like your little Roman!!" Madda hatefully shrieked.

"I'll have to bathe my baby in the basement!!" Jolana roared like a dragon.

"It can't go on like this!!" raged Borek, drunk with his own voice and the intoxication of his hatred.

"You think we're cattle!!!" Bogan furiously shouted, and Alex shouted him down with his deep voice, well exercised at district podiums devoid of microphones: "We-are-gathered!-here!-today!-unanimously!-to request!-fair!-firm!-revolutionary!-uncompromising! ..." Already they were all united in the indestructible unanimity of hatred for the ones on the second floor.

Julda Serafin climbed the stairs and stepped to the side of the landing. Behind him appeared His Serene Highness the director himself.

–that's the one who has three rooms and all our water, the one who rules and wallows and lives off our hard labor, the one who drives his ass around in cars and only looks at papers all day long and goes around in a white shirt and sows a thousand other provocations –

(–how many people since Creation have been killed just for water, of all mortal sins? And slaughtered–)

–Comrade Director Dr. Evžen Gráf.

(To be continued)

BESIEGED

(An Illustrated Novel in Installments)

> *In helmets and high boots, or only in hats and half naked,*
> *they will destroy us by fire and sword. It will be very beautiful.*
> *We could not wish for a better end ...*
> Jean Genet

Reclining in his deep easy chair, with his hands resting comfortably upon the cool blue satin, his head lightly sunk in the high, soft headrest, and his eyes half closed, Dr. Evžen Gráf luxuriated in the simple joy of relaxation. A difficult day behind us. More difficult ones ahead. Snooze a little while, Evžen.

Then suddenly from the floor below, a heavy wooden thump and then another. What am I supposed to do, sleep more quietly? Boom. Boom. Boom. Boom. What is that kid downstairs doing, that ... Borek Trojan, what's he doing down there? Boom. Boom. Boom. Boom. Boom. Working off his excess energy, I guess. Youth ... Boom. It doesn't concern you. He'll soon grow tired of it. Take it easy. Boom. Boom. Boom. More? So, there you have it. Noise is a simply necessity for them. Just like silence for me. Why doesn't Roman make any noise? At sixteen ... That glass bottle in his briefcase ... ether. At sixteen! Talk to him. Hopeless. He'd only get more stubborn. The need to rebel. He won't get his hands on any cocaine. One of the few advantages of socialism. We drank absinthe in our day. Can't understand the young ... The only thing to do is try to help them.

Crack! – Zita slams the bathroom door. She's been so nervous lately. The summer's been too hot. Seems to keep getting hotter. Both of us prefer the winter. That first time in the Alps... "The snow is really blue..." enchanted, exhilarated, calm. How she laughed ... snow in her hair. In actuality the snow was violet.

Have to pee. Too often. Prostate? Probably not yet ... Drink less. An apple's enough in the evening. Peel the tough, neurotic rind from the sweet kernel of simple nature: the slow buildup of pressure in the bladder, the urge to urinate, aping the libido's curve, until it is a burning necessity, exploding orgiastically with the sweet numbness of satiation, drifting into soothing relief. What was the name of that Renaissance thinker from Feuchtwanger's *The Ugly Duchess*, with his seven delights: eating, drinking, relieving oneself after eating, relieving oneself after drinking, bathing, eroticism, and the seventh, the greatest – sleep ...

The ceiling thundered with an insane stomping right above his head. Doop. Doop. Doopity doopity doop. The Serafins. They're probably jumping a meter off the ground. A man's the only one who can stomp like that. Someone up there's intentionally being cruel. Doop. Doop. Doop. Doop. Alex is not a good person. With his disposition, world view, belief system, or rather fanatical disbelief. Please let me sleep.

It keeps intruding. Why do you keep listening? Strange sounds ... he's up there with a girl. With Madda. His sister. The burning blood of the Borgias was satiated only with itself, writes Klabund. And he tells how Lucrezia, after seeing her first bullfight and learning that the bull must die, had asked her father Rodrigo to let the bull enjoy one last heifer. The bull then straddled three. Alexander VI was certainly a great Pope and statesman. He divided up the South American continent wisely, moderately, and thoroughly between the rival powers in such a way that the division remained in force for centuries. Compared to him, the United Nations and the Security Council are pitiful bunglers.

What's he doing up there with her? It bothers you, doesn't it, Evžen. Oui, c'est vrai. That Alex ... a brutal boy, of barbaric proportions, his insolent, mocking glance, his virile stench ... Before each man was executed, Lucrezia di Borgia would let three nuns into his cell and watch them from the window. She would have him sent for. And she would participate in his execution. Stretch it out. Spice it up with torture ... *The taut muscles of his back convulse and chafe against the wooden post soaked with his own burning sweat   Groaning as during orgasmic pleasure   His twitching arms are drawn and chained to the singed beam   Look*

This gives you pleasure   Me too   Just look

Enough. The complicated activating apparatus of a decrepit man, right, Evžen, old boy? The ancient Hebrews would arouse themselves without allowing things to take their natural course and thereby did they preserve their manhood well into old age. Shem lived five hundred years after begetting Arphaxad, and he had sons and daughters. Arphaxad was thirty-five when he begat Salah. And after siring Salah, Arphaxad lived four hundred and three more years, and he had sons and daughters ... that's what it says in Genesis. An interesting hypothesis is that years were shorter then, because they counted them according to the orbit of a heavenly body unknown to us today and which, according to another hypothesis, then crashed into the Earth, creating Australia, which would account for the completely different geological composition of that truly deformed continent. Fantastic, of course. But didn't they recently find the remains of an ancient vessel on the biblical mount of Ararat? Of course, it doesn't have to be Noah's ark. But no matter whose it was, how did it get three hundred meters above sea-level in a place snow-covered all year round? In other respects, we must consider the problematic treatment of –

BANG! BANG! BANG! BANG! Awful metal blows from somewhere above my head. The Tušls? What's going on? BANG! BANG! Like someone up there beating a heavy BANG! blunt metal instrument on hollow metal ... BANG! the pipes? BANG! BANG! But that's a little overdoing it, n'est-ce pas? BANG! BANG! BANG! BANG! Now they're going at one another. Somewhere on the stairs ...

They don't intend to grant you any sleep, poor Eugene. It probably wouldn't do you any good to go and ask them. They don't like you. How can I win their friendship? ... The only thing to do is try to help them. It's too hot this afternoon.

Relax. Waves of fatigue are flowing from your back ... your head ... your arms ... your forearms ... hands ... fingers ... fingertips ...

"Roman! – Can you hear me?" Zita calls him from the bathroom. "Go and see what's going on upstairs..." Roman walks down the hallway. Out. He leaves the door ajar. You should have closed it, son, it'll be even louder now.

Entspannung. Disconnect. Relax each muscle in succession. A piece of cake. Just think about them. Disconnect. The muscles of the forehead first. Imagine them. One after the other. Now the left temple. Flowing, slowly, calmly. The right temple. More. Completely. It just takes a little willpower. Now the facial muscles, the left cheek. Roman is back. And Zita is leaving the bathroom. Roman doesn't want to tell her anything. Is Zita coming here? No. She's walking down the hall. Out. The door is still open. The yelling keeps getting louder.

Please let me sleep. I'm exhausted. Tomorrow. Domani, domani. They're yelling at Zita. How they hate her. How they hate us. How to persuade them? How to help them? Zita's coming back down the stairs. Walking back down the hallway. That's not Zita! They're invading——

"Excuse me, please," says Julda Serafin from the doorway. "Your door was open, so I took the liberty..."

"My door is always open. What's going on up there?"

"My brother Alex has seduced my sister Madda. Now we're asking for your help."

"How can I help you?"

"Take my sister in. I beg you."

"Of course, such a solution–" an unclean girl in our apartment. For who knows how long ... But she can't sleep with Alex anymore ... But Roman's reaching puberty, and in the same apartment ... But it's better than ether ... But an unclean girl in our apartment ... "–is no solution, of course."

"I don't know where else to put my sister. She can't stay on the first floor, not with Teo and not with Borek in the itinerants quarters. The Tušls have just one room on the third floor, and they're expecting a baby. And on the second floor you have three rooms..."

"There isn't any way to swap?"

"Only if Alex moved in with Borek Trojan downstairs, but I asked him and he said no."

"We could have him thrown right out. He's committed a punishable offence. I'll call the police–"

"No, please don't. Who would that help?"

It wouldn't work, besides. He's indispensable to the factory. Unlike the director. One of the disadvantages of socialism. "Tomorrow I'll call a meeting of the factory administration and the individual sections. I'll telephone the People's Committee chairman."

"But we need help right now. It's evening."

"Don't you have a relative she could..."

"No, we don't. I'm asking you as a decent human being."

Below the belt. "The factory director is not required to solve such situations to the detriment of his own family."

"I'm asking you to be charitable."

We go upstairs. Beware of acting on your first impulse, warns Talleyrand, it's usually the noblest. Why is everyone half naked? Who scratched this girl all bloody? I don't understand a thing. The only thing to do is help them. They look at me with hatred. I'm not the one who scratched her up, my friends! – Guilty nevertheless, confused, for some reason anxious. Zita's trembling hand in mine.

"Okay, enough. Alex Serafin, for the time being I will refrain from filing a criminal complaint, at your brother's request. Tomorrow you will answer to the factory administration and the individual sections."

"Not tomorrow," Alex grinned. "I've got to work on that transformer."

"Miss Serafinová, please pack a few essential items. You'll stay with us for a couple of days. The rest of you ... I think it's been enough for one day."

"Comrade Director..." Bogan Tušl commenced his apartment tirade: "We've arrived at a solution whereby an apartment for me would satisfy all four petitioners–"

"I will not hear a petition from the stairs except for the purpose of information. Of course, you may submit proposals through my office. Good night."

Zita's been upset for a long time.

"If only you had seen the girl up there..."

"I saw her, darling. A few drops of hydrogen peroxide and a couple of poultices will make it all better."

"Will she be having supper with us?"

"If you want ... Why not? It might be amusing. But first let's drive her into the bathroom."

"And tonight? Roman..."

"Roman's sixteen, Madda's nineteen. Don't worry, I've thought of that, as well. There's no big difference between living in the same building and living in the same apartment."

Footsteps on the stairs. She's here. A knock at the door. Zita's trembling. Why didn't she ring the doorbell? She's knocking at the door, and Zita's going to open it.

A truly amusing supper. The girl comes straight from the bathroom, late and for some reason in a huff. Roman avoids her gaze but obviously doesn't see his persistently observed plate. "Roman, you've got your sleeve in the compote."

"Would you like rice or potatoes?" Zita kindly asks the girl.

"Whatever you have," the girl converses.

"I always have rice with fish," I try to explain, "but Zita and Roman prefer potatoes."

"Aha," the girl converses with her mouth crammed full of the peach she's just stuffed in it.

"Which would you prefer?" Zita tries again.

"I'll eat whatever you've got," the girl converses.

Let's hope she only means today's side dish. An enormous appetite. Pleasantly infectious. That's the reason a restaurant in Stockholm pays a young woman to overeat in front of the guests. But Madda really is hungry. Nothing to laugh at. Rather compassion. A guilty conscience. As well as envy, eh, old man? You don't allow youself to eat like that anymore. Never. Never's a horrible word. Connoting death. Connoting freedom. "Roman, you haven't touched a thing."

"Lfkhm," he says. Is he on ether? You must admit that even without a hint of table manners, Madda's a more agreeable dining companion. She's scrubbed pink. Zita worked on her nearly half an hour. She even put an old ribbon in her wet hair. A small, hungry, gentle girl with eyes cast down upon her plate. An hour ago bloody incest with her barbarous brother.

"Anybody like some more wine?" We all have some.

That night Zita's still upset. Her eyes glisten in the darkness. She drinks too much. More and more. She hides the empty bottles in her suitcase. When I returned from Paris, I found six of them in there. Three liters of cognac in four days. I dread the next time I have to leave you alone.

"I'll never forget what I saw on the stairs..." she whispers over and over. "How they were all standing around her ... Do you know where she had teeth marks on her? When I washed her in the bathroom..." So this is what's upsetting her. Just like that time in Opatija. That woman who'd fallen off a steep cliff, and all around her an agitated crowd. "Let me through, I'm a doctor–" Zita lied and knelt down right beside her. Why did you make that up?

My dear neurotic one. Your body is more dear to me than my own. "Hold me tight..." she whimpers. I entwine myself all around her as if I were taking her prisoner, as if I wanted to shield her, eclipse her, and submerge myself in her. Hide her in myself. She loves this more than making love itself. She's told me so.

She turns her face away. She stares into the darkness. What does she want there, what does she descry? Strangely disturbed. What does she see there? Don't flee. Her sobbing, which I love above all else in the whole world. She suddenly falls asleep. At least her eyes are closed and her breathing regular. Is she asleep? She doesn't answer.

Silence at last. Salutary silence. Sleep, dear Evžen. Thanks for your permission, sir. A difficult day behind us. More difficult ones ahead. And growing fewer. Between the trunks, the first rays of light are getting through, the forest is coming to an end. The summit. *Über allen Gipfeln ist Ruh*. Over all summits there is peace. Still five more years. I'm useful. Just five more years.

Tomorrow. A summer morning in the cruel heart of raging Europe. The morning light upon the wall across the room. Illuminating the Tibetan rug that hangs there. Warming the colorful tones of the bright red, yellow, and blue vertical lines of the unforgivingly geometrical painting by Richard Paul Lohse, *Rhythmic Progression*. What does the small black square in the lower right-hand corner of the canvas mean? A period? At the end of what?

Tomorrow. A summer morning in a forgotten corner of expiring Europe. A glass of milk. Sunlight on the sidewalk. Leafy trees. Dew on a patch of grass ... Life's little pleasures.

Fifty-five: a senatorial age. Rule and rest. It's fun. I like the wine. Noble, ripe apples. I display kindness. I sleep with a beautiful young wife. I own a house on a river. A good bed. The simple pleasure of repose –

Suddenly, a hoarse screech from the darkness. Like an animal ... It's that girl, that outsider. She's already over the wall. They're above and below. Advancing.

WHO'S WHO
Evžen Gráf (55)

In the final year of the last great European peace, when horse-drawn carriages trundled through Prague, when ladies wore lorgnettes of gold, and gentlemen carried in their vest pockets 20-crown gold pieces bearing the reigning emperor's portrait, on the second floor of the old patrician house belonging to the Gráfs, whose roots went back to the 11th century, the great-great-grandson of the Lobkowitz estate administrator, great-grandson of a tenant farmer of the Lobkowitz farmstead Golden Valley, grandson of a Prague dealer in cloth, and the eldest son of a history teacher at the C & K Gymnasium, Evžen Gráf would sit at the window above the Havelská Street Market, hunched over a French textbook.

"You should go out and play a while," his father repeated absent-mindedly, and over an oval saucer of Domažlice cottage-cheese rolls renewed his neverending argument with his brother Rudolf and his uncle Anselm, in which he defended the idea of a national Czech monarchy under an enlightened Russian Romanov against his brother's Federation of Free Danubian Republics based upon the pattern of the North American states and his uncle's moderately reformed Hapsburg Empire. Evžen walked up to the table for some more cottage-cheese rolls, listening to the three irreconcilables with equal amounts of moderate affection and moderate derision. *Vous avez raison – à la maison.* Cottage cheese disgusted him, but he ate it regularly and in abundance.

Naturally, everything turned out quite different. Rudolf the Americano-phile remained in Soviet Russia as a regimental doctor and then soon became the Deputy Health Minister in one of the Caucasian republics; Uncle Anselm turned a profit of seven million crowns in the post-empire boom, then lost nine million in the subsequent depression. And all the Gráfs lost their entire life savings. Naturally, everything eventually worked itself out. Evžen graduated the *gymnasium* as valedictorian of his class and enrolled in the natural sciences (Father wanted him to study philosophy, Mother theology) at Europe's venerable Charles University. He was still a virgin, but he took a lively interest in the words of Christ, Jan Hus, Thomas Aquinas, Aristotle, Kant, Confucius, Tolstoy, Lincoln, Lao-tzu, Leibnitz, Rousseau, Mohammed, Masaryk, Descartes, Darwin, Marx, and Jaroslav Hašek, and with respect to everything he found whole-hearted sympathy and ironic skepticism.

"Gentle, tender, and so good..." Miss Mimi (originally Emilka) Sedlák-ová, seven years his senior, whispered to him as they left the Olšanský Cemetery, her Papa Sedlák had bought a golden harp for 6,999 crowns that very afternoon, "...one day I might be able to love you..." In the Paris Café, Evžen spoke to her in French, which she did not understand but expressly asked to hear. She always ordered the purple liqueur Parfait Amour and after every sip would add some sugar. On the day she got engaged to Bruno Rafajem, an artillery captain ("Perhaps you'll under-stand..." she wrote him in a farewell letter, "but it would have been too beautiful..."), Evžen went to Neff's Hardware and bought a razor made of real Sheffield steel, placed the razor on the edge of the bathtub, beside a bottle of Parfait Amour, a pack of Parisienne cigarettes, eight cream cakes from a baker called Myšák, and Baudelaire's *Les fleurs du mal*, and began to fill the bathtub with hot water. Four hours later, in his so-called healing waters, French dictionary in hand, Evžen fell asleep exhausted by the hot water. By morning the dictionary was soaked completely through, and the cream cakes were slightly off, but still entirely edible. *Cela ne fait rien.*

Even before American jazz made its way to Europe, Evžen had begun to study English and to learn the Charleston with his colleague Joan (originally Jarunka) Dvořáková. In the empty apartment (Mother and Father had borrowed a thousand crowns from brother Norbert and off they'd gone, as if in a dream, to Paris, third-class, for five days) Evžen plugged away six hours at the record player. Joan, however, only allowed a kiss of her hand, and when at ten o'clock the neighbors up above and down below began to beat upon the ceiling and the floor, Evžen took the record off and walked with Joan to Spořilov, speaking English: "Was it not wonderful?"

"Lovely, indeed." He never learned to dance, but soon he was able to read English.

"For you, fifty crowns," the prostitute named Riri bluffed (originally Růža, normally she took twenty, and at home in Modřany she did it happily for five) when Evžen, on the strength of four gins, an illustrated edition of *Aphrodite* by Pierre Louÿs, and an hour of walking around the Powder Gate, was brave enough to suggest a rendezvous. The taxi to Modřany came to sixteen crowns, and Evžen gave the *chauffeur* (the "driver" or the "cabman," it was enough to make him, despite everything, horrified) a blue twenty-crown note and simultaneously to Riri a red fifty-crowner, because he felt quite wretched and wanted to go right back to Prague.

Riri, though, who'd never ridden in a cab, did not intend to give up this chance of advertising her life's success, and rather roughly shoved poor Evžen through the village to her ice-cold little room above a barn. *Cela ne fait rien.* At three and twenty Evžen was a handsome lad, but when he refused to part with his attire, the prostitute employed the heavy, Syrian camel whip a certain writer of ill fame had left with her, and Evžen got a taste of brief, intense delight. Evžen then spent five more hours at the village train stop, pacing through November mud awaiting the arrival of the morning local. For many years thereafter, Evžen traveled to Modřany four times every annum.

As a doctor Rerum Naturalum, officer-cadet Evžen Gráf signed on with the 43rd Infantry Regiment, in Brno-Židenice. The second day, he gave his hungrier comrades-in-arms his quarter-kilo portion of beef (which he'd never liked, yet always eaten), and when later he also gave out Viktoria cigarettes and Lidka chocolate, sincerely wanting to become their boon companion, they threw a blanket over him one night and beat him so badly that he lay four days in sick bay and was then assigned as medical officer for the 2nd Company. With guilt-ridden sympathy, he watched from a shaded sick-bay window as his sweaty comrades suffered on the hot, sandy training ground.

In view of the company's improper behavior, the regimental commander, Alois Páral, had broken glass cemented atop the wall surrounding the barracks, but Židenice's skillful lasses flung a blanket over the shards of glass and, after surmounting the wall, they sneaked up to the barracks, where they used honey to glue the blanket to a window and softly shattered the pane. Beneath his blanket, tautly drawn above his bony knees, Evžen listened to the squeaking of his comrades' nearby bunks – extremely aroused but motionless – until the infamous and enraged Mrs. Rudka at last worked her way into the bivouac erected by his knees, and for the second time Evžen experienced complete and utter gratification. By morning all had been revealed, and Evžen was quite unjustly discharged. *Cela ne fait rien.* He recommenced civilian life an ardent antimilitarist and inveterate pacifist, but at the sight of a barracks or a marching unit he felt not only quite revolted but also oddly aroused.

During the Depression, RNDr. Evžen Gráf was forced to leave his native city and journey north 27 kilometers to the town of Kralupy, where he joined the chemical labs of Roubitschek & Roubíček. As employee without peer, Evžen gained the favor of both his bosses and advanced apace. He went for walks along the placid hills above the Vltava, and every month he deposited 500, 600, and then 750 crowns (whose purchasing power of course diminished over time) into a passbook savings account with Anglobanka.

He still could not decide whether or not to start a family, but he took a lively interest in the words of Hegel, Bergson, Kierkegaard, Przybyszewski, Wilson, Nietzsche, Lenin, Beneš, Freud, Engliš, Trotsky, Ogden, Wells, Avenarius, Mach, Pearson, Schlick, Croce, Henlein, Hayakawa, Rosenberg, Gandhi, and Adolf Hitler, and with respect to everything he found wholehearted sympathy and ironic skepticism. Nevertheless, not long after Hitler's seizure of the Sudetenland, Evžen sought to systematically expand his literary German through ardent conversations with the Kralupy Germans, sincerely wanting to become their boon companion. But one night at a firemen's ball a group of German youths beat the living daylights out of Evžen; soon, however, he had learned to speak their language fluently.

Upon the German invasion of 1939 (every month now he deposited 800 crowns into a passbook savings account with Dresdner Bank), Dr. Evžen Gráf was forced to move a further 39 kilometers from his native city to the town of Roudnice to start work as a Betriebsleiter, managing a tiny factory producing typewriter ribbons. As employee without peer, he quickly gained the favor of the factory owner Drábek and the Treuhänder Fleischmann, as well as a Prague relative of the original owner, Silbernagel, who had emigrated to Venezuela. *Mit dem Hute in der Hand gehst du durch das ganze Land,* With your hat in your hand you walk through the entire land. Evžen went for walks along the placid hills above the Elbe and every month he deposited 600, 700, then 850 crowns (whose purchasing power of course diminished over time) into a passbook savings account with Živnobanka.

"That was a real lady," Uncle Edward whispered to him as they left the Olšanský Cemetery, where they had lowered Evžen's mother into her first-class grave. Evžen genuinely mourned her, even though they'd never been too close (the Gráfs employed a maid and governess, and Mother stayed at home only with friends or a migraine), the tearful Evžen summoned up the erect woman with the antique cameo ring, who was always exacting and with whom, from the age of ten, he was allowed to speak only French. "And now it's time you were married, my boy," said Uncle Robert. Overwhelmed by a strange certainty that something was departing him forever, leaving behind it only apprehension for the future, Evžen buried his foot in a pile of fallen leaves.

With respect to his mother's funeral, there were many matters to be settled. Evžen sold his mother's personal effects at half their value (the gold lorgnette was the only thing he could not part with) and he took the opportunity to marry Zita Šlechtová, a lass of eighteen years of age, that is, his junior by some twenty years; the Šlechtas and the Gráfs, however, had been acquainted more than eighty years. A year before the end of World War II, a son was born to the newlyweds, and Evžen chose the Russian but acceptably European name of Roman, then threw himself into the study of the Cyrillic alphabet.

"You should go out and play a while," his father repeated absent-mindedly to the newlyweds, and over an octagonal tray of walnut strudel, a Šlechta delicacy, he renewed his neverending argument with Brother Max and his new brother-in-law, in which he defended the idea of an independent republic under the protection of the League of Nations against his brother's partiality to the Soviet Union and his brother-in-law's idea of a Union of Central European Republics with the lifetime president Otto Hapsburg. Evžen walked up to the table for some more walnut strudel, listening to the three irreconcilables with equal amounts of moderate affection and moderate derision. *Vous avez raison – à la maison.* He hated walnuts, but ever since the wedding ate them regularly and in abundance.

Naturally, everything turned out quite different. Pro-Soviet Max soon emigrated to the United States, founded a fantastically thriving laundromat, and soon obtained an influential municipal position in Akron, Ohio; his brother-in-law was wrongfully accused of German collaboration and dispossessed of all his property; and with the currency reform of 1945, all the Gráfs and Šlechtas lost their entire life savings. Naturally, everything eventually worked itself out, and revolutionary events forced Evžen and his family to move a further 20 kilometers from his native city to Bohušovice nad Ohří, where he signed on as production manager at a factory that made artificial flowers. *Cela ne fait rien – vse rovno*, it's all the same, as the Russians say. As employee without peer, he quickly gained the favor not only of the original owner, Weber, and the trustee, Vepřek, but even of the new director, Comrade Horník. Zita passionately longed to go back home to Prague and see the real countryside of Šumava, to have another child or two and then to never have any again, to buy a mastiff and poison the cat. Evžen listened to her courteously, ironically recalled her previous wishes and foresaw her future ones, and simultaneously caressed her beautiful ashen hair until she yawned and fell asleep. *Cela ne fait rien.* They went for walks along the placid hills above the Ohří and every month deposited 700, 750, and then 900 crowns (whose purchasing power of course diminished over time) into a passbook savings account with the postal service. Already Evžen spoke Russian fluently and simultaneously taught his little Roman the Cyrillic and the Western alphabets.

"That was a real gentleman," Uncle Alfred whispered to him as they left the Olšanský Cemetery, where they had lowered Evžen's father into his second-class grave. Evžen genuinely mourned him, even though they'd never been too close (his work at school and studies at home took all his father's time), and the tearful Evžen summoned up the erect man with the Masaryk pince-nez, habitual black clothing, exhortations with regard to national feeling and democracy (in 1945 he was wrongfully suspended for alleged Nazi collaboration and in 1948 imprisoned for echoing at a private party of his former students former President Masaryk's motto, "Truth prevails!"). Overwhelmed by a strange certainty that something was departing him forever, leaving behind it only apprehension for the future, Evžen sadly sniffled.

With respect to his father's funeral, there were many matters to be settled. Evžen sold his father's personal effects at half their value (Jirásek's collected works was the only thing he could not part with) and he took the opportunity to once again schedule a rendezvous with Riri, who now was working as the chief personnel officer for a certain vital ministry. She was wearing a leather jacket and her hair hung down like wires. Laughing, she dismissed his invitation for a glass of vodka at the Moscow Restaurant, and in her own apartment in an old, patrician house on Havelská Street she produced a nationalized bottle of Courvoisier VSOP. Evžen committed his first and last adultery, left, and went to pray (although he'd never believed in God), taking a tram rather than walking to St. Havel's Church on Havelská Street, in case Riri was watching from the window.

"You should go out and play a while," Evžen repeated absentmindedly to four-year-old Roman, and over a Bakelite tray of marmalade pastries (cottage cheese was rationed and nuts were only for Christmas) he renewed his neverending argument with brother Albert and brother-in-law Otto, in which he defended the idea of Czechoslovakia as a bridge between East and West against his brother's American and his brother-in-law's Soviet political compromises. With a distracted expression, Roman walked up to the table for some more pastries. The child did not like marmalade, but you could get him to eat it.

Naturally, everything turned out quite different. Procommunist Otto became a significant party functionary, then suddenly overnight an extended arm of an anticommunist center, and he was rehabilitated only long after his death; anticommunist Albert soon became quite intimate with Riri, then assumed the post of general manager in an important branch of industry; and with the currency reform of 1953, all the Gráfs and all the Šlechtas lost their entire life savings. Naturally, everything eventually worked itself out, and revolutionary events forced Evžen and his family to move a further 30 kilometers from his native city to Ústí nad Labem, where he signed on as chief of engineering at national enterprise Cottex.

As employee without peer, he quickly gained the favor not only of the prewar owner, the wartime occupier, and the postwar trustee, but also of the entire procession of workers' managers, who year after year appeared and then quickly disappeared. He and his family went for walks along the placid hills above the Elbe (in a direction away from Prague, right toward the German border) and every month had deducted from his paycheck and placed into the factory savings association 800, 920, and then 950 crowns (whose purchasing power of course diminished over time). The more sincerely Evžen tried to acquire friends, the more he met with hatred.

Evžen harbored powerful sympathies with French-style parliamentary rule, Anglo-American democracy, the Soviet system, and European federation, along with a powerful distrust of French-style parliamentary rule, Anglo-American democracy, the Soviet system, and European federation. He showed a ongoing interest in the words of Stalin, Pius XII, Husserl, Sartre, Einstein, Nehru, Jaspers, Tito, Fromm, Camus, Lukács, Maritain, Kennedy, Khrushchev, John XXIII, Fidel Castro, Josue de Castro, Horney, Nasser, Schweitzer, Nkrumah, Russell, Paul VI, Sukarno, Adorno, de Gaulle, Wolfgang Kraus, Ginsberg, Mao Tse-Tung, Malcolm X, James Bond, and Vladimír Páral, and with respect to everything he found whole-hearted sympathy and resigned disagreement. *Vous avez raison – à la maison.* Evžen procured himself a Chinese textbook.

Evžen Gráf loved apples and actually ate them, half a kilo daily. He would line them up on the sideboard and then each day he would examine them and eat the one that was beginning to rot. He thus consumed twenty thousand kilograms of rotting apples.

That was a Tuesday I'll not soon forget.

In the morning at the slaughterhouse, I saw ten patients, only acute ones – the rest I rescheduled for the next day. And I sent perhaps eight of those right to the health center – I didn't have the energy.

But on the other hand, the devil's in my blood. That Thursday with Alex Serafin ... I thought of him continuously. The way he drove me around. His "flowers" – the potatoes will last till the end of the month. I smoke to eliminate the constant taste of St. Raphael inside my mouth. I'm once again inhaling thirty cigarettes a day. And after a year of peaceful slumber, suddenly I can't fall asleep and keep waking up at four in the morning. It's not good to be alone, someone once said. And a woman alone is above all sad.

In love at twenty-eight – ridiculous. The repairman drove the little doctor around in the company car, gave her potatoes and a bottle of vermouth, all of which cost him not a single crown. He was so boyishly shy when he asked me outside my building: "May I carry them upstairs for you?" And then right beside the bed, he kissed me on the hand and took his leave. That was Thursday. Friday nothing. Saturday nothing. Sunday nothing, of course. But after all, he knows where I live – ridiculous. He's surely got whole flocks of women ...

Shame slapped me in the face when on Monday I came in to the examining room of Cottex having decided to send Nurse Jandová for some distilled water, and then call him when she'd gone. "You've got a package," Nurse Jandová said a second before I spoke. Two kilos of Spanish blood oranges and a note: "Your A. S. is waiting for your voice on extension 99." Alex Serafin ... he called! He made me wait four days. Or is he really that timid ... I'll have to take things into my own hands. Invite him over. But where? Not my apartment, certainly! A café, pastry shop, pool ...

So now today, instead of my net bag, which for a year has been sufficient for my yogurts, milk, bread and butter, I've brought along a huge black satchel: Portuguese sardines (I've been denying myself for over a year), Hungarian salami (perhaps I can afford that too), chocolate-covered cherries (you only live once), a carton of Pall Malls (the link between smoking and lung cancer has not been substantiated), a bottle of red Rioja Coronila (the oranges Alex – I mean Mr. Serafin – sent me are also from Spain), and a bottle of Hungarian Egri Bikaver wine (Bull's Blood ... It's already terribly hot before ten in the morning). But this of course doesn't mean that ... I would ... It's just that one should always have a toothsome morsel on hand at home! Some makeup, too, my skin has been neglected for so long that it's a horror to look at. And then some new records – oh, my sweethearts Dvořák and Debussy! As well as something lighter: "Rhythm Is My Uncle," "Waiting for Love," "Launch the Salvo," and "Shake."

I left the slaughterhouse examining room early and arrived at the Cottex examining room late. Those morons won't go off the deep end. All they care about is constructing their cottages on the river Elbe while drawing sick pay. Nurse Jandová stared with astonishment at my black satchel. What are you looking at, you owl? "Okay, let's go! How many are there?"

"Just one ... When you didn't show up for so long, I told them you had business at the local clinic ... Remember when Mr. Gráf got angry because we kept the workers from the boiler-room waiting half the day ... So at eleven I sent them all away."

Well, Jesus, it's nearly noon, for crying out loud! There's nothing better than training new staff. "Well, send him in, he's been so patient."

"Patient he is, extremely."

A yellow-haired fellow wearing strange attire made of white material that's obviously seen better days, but clean.

"Strip to the waist and tell me where it hurts." Just because I got here late doesn't mean I can't leave early. I have to straighten up a bit at home. Why isn't he undressing? Hairy is nice.

"I came to see you on behalf of Mrs. Seligová." Interesting voice, he probably sings somewhere.

"Who's that? And why didn't she come herself?"

"She's ashamed."

"But! Doesn't your conscience bother you that you ... ahem ... placed her in this shameful condition?"

"She's ashamed because she's never been to a doctor before and doesn't speak Czech that well. And my conscience won't allow me to let her suffer."

"So what's wrong with her?"

"I don't really know. Some sort of pains."

"But I can't make housecalls ... Have her call emergency services."

"She's never done that. That's why I'm asking you for help."

"So why don't you call emergency services for her?"

"She'd be afraid and claim that nothing was the matter."

"Well, what then, for crying out loud..."

"I'd like you to come with me to see her – don't, however, say you're a doctor – then examine her without her knowledge and arrange for treatment."

"But only the doctor assigned to her place of residence can do that."

"I've already asked him, he just brushes me aside. He's not a good person."

And I am? A banal, competent nobody, but there's something special in this man, something ... something ...

"Are you a relative of this Mrs... . Mrs... ."

"Seligová? No, I just help her out. My name is Serafin."

"Serafin! Do you have a brother here?"

"But that's the one on Thursday … who," Nurse Jandová let me know unnecessarily. "This is Julda Serafin."

"Your brother Alex made a very pleasant impression on me."

"He's good at that," Julda Serafin sighed. "Dangerously pleasant."

"He was here on Thursday…"

"I often don't come till after he does," Julda sighed a second time. "Unfortunately…"

"Doctor, telephone!" Nurse Jandová announced.

Monika! Once again she's in a pickle. "…at least a fifty or at least a twenty or even five," Monika gabbled into the telephone, "or at least make me some fried bread and tea, I'm totally broke, just imagine, like a silly goose last night I…"

I placed the receiver on the table. Monika will go on talking for half an hour. She still hasn't returned my extra house key, so she'll be at my place this afternoon. One should always have a toothsome morsel on hand at home!

I looked at my bulging black satchel and at Alex's brother's yellow head of hair (and his fabulously fresh skin and sky-blue eyes). What was I thinking, a café or pastry shop or pool? A small party of four: Monika and me and the Serafin brothers! At least in a group I'll control myself, and Monika really knows how to get things going. "I'd be glad to see your patient, Mr. Serafin, but you'll have to let me introduce you to a girlfriend of mine."

"If it will make you happy…" he said softly. Oh, both brothers are gentlemen.

I lifted the receiver again. "…and I said, are you going to take your hand away or not, and then he grabbed me by the other leg…" Monika was still gabbling into the telephone receiver. "Okay," I cut in, "come to my place this evening." "Why evening? I'm hungry now!"

"Okay, this afternoon," I said concurrently to Monika and Julda.

"At four!" yelled Monika into the telephone.

"At four?" I looked at Julda pleadingly.

He laughed and nodded, and already I was dialing extension 99. Alex said he'd be "extraordinarily glad" to come at four. My mood improved tremendously.

The gentleman in white was carrying my satchel for me through the courtyard. Outside it was hot as Palestine, a breeze stirred up the beige dust.

Hemmed in among the monstrous pipelines, high-tension pylons, and factory cables, the former rectory gave the impression of a ghetto. In a dusty, arid garden an unbelievable number of soiled, naked, dark-skinned children with dark hair and shining black eyes, as in the paintings of Zurbaran, were toddling around. My former husband stubbornly refused to have any children with me and his sex life consisted more of time spent in the bathroom putting on those tasteless condoms than in bed with me playing games of so-called love.

These dear hearts were delightful. They grabbed me by the skirt and asked me to pick them up, how touching ... I realized I'd never kissed a child in my life ... and they returned my kisses with sweet slobbers.

"Let's see the satchel!..." and with a smile Julda handed it to me, already opened. In a minute, all the chocolate-covered cherries disappeared. Chocolate only ruins your figure, anyway.

"Are you a princess?" a little girl asked completely seriously, and then she introduced herself: "I'm Helenka Růžičková."

As I knelt down to her, the gray little street urchins grabbed one of my sandals and ran off behind the house screaming. Let's not get carried away, my dears ... "Don't worry," Julda laughed, "they only want to keep you here because they like you."

"Give me a shoe, too," said Helenka Růžičková, "I'll guard it better than the boys will." And the girl received my other sweaty sandal like a sacrament and pressed it to the little silver medallion on her chest.

Thus barefoot into biblical indigence, like in that film from Italy – that backward south of theirs. On cracked stone floors beneath limestone ceilings, the tortured wood of horrid furniture, an ancient sewing machine among some bags of something, shovels against the wall, a bathtub made of tin, two scythes, a derelict bicycle, and tin buckets everywhere, one shouldn't look into them, and everywhere a million flies.

Mrs. Seligová, a translucent old woman, was in such a state of undernourishment she should have long ago been hospitalized.

"Why doesn't she eat?" I whispered to Julda.

"Her retirement pay is only a hundred and ninety crowns a month, and most of that she gives her mother, two sisters, and..."

"Tomorrow she's going to the hospital. And now she needs some bullion and biscuits. Can someone here prepare it for her?"

"Let's go see the neighbors."

About ten neighbors filled a large room. Were they to come to my examining room, I'd have to work till midnight. I sensed Julda's eyes on my face and went to work. Fitting punishment for playing hooky this morning at the slaughterhouse and Cottex. Luckily, I have a pad of pre-stamped prescriptions.

"Why don't you see a doctor?" I asked them. "It doesn't cost you anything!"

They smiled and stared somewhere past me.

"How many children do you have?"

"Nine."

"What did you have for lunch?"

They smiled and stared somewhere past me. The prescription pad was quickly gone, and so I gave the cardboard backing to the little girl to play with.

"You wouldn't have a pinch of tobacco, would you?" asked a white-haired patriarch with his feet in a tub.

"Don't tell me you have to beg!"

"My retirement pay is a hundred and seventy crowns, dear girl. That's not an awful lot."

"There has to be a breadwinner in this family ... After all, with nine children there should be a family allowance of a couple thousand crowns a month..."

"Our father ran away," the little girl said, and she threw the cardboard backing at my feet.

"Well, then you'll have to pursue a legal course of action ... Meanwhile, submit a request to the Social Security Department..."

They laughed right in my face – an awful feeling.

"Let's see the satchel..." and Julda handed it to me, already open. What good will two tins of sardines, a piece of Hungarian salami, and a couple bottles of red wine do? I gave the old man all my Pall Malls, too. I think they could probably use the Dvořák and Debussy, as well ...

"Why don't these people respond? The worst part is, they look completely satisfied!"

"Beati mites, quia ipsi hereditabunt terram," Julda said with a smile, and then I got so angry at him: along with everything, to sit here listening to quotations in this backward, pitiful house, with its urine smell and swarms of exasperating flies –" You'll have to excuse me, Mr. Serafin, my college Latin was oriented in a somewhat different direction."

"Blessed are the weak: for they shall inherit the earth."

"Okay, fine. But now let's go find the children. They have my sandals. I thought you wanted me to send a relative of yours to a spa or to prescribe some drugs – but you've arranged a regular spine-tingler for me."

"Spine-tingler? What's that mean?" Julda's eyes are those of a child.

"Just payback for your church Latin. It means that somehow I'm even happy or something."

"Beati misericordes, quoniam ipsi misericordia afficientur."

"If you could be so kind to once again..."

"Blessed are the merciful: for they shall obtain mercy."

The children wouldn't return my sandals for quite some time. I unrestrainedly gratified my repressed maternal instincts. Why didn't I get myself knocked up by that imbecile before I kicked him out? Children are heavenly. Now, don't start bawling like an old whore.

At home lying in my bed Monika, wearing black bra and panties, and Alex beside her in his strange black sweater – it wasn't a sweater, he'd just put on a shirt.

"It's broiling in here..." he whispered, and he tossed her garter belt from his lap onto the floor.

"Let's see what's in your satchel!" Monika exclaimed.

"I see you've already introduced yourselves..." I pointedly remarked. Five-thirty – in ninety minutes they'd become remarkably well acquainted.

"What are you going to make for supper?" Monika inquired, and it was with great disappointment that she dropped my empty satchel behind the bed.

"Instead of ... talking to Alex, if you'd only scrubbed some potatoes, we could cook them now. I'd like to introduce you to my friend Julda Serafin."

"The pleasure's mine, and otherwise there's nothing in the house at all? All I found was one yogurt and three cloves of garlic!" Monika complained.

"We really couldn't wait for you guys..." Alex said sweetly. And having conquered Monika – a tiresomely easy task – he reoriented himself to me with astonishing facility.

"I hope you didn't get bored waiting. I was with your brother Julda at the former rectory."

"Julda's lots of fun," Alex grinned.

"Dr. Zíbrtová liked it there," said Julda softly. "She helped those people."

"Call me Dáša."

"Because I care for you, Dáša, I have to warn you about those people," Alex said. "Give them a finger, they'll take your whole hand. Are you expecting their gratitude just for a couple of prescriptions? I'll bet a bottle of Raphael they won't even try to fill them. As long as you haven't prescribed them spiritus vini – but oddly enough, they always have enough of that."

"Why do you speak so badly of them?" Julda asked his brother. "What harm have they done you?"

"What harm?!" Alex was getting worked up. "Don't give me any of this poor wronged souls business – those drunks, those criminals, those smugglers, those whores! Of course, dear Dáša, you don't realize that the ancient paralytic prostitutes his grandsons to German homosexual tourists down at the docks. Ten crowns or three marks a go. And extra for special services, for example–"

"That's a lie!" yelled Julda.

"I've never been to the docks," I said, "I find it hard to believe, however, that those children I was holding in my arms..."

"...were making fun of you before you'd even turned around," he interrupted. "Another cow who fell for Grandpa's bait – that's what they're saying about you now!"

"Dáša gets taken in by everything," Monika announced. "But maybe we should start thinking about supper. And to start, a little aperitif. Where have you hidden the cognac?"

"The cognac's gone," I announced.

"Here you've been jabbering on about some little brats, and meanwhile all the stores are closing!" Monika was truly alarmed. "You want to sit here dry?!"

"I have a car downstairs," Alex jumped in. "I'll go get something – Hey, know what? Let's go to the Palace instead!"

"Can't you sit for even a moment without alcohol?" Julda said softly.

"I can, but it's annoying. To the Palace! –" Monika shrieked, and still lying on the bed she looked around for her garters. Instead of his own shirt, Alex had put on Monika's black chemise. So this is the gentleman I wanted to be with tonight –

"I'm staying here," said Julda. "And Dáša's tired."

"Just get a couple cognacs in her," chuckled Monika, putting on her garter belts. "Remember that time in the Grand Hotel, up on the stairs, Dáša–"

"Shut up!" I begged her. "Give me back my key, once and for all, and get out."

"Well okay, let's sit here a while," said Alex, and he angrily kicked the chemise under the bed.

"Traitor! Shame on you!" Monika shrieked. "What are you going to trample on next? I've already put it on twice–"

"I thought you wanted to go to the Palace, Alex," Julda reminded his brother.

"Dáša invited me, so I'm staying here!" Alex growled.

"As you wish. Dáša, perhaps Mrs. Seligová's story will be of interest to you," Julda said. "Her father was a colonel on the General Staff–"

"Yeah, and her mother was the Grand Duchess of Luxembourg!" Alex shouted. "Oh yeah, this is going to be fun!"

"A little different kind of fun than you had planned!" Julda shouted back.

"You wouldn't know fun if it bit you in the ass!" Alex shrieked.

"And you know how to make a whorehouse out of anything!" Julda yelled.

"You idiot! You impotent monk!!!" Alex roared.

"You shameless, incestuous animal!!" Julda thundered. In a flash, Alex pushed the chairs aside, Julda rushed him, and the two brothers tussled around on the floor. I think I even took a punch before I managed to tear them apart.

Monika was already dressed and waiting by the door. "Stop it, Alex, and at least drive me to the city. This place has gone to seed."

"That would probably be best," I added.

Angry, Alex stood up and disappeared without a word. "I hope you're not trying to give me the slip –" we heard Monika through the open window and then the roar of the engine.

"I'll go, too," Julda said softly. "You need to rest. And please forgive my anger."

"No, you forgive me ... I'm the one who arranged all this. You know, at first I wanted ... but this is better. Much better."

"Beati mundi corde, quoniam ipsi Deum videbunt."

"That's something about the heart..."

"Blessed are the pure of heart: for they will see God." And Julda Serafin kissed Dáša Zíbrtová on the shoulder and left the apartment, walked across the street, and headed south, where the houses, gardens, and fields ended and where in the bare, severe biblical landscape, dead mountains of trash rose up.

The day was ending in bloody tatters. Julda was on his knees in the burning desert dust, Lord, have mercy on them *The extended, begging arms of a naked crowd   Cracked lips   Flies in the corner of their eyes*

Drive the puss from their sores with your lips, kiss them   Thrown in after them to beasts in the ring   Flayed for them with burning iron   Torn to pieces by their dogs   Stoned   In agony for you all

WHO'S WHO

Julda Serafin (37)

In those distant times before the Second World War, the Serafin brothers were the pride of Father Gott's choir at the Holiest Trinity Church.

The first time tenth-grader Julda, the best student of Latin and the poorest child in the class, went to the magnificent riverside villa of Madame

Rapantová to tutor her daughter Jitka in Latin twice a week, he joined the lonely lady for afternoon tea and for nearly an hour partook of savory delicacies he'd never seen before, while the young Jitka had to walk in the garden down below. Julda felt increasingly anxious and strangely uncomfortable. Madame kept prolonging their sybaritic teas on the terrace, to the detriment of Jitka's Latin. Then one afternoon Madame prepared their tea inside her bedchamber and compelled the young man to drink some wine. When Madame bared her breast and pressed Julda's palm to her burning body, young Julda spied upon the wall above her head a tiny black crucifix, tore himself away, and fled in tears. In the garden, pale Jitka blocked his path, knitting needle in hand. She knew everything and was prepared to stab both Julda and herself. In feverish gratitude, the pale young girl kissed the boy on his forehead and in childish majesty placed his palm against her flat chest. As if floating on air, in his pocket the girl's knitting needle and in his eyes tears of burning joy, Julda walked along the gardeny road the five kilometers down to the city, whose towers reverberated with tintinnabular bells.

Young Julda had discovered that goodness is its own reward.

From the choir Julda Serafin made the cathedral's golden baroque magnificence vibrate with his pure and gentle voice, and with gratitude and unending joy he realized that it is possible to serve easily and sweetly, both heaven and people here on earth.

"We should have taught you German and how to use a shovel rather than Latin and the wisdom of the ages," sighed the eighth-grade classical *gymnasium* teacher when they closed the Czech university and the students went to work as factory assistants for the war machine. "You taught me how to sing..." said Julda with a smile, and instead of entering the Department of Theology he cheerfully started work at the First Brno Machine Works.

With absolutely no interest in machines, more engaging work, or better pay, and becoming ever more obliging and good, Julda finally sank to the lowest paid as well as easiest position – assistant to the crane operator in the pig-iron warehouse. During the long hours when there was nothing to do, Julda would lend the warehouse manager his beautiful handwriting, and since he stubbornly refused to learn to type or use an adding machine, having no desire to become a warehouseman, he lay instead out in the sun between the enormous rusting metal casts, enduring the hours by watching clouds pass overhead.

Considered by most a thoroughgoing idiot, Julda did not have the honor of being trusted and was not called upon to serve in the Student Defense Unit (the members of which were brutally murdered after sabotage was discovered) nor was he made a stool pigeon for the administration or the Gestapo (all the stool pigeons were brutally murdered after the liberation). During air raids, Julda would not go down into the bunkers because he didn't like the musty smell or the unchaste mischief that transpired in the dark. He trustingly raised his eyes heavenward, unable to distinguish American from Soviet aircraft – all of them wore stars. And the force of an explosion that knocked down heavy gates and four specially trained national guardsmen, as well as a highly experienced Luftwaffe anti-air defenseman, merely knocked Julda to his knees. Julda sent out a short (so-called projectile) prayer of gratitude and then immediately set to work digging the victims out from under the collapsed bunker (all were dead).

When he learned that the end of the war meant he didn't have to work in the First Brno Machine Works anymore (they offered him the post of warehouse manager) and when that very same day he saw a poster reading "Help the Czech Border Regions!" he departed with a buoyant heart and suitcase to a northern border station called Good Water, because he liked the name when he saw it on the train schedule. He cheerfully signed on as assistant forester. On August 6th, 1945, when over Hiroshima an atomic cloud developed and, fearing an atomic chain reaction, people left their homes, Julda was feeding black squirrels out of his hand.

The magnificent national solidarity forged during the German occupation quickly came to nothing in the subsequent battles over easy money. *Perdidistis utilitatem calamitatis.* In the strengthening political whirlwind war-time politicians were imprisoned one by one and then, if necessary, executed, followed by pre-war ones, then post-war anti-communists, and then the hanging of the General Secretary of the Communist Party himself. Julda meanwhile lived in his forest with his goat in an abandoned German house, he stripped bark from trees, improved the forest paths, dried hay (not caring for money, he only did the easier work), filled feed-troughs with chestnuts and salt, collected raspberries, blueberries, and mushrooms, lay in the sun, and learned to understand the songs of birds. He lived eleven God-fearing years in the forest.

In August 1956 he completed his thirty-third year. The age at which a man must do something or die. He longed to be more useful to people and all night under an ancient fir tree he implored the heavens to give him a sign. The following day the gamekeeper's wife delivered a summons for him to appear at the local court in Ústí, establishing him as legal guardian of his fifteen-year-old sister Madda, of whom heretofore he had no idea and who, in the opinion of the court, "was not living the proper life of a socialist citizen." Julda kissed the hand of the gamekeeper's wife, packed his suitcase in a thrice (he had, somehow or other, fewer things than he'd come with), and gladly signed on as a tour guide in Ústí, on a bus that for three crowns drove tourists from the town up into the woods.

He spent his free time searching for his little sister, who was missing. Surprised at the quantity of cars, strange antennas on the rooftops of new buildings (only later did he learn of the invention of television, but never did he miss it), four times daily he would journey through the former German, now half-destroyed communities, whose new residents had without delay torn down the crosses and statues of saints on the village commons and in the fields and then, as if exhausted by the effort, had let their cheaply acquired houses fall into serious disrepair. Julda searched untiringly in taprooms, cafeterias, and taverns, coffee houses, hospitals, train stations, and docks, filled with pain at the sight of moral destitution and a burning longing and resolve to be of help, to be effective. *Tu es Deus fortitudo mea.*

When he finally did find his little sister, he acquired by the grace of Teo, house manager of building No. 2000, the empty formerly men's one-room flat intended for the employees of national enterprise Cottex. With an easy heart he renounced his tour-guide job and therewith his solitary moments in the forest, and signed on at Cottex as a fireman. As one of few employees with a high-school education, always obliging and good, Julda was offered the positions of transportation director, librarian, planner, and paid chair of the Works Committee, as well as a whole slew of various courses at various technical colleges and schools. Indifferent to money, Julda remained a fireman. With his fire extinguisher, he loitered around the welders during explosive operations (he only did the easier work), in summer he would water the lawn with the fire hose, in winter he would spread salt and look dreamily toward the bright mountains in the south.

Being practically without needs of his own, he gladly helped out his little sister, later his wonderfully prosperous brother as well, and everyone he knew or didn't, he would stop to say hello, baby-sit, and visit the ill. *Per eum, cum eo, in eo omnia.* Except for the youngest children, everyone considered him a thoroughgoing idiot.

(A June of shady alders on the riverbank, of quiet afternoons beneath the old linden, of girls laughing beside a fountain and the cooling breath of the garden bower ...): Among the stumps of rotted trees, the trampled grass retired from sight beneath three thousand naked, sweaty bodies lying as if slaughtered by the murderous heat, coagulating into a sizzling, oil-covered throng of pungent odors. With his blue Air France bag first against his belly, then under his arm, and finally over his shoulder, Roman Gráf meandered along the kilometer-long Elbe swimming area, pursued by longing and struck numb with a painful discomfort concerning the bodies and himself.

Atop an outlandish checkered blanket, like something from a ski lodge, lay a female student also totally alone in this crazy mummery – I sort of squatted down next to her, not to crowd her, but not really too far away, so that it'd be clear I was sort of interested. Lately, as a matter of fact, I've been totally obsessed with sex.

Of course she gave me one of those looks that says: "What do you think you're doing?" and so then you have to be cocky and sit down right next to her and say stuff like, it sure is hot today, or ask her if you could take her picture or what time it is, and it's this insane silliness that really gets me down. Why can't you simply smile at one another, for instance, maybe nothing would come of it, or on the other hand maybe love like a bolt from the blue, but that's not what I'm talking about. We're all so fed up with everyone, people should find a moment just to maybe smile at one other and then go on with their business. But everybody's really waiting for you to crowd them, sweet talk them, violate them, and then be fed up with them – and if you don't do that, they think you're simply a cretin. Isn't that what this girl on the impossible ski blanket – purple squares and green stripes! – has just made plain?

With a belittling arch of his eyebrows, Roman rose, contemptuously stepped over the girl's legs and, ostentatiously holding his flight bag in both hands, walked on in disgust.

And at the end of the swimming area, by the Yacht Club's wire fence, half of our class is piled beneath the linden tree, of course. All year they keep eagerly assuring one another that they can't wait for summer recess to get away from school and all those stupid faces – but hardly has vacation begun when everyone goes on a work brigade together and then always in the same herd to one tiny spot of the entire enormous swimming area, next to the fence beneath the dug-up, pissed-on linden tree.

"Czarevitch!" They call me Czarevitch because they know I hate it and because my dad's the director.

"Who said you could be here, you ghoul!"

"Hey look, he's got a cutesy little purse!"

That's the extent of their communication abilities – to tell you to your face you're a cretin. Even though *they're* the ones with the miserable imitation jeans with cretinous leather tags and labels – THE RIFLE or OHIO – that some co-op of disabled people from Smržovka put on them, and they're okay because *they all* have them. But when *you* have a real bag from Air France, which a real stewardess personally bestowed upon you in a real Air France caravel, and which just happens to be just perfect for the beach, then you're the cretin because the only one who has one is *you*. But then I thought that maybe it *looked like* I was trying to show off, and suddenly I was soaked with sweat, which always happens to me in uncom-fortable situations, which means I'm almost constantly covered with sweat.

"So Czarevitch, you got a girl yet?" said Tomek, and everyone was already laughing at me, they were *already* laughing before he'd said a thing, and they would have kept on laughing even if I made a stinging reply, because they don't listen to me anymore. In our class Tomek – and no one else – has a monopoly on being witty, apparently a monopoly for all time. The only thing you're expected to do is blush and stammer, whereby you confirm your status as a cretin.

And while he was talking, with those dirty paws of his, Tomek was calmly pulling at his jockstrap beneath his shorts, he was practically sloshing around in there – I just can't communicate with my class, and the harder I try the more impossible it becomes. And this leads to my congenital nervous instability, as my old man's famous psychiatrist puts it, when he pretended he wasn't examining me at all and jabbered on about communication, a word for cretins, after all there's process, there's connection, and there's speech.

Roman Gráf plomped down some distance from his classmates, it wasn't that he conspicuously moved away from them but rather that he stayed off to the side and suffered the heat with an ostentatious display of his contempt, boredom, and infinite fatigue.

Then I suddenly found the entire swimming area disgusting, all these bodies spread out, everyone more undressed than if they were completely naked – what insane silliness. Why can't they go ahead and agree to swim without bathing suits, like they do at Rujen. Who could possibly mind? It's crazy how everybody always wants something, but for some ridiculous reason it never comes about. Like for instance war: except for a few imbecilic generals, nobody ever wants to go to war – but it always happens anyway.

That probably occurred to me when I saw some soldiers going into the water from the towpath. There on the grass were their horrid boots, which looked like they were made to climb the Pamir Mountains or something, and those poor souls had draped their awful footwraps over their boots to dry in the sun – my God, they had to serve as radar operators, on jets, and with Geiger counters and at the same time wear those cloth footwraps! – it's simply mind-numbing.

The army completely depresses me. On the way to school I pass some barracks, and when I see those prison bunks made of metal pipes ... Two years! Why can't I be a girl ... I'd do much better sexually as well. When I'm a soldier, I'll hate the girls ... I'll have to march all sweaty and exhausted through the streets and along sidewalks past done-up girls just coming from a swim and: "Hey, look at that one at the end dragging his leg!" And we're supposed to shed blood for those dumb clucks! That's oppressive.

But maybe you could even shed blood for the stupid girls at the swimming area or maybe even for that idiot Tomek or simply for no reason at all, and at the same time actually be *happy* – if only so that people took you seriously for just a moment. Otherwise you're simply hopeless. But how do you go about it? The ancient Spartans wouldn't leave their boys in the lurch like this, they even *organized* it for *all* of them like a sort of graduation: when the boys had reached a certain age, they were stood in front of some priestess and whipped. A single afternoon suddenly turned the boys into men, and no one could call them cretins anymore.

So I stumbled away from the swimming area and it wasn't till I boarded the bus that I realized I hadn't swum at all. The bus to town was practically empty, whereas the buses going the opposite direction were understandably packed to the roof. Who'd leave the beach so early? Somehow I always end up where nobody else is.

When I got home I fell ill with the longing to take a shower and wash that morning away. I constantly keep on washing myself, and my skin is cracking from it, it's probably due to psychological reasons, if that tells you anything.

As a rule, I never take a bath in the bathtub, because I can't bear the feeling of sitting up to my neck in my own filth, and I almost constantly have the same feeling everywhere else as well. I'd say that I'm a fairly serious neurotic and psychopath. I sit in the bathtub, take the shower nozzle in my hand, spray water onto my shoulders, and the water washes everything off me. I can do this five hours at a time or longer.

Until whenever Mama decides to throw me out of the bathroom. Already she's banging on the door, "You've been in there forever, Roman!" Then I have to crawl out and meet my mother in the doorway. We seem to meet only in doorways, always when one is going in a different direction than the other. When no one's going anywhere, each of us sits in a different room.

Mama jokingly casts her eyes down when she sees me in just my underwear, and I raise my arms to cover my chest as if I were ashamed. But there's nothing Oedipal in all this, it's just that, as a matter of fact, Mama is such a beautiful woman. Instead I feel sort of sorry for her because, for some crazy reason, I think that she, for some unfortunate reason, feels sorry for me. This is a hell of a psychological mess, isn't it. Well, I just keep on fumbling through it all.

Then in the next doorway I run into the old man. It's a good thing we have so many doors, otherwise we'd have to write letters to one another.

"So, Roman?"

"Nothing, Papa."

Some interview, huh. Then I go to one room and the old man goes to another, two doors slam shut, then silence. The next time we see each other will be in a couple of hours. This simply devastates me. The silence here is HORRIBLE – *To live in a one-room flat   In a small, single-story earthen house   An enormous earthen oven taking up half the floor   Lots of brothers   Little sisters always underfoot, sisters you have to hug   There's always plenty of chattering, screaming, laughing, jostling, rolling on top of one other   And you're never alone*

The silence is dreadful. But worse is the longing of my skin, the insane need to be *touched*, any sort of contact, just as long as it's human and warm, I don't exactly mean sex, but *any* kind of contact, which is the final means of communication, when process, connection, and speech no longer exist ... A shower can never take its place. Out of utter desperation I experimented with ether, but then your head feels as if it's made of glass, and the vomiting afterwards is horrid.

I am infernal, one of those South American bearded men, and I'm lead-ing a group through the jungle   We're going to protect the brown people   They're shooting all around us   I'm seriously wounded   We've driven those bastards back   People are taking us into their huts   Hovels made of clay and banana leaves   (They're insanely grateful to us for protecting them)   They're little brown people with black eyes   They have all these little kids around, and we play with them on their hard clay floors   And then pow! – pow!   The bastards have returned.   Let's get 'em   The bastards overpower them and take us captive   They drag us out of the hut   The ones inside won't let us go, they grab us around the waist   The bastards pull us out   The dark ones pull us in again.

"Roman! – can't you hear me?" Mama's calling from the bathroom. "Go see what's going on upstairs..."

There was a dreadful racket on the stairs and when I walked up, I saw an insane scene on the third floor – screaming and gesticulating, Borek Trojan from the itinerants quarters half-naked, Alex Serafin almost naked and horribly scratched up, and Madda –

–barefoot, wearing only a chemise, incomparably more naked than all those exhibitionists on the beach, scratched and bloodied like after a battle, and so insanely beautiful that my entire body was set aflame.

I cleared out of there. I couldn't even say a word to Mama. Orange circles spun before my eyes. Upstairs they went on shouting, and then I realized they were shouting at Mama, who'd gone up there to take a look herself – those swine were yelling at my mother, three rude, contemptible bastards against one weak, delicate woman, I heard every word through the laid-to-ruin gates, I banged myself against the couch and couldn't go up there again, in my mind I was stabbing a knife into their kidneys with such skill that the victim instantly falls, but I still couldn't make myself get up, I know that I'm a chicken-shit and hate myself for it, at that moment like never before, but I just kept lying here on the couch –

Then the old man went up, and everything quickly quieted down. An hour later, though, my legs still shook, like after a long run, and then when I went to take a shower, I looked at least ten years older and found a new gray hair.

So Madda's going to come stay with us!

At dinner I stared at her constantly and didn't have any idea what I was eating. Mama had scrubbed her so much that she didn't glisten as she had on the stairs, almost as if she weren't tan anymore, but now, on the other hand, you could really see her sensational skin, and she's only three years older than I am. She sat across from me like a totally normal girl, it was crazy, just as if nothing had happened – and just a moment ago she and her horrid older brother had been in bed biting each other! She stuffed herself, wiped her mouth with her arm, and: "Okay, I'm off to bed." And she quietly left! She totally floored me.

Infernally aroused, I ran to the library to confer with Van de Velde, I've read his *Perfect Marriage* backwards and forwards. Let's see: "Love biting – An analysis of the feeling of delight in the bitten party – Two further theories of love biting – The use of force by the man as equivalent to love biting – A component of sexual hatred in this use of force" – Criminy, there's a whole system for it!

"For example, bruises on the woman's arms show that the man was truly captivated. Here we see a trait of the sex life of animals: the female's need for subjugation by force ... For this reason, a certain amount of ferocity and inconsiderateness – actual or only apparent – is often wel-comed as an expression of this force factor. This is the source of biting the arms, sides, and butt."

It made me dizzy, but I couldn't tear myself away: "Cases such as Edith with the neck of a swan, who according to Heine's poem recognized King Harold in a pile of bodies on the battlefield at Hastings by the scar on his shoulder caused by his lover's passionate biting, are relatively rare."

"Biting during the sexual act may arise from sexual hatred rather than sexual love. The fact that in a sexual relationship elemental aversion asserts itself in the same way as attraction will escape only the most superficial observer. Behind love hatred is always lurking."

They call it love and making love – but really it's a horror story. No wonder I feel like such an outsider to the erotic sphere.

Van de Velde always ends up getting me depressed. First he whips out twenty aphorisms, like for instance: "There is joy in perfection. Spinoza." And then he'll fire off: "Also quick, springy pats, especially on the loins and in the area of the sacral bone, may produce a fairly strong erotic feeling, even stronger that petrisage (kneading)." This completely unglues me.

I spent nearly an hour washing myself, but I still couldn't fall asleep. Madda's sleeping in the kitchen alcove, just on the other side of my wall ... I held my breath to try to hear her breathing. At supper she practically didn't notice me at all. Would it have been appropriate to shake her hand?

Those bastards pull me out of the hut and the brown ones drag me back inside again   There's more of them, and they're more powerful   The head of the gang is Alex Serafin, completely naked, dark and covered with hair   I bite him and give him hell   But finally they capture me   They lash a beam to my shoulders and tie my hands to the ends of it, so I'm like Christ walking up to Golgotha in that film Ave Maria   *They throw me into a barn along with the other prisoners, but all they have is their ankles chained to the wall   I'm alone standing in the middle with my arms extended   Then they bring in these circus performers   A fat one stretches the bars until they're sort of egg shaped, then a woman steps through this gateway, right toward me   She comes closer and closer, and I just keep standing there with this beam on my shoulders   It's Jeanne Moreau   She walks up and kisses me   No, it's Brigitte Bardot   No, it's Madda   She rips the front of my shirt   With a twitch, I signal to her that I can't do anything with my hands   She simply smiles   And rips her own shirt down the front   The performer turns away with understanding   We sink into the straw on the hot clay floor   Her teeth*

The entire next day, before Madda came home from the factory and who knows where else, Mother and Father and I discussed how to make things easiest here for Madda. As Dad put it, a regular diplomatic code of conduct: so she could eat with us and not pay anything, for it or anything else, so that we don't offend her in the least. If she wants, she'll eat with us every day, we don't eat everything anyway, and we could even adjust our meal times to better suit her, but if it embarrasses her, we'll leave a plate of food on her table, and if she wants to pay, we'll let it pass without comment or, so as not to offend her – this we absolutely cannot do! – we'll accept a small amount from her, and this we discussed for the longest time, because a really small amount would offend her, but on the other hand a large amount would worry her, since she makes so awfully little at the factory.

But Madda totally took us in. You might say, pissed on us. She flitted in whenever she felt like it, at five in the afternoon or eleven at night, ran straight for the dining room saying she was hungry, she even banged her knife on her plate like at some dive when the service is lousy, and she was always the first to load up her plate, and before she'd finished that – she didn't even register us – already she was taking seconds ... for the first time ever we didn't have enough to eat, and Mama was making enough for a troop of parachutists. And after supper she says: "There wouldn't be anything else, would there?" and poor Mama goes and makes her omelets or scrambled eggs and I take it to her on her plate, that girl was practically *hunting* us. And then she'd gobble down the plate of food so nonchalantly that Mama didn't dare stop giving it to her. Our worries about how large an amount to ask her for were completely beside the point, Madda simply *neglected* the question of payment, and before bed she even had the nerve to raid our refrigerator and pantry and always eat the most expensive things. It was simply mind-numbing.

On the one hand, you have to hand it to her and even envy her the way she settled in with us. Had I been in her place, I'd have stayed out till midnight or spent the entire day in that little kitchen alcove. She's not even *a tiny bit* afraid.

But if all she'd done was settle in with us without being afraid, we'd all have been happy, but she basically *plundered* us. The only thing she did in her kitchen alcove was sleep, otherwise – except for the master bedroom and my room (still!) – she went wherever she felt like. Soon we couldn't even get into the bathroom, when Madda wasn't stuffing herself she sat in the tub – that girl would constantly sit in the tub, for three hours! – after a while she started stuffing herself even in the bathtub. We gave her her own towel, but she'd use all the towels – how can someone dry herself with four towels? – of course her favorite towel was Mama's big, extremely fluffy towel, because Mama has especially sensitive skin. And as a rule she'd always throw the towels down on the floor.

Her favorite thing was to pace the bedroom hallway. What could interest her so much there? Could she really like those small, dark English engravings I like so much? I carefully opened the door a crack – the girl was standing right behind it staring straight at me! She didn't move a muscle, so I abruptly closed the door, suddenly covered with sweat. What would I do if she burst in here after me? ...

She's everywhere. I smell her everywhere, she gives off a scent irrespective of her furious bathing, and that scent roams the apartment, seeps through the walls, driving me crazy, I couldn't take it and would always put cologne on twice a day, under my arms and on my neck, and now I pour it right from the bottle onto my chest and constantly pour it into my handkerchief for my nose, but nothing helps. She's creeping through the hallway again. And now, once again, she's standing before my door, the ultimate door.

(To be continued)

CONQUERORS

They finally withdrew.

It took them almost three hours to get ready for a night at their hovel on the river. Food enough for a week, five sweaters and four pairs of sunglasses for three people, and a glass coffee pot, Old Man Gráf still had to come back in for some flypaper. The car started, and then silence.

Madda kicked her sandals off, bounded up and yanked a length of Hungarian salami down from a hook in the pantry, passionately sliced into it with a large butcher's knife and, munching on the fat cylinder of captured meat, with the white moldy skin still on it, she stuffed the pockets of her jeans with tomatoes from the fridge.

Barefoot into the seized territory: we've already been in the dining room, of course only in that little chair next to the door under the ceaseless fire of their fucking pleasantries: "Would you like some more potatoes? Will you be wanting more compote?" Okay, fork over whatever you want to stuff into me, and no conversation. Then they make a song and dance about their tiny portions: fifty little plates and on each one a puny piece of shit. One sickly chicken for four people! When I don't have enough money, I make a batch of potato pancakes, and everyone gets a liter of milk. And when I have enough, I buy a goose that's at least been fed, or a side of bacon. The manners of the nobility: with half a dozen spoons chase a single mouthful around a painted plate ...

Which they probably even got at the hard-currency store – Madda knelt in front of the open sideboard and scrupulously counted all the painted porcelain. We'll see what we can do with these. She put in her mouth a tomato slightly larger than her oral cavity, poked it with her finger so she could breathe and begin to chew it and, with two streams of pip-laden juice squirting from the corners of her mouth onto her chest, she went to where we haven't been yet.

Young Master Roman's room – good God, that moron even has a piano in here! The Works Committee doesn't have the money for one but this boy does. In any event, he's an incredible moron. Once he hustled out of the bathroom and said: "Excuse me for walking around like this in front of you." And he had a towel around his waist! I'll bet he doesn't have anything down there yet. His little body's all white and delicate ...

Boxing gloves above his bed. Perhaps he could be the champion if before the bell his opponent began to giggle and then fell down in spasms of laughter. Good God, he's got enough books to fill a library! He couldn't have read them all himself ... although he's enough of a moron. They're probably from school. Yeah, from school! Bau-de-lai-re – that has to be something about bordellos. Obviously, right on the cover is a stark naked girl. "Aphrodite" – that's some kind of skin cream, isn't it? And inside a stark-naked whore. I'd bet my life he hasn't had a girl yet.

Why does a stupid, sixteen-year-old, snot-nosed punk need a rug and two chairs like in an office, and a piano all to himself? You live here like a pig in shit. Okay, but come the revolution, at least we'll know where to start.

Zita and Evžen's baby-blue bedroom took Madda's breath away. She unconsciously wiped her bare feet on the threshold and tiptoed in.

Outside somewhere the fierce sun roared down from incredibly far away. Here in the green twilight of the lowered shutters and thick cream-colored shades a soothing coolness rose from the resplendently blue, almost luminous, bedding. Madda went over to the bed and lightly tested its softness, first with her finger, then with her hand, and finally with all her strength, the way they test the fenders of American limousines. A regular trampoline. Here you could – with difficulty she suppressed the urge to fling herself onto the bed and bury her whole body into it.

On the left was Zita's partially opened closet, stuffed as if by a steam press, on the right a huge three-section mirror. In a couple of seconds Madda was completely naked, and here's the underwear of Lady Gráfová. Her panties are a little loose, but both of us wear C-cup bras. I'd like to see her naked.

A classic, black, two-piece outfit with a white blouse and rich lace scarf still smelling of lilac – where are your handbags, old lady? black ... white ... or silver?

A dress of gray brocade with a low, rounded décolleté and a black ornamental extension. Breasts served up like this must really make men drool.

A black dress with a long bodice sewn with strass and finished with fringe, a rounded décolleté, somewhat deeper in back, and slits up the sides.

And a blue airy chiffon shirtdress sewn with large pearls, with a high stiff collar almost to the chin, which ties in the back with a ribbon – just like in a fairy tale.

And in a perfect blue fairy tale Madda circled the room: the room grows larger as she opens the door, you almost float along the carpet barefoot, how the thin, elegant, delicate glass tinkles, and white Cinzano from crystal, enormous chocolates in striped tinfoil, and here's a Chinese fan, oh! And golden eyeglasses with a golden handle studded with precious stones, and here's a long cigarette holder made of meerschaum, and blue cloudlets of perfumed tobacco, and the purple liqueur *Parfait Amour*, like honey the heavy golden Courvoisier cognac flows into the massive, dark-gray glass. On the way back, Madda's already dancing from room to room, behind her a series of parlors and a ballroom, you can watch TV from bed, and the sweet face of a singer in a radiant hairdo floats out from the screen, dancing in arctic, variety-show scenery between bands of rotating, silvery glass, snow-covered balustrades, and clusters of white plastic orchids, kneeling girls atop a glittering glass staircase all in white in the receding gleam of rotating, burnished prisms, arms outstretched toward the mirrored altar

of my throne   On which I can lie down as well as sit   No one may ascend to me along the glass staircase   They must remain below, among the rabble, at most they may merely look   But even to look they must be properly arrayed   All in white   Šmudla, Tarzan, Robek, Borek dressed in white to the neck   The girls   Expel the girls   Expel the boys as well   Whip them with thick high-tension wire   Alex in white down to his ankles, like an acolyte   Not even a hair may peep from his high neckline, and he must be shaved   Scrape it off with a brick

Tie Old Man Gráf and his old lady Gráfová to a pole downstairs   Or maybe they can serve iced drinks to me   But no one may ascend the glass staircase   And take the wire to the Gráfs, across their heads   I'd barely walked into their apartment and they drove me into the bathroom like some street whore   So I wouldn't stink the way I did at Secký's house   Like a mangy mutt

So, both Gráfs and both Seckýs into a bathtub filled with napalm   Or better yet something that burns very slowly   But do it somewhere in the basement   Everything here must be clean   And all around me, pavilions made of glass and blue metal   And ornaments of cream   And from eternal springs warm rain shoots forth   Swans sleep in the grass   No one may ascend to me up here   Just whispered music, very cool and very slow

The Gráfs' boy   Roman Gráf   Czarevitch   The skin over his entire body is like the skin men have only behind their ears   You may ascend to me   We'll hold each other's hand   I'll play with you   And then most likely I'll devour you

Reclining on the luminous pillows, Madda pressed her chin down to her collarbone so that she could regard her smooth breasts gleaming with perspiration and the taut skin of her nervous stomach. Softly purring, with her index finger she slowly soothed herself into blissful unconsciousness.

During a week of morning shifts, whole long afternoons are free, and all this week the merciless afternoon sun beat down upon the closed green shutters. Madda couldn't endure her stuffy kitchen alcove one more minute. In that hole for pitiful, exploited servant girls of erstwhile nobles, whose hands we had to kiss – why didn't they liquidate the nobility long ago? I think the last revolution was just a feeble little tea party. Because they're all still here making serving wenches out of people. Which people let them do!

"Lately we've been going through an unusually large number of towels," the baroness assayed with arrogance. To wash off your filth! Madda looked furiously into the nervous eyes of Zita Gráfová. So here it is, a pitched battle.

"What's that got to do with me?" Madda snarled through clenched teeth, aiming the blow at the old woman's twitching face. "I neither have nor need your stupid towels!"

A clear K.O. She immediately apologized and asked if I'd like a snack, and so I had her make steak tartare – The old lady makes it out of real sirloin, no less, not grinding it in a machine, but honestly pounding it with a knife – "With lots of onions!" The old lady flew into the kitchen, clearly glad to have gotten off so easy. Better they make a scullery maid of Her Ladyship than a serving wench of me.

Hour after hour, the sun beat down upon the closed green shutters, it was stifling on the second floor. Madda relocated herself from the alcove to the bathroom, and the murmur of the shower was almost constant. It's best to fill the tub up to your neck and then to aim the shower head up toward the ceiling so a warm rain falls on you in the tub.

A diffident knock at the bathroom door. "Yes?!" Madda shouted. "Sorry…" someone quickly said, and another hour of silence like the grave. I simply adore bathing in the rain.

Madda had become fond of the long dark hallway with tall white doors, and wonderfully fresh from her overbathing, she paced back and forth through the hallway like a well-rested tigress in a cage, stretched and crept, skipped and practiced the Charleston, the Dutchman, the letkis, and the twist.

I see the Gráfs less and less often, and when I do it's always such a riot. "Excuse me, sorry…" Old Man Gráf snivels when I burst in on him in the crapper where he sits enthroned – that stupid ass apologized to me yet! – he immediately flushed and cleared out. It seems I frightened him so much he didn't even finish crapping. And another time, when I was practicing the twist outside his door, he came out and bleated, "Pardon–" and immediately crawled back into his room, even though he obviously wanted to come out! They've learned to get the hell out of the way when they see me, even from a distance.

During a week of afternoon shifts, only the mornings are free, and most of the time she sleeps away. Madda slept twelve hours a day and spent another hour lounging around in her cubbyhole. The Gráfs were out and the food divinely accessible.

Well rested and fed, she languidly crept through the quiet apartment in the heat and the green gloaming of the shuttered windows. Shadows from the sprawling philodendrons near the windows passed over her naked shoulders and breasts, Madda knelt, languorously rubbed her fingers in the damp, redolent soil, and rubbed her face against the damp tropical leaves.

Soft coughing behind a tall white door. Roman is home! Madda walked the length of hallway, without any haste put on her bikini, walked back down the hallway, flicked the branches of the ficus, and entered the white door.

"What are you doing, Roman…" He almost fell down beneath his table and quickly shoved a book into a drawer. Just as if he were in school! "Show me what you've got…" A book with dirty pictures, of course.

"You're home…" He stuttered.

"This week I work afternoons, you know."

"Oh yeah. I see."

So he wasn't exactly talkative, but he's got a nice little den here, sort of gentle and … What are those boxing gloves doing here?

"What are those boxing gloves doing here?"

"Nothing … Just … Mama once b-b-bought…"

God, he's actually stuttering! That blue-striped sailor's shirt really suits him. He has such soft, smooth skin. He blushed, oh-la-la!

"Come on, let's box!" I say to him.

"But I can't…"

"Afraid I'll beat you? You are, aren't you?"

"No, that's not it at all … But you can't expect me to fight a girl…"

"I'm three years older, aren't I? Come on, let's go, put 'em on already!"

He obeyed and we boxed. Lord, what a match! If he were smart, he would have given the gloves to me, because bare fists against boxing gloves will always win. And he was so afraid to punch me that he sort of stroked me instead of hitting me.

He got a little braver at the end, but was never the least bit dangerous. I liked just playing with him like that … until he punched me on my left breast, it wasn't a real punch, but women are sensitive there, so then I put him in this hold and there he was on his back.

"One–two–three–four–five–"

Roman Gráf lay on his back, and Madda counted slower and slower until she stopped. The game aroused her, and she softly purred, then suddenly bit him lightly on his chin, shoulders, and earlobes. Roman no longer struggled to free himself from her tightening grip, and with his arms, with their fragile wrists in the heavy shackles of the boxing gloves, he embraced the body towering above him.

I've never been given a virgin before   I've had to help myself   Don't worry, my white little boy   We'll just play together

I've waited for You an insanely long time   I've read about You and seen You in the movies   I've looked for You at the swimming area, in the crowd I find so appalling

You're strong and fearless   You'll lead me there   They'll take us together

The skin over your entire body is like the skin men have only behind their ears   And behind your ears there's a membrane   You're sweet and good enough to eat   And in a minute I'm going to eat you whole   You'll like it

I hated You to death   I was afraid of You   I knew that You would come   You are a catastrophe   We knew that You would come   For a thousand years   Now that you have finally come I'm calm   You had to come   I suspected it

I knew it   I know it

My young and gentle, blue, sugar-coated czarevitch   You may ascend the glass staircase   We will float together in the luxurious, warm, restorative sea   And you will lead me to your silver television land   Does it hurt too much?   You'll get used to it   It's already getting better   Now it's completely fine   Come on

It has to hurt   I read about it   I want it to hurt   I try to pinch Your arm Teach me   What marvelous teeth you have, Edith with the neck of a swan So you'll recognize me by my scar in the pile of corpses on the battlefield

Your flesh is like a chicken's   I adore white meat   You'll have to endure it   My poor young blue fawn lying on your side

I want your warm rain on my face

I want to be allowed to bleed to death for You   You put my boxing gloves on me   I shall never take them off now

An enormous knife glimmered in Jolana's hand, the edge continuously cutting into the board as she sliced bread, horse salami, bacon, onions, and peppers, everything cut into cubes. Then she wiped the sweat from her brow, sprinkled everything abundantly with salt, paprika, and pepper, and sank her bare arms (she was wearing just panties and bra) up to her elbows in the heap of food and molded it into ten-inch pyramids. She finally covered it all in peanut oil and served it on a board without utensils.

In worn boxer shorts, which had been once khaki-colored and had a slit in front that went up to his waist, his naked back to the cooling breeze from the window, Bogan Tušl greedily watched the food. "Remember when we discovered this dish?"

"I was still living with Jiřina Háková ... We made about a quarter of this."

"The more you eat the more you want..." Bogan grinned and took a long pull of beer from a two-liter can. The set of seven glass beer mugs, each with five golden bands, is under the bed, still wrapped from when we bought it, there isn't any room for them here, so we'll unwrap them when we move into our new apartment. Just like the set of three blue rugs for the bedroom (when we get one), the table made of stained oak for four, extendable to six, for the dining room – when we get one – and the blue baby crib with bars for the children's room WHEN WE HAVE THEM – meanwhile the rolled-up rugs and table top, along with the blue chandelier and the silver table lamp (all still wrapped up) in the crib, the table legs still wrapped in gray paper tied with twine, along with the five golden picture frames, beneath the crib, which has a still unused ironing board leaning against it (for now we iron on a blanket on the communal table), with golden curtain rods for our future windows, everything of ours is FOR NOW and NOT UNTIL, a tiny room reduced to the mobilization closeness of a wartime bivouac, and everything still wrapped up like explosives for destroying a besieged fortress.

"Ready!" Jolana finally called, and she blew her hair off her forehead. Bogan was already laying into the dish. "First wash your hands!" Jolana merrily shouted. Bogan turned the handle of the faucet above the sink on the wall: a few rusty drops, loud rattling, then nothing. In the silence from the Gráfs below they heard the sound of the shower, like silver flames.

"There are limits to everything," Jolana said, and she swallowed hard, "and they've..."

"To my lecture on the significance of the October Revolution," Bogan wheezed after stomping on the floor for an extended period of time and beating the pipe with his wrench, "I added a long part in which the muzhiks sat countesses on their bare asses on a burning hot stove. It wasn't in the lecture notes, but everybody loved it."

"Es kommt der Tag," Jolana said (she'd eagerly begun to study German, hoping to receive the language bonus of 80 crowns a month, but in the meantime they'd abolished the bonus), the day had come, and the couple laid into the dish.

"I didn't..." Jolana grunted when she couldn't eat any more and was now only picking out the bacon and salami cubes and pushing them to the edge of the board, "...make very much today..."

"It's just that it's so hot..." Bogan grunted as under the table he unfastened three cotton buttons sewn horizontally on the band of his underwear, and in one powerful gulp he drank the last of the beer.

After supper cognac on the veranda   Each with his own room   We'll gather in the dining room and then go our separate ways   Separate bedrooms   I wait with a cigarette by the window overlooking the garden to see if my lover is coming today   He who desires knocks at the door   We go our separate ways in the middle of the night   To come back together again the next evening   Eternal lovers protected by walls

Dusk came in through the open window, but the lowered temperature in the room was barely perceptible.

"There were so many things I wanted to do today..." Jolana whispered, "but not anymore..."

"Come on, let's go do something ... really nice together..."

"Really beautiful..."

"Now that we can do it without ... it's really wonderful. I'm only afraid that later we'll miss it..."

"Why couldn't we have another child..."

"That's hardly something we can decide right now. But ... Only in the last few weeks have I realized what making love could really be like."

"Without fear..."

"Only a few more weeks–"

Jolana quickly undressed and stood there naked. Bogan had barely managed to get up from his chair. "Let's never forget this..." he whispered tremulously, and he impatiently began caressing his wife's tumescent womb.

"What making love could really be like–" he groaned toward morning into her wild, delirious face. Her ravenous insatiability was finally allayed.

The following day, D day, an hour before H 06:00, the long-prepared general offensive was begun. Strategic targets: apartment and advancement. Tactical target: in order to increase pressure, Madda must leave the Gráfs'. Open fire on Gráf with all available weapons. Engage all reserves. Burn all bridges. Total warfare until the final victory.

5:52 ... "It's difficult for me to say this, Comrade," Bogan said to Comrade Abrt (a member of the Works Organization Committee of the Communist Party of Czechoslovakia), "but Comrade Gráf has morally failed us. Really, you still haven't heard? With Madda Serafinová ... Exactly, and at his age! People are judging him harshly."

5:54 ... "It's difficult for me to say this, Anička," Jolana said to Comrade Jelínková (an unusually efficient loudspeaker, whose effective range is the entire factory, is in the office with Comrades Bárta and Caha, the companion of Comrade Dolejší, all three members of the Works Organization Committee of the Communist Party of Czechoslovakia), "but these orgies at the Gráfs' ... You really haven't heard about them? Well, it's mainly Gráfová with Madda, while Gráf just watches, he needs to do that to get himself into condition, if you know what I mean ... You know, at his age..."

6:08 ... Taking full advantage of the planning department for the entire day, Bogan hung up the telephone and from a locked drawer took out a carefully hidden item disguised with the inscription DISCARDED DUPLI-CATE, along with a great deal of explosive material (the Company Board revises slightly – and highly secretively – the announcement of results attained in order to retain resources. Usually it's sufficient to transfer a couple of production percentage points to the following month, by a single day for example, nothing's actually lost, but it's all quite punishable), plugged in the electric adding machine, and at 9:42 had already thoroughly paraphrased the bombshell in six drafts, on the packages he wrote DISTRICT COMMITTEE, MUNICIPAL COMMITTEE OF THE COM-MUNIST PARTY OF CZECHOSLOVAKIA, both prosecutors' offices, and the National Bank, signature illegible.

6:37 ... By hinting at the backlog from the quarterly price restructuring, Jolana easily got her boss to give her a day off and from the anxiously hidden item disguised with the inscription SUBSIDIARY CALCULATIONS took out and on the typewriter made five copies of the explosive material processed earlier about a certain illegal price adjustment at the order of Comrade Dr. E. Gráf, the company director, on the packages the District and Regional Commissions of National Inquiry, the Ministry, and the Association, typed signature: Administrative Collective III.

10:44 ... The Chair of the Works Council of the Revolutionary Trade Union Movement, Comrade Schejbal, is informed that the collapsible kayak has still not been returned, 11 (!) months ago it was lent to Comrade Director Gráf. The objection that "the kayak was full of holes and immediately sank to the bottom" was categorically rejected, his knowledge of Comrade Schejbal's evening at Comrade Gráf's cottage on the river was tellingly hinted at, and the kayak was immediately requested for the Works

Organization ČSM (additionally, the support of the chair of the Works Organization ZO ČSM was obtained).

11:06 ... A question was raised in the auditing department concerning an invoice relating to the painting of the director's apartment, and it was indicated that the impulse for the investigation came from the "comrades of the City Council."

11:28 ... The transportation department was asked for information regarding Dr. Gráf's excursions in the company vehicle and was cautioned that "we're already looking into it."

11:53 ... The office messenger Comrade Alžběta Švarcová was interrogated about the method of payment for Mr. Gráf's coffee as well as compensation for 30 open-faced sandwiches and 2 bottles of white wine during the visit of the divisional delegation from Guinea, it was suggested she carefully note everything in writing, and this matter was offered in connection with her request for transfer to the packaging warehouse due to her short-windedness and the varicose veins in her right leg – Comrade A. Švarcová eagerly agreed.

12:11 ... A lively interest was aroused in the Chair of the Social Committee, Comrade Věra Netuková, regarding 6 missing packages that were to have been distributed at last year's children's holiday party, all the packages had been brought by Zita Gráfová in her private vehicle – V. Netuková enthusiastically promised direct and energetic intervention on location at Zita Gráfová's apartment.

12:12 ... 12:57 ... 13:08 ... 13:51 ... 14:03 ... 14:12 ... salvo after salvo till the sky turned black with smoke.

Zita Gráfová came out of building No. 2000 into beige clouds of dust, she was wearing a low-cut baby-blue dress of tussah silk with a white ribbon like a diamond in her gel-stiffened hair. Behind her, Roman Gráf in a shiny dark-gray suit of raw silk, like Prince Philip in a movie magazine, with one white handkerchief in his pocket and another in his hand, their white slippers and black patent-leather shoes took three fastidious little steps along the rough ground between building and street and then sank into the pillows of the car, Zita at the wheel and Roman beside her holding handkerchief to mouth, magisterially displeased, more like a pair of perverse lovers than mother and son – fragile iridescent birds ridiculously colorful in the beige dust, against a background of cracked facades, boarded-up windows, and wooden fences on OUR street – Bogan and Jolana are firmly holding sweaty hands. We are better. And stronger.

Bogan got up from the floor and raised his champagne glass (which he used as an acoustic amplifier, alternating with Jolana to listen in on the Gráfs' activities – surprisingly enough, Madda scarcely moves at all) as if to make a toast, "The first champagne in this glass will be to toast our new apartment!"

"In the meantime at least a down payment..." Jolana laughed, unwrapped an identical glass from tissue paper, and raised it. In the empty glasses the sun sparkled, and the couple drank the light.

"How do you dance with a glass in your hand..." Jolana wondered.

"Probably like this..."

"You know how to hold me so well..."

"I can't hold you any other way..."

"I'm so happy I have you..."

Bogan bowed, kissed his wife's hand, and felt Jolana's kiss on his neck.

Later in the evening Bogan scribbled on a piece of paper REVENGE FOR MADDA BEGINS — THE BLACK RIDERS, he wrapped the paper around a lump of glassmaker's slag, crept out in front of the house, threw the missive through a closed window on the second floor, a direct hit, the clatter of glass, Bogan hid behind a fire hydrant, where he smoked two cigarettes in peace then calmly took a circuitous route home, his bed still warm. An inquiring glance from a drowsy Jolana. "Fine and now go beddy-bye..." he whispered, and he pressed her warm cheek to the pillow with his. What else could those hooligans do to that old moneybags who smacked our girl?

In the cool of the electrical equipment warehouse, comfortably spread out on torn bales of insulation material, with imperceptible interest Alex Serafin listened to Bogan's question (regarding cables not corresponding to specifications and Gráf's implicated guilt) between two swigs from a chilled bottle, and he only half-heartedly promised to be a witness. "That's pretty weak," he sleepily responded. "Think of something better, Tušl." And Julda Serafin, calmly sweeping damp sawdust over the floor of the large firehouse, forthrightly refused to participate in anything against Dr. Gráf. "Your heart is full of hatred..." he said as if it pained him.

On the other hand, Borek Trojan enthusiastically joined the residents' petition for the "radical elimination of this swinishness." After two years in the itinerants quarters, he was beginning to get his bearings, perhaps too late, but nevertheless with vigor, which could in time become even dangerous. That night Bogan threw a dead rat through the still unrepaired second-floor window, with a Black Riders business card stuck through its rotting tail.

At exactly noon a white-hot Madda Serafinová drove through the courtyard on a red fuel-cell cart, and the men waved to her from the doors of the workshops –

"That T-shirt–" Jolana whispered, she was hiding behind the philodendron next to Bogan's office window.

"It suits her," Bogan whispered hoarsely.

"I know that T-shirt … Gráfová was wearing it on her trip to the Brno trade fair!"

"So you're saying that those two tramps…"

"That we didn't just make it up."

– Madda laughed, waved in all directions, and slowly drove through the courtyard like a countess in her carriage along the tree-lined avenue of an English park.

The Tušls slept during the evening, and just before midnight the alarm clock rang.

"Here," said Bogan, and he handed Jolana a half-meter-long glass pipe.

"What's this?"

"A blowgun. In New Guinea they still kill people with it. The ammunition's in the bag.

"And this … a bow?"

"Along with three metal arrows. And this catapult will come in handy."

"Isn't this a bit… primitive?"

"It is. But it's been proven by a few hundred years' use."

And with the catapult, blowgun, bow and arrows they crept out into the warm night.

WHAT IS RED

men, flesh, blood, conquerors, youth, hunger, the jungle, the interior, the ghetto, erections, rape, sadism, rivers, deserts, motors, east and south, curiosity, morning, fires, states of agitation (of cells, biological or fuel), barbarity, typhoons, revolutions, bread, wolves, settlements around castles, oil wells, war, excess pressure, salt, technology, machine guns, debt, spring and summer, ravines, the longing for freedom, grass, force, natives, aggression, gothic architecture, freshness, volcanoes, jazz, intuition, will, fanaticism, hatred, black, insults, anger, sex, longing, the beginning

On the highest shelf, lounging atop bales of insulation material, whose paper wrapping he'd torn open for the pleasure of exposing his naked skin to the soft, smooth cottony wadding, Alex Serafin looked out lazily from his basement electrical equipment warehouse through a narrow window at the level of the factory courtyard and rested his legs against the hot mass of heavy pipe along the ceiling. Through the window he saw only the feet and legs of people outside – the rest is merely appendix, right? – and he passionately loved the heat.

In the darkness below, by the door, a white coat appeared along with a shrill female voice that said: "Comrade Director is sending a car for you. You have to go immediately!

"But my little girl–"

"You have to go *immediately*. And stop that little girl business!"

"Excuse me, Comrade, I wouldn't dare be so bold, but I don't think I can climb down from here ... could you help me out a bit? If only you'd be so kind as to push that bale a bit to the side ... not that one, that one ... And now that one, too ... And then that one just a little ... And then..."

The young office worker climbed up the shelves as if up a ladder, all the way up to Alex, and assiduously toiled away until her glasses fogged over. Alex grabbed her around the shoulders and waist and pulled her into his warm berth. "What are you doing – Who do you think you are – How dare you – Ow! – Help!" Alex laughed into the girl's red, exasperated face, on which drops of sweat sprang up. He amused himself with her little body, which was more like a boy's than a woman's, and besides, nine a.m.'s too early for an orgasm – and when he'd had his fill of the little office mouse, he shoved her through the window into the courtyard, fastened the strap of his overalls, and with a snort climbed down from his shelf.

In front of a shard of mirror he slowly shaved with an Elektrostar razor, poured an entire bottle of delicate Barberina cologne (a freshly opened box of two hundred bottles, a gift from a colleague at Cosmopharma, lay on a lower shelf, beside a coil of hard-to-come-by bronze electrical outlets from a colleague at Armokov) on his face, shoulders, chest, and back, and delicately worked two layers of Barbus skin cream into his face, and with an ensemble of combs and brushes and a layer of brilliantine, created a shiny Hollywood hair-do, onto which he placed his hat, blackened by lime and tar.

In the courtyard Alex threw four bundles of electric cable into the back seat of the waiting car and drove off to May Day Street, where by order of the local authorities national enterprises Cottex, Cosmopharma, and Armokov were cooperating in the construction of a nursery. In the coolness of the building Alex drank beer from the bottle and lingered in heartfelt conversation with the men of Cottex, over whom he managed to exercise some control, and while walking across the site he proceeded to berate one after the other: the funder's representative, the nursery's designated directress, and representatives from various departments, boards, and administrations. And when a certain four-eyes with a prominent facial tick tried to bore him with some building designs, he peremptorily shoved the papers aside, kicked the idiot out with the threat "with such faggots we might as well shit on the whole thing!" and whistled to his apprentice. He tossed into the car two more lengths of cable, and took off with the apprentice to the Green Tree Tavern, whose owner wanted to increase his takings with a Bengal Night in the restaurant's garden.

The apprentice climbed like a chimpanzee along the tops of the chestnut trees stringing up the cable they'd brought with them. Over a cloudy bottle of Cinzano Bitter, Alex continued his heartfelt conversation with the owner, was handed three hundred crowns, and asked for fifty more.

"I hope they don't go on us, Mr. Serafin–" the apprentice whispered from the tree.

"What do you mean 'on us'? You mean 'on him', right? After all, it's his Bengal Night–" and Alex handed fifty crowns to the overjoyed apprentice and left Střekov wondering whether he should moonlight at the architect Švajn's (who for five crowns each wanted red lights installed at various heights above his couch, so that he could control them from a single place beneath the couch), or install a refrigerator in the dairy, or go sunbathing in the woods or swimming in the river. Steering with one finger, Alex sang and recklessly varied the car's speed, bounced up and down on the seat, and smacked his lips at himself in the mirror. The sun was shining and – what to do with the rest of this Thursday – at the intersection, stop:

West, gentlemen, Herren, Messieurs, in the direction of the city, and for nothing pick up one hundred crowns for my private moonlighting enterprise, tax free, risk free, and without the hysterical reliability of the rush-rush Occident's psychopharmacology?

East, comrades, tovarishchi, Genossen, in the direction of the plant, to lie around in the electrical equipment warehouse with a bottle of beer observing the accumulation of overtime in the soothing nirvana of the somnolent Orient?

South, monsignors, prophets, lamas, in the direction of the dead hills of earthworks and dumps, climb out of the vehicle, fall to your knees, and call upon Light, which has been here for eons, and then Darkness, deeper than before the first day of Creation?

Wherever you please –

In a surge of vital energy, Alex drummed away on the steering wheel of the company car until he convulsed in a spasm of laughter, he tore through the intersection and set out on a hunt – hunting is the primary and supreme faculty of the erect intelligent mammal – for Dr. Dáša Zíbrtová. Let the intelligent mammal hunt and suckle – other activities merely hinder and bore him tremendously. Driving past building No. 2000, Alex let go of the steering wheel and sprightly thumbed his nose at Teo's lime-covered window, what's up, you old paralytic!

Dáša Zíbrtová was pacing the examination room, she waved her hands above the blue flame of a gas burner in the antiseptic odor, and her voice trembled with rapture, "...your brother is simply an amazing, wonderful person ... You know, it's as if there was something radiating from him ... something like ... Those folks at the old rectory look up to him as to a saint ... And Julda is a saint ... If only you could have seen those children ... Something possessed me there ... something ... something like satori, you understand, like enlightenment, you know, I always wanted to be a neurosurgeon, I only took this job because it was pensionable, but at that moment ... but since that moment I've known that being a doctor is chiefly a mission ... to help people ... to serve..."

Dáša was practically choking on her two days of goodness, and Nurse Jandová was almost crying with emotion, when Alex sighed piously and shot a glance at the waiting-room couch: should I do her here or in her apartment?

"...so that everyone..." Dáša whispered, and the back of her white coat darkened with sweat, "one another and everyone together ... somehow ... with a pure heart..."

Et cetera, et cetera, she jabbered on and on and kept harping on those two biblical slogans she'd managed to pick up from Julda over the course of a single afternoon, a disheveled, wilting old woman with drooping breasts, a roll of fat below her belly, and an office-fattened ass, what could you possibly have to declare to mankind, you pathetic nonentity who, like an automatic washing machine, serial number NX-43826B, came off an assembly line for the manufacture of grave robbers, two hundred a year in this mini-country alone, you exemplary daughter of this fucked-up continent on which from sea to sea herds howl about civilization, democracy, and the general welfare of mankind, and continually deify their butchers (because the cattlemen candidates laughingly blink their eyes behind their dark glasses and express their views in books and bore you on television), inviting them to greater and greater defeats, and from the soil overmanured with their imbecilic flesh will grow the tubercular lily of European civilization, to be smashed and ripped out again and again by the wild boar of victorious barbarity, so often that it seemed the lily itself yearned for such an existence and its bulb (if lilies have bulbs) roared for coitus with the boar's snout. "How perfectly I understand you, dear Dášenka..." Alex sniffled, and he kissed the tips of her fingers, which were damp with excitement.

"How beautiful is the earth, and yet there are so many unhappy people on it..." Dáša grew impassioned (standing near an old oak tree on Střížovický Hill). "But the Lord wishes us all to be happy," Alex objected delicately, and he offered her his hand so she could descend from the pulpit-shaped rock.

"What a horrible thought that millions of children will never taste this fruit..." Dáša sighed (over Alex's Lufthansa bag full of enormous ripe peaches). "Go ahead and eat them, they're good, and tomorrow they'll begin to rot," said Alex with a smile, and with his fingers he wiped the sweet and sticky juice spurting from the corners of her mouth.

"So innocent and magical and gentle..." Dáša grew impassioned (on the sandy park path along which she was pulling a caravan of uniformed children from the nursery). "It is written: Be fruitful and multiply..." Alex pointed out with a poker face: "Oh, how I'd run home from work if you were there waiting for me like the Madonna with a child in your arms..." "I'd like two..."

"Living alone is probably a sin..." whispered Dáša (after her fourth glass of St. Raphael, sitting at a booth in the atmospheric wine bar Družba). "You've been given a great mission not only as a physician but also as a woman..." whispered Alex, kissing Dáša's wrist, and with a deftly placed finger he verified her quickened pulse. And a moment later he registered Dáša's first answer – a reply in kind, finger for finger.

A few lies, a few Brazil nuts, a few Negro rhythms from the primeval rain forests, and a little alcohol, a few caresses of the appropriate erogenous zones – scarcely a single daughter of Europe could resist – with ice princesses and *gymnasium* students you'd have to add a bit more drivel and hence 2-3 days of tedium:

"Do you believe in friendship between a man and a woman?"

"Of course, but isn't love more beautiful?"

"I yearn to simply hold hands like this and dream..."

"And not notice how the other suffers..."

"But that's exactly what true love is!"

"True love means giving!"

"It's those things everything always ends up at..."

"Everything on earth begins with those things..."

Et cetera, et cetera, and et cetera.

"I feel so tired ... So weak..." whispered Dáša, yielding more and more to Alex the more brutally he gripped her in his gorilla-like arms, "...and so happy..." Alex emitted a short laugh, threw her down on her back, and clung to the nape of her neck like a leech.

She was born from ignorance of birth control or to keep the partner, to get an apartment, or as a prosthesis for long-extinct connubial love here in the geographic center of Europe, so that she could live out her statistical mean of 71.4 years   That is, of course, if it is not decided to cleanse this corner with thermonuclear war

How I would like to climb to the top of a mountain with you   I can no longer bear seeing the abyss again   I've feared it all my life   Until I fall I will only look up

Into a metal shaker place the following ingredients in the following order: 2 cl of separated, pasteurized mother's milk with an antibiotic additive   2 cl of mustard gas   .1 cl of pulpy, ancient wine from the cellar of Emperor Diocletian   10 cl of fresh blood   1 white yolk of a standar-dized egg produced in the super-incubator of an industrially produced chicken that's seen neither grass nor sun   2 balls of pink urinal deodorant   5 cl of cognac, whisky, or vodka   On the tip of a knife Christ, Marx, J. P. Sartre, and James Bond   Add lots of ice and shake until well mixed, diluted, and chilled   Serve with a plastic straw in a slender glass garnished around the rim with dust from the desert of Vanitas vanitatum as the European Cocktail for half a billion people

First I didn't want to, then I did   Or was it first I wanted to, then didn't?   They released us from school empty-headed   To be always afraid makes one neurotic   Why doesn't someone lead us

I want to believe   Whether it's one thing or another   But when I don't know

Everything is incredibly complicated   I want to give

But I take, since it's as simple as a slap on the face   So give, give already   More   More   And much much more

I want to be good and to do good things

But this makes me feel good, too   Just keep doing that good deed to me   Just a little lower   Abase yourself if it makes you feel good   And I will gladly defile you

I want to be cleansed

That's what bathrooms are for   They didn't have them in Palestine

I want to live far away from here   Where there is safety and there won't be any wars   A student song on the white beaches of the Pacific Ocean

We took them over long ago   "In the ten days following the release of the album containing the Rolling Stones' latest hit, 600,000 of them were sold. The song is called 'Their Satanic Majesties' Request'"

Dressed in the better of his two nylon shirts (twice specially washed in a bath of laundry detergent and soap flakes, with a dash of an expensive concentrate of a Swiss optically-activated cleaning preparation – made from laboratory chemicals – and finally rinsed for an hour under running water), a recently purchased, luxurious, forty-crown silver-gray tie, a suit same-day dry-cleaned, and shoes left overnight under his cot with six coats of polish liberally applied, more finish than actual leather, and the shine lasted for maybe an hour, a thoroughgoing man of society, except that the safety pin holding up his underwear with the elastic long ago worn out was poking him in the side a bit, but if it comes to disrobing, everything will come off together, besides it'll be dark in the forest pit by then.

On the terrace of the Větruše restaurant Borek pulled out his cuff with its black-and-silver cufflink (70 crowns), took a sip of white wine from his glass, which he held with an ostentatiously extended pinky, and cheerfully smiled at the person across from him: Yveta (daughter of the director of the Meat Association and member of the local government) is a society girl out of a magazine of a *dream*, the first one I really want to have. My blue antelope.

"...the Alps best. But the most beautiful days were in Avignon, enchanting afternoons in old fortresses ... and then of course Paris. Papa knows this Malaysian restaurant near the Odeon, never in my life have I eaten such fabulous prawns..." Yveta prattled on and on, and from the great aquamarine of her ring (worth three months of Borek's pay) a beam shot out a bright blue arrow.

"... I on the other hand prefer the white wine *Blanc de Blanc*, you know, the one with the *golden foil. Last year in Monte Carlo we drank it on the terrace of that famous café in Cap d'Antibes,*" said Borek as he stood at home in front of the shaving mirror, he spoke in a soft, carefully studied voice meant to sound tender and somewhat weary. *"That was where Sam Spiegel was anchored, you know, the producer of* The African Queen. *And right next to him that old creole Niarchose, he's sixty-five years old by now. And in Greece he has his own private island called Spetsopoula..."*

"I read that somewhere too, wasn't it in *Life* last year? I don't know Monaco, that trip we only went to Menton and Cap d'Antibes."

"I couldn't exist without the sea..." mumbled Borek, and he made a firm resolution to see it the year after next, even if it meant not eating for a whole year – God, a wagon carrying industrial fructose just arrived at the factory, just recrystallize it a couple times and you've got supper for free, it's got enough calories, and you can steal a few turnips or radishes ...

"You don't speak French, do you?"

"Studying the language of a puny country is a waste of time."

"God, you engineers are a bunch of barbarians. You could use a bit more education."

"I know technology, and that's the only kind of education worth anything anymore.

"But education is something totally different, it's culture and music and … Do you play anything? Like the piano? …"

I don't know how I'd squeeze a piano in among five beds in the itinerants quarters. "I used to play, but I stopped … Do you play?"

"I love to play! You don't know what you're missing…"

"French and the piano … Every butcher's daughter used to have to know both of those if she wanted to get married. The main thing of course was the butchery."

"Why do you go off at me when all I'm trying to do is explain … that you don't say 'Niarchose,' for example."

"What do you say?"

"Niarcha. And you also pronounce Antibes wrong."

"Is that important?"

"No, it's not … but some things you'll never understand. After all, what is really important in life?"

"One thing."

"Technology?"

"That too, very important. But most important is something else…"

"?"

"Hunger. But you'll never understand that. Have you ever been hungry in your life?"

"Hungry? … Wait, let me think … I don't think so … No, wait! Once when I was little … We were having veal cutlets for lunch, which I loathe to death, and so I refused to eat and ran upstairs to my room. And when I came down for supper I was really, really starving!"

"Even for the veal?"

"They made me a steak, so I wouldn't get upset. After all, my parents aren't sadists."

"Not to their family members. Care to dance?"

(Dancing: the woman allows herself to be led, subordinates herself, and gratefully embraces her abductor.)

"Not so far away…" On the dance floor Yveta laughed.

"I love you."

"Oh."

"And I really need you. And want you."

"The latter is very … obvious."

"Why should I hide it?"

"My little barbarian ... Are you trying to squeeze your cufflinks between my vertebrae?"

"I can't think of a snappy comeback just now."

"But love should be merry, yes?"

"I'm focused on its core rather than its covering."

"You're a surly, enraged, starving animal."

"That's why you like dancing with me."

"Of course ... It amuses me."

"To see me suffering–"

"Indeed."

"How I writhe before you–"

"You mean when you dance? Indeed."

"We don't just have to dance all the time, you know."

"You want to go for a little walk?"

"I was just going to suggest that."

Beyond the asphalt roadway, the dark forest roared. And in the forest the warm pit for the body of the blue antelope. Just past the first trees, Yveta came to a sudden halt. She quickly allowed herself to be embraced and kissed. Frail and gentle ...

"My blue princess..."

"My beast with red eyes ... And red ears."

"Let's go a little further ... I'll show you this marvelous view..."

"It's not proper for butchers' daughters to go into the forest at night ... with savage men with improprietous intentions."

"Do you really get so much pleasure from making fun of me?"

"Maybe ... actually, yes ... It gives me a little *frisson* ... I like you better here than at the table..."

"The princess leaves the castle by the servants' entrance and beyond the wall gives herself to the slave."

"She doesn't give herself to him. Just dallies with him."

"You're a monster."

"You're the monster. Don't you understand that love is the best game of all? Do we have to be like the baker and his wife on the stove? If you profess your love for technology so much ... you must know what necking is, for example?"

"Teach me."

"Read the Kinsey Report."

"It's too dark for reading. It's too dark here for your..."

"Necking is when ... Here, I'll put it in your language: You can do whatever you want above the waist, but below, nothing. Kinsey of course formulates it somewhat more elegantly."

"You mean like this?"

"You're quick. But Kinsey hints at other possibilities."

"This too?"

"I don't have my copy at hand, but I think that as well."

"And this…"

"Kinsey would be proud of you."

"And this–"

"Yes. Yes … … … … … … … Let go. Not that. That's what Kinsey calls 'petting.'"

"I've had enough of Kinsey!"

"Well, I haven't. You're spoiling the game. No. No! Enough. Let go of me."

"No."

"Borek – Engineer Trojan!"

"I'm not letting you go yet. Now I'm going to be the teacher."

"Wasn't it nicer a minute ago? The game…"

"In a minute it'll be even nicer. Damn it, just come with me a little bit further!"

"Do I detect a new tone?"

"You'll detect a whole keyboard in a minute!"

"Okay. I suspected as much … *bon*. Let me at least go behind that tree–"

"You're not getting away from me now."

"Look, I really have to go!"

"I'll go with you."

"You idiot. What do you guys say in the factory – I have to drain the lizard?"

"Oh … I'm sorry, I'm … Go ahead, I'll turn around."

Borek pressed his forehead against the trunk of a tree, behind him he heard light steps, grass rustling, and then loud steps on the asphalt. He spun around: Yveta's dress flashed in front of the dark facade of the restaurant and darkened in the lit entrance.

Inside, at the table, sitting over the remainder of the wine, only Borek spoke. Yveta wasn't answering, she just stared at her tiny golden watch, tapping its thick convex crystal with a polished nail.

"Taxi's here, miss," said the waiter.

"Give me a fifty," Yveta said to Borek. "I didn't bring any money." And as she stood up: "I'll return it to you by mail. Goodbye." She disappeared.

Fifty crowns plus a hundred and forty for dinner and wine – looks like I start the fructose tomorrow. Don't go skating on thin ice … By foot and as slowly as possible, Borek set out on yet another night retreat, from anxiety, from fear of himself alone among five empty cots.

And once again, like the wild dingo, he goes back through the burning, overcrowded, afternoon city streets, through the evening and the night, with his soaking shirt stuck to his hot body with stinging sweat, his underwear, held up by only a safety pin, slipping down his damp sides, the pin chafes his skin and draws blood, and the socks, worn out since last year, flow around his feet rather than clothing them inside the single pair of shoes he owns, which had cost a third of his monthly pay, which itself barely suffices for subsistence – am I to be forever starving, thirsting, unsated?!

Five fat pigs get out of a big limousine and charge into the Palace Restaurant. On the menu in the window: Palace Surprise 12.40 crowns. Calf's liver with pineapple 17.20 crowns. Chateaubriand for two 33.80 crowns. There's somebody just like me, a twenty-five-year-old wearing a long, silver-gray, silk Parisian-cut jacket opening the door of a low white convertible for a beautiful blonde wearing a blue minidress. The young woman ostentatiously kisses a young man in a white suit leaning back against a wall and looking indifferently into the faces of passersby. A guy driving his girlfriend around. They go into the house. The girl at the window. Two little girls. The girl alone. One more. Another. And another.

In the display window of Primo, "exclusive accessories for men," a white shirt made of Dutch nylon, which costs a laughable 150 crowns, is still screaming out. "You should have at least two of those," Yveta concluded on our first walk, thank you for pointing that out, Mademoiselle Goat de Frigidbourg, I have two white shirts *altogether*, I'd have a few more but they cost money. Funny, isn't it.

At least sell those provocative rags somewhere in the back, you whores, in the basement or passageway like they used to sell alcohol in the U. S. and now marijuana and LSD, since that fucks you up just looking at it, as does for instance a villa with too many rooms or an excessively beautiful car, we still don't have these things, get it? But we still live among them, and so we yearn to come in contact with them, and so of course it's true that more and more often it happens that people start smashing windows that are too high or overturning cars that're too nice and then lighting them on fire, and it's not even all that uncommon for an upstanding citizen to get his face bashed in –

Car after car emerges from the blue twilight and joins the long chain of cars in front of the House of Culture. Headlights go out, doors slam: A princess in a long white dress with gloves to the elbow. A princess in a radiant orange dress with a white diadem. Two princesses all in silver. Twenty-nine princesses. Little princes in black with bow ties close the doors

– how can a bitch younger than me own a car worth four times my annual salary?! – The procession walks through the glass foyer and, between two white statues, ascends the marble staircase.

Out from behind the statue on the left runs a bespectacled moron with a shiny black collar and bow tie. How could he tell I didn't belong here?

"Invitation only, please. This is a private party for our school."

"But I..."

"You couldn't go in like that anyway ... Good evening, Comrade Professor, good evening, Madame. Allow me..." And the little prince ascended the staircase arm in arm with a princess in golden slippers.

Out from behind the statue on the right runs an identical bespectacled moron with a shiny collar, but this time around his neck he had a four-in-hand.

"Invitation only, please. This is a private–"

"I know, but I'm a special case."

"You couldn't go in like that anyway..."

"I have an important message for the organizer. But I'd rather not–" Borek shoved the little prince back behind his statue and went back down the staircase, around the corner, and down the corridor to the little green doors of the distribution center, I was here on a work brigade once and toiled away my whole vacation for four crowns an hour, this is *My Avignon, Menton, and Cap d'Antibes* –

"Then perhaps you could..." The young man's pink face was smooth and fresh as a refined little girl's, as Yveta's, and smelled of expensive cologne rather than salicylic acid –

"I'm going–" Borek stomped on the toe of the young man's shoe and, as the prince bent over in pain, he drove his knee sharply into his belly, twice and then once again, that's for recognizing I didn't belong here.

He stepped over the writhing body and took a detour through the café on the second floor and into the gallery above the Great Hall. Even before the couples downstairs had stepped forward for the first dance, it was painfully obvious to Borek that he couldn't go down there among those people. Even with an invitation pasted to his forehead he would have stood out like a coyote in a space suit. The hall resounded with a waltz, which I love above all other rhythms, and the couples set off, separated, alternated, and again found each other with the precision of porcelain dancers behind the glass of a rococo musical clock.

Coarse shouting and rude laughter came from behind the door to my room – inside four strange men were on my cots.

"Get lost–" thundered an enormous red square sitting on my bed with his column-like legs pressing down on the lid of my suitcase.

"What do you want?" asked a powerful, bronze, gray-haired man recalling a photo of a Congolese mercenary colonel.

"I live here."

"Really? By yourself?" squeaked a fat white ball who reluctantly stopped digging through my closet.

The fourth, a beautiful pale youth who was leafing through my magazine, gave me a hostile glance and then went back to perusing my pictures.

Itinerant workers had arrived. Borek quickly lost his cot (taken by the head of the group, Olda, the mercenary colonel), his forty-crown silver tie (swiped by the squeaking white ball, Valtr), his physical safety (after three beers, Dízlák, the red square, started fighting, and he drank ten beers a day, up to thirty in sunny weather, and this year summer's been marvelous), and his nocturnal peace (the beautiful, pale youth suffered from a strange disease, and his attacks shattered the night into frantic shards). The men lived their own lives.

For a while Borek stood in the afternoon heat in front of the door to his room, from inside he could hear harsh singing and suddenly a metal crash – probably the tin wardrobe thrown against the metal bed, or perhaps the other way 'round – Borek cursed the world from the day he was born, emphasizing this painful event, and disappeared down into the basement – in the darkness something flashed white on the coal stove, a naked female figure and Madda's cruel glance, Roman Gráf on his knees before her, his childishly angular butt swaying, so that little shit finally got the whore, I begrudge you her and even more the room you have to yourself –

Languidly, Borek left, and dropped down on the steps in front of the building, he took his burning shoes off and drove his bare feet into a drift of hot beige dust.

Footsteps came from behind him, at eye-level an exquisitely turned-out pair of pale, female knees and a waft of fresh fragrance.

"You look as if you were at the beach," said Mrs. Zita Gráfová somewhere high above him.

"Like at Menton or Cap d'Antibes..."

Madame Zita laughed, corrected Borek's faulty pronunciation of Antibes, and with a smile said: "It seems pretty lively down in your room now."

She stepped over Borek's legs and in a cloudlet of fresh fragrance – 1 ml of magnificent perfume and 300 ml of cool water, most of all I'm THIRSTY – she lowered herself onto the cushion of her car, started it up (so now Monsieur Roman de Gráf can get up from the stove and continue his petting in the three empty rooms on the second floor), and sped away, and to top off this delightful encounter, Madame de Gráfová spewed a cloud of exhaust fumes into Borek's face – there are moments when a man realizes he could kill even a woman.

I'M THIRSTY, perhaps I could at least go home and get a drink of water from the faucet – Borek deftly slipped on his shoes, crossed himself in front of his door, took a deep breath, and burst into his room.

With great delight, the red square, Dízlák (a quick guess: twenty beers), rushed at him with a chair leg in his hand and boing! boing! Borek was much lighter but also more nimble, and hop! hop! over the cot, and just as Dízlák, braying with excitement, was slowly turning around, whack! whack! into his side and then his shin.

"That a way, boys!" squeaked the tie thief, Valtr, as he rolled his round white paunch on Borek's cot (as a rule he always lay on someone's else's cot so he wouldn't have to make his own) and leaned his fat face on his chubby little hand as if he were in a box at the Colosseum.

In a cloud of golden dust, completely naked and beautiful, like an ancient little god, the boss, Olda, slowly smoked a perfumed cigarette and with a lightly amused expression observed the contest through blue cloudlets of smoke. "Stop!" he ordered the pale youth, Stěpa, who, with a cunning smile, was about to help the not especially successful Dízlák in his fight with Borek.

The contest ended in a draw, "…'cause it's too fuckin' hot," wheezed Dízlák as he sat down and with a snort touched the kidney that Borek had kicked.

Borek spat blood onto the floor and with his head held high walked over to the sink on the wall, he opened the faucet all the way and stuck his entire head into the briskly spurting cone of water. I declare the spring conquered.

"You wouldn't be guzzling water, would you?" Valtr said with disgust.

"Go get beer–" snorted Dízlák.

"Everyone cough up four crowns," Olda decided, "and you'll drink with us. What do they call you?"

"Borek Trojan. Borek–"

"I'm Olda, this is Dízlák, Valtr, Stěpa. Jug!"

"Jug" referred to the twenty-liter tin can they used to carry back beer from the Corner Pub. They were already putting down their four crowns apiece.

"I'll buy–" said Borek.

"Great!" snorted Valtr, and he took someone's five-crown piece from the table.

"Bullshit, we know you don't make shit," said Dízlák.

"Well, if he really wants to–" Valtr protested.

"We invited him," Olda concluded, and he lit another golden-tipped cigarette on the burning butt of the previous one.

And so Borek took the can and went to get the money on the table.

"We can't send an engineer for beer–" said Dízlák.

"The youngest goes," said Olda. "Stěpa."

"If the engineer wants to..." Stěpa grinned.

"Nonsense. Get up," said Olda. The pale Stěpa turned red, grabbed the can from Borek, and disappeared.

Liter after liter of cold beer passed from mouth to mouth – Borek quickly learned to drink it. The men lived their own lives. At Cottex they were welding the iron structure of the new storage shed, and the rhythm of each day's work was entirely up to them, on Friday they finished at nine in the evening and then didn't even get up on Saturday. From the tavern, the cinema, or a dance, they came home to the itinerants quarters as if it were another bar without a closing time. They either worked, slept, or lived it up – there was no fourth activity, but they drained these three to the dregs and then started breaking things. In the pockets of their rarely removed overalls were rolls of bills, and in a week we get paid again, strong as horses, but smart and wild, free from all familial (the 500-km trip home they undertook but once a month, and not every month), official (they were subordinate to a different, distant, powerful company called Hydrokov), local ("When we polish off the work here in Ústí, we'll go to Pardubice, then Brno and Košice, we'll never come back to this shithole!"), temporal ("It'll get done when it gets done!"), subsistent ("Hey boys, should we renew our contract with Hydrokov or move on to Průmkov? Stavkov is begging us again, too"), emotional ("Go fuck yourself!"), and other ties, an entirely casual disposition towards themselves and their strengths, the last *condottieri* of this dull century and continent, as free as one can imagine.

The brutal July sun beat against the window, the burning air quivered above the tin sill, and through the window came a beige cloud of dust whipped up by heavy trucks, along with the sweetish odor of tar from melting roofs.

Olda finished writing a letter to his beautiful young wife (he had several of them), wet his hair, sat down on his cot with the golden tip of another perfumed cigarette between his teeth, and stretching out, with his hands behind his head, he blew cloudlets of blue smoke up toward the ceiling. Valtr was removing the wrapping of the new brass lighter he'd acquired that night at the bus station, and out of boredom Dízlák was bending the metal tubing of the cots. On the table was a second "jug," still full, we've already had our fill, the day's work is done but it's still too early to go to bed, ghastly boredom in this shithole where nothing's going on, let something happen, what are we, prisoners sitting around on our cots all day? Throw something our way, let something happen, AND QUICK, or we'll throw each other around and someone'll get hurt, we don't have a piano or a yacht, or even a stupid television set or a bathroom like you do, so at least give us something from all that you've had for a thousand years, and that your little bastards will have for another thousand years, let something happen, TO US – here and now!

"A girl–" Stěpa gasped from in front of the window, and the nape of his white neck quickly turned blood-red. "Where–" shouted Borek, and he was already racing toward the window, Valtr and Dízlák looked up, and Olda intensely smoked on. Like two white moths there in the heat of the burning desert was Madda tottering along in a white minidress with Mr. Roman Gráf beside her, wearing white silk, arm in arm like a viscount with his comtesse strolling through their orangerie.

In profile Stěpa's quickly whitening face looked cruel, he glanced at Borek and they came to a decision, their mutual grudges forgotten, at least for the duration of this campaign, which was already underway.

"Madda..." Borek called from the window, "could you come here for a second–"

"We've run out of matches–" Stěpa called.

"Go buy some!" Madda yelled back.

"Come on, at least give us a light ... please..." Borek pleaded.

"Don't be a swine–" Stěpa shouted to the entire street. "Mr. Gráf, talk to her–"

"They're capable of going on like this all afternoon," Madda said to Roman, annoyed as on her fantastically high white heels she nobly swayed her way over to the window.

Stěpa (a nonsmoker) quickly took a cigarette from Olda, firmly closed his lips around the rigid tip, and stood in the window.

"Well, at least bend down here, you nitwit," Madda said as with proprietary nonchalance she pulled from Roman's pocket his engraved silver lighter.

"You're not even going to let me hold the stupid thing?" said Stěpa, now completely white and slowly leaning out toward Madda.

"I don't think so. Inhale, you nitwit, it's not going to burn by itself. What the, Ow! Let go!–"

Naturally, Stěpa did not let go, but rather the opposite (with his other hand, and then with the four hands of the other two vigorous young men, and despite her resistance), he quickly pulled her into our room. Roman Gráf offered only a feeble, cursory defense, took a couple of random blows to the face himself, including one to the chin, and lay down in the beige dust beneath the window – the window slammed shut. Dízlák let go of his metal tubing, Olda tossed away his unfinished cigarette, and Valtr eagerly threw himself on his new engraved silver lighter. Who wouldn't have shouted at a time like this? So all of us started shouting.

Suddenly a light tapping came from the ceiling, a weak thin chirping against the massive roar going on in here, but surprisingly everyone was listening to it ... And Borek started jabbing at the ceiling with a broom. Olda started throwing at the ceiling, one after another, both of our plastic plates, when they fell he picked them up and hurled them again, like discuses; the bed-piping virtuoso, Dízlák, joined in on the plaster of the ceiling until it started cracking, and it began to snow in the itinerants quarters. The indignant, concentrated counteroffensive from below lasted much longer than the brief, cheeky assault from above and came to an end when Madda resisted.

Stěpa ripped the covers off two of the cots, deftly nailed them to the upper frame of the window, and the blood once again returned to his skin. In the darkness Olda was no longer smoking ... And even Valtr had forgotten about his newest lighter.

This is ours   Meat and games   You say that at this very moment someone somewhere is playing Mozart and Mahler   That the spirit of Lincoln and Comenius and Gandhi and all sorts of spirits are alive   Well then, you go talk to them, since that's what you've been taught   No one has taught us that language   Those gentlemen do not amuse us Nevertheless, we shall win   That's why we'll win   So go on

Let me go   You're dirty, hairy, you stink, you're repulsive. I don't want to

We're just like you   So let's go   Stop jabbering   You're starting to like it, aren't you   You see   So stop jabbering

What a fuss the poor girl makes when the right fellow takes her properly into his hands   The devil take it   That's it   So give up and come to daddy

So give up and come to daddy

We'll take what we want   We'll be victorious

(To be continued)

BESIEGED

"Yes, dear," said Zita Gráfová.

"But you're not listening to me at all," said Evžen Gráf, with soft reproach.

"No, dear."

"Is something wrong? Do you have a headache?"

"Yes, dear. No, dear."

"Why don't you want to tell me?"

"I've told you everything you've asked about: something's wrong, I don't have a headache."

"What's wrong?"

"Absolutely nothing."

"I can't say you've put me completely at ease…"

"But you're the one who wanted to put *me* at ease … oh, forgive me."

"No, you forgive me."

"How does that song go? Let's forgive each other for what we did. What we did? Nothing's what we did…" Zita sang, and in the stuffy darkness of the shuttered room she waved her hands languidly in time to the beat.

"Dear, just so I don't forget: I put in the sideboard–"

"If–you–tell–me–today–for–the–eighth–time–that–you–put–a–new–tube–of–Librium–in–the–sideboard–"

"Oh, forgive me, have I really already…"

"Seven times today. Do you know that joke about Meprobamate?"

"Librium is better."

"Doctor, will Librium really keep me from wetting the bed at night? No, but you won't care about it anymore."

"Ha ha." Evžen's was a sad laugh, and Zita got up from her armchair. "Are you going to take another bath?" asked Evžen. "No, I'm going to hang myself," said Zita. "Ha ha." Evžen's was a sad laugh, and Zita went to take a bath. As she was closing the door she looked back: huddled up in his armchair with his hands joined across his belly – seen from behind, where I can see only his head and elbows protruding, Evžen looks like a venerable English lady in her chair crocheting a blanket. Do ladies crochet blankets? But Evžen even looks like that from the front … Why do I torment him so? And why doesn't he torment me?

It's too hot this afternoon. Too hot this whole summer. It seems to keep getting warmer … We both prefer winter. That first time in the Alps …

"The snow is rather violet..." lively, merry, happy. How he laughed ... then. Then and only then were we the same age. Both young. The snow was actually blue.

Okay, another bath. My hair's still wet from the last one. My hair's all curls ... like a terrier's. Or a poodle's? An airedale's. What does an airedale look like? Like Evžen. So then: a lady or a dog? He's noble: like a lady. He adores me – like a dog.

"Ruff! Ruff!" Zita barked as she shuffled listlessly down the long corridor past the tall white doors. Where's Roman again? Gone. He's right to. Should I have something to eat? I'm not hungry. *Cela ne fait rien*: it doesn't matter, it doesn't mean a thing. When you've already taken a bath and are going to take another ... On her way to the bathroom, without the slightest enjoyment, she ate a thin slice of cold ham, in the bathroom, without any feeling at all, she took off her clothes and impatiently turned the faucet on full.

With indefatigable care, Evžen had installed a bookshelf above the tub. We both read in the bath: two venerable English ladies.

"...it was as if fragments of music were flickering through Hummel's strained face. Caldwell perceived his old friend through a tissue of worn-out joints, worn threads, dreary carbon-coated metal: What is this, are we disintegrating?" It seems like we are to me, Mister Updike. You've written a scrupulously beautiful book about how you loved your father. I loved mine, too. Both of them died. Mine, twelve years ago. Your book ends with that. Then what?

Boom. Boom. Boom. Boom. That's from downstairs, from the itinerants quarters. Boom. Boom. Boom. Boom. Boom. That guy lives down there ... Borek Trojan. Alone ... Boom. A young man with a blazing body. Why does he look so much like the St. Sebastian at St. Petr's? ...

Doop. Doop. Doopity doopity doop. That's from above, from the Serafins'. Julda wouldn't stomp like that. It's probably Madda ... There's something in that girl's eyes that ... something. Doop. Doop. Doop. Doop. That's Alex: the sardonic gorilla from a primeval rain forest the sun never penetrates. When he was installing our television antenna, he practically tried to rape me. Evžen arrived just in time. Ruff! Ruff! Yes, dear.

BANG! BANG! BANG! BANG! Upstairs again, this time from the Tušls'. A regular orchestra. BANG! BANG! That young Tušlová is expecting a baby. When I was expecting Roman I was in a spacious, quiet country house ... BANG! They took him from me right after I gave birth. Evžen wasn't there. I was deprived of so much ... BANG! *To give birth in a corner on a pile of rags with your husband and your flock of children In a little, single-story earthen house Among a thousand other lookalike hovels in a ghetto where everyone lives together in a single room and only human things, the most human, live magnificently* BANG! BANG! *far away from our port, where we just sit there drunk waiting for a boat that has long ago departed* BANG! BANG! BANG! BANG! *in a ghetto where people live out plots –*

Ridiculously overbathed, Zita Gráfová walked out into the street and was immediately seized by the heat, flames shot up from the beige desert dust, and her clothes blazed up. Go deeper, ye flames, and burn the carbon coating off my dreary metal –

"Hold me tight..." Zita pleaded in Evžen's embrace. When Evžen squeezes me hard as he can, it's just a comforting caress. He's good ... he's tender ... On Saturday we're going out to our house on the river. On Saturday it always rains. We walk through the wet grass along the river. Silver circles on dark water. A metal lantern above the entrance. The calming aroma of drying clothes. The window on the veranda misted over. Slow, quiet music. Evžen walks by quietly in his velvet slippers. I love the leather armchair we inherited from Father. And a glass of cognac. The cool glass between my fingers. A tender, pleasurable warmth sets in. Raindrops softly flow down the picture window.

That awful scene on the stairs! ... The Serafins, the Tušls, and Borek Trojan ... stood in front of me practically naked and shouted their hatred right in my face. And their blood ... Madda, a girl from the ghetto, came into our port.

Agitated, thankful, and happy, I bathed Madda in the bathtub like my own daughter. No. Like a companion. A sister. A happier sister. Beneath her long, beautiful eyelashes she has radiant eyes, and on her neck warm, svelte muscles. I couldn't keep myself from kissing the bloody slash on her shoulder. Her humiliated and disgraced majesty. Humiliated? Really? I had a maid once. I envied her when ... Or Žofka when she was nursing Roman ... oh, how I envied her! I've envied all of them. My entire life.

Madda, a girl from the ghetto, burst into our port. Magnificently ravenous. As if only with her arrival did my kitchen acquire a true meaning. But so ravenous it became frightening. *Sunt certi denique fines* ... Voracious. Greedy. Insatiable. It wasn't simply hunger that compelled her to smoke our by no means inexpensive Dutch cigarettes, drink our Courvoisier, my white Cinzano, and even Evžen's beloved purple *Parfait Amour* ...

Madda is aggressive. And decidedly audacious: when I'm not around she tries on my clothes, even my underwear ... Once I caught her counting our plates ... Always on the offensive: she pushes us, occupies us, plunders us. We tolerate it all the time. We only know how to retreat. We're altruists – indifferent to ourselves. It's absurd to do good: I gave Madda one of my

T-shirts, it was practically new, I'd only worn it once – Madda grabbed it out of my hand and instead of thanking me, her head swelled. That night her friends, the "Black Riders," smashed a window in the dining room.

She has Roman completely under her thumb. She simply plucked him. My poor boy ... Werther in Levis. Gentle, sensitive, intelligent, passive, basically unathletic – like me. It was a waste to buy him those boxing gloves. He hung them above his bed to make me happy. He's never put them on. He must hate them.

He hates violence just like me ... but at the same time finds it oddly attractive – like me? Like me, he submits to it. Like all of us here and in all the blue ports submit to the red people of the ghetto. There are more of them. Infinitely more. Catastrophe is imminent. Our catastrophe. Their victory. Our extinction.

My poor little son ... He hides his anxiety beneath our traditional mask: he pretends to be disgusted, haughty, ironic, cold ... The way I hide it? I silence it. At least for the moment –

"Yes, dear." "No, of course not." Evžen's looking into my eyes, full of fear: he knows I'll drink myself silly as soon as he leaves. Well, I will drink myself silly. "Yes, dear."

Zita stood by the window, and her eyes shone. Down on the street, the chauffeur was opening the door to the black company limousine, Evžen wearily sank down into the back seat, the chauffeur closed the door, walked around the car, got in, and quietly drove off. The husband is off on a business trip, and what about you, young lady?

Zita stood by the window, and her eyes shone. This moment is always the best. Then she carefully pulled down all the shutters, took off her shoes, and walked barefoot through the apartment several times, waving her hands until she felt a bit tired. She came into the bedroom with a bottle of Ronda in each hand and a crystal gin glass between her teeth. With her fingernail she peeled the covering off the stopper. Ow! The nail broke. In a minute nothing will hurt anymore.

Ronda is a white Cuban rum made from sugar cane. "7 Años" – seven-year. "La Habana, Cuba" – genuine. The proper drink for the spouse of the port's governor. "Grados 44 a 15 T." Then a clever sailor's trick – this sissy crystal glass doesn't go. Zita got up from the rumpled bed and went to get a crude green mustard glass. With her teeth she pulled out the orange, fluted stopper – a girl biting into an orange – and to the murmuring of the bubbles in the neck – the clinking of the anchor chain – poured her first glass up to the rim. No need to hurry. Nor economize. "750 gramos." Times two is 1,500 gramos, enough fuel to get to hell.

We know how to drink, us port people, our glass is our amigo, ami, lieb Freund, over the rim of our glass we look out from the shade of our white loggia

onto the square and the market of our workaday world   Behind us deathly silence   At our feet din and clamor   People below are fighting   For now they're fighting among themselves   They're looking up here   The mother ship on the blue sea   Danger doesn't threaten us from the cool sea   It comes from the hot interior   They're looking at us   Dressed in rags   Girls in black dresses frayed at the bottom   Men in worn coats spread over sweaty naked bodies

Naked children with swarms of flies in their eye sockets   All of them nearly naked

Veined hands brushing hard crumbs of bread from our doorstep Toothless mouths chewing in vain   They're hungry   And from this hunger terror begins   They scream   They shout their hatred right in my face

They're coming closer   Where are our blue soldiers?   We have more admirals than deck hands   Fire and black smoke erupt from the white palace of the naval department   The white villas on the shore are burning The people from the ghetto are stirring

Moving forward   Surging   They're trampling our lawns   They're rushing up the steps   They're smashing through the gate   But why are they breaking the vases in the atrium   Why are they snapping the branches of the young oleanders?

Strange sounds from the other side of the wall, Zita went rigid, the glass at her lips, and then quietly stood up. Is there someone on the other side of the wall – in the next room?

Zita laboriously and forcefully blinked and pinched her chin until she felt something: there were two voices coming from Roman's room: Roman's and Madda's.

They're in there together. Are they talking? No ... Roman is sobbing ... She's hurting him, my son, she, that – Zita dashed to the wall and pressed her ear against it. The sounds continued. The anxious contraction of her face muscles loosened, the corners of her mouth drooped into an arc of disgust and then extended into a bitter grimace.

"When happiness reaches its peak, it turns into groaning," says Larose in that cruel play by the master of blood Michel de Ghelderode. "Can't we express pain and pleasure just the same?" Marguerite asks him, and Larose convinces her: "Of course! Pleasure is simply an abbreviated form of torture. But it's odd that this interests you. Doesn't a woman know all this?"

Larose is right. He's wise. Larose is a hangman, and Marguerite loves him. And with pleasure will die by his hand ...

To meditate at the wall behind which my own son – But what can I do? It would be at most a disturbance. Just for now. My poor little son. She just plucked you up by the roots and now, unruffled, she's devouring you – both of us. I'd come to your aid if I thought you deserved it ... But I don't know. I doubt it. I don't believe it. And I wouldn't want to live to see you two uniting against me.

But when it sounds so horrible, as if she were strangling you rather than making love! Does love have a Janus face or only one, the punishing, yelling one ... At night Madda's friends, the "Black Riders," threw a rotting rat into our bedroom. The first corpse ...

And so I lost my only son and dared embrace him only several days later, when they brought him upstairs unconscious. Someone had hit him in the face, and he lay in the dust of the street right below the window of the itinerants quarters, that ghetto of roaring red devils beneath us, from where – when I had been washing Roman's face, putting on a compress and trying to get some peace and quiet for Roman by tapping hesitantly on the floor – there was such a racket in reply, as if they were stomping on the very ground beneath our feet.

That night a steel arrow flew in through the window and embedded itself in the bed.

> Two mice are talking:
> "There's a cat in front of the hole!!"
> "So what does he want?"

WHO'S WHO
Zita Gráfová (35)

A barefoot, dark-haired little girl in a frock, without panties, sitting beneath a boulder where the wind has created smooth, even drifts of beige sand, uses her hands to shovel the sand over her legs, leans back and shovels more of it further up her little body, all the way up to her chin (beneath the loving gaze of her parents and Odette, her governess, on beaches in Deauville,

Bournemouth, Ostend, and Sylt). The Šlechtas avoided the burning sun of the South.

"Under all circumstances, you must preserve that which we imperfectly refer to as taste," with a smile her father tried to impress this upon her, as well as French, "always, even when – quand même." Zita grew up surrounded with all the attention anyone could desire, but she rarely saw her parents. Her mother suffered nervous breakdowns and spent most days in her room behind eternally shuttered windows. "Here's a crown, now go play somewhere else, little girl," she once said to Zita when she was playing with some children near the entrance to the ancient house in Malá Strana (above the door was the Šlechtas' family emblem – a white goose), at first she tried to chase Zita away, because she didn't recognize her own daughter in the dirt-covered girl.

The immensely devoted governess, Mademoiselle Odette, practically replaced Zita's mother, and other than her, Zita loved only her father. Dr. Eduard Šlechta, the last descendent of a once wealthy old Prague family, had received a marvelous European education (Sorbonne–Heidelberg–Oxford), after which he resigned himself to a scientific career as well as to the management of his family's wealth and lived as a *rentier* (pronounced rant-yay). He wore nothing but gray suits, a rich selection of them to be sure, and always had a fresh flower in his lapel.

Zita had gone to three different schools, all select, and she'd left them all uncompleted (a French *lycée*, a classical *gymnasium*, and a French *gymnasium* for girls). At a loss as to how to spend her abundant free time, the little girl threw herself into the reading of the *Lives of the Saints and Martyrs*, and lying on the cool silk pillows of the silver-blue chaise lounge, she breathlessly devoured detailed, illustrated descriptions of breast lashings and lacerations with an iron spider, of pouring liquid lead down throats, of red-hot irons and baths of burning oil.

Through an act of charity by the benevolent women of Prague, carefully selected indigent students could once a week have lunch at their benefactor's table. Every Friday the high-school student Karel Vlasák, the son of an unemployed drunk, would arrive, and after Odette and the serving woman had scrubbed his hands in the kitchen with All-Away brand lye soap, he would sit down at table next to Zita. The surly youth responded to Zita's charity with viciousness: during dessert alone with Zita in the dining room, he roughly forced her to strip and then he bit through her earlobe. This indelible experience engraved itself quite deeply into the sensitive girl's mind and filled her with conflicting emotions which were, however, deeply arousing.

The fourteen-year-old Zita learned of her country's defeat a few days after the occupation of Prague by German soldiers. "Taste must be preserved," her father quietly noted, "quand même..." and with the help of two owned and three borrowed automobiles the Šlechtas relocated to their uncle Petr Ludvík's country estate in picturesque Podbrdí.

The summer of 1939 turned out to be a splendid one. Zita wore an elegant straw hat with a pale blue ribbon fluttering down to her shoulders and rode at Uncle Peter Ludvík's side in a light carriage through his ancestral lands on his daily rounds of his fields, forests, and ponds, and on his visits to his deferential tenants. However, the jovial boisterousness and animal hedonism of the robust Petr Ludvík – who passionately liked to palpate the shoulders of his calves, choose one, have it killed on the spot, and with his bare hands rip out the steaming cutlets – soon put Zita off the daily rounds. She would meander through the spacious silence of the white house and spend most of her time reading in the arbor.

The war years calmly drifted by, and only seldom would Father bring political news from Prague. "The longer it lasts, the worse..." he'd mutter softly, and his long white fingers warmed a massive dark-gray glass, "cela va au pire..." he'd add, and sadly smiling he would lightly run his hand across her proffered face, the girl would beg for this rare caress from her eternally distant father.

Zita first became aware of her body when she was reading *The Unknown Martyr* by Francesco Perri. The description of "the punishment of Levit's wife" (she was pitched into a grotto, and one by one the men around the fire rose and went to her, and finally she was tied naked to the back of a donkey and sent out into the night, where she met Christ) threw her into horrible turmoil alternating with religious exultation: before her mirror Zita drew Christ's five wounds with lipstick on her bare body and then she spent the entire night enraptured, with a light fever. "I'm not elect, my wounds don't hurt at all–" she desperately screamed the following morning into the bewhiskered face of the kindhearted local doctor (and great hunter besides), who with warm soapy water washed the stigmata from her body and prescribed a tablespoon of Xeres sherry or Malaga wine before each meal, as well as a bland diet. "But best of all would be to have her married–" he whispered to her father. The doctor's whisper resounded more loudly than the raised (and exceptionally so) voice of the Šlechtas.

In view of these events, her father began to devote immeasurably greater attention to Zita, not infrequently as much as an hour a day. She was allowed to sit in Father's leather armchair in his study and rapturously follow her slender, beautiful father as he silently paced the rug in his velvet slippers or stood by the French windows looking out upon the old garden, his long, white, delicate fingers gripping the brass-wrought handle and his forehead pressed against the misty glass softly narrating stories of the great loves of world literature. When her father later asked his daughter, for reasons of consequence, to marry a man he'd chosen, she agreed unhesitatingly and without expressing the slightest wish to see her fiancé. She saw him for the first time just before the wedding, a deed for which she'd mentally prepared herself as for a heroic feat, like Judith's visit to the tent of Holofernes.

During her defloration by the young and handsome Dr. Evžen Gráf, she felt only pain and fear of pregnancy. Immediately after the act, when her sudden pallor frightened him, her husband assured her that it rarely came to that. The following morning Zita paced the rug of Father's study and smoked two of his Egyptian cigarettes, as rain flowed softly down the large windows. "I'm a woman..." she whispered over and over, "I'm a woman..." It was the most beautiful moment of her marriage, in which she never achieved total gratification. Ten months later, a son was born for whom as a girl she'd already dreamed up the name Šebestien, after her beloved saint with arrows protruding from his bound, youthful body. The Soviet era had arrived, however, and they christened him, in fine Russophile fashion, Roman.

Roman was nursed by a robust maid named Žofka, and Zita painfully envied her this delight that was denied to her, as well as Žofka's moans of consummated love (with the driver Ferdinand in the arbor beneath Zita's bedroom window). With the political coup of February 1948, the Šlechtas lost all their property. Zita's father refused to emigrate and soon died in the family's Malá Strana house, which had already been expropriated and allocated to national enterprise Prague Pastry Factory as a baking student boarding house. Before his final breath, he indicated to the weeping Zita that she should step closer. He laboriously sat up on his deathbed and with his final strength whispered to his daughter: "Cela va au pire ... quand même." With these words Dr. Eduard Šlechta, who'd received a marvelous European education (Sorbonne–Heidelberg–Oxford), departed from this world, and his spouse, even though during their final years she had exchanged few words with her husband, departed of her own free will shortly thereafter.

Zita resolutely entered into the spirit of the new straitened circumstances and stalwartly followed her husband to his new places of employment in Bohušovice nad Ohří and Ústí nad Labem, always trying to impart coziness and taste (without tremendous success) to their new homes and to help her husband with his exhausting work. She variously worked as secretary, translator, and librarian. She organized children's gift exchanges at the factory, bus trips to the mountains or Prague theaters, and student musical groups (without tremendous success). During factory-wide meetings, she took charge of the cultural interludes of poetry or piano recitals (without tremendous response), and with a peaceful mind she came to terms with the necessity of doing all the household chores herself, without servants, including caring for the child, accepting devotedly the difficult task of a working mother plus the ceremonial duties of the factory director's wife (without tremendous ambition).

Her trip to Greece was an amazing experience for Zita, and it had been facilitated by the kindness of Evžen's long-time acquaintance Růžena (whom he referred to jokingly as Riri). This act of kindness was indeed unusual, for in that year of great political trials in Prague only two families of Czech tourists arrived in Greece (the Gráfs and the daughter of the Vice-Minister, with her beautifully built cousin. They, however, as they never tired of pointing out, were there on a study retreat, although they spent all their days swimming and all their evenings in the bar. That same year the Vice-Minister was executed). A wonderstruck Zita discovered the South.

On the very first day (the Gráfs arrived in Athens at 16:52), Zita went for a walk quite far from the hotel, and when she wandered into one of the poorer parts of town, her widened eyes drank in the scenes of biblical simplicity and elemental humanity, houses overcrowded with bursting families living side-by-side with domestic animals, old women dressed in black standing near low, burning white walls, barefoot girls in close-fitting one-piece dresses made of coarse black cloth frayed at the bottom, the bustle of naked children and of donkeys with swarms of flies in their eye sockets, dry, veined hands sweeping up hard crumbs of bread from stone doorsteps and placing them one by one into toothless mouths chewing in vain. For the first time in her life Zita had seen hunger and bowed down before its majesty.

The last afternoon was unforgettable. As Evžen saw to the formalities of departure, Zita discovered the poorest ghetto. Four men, dressed horribly, with nothing but overcoats draped over their sweaty, naked bodies, dragged a beautiful girl into some kind of adobe-and-corrugated-tin shanty. Terrified, Zita listened from the broken-down gate to the cruel sounds that continued for perhaps an hour, and when the girl finally emerged, erect, head held high, Zita barely suppressed a burning desire to touch her and kiss her.

Singing softly to himself, with his rice broom Julda Serafin swept the dim floor of the large, low factory firehouse, he scattered fragrant white wood shavings along the wide concrete floor, and when they'd absorbed all the unclean earth he swept them up, swelling and grayed, as if wearied by the filth they'd had to devour, and then he wheeled them to the boiler room, where the wood, having served to its last fiber, was burned to ashes in the cleansing flame.

In the luminous square of the open gate a white coat appeared and a girl's shrill voice called out: "Comrade Director orders you to go water the flower bed beneath the manager's office!"

"But my daughter–"

"*Immediately.* And stop that daughter business!"

"Forgive me, Comrade, but I've already watered that flower bed today. However, if you want, I'll gladly water it again. In the summer you should always water flowers in the morning, because cold water in hot air ruins them. But as you wish."

"... Okay, forget about it if it'll ruin them ... I've been in the canteen since morning and Mr. Gráf called me..."

"I probably didn't give them enough water. Otherwise you would have noticed the freshness of the gladioluses."

"Yes, I ... Forgive me."

"No, please forgive me for making you undertake the trip to see me."

Julda swept up the remaining wood shavings, wheeled them over to the boiler room, and then pushed the heavy fire extinguisher over to the third workshop, where there was an explosive environment and where they'd be welding today. For five hours he stood there silently at his rescue station and observed the welders crawling around the construction site with the bright flames of their oxyacetylene torches.

Julda longed to be of service to them, even though he understood that they were much better off not needing his intervention, just as we do not wish for sin although we long for the virtue of its expiation– "Julda, what are you still hanging around here for?" the afternoon foreman yelled at him, "the welders knocked off a long time ago–" "I was waiting for them to dismiss me..." "Jesus, are you a fool!"

Julda patiently smiled and wheeled the fire extinguisher back to the firehouse, where he carefully deposited it, then he washed his hands and face in the water tank (he rarely washed his entire body, for he hated his own nakedness, but his light work rarely got him dirty) and without even changing (the burlap work clothes the factory gave him free of charge looked almost civilian after years of wear and washing) he set out for town. His sister Madda was causing him ever greater worries and ever deeper sorrow.

"Madda? That bitch Serafinová?" said a thin, severely wrinkled, spiteful girl with gray, worn-out skin. There, on the second floor of the Grand Café, she blew cigarette smoke right into Julda's face and continued, "She's been leading us by the nose for a long time now, and she only goes for married guys. You seriously wanna go there? ... Sure, I'll gladly tell you his name, Secký, he's an engineer at Cottex, drives a blue convertible and lives in Klíše–"

"I know where he lives," Julda sighed. "I once delivered a box to him from the train station ... And I thank you for the information, Miss."

Julda proceeded through the bustling streets of the evening town, stepping out of everyone's way, often going off the sidewalk into the street. They were all rushing around without ever reaching their goals, they crowd around store windows stuffed with superfluous goods, colorful trinkets of vanity, and they all sacrifice their lives trying to acquire them, lives from which so much light could shine forth ...

Out of the blue twilight emerges car after car, glittering like a Pharaoh's chariot but actually made of the thinnest steel. Beautiful young people climb out, dressed as if for a wedding or church, and charge up the marble stairs of the House of Culture, that soulless, mass-produced quasi-culture for poor, seduced sheep, sprinkled into their trough as just the entertaining appendix of an omnipotent but unsuccessful economics, the house of soulless dancing to the primitive music of the primeval rain forest, the house of flirts and scarlet lust, without happiness or blessings – across the street, in its shadow, mourns the Archdeacon Church, completely forgotten.

Julda immediately decided to bring the a bouquet of gladioluses to the Archdeacon Church the following afternoon, perhaps the girl at work will forgive me, and he set out to the garden suburb of Klíše to see Madda.

He silently climbed the blue building's wide staircase to the second floor and rang at the tall white door bearing two nameplates: Eng. F. Secký and Eng. H. Secká. You have a wife, my friend, why do you desire my sister as well?

The doorbell resounded from somewhere in the depths of the apartment, and again. No one answered for a long time. Finally, the door opened just a bit, with the chain secured, and an ill-humored face peeped out.

"Ah – Julda!" said Frank Secký, yawning. "What do you want – oh yeah, I still haven't given you those five crowns for picking up that box at the train station ... Okay. Stop by Sunday, I don't have any change on me right now."

"I'm not asking anything for that. It was during working hours, for which I'm already paid. I've come here with regard to my sister, Magdalena."

"Jesus, who's that? Oh, Madda. Well, what's this all about?"

"Can I come in?"

"Well, you see, right now ... I've got some ... work to do. And I don't have time."

"You found time to lead my sister into temptation."

"Has she said anything to you?"

"No, but I have heard that you have been seducing her."

"Come on, you sound like a book."

"In which it is written: It were better for him that a millstone were hanged about his neck, and he cast into the sea than that he should offend one of these little ones..."

"What was that about the sea? I wouldn't mind taking a dip right about now. Without the stone, of course. Now, would you like to make any further, similarly significant announcements? Make it quick. You're starting to bore me."

"You have a wife, why do you desire my sister as well?"

"I'm not the one doing the desiring, pal. The girl's eager herself, right down in her crotch. I got bored with her ... and when something starts to bore me it exists for me less than if it had never existed at all – it anti-exists, which for me is a repulsive, subhuman form of minus-nothing, a negative, far below the x-axis of my coordinate system. However, let us go from theoretical toasts to the more bracing fare of the practical, and out of pure love for my neighbor I offer you this tip: when Madda still existed for me, she was on her way from the itinerants quarters when she climbed through my window. She was barefoot – her seducer's name is Borek Trojan – *salve*!"

Frank Secký slammed the door, and Julda heard a woman's voice: "Who was that?" and Frank's answer: "No one, someone from the factory ... an idiot."

In the heat of the itinerants quarters four workers were sleeping on their cots and on the fifth, spread out over a magazine pruriently depicting abject nakedness in garish colors on expensive glossy paper, lay Borek Trojan, himself abjectly naked.

"So you've read all the beautiful and wise books, and the only thing left is that..." said Julda softly, and he fastidiously pointed to Borek's *Life* magazine.

"I'm using it to learn English," Borek growled, and he snapped it shut. On the cover was another naked whore climbing down a ladder into the sea. A ruby around the strumpet's neck –

"Aren't Shakespeare, Byron, Browning, Keats, Dickens, Chesterton, and Greene in English?"

"Well yes, but this is spoken English, that is, American English, which you need ... " chattered the pitiful young man.

"And if you want to learn English, I mean American English, you need that?" Another fastidious gesture toward the cover.

"This is the most popular magazine in the world. Millions of copies ... all those people can't be morons!"

"I read in the newspaper that the most translated book in the world is the Bible. Shouldn't it then be the most read? And for two thousand years?"

"Okay, get me an English Bible and I'll use it to learn English!"

"Who gave that to you?"

"This? I just ... got it myself."

"Well couldn't you ... get a Bible yourself? Or Shakespeare, Byron, Browning, Keats, Chesterton, Greene..."

"Probably, but this is opium for us poor folk, like the Bible is for you."

"Have you read the Bible?"

"Me? Well, I haven't exactly read it, but..."

"But you know it's opium..."

"Well, of course, everybody knows that, it's been completely refuted by science, and people need opium. Drugs are what make us different from animals."

"And why did you choose precisely this drug?" Julda made another fastidious gesture toward the almost completely naked woman poised on the side of the white yacht.

"So I can at least see it in a picture, because I'll never come near it any other way, get it? Because I'm hungry – okay? I own just one decent suit and two white shirts, and one's already fraying at the collar – here I have a hundred white and green and purple tuxedos with diamond cufflinks. Today my breakfast was tap water, lunch was garlic salami and my ration of milk, and for supper I'm having recrystallized fructose, a stolen turnip and, thanks to the compassion of these workers, a swallow of warm beer – here I have glass bowls with mountains of fantastic food and a golden bottle of *Blanc de Blanc* in a silver ice bucket, I've been living for two years in this repulsive room with whoever happens to come along, my own straw-stuffed cot barely belongs to me – here I have a white bedroom, a blue bathroom, a red dining room, a library made of natural wood, and a bar with white swivel stools on a green carpet – all this on a yacht anchored at Monte Carlo ... Mainly I read it out of anger at all the stuff other people have. And in the belief that some day I too will be able to get a piece of it."

"I'm sure you'll get a lot if you care so much about it..." Julda sighed, "but don't you wish that wasn't all you cared about?"

"I care about a proper apartment, decent clothes, about seeing the sea ... Later a car and ... a sailboat ... at least for the Elbe."

"You'll get all of that soon … I know you. But I'm afraid, my son, that you will never be happier than you are right now, there on your straw-stuffed mattress…"

"You think I'm happy now? How could I possibly be happy now?"

"And why do you think you'd be happy with a sailboat on the Elbe? What if it rains? And what about when the river freezes?"

"Boy, he sure can talk!" Valtr interrupted, laughing. Borek's voice, which had reached the screaming point, had woken him up, and he was observing them across the round, downy protuberance of his belly. "He's not by chance from the Church, is he? I was in prison with a priest who'd abused a little girl. Sexually, I mean, just so you know what I'm talking about."

"But he wasn't in prison with those who have caused the death of thousands of girls, boys, men, women, and the elderly," said Julda softly. "Those to whom you bow down and encourage with your applause. Borek, what did you do to Madda?"

"To Madda? Me? … I didn't do anything. Seriously."

"Engineer Secký told me–"

"Him?! That pig – he's the one who drove her away in his car. He's an asshole. But now Mr. Roman Gráf is plowing her field. I caught them in the basement petting on the coal stove."

"What's petting?" asked a frightened Julda.

"Someday, when you're finally finished reading the Bible, take a look at the Kinsey Report."

"What's that?"

"It's also a very much translated and widely read book. Petting is … I don't know exactly what it is, but I know for certain that compared with that, this magazine is Sunday reading for pious schoolchildren."

"With Roman Gráf…" Julda whispered, astonished, "but he's still a child … It wasn't long ago I used to buy him marbles…"

Then wearily up to the second floor, ringing the doorbell again and waiting at the door they'll never permit me to enter.

"Our Roman…" said Dr. Gráf, it didn't sound like a question, there wasn't even any shock or moral indignation in his voice, just infinite weariness, and if there was any affability it was only verbal, and derisive at that. "Well, I guess at sixteen boys become men…"

"That's all you have to say?"

"I don't like it any more than you do … but we're helpless in the face of … When the blood speaks…"

"Then the Word must shout!"

"That's what happened: biology shouted, or roared rather. And its voice is quite powerful!"

"Doctor, you amaze me ... Such an educated person, and all you can do is shrug your shoulders ... You're his father, after all!"

"That's more blood than word. Leave me alone now. And leave them alone ... they're young. Let's think about how we can help them."

"Help them sin together on the stove in the basement?"

"There too? That surprises me, since they've already done it here–"

"In your apartment? And maybe even in your own matrimonial bed?!"

"Stop trying to torment me ... that doesn't work anymore. Too many words have betrayed me, and I've already shed too much blood along the way ... And it's too hot today for an argument. I want to sleep. Besides, isn't Madda three years older than my son ... and a thousand years more vital ... And isn't she the prime mover in all this? Enough already. I'll have a talk with my son."

"Reproach her for it, that tigress – you're afraid of her, aren't you?" whispered a pale Zita Gráfová. There was spite in her voice, and her eyes sparkled. "It was her ... she tore my son from me, he just sobs and she devours him, unruffled ... Next she'll start on me ... She'll devour us all ... She'll bite you, bite you to death, just in passing, if you annoy her."

And Madda shamelessly stretched out before Julda in all the triumphant nakedness of youth: "Jesus, you can really be annoying!"

"Couldn't you leave Jesus out of this?" said Julda softly.

"And now you're going to watch every one of my words like a cop. Just admit it, you're terribly annoying!"

Julda trudged through the hot beige dust of the street, past cracked facades with boarded-up windows, wire fences, and endless warehouse walls, along little side streets with smaller and smaller buildings and wretched gardens with poor, depleted soil where the earth has refused to provide nourishment and has hardened to stone, still further on toward the south, tired and exhausted, like those wood shavings, first bright white, then gray and swelling with the filth they've had to ingest, and then longing only for the purifying flame and eternal rest, all the way to the southern part of town, where out of the hard, bare, biblical landscape dead mountains of earth and trash rise up, and then down on his knees in the burning desert dust, Lord, forgive them, for they know not what they do, *beguiled by sin From blind eyes hatred Stones in their hands, placed there by the devil Thin sharp arrows of Satan's ridicule Cudgels of carnal rage in outthrust arms The stones and arrows are cast I will gladly place my chest in their path and die for you To wrest your bodies from their clutches and offer mine instead And after you I will enter into the kingdom of eternal bliss*

"You've come at a very inconvenient time." Dáša Zíbrtová grimaced. "I'm leaving in three minutes." She rushed around the empty examining room (her hours had just ended), waving her hands to dry her freshly painted nails, applying lipstick, sleeking back her hair over and over.

"Where are you rushing off to?"

"I'm going with Alex to Teplice and then ... Today's going to be marvelous–"

"Dáša, do not go!"

"Are you crazy?! I've been looking forward to this, saving for it all week long. Alex didn't want to let me ... but this time I'm paying, and he's going to make it up to me!"

"You cannot."

"Forgive me, but–"

"Please ... it's for your own good. Because I love you."

"A rather inopportune moment for a declaration, isn't it!"

"I didn't mean it that way. Let's go to the old rectory ... the children keep asking about you. They need you–"

"But I need something, too. Alex–" Dáša snatched the telephone receiver from its cradle. "I'm on my way..." she breathed into the receiver. "I'm on my way," she said to Julda, and then added ironically: "Say hello to the children for me. I have a strong suspicion there'll be one more in nine months."

Julda grabbed her firmly by the shoulders and shook her. "You cannot do that!"

"Let go of me – now!"

"No. Because right now you're longing not for motherhood but for sin. I will not let you go."

"Mr. Serafin! I'm asking you for the last time–"

"Are you really that blind? Do you really believe he loves you? That he longs to take you to wife? Can't you see that after he's had you once, he's bored with you? And now, at your request, he'll disgrace you a few more times?"

"You can't say that – No! That's not true! No! No!"

"You know it well enough yourself. Why do you keep trying to deceive yourself? Take a look in the mirror – is this a woman men long for because of her beauty?"

"Ouch – that was cruel..."

"He holds you lower than an animal. He takes you like a glass of water whenever he feels like it – and you're going to pay for this service?"

"I know I'm ugly ... But I want to forget about it – at least for a moment – and Alex will give me that moment!"

"A moment of delight, a mouthful of meat impaled on the fork of contempt ... Ten minutes! An hour! Two! And then days and weeks of humiliation, desperation, and hopelessness. Long nights ... and years. You waited a week for his permission to come to him a second time. How many weeks will you wait for admittance a third time?"

"Worse than anything is loneliness..."

The telephone rang. Dáša reached for it and then let her hand fall. Julda gently led her over to the examining couch and sat her on its cool white cover.

The telephone rang into the heat of the examining room. A third time. A fourth.

Dáša shuddered and then suddenly tried to dash to the telephone, but Julda held her back by force.

The telephone rang a fifth time, a sixth, a seventh, a brief eighth, then silence.

"And now..." she said bitterly. "What do I have now?"

"Purity."

"And what do I do with that? What good is it?"

"It will fill your days with light. Days and weeks ... and years. There is strength in purity – hope, eternal grace, and the joy of the humble."

Dáša placed her head in Julda's lap, and her shoulders shook with sobs. "At least you won't abandon me–"

"I won't abandon you," whispered Julda, and he stroked her thinning hair and trembling, sweat-covered neck. "Don't be afraid. There's nothing to fear. You're young and able, you've received a wonderful education, and there are so many things you can accomplish. You can do it and thereby achieve happiness, a happiness for which there is no division between day and night, between years, an immense happiness that will not grow old, will not subside, will never end. You must believe – and you must believe in yourself."

In the window suddenly a black silhouette. "Dáša ... are you there?" Alex's voice from outside ... *looking for one who seeks.*

Dáša moaned and dropped down from the bed onto the floor, wedged herself between Julda's legs, and pressed them against the sides of her head. "Squeeze me, crush me ... Just don't let me hear him–"

A loud knocking at the window. Again, louder. A third time, even louder.

Dáša was kneeling, trembling, shuddering, swaying, she pulled Julda's legs close around her, then pushed them away, she rubbed her face against them, pressed herself against them, howled, tried to pull Julda down to her, then tried to knock him over, she writhed, jumped up again, then sank back down. Julda held her firmly and with his free hand he caressed her sweat-soaked neck.

Then a moment of silence, footsteps, the sound of an engine starting and the honk of a horn cut through the silence – but Alex still hadn't left – and Dáša bit into Julda's leg, to keep from shouting. Then the car drove off.

With a moistened cotton swab Julda carefully wiped Dáša's temples as she lay unmoving on her back. "No water..." she whispered, "alcohol–"

"Water will do," he smiled.

"And now," she said when she'd pulled herself together and stood up, "I'll give myself an injection of something that will keep me calm."

"Don't. You know better than I do why not."

"So I can't even have a tablet? At least half of one ... at least Pheno-barbital – after all, they prescribe it for children ... Then what am I allowed to take?"

"Have some water. Your lips are chapped."

"And bitten ... That was hell–"

"You came through it. Ex orco–"

"Through hell? ... But where to?"

"Into the light, Doctor."

"Into the light ... Shall we go? I'd like it very much if you'd see me home. It's too tempting here, a whole pharmacy."

And Julda accompanied Dr. Dáša Zíbrtová home, and not a word was uttered on the way.

"Do you still need me?" he whispered at her door.

"No. I want to be alone now. I'm going to sleep ... for the first time this week without barbituates. I'm already better again. Much better..."

"Godspeed, Dáša."

"Goodbye. Won't you give me your hand–" Dáša bowed and kissed Julda's hand.

Julda took a circuitous route through the streets, making larger and larger circles, as if he couldn't get enough of his journey through the beige dust, and to the surprise of pedestrians he was softly singing.

In front of building No. 2000 he glanced timidly at Teo's window, unable to see through the cloudy glass covered with lime. Teo, however, could see him through the window, and Julda smiled cheerfully to himself. Out from the shadows in the corridor rushed a boy, his face distorted with rage: "Thanks a lot, Mr. Serafin!"

"But my little Románek ... my son..."

"I'm not Románek anymore, and you're not my father, you ... you ... you fucking squealer!"

"But Roman, I just..." But Roman Gráf was no longer listening.

Julda sighed and trudged heavily up to the third floor, he knelt down facing the window in his room and prayed a long, long time, then he removed his burlap work shirt, untied a blackened, knotted rope that lay against his bare body, whipped his shoulders, back, and chest, retied the rope around his waist, and put his burlap shirt back on. He wanted a drink of water, but there wasn't any, and then after a longer prayer he lay down, crossed himself, and immediately fell asleep, a light smile on his slightly parted lips.

WHAT IS BLUE

women, spirit, words, being besieged, age, satiety, parks, coasts, ports, post-coital gratification, onanism, masochism, lakes, mountains, stabilizers, west and north, wisdom, afternoons, ice, states of rest (of cells, biological or fuel), culture, calm weather, democracy, ice cream, dogs, palaces, pumps, peace, low pressure, sugar, art, long-range guided anti-missile systems, savings, fall and winter, combs, freedom, garden flowers, rational persuasion, colonists, submission, rococo, fatigue, sediment, Mozart, ratios, knowledge, wisdom, love, white paint, anecdotes, quiet, eroticism, indifference, literature, the end

I'm no longer alone! And now I don't have to go through all that psychological mumbo-jumbo and all ninety-nine of my complexes! Soon I won't need to take baths at all! No more neurotic and no more psychopath! Papa's famous psychiatrist, who keeps going on about communication – and who took five hundred crowns for mine – is a complete dimwit! All that hocus-pocus about communication is just stupid, process, communication, and speech simply exist! Like highways, rivers, air! Did I really take ether? That must have been someone else! And Van de Velde's a nitwit! Love is something completely different – whoever says I'm an outsider to the erotic sphere is an idiot and a moron.

With a red face and boxing gloves on his sore hands, Roman Gráf danced in front of the mattress he'd leaned up against the wall and threw punch after punch right into it. It's already going much better, really, a week ago five minutes of this physical exercise and I was completely out of breath, but now I'm breathing like a horse and I've been hacking away for eleven minutes! He threw punch after punch into the mattress of his boy's-size bed, some of them would even have knocked out a rabbit (that is, if it were hung up by its legs right next to a brick wall).

And it's all because of her. Madda ... my squaw. Gentlemen, I've got a girl! And what a girl! If only you could see her naked, or only one of her shoulders, or even just an elbow or a knee – she's really got marvelous knees – but you'd only need to see her little toe or just her little toenail ... I love her madly, and that's a fact.

But it's not just a matter of her body – Madda's really insanely marvelous – it's a matter of the entire package, if you know what I mean. But maybe you don't. She's amazing. She can be so happy ... When I took her to Karlovy Vary, she was just like a little girl, she caressed the metal columns of the Garden Colonnade, stuck her face into a spring, which is of course absolutely against the rules, and when she saw a swan on the grass she grabbed it by the wing and kissed it on its beak ...

And then she went with me to the swimming area. At first she didn't want to go, no, not a bit. And when Madda doesn't want to do something – or, on the other hand, when she does want to do something – she's not to be denied. But I plucked up my courage and begged her for at least a week, at least three hours a day, and I kept giving her money – I was *obsessed* with the idea that Madda go with me to the swimming area. Into that crowd and in front of my whole class, no longer a cretin, but simply a man with his girl. No, more than that – simply to be like anybody else who *belongs* there, just so they *notice* me ... that was the last complex of those ninety-nine of mine, and it was a persistent one, like a leech, or more like cancer.

Of course, Madda didn't want to go because it's all a bunch of nonsense, but I pleaded with her and promised that we'd just go there for a minute and then move on to the Svět Café for champagne (Madda drinks only real French champagne at a hundred and forty crowns a bottle, and she drank two of them more or less herself, she's simply fantastic), and I had to drive her to the swimming area in Papa's car because she didn't want to take the streetcar. Of course, I don't have a driver's license.

And so we strode through like royalty, Madda in front and me right behind her, so everyone would see that we belonged together, and also so I could see how everyone turned to look at her – did I tell you Madda looks like a goddess? Exactly like goddess! – And so, like royalty we proceeded through the crowd, completely normally, and there was an enormous response – did I already tell you she looks like a goddess? – straight through the entire area all the way up to the wire fence of the Yacht Club, where, naturally, half our class was in a group beneath the dug-up and urinated-on linden.

And my class acted like it was nothing! They're so lame, simply lame: since the whole world knew I *didn't* have a girl, everyone asked whether I had a girl now, when *they can very well see that I have one*, like it was nothing. But this doesn't bother me anymore. I'm already above all that now. And so I drove my girl to the Svĕt Café on the square, and it was great, we had two more bottles of French champagne and then a bunch of gin fizzes at the bar (Madda loves lots of ice in her gin fizz), we danced like devils, and Madda played songs for the whole bar, she knows exactly what she wants (Madda loves soft music, really cool and really slow) and always gets it. Well, I really drank myself under the table – I spent the rest of the money I was saving for Yugoslavia, but I wouldn't have gone there anyway if Madda couldn't go – and Madda had to take me home in a taxi – she's amazing – and Mama had to come the next day on the tram to get the car.

The following day I felt pretty bad ... Lately I've been really lethargic ... and I eat like I was starving, like I'd never eaten in my life. And I'm always tired ... probably from the boxing, since I'm not used to doing any sports ... Today I fell asleep right after breakfast and slept like the dead till lunch.

Because Madda was away. When I'm with Madda it's wonderfully different, it has to be different because she's divinely fit day and night, constantly. It's as if she were younger than me by at least a thousand years. Madda's amazing. Van de Velde's right about one thing: love is definitely a thriller. You've gotta be brave ... And happy that you can give. So that the most brutish thing is actually gentle, like those sad and misty blues. But also sublime and beautiful.

Those guys pulled her in through the window right before my eyes ... I came to only when I heard their terrible racket down below, and Mama was applying compresses to my banged-up face. The floor of our apartment was thundering right beneath our feet like an earthquake, WHAT ARE THEY DOING TO HER DOWN THERE – *A thousand red devils are frolicking around my love to an insane* biggest beat never before heard *They're whipping each other and shrieking and SHOUTING*

They're taking turns, one at a time, on top of her   There's a million of them   A billion   Billions of insane termites   Destroyers and omnivores

They're gnawing their way into the building's foundation   Each one bites off just a tiny piece   But there are billions of them, more and more They're terribly fertile and multiply like crazy   They gnaw away day and night   The building is collapsing

Meanwhile Madda calmly takes a bite of raw meat   She'll survive everything   I shall die   Because I want to   Just one final wish for the condemned man: that I may die for her   That she take pleasure from my pain

"Románek ... My son..." cried Mother, and she wiped off my blood, I had to comfort her, and finally I almost succeeded, then everything was fine between her and me like it hasn't been for a terribly long time, like when I was still a little brat. Mama was almost cheerful and then brought me a bottle of Ronda, that white Cuban rum, and poured me a full glass! Lord, I could get used to this! "You're now a man, Roman." That's what Mama said to me!

The racket in the itinerants quarters abated but didn't stop, so we put on the stereo and started to dance! You always have the most unrestrained fun when all is lost. Mama dances wonderfully, even to rock, which she didn't know but learned really quickly and then wanted to dance to nothing else. She really has a talent for it. Papa shook his head derisively, but we could see he liked it, and he even decided to smoke an enormous cigar, which he only does on very special occasions, an original Cuban H. Upmann in an aluminum tube, which you light with a piece of palm tree bark, "...or with a hundred-dollar bill," joked Father. He also took a drink and toasted with me as if I were one of the guys. A regular Havana carnival! The racket on the first floor moved up to the second.

Madda didn't come out of the itinerants quarters till late that evening, she took a shower and came to dinner absolutely O. K., as if she'd been somewhere sunning herself all afternoon. She had a scratch here and there, but her skin was wonderfully fresh – she even seemed *cheerful* ... and if she normally ate for three, this time she ate twice as much as normal.

I didn't dare ask her what all went on down there, Madda simply *passed over it in silence* ... But since that day – or am I just imagining things? – there's been something wild in her eyes, even during lovemaking, especially during lovemaking ... And she's impatient, irritable, mean ... and cruel.

And unfair. "Your parents are ... blue cretins!" she said contemptuously when I tried to explain to her that Papa really couldn't give us his company car to go to Prague (Madda and I banged up our car on the way back from our best, and last, trip to Karlovy Vary).

"Alex takes off with your fucking company car whenever he wants!"

"Papa can't do a lot of the things that Alex does every day..."

"Like I said, you're all a bunch of cretins. Do you at least have some sort of *love?*"

Money began to be a problem. Usually Papa gives me a hundred a month for pocket money, and more if I need it, and Mama sometimes gives me a hundred for no good reason at all. I never spent it all, so money was never a problem for me, I almost didn't even *notice* it. But with Madda I could probably spend a million crowns a month ... she has an unfailing sense, goes right for the most expensive thing, but that's the least of it. She always has to pay musicians, at the bar she pays only with hundred-crown notes and never wants change, she even gave the cab driver a hundred and refused the change, although the trip from town costs only twelve crowns. In Paris Papa had taught me how to give tips, as a rule just ten percent, anything less is a *faux pas* and more makes it look like you've got an inferiority complex – when Madda admitted to me she'd never ridden in a taxi before, I thought that maybe with all this swaggering she was treating her own complex, and I was *touched*, you see, because I treat my complex by walking around with her at the swimming area, and she's treating hers by riding around in taxis and eating in first-class restaurants, so we're *indispensable* to each other – but as I get to know her more, I realize that Madda's simply incapable of any kind of complex, she's *ridiculously* healthy – and this tossing around of my hundred-crown notes is her intoxication, her ultimate intoxication, and it's called *plundering*.

"Well, tell your old man to give you more–" she constantly says to me, and I can't get it through her head that we don't have a hundred-crown note mine, she has the fantastic idea we make at least twenty thousand crowns a month, but Mama and Papa together make just six.

So Madda decided we should sell some of our china, and we started with the dessert service that belonged to my Malá Strana grandfather, a Šlechta, which we never use anyway. They were stupid, ancient pieces of junk, but the grape motif was pretty … For the fourteen-piece set, the stupid bitch at Tuzex offered me a lousy fifty-crown voucher – this china's worth *at least* a hundred dollars and probably more, according to what I've seen in various antique shops … But Madda bawled me out horribly, disappeared with the set somewhere, then never mentioned it again.

Mama noticed right away but didn't blame me, which actually was worse than if she'd broken my jaw. "That was from my dowry…" is all she said, "and I really liked those grapes…" Then we both started crying … but this time no dancing to the stereo, no Havana carnival … Never again. I'll never forget that look of hers, as if she simply wanted to say that we were overwhelmed. I understood her – that look of hers – immensely sad and nearly wild from the sadness. After that, Madda sold things by herself: damask tablecloths, some Uhland poems written on flameproof paper in gilded leather, Dad's antique coin, and the golden lorgnette he'd inherited from Grandma on Havelská Street … but this she didn't sell, she hid it among her underwear, it fell out once when we were getting dressed after sex. I pretended not to see.

Even though I like Madda more and more, there are some things I just don't understand. Like about those workers who did that horrible thing to her: she jokes around and laughs with them like it was nothing ... All those people understand each other better than my folks understand each other, for example, they're horribly cruel to one another – although no less than my folks, but they always have to preserve that stupid *bon ton* – but at the same time they somehow stick together. Madda's people are the opposite color from us: they're red, and I hate them. Because I'd like to join them, but I'll never be able to.

On the other hand, a mere office worker, let alone an intellectual, is enough to incite Madda's hatred. But she hasn't had much experience with intellectuals.

"That's the biggest swine in Ústí," she told me once when we saw Frank Secký, Father's deputy, on the town square.

"You say that killing him wouldn't be enough..."

"Not by a long shot – Hey, go up to him and tell him what I just said about him–"

"You think that'll have any effect? He's been aware of that for some time now, and he's pretty proud of it."

"My buddies wanted to set his flat on fire ... I had to talk them out of it. You'd never do that, would you?"

"Kill him or tell him what you just said about him?"

"As if you could ever kill anybody ... you little lamb..." and Madda burst out laughing. At that moment I hated her. Behind love hatred is always lurking ... I ran after Frank Secký, who was just getting into his car.

"You're the biggest swine on the planet–" I yelled right into his face.

"Get out of here..." Frank quickly glanced around. "Is that what your father says about me?"

"Madda Serafinová. And me."

"My extremely young friend," Frank Secký said softly, "absolutely no one can offend me, least of all Miss Madda Serafinová..."

I stood above him, suddenly very dizzy from the sudden realization that I was in fact quite *capable* of murdering him. If Madda really wanted me to –

I didn't hear what Frank was saying, and I didn't even notice him driving off. When Madda came up to me, all I felt were her fingers in my ,palm, and I firmly squeezed her hand, *to be permitted to bleed to death for You* – you'll put my boxing gloves on me. The boy will put the dagger into his hand himself.

I have my beautiful, pure little boy, with a body like a greyhound and with tender white hands like those of a priest, we fall asleep together holding hands, we sit together on the terrace over iced gin fizzes and listen to music that's cool and slow, we lead each other by the hand through pavilions made of glass and blue metal, where eternal springs of healthful water rain upwards – transported, Madda sighed and took off running from the Garden Colonnade toward a pond, on the lawn she caught up with a swan and grabbed it by its wing.

"You're my bleu blues..." she whispered to Roman as they were leaving Karlovy Vary that evening (colored lights shone just beneath the surface of an artificial pond), she hugged him around his shoulders then leaned forward and kissed the membrane behind his ear, Roman returned Madda's kisses and didn't quite make it around the bend just before Teplice, but that's okay, as long as there's *love* it's all easy, and we came home in a taxi, Lord, I always thought you could only take taxis in town, but they travel between towns, too –

And from the car straight to the bath, and from the bath straight to the dinner table, and from the dinner table I go and roll around on my little feather bed, and then my sweet, gentle czarevitch is shyly scratching at my door. And in the morning, breakfast as big as other people's Sunday dinners, and from the table straight to the bath, the whole bathroom to myself, a whole room to myself, a whole apartment to myself, in one room my little white fawn waits patiently until I'm in the mood for him, for his patient lovemaking, he'd have himself cut in pieces just to give me pleasure, he'll wait an hour and then last five minutes and then right back to the swimming area, pastry shop, café, and in the evening we'll take a cab to a bar, iced champagne from Paris and lots of iced gin fizzes. Then to the bathroom and the dinner table – Madda stood before the mirror in the bathroom, shook her head hard, and with her fingers held her eyelids open the way we do when we're really drunk and trying to see something stable through all the stupid spinning and whirling – girl, I can't see anything anymore! It's nothing, girl, you just need a little drink – and Madda lethargically reached toward the glass shelf, a little bottle flew down into the washbasin, and now I'm holding another, what is it: *Renaissance*, must be the name of a restaurant and therefore something to drink, Madda unscrewed the golden cap, YUCK, it's some kind of nasty aftershave.

Why are you drinking from the bottle in the bathroom, girl, when you've got a pilfered bottle of purple Tuzex *Parfait Amour* under your bed. I don't know, girl, maybe I don't like it anymore, good God, why am I suddenly so tired? Probably from stuffing yourself, girl. But already I'm eating less and less, what happened to those times when I would eat four omelets after dinner and a plate of ham on top of that? Now I'm just sucking it in, and that's supposed to make you happy? Am I happy? No, I'm not! So it's a swindle! It's probably from drinking too much, girl, you know, like those slobbering wrecks downstairs at the Svět Café. I don't want it anymore. And why am I suddenly so nervous and gone to seed?

But with your store of charms you've got positively everything you've always wanted, girl, and everything you could possibly think of wanting – you're right, girl, but if it's suddenly no fun anymore ... The thrill is gone.

And so Roman and I trudge on like overcooked noodles through the dust of the street (it's a pain in the ass to walk when your car's broken), these worthless, nasty, dirty streets that hate me now as if I were a hyena, out of envy, they envy me my white minidress and my czarevitch beside me wearing a white silk suit – buzz off, you losers.

"Don't be a swine–" Stěpa shouted from the window of the itinerants quarters, and beside him stood Borek Trojan, they're capable of going on like this all afternoon, so I gave them a light with our silver lighter, it didn't want to light, maybe I should have gotten a gas one, and gold would have gone better with my skin –

"Let go!"

Suddenly I'm in their den, and they're facing me, feverish, coming at me, boys, please, we work together at the plant, we're buddies, after all. Dízlák runs on beer instead of fuel, that criminal Valtr, the bat Stěpa, and their boss Olda – a schoolgirl's dream – Borek, you too ... Already Madda is powerless and besieged in the circle of men.

(To be continued)

CONQUERORS

Well, I'm going to get something out of this moment, which is starting to drag on, I'm not going to play the pitiful victim and I'm not going to be a doll either, what can I do when nothing can be done. I can bite better than you, I'm the sister of Alex the Devil, you're repulsive, fat Valtr, and all you can do is drag it out, Borek's in and out like that, you need a couple of years with a woman first, little Onan, Stěpa's a mean, pitiful animal, and

Olda, Olda ... "Olda ... Olda ... Olda – – oh-yes-yes! oh-yes-yes! oh-yes-yes! YES!"

And suddenly for the first time in my life I had one, that devil Olda gave it to me. My first one not till I was nineteen – that's crazy: then what was all that before? – "... Olda ... Olinek ... Oldříšek..." – and what about my bleu blues? That should probably remain music ... or I just imagined it.

Then Madda walked up to the second floor as if she were in a hotel, I live neither here nor there, a bath (because the boys downstairs don't have a shower) and dinner (you're stupid if you give, but stupider if you don't take), suddenly I have my old appetite back, Madda devoured the veal and rice and ordered "an omelet with brains" (right now the boys downstairs are cooking cured meat in a pot, I'll have some with Olda later) and drank two cans of Lebanese orange juice (and now a can of beer), dismissed Roman with a contemptuous glance, and quickly fell asleep with thoughts of her man Olda.

Roman, Roman, Roman ... czarevitch, but now without *love*. And without a car – ours is broken, and he says we can't use the company car. Then why is Old Man Gráf the director if the director's car doesn't belong to him?! They're a bunch of nitwits ... blue cretins. I should be the director.

But without *love* it's really annoying: when I have money I pay, and when I don't I sit at home? Or maybe I could bring some in, so I pilfered those painted plates. Roman says they're worth a hundred *dollars*, do dollars really exist? In Ústí no one's ever seen them, not even the boys at the docks. And at Tuzex they offered Roman a *fifty-crown voucher* for those shards, what a girl would have to do to make that – and that idiot didn't take it! So I took those plates myself to this waiter in the Staročeský Alehouse where they break a lot of glass, the waiter pulled a long face but finally plonked down forty crowns. I'd say he got a deal.

And then a few of Gráfová's rags, an old tome, and a Roman coin that hasn't been used for two thousand years and doesn't even fit into a vending machine – so why do these nitwits keep them locked up at home? And would you believe you can find even bigger nitwits who'll pay for these things? I'll bet I could become an economist in a second – and maybe a better one that those morons with all their degrees.

But on the other hand, since people pay for this junk, it must be worth something, like for instance Gráfová's golden eyeglasses with one gem right next to another, even though the gems are pretty puny – gold's worth something, I'm sure of that, and it's really vulgar that bourgeois like the Gráfs have so many golden things at home – God, if you only saw Gráfová's jewelry! – and they don't even do anything with it, why don't they use it to import oranges so they'd be cheaper for poor children, or they could buy poor newlyweds furniture or something, couldn't they, or they should nationalize these jewels and give out holiday vouchers to everyone so you could use them for fourteen days or something, because gold after all is really cool. So I still haven't sold those golden glasses yet, even though there'd be plenty of buyers and considering my business talents – for now, I've hidden them among my underwear. My first jewelry ... they'd look a lot better on me, I've got the figure for them, after all.

And I almost lost them ... well, not exactly. When I was going through the pile looking for some clean panties, the golden glasses fell out onto the floor and one lens cracked. But that's okay, because my eyes are good, I don't need glasses. Roman saw them but pretended he didn't ... and that started to bug me. Most people would be outraged – you stole our glasses, give them back and just be glad I don't smack you 'cross the jaw – but not little Roman, he pretends it's nothing, just to show you how well he's been brought up and how noble he is ... If you took his shoes off and set the roof over his head on fire, he'd just look at you sadly so you could see how noble he was and how far above you he stood. It makes me want to vomit. He's really getting on my nerves – he's like a stupid sheep.

Románek, my *blue* blues. My pitiful little thing. I don't know if I love you anymore when you're not at all a man, I've got a muddle in my head, there's only one thing I know for sure: Olda.

On Saturday afternoon Madda sent Roman off with his parents to their house on the river for the weekend, she pulled the white minidress over her bare body, and hour after hour walked around building No. 2000 and up and down the street in front of it. She'd sit down on the steps, get up again, go out, come back, grow damp with waxing desire, pace back and forth until she could no longer feel her legs, and went on and on till nightfall.

Olda buzzed in from his trip to his beautiful young wife, in the itinerants quarters he just threw off his overalls, grabbed a pair of clean underwear, a white shirt, and a black leather tie, a well-made black suit, and took off for the station to go see his other beautiful wife.

On the first floor, the lime-covered window opened a little, and the sad, ancient face of Teo looked out over the darkening street.

"Go home, little girl. It's time for bed."

Madda defiantly shook her head, ran up to the second floor, I'll just have a shot of something, scrape up a hundred crowns, and go to the Svět Café on the square –

"What are you looking for in the sideboard?" Madda heard a familiar, derisive voice. "Strawberry marmalade? I wouldn't mind a lick."

Alex! – I forgot to close the door ...

"Buzz off, Alex. I'm in a hurry."

"When you're in a hurry, sit down for a moment, goes an old Russian proverb, and on the other hand we who speak Latin say: Festina lente!" Alex laughed and quietly closed the door behind him. "We'll hurry together then, okay?"

"Alex–"

"So break out the marmalade. Courvoisier? Gratias! VSOP? Hosanna!"

"Alex, dear brother ... please, no."

"Madda, dear sister ... please, yes. And besides please, I'll beat you again, too. Hallelujah!"

How the thin, refined glass tinkles, and from the crystal white Cinzano – blue cloudlets of perfumed tobacco – the heady, golden Courvoisier rolls like honey into the massive, dark-gray glass, the purple *Parfait Amour* phosphoresces, and the Cuban Ronda throws out angry white flashes, the room gets bigger when the door is opened, and barefoot (when he was taking off his shoes Alex knocked over the little flower stand and as punishment threw his moccasin through the glass of the sideboard) you practically float along the carpet (the WC already seemed to Madda unnecessarily far away), the rooms behind you form the main avenue of the conquered port (Alex was swinging the chandelier, something fell, and Madda knocked over the refrigerator), may the parasites perish, Madda broke the Japanese tea service and Alex, irritated by the flameproof nylon curtains, poured Ronda on the tablecloth and set it on fire, behind the blue flames Madda paraded around in Zita's blue chiffon dress and with his feet Alex was marking up the phosphorescent beds. "Put on something white–" Alex ordered, and Madda joyfully pulled out the piece of clothing that hung at the end of the overstuffed closet and put on Zita's wedding dress.

Don't you hate being woken out of the best sleep you've ever had? The Gráfs and Roman were standing over us yelling – some squealer must have ratted on us, it's only noon after all! – their faces were greener than ours after a party.

For reinforcement they'd even brought Julda, and I've never heard so much ridiculous drivel all at once, we were just having fun, so a couple things got broken, I'll pay for them, and with better currency than *love*, better than gold and steel, you degenerate asses. But Julda, you disappointed me when you joined those blue cretins against me, I know they hate us, but what about you, are you poor in a different way than me? You betrayed me, Julda, and that will not easily be forgotten –

And so I moved back to the former men's one-room flat on the third floor, to the cot stuffed with straw, and instead of a bathroom just a faucet on the wall that doesn't work ... either way, I live neither here nor there, is this really any way to live? So now we'll be living again like we didn't really live before. But Alex has to leave. He'll go to the itinerants quarters on the first floor.

Alex just laughed, packed his little suitcase in a trice, and in his one suit (that devil, with all those jobs on the side, makes at least six thousand a month) he affably shook our hands to go:

"So long! See you, old wringer, and God be with you! Goodbye and Aufwiederschauen – I'm not going far."

"This is obscene," Borek Trojan blurted out in a voice quaking with indignation upon coming back from work to find his cot occupied by Alex Serafin.

"There's six of us for five cots," declared Alex, comfortably ensconced on his captured cot, "and if I have to fight for a bed, I'd rather fight with you than with Dízlák, for instance. Try seeing things from my perspective, my pitiful young friend..."

"So, you're not going to clear out!" screamed Borek. Instead of answering, Alex slowly raised his fist to his shoulder, and as he flexed his gorilla-like arm, up sprang a monstrous bicep the size of Borek's thigh.

Choking with rage, Borek went around the room picking up his clothes (Alex had also occupied Borek's decimeter of space in the common metal wardrobe), hung them on a nail on the wall, and looked for his dress shoes under the cot. Then, during the night, he broke into the Gráfs' fenced-in yard, dug up several kilos of potatoes, enough to fill up four large bags, and fell asleep at Alex's feet, resting his head on his battered suitcase.

Since Alex arrived, there hasn't been much sleeping in the itinerants quarters. Via various automobiles, Alex brought all sorts of women and always a sea of alcohol, the border between night and day collapsed, the walls themselves blanched at the wild spectacles, and Stěpa started howling even at noon.

Alex required several pogroms a day, and with the skill of a great contriver he arranged them into connected chains. He distracted himself with them all day and into the following morning – he lived for his art alone. Beneath Valtr's pillow he planted Stěpa's inviolable photos of actresses, he persuaded Valtr that Stěpa had called him a dirty thief, he got them both together and turned over Valtr's pillow – free-for-all wrestling. Olda found his golden-tipped cigarettes in Dízlák's coat pocket – *corrida*. And Olda found his pictures of his beautiful young wives among Stěpa's actresses, and at the same time Borek found the remnants of his *Life* magazine – which had recently disappeared. Stěpa found his paycheck in Valtr's shoe, and Valtr his lighter crushed beneath the leg of Dízlák's bed – a rodeo in a volcano.

"You're doing this on purpose!" Borek screamed in Alex's face, and smiling, Alex hoisted Borek with his powerful arms, threw him at the other men, and with a series of powerful blows went to work on the squirming ball huddled on the floor.

You couldn't even go home anymore – and there was no reason to. Food, drinks, and cigarettes were stolen as soon as you crossed the threshold, and to top it off, last Saturday night Dízlák ripped the faucet from the wall. After the flooding, the place dried up completely. At night, Borek took his bag down to the basement.

Unwashed, sweaty, without a crown, hungry, thirsty, sexually unsatiated, and furious, Borek sat in the brutal sun on the steps in front of our building of insanity and ran his bare feet through a drift of hot beige dust, his own method of cleansing and probably the way the Bedouins wash themselves in the desert – A shiny blue-and-silver car drove up in a cloud, and out climbed:

Comrade Dr. Evžen Gráf, the factory director ("You've really settled in here, haven't you–"), his indulgent smile was like a dagger thrust into my kidney. "Good afternoon, Comrade Director."

Madame Zita Gráfová, his wife ("Just like at the beach – have you learned how to pronounce Antibes yet?"), a needle into my trigeminal nerve, and she spins it around a bit. "I'm trying, Mrs. Gráfová."

Dauphin Roman, the offspring (a brief imbecilic smile, then back to haughty disdain), lets off a hydrogen sulfide fart right in my face.

Three sets of knees drift by above my head into the apartment THAT BELONGS TO THEM ALONE on the second floor, into that spacious suite of grottos, which they've conquered and defended for time eternal in an eternally ferocious battle to divide up this residential cliff with its grottos of very unequal sizes. The sly vulture Evžen sits at the entrance and first wisely pecks the enemy in the eyes; inside, the ferret Zita untiringly bustles about and lines the cave with pillows so that the young Crown Prince won't bang his little butt against the hard rock of the cliff and can grow into his inheritance, pampered and healthy without the just deserts of battle – what chance could the simple-minded female Madda, the desperate hound-dog

Tušl, with his young bitch, or me, a lousy dingo, a lonely dog of the prairies, have against this?

With his toes Borek Trojan grasped some grains of sand and thought about the Gráfs' lunch, which was being served right now, that's for sure:

"Just think, that urchin Trojan wants to live like us!" jokes Dr. Gráf at the head of the table (everyone laughs, chicken à la peacock and peacock à la l'Empereur Nero, fed only on almonds on the island of Chios; as an appetizer, Ostean murena fed on the flesh of slaves, and apricots in wine).

"That boy out there said sitting like that in the dust in front of the building made him feel as if he were in Menton or Cap d'Antibes – and he can't even *pronounce* Antibes!" giggled Madame Zita (as she served cream cake Imperial, with pineapples, pistachios, agar-agar, saffron, anise, New Guinea pepper, all to the accompaniment of a music box and a nine-color water fountain. As she was cutting the cake, accompanied by an eight-color pyrotechnic display, from inside the cake a naked, singing slave boy appears, everyone pours Hennessey VSOP cognac on him and sets him on fire, the little slave boy writhes to the sound of his own heartrending shrieks and burns to a crisp. Around the table laughter).

"That poor Trojan thought he was going to have our maid Madda before I did!" whinnied Gráf, Jr. (laughter, and Pommery & Greno Champagne is served along with an assortment of cheeses, Yemen coffee, hundred-year-old cognac, followed by a digestive liqueur called Nuncius).

"Will you be wanting that nubile young slave boy for your afternoon siesta again?" Mr. Gráf smiles indulgently at Mrs. Gráfová.

"I think I'll have him whipped in the stable instead – he's soiled my last rug – and then I'll have them pour salt on his back. I have a taste for something lighter today, perhaps a Brit or suchlike, since it's so hot this afternoon."

"I'll see to it, dear. And you, little Roman, will you be wanting Madda again today?" the father turns lovingly to his son.

"I've grown weary of her," yawns young Master Gráf. "Unless we could liven it up a bit…"

"Just say the word, son…"

"I could do her on top of a cage with that Trojan creature in it. To add a certain *frisson*…"

"But won't those bars be hard on your dear knees, my little imp?" Mrs. Gráfová asks affectionately as she caresses his cheek.

On a scabby, mangy mare at the head of the red ghetto troops, I invade the blues' besieged port   Across the forbidden lawns into the shaded atria with burbling water fountains   We plunge into the aristocracy's bedrooms   Let four comtesses from Versailles disrobe me   A bottle of chilled Blanc de Blanc *at the bedside   Let the princess plunk on the harp a little before her striptease   I'll do her on the silver brocade of the bed bearing the crown and the coat of arms   Rose petals rain down from the ceiling, coloring the sheets blood-red*

Then   the princess washes my member with blue, perfumed water from a marble fountain   And with a snap of my fingers I order the admiralty palace burnt to the ground   Instead of their eternal "Feuer!!" and "Los!" the blue, puppet-like officers chatter "Comment allez-vous, Madame, Mademoiselle, Monsieur?" – hang them by their epaulettes and put their stars, medals, and orders on their tongues and melt them in the flame of a gas lamp   Give the white villas on the shore to the troops as spoils   The vases and atria will be toilets for our men   And our mares shall dine on the shoots of the oleanders

They're not even strong enough to resist   There are more of us   Billions   Like termites   The enemy's aircraft carrier, far out at sea, is occupied with a sociological investigation and elections on deck   They're voting on who will fire   For us it's a reward   For them punishment   They want it to be democratic   They'll drown themselves   And our termites will eat through their weirs and dams   And above the former port the sea will seize the jungle

"Excuse me..." a soft voice says almost apologetically, footsteps behind me and refined, exquisitely turned female knees glide past. Zita Gráfová stepped over Borek's legs, and as she sat down in the car she looked back again at Borek as if guiltily ... as if pleadingly ... as if ... like a woman.

And Borek Trojan fixed his yellow-gray pupils on her, wide with the cruel clearsightedness of prehuman instinct.

"...the situation has become unsustainable. We will not allow ourselves to be oppressed forever!" thundered the speaker. "No more oppression!" roared the masses below him, and they began to chant in time with the swinging of his arm, "No–more–oppression! No–more–oppression! No–more–oppression!" which gave way to frenetic applause.

Bogan Tušl had called a meeting of the residents of building No. 2000 on the steps between the second and third floors. Naturally, none of the Gráfs came, but those present – Jolana Tušlová, Alex and Madda Serafin, and Borek Trojan – saw to it, under Bogan's effective direction, that every word reached the second floor. Only Julda Serafin was silent, but he's an idiot. The cruel, unjustified reprisals taken against Madda Serafinová, which deprived Alex Serafin of a room and Borek Trojan of a bed, are the final drop of bitterness with which the cup of our patience runneth over. And since the Gráfs have not responded to our polite requests –

"Effective immediately I hereby proclaim a state of emergency throughout the building! With your assistance I call for the implementation of the following measures! Cut off the main water line! Board up the main entrance to the building, we'll enter through the window of the itinerants quarters! Cut off the electric power! This I submit for your reflection–"

The masses of course long not for reflection, as Bogan Tušl sensed with the quickened instincts of a rapist in the act, but for firm leadership and most of all a pogrom. And thus to his heart's content he molded the minds of his listeners like a dictator, the dictator of the red ghetto in an all-out anti-blue war – the great manipulator of the willingly ravished masses.

"Does anyone else have a better suggestion?!" shouted Bogan in a tone that brooked no response.

Nevertheless, someone dared – Julda Serafin. "You speak with much anger and little reason..." he spoke softly into the unfriendly silence. "Things cannot be resolved this way. One must act with patience–"

A hostile silence suddenly turned into a hostile uproar, Bogan secured silence with a mere wave of his hand and shouted: "Until they throw us all out?! Until everyone loses his bed?!"

"Julda's a traitor–" shrieked Madda. "Let's go to the basement and shut off the water!"

"Turn off the electricity!" thundered Alex.

"Break down the gate!" raged Borek Trojan.

After Julda was knocked down from behind by several arms, he disappeared from the scene, silenced for good. Meanwhile, Bogan Tušl formulated the fundamental subsistence demand on behalf of all of us gathered here today:

"A–FLAT–FOR–THE–TUŠLS!! This is the situation! Alex Serafin and Borek Trojan will move into the room vacated by the Tušls! This will liberate one cot for a worker in the itinerants quarters! A–flat–for–the–Tušls–will–satisfy–four–petitioners! A–FLAT–FOR–THE–TUŠLS!! A–FLAT–FOR–THE–TUŠLS!!" The masses wildly screamed the slogan of their freedom, the harbinger of their happy future. A–FLAT–FOR–THE–TUŠLS!!" They thundered their sacred claim to the justice of history.

His Serene Highness finally bowed before the will of the people. "You are to report immediately to the director–" said a shrill female voice over the telephone, and even after the girl had hung up, Bogan gripped the receiver as if it were a marshal's swagger stick. The sun gilded the forms, documents, and adding machine, my victorious weapon, and covered Bogan's shoulders and chest in gold. The Austerlitz sun of victory –

"Don't let him trick you–" whispered Jolana, pale with excitement.

"I'll crush him," was all Bogan said, and he exited into the dark hallway of the White House and slowly made his way along the lighted rectangles of the forty glass-paneled office doors. It looked as if the silhouettes behind the doors had frozen into a lane of statues leading to the Arc de Triomphe. A–FLAT–FOR–THE–TUŠLS–

"You're to wait a moment," said the girl in the waiting room, who was wearing a white coat, and without a word Bogan sat down in the visitor's chair. This is the last time I'll wait.

The moment stretched into minute upon minute, and the heat in the waiting room perceptibly rose. Gráf's old trick – let him stew in his own juices to soften him up … Nevertheless, Bogan grew uneasy, and his thoughts quickly ran through a succession of distinct operations: the falsification of the monthly output – both committees, the Prosecutor's Office, and the bank; they might be here already. The to-do about pricing – the people's audit, the Ministry and the Union, they'll take their time. The collapsible kayak – that's nothing. Painting his flat and the business trips – also slight. The six lost holiday gifts … Maybe that wasn't such a good idea.

The moment had turned into forty-six minutes when Bogan was shown into the director's office. Gráf did not reply to Bogan's greeting, nor did he even offer Bogan a chair – but looking down at you from above corresponds to my position of power …

"Enough already," Director Gráf said after an endless period of time, during which he'd calmly finished reading the local daily, *The Vanguard*, lit a cigarette, called and ordered three box seats to *Swan Lake* (Gráf's typical improvisations, but no one buys it, least of all me). He suddenly opened a drawer, fastidiously pulled out my metal arrow, and threw it on the floor at my feet. "I'm returning your toy. And now."

"And now."

"In response to your allegations, the first commission arrives tomorrow at ten, I think they're from the Public Prosecutor's office. A review by the State Bank has been announced for Wednesday, and one by the City Council for Thursday. After Sunday there will be considerably more – you know best whom you've invited."

"But now–"

"You are to see to everything. Explain it to them however you want. It is now your affair."

"My affair?"

"Yes, it is now your affair." The director grinned, and with a ruler he slowly pushed along the table toward Tušl, a decimeter closer, three keys on a keychain. "As is this flat. Two rooms in Všebořice, a balcony, central heating, hot water, gas. But I'm not giving you official permission yet. You'll move in without authorization. Moving expenses will not be reimbursed."

"...without authorization?"

"Yes, unofficially and illegally. So you can be moved out. In the event your work with these commissions fails. You'll receive authorization only when you've dealt with them successfully."

"But what guarantee..."

"The logic of the matter. Think it over a moment." And the director buried his nose in the pages of the local weekly, *North*.

"Please understand, Comrade Director, I really want to believe you, but..."

"You have no other choice. Except to call another meeting on the stairs. If you do, I'll have you moved out to the old rectory for systematically disturbing our socialist communal living quarters. Need I remind you that you're now living in a former women's one-room flat illegally and without authorization? You can be moved out now."

"And you can be sued. If the commissions confirm my accusations—"

"You're a capable official." The director yawned. "But politically you're simply ... well, let's just say childish. Our little archer. What is it you wish to show these weary people? They know as well as us that we do just what almost every company in the district, region, and country does. The commissions will arrive with this opinion from the very beginning. Our organizations will naturally support them – do you think someone's going to let his bonus be taken away just because you want a flat? Finally, as has happened so often before, it will degenerate into a witchhunt for an informer. He will be uncovered. My young lawyer has already promised ... to break your jaw. He's a weight-lifter, you know."

"But we're not talking about an informer—"

"Then why did he befoul his own company? His collective?"

"He acted according to the letter of the law. In the interests of the Party and the People. And justice."

"We have proof he acted out of base motives: for personal revenge."

"Why would he seek revenge?"

"He's morally degenerate ... because I lowered his merit pay by eighty-three crowns. And reduced his wife's bonus by twenty crowns."

"But you didn't reduce my merit pay ... or Jolana's..."

"Oh, but I did. Both of yours."

"Then you must have done it today – otherwise I'd have known about it. And isn't that a low and base motive, when a director punishes employees for making justified criticisms?"

"Except that the director did this *before* the allegations were made. Are you any good with calendars?" And with a ruler the director pushed toward the reddening employee two completed forms, one merit-pay reduction and one bonus reduction, dated almost a month ago ...

"You made these today! And backdated them!"

"Litera scripta manet, which only litera pressa – or, there's no disputing stamps."

"That's really low ... but be careful: Let's allow that they're dated, but at the same time we have to allow that these two pieces of paper have been in your desk a month. And so my base motives don't hold. I simply didn't know about it – I couldn't have broken into your desk, now, could I?"

"Of course you could. And not only mine. How else could you have gathered so much secret information – it couldn't all have been in your own desk. And how could such a clever informer, who broke into so much confidential information, miss a reduction of his own salary? The girl behind the door caught you in here twice."

"So you're going to accuse me of breaking into your desk..."

"What's funny is that you'll break into it again in three minutes..."

"I'm going to break into your desk right now..."

"Naturally. How else did you intend to take these keys–" and with a ruler the director pushed them along the table another decimeter closer to the pale employee – "for your unauthorized, unofficial, and illegal move? Would you prefer to obtain them at a factory-wide meeting to the accompaniment of a brass band? Take them, my pitiful young archer, or in three minutes I'll lock them in the vault. And instead of you, our old soldier Frank Secký will attend to the commissions, you'll go live at the rectory, and I'll take those eighty-three crowns from you to teach you a lesson."

"I'll take them," Bogan smiled bitterly. "It's still a bunch of tomfoolery. Right now I'm supposed to be breaking into your desk, you're secretly reducing my pay, and I'm supposed to testify in your favor..."

"Such inconsistencies are known as dialectics. That is tails. Heads is shining you in the face: with your attempted treachery you've gained a flat you couldn't have achieved through loyalty."

"I'm taking them," said Tušl, and he reached out his hand for the keys, but with a sudden movement of his ruler, the director moved them half a meter beyond Tušl's reach.

"There are still two catches," said the director affably.

"Even this has a catch, even this unauthorized, unofficial, illegal–"

"Two catches. But of course you'd take the keys even if there were sixty-five. However, there are only two. First: the room on the third floor vacated by your move must remain empty. On principle, I will not tolerate rape in my building."

"But I promised Alex and Trojan…"

"You'll just have to discuss it amongst yourselves, this time with only your own conscience to rely on, my young demagogue. So, can you arrange it?"

"It'll be difficult … but I'll arrange it."

"Locking the door isn't enough. You'll need to do it scientifically…"

"I'll arrange it. And the other catch?"

"You'll replace my broken window. At exactly five-thirty this afternoon."

"Okay. Anything else?"

"Perhaps some thanks are in order."

"Thank you. I sincerely thank you. Really. Thank you very much."

"If you do what's germane … In two years Abrt is going to retire. I'd like to begin training a new economic deputy … You're a capable official, and if you're quick on the uptake…"

"Comrade Director … Dr. … You'll be completely satisfied with me. I…"

"Will you do what's germane?"

"I will!"

"Let's try it then. Say: Danke sehr."

"Danka sarah."

"Ouch, you're turning it into Yiddish. We should try French; that'll be even funnier. And before I forget – you'll be studying technical engineering in the evenings, for six years, evening classes will be of more avail to you than throwing rats through my window. For that, say: merci mille fois!"

"Mersimilfoa."

"That means – *cela veut dire* – a thousand thanks. C'est ça, parfaitement … No, don't try to repeat that. I don't think I could take your nasals. Out!"

"I'll ring at your place at precisely five-thirty with a pane of glass beneath my arm!" Bogan called out and he stood at attention.

"Naturellement." Dr. Evžen Gráf smiled and once again called Bogan back from the door: "Tušl – you forgot your arrow–"

And with the metal arrow hidden in his trouser leg, Bogan Tušl limped as if from a serious wound down the dark hallway of the White House and rejoiced in his mind, WE HAVE A FLAT, our own flat completely to ourselves and our baby who's soon to arrive, each will have his own room, *after lunch we'll have cognac on the balcony   We'll meet in the dining room and then disperse   I'll wait by the window with a cigarette to see if my beloved is coming* she's already knocking, in my flat with my wife, we have a flat, we have a flat, we have a flat, A–FLAT–FOR–THE–TUŠLS ... we've arrived!! I have a flat... and in two years I'll be a deputy, life is marvelous, miracles do happen, I have a flat – and the lighted rectangles of the glass panels of the forty office doors arched up into the canopy of the sky, and the stars mounted this new galaxy and with childlike rejoicing descended into Bogan's lap.

(To be continued)

BESIEGED

Reclining in his laminated armchair, his hands resting lightly on the chair's cool plastic, the back of his head against the headrest, his eyes closed, Assistant Economic Deputy Bogan Tušl savored the simple joy of relaxation. A difficult day behind us. More difficult ones ahead. At least we can sleep – right now and as long as possible ...

Suddenly from the floor below, a powerful, wooden blow, and then another. Am I supposed to be quieter still? Boom. Boom. Boom. Boom. What are those people doing down there ... I have to be polite to them. As long as I still don't have authorization. Boom. Boom. Boom. Boom. The commissions have already stopped coming. To the flat and to the plant. It's over. Boom.

Crash! Jolana bangs the bathroom door. It doesn't close properly. She's getting more nervous every day. There's been too much the last few weeks. When the Housing Administration Committee barged in here ... quite an unpleasant scene. The ones from the People's Committee were more decent. But they didn't have to send the police after us. The worst was the building manager. They've used up all their ammunition. So have I. A truce due to mutual exhaustion. Nothing more should happen now.

Sleep ... I don't sleep much anymore. Six years of correspondence training. Six years of nights sitting over textbooks. Then Deputy. Deputies take their work home. I'll have to read thousands of stupid pages. It used to be wonderful to lock my desk at two and be done ... A manager's work is never done. He runs with a water pistol from fire to fire, putting out only the biggest ones. The danger of third-degree burns. A bigger salary ... there won't be time to spend it. Personal power ... the deputy experiences it only at the director's rear.

The ceiling directly above his head resounded with insane stomping. Doop. Doop. Doopity doopity doop. Now who's that? They must be jumping a meter off the ground. I have to be polite to them. Even when I get authorization. I can't even allow myself ... In the building nothing at all.

My subordinates hate me. I want more work out of them. But I must admit ... I can't work any more myself. There's no way back. Only upward. They're whispering all sorts of things. About Jolana, too. It used to be wonderful to lock the desk at two and go see friends ... Never again. There won't be time. Or even the desire.

And the new boss, Deputy Abrt, has completely stopped working. He's got two years till retirement ... He doesn't tell me the main things, the important ones ... Why should he? He's keeping them for himself. With an efficient coolie like me, it could be another five years before he retires ... A horrible thought. But I can't act against him. Not even in a year. Not even in two.

To be a fish warden at a pond in southern Bohemia   Walking every day along the embankment beneath the ancient oaks   Catching carp, pike, tench, perch   Observing the quiet surface of the water with a pipe between my teeth   And in the evening to the tavern, where everyone is glad to see you   To live alone with just a dog in a small house on the edge of a pine forest

BANG! BANG! BANG! BANG! Horrible metallic banging from somewhere to the left. Thirty-six tenants in this building. Be polite to all of them ... BANG! To all thirty-six. BANG! BANG! BANG! BANG! BANG! BANG! Let me sleep, I beg you.

Well, I have a flat. Our blue rug has finally found its floor, and the blue chandelier its ceiling. But the light is pitifully weak. The table, made of red oak, wobbles on its screwed-in legs. It looked better packed up. The child's crib on the other side of the wall. That'll bring more work. Where are we going to hang the diapers? And till the baby grows up, we won't be able to go anywhere at night. Besides, there won't be time. Our five golden picture frames have finally found their pictures.

Brrrrnk! – brnk! – brrrrrrrrrrnk! – Someone's at the door. They've come again to throw us out. But they've been misinformed. It won't work anymore. But I have to be polite to them.

"...your radio's blaring like it was out in the yard somewhere!" hissed a repulsive four-eyes in a grubby robe.

"Excuse me, I'm sorry ... I didn't realize ... Jolana! Turn down the radio!"

"But I just..." and Jolana appeared, disheveled, wearing only her chemise, at least in front of people she could – "turned it down..."

"Then turn it off!"

"You're living in an apartment building, for crying out loud. At night I can even hear you snoring!" barked the repulsive character in place of thanks, our dear, respected neighbor.

On the table our traditional celebratory meal. We've been celebrating victory a while now. It's a celebratory spread we've laid out numerous times: for getting rid of the commissions that came to get rid of us. For lacquering the floor. For painting the walls. For hanging the curtains. Twice for feeling sleepy. The last time for feeling totally exhausted.

"Remember what we said a few weeks ago," says Jolana, trying to be emotional, "with the first champagne in this glass, we'll toast our flat!"

"Yes, dear." The glasses have finally found their champagne. Jolana must have overchilled it. It doesn't fizz at all ...

"How do you dance with a glass in your hand ... do you remember?"

"Probably like this..." That's what I said last time.

"You know how to hold me so well..." Jolana lies charitably. Because of her six-month belly, I can't quite reach her.

"I can't hold you any other way..." Some things can't bear repeating.

"I'm so happy I have you..." Jolana remembers what she said last time.

"Yes, dear. But let's go sit down. With that belly of yours..."

"Yes, dear."

On the table was our traditional victory meal. The pyramid of food today is almost half a meter high. Poor Jolana overdid it. Instead of squares of bread and horse salami she's bought white rolls and real ham, instead of peanut oil, Greek olive oil, and instead of onions – what's this? – real olives. A bitter fruit with a stony pit. We can't really be expected to eat this.

"Remember when we said..." Jolana tries to liven things up, "there are two kinds of people? Those with a flat and those without. And between them a barbed-wire fence ... Now we're on the other side!"

"We've won the battle." We're on the other side. Before we were outside. Now we're in.

"Do you like it, dear?" asks Jolana as she separates out the olives and oily ham and pushes them toward the edge of the board. She can't eat it either.

"Yes, dear. Do you?

"If you do, I do too. More champagne?"

"It's kind of rich ... how about some beer first."

And Jolana brings out on a tray our seven-piece beer service, with five golden bands on each glass. We've lived to see the day ... but you can't mix champagne and beer and expect to go unpunished. The triumphal procession ends at the toilet.

Cognac on the veranda after dinner – On our balcony, 2 x 0.5 meters, we'd have to drink it standing up. When Jolana goes out there for five minutes to hang laundry, she returns covered in soot. Besides, drinking alcohol before thirty-five tenants and the entire neighborhood is social suicide.

Jolana is thoughtful, she doesn't even rub it in. We'll probably even love each other differently. They say love is compassion. The director told me this.

"Come on. Let's do something together ... something really nice..." whispers Jolana. This, however, is not thoughtful of her. If only she could see herself ... If only we'd waited on the child ... If only I hadn't married her and was now single ...

"We only have a few days left..." whispers Jolana, exhausted.

"How making love can be..." Bogan whispers sadly when the mechanical pleasure, as if from a hollow log, finally drags itself up to bring an end to the toil.

Through the open window blows a cold wind from a sky strewn with immensities. Lying on his back, Bogan tries in vain to find the Milky Way and soon gives up. I'm simply tired. I'm thirty-five already: the whistle's blown for the second half to begin.

Jolana wants to fall asleep with my hand in hers, but soon lets go. She's simply tired. The summit achieved. We've both had enough. A difficult day behind us. More difficult ones ahead. And it was too hot this afternoon. Please, let us sleep.

But what's beyond the summit? ... There's nothing more above it. And beyond it ... For there to be a peak, there must be an abyss around it. But ... then what's going to happen now? Since FOR NOW has ended and NOT UNTIL has arrived – – –

Covered in a cold sweat bursting from all his pores, in terror Bogan sat up in bed in a sudden flash of satori ("a sudden illumination, a sudden awakening, or simply a kick in the eye," as Jack Kerouac explains it) or rather some kind of evil anti-satori, because it was ice-cold and congealing, and with exhausted anger he looked up toward the mockingly winking, merciless stars.

Then his exhausted anger reached out its front paws and calmly rested its muzzle on them, well, little stars, we're safely far away from one another, you're there and I'm here. We've used up all our ammunition and now, out of mutual exhaustion, we have a permanent, quiet truce. It could be worse, although it could be better, but it's simply turned out like this.

I will not cry. I have a good wife. Body of my body. I embrace her sleeping form, and in her sleep she embraces me. We take shelter in each other, shield each other, and together we will slowly submerge. We will die together the way we've lived together. My dear neurotic one. I'll become neurotic myself. Tomorrow: an unpleasant day awaits us.

I'm thirty-five years old. Still twenty-five years to retirement. These last twenty-five flew by in a single feverish day. Now only the second and final feverish day remains.

Thirty-five: a man's best years. The path to power is open. Scheme and rule. I'm enjoying myself. I have a good wife. A comfortable flat with all the amenities. I gather my honors from the eyes of my subordinates. I'm useful. I'm on my way up.

Tomorrow an unpleasant day awaits us. Once again into that awful building. I'll never be rid of it. Those people there … they're dangerous.

The following day at 12:00, when everyone's at work or sleeping, the Tušls arrive at building No. 2000 in a loaded pickup truck. (Old Teo looks out the first-floor window – why didn't we ever have a talk with him? … There was never time.) Non-Cottex workers (hired from Cosmopharma, ours wouldn't have done it) took five cases out of the truck and carried them up the stairs to the third floor (this is where it all began …), to the former women's one-room flat, each case 300 kilograms, as well as welding equipment, tracks, and other necessities. The actual work we have to do ourselves. Even the hired men refused to do it. Each one gets fifty crowns and takes them with disgust. "Okay, beat it—"

"This is where it all began…" Jolana whispers between the cases in her old women's one-room flat. "Remember how I played the accordion here with Jiřka Háková…"

"Why don't you think instead about the time you threw Jiřka's shoes out the window, at her head … come on, let's go, let's get this off our backs…"

In the spaces between the cases (which are filled with bricks) are two sets of tracks running across each other, quickly weld them into the shape of an X, meanwhile Jolana removes the putty from around the window pane, unglazes the window (the glass is broken), and boards it up, then I remove the water pipe from the wall, close the water main, rip out the electrical installation, and then together we put the WC out of commission. In case of an unauthorized move-in, the room must be completely uninhabitable and technically secured, to be at the disposal of the plant administration. To ensure success, I'll do it scientifically. Finally I'll bang on the pipe with this wrench – now we're on the defense.

Suddenly a knocking at the door – good God, they're back from work already?

"Who's in there?" thunders Alex Serafin.

"This flat is ours!!" roars Borek Trojan.

Until now our main allies, from now on our mortal enemies. Is this also dialectics? We would have already lost a continuation of the revolution on the stairs. Otherwise we control all means of power.

"What are we going to do?" Jolana whispers anxiously.

"We'll wait until they leave..."

"They're not going to leave..."

"We'll hold out until ... we'll hold out."

Outside, shouting and blows to the door; inside, as if trapped, the Tušls are besieged.

After Tušl's departure from the director's office, Dr. Gráf asked his secretary to call Engineer Secký. He softly returned the receiver to its cradle and slowly placed his manicured white hands, with their beautiful, slender fingers, upon his red oak desk.

Bogan Tušl. Now we've got him on a leash. When he came here: young, self-confident, superior, triumphant. But didn't he indeed triumph in the end? I only punished him for his defiant youth. Like he did me for the weakness of my years. How can I halt the impending deluge of the rabble? By integrating their elite. With some it'll work. With a hundred, a thousand, with a whole social layer. But with a dense, undivided billion?

The telephone hummed (he'd had it specially deadened and the sound linearized by a colleague from the communications department): "Technology Deputy Secký is here."

"Two minutes." In other places, whoever wants to barges into the director's office without even knocking. I run things the old way. No one may call me directly. At the Vatican, nobody calls at all during business hours. American experts are amazed at what they call the administrative *efficacy* of the Papal See. It must be interesting to be a cardinal. Or better yet his librarian. Pablo Casals betrayed the secret of his vitality at ninety years of age: Rest at inopportune moments! That's what I do, even though I'm not keen on being ninety. A terrible thought.

"Engineer Trojan is here," hummed the telephone.

"I don't have time for him–"

"But he says it's urgent..."

"–or the appetite."

Borek Trojan. Another one of them ... He wants me to give him such a trifle: a flat, a raise, a promotion ... He wants the whole world. He's driving me crazy. He looks at me with mockery, condescension, hatred – with just a glance he *buries me alive* ... They're all rebelling against me. One after another, endlessly. Every day there's more of them. The pressure keeps increasing ... until one day it will burst. What will burst? You, of course, my dear Evžen. But hasn't it been bursting continuously for a thousand years? This moment is still mine ... as long as I can still have the rebel thrown out. One of the advantages of power. Well, let's return to Bogan Tušl. That's nicer. He's already eating out of my hand.

Evžen Gráf pressed a button and Frank Secký entered.

"Have a seat," said Evžen.

"Did it work?" inquired Frank.

"He even thanked me for it in several different languages."

"You got him cheaply. We couldn't have kept that flat in Všebořice for long anyway."

"And Tušl's boarding up the former women's flat, as well."

"Great. For how long?"

"He's doing it scientifically."

"Even better. Tušl's a capable rascal."

"He's going to be your colleague."

"But? ... After Abrt, right?"

"Do you think you'll get along with him?"

"I get along with absolutely everybody. Congratulations, Evžen, you're pretty clever. A clever gardener always gets himself a nasty dog."

"Thanks, Frank. Are you coming on Thursday?"

"With pleasure, thank you."

"I've received a denunciation of you from some moral delinquent. It peaked my interest at first, but the style is so pitiful – go ahead and read it yourself."

"Thanks. It's so long ... Okay, I'll take a look at it."

After Technology Deputy Secký, the factory doctor Dáša Zíbrtová and the fireman Serafin, an "urgent matter." Amused, Director Gráf ordered that they be shown in.

"...because the situation at the former rectory is crying out to heaven," concluded our physician. She doesn't look especially good, even though Zita's a little older ... Why doesn't she take care of herself a bit? She should prescribe herself some exercise. Unless she's expecting to find it in that.

"...and there are children there. We can't allow them to suffer," concluded Julda Serafin, our local missionary. If only he knew he was being watched more closely than I am. But how did these two get together ...

"As you know, the current precarious situation must first be resolved..." The director rather casually emitted his usual protective cloud, and at the end of his standard speech he added maliciously, "I'm concerned about the necessity of moving the Tušls to the rectory. It's not completely certain yet, but you can let them know about it."

"You want to seek revenge on them," said Julda Serafin. The sight of forthright people is ... indecent. At the very least, it's not *comme il faut*.

"Do you think I'd have reason to?" The director grinned.

"Vengence is mine, sayeth the Lord..." said Julda, and the director ostentatiously yawned, it's too hot for theological discussions, you Christians think everything's so simple: let's all join hands and be nice to each other like little children. But what if the devil gets a hold of one of those millions of children and kicks the neighboring child in the shins? Or somebody shoots a metal arrow through his window and tosses in a rat? Perpetual Christian sermonizing really gets annoying too. A worldly prelate is more likely to win me over with a glass of cognac in the art gallery of the bishop's palace ...

"You stay here–" said Evžen Gráf, in a suddenly peevish mood, to Dáša Zíbrtová when both visitors apologetically rose to leave. And with a sudden regret over something lost, he looked at the back of the retreating Julda. Turned to faith by the factory fireman ... what would remain of Fellini's films if instead of Claudia Cardinale at the mystic fountain, a fireman was beckoning to the viewers from an office?

"You haven't been to see me in a while..." said Dáša.

"You know what they say: doctor, lawyer, hangman ... But you haven't been to see us in a while either."

"I'd be glad to come and see you."

"Come see us like you used to. Every Thursday, Zita's jour fixe. Roman worries me. Pale, tired, lethargic..."

"Typical for his age."

"Is sexual exhaustion typical for his age as well?"

"Perhaps you're simplifying things. Those are common post-pubescent difficulties, you just have to..."

Make sure the little tyke eats well, gets plenty of sleep, and listens to Mama and Papa. Medicine hasn't made much progress since Hippocrates – Evžen Gráf sighed and regretted the fact he'd detained Dáša at all and moreover invited her to resume her usual Thursday visits. Not long ago it was almost fun ... "Has a cure for cancer been invented yet?"

"Not yet."

"Or the flu?"

"Not yet."

"The common cold?"

"Not yet."

"Not even the common cold? So what's the secret of life?"

"That's been known for two thousand years already."

"Well, despite my abundant reading, I somehow seemed to have missed it."

"The sowing of a seed and a miracle."

For once, the humming of the telephone came just at the right time, a powerful man from the tallest building in the city was calling, setting in motion the director's efficiently speculative mind – the doctor had already left, and the powerful man has finished speaking – with increasing speed. Once again it's all on the line –

Hardly have I painstakingly and ingeniously established my equilibrium when once again it's destroyed and dispersed. This insane masquerade of the ages. And blood. I don't envy you youngsters the remainder of this millennium. Keep it. It no longer amuses me.

I just need five more years. If only I were those five years older – *to be an old man sleeping with the rabble beneath the palace ramparts   Wearing just a coat made from a single piece of material and owning just a pair of bast shoes and a walking stick   In the morning only a drink from the well and then sit day after day in the marketplace   Just looking   Living on alms   The fewer the better   Not even looking anymore   Not thinking, not dreaming   Just lingering and softly fading away   Dying unobserved*

I no longer desire anything: fulfilled, sated, abated. The only thing left is waiting for death. Come, Eternal One. All of us are calling You. My son Roman has stepped forward to meet You. My wife Zita is calling You. Life is ... unhealthy, of course. Life is the instinct for self-gratification, the death instinct. A coup de grâce – a merciful blow to the fulfilled, sated, abated. Who said that? Freud? It doesn't matter. Why does fulfillment pummel and weaken a person? It's not logical ... Or is it perhaps logic of a higher order? After all, the living live precisely through fulfillment ... The death instinct.

Zita Gráfová drove up to building No. 2000, turned off the engine, and gathered the strength she needed to get out of the car and climb the stairs to the second floor. What am I going to do there? What am I doing here? Life: at every intersection choose the path of least nonsense. You'll surely soon go crazy.

Sitting on the steps in front of the building like an Athenian beggar with his bare feet buried in the dust, Engineer Borek Trojan. The young man with the blazing body, so similar to St. Sebastian ... the one who keeps banging the broom on the floor from down below. Boom. Boom. Boom. He's looking under my skirt. Boom.

Two thousand years of evolution seem to have escaped him and his friends from the itinerants quarters. They say he sleeps with Alex Serafin in the same cot, and the gap between them is sealed with women. Women morning, noon, and night. A constant flow. They live only for the fulfillment of their eternal appetites: like animals running free in the jungle. For pleasure alone: like the courtiers of Louis XV. *Après nous la deluge.*

"Bring the materiel over here–" Alex calls as he opens the sides of the truck and empties women onto the street like coal through a basement window. To chase them through the door would be a waste of time.

"Come here, little one–" mumbles Valtr, his mouth full of cured meat, with his right hand he's holding the meat and in his other paw his first victim, meat in one and meat in the other (the racket grows louder in the room, beer and cured meat, but no bread, was being served up).

"Leave that one for me–" Dízlák bawls at him (the racket in the room grows louder, a plump waitress is being served up, and the men are fighting over her).

"That one's for me–" shrieks Borek (the racket in the room grows louder, an old whore from the docks is being served up along with beer and cured meat, the men who haven't copulated yet are practicing by pounding on the ceiling).

"Hand her over–" squawks Stěpa (the racket in the room grows louder, a young produce clerk is being served up, the boss, Olda, sinks his teeth into her side and drags her away to a corner).

"This meat is mine–" yells Alex Serafin (Madda Serafinová is being portioned out on the set of grape motif dessert plates from my dowry, along with beer and cured meat, the men are tossing aside their uneaten courses and pouncing on dessert, they fight on the floor and the racket in the room grows even louder).

"How about a little entertainment for a change–" yawns a bored Borek Trojan (everyone shrieks in approbation, and they throw the women out the window and start beating on the ceiling, our floor, and yelling in unison, fortissimo:) "Death–to–all–decent–people!"

Thursday afternoon, my *jour fixe*. My husband wants it that way. The guests showed up today in full force: Frank Secký, Evžen's deputy, and Dáša Zíbrtová, the factory physician who works half-time (we share her with the slaughterhouse): my salon in its full glory. A salon of din and patter.

"The heat's insane," Frank converses as he pours himself a third glass of our Courvoisier (perhaps to indicate its necessity, as well as appeal to Evžen that he needs a pay raise).

"Mhm," Evžen converses from his chair (from behind, the front, the side, and above: an old and venerable English lady. Why isn't he embroidering something?).

"You should do something for those people at the rectory, sir. At least for the children..." urges the importunate Dáša Zíbrtová (usually she drinks my white Cinzano like water, today for a change she's drinking water like Cinzano, she's had a religious epiphany and stopped going to the hairdresser's).

"It'll probably cool off soon," adds Evžen, expressing his aversion to this deviation in the conversation (after all, it's ladies who talk exclusively about the weather).

"It's July," I utter laughingly (why aren't I embroidering something?).

Thursday is my *jour*: we're bored. My husband wants it that way. We'll play two rubbers of bridge, the guests will rise and leave, to the relief of everybody. See you next Thursday. One more afternoon of a sad, elderly lady. The things one could experience in these four hours.

"Hold me tight..." I plead in Evžen's embrace. Take me prisoner, shield me, eclipse me, let's submerge ourselves together. Hide me completely in yourself from the horror all around –

–those noises on the other side of the wall: Roman with Madda. No: Madda with Roman. Of the two of them she's the man –

–when Evžen squeezes me as hard he can, it's just a comforting caress. Neither of us is the man. Two old, venerable, English lesbian ladies: frugal, peaceful, apologetic, blameworthy, comfortable, hygienic, and thus – nothing here about love!! – deeply perverse. Roman, my son, I envy you your wild man –

"Yes, dear." Evžen's no longer anxious, he's certain I'll start boozing as soon as he's gone. "Yes, dear," of course I'll start boozing. He's gone. So what about you, young lady? Señor Ronda arrives, "7 Años," we've known Mister Alcohol seven years now, "750 gramos" times two is 1,500 gramos – should I try cutting it with Librium? – considerably more than enough for one aging lady. How long can you endure this without going insane? So this isn't insanity yet? Oh, what a relief!

Zita Gráfová trudged through the desert dust toward the bus stop and for a long time could not get on board, only thanks to our brokendown car have I learned that you're supposed to enter through the rear door, the crowd saved me by pulling me into its firm embrace and pressing me tight, and off we went. I've never been embraced by more than one man at a time, and all of these here are squeezing so tightly I'm losing my breath, like a ride to hell *toward the mercenaries' garrison deep in the jungle   To the burning sands of the training ground surrounded by a square of low buildings made of gray, white-hot clay   I've been assigned to one squad, for all purposes   The conquest is carried out in their quarters   There's only five cots here, a tin wardrobe, a table, a single chair, a faucet on the wall, and six half-naked men   The leader of the squad is Sergeant Olda (the inspecting officer, Alex Serafin, at his side, holding a whip)   Privates Dízlák, Valtr, Stěpa   And Officer Cadet Borek Trojan   I go from hand to hand*

These are men of action   They truly do not coddle me   But during the breaks they let me have some cured meat and a swallow of tepid beer   Above me the men bellow   They're cruel, but I deserve it   The night is endless   In the morning I drag myself to the window   In heavy boots around the training ground, half-naked men are marching through the morning mist   Acrid, pungent sweat

The men topple from exhaustion   The sergeants raise them with kicks and blows

Commandant Alex is still not satisfied   My cadet is guilty of something   They tie him to a column in front of a squad of archers   Aim   The bows are drawn   Fire   Five arrows soar in an arc and bury themselves in the cadet's bared body

Borek! – Another command and five more arrows, oh, Borek ...

Only at dusk am I allowed to untie him and nurse him   His cracked lips lap water from my palms   My young man   He soon begins to recover consciousness   As soon as he comes around, he begins to torment me   He orders me to wash his feet and dry them with my hair   He doesn't see that this arouses me   Already he's completely well   He whips me to pass the time   I'm happy and my mouth gasps for the whip   Isn't whipping a display of personal affection

Zita Gráfová went back into building No. 2000 and then came out, her anticipation of seeing Borek Trojan grew stronger, then turned to disappointment when she didn't see him, and then turned to neuroticism when she saw him and didn't have anything to say – his faulty pronunciation of Antibes hardly serves as a possible topic of conversation, I would love to talk with You, my young cadet, and I have oh so much I long to tell You ...

How You excite me. I'd love to taste Your kisses. What would they be like? Clumsy and forceful. My St. Sebastian. To see Your wide pupils, like those of a magnificent young animal, hovering just above my face ... It would be a sin. I'm a married woman. Oh. An old, venerable, English, lesbian, perverse lady. Ruff! Ruff!

Zita Gráfová trudged through the beige desert dust and prayed to building No. 2000 that it bestow upon her the sight of her beloved, please, please, at least for a moment ... And on the ground floor the lime-covered window of the former shop opened, and peeping through the crack Teo's severe, ancient face – oh, forgive me, old man, for what I have not yet committed ... Religion is cruel: a covetous look qualifies as fornication, and it recommends that you prophylactically pluck out your eye. But the world is far crueler.

Before the mirror applying my skin cream ... In the bathtub washing my chest with a tender Greek sponge ... At the window ... Moments of a strange bliss, of deep agitation ... Oh, I'm even singing to myself like I did in my youth! In my youth ... I've only read about that. Where do these things come from? Is it poetry or atavism? But it's good, girls, you know. I've fallen in love with a barefoot Greek boy ... Aren't you curious where you're going to spend the night with him?

And then one day it happened. *Fiat lux* – and then there was light. *Fiat amor* – the boy looked at me with love. I'm rejoicing – I'm choking – I'm raving –

The car's been repaired, my boy Roman, in the voluptuous embrace of his husband, Madda, barely speaks to me and avoids even looking at me – Borek, the barefoot Greek boy, looked at me with love. It's as if fate bestowed upon me another boy in exchange for the one I lost.

To sleep with an employee of Evžen's firm. With a fellow from the itinerants quarters a little older than my son. To tarnish myself. To disgrace my family. To harm my husband's name. To be unfaithful. To betray Evžen – my good, tender, noble husband. And everything that I love and all that makes up my life, my tradition, my style. My self-respect and my honor. My faith.

An end to our walks along the river. To our house on the river. To evenings with Evžen, with glasses of cognac in our hands, as rain flows down our picture window. To our compassionate – isn't love compassion? – embraces.

But if you want a drink, must you jump in the river?

But even if all this were to disappear ... Isn't love, at least for a year or a month or for only a week – isn't all that old rubbish worth it? Let everything else be destroyed – even for just a single night. Then what? Well, the morning and a new day. It doesn't belong to me anyway. And the deluge? It'll come anyway.

Our family's aristocratic taste for catastrophe. Or is it an instinct for self-destruction? Or perhaps it's simply a natural human longing: to allow yourself to be wiped out by a single act.

In this case a sweet one. I can already feel the taste of Your kisses on my lips, my clumsy, violent boy. My St. Sebastian. My deluge. It will come in time. But before – – –

But how to bring about this pleasure? This hope – How do I embark on it ... How do I give You a hint that I want You ... And now, a more practical question: where?

Not in the apartment. And surely not in the itinerants quarters. Somewhere outside ... not in the park ... by the river, in the woods, out of town, in a secluded spot. And definitely at night.

This must be thought through. Coldly. Organized: like a conspiracy. Like a murder: He'll drive somewhere out of town, inconspicuously. I'll secure an alibi beforehand. We'll walk for a long time through the dark, breathlessly. Anxiously avoiding other people, buildings, highways. Always on guard. Cautiously advancing. Hiding quickly when there's a chance of being seen. Furtively stealing to the chosen spot. And there, without witnesses and beneath a veil of darkness –

Which one of us will be the murderer?

(To be continued)

CONQUERORS

Torn from sleep by a blaring alarm clock, a searing erection, an excruciating hunger and a burning thirst, Borek Trojan unwound himself from the scratchy burlap bags he was sleeping in on the cement floor of the basement (his only consolation: he couldn't sink any lower) of building No. 2000, which is becoming LESS and LESS mine, in the itinerants quarters I lost my bed and now the liberated room on the third floor, which had been promised to us, has been appropriated, Bogan Tušl and his pregnant cow Jolana played a dirty trick and stole it from us by force and by using big-shot legal tricks, they betrayed us for a flat, which His Majesty circumspectly, but improperly, gave to them – the Tušls are gone, written off as if they'd died, and what's worse: they're now against us, on the side of the blue enemy, they've become blue themselves.

In anger Borek Trojan kicked at the dusty burlap bags, and instead of washing he hopped barefoot across the cold cement floor, there's not even a stupid faucet here and and so I'm out my breakfast – suddenly his eyes fell on the T-shaped pipe of the building's water main. He bent down to it, quickly turned the stop-valve, and from the pipe spouted a powerful stream of water, Borek frolicked naked in his newly established water fountain, and by turning the knob he manipulated the building's water supply at will, like Neptune – when he'd drunk and bathed his fill, in a sudden flash of inspiration he turned off the main valve, thereby depriving the entire building of water. I'm taking over command from the traitorous Tušls, and from this moment on I control the water supply. I declare the water supply conquered.

The blue-gray outline of the factory, tower, concourse, and warehouse, resembling in the morning mist an aircraft carrier at anchor ... The places it could sail to under determined and virile leadership – "Of course, of course..." standing near his window with a weary smile was Borek's boss, the sterile chieftain of technology and impotent ship's officer, he had given the job of filling out the salary lists, doing the calculations, and completing a small chart to the horny chemical engineer with practical experience, inventiveness, and lots of ideas – they're steering our ship toward the sand.

With two hundred and fifty grams of garlic salami and five hundred cubic centimeters of milk ration in his flat, rumbling stomach, increasingly slimmer (what's the sculptural grace of an ancient Greek youth when you're hungry), Borek stole up a metal ladder to the third floor through a hole in the ceiling to the water tank (Water Lord of both the factory and the building), and from there up the fire escape to the steel roof. He stripped down and on the soft, blazing asphalt spread out his overalls in the shape of his body and lay down on them to sleep (large predators sleep at noon). Rested and volcanically fresh, at 14:00 he set out on his daily hunting route, like a wild dingo in heat, through the burning, overcrowded afternoon streets, till nightfall, even more hungry, sexually unsated, and furious –

Through the glass doors of Primo, "exclusive accessories for men," emerges Yveta (daughter of the director of the local meat factory and a member of the local government, the one who owes me fifty crowns for a taxi from the Větruše restaurant, a trifling sum – what I make in ten hours – she never returned nor intended to, with the money she saved on the taxi the girl will buy herself a bottle of eau de cologne), arm in arm with a peculiar, bespectacled moron of studied elegance, who carried in his free hand an enormous white package, at least four white shirts of Dutch nylon with wide stripes à 150 crowns apiece (600 crowns in all: it takes me more than fourteen days to earn that much). To increase the amount of her modest pocket money, does Mademoiselle Yvette get a commission from the Dutch tailors or from Primo for chasing her suitors here in droves? And how far has she allowed this young monsieur to go, provided her cultivated emotional impulses have already matured from the necking to the petting stage? And the deputy Frank Secký (who makes 3,800 crowns a month and kindly calls me his "colleague"), that is, my other boss (otherwise at Cottex who's my boss depends on where I'm working), like a prince in his shiny blue convertible (42,000, my pay for four years) drives down the main avenue with his ceremonial wife, Eng. Helena (who makes 2,400 crowns – the boss of the product development lab, who during her tenure here has coiled up like a petrified snail from the Diluvial Period), all the while shooting glances at the girls lining both sides of the streets, chase the scum *onto the bus   Take them out to the middle of the forest   To a military training camp   Assign one Madame or Mademoiselle to each squad room for all purposes, like a barracks sutler*

I'll have one like a cleaning woman to clean my shoes and feet   She can sleep under my bed curled up like a dog   And polish my riding crop daily with her hair –

On the sidewalk and in the street a herd of antelope, and not one of them is mine. Zita Gráfová looked at me so strangely out in front of the building – what I wouldn't give for a little gentleness …

Long before 21:00, Borek was pacing back and forth at the bus station, impatiently looking at his watch. The gray bus didn't arrive till nine-thirty, and Borek struggled through to the rear of the car, to his corner with the concave ceiling, this time the girl didn't even look up from her seat as he stood above her, trembling, for three whole endless stops. Suddenly the bus halted at the square, as the girl was getting off she passed Borek and he caressed her breast with his readied palm, the girl got off and Borek, with his palm to his lips – tomorrow at the same time – rode all the way to the bridge across the Elbe.

At the docks, men's shadows waited for women who would never arrive. And the train station came to life for only a moment with the arrival of the train from Prague, the waiting men quickly divvied up their wives, none was left, and once again the place was empty, sleep in the waiting room, the tracks are empty and in the silent hall the fluttering sound of the fluorescent lights like snow falling in a graveyard.

21:56 – too early to go sleep beneath the sacks in the basement, Borek set out along the forest road up to Větruše, you've got to get tired somehow, maybe a good hike will do it … On the café terrace music, laughter, the clink of glass and silverware, and all around couples between tree trunks approaching from and receding into the darkness, people, why do you think I should like you – Borek walked through the dark facade of the forest and sat down in his hunting pit, where the only thing he'd caught so far was a kick in the groin. In the sky a jungle of stars above the jungle of earth, on which love is prey, the perfect prey for the conqueror. Zita Gráfová. Zita. Z-I-T-A. Zitushka, Zítěnka – no, that won't do, that would be completely … completely. The first success of my love life: a woman finally looked at me! Yveta looked at me, too … the scabby Slávka from the warehouse, too, and in Brno, long ago … But until now no woman – VICTORY! I AM DESIRED –

And Borek ran up out of the pit, threw himself onto the grass, and pushing off with his arms and legs rolled with laughter down the slope and beneath the little bridge, he drank from the stream, champed at branches, and with his mouth full of leaves raised his fists to his chest and set off running down the silvery-black, tiger-striped asphalt to the city, like a birthday cake waiting in the valley, rumpled and pressed against the arm of the dark river embracing it. With Indian steps – one hundred running, one hundred walking – Borek proceeded toward the city along asphalt, concrete, and paving stone.

Already, from afar, he could hear the racket and roar coming from the first floor of building No. 2000 out into the dark street, on the second floor curtains a tender, bluish glow – Zita's in there lying on her wide bed – and soft music wafted out. Borek walked through the hallway and out the back gate into the yard, crept through a loosened slat in the fence into the neighboring garden, appropriated his eggs along with a couple of turnips, in his basement he sucked out the eggs, ate some of his recrystallized fructose, the turnips would serve as both his beverage and his toothbrush, he hung his clothes on the pipe valves, rubbed his body (maybe someday she'll even see it – –) with burning salicylic acid, lay down naked beneath his sacks, and happily fell asleep gripping the handle of his switchblade in his hot palm.

Someone was shaking him, tearing him brutally from his sleep, the wire-encased basement light bulb was shining on the cement walls, and Borek spied someone's hand on his shoulder, he quickly scrunched down and at the same time pressed the button on the handle of his switchblade, then he jumped up naked from the sacks flashing the bare blade – In the feeble light, Alex Serafin towered over him.

"That's a nice little stabber you got there. Imported, right?" Alex grinned. "Put it away and come with me. There's just been a fuck-up in the itinerants quarters, and I have no desire to breakfast with the police ... I'm always in a sentimental mood in the morning."

"I'm not going up there."

"Me neither. Remember when Comrade Tušl, a member of the factory administration, promised us the room on the third floor after they moved out? It's vacant, so now we can move in."

"Now? ... But the door's nailed shut..."

"No time like the present. We'll un-nail it. Come on. I took the liberty of bringing along your stuff–"

At Alex's feet stood two little suitcases, one of them Borek's. Borek quickly dressed, and they both ran swiftly up the steps to the third floor. Alex took a pair of pliers and a chisel out of his suitcase, and the door barricaded by Tušl – the symbol of his betrayal of us all – began to moan and whine. Madda stuck her head out of the door across the hall, a poker in her hand and Julda Serafin behind her:

"What are you doing? Stop it ... This will come to no good..."

"You two live nicely in your double room..." Borek panted as he tore nails from the wooden beams. "Why shouldn't we have our own double room, as well?"

"But nothing is solved by force..." whispered Julda.

"According to whom?" said Borek as he pulled out another nail.

"Don't just stand there jabbering," Madda said to Julda, and she walked across the corridor, stood next to the men hard at work, and began to pry a board loose with her poker, which bent, but the door soon gave way.

Inside, the light didn't work (Tušl had torn the switch and its case out of the wall), and in the cone of the flashlight there were enormous cases on the floor of the one-time women's, and then the Tušls' flat, and between them – is this really possible? ... Tracks! ... To what meanness can blue hatred sink? – Alex ripped the boards from the window, and the moonlight silvered Engineer Borek Trojan's first flat.

Of course, half Alex's – but who wouldn't rather live with one devil than five? When it began to grow light, the new tenants discovered that the cases contained nothing but bricks, and with the help of their neighbors across the hall ("Well, you can't sleep on the floor..." sighed Julda, Madda swept up the broken bits), they formed a chain like bricklayers at a construction site, brick after brick went hand to hand and out the window into the morning mist.

"We don't need to fix the water pipe," said Alex Serafin, the head of the new household, "the water barely makes it up this far anyway. We don't need a shitter either, having as we do a window, a board beneath it will add comfort to the shitting. And we won't even disturb the efficient air-conditioning system of Tušl and Company by fixing the window. I could chase down some of my underlings to fix the electricity – but that can wait till fall. We'll live here natural and healthy."

"We'll also get used to these tracks." Borek rejoiced as he tossed the remnants of the cases out the window. "I read that in the U. S. forty-six people die every year tripping over rugs..."

"This evening we'll organize a little celebration in our family circle," said Alex. "Hey, kid, do you have a girl?"

"Maybe ... I'm beginning to have one..."

"Never mind. I just want to preserve the natural character of our soirée. Should I bring Bubička, Panda or–"

"Mr. Serafin, don't you think it'd be better to ... actually live here a while first? I mean, for a change."

"You might have something there, kid. And you can call me Alex. But that's it, no other familiarities – don't forget that I can kick your ass!"

"I've got a pretty nice little knife." Borek smiled as he placed his palm on his switchblade. "Imported–" and with a press of the button out shot the wonderful blade of Solingen steel.

Alex smiled back. "Okay, you can address me informally. I'm starting to like you, kid – sorry, Borek. I'll be your advisor and teacher. Lesson number one: man is Lord of Creation and therefore on principle does not clean his flat. Throw away that broom – we'll get a maid."

"You think the deputy of Deputy Tušl's going to send us one, or how about Director Gráf himself?"

"The great I myself will bring her here *personally*. At first she'll be rather clumsy – she studied medicine, the poor thing – but with the proper training we'll raise her to a level just below human."

In his electrical equipment warehouse, foreman Alex irritably dispersed his staff members by making it known he wasn't to be spoken to today and everyone could go to ... yes, there, and he climbed up to his top shelf and drank two beers while looking sleepily out the window into the courtyard. He stretched himself out all snug on the soft cottony insulation and after the previous night's exertions fell into a restorative sleep.

Shortly after noon, in a recumbent position, he received a police officer acquaintance of his concerning some sort of rape that had occurred in the itinerants quarters the previous night, from which Alex distanced himself with disgust, promised the police officer to fix his TV antenna to get rid of "that drunken doppelganger or whatever it is," which in professional circles is called a "ghost," the men had a beer, and then Alex climbed down from his shelf, shaved twice with his Elektrostar razor, and with an ingenious combination of emollients (Barberina cologne and Barbus lotion) secured for his skin (from forehead to knees) a photogenic attraction and cheerful kissability.

"Alex–" In her examining room Dr. Dáša Zíbrtová panicked and broke out in an obvious sweat. "I no longer have anything to say to you, Mr. Serafin."

"I know. We're finished. With all that ... evil..." Alex said slowly and extremely softly. "You've begun a new life. I'd like to start one, too. I came to say goodbye ... forever. And to ask your forgiveness."

Boy, did her eyeballs goggle! But you've gone downhill, girl, with all this church business. Even in the religious paintings the heads beheaded martyrs carry beneath their arms are neatly combed – how can a hag of your age allow herself to stop going to the hairdresser's? And your skin – just horrible. But perfect for scrubbing the floor. *Dixi.*

"...because my eyes have been opened, I've seen that ... that ... simply doing good is the greatest good that ... that..."

Listening to her with disgust, Alex assiduously sniffled with ostentatious emotion, and not finding even after ten minutes of her babbling the desired drift toward the topic of himself – Julda's really done a job this time, but never mind, you've turned blue on me, girl, but soon you'll be red again – Alex decided to kneel before her (which will undoubtedly speed up the enlistment of our cleaning woman and reduce the amount of this unbearable babbling) and to this end picked out a corner of the foam rubber doormat to forego the necessity of kneeling on hard tile. The mat, however, was inconveniently located, and so he ended up kneeling right in front of the cabinet containing all the poisons, but in so much literature such a detail is lost.

Dáša Zíbrtová gushed on, women don't say only what they know, and this one doesn't know a thing, she gabbles nonstop with the appropriate biblical quote dropped almost like a bon mot, bene, but I can take just one or two, not fifty-two, moreover, quotes must be cited verbatim, do you know what *cit, citas, citare, citavi, citatum* means, you goose? You're better acquainted with *fasciculus seminaris* or glans, penis, clitoridis, aren't you? Don't worry, we'll get to that, but how sad it is to spend your afternoon siesta listening to biblical Czech from the mouth of an uneducated bone cutter! But somebody's got to clean our floor.

Alex examined the opiates and other paraphernalia behind the poison cabinet's glass, they could be made to turn a profit, na gut, man wird seh'n, and he negligently listened to Dáša's enthusiastic effusions ("...whosoever shall not receive the kingdom of God as a little child shall in no wise enter therein. Whosoever therefore shall humble himself as this little child, that one is greatest in the kingdom of heaven..."), you can humble yourself till kingdom come, if you're walking on stilts how will you scrape the floor ("...whosoever shall receive one of such children in my name, receiveth me..."), but you know I'll be receiving you again, girl, but verily in my name, and we'll partake of the sweetness of this movement together, and you'll be lying on your back groaning in gratitude, okay, isn't that enough already?

But she gushed on and on, spouting those heartrending scraps of knowledge snatched from old texts on the run, without experiencing them at all, you've fucked everything up in your fucked-up Europe, you pitiful daughter of a self-sterilizing continent that even imports from its younger brother overseas a condensed *Reader's Digest* paperback version of the Bible for easier consumption, with color illustrations by Walt Disney, if possible, and a plastic cover so you can have your religious conversion in the bathtub if you like, since you spend the rest of your free time in front of the television, couldn't you shorten this a bit, too?

But what one won't do for a clean flat, and so Alex summoned his most refined rhetorical strategies, the Secret of successful ambassadors at an audience with a mighty king or with an Indispensable Associate is, in brief: To say nothing at all – everyone is interested only in what he himself is saying, and you will gain the reputation of a wise (moreover, a terrifically smart, amusing, profound, and absolutely magnificent) companion by simply yodeling according to the following model:

"Exactly!"

"Really? Only now do I actually realize it…"

"Only in your version does it start to make sense…"

"Yes, that's exactly it!"

"You're simply wonderful!"

"You put that amazingly well!"

"You know, you're right, you're totally right!"

"Absolutely!"

"Of course not!"

"Tremendous!"

If the goal of the dialogue (even though this method may also be used with large groups) is coitus, it is necessary (as long as, of course, you don't fall asleep from the tedious torrent issuing from your interlocutor, since the object thus treated quickly loses self control and a sense of time) to shift the conversation (monologue) gradually to the erotic sphere, for example:

"In your fervor you're simply … beautiful…" (in a strained voice, and "beautiful" should acoustically taper off).

"You cannot – No! That's not true! No! No!"

"You know it's true yourself. Why do you try to deceive yourself?"

"Alex, please, not that…"

"Look at yourself in the mirror–" and Alex rose with relief, his left leg having fallen asleep from kneeling.

"I know I'm hideous…"

"You're not, my love. Just look … You're beautiful … how can anyone not see that?"

"…but I want to forget about that…"

"Step closer and look once more … I can see it, and I'll show you…"

"…at least for a moment. Will you give me that moment?"

"I'll give you anything–"

In the window suddenly a pale silhouette. "Doctor, are you there?" Julda's voice came from outside. The shepherd is herding his sheep.

Alex embraced Dáša firmly with one arm, with the other he placed his palm on the back of her head and his fingers slowly crept toward her control button (every animal has one in a different spot: the bull in its nostrils, the horse between the ears, the snake just behind the head, the fish in the gills, and Dáša Zíbrtová:) below the earlobe, and Dáša, trembling violently, placed her head on Alex's shoulder.

A loud knocking on the window. Again, louder. A third time, even louder.

Alex quickly and firmly snatched up the swaying Dáša (a combination of caressing and force is the preferred method of controlling domestic animals and women, which has been enriched with slogans by subsequently stubborn women, masses, and nations) in both arms, carried her a couple of steps, knocked his foot against the cool white cover of the examining table, and laid her on a soft mattress of African grass.

The knocking at the window became a banging and shaking of the window panes, but the doctor no longer noticed it.

Move the sole of his shoe like a tightrope walker, right heel just in front of the tip of the left foot, and then bring the left foot along the ankle of the right leg and transfer onto it the weight of the body as soon as the left heel is resting firmly in front of the tip of the right foot, Borek Trojan was walking with arms outspread like an angel along the tracks welded into the shape of an X on the floor of his one-room flat on the third floor, a perfect form of yoga, which tremendously improves concentration (these tracks are coming with me when I get my own apartment or house, just like Balzac's scratched-up desk, which accompanied him from his attic room all the way to his Parisian palace), mentally he was calculating that if on average Zita left the house and came back twice a day, this would make a total of four one-minute passages through the front gate, for a total of only four minutes of exposure time – a hopelessly small amount of time for making contact. How could one increase this exposure or how –

Vigorous pounding on the door, which then opened all by itself, a Cottex housing official backed by a police officer.

"Are you Borek Trojan?"

"Yes, but–"

"Pack your stuff and clear out!"

"Excuse me, but I–"

"What else do you want us to excuse you for? You broke in here in the middle of night like a thief, you broke the door ... where are the cases that were here?! They were filled with valuable material from the factory, and you'll pay for every last bit of it!"

"They were only filled with bricks..."

"Then you admit to opening the cases without permission from national enterprise Cottex. And you broke the window! What are these tracks on the floor?! And the toilet's been smashed to smithereens! Do you know what all this is going to cost you?!"

"It was already broken before we moved in here ... Tušl did it."

"Oh, please, why would the assistant to the deputy tear up the place like this? Only a vandal could have done this! The light switch has been ripped out of the wall! What did you do with the sink?!"

"I'm telling you, it really was like this when we got here..."

"So, it was already like this? Well, that's just great! So why didn't you report it? You'll pay for everything down to the last heller! And you'll go before the court! Let's go: pack up your stuff and clear out. Now!"

"But I have nowhere to go."

"The company assigned you to the quarters on the first floor. You have no reason to be here. Now, get on down the stairs–"

"The itinerant workers are living there now."

"So all of a sudden they're not good enough for you?! You lived with them for two weeks, didn't you? So Mr. Engineer is too good to live with common workers, huh? You should be thankful, you bastard, that we've given you the opportunity to become familiar with the collective's comrades – so get your stuff! Or do you want us to pack your suitcase for you?!"

With burning tears of rage, Borek collected his few things as slowly as possible, as if he couldn't part with his very first one-room flat, which we've held onto for barely fifteen hours, my first room, half of which belonged entirely to me –

"Why the fuck are you taking so long?! Get going!!"

–place my switchblade on top.

Goodbye, little flat, goodbye and farewell – I shall return ... And with his cardboard suitcase, Borek exited past the housing official and the police officer.

On the stairs he suddenly heard voices coming from below, on the steps appeared the company doctor, Dáša Zíbrtová, and behind her Alex Serafin.

"Borek, where are you going now, you antsy pants?" blared Alex. "Did they give us the first floor instead of that crappy place upstairs? Well, I could get used to that!"

"They've thrown us out," Borek informed his roommate."

"It can't be that bad," said Alex. When he caught sight of the police officer he greeted him merrily, saying, "Frantík, you still haven't spoken with the boss yet, have you? I already discussed it with him this morning, he'll explain the whole thing."

"I didn't realize you were in on this." The police officer apologized to Alex, then saluted him and disappeared.

"Well, let's go, Borek. I'm bringing you a visitor," said Alex, smiling.

"Do you two know each other? Dáša Borek, Borek Dáša. You should like one another. We're not going to stand here on the stairs, are we?"

"Sorry, Comrade Serafin, you can't go upstairs!" said the housing official. "I have a written order from the factory administration–"

"Well, let's have a look at it under the light," said Alex, already walking upstairs, and pressed on by Alex's body the four went up to the one-room flat on the third floor. Alex closed the door behind them: "All right, let's see the order!"

The official handed it to him, Alex read the document with a smile on his face, folded it, ripped it in half, and shoved the pieces into the back pocket of his black trousers. "The next correspondence regarding this matter will be accepted only on paper of lower quality. This paper doesn't tear well and cuts into your butt."

"I'm required to inform you," stated the official, "that you must immediately and without delay–"

"Get out," Alex told him patiently.

"I will not budge from this spot until," said the official, "you vacate–"

Alex displayed to him his enormous palm with its powerful fingers, then he turned it over and thoughtfully examined his knuckles, covered with black tufts of hair, slowly raised his hand to the level of the official's face, and started moving all his fingers as if he were snatching at butterflies fluttering around the official's head, and since the official was still boring him, Alex grabbed him by the nose, twisted it until the cartilage started cracking, led the official – suddenly fully compliant and whining beseechingly – out into the hallway, where he launched him down the stairs with a tremendous kick to the coccyx, that spot where till recently – geologically speaking – humans grew tails from their hairy animal butts.

"We'll have some peace for a couple of days." Alex sighed as he wiped his soiled hand on his pants. "But they'll come crawling back before too long. Nowadays the authorities are ubiquitous, you can't get rid of them. But never mind. So, Dášenka, my pup, will you make us something for supper? Dáša's wonderful. Just think, Borek, she's offered to help us out a little here. There's your broom, dear, over there in the corner. Isn't she magnificent? Already I'm almost in love with her."

The Tušls obviously didn't have enough time to remove the electrical outlet, Dáša joyfully opened up the little suitcase she'd brought, in addition to her large black satchel, and a hot plate appeared, a flitch of cured meat (Alex's main source of food, morning, noon, and night: approximately a kilo per day), five tins of Portuguese sardines, a staff of salami, a kilo of chocolate-covered cherries, a carton of Pall Malls, two bottles of Rioja Coronila red wine and two more of Bull's Blood, a Japanese transistor radio, and a portable record player with some records: "Rhythm Is My Uncle," "Waiting for Love," "Fire the Guns," and "Shake," as well as some Dvořák and Debussy or whatever it says in French, a white tablecloth, silverware, saltcellar, and a small slender vase.

A block of cured meat floated in the boiling pot, and by the time Borek returned with beer, Dáša had scrubbed the floor and Alex was lying on his cot gently stroking her neck and scratching her lovingly behind the ears. Dáša laughingly snapped at Alex's hand, as happy as a tick, or rather, as happy as a tick's favorite quadruped.

Alex knows how to handle women, Borek reflected as he and Alex lay back on their cots, each with a piece of meat in his hand, Dáša merrily fluttering about, he's in clover when he's always got a lover at his disposal – but what about Zita and her daily four-minute exposure. How can I approach her? How would Alex approach her?

"Knock her over onto her back," suggested our teacher and counselor when Dáša went to take the trash out.

"Yeah, I know that – But what about before..."

"Well, first observe her inconspicuously, then follow, chase, pounce, seize, then do the deed."

"You make it sound so simple."

"I've explained the general plan, you develop the individual branches, which are merely little strokes, but look what world literature has manufactured out of them. Have you ever read Shakespeare?"

"No! I'm just a dumb engineer who reads magazines."

"You'll find it there too," said Alex, "and in the newspaper – what else is politics? – or most concisely in *Hunter's Monthly*."

"What about hunters?" asked Dáša, returning with the empty garbage can.

"I was just telling Borek that you're my little doe..." Alex laughed.

"Are you going to shoot me then?" Dáša laughed.

"Later, dear..." Alex guffawed, and he pulled Dáša over to him on the bed, the garbage can still in her hand.

"Later, dear..." whispered Dáša with an apologetic glance at Borek.

"Oh yeah," said Alex. "Hey, Dáša, give Borek twenty-five crowns to go to the movies ... take it, Borek, take it and don't be ashamed!"

"But I can't..." Borek stuttered over Dáša's twenty-five crowns, which she was holding out to him most willingly.

"Dáša makes more than you. Probably twice as much, right dear? So take it…"

"But … I can't take money from a woman…"

"Just take it, Borek." Alex laughed. "If you want to be a hunter…"

And Borek, blushing and embarrassed, slowly and diffidently but ultimately snatched Dáša's tribute to love.

The door on the second floor, the white gate to Zita's fortress, stands there mute and imposing minute after minute, for another thousand years. How do I take the fortress? How do I hunt the beast?

Inconspicuously observe, follow, chase, pounce, seize, then do the deed. INCONSPICUOUS OBSERVATION, that's done – the antelope: beautiful, noble, tender, fragile, delightful. Her exquisitely turned white knees – FOLLOW, chase, pounce, seize, then do the deed.

FOLLOW … four minutes a day on the way to the front gate – the fortress gate, what can you do in four minutes, which are, moreover, divided into four one-minute runs – Damn it, what does she do, fall from the sky in front of the gate …

Carefully shaven and with a drop of Soviet cologne behind each ear, Borek stood by the front gate in the afternoon keeping his eye on the stairs. When he heard the clatter of women's shoes, he ran far down the street, then dashed back, flustered, when Zita's blue dress swished through the gate.

"Good afternoon…"

"Good afternoon … Mr. Trojan…"

Is it just me or did she really slow her pace a little … is she looking at me curiously or does it only seem that way …

"Excuse me, but I have to…" Zita blurts out.

"Yes, of course … Sorry…"

"You've no reason to be sorry. Nothing's happened!" Zita suddenly stops, then rushes to her car, gets in, starts it up – will she look back again? No. But maybe in the mirror … She's gone.

So I'll have to wait again until tomorrow afternoon. Zita doesn't fall from the sky right in front of the gate – she comes in a car, so she's just as unobtainable for a pedestrian as if she'd really fallen from the sky. I can't FOLLOW birds in the sky, can I? Because of a stupid car – It's in your way, huh? So how can I get rid of it? It's really very simple … Pick it up and carry it off beneath your arm –

!!! Actually, that's not such a bad idea – – The next evening Borek took another twenty-five crowns from Dáša, but without all that bothersome hesitation, at the Corner Pub he had an inexpensive (extraordinary expenditures are approaching–), although substantial (–and the need for physical potency) supper and sat near the pool table till dark, we'll have a small shot of rum for courage and then walk quietly down our street ... Zita's car stood in front of the building. Borek pulled out his dagger and slashed the tires the way one slashes the tendons of an antelope's leg.

Then in the bright afternoon sun he stood in front of the gate, carefully shaven and with a drop of cologne behind each ear, the car was already gone and he heard the clatter of women's shoes from upstairs.

"Good afternoon, Mrs. ... Zita."

"Good afternoon ... Borek. May I call you that?"

"Yes ... of course ... It'd make me happy..."

"It's such a beautiful name..."

"You have a beautiful name, too ... Zita, the name of our last empress."

"Yes ... You know, my father actually named me after her. But don't think I'm old enough to remember the empress!"

"Her great-granddaughter at the most!"

WE LAUGH AND WALK DOWN THE STREET TOGETHER –

This first time I'll only walk to the corner. Tomorrow ...

... the freshly shod car stands in front of the building laughing its heart out with its silver wheels ... the DAGGER – no, you can't slash the tires in the middle of the afternoon right in front of the building, and after another slashing the director would have it guarded. Or he'd take the trouble to put it into a garage –

The clatter of women's shoes on the stairs.

"Good afternoon, Mrs. Gráfová..."

"Good afternoon, Borek ... You look sad today ... Has something happened?" My unobtainable blue love – observe her inconspicuously, then follow, CHASE, pounce, seize, and do the deed. Forgive me, but I must –

"If I told you ... you'd laugh at me..."

"I won't laugh at you. I promise."

"I – But it's really funny. To you ... it'll be funny."

"But yesterday we laughed together ... You can trust me, Borek. I beg you..."

"It was so nice yesterday walking with you that little bit ... I was looking forward to it again today ... But you're in a hurry. I'm sorry for detaining you."

"Why can't we walk together again today?"

"Because you're going by car. Why would you walk..."

"Well, I walked yesterday because the other night someone..."

"I know." Why is she looking at me like that? The whole street knows about it, after all ... this street has always been a little rough.

Zita took a step back, paled, slightly turned and leaned her white hand upon the gate. "Borek ... That little walk really meant so much to you..."

"More than you can imagine."

"Oh – I'm feeling a little ... weak. Okay, I'm better now. Borek. Borek – Will you give me the pleasure of getting in with me? I'll take you wherever you want."

"I rather doubt it."

"I have a full tank."

"Is that enough to make it to Cap d'Antibes?

WE LAUGH AND DRIVE DOWN THE STREET TOGETHER –

She parks at the square and we separate for two hours, Zita goes shopping and I wait by the car for my lover ... She's fabulous. Really special ... she has everything I don't. Here is a complete, closed world where even the stars in the sky are different. A world already forgotten ...

On the way back, we take a rather long detour and we both pretend it's nothing. Zita's profile looks like the Empress's on the old silver coins. We don't speak. Of course she thinks I'm a dolt.

"It'd be nice to go home via the Krušné Mountains..." I say.

"If our town wasn't in the way. And our street..."

"It's too bad the car's so transparent–"

Ouch, that was a bit much. Zita stiffens and avoids my glance, even in the mirror, she doesn't say another word, in front of our building she simply nods goodbye and waits until I disappear, the following day she goes with Roman, and the day after that with her husband, and the day after that with the whole family – finished. The fortress's white gate has been bolted.

We meet at the gate, on the street. "Good afternoon, Mrs. Gráfová..." "Good afternoon, Borek" – I already know where she parks almost every afternoon around four o'clock – "Good afternoon, Mrs. Gráfová." "Good afternoon, Borek" – and I learn more the less I watch everything simultaneously.

They all come home separately: Madda walks around the building like I do, we avoid each other's eyes when we meet; Roman runs downstairs, and Madda hides from him around a corner; Olda comes out of the itinerants quarters, and Madda quietly follows him; Stěpa leans out the window, then jumps out and joins the convoy – "Good afternoon, Mrs. Gráfová." "Good afternoon, Borek..." – The Gráfs are going to their riverside house. I've already seen it: an elegant little house on the river bank, with a metal lantern above the entrance and a picture window looking out onto the garden toward the river ... The fortress's tall white gate stands there silently day after day and night after night.

"Good afternoon, Mrs. Gráfová–"

"...Would you like a ride into town?"

"I certainly would. Thanks. Mrs. Gráfová, I..."

"I've been seeing you ... everywhere."

"I'm sorry, but I ... How can I tell you this–"

"Don't – Oh ... I'm not quite myself today."

The silver profile of the last empress, we're both afraid to look in the mirror between us, before us ... Where's she driving me? ... Suddenly she brakes and comes to a stop.

"May I once again ... ride with you back home? I'd be glad to wait..."

"How long?" Why is she suddenly so pale? What did that question mean? After all, she's the one who decides ...

Zita hastily steps out and locks the car, she still hasn't told me when to be back here for the ride home, she quickly walks down a narrow street, I wait helplessly by the car, Zita, you don't want me beside you anymore. Zita looks back and disappears around the corner, she's gone and I don't know what to do, she looked back, was that an invitation?

I run after her – she's going into the Archdeacon Church! – Why didn't she tell me when she – "How long?" SHE asked ME, everyone longs for his own destruction, why a church? Because it'll definitely be empty, a church isn't transparent like a car, and where else can the director's wife go in such a small town, Zita is UNDOUBTEDLY THINKING EXACTLY like me, but isn't visiting a church in a small town a bit risky for the director's wife, but if Zita is undoubtedly thinking exactly like me, then she wants the SAME THING I want –

Borek walked around the church in ever-narrowing circles, the beautifully functioning hunting mechanism suddenly begins to disgust its designer – but this is what our forefather the orangutan was or, long before him, the first copulation-capable protozoan – a mere service technician, am I really MERELY a service technician, what are we, for God's sake (but that's already been scientifically refuted) are we really STILL just wild animals?

In ever-narrowing circles Borek walked around the church, the final desperate refuge of the pursued blue antelope, inconspicuously observe *I would love to kiss Your ankles* follow *sit with You on the terrace, laugh and drink orange juice through a straw* chase *in a white wicker chair with a mandolin beneath Your window, until You awake* POUNCE, seize, and do the deed.

Zita is kneeling in a pew off to the side, pitiful, crouching, silent, forgive me, my dear, white gladioluses in tall silver vases and an image of the Madonna baring her breast, her heart fully exposed for two thousand years, and she stepped down from the white pedestal to the pew made of dark wood as into an open coffin – or a bed? – good Lord, I can't see any difference anymore! –

Here every step toward her sounds like a rifle shot, Zita stares straight ahead and her white profile is now just the profile of a sad, pursued woman.

"Excuse me, Mrs... ."

"When you were still a child, I read a wonderful old story. The hero was just like you, his name was Julien Sorel, hers was Mme. de Rênal. A story of great love and passion..." she whispered into her clasped hands.

"I saw the movie, it was called *The Red and the Black*. Gérard Philipe played Julien, Danielle Darrieux played Mme. de Rênal."

"Julien went to the seminary..."

"He wanted to be a bishop."

"A beautiful young woman entered his life, Mathilde de la Mole..."

"But he loved Mme. de Rênal and came back to her. He came to get her in the church and – No!"

"And in the church he shot her."

"Then he was executed ... A terrible story..."

"And beautiful–" Zita rose, and as she was leaving the church, she suddenly spun around, her face chalk white: "Borek – I love you, I love you, I love you–" and then all he saw was her trembling back, she's crying ... she's running, escaping, fleeing ... I fled to the river and paced back and forth there all through the night.

The next afternoon Zita did not respond to my greeting and drove off in her car. I took the streetcar into town to look for her and found her car parked on the square, I hid and watched the car for some three hours and when Zita suddenly emerged from the crowd I ran toward her, Zita wanted to slam the door, but I held it open. "Why are you running away from me?"

"And why aren't you running away from me?"

"Because I love you–"

"Like in the movie? But I'm not Danielle Darrieux."

"You're more beautiful..."

"*The Red and the Black* in Ústí nad Labem, or Stendhal à la Czech. Let go of the door, Mr. Trojan! I still have to do the laundry and fix dinner."

Mme. de Rênal drove off in a cloud of exhaust fumes and cruelly bolted the white fortress gate.

Every day he walks by their white door, upstairs and downstairs – it seems to be closed more and more.

"Your disappearing act seems a bit conscientious for just twenty-five crowns." Alex grinned as he ripped off a piece of cured meat with his teeth and handed Dáša the vase she'd brought from home, for her to pour him some more beer.

"I'm off observing. Besides, I'm in love."

"Remember my advice. Observe, follow–"

"I'm already up to CHASE, and it doesn't seem to be working anymore."

"Then it's high time to go to pounce, seize, and then the sweet deed. Dulcia sunt praemia Veneris…"

"Is that something about women's problems?" Dáša interjected to draw Alex's attention, which was becoming harder and harder to do. Alex was acting downright rude to her. He'd actually made a servant out of her – and she adored him for it all the more. The paradoxes of this relationship were starting to be somewhat insane.

"Run down to the post office and send a special-priority telegram!" Alex yelled at Dáša.

"Okay, to whom?"

"Charles University!"

"I can still remember the address. And what is the telegram to say?"

"Tell them to return your tuition – Dummkopf!"

"Don't be angry with me, Lexi dear, I just…"

"Don't call! – me! – Lexi! – Du Mistvieh!"

"Forgive me, I just … Excuse me, what's a mistvy?"

"But you told me you were studying German – Du Trottl!"

"I'm studying it because of you, because you love the language, I'm only up to chapter eight…"

"Before she was twenty-eight, Dr. Zíbrtová began studying foreign languages: Latin, Greek, and French … before the war. German – during the war and now. English from the war until the victory of socialism. During the victorious socialism Russian, of course, and now she's having a look at Italian and Swedish – are there any more languages in Europe? – naturally she couldn't make herself understood in any of them. You're a perfect example of the population of this rotting appendix to Asia. I will call you Europa."

"That's a beautiful name. And since you're the one who gave it to me ... Europa is a girl riding on a bull..."

"Ja, das war noch damals, when Europa was still a little girl. Now she's just a withered old woman. Europa Zíbrtová! Take off my shoes."

And Dáša actually removed his shoes ...

Their relationship is utterly distasteful – I'm still walking by Zita's door, upstairs and downstairs – but wouldn't it be better to do something other than slam the door to love that's been declared and avowed? What is love, after all ... isn't it continuation, growth ... And the method: observe, follow, chase, pounce, seize, and do the deed. Oh, that's painful ... but I didn't create this world, I arrived when this method had been in effect for thousands of years ... Love is prey and everyone longs for his own destruction – let's not want them to expose their necks themselves ...

The white gate of Zita's fortress is locked behind nine locks, silent, and Your drawbridge is up – I don't want you to take off my shoes, I *want to kiss Your ankles* –

The drawbridge chains rattled – or did I just imagine it? – and the white gate moved – has this destructive love for You driven me insane – yes, the chains actually rattled (of course it wasn't the chains on the drawbridge but the chain on the Gráfs' door), and the door opened a crack (at that moment I was struck with the insane realization that Roman and the old man were in Prague, insane because it occurred at that very moment, but it wasn't my fault, it emerged of itself–) and a dark crevice formed between the white wood of the doorjamb and the door.

"Why are you standing there?" asked Zita.

"And why are you..."

"Come in quickly–" and she took me by the hand, our first contact, it was she who did it, and I pounced immediately – OUCH, it's cruel to POUNCE, seize, and do the deed – into the fortress.

I crept through the dark hallway with my heart pounding in my temples, red circles behind my eyelids, I held (consciously! Why?!) my breath, feeling an awful fear and terror and at the same time, however, an insane capability to accomplish anything (good God! Why ANYTHING?!), and involuntarily (was it really involuntary? ... But that would be ghastly–) I touched the dagger in my pocket and at that moment was struck with the insane realization that I was in the apartment with the victim I had been stalking, dangerous and ready for action, because for the next few hours there was no chance of interruption, no one knew of my relationship with the victim, no witnesses, no motive for the police, the dagger readied in my pocket, insane because at precisely that moment, but I'm not responsible for it, it emerged of itself, I realized I was standing there like A MURDERER, insane because as a murderer I could not act otherwise, even though I had come as a lover, like A MURDERER OR A LOVER – insane because I no longer saw any difference.

"Are you going to keep standing there in the foyer?" said Zita, and when I followed her into the apartment she added: "We can address each other familiarly, of course, only this one afternoon."

"As you wish, Mrs... . I mean, Zita..."

"Won't you have a seat. Cognac? – Or would you like me to whip you up a bacon omelet or something? I don't remember what Mme. de Rênal fed Julien in the movie."

"They sat together around a little garden table..."

"And the husband urged her on. I've got a garden table at the riverside house – should I go get it?"

Mocking, scornful, malicious, haughty, cruel: Empress Zita the Last.

"If I remember correctly, Julien came in the evening ... I apologize for coming so early in the afternoon."

"In the movie was Julien so arrogant?"

"In the movie Julien went straight to the point, which is, as you know, a rule of filmmaking."

"So in twenty minutes I'll see you as a seminarian. I'm looking forward to seeing your delightful little black cap."

"In half an hour I'll climb up a ladder into the bedroom – of Miss Mathilda de la Mole."

"But you'll come crawling!"

"With a revolver in my hand."

"They'll finally hang you."

"And then I'll hop down for a beer at the Svĕt Café. Mme. de Rênal died."

"But before that – –"

"Zita..."

"Mr. Trojan? Let go of my robe, I don't have anything on underneath. And lie down!" SEIZE, and do the deed.

"Ouch – you're cruel. I only invited you in for a cognac and a bacon omelet – please be so good as to notice the nuance: I didn't let you in here to be just an ordinary billy goat – OUCH!"

One more slap to this cruel and hurtful face, you, Madame, are worse than Alex the Devil himself in rut – Zita tore herself from my grip and now she's running from the room, should I go after her or must I leave the fortress forever – I'm not going to sit in this dining room alone.

Zita locked herself in the next room, and the white door stands unmoving before me, somewhat lower than the white gate but just as white, shiny, smooth, sturdy – and inaccessible.

I have no idea how long I stood there, I only know, I remember only – or did I only imagine it? – that that final white gate moved and opened and between the white wood a dark crevice. And already completely insane, I mumbled those words inspired by madness, THE DEED, those ghastly words, not the words of a lover – the words of a murderer.

My clumsy, violent fellow   Replacement for my son   Native of the hot interior   Red devil from the roaring ghetto   Enter my blue port   Sebastian, that's what I wanted to call my son   They never let me do anything   My saint not in heaven but rather here with me on earth   With my teeth I pull the arrows from Your body and I kiss every inch of it   My cadet from the barracks in the jungle   Throw off those heavy boots   My barefoot Greek youth   Allow me to wipe your feet with my hair   Mme. de Rênal kissed Julien's

I want to kiss Your ankles   You stand upon a white pedestal like a statue of the gentle Madonna   I will call You Berenike   I see what You see, the blue port overlooking the blue inlet   I follow you into it   And together music like the soft whisper of the rippling sea

And together we'll set fire to our white villa   Let the entire shore go up in flames   Burn the carbon coating on my tired metal   Stigmatize me with my blood   Here no one will wash it off   Because I am elect, You have chosen me

The stars tumbled to the earth and the earth spurted up to the stars   Let us go together along the transgalactic, nickel-plated autobahn   Antarctica will become a burning continent   Take your prey   And give me mine

I penetrated Your fortress   We are together in the jungle   I'm a wild dingo and I will now tear You apart   Look at me, my blue antelope

Another bottle, Señor Ronda   Only please, no Librium, I no longer want cold, blue poison   A full tank of gas for a trip all the way to hell   Run me over   Plunder me   Beat me   Fill me   Assault me and break me   My love

Love of mine

My catastrophe   My deluge

(To be continued)

BESIEGED

Everything assumed a new, arousing import. Soap: so I'll be appealing to you, Borek. Armchair: I am the armchair and You sit in me. Cigarette: I am the cigarette, You the match and the all-consuming, purifying flame, You are the air and I the humble ash falling gratefully to the ground. I am the lamp and You the electric current. I am the dough and You the kneading hand. I am the meat and you the knife of my evisceration –

Zita Gráfová proceeded through the beige desert dust of our street, aware of her body, shoulders, breasts, hips, thighs, and knees, her sex, her happiness, her victory. Our house is now a house of celebration –

Roman, my son. I no longer feel sorry for you. Neither of us is pitiful any longer: men have found us both. Now we both are happy newlyweds–

Evžen sits patiently in his easy chair trying not to look me in the eye. Is he patient or simply uninterested?

"I would just like to say that you can count on me under any circumstance and that I love you," my husband, Dr. Evžen Gráf, decides to tell me right now. Is this old man really my husband? What a sad thought.

"Why did you decide to say this to me right now?"

"Now is as good as any other time."

"You say that so lightly, so conversationally…"

"Yes, dear." He smiles and returns to his book. Is this refinement or mere indifference, nobility or just plain stupidity?

But it no longer matters. No more Ruff! Ruff! No longer am I an old, venerable, English, perverse, lesbian lady. I'm a woman in love with a man. With my boy –

I'm happy: I feel like a serving woman going out with her soldier. After lunch I quickly and carelessly wash the dishes. Dance a bit while cleaning up, smash! – damn! there goes another plate. Quickly sweep the pieces up before Madame discovers and doesn't let me go out.

The less time in the kitchen, the more before the mirror. I steal some of Madame's powder and rouge. I'm giggling. And in the kitchen I pilfer two veal cutlets intended for Sunday dinner. My soldier is ravenous. I put the meat in a plastic bag, wrap it in a red, flowered handkerchief, and quietly – so as not to wake Madame and Monsieur – oh so quietly creep through the apartment and out the door.

We meet behind the slaughterhouse fence. A sweet kiss and without excess words we climb through a broken board. Borek holds the board above my head like a curtain into a theater box. Inside, enormous cement pipes are scattered about the high grass. My soldier clumsily undoes my blouse while I slip off my skirt. After making love we laugh together, we eat cold veal with our hands from the flowered handkerchief spread out on my lap, we wipe our hands in the grass and make love again. We look at my watch, Borek lights a match to see, goodness, it's that late already? I should be home! Quickly I tie the flowered handkerchief around my head and rush home, softly I unlock the door and silently slip into the kitchen ... Thank goodness! They didn't notice I'd come home late.

If I'm careful, I can go right back out the following afternoon. With a basket of laundry I pretend to go up to the attic. I place the basket on the floor in front of Borek's door and softly knock – my lover opens, we both lift the basket, one handle each, and quickly pull it inside.

Is there any greater pleasure than introducing a boy to the ways of love?

Suddenly a quick, light tapping on the door, it doesn't lock and already it's opening – I'm dying with fear – "Don't worry." Borek laughs and without undue haste pulls on just his underwear. "It's only our Dáša..."

We both greet the new arrival – she's carrying two shopping bags, and I'm dressed in just a blanket and wristwatch–

"Good afternoon, Mrs. Gráfová."

"Good afternoon, Doctor."

Should I leave now or in five minutes? I should at least stay to have a five-minute conversation with a member of my Thursday salon, my *jour fixe* ... this might be horrible, but I begin to laugh! Besides, I have the whole afternoon free and no great desire to go back downstairs to the kitchen.

And so Dáša and I became friends – in half an hour, more than we'd spent over the last five years, and I helped her clean up a little. After all, you can't just sit there naked on the bed and watch your friend wash the floor of your lover's room – so we quickly washed it together. Borek happily divided the floor in two for us, each with her own half – he gave me the smaller half, my sweet boy, and the one less tramped upon – and the work just sailed along. Finally when Dáša and I, down on our hands and knees, began banging our heads into each other the way children do when they're pretending to be rams, and Borek as the shepherd began whistling through a comb and pinching me in the side, I began crying out joyfully – I'd give a hundred of my *jours fixes* for one afternoon like this.

Is it perverted to play at being a cleaning woman or is it the happiness of an abducted Sabine? Do I prefer being a lazy odalisque in a harem or a loving slave indispensable to my master? In which of these situations is there more love? Or more excitement ...

Zita waited in Borek's room for him to come home, walking back and forth along the tracks on the floor and sighing over her lover's pitiful possessions, the poor boy irons his trousers with the weight of his body on the mattress ... and now with the weight of mine as well ... She fearfully removed the black leather belt from Borek's pants, this embraces You around Your waist, my love, my cruel cadet from the barracks in the jungle, and she fastened the belt around her own waist and tightened it firmly, that hurts a bit, she unfastened the man's black leather, doubled it over on itself, and with the loop experimentally whipped herself on the arm, then again, harder, blows give things shape –

My lover sees me from the door that doesn't lock, and he's at my side in a trice – no longer the boy lover of a married woman, but a soldier released from his barracks rescuing a woman from hunger. What we're doing together, that's love.

And then I have to go home, downstairs somewhere ...

"The heat's insane," converses Frank Secký, vigilantly and calmly he pours himself another glass of our Courvoisier, well, my dear little eunuch, if that's what makes you euphoric ...

"It'll probably cool off soon..." converses Evžen, the old, venerable, English, lesbian, perverted, tired, abandoned lady ...

I look at them. I see right through them. They're made of glass. Inside: a few worn-out contrivances, a few well-rehearsed tricks from the areas of administrative machinations, bridge, and local politics, concern over a couple more crowns that they don't need, a bit of fear and a bit of protective cynicism, fatigue without being able to sleep, satiety without good digestion, jokiness without laughter and seriousness without real seriousness – they're frigid. Annulled and annulling. They're dead.

In the afternoon, on the third floor, with my plastic comb I comb Borek's short, fabulously thick hair, coarse and warm like animal fur. Electric sparks jump into the air. Slowly I move onto his knees, dynamite in clasped hands. His kisses are more clumsy and more violent, his dilated pupils flame and burn into mine, I want to burn even more – I slip the comb beneath my robe so that the teeth are against the small of my back, I want my love to burn –

Before I die.

CONQUERORS

Through the white door of Zita's bedroom, leave the innermost fortress gate open behind us, now no one will close it before us, we've conquered the port and the citadel itself – Borek Trojan slowly walked naked (honor to his victory uniform!) down the hallway, around potted philodendrons and palm trees, and entered the bathroom of the apartment on the second floor, filled the tub with warm water, and lowered himself into it the way the usurper of a fallen empire lowers himself onto the throne. I declare the port conquered.

"Don't drown on me, darling," whispers the fallen Empress Zita, and she knocks on the door to OUR bathing salon FROM OUTSIDE. "Aren't you hungry?"

"Yes I am, but I'm even thirstier."

"Okay, just a minute..." Your Majesty and Highness, I will serve you immediately.

And the naked slave girl Zita brings a goblet of red wine, don't take it from her right away, let her stand a moment on the cold, wet tiles ... Wine tastes good in the bathtub. "Thanks. And now something to eat."

"Would you like steak?"

"That will do."

"Well done or rare?"

"Blood through and through."

And so I'm eating steak in Zita's dining room (for some reason she hasn't mentioned the bacon omelet she offered me originally), in the same dining room where an hour ago I was sitting alone, abandoned and in despair –

"Give me another. And more wine!"

After the food the woman, she follows me to my conquered bed, meek, yearning, grateful for whatever I deign to bestow upon her, of course the bestowing is upon myself, I take her, and therefore get even more, how marvelous love is down here on earth ... We can't get enough, I of my triumph, she of her defeat, I gratefully kiss her hands and she gratefully kisses mine, we love each other even beyond fatigue, even beyond the pulsating sphere of the body. The universe is cut in two, the two halves sheathed into one another, forming over the bodies an arch of victory –

"My darling..."

"My darling..."

The greater the love, the fewer words you need. After all, perfect understanding and blending, silence says it all. We take our leave from one another over a shared crystal glass of *Parfait Amour* (the purple liqueur from the Dutch firm Bols).

That night Borek Trojan did not go to sleep for a long time, he walked up and down our street through drifts of beige dust, falling into the darkness and then lifted up into the heights by the illuminated discharge tubes, he crept through the silver, moonlit desert, past the dark building with lights on the second floor, as if he were walking past his yacht into his kingdom of happiness, into his conquered land of milk and honey

And the next evening out of town and higher still (with a detour around the boring bourgeois tavern Větruše), into the black forest, in the car at my side the conquered woman, to the sound of the music of the ether, behind glass on pillows along the asphalt, tiger-striped witht the shadows of trunks, the triumphal entrance of the mangy dingo into the jungle, I lead her by the hand up the grassy slope to my pit like an offering to my pagan site of sacrifice, the forest altar of the god Myself, and rapaciously I lower myself onto my offering.

"Bite the grass–" I order, as my ritual commands.

"Okay, but why..."

"Because I too have chewed the grass here ... Out of pain."

"Let me feel that pain as well, I want to experience everything with you – I beg you..."

It was just as I had marvelously feared – above the jungle of the earth and my captured blue antelope, the jungle of the stars exalts, and I am master of all this swirling, the world is my prey and I am the flame, the burning plasma, rising slowly into the universe –

Outside the door of the former women's one-room flat on the third floor of building No. 2000, Alex Serafin toiled away with a pair of pliers, a chisel, and three screwdrivers. "Those bastards–" he angrily hissed, "they screwed them down even more today!" In his battle with the bolts, hasps, and hooks, his sister Madda was a great deal of help, while his brother Julda Serafin just sighed and brought bread and butter to the perpetual conquerors.

"Alex, if you'd go back to the first floor, Borek could live with me in my room and once again we would have peace and quiet..." Julda repeated until Alex chased him away with the poker. Meanwhile Borek set about with gusto pulling nails from the fortress gate. "I hope those bastards didn't expect us to kneel down before this door, start crying, and then go back to sleep in the basement!"

What caused the most trouble were the iron rods put through the bar across the door and anchored with bent nails, whose heads were then pounded through the wood on both sides. Borek and Alex didn't break into their flat until the early hours of the morning, in the early hours of the afternoon the sleeping wood-fighters (the door looked like a captured Turkish flag in the Montenegrin palace of the Black Mountain King Nikola) were approached once again by the housing official bearing two more richly stamped decrees, from bed Alex kicked him wearily in the kidney, the official cried out in pain and pointed out the fact that he had three children to provide for, fled from Borek's West German dagger as it approached his ear, and then for a long time plaintively pleaded with them outside the door ...

"What diehards," Alex sighed as he rubbed his stubbed toe against his other leg, "the first of the twenty-five superpowers on this planet is the bureaucracy, no one will snatch the world from its briefcase. Damn it, where's Europa with our meat?!"

Europa Zíbrtová was whispering with someone in the hallway, Alex's hearing quickened and suddenly (the voice of that someone was growing audible behind the broken door, it was the voice of Julda Serafin) he sprang out of bed shouting, ran out into the hallway, his shouting continued and grew louder, Julda shouted back at him, exasperated, with his high, choir-practiced voice, then a few smacks, after which Alex dragged Europa into the room by her hair shouting: "And here's another!" Smack! Smack! Smack! Borek counted three of them and turned away, interfering between these two would mean placing your life in danger, and once when Borek tried to stand up for her, Europa herself drove him away and took more slaps ...

"And one more for good measure!" Smack! "And one more to make up–" Alex yelled, and he went on beating Dáša, "you're really starting to get on my nerves, Europa, and if I catch you one more time with Julda – How many times have you come to a decision between the two of us, and always the same decision: the exact opposite of the one before! You think I have high-tension wires instead of nerves?! What exactly do you want? Borek, what must something be to still be alive?"

"Highly organized matter manifesting goal-oriented impulses."

"So I guess our Europa is no longer alive since her impulses are zig-zaging all over the place, from paradise to kingdom confound it – if only they'd taken you straight from the cradle and made you work somewhere on a rice plantation, where you belong and to where you're being called, liebe Europa, and all the more insistently – but instead of that they taught you some scraps of philosophy and foreign languages, how to ride the streetcar and read novels, jabber about democracy, smoke and talk on the telephone – anything else? – and all of it miserably. You don't even know how to use the telephone!"

"But when I called you this morning..." Dáša tearfully objected.

"You asked whether you should buy nine rolls or a dozen. Does one really say 'nine' into a telephone?"

"Well, how then?"

"'Niner,' of course, because 'nine' can sound like 'five.' They didn't teach you that at Charles University, did they? Well, our instructors taught us that at trade school, and in two languages, too. How do you say 'two' in German?"

"Zwei..." whispered Dáša.

"And how do you say it over the telephone?"

"Zweiner?" Dáša hesitantly attempted.

"Zweiner! That's ridiculous – Zwo! Zwo! Zwo! Run around the room and yell zwo!"

And Europa Zíbrtová dutifully did her German lesson double-time...

The next day Jolana Tušlová appeared – we couldn't for the life of us believe that this picture of arrogance was being sketched on our retinas – to ask us for a little favor: whether we would be so kind as to move back down to the itinerants quarters.

"The only thing you have going for you," Borek Trojan told her after much swallowing of saliva, "is your delicate condition. So clear out as fast as your condition will allow–"

And since we considerately did not throw her down the stairs, the next day the blue deserter himself – it can't be, this is just too much, I placed the switchblade on my open palm and pressed the button – the traitor and felon Bogan Tušl came crawling back, he who's been living at our expense – haven't many people died for lesser offenses?

The assistant deputy director was wearing a white nylon shirt stuck to his chest with sweat and was softly begging – where did you leave the voice you used on the stairs? – and promising much more than he could have collected for his perfidy. Why is this pitiful little room so important to him? Obviously, you don't want to disappoint them with this, your first special management task, your first dirty little duty, and you will be committing so many other, bigger ones just to hold on to your seat, your lackey's seat in front of the boss's door – behind that door the boss sits in yet another lackey's seat in front of the door of yet another lackey, what have you guys done to our wonderful aircraft carrier, to that magnificent metallic toy for men – already and for life the blue lackey of blue lackeys. This is not an ori-

ginal thought, but it's true: on this fucked-up continent, in the twentieth
century, the lower you are the freer you are, and I will never be a lackey –

Mr. Gráf's lackey went away empty-handed, but he promised he'd
come back soon – before he came back, however, Mrs. Gráfová showed up
and came more often than he did.

I'm lying on my cot, my hands behind my head, and barefoot Zita is
stepping over the tracks on the floor, bringing me some French red wine,
Paul Robert, and that book about Julien by Monsieur Stendhal, gifts from
blue France, and bloody pieces of flesh from northern Bohemia, along with
her love and tenderness – why is there so much between us, my dear, why
must we make love on the edge of a barrier and meet at the crest of a
barricade ...

"Stab me–" pleads Zita, "beat me, kill me, if you have the urge to..."

"I do."

I throw away the half-eaten beef and push aside the unfinished wine,
what else can we have, something even more exciting, I reach my hand out
for the fallen empress, I wonder how she'd burn, you want to be beaten?
Then you'll be beaten. Isn't hatred always lurking behind love?

BESIEGED: CONQUERORS AND LOVERS

Zita stood by the wall in the darkness of her apartment hallway, pressing
her knees, thighs, arms, and her entire body against the vertical metal tube
of the water main, waiting for Borek's signal from upstairs, at his signal she
rubbed her face against the pipe, already hot from her kisses, stroked it, and
ran her lips along it ... What have you done to me, you cruel cadet. My
barefoot Greek boy. Which one of us is St. Sebastian now? My body is
bristling with Your arrows like a porcupine. But my skin longs insatiably for
more. My meat provides You with new draughts of blood. Fire into me, my
archer! Be cruel and aim carefully. I cannot wait ... the drumroll!

Borek lay with his hands behind his head on his cot in his room on the
third floor, his bare feet resting on the vertical metal pipe of the water main,
I have only to drum upon it four times with the pliers, like a mallet on a
gong, BANG! and in a moment my prisoner will stand before me ready to
endure and subject herself to whatever my aroused imagination comes up
with, she will gratefully and passionately subject herself to absolutely
anything –

BANG! BANG! BANG! BANG!

Only at sundown did Zita descend from the third floor back home to her second-floor apartment. She tottered down the stairs as if broken on the wheel. Crucified, burned at the stake. Oh, how my skin burns! But oh, how I burned! How many of Your arrows am I leaving with?! The feeling after a beating is sweet, like a resurrection. Call me back soon to your house of pain, my dear. Oh, how good I am at burning! And at being happy –

Sated with meat and wine, with red circles behind his eyelids and the last traces of pleasure in his body, Borek slowly walked along our nighttime street, turning up beige dust with each step, like on the beach at night, on the Riviera, in front of the Grand Balmoral Hotel, and sovereignly serene he looks up into the August sky striated with meteorites of wishes fulfilled.

Just before 23:00, Zita exited building No. 2000, unlocked her car, and started it up. Slowly, silently. Like a murderer. A suicide. A participant in a witch's sabbath in the woods by a river. Didn't you forget your broom? I drive down the street, turn, and brake. Borek jumps in. We don't speak. Does one make jokes in the sacristy before a pontifical black mass? We drive quickly through town, past the respectably sleeping windows. Why respectably? All you can see in them is darkness. What does respectability do in the dark? At night the city is silver. As are the garbage cans, the kicked-in door of the grocery store, and the sewer grates. Overflowing wastepaper baskets look like baskets of flowers. The arch of the bridge looks like a sleeping brontosaurus, we drive into its maw. The asphalt road along the river is reserved for us alone. The trees are bathed in snow-white moonlight. We drive into a small clearing and stop. We leave our clothing in the car. On my shoulders I feel a cool breeze as if thousands of eyes were staring at me. I feel like I'm in a pillory. It feels good. Beneath the moon, that womanish star. I'm waiting, my dear executioner. I want to die here and now –

Borek led Zita across the grass toward the bank, and when they reached the towpath he forced her to run, run with me, my dear, and laugh, more, more, more, I practically had to throw her into the water, she went quickly under and I pulled her up by her hair, up above the black surface of the water. Look around, my love, we're swimming here among the stars, and whoever's first to swim to the moon – and finally she began to laugh with me, we raced and splashed water at each other like kissing water cyclists, Zita whooped and screamed like a little girl, I tickled her under the water, she squealed and giggled and her eyes sparkled behind her wet hair, when we climbed out of the water she was a happy, lively schoolgirl – stay like that! She'll stay that way – you may not grow old on me, and why are you always talking about dying, you're not allowed to die for me – if she's not allowed to die for ME, then she cannot die … Zita, I love you! And we joyfully fooled around on the grass until it began to grow light, we were still too excited to go home, so we reclined the car seats and lay down and you know what! We fell asleep! If you're in a mess, you might as well make it a good one, so at six in the morning we buzzed along the river, which was emerging through its diaper of mist, and parked right on the square, boom! And for breakfast we went to the milk bar downstairs at the Svět Café, cocoa and hot dogs with horseradish and carp in mayonnaise, since we'd just come from the riverside, at our counter two old men were having beer with beer and no bread, and they started to look my girl Zita over, and boy! They started hitting on her! And Zita laughed and drove straight to the office and I hitchhiked to work at the factory. We had a date at two at my place. I live close to the factory, and if I run –

"Beat me again," says Corinda, wrote Langston Hughes and said Zita to Borek, "No–" answered Borek, and he threw his black leather to the ground, "–no more."

"I want pain and pleasure from your hand – if they're both from you, I don't feel any difference."

"But I don't want to cause you pain! Because now your pain is my pain!"

"It wasn't like that before, was it…"

"No, it wasn't, not till now. Why is that?"

"I wonder."

Because I began to love you.

And I you. And we both recognized it.

I matured from sex to eroticism, and then on to love –

Backwards program, isn't it? But thanks. At least the best awaits us.

My hatred has been satisfied and has yielded to love.

And my yearning for cruel delight has ceded its place to happiness – I no longer need to suffer.

Everyone needs love, and it can be had. Its price: love me!

Try it, and we'll learn together …

Love is not prey, even the world is not prey … Love is not a sacrifice, it's not even a gift. Love is one hand presented to another, and these two hands join and squeeze.

Who would long for his own destruction?

On the contrary, we long for kisses.

In love there are no victors ...
... and no defeated.
Love is not meat –
... but rather grass, milk, and air.
And music.
And music.

"Give me that broom," said Borek to Zita.
"No. Sweeping is women's work."
"I'll do it today myself."
"I'll do it."
"Then let's do it together..." and our hands meet on the broom handle and we sweep under the bed and between the tracks.

Whenever we feel like it, we knock on the pipe that connects our two stories, I with the pliers BANG! and I with the scissors Clink! in the morning, in the evening, and in the middle of the night, these are our long telegrams to one another, it's always the same telegram with just three words: I LOVE YOU. And our building resounds with the happiness of metal, and our happiness extends for miles around, and wherever we go, into town or to the factory, we both carry around the end of our shared pipe, and all day and all night this pipe sends out and receives our mutual message to one another – we love each other and are always together.

CONQUERORS

"–OUCH..." Delerious, Madda opened her eyes, Olda was floating in a red haze above her and in her and then suddenly dissappeared. "Olda–"

Olda stood by the window with his back toward Madda, smoking a perfumed, golden-tipped cigarette.

"Olda, darling ... come lie with me..."

"It's late. Get out of here! Here, wipe yourself off – and scram," said Olda, gripping the rigid cigarette between his teeth and throwing Madda his coveralls, Madda snatched them up from the ground and wiped herself off, the cloth was soaked with diesel fuel, oil, and grease and it left black smudges and dark little balls all over her body, I'm dirty, dirty again just like with the boys from Robko's gang in the wet leaves under the bench in the park outside the chemical factory ... Madda got up with difficulty, pulled her dress over her head, and stumbled out of the itinerants quarters into the hallway.

"Maddička–" whispered a pale Stěpa lurking behind the door, he grabbed her greedily by the elbow and pulled her toward him, Madda pushed him away with her free hand, get out of the way, you shithead, Stěpa pressed against her more and more insistently till Madda rammed her fingers in his eyes, forced him to his knees, and then pushed him over onto the ground. This building really is insane –

Up on the stairs Czarevitch Roman was on the lookout, everyone go to hell –

"Madda ... please..." whimpered the young Gráf.

"Scram," said Madda witheringly. "I don't even want to look at you."

This building is a regular loony bin. In our room on the third floor Julda's kneeling by the window, hands clasped in prayer, it's hard to know whether to cry or burst out laughing, and all of you can kiss my you know what. Madda pulled her dress off over her head and turned on the faucet, no water of course came out, Madda angrily kicked the sink and yelped in pain over her stubbed big toe.

"Where've you been, dear sister?" Julda asked.

"Better not to ask, dear brother!" Madda answered, then stripped the sheet off her bed and began wiping her burning, scratched-up skin with the corner of it, s-s-sss, that stings, oweee!

"You're dirty..." said Julda.

"Really? No! And how can you tell?"

"I can see it. I can feel it..."

"Then fix me up a bathroom with a whirlpool so you don't have to smell me. Nitwit!"

"I prayed for you."

"Well, I thank you very kindly, sir. Right now I'm hungry."

Julda sighed, got up, cut Madda a piece of bread and spread it with yeast paste. "But first get dressed. That's no way to eat bread."

"Should I put on the evening robe with flounces – I'll bet you put that shit all over it, didn't you?! Ugh, that horrible yeast again! ... You want to starve me to death, don't you! Didn't you get paid today? Then why didn't you buy any meat? At least some garlic salami, the kind for eighteen crowns..."

"You received your salary, as well. And there are people less fortunate than us."

"You gave it to that stupid rectory again?! – Shit, you're a fireman who makes nine hundred crowns a month and yet you maintain a whole colony of lousy urchins – Jesus Christ, my brother's a nitwit!"

"Must you take the Lord's name in vain?"

"Must you be such a cretin, for God's sake?!"

Julda sighed, turned his back to Madda, and knelt down once again, that's the second time today a guy has turned his back on me, even though this one's not even a guy, and the other one's too much of one, damn it, won't someone at least speak to me like a human being, "Julda–" Madda angrily screeched, "come here and talk with me!"

"Your heart is full of malice. Come kneel beside me and we'll pray together..."

"I'm supposed to stuff my craw with yeast and then thank God for it, that's your plan for the evening! You nitwit! Julda, know what I'm doing right now? I'm poking around in your pants pocket. Don't you even want to see? And hey, five crowns ... Julda, I'm taking these five crowns from you, five crowns that you had and that you don't have anymore, now they're mine ... Julda, don't you even want to see? I guess not. And look, Julda, when I was taking them out, I tore the pocket a little, you under-stand, and now I'm running my nail along the seam, and this pocket is going to keep ripping more and more – Julda!!"

But he doesn't even turn around, he just keeps babbling to his knapsack, this is horrible, if you killed him he'd just thank you for it ... this building is full of loonies, really dangerous ones.

Madda tossed and turned beneath her scratchy blanket, and from the street below came the soft sound of a harmonica that every night Czarevitch Roman, the moron, uses to send me a message, my clean, beautiful boy with a body like a greyhound and the delicate white hands of a priest, but he can't do anything with them, they're both left hands – Olda has two right ones, and instead of a harmonica he plays me, I was probably made for bulldogs or Great Danes instead of greyhounds or pugs, *my bleu blues* ... I'm probably just hearing things, it's just music, *cool* and *slow* and *far away* like the Far West with its clean, blue Indian lakes, the Far Far West, which doesn't exist, never has and never will.

Oh-yo-yo-, Olda goes wild on top of me like the devil himself and his eyes swim so close above mine, they run together and I see the single eye of a mean gray wolf, oh-yo-yo-, then he lifts himself up on his hands and looks just like a middleweight boxer, dark and muscular, and those muscles play across his chest, like when the wind blows through high grass, oh-yo-yo-, Stěpa was pretending to be asleep but now he's staring at us brazenly, Olda should throw him out, but I don't care, oh-yo-yo-, this is my kind of music, this is what I was made for, this makes my body feel good, then why am I crying – it must be from all this kindness, oh-yo-yo- oh-yo-yo- oh-yo-yo- oh-yo-yo- YO YO YO – – and then he soiled me and got rude and cruel, to Olda I'm like the wind or yesterday's newspaper.

Roman Gráfovich is waiting for me on the stairs again, he stands there like the police, like a prosecutor, guard, and executioner, you, my boy, can take that eternal love of yours and stick it, you never satisfy me and I'm constantly hungry, you take from me my equanimity and balance, your very existence gets on my nerves, you make me feel like a vulgar, dirty whore, or at least remind me of it, should I go to a convent for seven years and then hold your hand and walk through the park like a nice girl? That face of yours and those sincere little eyes burn into me like a glowing cigarette, your eyes are like a rearview mirror and I see a whore in them, it's me, I never asked you to show me this reflection nor will I allow you to, I've had it up to here with you, my little blue junior, I can't stand you anymore, you're driving me crazy and I've had enough of this loony bin from basement to attic, I WANT TO SEE THIS BLUE SHACK FLYING THROUGH THE AIR –

"Get away from me, Roman, scram!"

"Madda, my dear. My squaw. I love you..."

"But I don't love you! I hate you!"

"Come with me..."

"You want to do it with me too, don't you! But I don't! Not with you, ever again."

"But why, Madda ... Madda..."

"Julda has convinced me that one should not have sexual intercourse."

"Come with me ... We'll just talk and I'll play for you..."

"No! I can't ... really, because ... Because Julda won't let me be with you."

BESIEGED

Julda made the sign of the cross on his forehead, his lips, and his chest, tapped his forehead on the floor beneath the window, rose, walked across the third-floor hallway of building No. 2000, and knocked on the door. Borek Trojan lay on his cot, his hands behind his head and his bare feet around the metal water pipe.

"Is Dr. Zíbrtová here?" Julda inquired softly.

"Europa? She's somewhere with that devil of hers," laughed Borek.

"The poor girl ... And even you I pity, Borek..."

"Me? But I feel fabulous now ... you yourself once told me that I'd never be as happy as I am right now on a mattress stuffed with straw. I'm starting to believe it."

"But that woman ... Mrs. Gráfová, you're bringing her unhappiness."

"That woman is happy with me."

"That woman can only be happy with her family. You're killing her."

"Not anymore."

"More and more certainly all the time."

"No! That's not true. And if it is ... then I'll die with her."

"She will die. You will live."

"Why do you want to separate us?"

"Life shall separate you. It's merely a matter of time. Think about it, what will become of the two of you in a year? In two years? Five?"

"Shut up, for God's sake! – You're a bad weather prophet, and a bad one at that. Why do you care about us? Leave us to our sinning – can love really be a sin? You don't even know what love is. You tiresome little fireman! Focus on something else, would you. Like those tracks you're standing on. How long do I have to live like this, not to mention like an outlaw in a constant state of jeopardy as well? One year? Two years? Five?"

"You must be patient, my son..."

"How long? One year? Two years? Five? Why should patience last longer than love?"

"You say love but you mean lust. Love is eternal and patience is the path thereto."

"And what if halfway along this path they kick me back down to the basement? What's better, lust on the third floor or patience in the basement. Anyway, you've annoyed me long enough. Dáša's not here. Sbohem, so long."

Julda sighed and went back downstairs, in front of the white door on the second floor he crossed himself and then rang the doorbell.

"What – is there a fire?" said Director Evžen Gráf.

"You know well enough yourself that fire's everywhere. I've come to see you about the living situation of Borek Trojan and my brother Alex. Why can't you make it possible for them to live like human beings?"

"Why don't they act like human beings?"

"Why don't you make it possible for them to live and act like human beings? Let them have that room."

"The factory housing administration takes care of these things."

"Is Bogan Tušl an employee of the factory housing administration?"

"Bogan Tušl is old enough to answer for his own actions."

"Actions to which you impelled him."

"I do not impel anything, I see to the successful running of the plant and all of its equipment."

"Does this include the people entrusted to you?"

"Certainly. Just like the observation of directives, regulations, and laws. Your two clients wrongfully, illicitly, and illegally broke the rules. Therefore, sanctions will follow until the original situation is restored."

"Is the placing of tracks in living quarters part of your legal sanctions or is that simply brutal lawlessness?"

"I know nothing about any tracks. But I most certainly know of the violent actions of these two in our building."

"Come with me, I'll show you the tracks."

"For now I can say only this: until the original situation is restored in this building, I refuse to concern myself with these matters. It's a question of chronological order. Just like my plans for the rest of the day: I've worked. Now I'm resting. Leave me alone. I want to sleep."

Roman appeared behind his father, his face pale and tense with anger. His wide eyes, fixed on Julda, glittered with hatred, and the boy slammed the door right in his face.

First thing next morning, even before the commencement of the workday, Julda lovingly watered the bed of white gladioluses below the window of the director's office and lingered over them in silent joy ... the sound of a siren woke him from his reverie. Julda watered all the lawns because the sky promised a sultry day, then he brought over a wheelbarrow of white sawdust from the joiner's shop and spread it on the cement floor of the factory fire station, sprinkled it with water, with a rice broom swept up the gray, swelling filth of the earth, wheeled it out to the boiler room, and silently watched it toss in the flames. Then he washed his hands and went to the office of the assistant economic deputy.

"You're pale, my son, and careworn. You toil too much and do not contemplate things," said Julda, and sitting behind a desk piled high with paper, Bogan Tušl rolled his eyes. "I've come to ask you, Bogan, to give up once and for all on Alex and Borek's room. Let them have it, and call off your officials."

"This matter is being dealt with by the factory housing administration."

"In a manner suggested to them by you. Who deals with the matter of basic human necessities?"

"The personnel department. Payroll. The factory dining hall. The factory dispensary. The factory library. The janitorial staff. Security – and it's security that's most qualified in this matter. Tell that to those two. They moved in by force. They will be moved out by force. That is all. Now scoot."

Julda had no further tasks that day and so sat down on a barrel by the door of the fire department ready for immediate intervention, which was not, however, required, and so he sat out the rest of his shift staring meditatively south toward the stark, luminous mountain range of junk heaps and dead earthworks, toward a harsh, naked landscape, which is probably what the Holy Land looks like now.

In front of building No. 2000, a blue-and-silver vehicle drove up in a cloud of desert dust, a glass coffin of futility for self-made fugitives who race down the road forgetting what a tree looks like, a flower in a field or a rose on a lawn, overlooking even themselves and appearing as blurred smudges as they flee from their very lives ... And isn't their frantic speed really just anxiety at the distance of the trip lying before them, which, to their horror, time does not shorten, but rather horribly perpetuates, as if they hadn't even begun, so that their goal is so distant as to be inconceivable?

Mrs. Zita Gráfová steps out of one of the glass doors, and booming from her car is music that sounds like animal shrieks, can't you even for a moment be alone without deafening yourself ...

"Do you need a ride somewhere?" said the pitiful woman cheerfully.

"Not me, my place is here in this building. Are you sure, Madame, where your place is?"

"Is that supposed to be witty? I live in this building, too, don't I?"

"On the second floor? Or the third?"

"I don't understand..."

"Rather, you don't want to understand. Where is a woman's place – with her husband and her son ... or with her sin up near the attic?"

"And in your grim interpretation, the attic is above the second floor."

"In your opinion, then, is hell all the way at the top?"

"In my opinion, heaven begins immediately above my ceiling. Coincidentally, same as you. Aren't we both on the third floor?"

"We're both on the third floor, but a horrible chasm separates our rooms. In this chasm I see flames!"

"Then you should be able to see that I'm already on fire. I'm better off in the fire than I would be in your cold heaven. Keep your loveless heaven! And if you have a heart, bow down before our flame."

"I hold my nose before your flame, Madame. It smells of sulfur!"

"I feel sorry for you. And I hate you!"

"I love you like a sister and feel sorry about your ruination."

Julda stood alone in the dust of the street and timidly looked at Teo's first-floor window, the shutter shook and through a chink a mound of cloud-colored pillows were revealed, Julda took the liberty of looking up above the pillows and he caught sight of ancient Teo's face and his fixed gaze – where was he looking? A mocking, challenging look on his face, Alex Serafin took a lengthy detour around the building, Teo was following him with his pensive gave.

Julda tried to grasp the strange, high-tension relationship between sin and truth, he himself being incapable of sin. But perhaps sin stigmatizes one more strongly than does virtue, and the prodigal son draws the father's attention more than the obedient one, perhaps even lust, sin, even anger are ways of being together, as night borders day, hatred and love, pain and bliss shine most radiantly only together in their eternal, indivisible unity. *Extrema se tangunt.* Death is known as dispassion, and dead he who is indifferent. Perhaps sin itself is closer to truth than deathly indifference. And maybe even the battle of good against evil is a union that cannot take place with silent indifference ...

Alex disappeared into the building, Teo closed his window, and Julda stood alone in the dust of the street in front of the building. No, someone's coming. A graceful girl with a clean face ...

"Good afternoon," said the girl. "You're not Mr. Julda Serafin, by any chance?"

"I am. And who are you, my daughter?"

"I'm Jana Rybářová. They sent me to you – and I recognized you immediately by the way you're dressed."

"How can I help you?"

"You see, Mr. Serafin, I'm a new employee at Cottex, I signed on to work in the laboratory right out of school and my problem is … In short, I have nowhere to live in Ústí. For a week now I've been commuting from Malešice, a little village beyond Most, and it takes two hours to get here by train in the morning and two hours in the evening to get home … And I've heard that in your building there's a women's one-room flat…"

"Yes, there is such a room, on the third floor. But two men are living there."

"Two men … in a room for women?"

"A few years ago two girls lived there, and then one of them got married. Only recently has she moved out, with her husband."

"And how did two men get in there?"

"They were living in very poor conditions, here on the first floor. And so one night they secretly moved into that room on the third floor."

"Just like that, without authorization? But that's not right."

"Indeed, it's not. That's why the administration wants to move them out."

"To where?"

"To where they were before.

"Where the conditions were poor?"

"Yes."

"But that's not right!"

"It's not … you're right."

"So let's put everything in order!"

"We'll have to work on it. You'll help us."

"I'd be glad to! I'll love it here, it's close to the factory and it's a big, lovely building…"

"It's rather old, my daughter…"

"But you could still do so much with it. But first we have to get things in order! It's not right for people to live in poor conditions! So that they have to move in at night like thieves! After all, in such a big, lovely building everyone's rooms should be lovely!"

"Beati esurientes et sitientes iustitiam, quoniam ipsi saturabantur," Julda said with a smile.

"That's Latin, right? Are you a lawyer? What does it mean?" asked the indefatigable Jana Rybářová.

"I'm just a fireman, my daughter, and it means: 'Blessed are they which do hunger and thirst after righteousness: for they shall be filled.'"

"Yes, there must be righteousness. And people must have somewhere to live. And don't forget about me–"

"I'm glad to help you in your hour of need. I myself shall move down to the first floor and you shall live on the third floor with my sister, Madda. Tomorrow I'll get permission and today I'll pack my things together. You can move in the day after tomorrow–" and refusing the girl's thanks, Julda cheerfully ran off into the building and up the stairs.

Behind the tortured wood of the door of the former women's one-room flat on the third floor came the sound of a woman moaning. Julda pricked up his hears – it's Dáša! – and without further ado he forced his way through the door. Dr. Zíbrtová was kneeling and scrubbing the floor between the tracks, her hair hung down into her tear-stained face.

"Doctor! I've been looking for you everywhere. Get up and come with me!"

"Julda ... I no longer have anywhere to go..."

"You've taken a fancy to your role as cleaning woman?"

"I love him ... your brother Alex. He's done worse than make me a cleaning woman – but I love him!"

"Do you love my brother or your own body in his embrace?"

"I love everything about him ... Even the blows he gives me..."

"And don't you love those blows most of all? Is the pain brought on by your lust satisfying that very lust?"

"Leave me alone ... go away. We've already said all there is to say to one another. I'm his because I want to be–"

"Because you want to be wrested from your very self! But I have enough strength to help you. Come with me. Doctor, get up!"

"No! No! No!"

"I shall help you–" and Julda grabbed Dáša under the arms and forcibly lifted her up, Dáša screamed, scratched, and kicked, but when in furious resistance she used the tracks to brace herself, Julda grabbed her by the hair and dragged her across the tracks, along the floor, and across the hallway into his room. Dáša shrieked, rolled around on the floor, and beat her fists against it like a maniac. "He calls me Europa – and I just want to be his!" she screamed like one possessed. "I want my devil – on me and in me!"

Julda crossed himself, ran his hands beneath his linen work shirt, felt the knot against his naked body, untied it, pulled out the blackened rope, folded it in two, and used it to whip the woman at his feet until she was comforted, silent, numb.

Then he carefully raised her by her elbows and placed her on his cot, Dáša slept like a child and Julda gently caressed her hair, looked around his room, and softly sighed, tonight I sleep here for the last time, after so many years here … But Madda and Jana Rybářová will like it here, I gladly cede my place and go downstairs to the itinerants quarters.

Julda pulled his suitcase from beneath his cot, packed his black holiday suit, black shoes, and white shirt, his razor, shaving soap and brush, towel, woolen cap, and well-thumbed Bible – that's everything except my old wool coat, in which I shall depart and in which I arrived oh so many years ago.

Madda straggled in towards evening, exhausted and quiet, stretched herself out on her bed with her clothes still on, and immediately fell asleep. Julda knelt at his spot by the window well into the evening and softly prayed for Borek, for the unfortunate Mrs. Gráfová, caught up in sin, for her deathly weary husband, Evžen Gráf, and for his prodigal son, Roman, for Dáša Zíbrtová, floundering and hounded, for the obstinate Bogan Tušl, his wife, Jolana, and their child soon to arrive, for the proud Frank Secký and his wife, Helena, for the charming girl Jana Rybářová, who longs for righteousness and human dignity and who the day after tomorrow will replace me here, for my no good brother, Alex, for the uneducated people at the old rectory and for their little ones, who are dearest to You and me, my Lord … Then he spread his woolen coat upon the floor at Dáša Zíbrtová's feet and contemplated whether today he had done everything he could have, yes, probably, and in silent joy – the just fall asleep satisfied, calmed, and consoled, without desire – he happily fell asleep.

In the middle of the night insistent knocking at the door, Julda sat up on his wool coat, Madda was breathing regularly, in a deep sleep, but the other bed was empty – where'd Dáša go? She probably left during the night and now was trying to get back in …

Outside the door stood Roman Gráf, his eyes downcast. Across the hall the sound of Dáša moaning – she's fled back to Alex!

"Let me in or I'll die," said Roman hoarsely. "I got to see Madda. During the day she chases me off and so at least when she's asleep … I need to caress her . . ." The boy's breath reeked of alcohol.

"You want to enter a girl's bedroom?" said Julda as he listened painfully to Dáša's husky moaning across the hall.

"I beg you!" shouted Roman Gráf.

"I will not let you in!" shouted Julda Serafin.

"You asshole, you bastard, you squealer!" Roman shrieked like one possessed. "Then I'll come for her another time and another way! And I'll kill you!!"

That's what the poor boy shouted before he angrily stomped back downstairs, it was as if the entire building was opening up, you could hear doors opening and sense the held breath of the eavesdroppers, you'd even be able to hear the fall of an apple, and the boy roared hatred from deep in his lungs and the entire building gorged on it like a single, monstrous ear.

Well, unfortunately I'm still here, just so you don't forget me – Roman Gráf, the most superfluous person on the planet, that fellow who's in everybody's way.

I bother my old man, who says it's my fault he can't take his afternoon nap. After all, as my father he has the responsibility of raising me, so instead of his afternoon nap he's constantly and sleepily staring at me for up to a half hour without saying a word, because what do we have to say to one another? Borek Trojan doesn't talk to me either when Papa's out and we meet in the hallway of our apartment, what kind of conversation am I supposed to have with Mama's beau – Borek's expression buries me deep beneath the lower geologic layers of our Czech basin, somewhere among the trilobites, and even lower, deep down to the Mesozoic, the Paleozoic, even the Azoic. "Go away," Madda says to me, my girl, beautiful as a goddess, my squaw, "I don't even want to look at you."

And my mother's not even my mother anymore, and I'm not her son anymore, Engineer Borek Trojan has displaced me the way sulphuric acid displaces sulfide in Kipp's device, which we just learned about in school. $BaS + H_2SO_4 = BaSO_4$ (that's those two coming together, with their electrons...) $+ H_2S$, that's smelly hydrogen sulfide, which to everyone's great relief escapes and disappears, Mama, how nice it was together with you in our BaS – but you've obviously gotten more than you could get from me.

Mama, please forgive me for still existing –

To my delight I'm getting more gray hairs, and when I count just the ones on my temples – just the ones that are *completely* gray, because the yellowish ones I figure have just been bleached by the sun – I have 27 completely gray hairs on my left temple and 42 on the right.

It's September and us kids are back in school. I've never been popular, not even close, at least that's what I imagined, and so I got some consolation from the fact that things couldn't get any worse – but things can always get much worse. We have a new and completely imbecilic French teacher who constantly fucks up the language that's supposed to be his bread and butter, and once when my eardrum was literally rent, I took the liberty of trying to correct him a little – can I help it if I go to Paris every year, a place he'll never be able to go, and is it really such a horrible crime to know something better than the teacher? – and the class turned the rest of the lesson into a free-for-all, they thought I was bragging about my poor Paris, of which I'm already ashamed, but they're always glad when they can find something against me, and then during gym class, when we were playing "shepherd" (a concentration camp invention of our gym teacher Sádi: two teams and two mats on opposite walls, the object is to get the ball to the other team's mat using whatever means possible, no holds barred) both teams showed more interest in me than in the pigskin. The only person who seemed to understand me was the history teacher, but that's just what I imagined until he took me into his office and whispered to me that I was like an Oxford student among philistines, he kept whispering more and more softly, that I was Ganymede and Orpheus and a beautiful, white youth among barbarians, and then he started rubbing my knee and his hand kept going higher ... so now I'm completely alone in this hole.

Madda keeps running away from me and I keep looking for her, I can't believe she's been able to forget about everything ... What does she do all that time downstairs in the itinerants quarters? I keep walking past the door down there and a lot of times I run into Stěpa, one of their gang, and we both wait for Madda, Stěpa amiably shortens the time by kicking me in the leg and then pretending nothing happened, he acts like he's leaving and then suddenly from behind he crushes my ankle with the sole of his shoe like he was crushing a bug ... and it *really* hurts. But what's worse is when the workers walk by and laugh in my face. I'd do absolutely anything to make them stop laughing at me, I could kill any one of them – but which, if Madda's already ... Kill someone and then they'll lead me *down the stairs through the open door   In front of the building   Into the middle of our street   My hands tied to a beam laid across my shoulders   Like Christ walking up to Golgotha in the movie* Viva Maria   *Everyone will line the sides of the street, horrified   Who would have thought this boy was capable of such a thing, they'll say   And keep staring at me*

Madda walks past and she too stops   And stares at me
The way she used to when we were still together –

How Madda's eyes sparkled that time on the square when she sent me to tell Frank Secký he was a pig ... and when she said her gang would kill him for her. Who am I supposed to go up to now, my squaw? Who has taken from us our lovemaking? Because I can't believe it would be you yourself.

No! It can't be you, you still love me. Who else? The old man – no way, on the contrary, he told me after an hour of throat-clearing and nose-blowing that a girl was in any case better than sniffing ether – no, not the old man, he's just weary of me. Mama – she doesn't take any interest in me at all, I'm just an impediment, when I slink into her apartment at night – because my apartment isn't mine anymore and I don't say "home" because

I don't want to start bawling – but I still live here, don't I ... Am I just supposed to disappear? How? Where? Mama still takes care of me and is terribly considerate, but that's just what crushes me the most. If only you'd throw me out, then I would have to defend myself and we could at least fight about it – wouldn't that be better than running away from one another?

And then there's Julda Serafin, Madda's goon. Julda complained about me to my parents, Julda's agitating against me and he keeps ratting on me ... but Julda's just a pitiful idiot.

I wake up, eat, go to school, which annoys me and where I annoy everyone else, eat again, take a shower, avoid my parents so they don't have to avoid me, hang around the building, and in the evening play my harmonica below Madda's window so I can at least *somehow* gain entrance to her ... but Madda doesn't even listen to my music anymore.

Somehow gain entrance to her, get INSIDE any way possible, because outside there's only cold and death, ENTERING INTO AN OPERATION means going in among people and warmth, whatever the entrance fee is I'll gladly pay, whether or not I even have it, just so finally everyone will begin to *register* me ... Otherwise you're completely superfluous. Otherwise you're absolutely dead. And all that's left to do is polish yourself off.

We're all going to die when the bomb falls. And sorry is he who has long before stopped living ... Get yourself a scar so at least you'll be recognizable among the mass of corpses on the battlefield. As a man and not just as the 2,876,943,215th victim.

The ancient Spartans organized whippings for their young men, in front of the priestess, that would be a much easier graduation exam, instead of nine o'clock in a black suit in the common room, it would be nine o'clock without clothing in the temple, that would be quicker than any exam and also a more enjoyable preparation than using Kipp's device to get that smelly hydrogen sulfide, taking miserable French with someone who's never in his life seen a Frenchman, and learning politically castrated history from Mr. Homo.

Other nations go at it more directly, like for instance the Dayaks, for them you become a man when you *make yourself a man* ... And surely at this very moment there's some guy from Oxford who has somewhere above his fireplace, among stuffed heads of antelopes and tigers, a pistol or a knife with an inconspicuous notch on the handle ... and till the day he dies, no more inferiority complexes, he just sits there by that fireplace with a glass of brandy, stares into the fire, and recalls the adventures of his magnificent youth.

Who did he kill? The enemy, of course. Simply *somebody* who had to die anyway. Like for instance Raskolnikov killing that old bag. Why? Just for himself ... Like Herostrates burning down the temple just so that people would *register* him. And who today knows about that temple? No one, but everybody knows about Herostrates. Or like Don Quixote jabbing his lance at a windmill ... and since then laughed at by everybody.

On Revolution Street they sell beautiful daggers with handles made of deer antler. Who buys them? What is the annual consumption of daggers in a small city? And what if the salesperson asks you what you need a dagger for? What's it to you, pal. Not a good idea, he could get angry and not sell it to you. A classmate of mine asked me ... he's from the country, afraid to walk home at night from the train station, he lives in this little village that has a prison nearby and every now and then the prisoners escape and he arrives by train, always at night ... That's no good either. I'm buying it just for the heck of it, after all it's for sale, isn't it? I want to give it to my father for his birthday, he's a forest ranger. I'll use it to open letters. Mama broke the key on a sardine can and sent me to buy one of these to open cans with ...

I stand in front of a window display of daggers and hate myself, what a chicken-shit I am. I guess that for me deciding to kill somebody is easier than buying a dagger ... because this is right now, and who knows when the other will be, obviously never ...

"Give me one of the ones in the window!" I said to the lady behind the counter.

"The one for twenty-five or the one for seventy?"

"The one for seventy..."

"That comes to eighty-two crowns ... Because we only sell it with the leather case–"

A man takes a dagger into his hand himself. So I bought it with the case. It has a beautiful handle made of deer antler ... my knightly lance. But no Don Quixote and no windmills ... there've been enough sad farces already.

All four itinerants were in the itinerants quarters, including Stěpa, but Madda's not in the building – I rejoiced: finally a new and *real* enemy, and not just Madda alone ...

And so I rejoiced and said to myself, let's go, boys, I buzzed into town on the streetcar to look for Madda, and after those long days I finally felt fine again, in my pocket I squeezed the deer antler and undid the button on the case so I could pull it instantly out, he'll shit himself from fright and run off and I'll lead my squaw away.

I started at the second floor of the Grand, where Madda always used to go before she met me. The frantic faces of her girlfriends, how they looked at me when I asked after Madda … They said she's sure to come at any moment and wouldn't I like to wait here and pay for something.

The faces were downing beer, so I gladly coughed up, then the girls asked for another couple of crowns for the jukebox and constantly played "Don, Diri Don," such a schmaltzy tune, over and over, grunting to it all the while. Those poor girls, a few of them wouldn't be bad if they'd take a bath now and then. And there weren't that many guys, so they danced with each other … Brother, if I'd only known earlier what it's like here – but I'd be the youngest.

Now I'm thinking only about *Madda*. And Madda hasn't come, outside it's already starting to get dark and the girls have already drunk a keg of beer on my tab, well prosit, to your health! Maybe Madda's home already, just walking around in front of the building, maybe she'd be happy to see me right now – but the girls won't let me go, they keep saying Madda's certain to show up, and so I sit there till closing time.

One girl, who the others called Mrcina, after whispering for a long time with the others, stumbled over to the telephone (I had to give her coins for it) and came right back. She said Madda was waiting for us in the park behind the chemical factory. And so we left, me and the six girls. They were pretty wasted from the beer and kept shouting all the way there, fortunately the streets are empty at this time.

In the park behind the chemical factory it was dark as hell, we came to a bench and everyone crowded onto it … The girls got really strange and then … I felt their coarse hands on me … it was really cruel and really disgusting. They kept laughing at me and I started bawling for the first time in front of someone else. Everyone considers me an absolute fool, everyone just pisses on me – no, I can't live like this,

"Get away from me, Roman. Scram," Madda said to me on the stairs. "I hate you."

That can't be true – – That can't be my Madda saying this, someone must have put an idea into her head – –

"Julda has convinced me…" said Madda.

"Julda won't let me be with you," said Madda.

– – and I understood I had to pull myself together right now or else I never would. If I don't do it now, in a couple days I'll be a crushed jellyfish. Julda Serafin. Now I have *my man*.

For courage I took a shot of Ronda, that white Cuban rum that Mama gave me that time when she said: "Now you're a man, Roman." That's what she said. Thanks, Mama, I'll take care of myself now, so you won't have to anymore, and I'll be out of your way.

With rum in my blood, my dagger in one pocket and my harmonica in the other, I set off upstairs to the third floor, I'd like to caress Madda one last time, then I won't be able to – I knocked on the door and *my man* came to open it.

I simply cannot stick a blade into somebody. Especially if he hasn't done anything to me.

"I will not let you in to see her!" shouted *my man*, but it was a really weak shout, it's not surprising that he won't let me into his room at night to see his sister, and so I yelled at him and screamed at the whole building like a madman, so that *my man* would pluck up a little courage and make my task a little easier – or was it so that someone from the building would come and make my task impossible?

Of course, nothing happened. I went back down to our apartment and my knees shook till morning, as if I'd run a marathon. And didn't finish. After all, I almost killed a person – –

In the morning I get up, have a piece of bundt cake and a cup of cocoa for breakfast, then walk to school. The acacias are starting to turn yellow, and the chestnut trees are turning red. The sun is shining on the paving stones. The streets smell of newspapers and coffee, and radios are playing in the windows. Children are walking to school with their little book bags on their backs, nudging each other and constantly laughing. I'm sixteen years old, the sun is starting to warm up – WHY FOR GOD'S SAKE AM I UNHAPPY WHEN I DIDN'T KILL MY MAN ... isn't it supposed to be the opposite?

My first class of the day is French – this time no commentary. Then physics, which I hate. History, where the teacher's already written me off. Chemistry – my mama was sulfide, and with an addition of sulphuric acid she becomes sulfate, and I'm a hydrogen sulfide fart, Kipp's device mostly just stinks, and in a test tube cations of the third analytic group congeal like clotted blood. And then two periods of gym with Comrade Sádi, who impatiently orders us to put the mats against the walls, as goals, which is completely superfluous because the only goal in this game is me, and there's no break when we have two periods of gym together. How happily and non-dysfunctionally everyone beats me for those ninety minutes – they simply don't trouble themselves about *their man*.

I went straight from school to the swimming area, without a bathing suit, I never really come here to swim. The bus was almost empty ... as was the grass from the bank all the way up to the wire fence of the Yacht Club, and under our class's dug-up linden tree. I used to bring Madda here, my beautiful goddess, my squaw ... even then my class didn't register me. Tomorrow they'll read about me in the newspaper. Do convicts get to swim? When I come back here many years from now, my body will be built up from working in the mines, and on my powerful, hairy chest I'll have an elaborate tattoo. The water's already cold. A deer spat in the river, and now I have a piece of his antler in my pocket. That deer died for me. Now I'm the one who's going to spit in the river.

The old man's home sleeping, and he's obviously afraid he'll have to have another heart-to-heart talk with me. Now you'll be getting enough sleep, Papa. Mama looks surprised to see me still hanging around. She's standing by the water pipe telegraphing her beau upstairs that the coast is still not clear, the old man will surely go away, but what do we do with this boy Roman, what do we do with this stupid boy ... Soon you'll all heave a sigh of relief and feel a lot better.

I wait for evening, I'm sucking down Ronda and all is well. Today was a useful day: it showed me vividly everything I do not want and how little I have to lose – I couldn't take many more such days. I wait for evening, I suck down the pale sailors' rum, and the first stars come out in the sky. The stars of bygone emperors and poets. Each one departed the best way he knew how. The heavens couldn't care less, they've seen it all too many times before. Now they just snicker and look forward to the moment when the bomb is triggered.

I walked down our street and with the darkness entered our building, it still wasn't very late. Old Teo was snoring in his first-floor apartment – With difficulty, ancient Teo climbed down from his pile of pillows and comforters, now he's listening by the door leading out to the stairs. Is he waiting to see what they'll do ... or does he know already? Then why did he climb down from his bedding? So that he could still hope ...

–and across the way, in the itinerants quarters, were sounds it's better not to hear –

"oh-yo-yo-, oh-yo-yo-" Madda howls with delight, and Olda raises himself up above her on his arms, the better to see her beneath him, moreover the light was on and from a neighboring bed Stěpa was watching them, on the verge of another paroxysm.

–and then I climb the stairs and hear laughter and amused voices coming from our second-floor apartment. It's Thursday, our *jour fixe*, so they're having Engineer Secký and Dr. Zíbrtová over to play bridge. I stamp my feet a bit, will something happen? Of course it won't. Unless I do it myself.

"One club," bids Zita Gráfová. "That's Roman on the stairs…"

"One diamond," bids Dáša Zíbrtová. "Where could he be going…"

"One heart," bids Evžen Gráf. "Yesterday he was threatening Julda."

"One spade," bids Frank Secký. "If only he'd rough that Julda up a bit."

"Two clubs," bids Zita. "I simply can't stand that Julda."

"Two spades," bids Dáša. "He's thoroughly revolting."

"Three clubs," bids Evžen. "That fellow bores me stiff."

"Three diamonds," bids Frank. "He's an idiot."

"Four clubs," bids Zita.

The third floor, the scene of the crime. *My man*'s door. From across the hall come voices and the sound of a quarrel. Why isn't Engineer Trojan with Mrs. Gráfová today? Several reasons: Mrs. Gráfová has her *jour fixe* today and so Engineer Trojan is using his free afternoon to renew his sexual energy. Another reason, the stupidest one, is that stupid boy Roman who's always in our way. I stamp a bit. Nothing bothers anybody.

My man's door. Will he open it again today? In one pocket I have my dagger in its case, unfastened long ago. In the other pocket my harmonica. What was Nero playing on when Rome was burning?

I knock on the door, *my man* opens it, I step inside – this astounding laxity when you're already totally fucked – my God, I wonder if he'll make me tea to top it all off – my God, maybe something will happen yet …

"Madda's not here," says Julda Serafin.

"I've come to see you," I say.

"I'd be glad to talk with you, my son. Won't you have a seat?"

"No! No, thank you…" At this rate I'll never kill him, if we keep going on like this we'll burst out bawling together and just like yesterday I'll go back downstairs, back home. In the morning I'll get up. I'll have a piece of bundt cake and a cup of cocoa for breakfast. Walk to school – NO! Not anymore.

"I've come to kill you," I say. This is horrible – I'm saying it in such a conversational tone: "Would you like some sugar with that, sir?" I should have started out shouting – when you're drunk everything goes better, but the rum by itself is weak … After all, you have *your man* right in front of you –

"I'm ready to die at any time." Julda Serafin smiles. "Why do you want to kill me, my son?"

"Because you're in my way! And don't call me your son!! Because you're in my way!!"

"I was just getting ready to leave. Jana Rybářová, a pure girl, will be living here in my place ... I'm just waiting for Madda, and then I'll be moving right down to the first floor – look: I've already packed my suitcase..."

I approach *my man*, I have to get real close to him since I don't have a revolver, just a short blade that I have to stick all the way into him ... maybe several times – The worst part is taking these steps directly toward him, because he keeps looking at me and smiling ... If only it were dark or if I could sneak up on him from behind ... I MUST DO SOMETHING, I pick up his suitcase, it's half empty, and I bang it against the table and shout, I shout desperately and with all my strength, maybe that will attract someone, my shouting, maybe someone will come yet, I shout as loud as I can and at the entire building – "This is all you have?! Who are you trying to kid?! It's practically empty!! But you won't trick me!! Asshole!! Bastard!! Squealer!!! Pig!!!"

Above the tracks in the former women's one-room flat on the third floor three men sitting on two cots have been haggling for two hours over this space.

"It's all a question of coming to an agreement! Why don't you want to agree to something?" shouts Bogan Tušl.

"I don't believe you anymore! You're a traitor and you're Old Man Gráf's flunky!" shouts Borek Trojan.

"Give us each a one-room flat with a balcony, then we'll come to an agreement!" blusters Alex Serafin.

"You can't be maximalists – be realists instead," insists Bogan.

"We want a place to live – is that maximalism? Like people – isn't that realism?" Borek shouts indignantly.

"Fork over two one-room flats with central heating!" Alex laughs as he takes a bite of meat.

"Wait a minute – shhhhh! What's going on out there..." says Bogan. They hear a horrible shouting from the room across the hall: Roman Gráf is bawling Julda out.

"If only he would sock him one instead," said Alex, "words won't do a thing..."

"If only he'd break him on a cross..." said Borek. "But seriously, it sounds like he's murdering him in there. Maybe we should..."

And Borek stood up, but Alex pulled him back down on the cot. "Maybe it's come down to a real thrashing," Alex laughs between draughts of beer. "That's the way it should be, we've got to have some fun around here. If only they'd hang his old man."

"Maybe he'll take one in the kisser," Borek agrees. "Two blue cretins in a fight..."

"A big scuffle would be just the thing right about now," whispers Bogan. "We could throw out Julda and that slut, you could take their place – aren't they living in a former men's one-room flat? – and administration could renew its claim to this place."

–I keep shouting more and more, I'm getting desperate, I can't do it any louder ... And now I understand that nothing is going to happen in this building unless I do it myself.

"Madda doesn't love you," says Julda, "and it's good that she's more sensible than you. You must reconcile yourself to this..."

Well, thanks, *my man*, that was just what I needed, I will stab you in the kidney, all the way up to the handle, as soon as you turn around a little, because now it's only your eyes that are stopping me, those eyes of yours cut into me because they're the eyes of a sheep, *my man* is wearing such an absurd work shirt issued free to all factory workers, with tin buttons, that top button is shiny as a little mirror and goggles at me like a fish eye, I will never forget that button, till my dying day, now I can't stab him, I don't see *my man*, just those sheep eyes and that fish eye blinding me like a searchlight –

And suddenly Julda Serafin gets up, turns his back to me, I can no longer see those three horrible eyes of his, I can look straight at him now, *my man* is kneeling by the window, folding his hands together, his kidney is just two meters away, just two steps, thrust out my arm, I can do anything now, I'm strong and courageous, above everything, like God alone with the stars –

Father, forgive them; for they know not what they do
You put those boxing gloves on me   A man takes a dagger into his
hand himself   Madda   My girl, beautiful as a goddess
My squaw   I could bleed for You
It wasn't long ago, my son, that I was buying you marbles   I will gladly
depart like the white sawdust, tired of all the evil I've had to devour   On to
meet the purifying flames   Rent for you by steel   I'm happy to die in your
stead   To wrest your bodies from their clutches and offer mine instead

I was afraid of this   It had to come   Madda, my catastrophe

Now I am no longer afraid   Look how brave I am, priestess in the temple   I don't even flinch   I will never again be afraid   Communication simply does not exist, just as there is no process and no speech

No longer will I have to learn bad French   No longer will I have to go to school   No longer will you have to raise me, Papa   Mama, I will no longer bother you

The Lord is calling me to him   I forgive you, my son   I will pray for you at His throne   Lord, I am not worthy

They will lead me down the center of our street   They'll open all the windows just because of me   Everyone will register me like never before   Madda, my love   You will look at me the way you used to when we were still together

Per eum, cum eo, in eo omnia   By my agony for you all

(To be continued)

"I think in a minute we'll witness a nice little murder." Alex grinned when the first shriek went through the building. "And in a few days we'll move into a better room." With relish he bit into the block of cured meat. Borek and Bogan looked at each other, in the eyes of both men intense concentration.

The bridge party on the second floor spilled out into the hallway. Zita feverishly mumbled her boy's name.

"Be careful, Madame, your son is not named Borek, but Roman," Dr. Evžen Gráf said to her icily.

"I'm afraid..." Dáša Zíbrtová whispered on the steps, she let go of the railing and sank down to her knees.

"Shouldn't we first call the police?" said Frank Secký, but he first finished his glass of Courvoisier VSOP, which the label boasted had been drunk by Emperor Napoleon.

"oh-yo-yo- oh-yo-yo- oh-yo-yo-!" Madda whimpered as she writhed and squirmed, "OH! OH! OH!" On his bed Stěpa howled in a new paroxysm. And downstairs on the first floor, ancient Teo left the door leading out to the stairs and with difficulty climbed back atop his mound of comforters piled up almost to the ceiling. Can so old a man still cry?

BESEIGED

Why during times of greatest pain is it possible to sit calmly in your armchair? Why don't you curl up like a wounded animal? Why don't you wail, groan, howl? After all, don't we express pain and pleasure just the same? Why is it that during times of greatest pain one doesn't sweat, shout, or writhe?

"Take another tablet," said Evžen Gráf to Zita Gráfová.

"Yes, dear."

I swallow another Librium. It's awful: it works.

And so we sit in our armchairs. Two old, venerable, English, perverse ... now just two old, shattered ladies. And I'm actually crocheting ... Sorry, but even murderers – my son is a murderer. OW. I am the mother of a murderer – yes, that doesn't hurt as much. Even imprisoned murderers are allowed to glue together paper bags or strip geese of their feathers. Light manual work. Roman will have a difficult – OW OW ow ow. Dressed in convict rags ... The way they led him away – that night. In chains – Lock me up, I'm the one who sinned –

"Sbohem, Mama," said Roman, "Goodbye." OWWW –

"You should eat something," says Evžen.

"I wonder what Roman ate today..."

"Forgive me."

"I'm crocheting something. They could be beating Roman right now – ow. He's bleeding – OW. That time they brought me to you, my dear, and I washed the blood off your face, now who's washing your OWWWWWW – Another Librium. Evžen takes them out of my hand. Dying would be too easy. I don't deserve to die yet. I have to swallow more pain. Why did you leave us, my son? You didn't want to be with us any longer, did you.

The days drift by. We consult a lawyer. Roman will probably get seven years. When he gets out he'll be twenty-three, that's still ... SEVEN YEARS – OW ow ow ow. In the afternoon I once again get beastly drunk. Humanly drunk.

The days drift by. Dáša is once again going to church and not to the hairdresser's. I stopped going, too, ever since that day. Dáša enticed me to go to church with her. I couldn't explain to her why I couldn't go to the Archdeacon Church ... we drove to the terminus at Všebořice. Between the high-rise blocks, where so many children were playing in the grass – ow. Down the asphalt highway to Skorotice. The church dominates the village.

One approaches it from below, it slowly rises up above old chestnut trees. How did such an enormous church come to be in such a small village? Around its walls is a small cemetery. Why here? I can no longer kneel on stone – but one quickly learns how. Maybe Roman is now – OW – I touched my forehead to the stone pavement. How comfortingly cool ... From one of the pews a woman wearing a kerchief gave me a flabbergasted look. You're making a sight of yourself, *ma chère*. I rose. In the nave was the Virgin Mary holding the Son of God in her lap, and I fled in terror from that cold church ... NEVER again will I hold my son in my lap–

A tablet of Librium, and in the local restaurant four double rums, standing. The bartender wouldn't pour me a fifth. I drove home through town and bought four bottles of Ronda. Dáša's praying. For Julda. Of course, since your son is a murderer, dear lady. Will she take another tablet?

The days drift by. Is it really October already? The leaves on the trees ... I can't see them. Roman's trial isn't until next year. The time he's serving now will count. Until then ... Until then what? He'll get seven years. Maybe only six and a half. Maybe as much as nine. He's a minor: the most he can get is ten years. Maybe only six and a half. Only? – Ow.

The days drift by. We sit in our armchairs and I actually crochet. Evžen's been behaving amazingly. I don't care anymore. Let's forgive each other for what we did. What we did? Nothing's what we did. We sit across from one another and behave amazingly: two wrecks. Made of glass. Inside: anxiety and a bad conscience. More than pain? I deserve searing torment – OW, after all, you told him about making love with Bor – You may never pronounce that name. A catastrophe has occurred and all you have left is your own extinguishing. Searing torment – but my husband untiringly supplies me with Librium. And it works awfully well.

What's left? I throw myself at Evžen. He takes me politely. Lovingly? Conscientiously. We sleep together ... at least we try to. It's horrible. It doesn't work. Wouldn't it be more horrible if it did? But it will never work. Librium is better.

Plus Ronda, of course. 750 gramos times two is 1,500 gramos plus a third bottle is awfully few gramos to drown my son. The murderer Roman Gráf. OW, ow. When will it stop hurting?

I don't comb my hair and I don't eat – will it do him any good? Dáša doesn't comb her hair either, but she cut hers off. She's always so practical about everything ... Who will it help if I don't get a permanent? Who will it hurt? I don't matter anymore. I don't bathe. I'm afraid of the bathroom – because Roman liked to sit in there for so long with the shower head in his hand. Or maybe it's because you're afraid to take off your clothes in front of the mirror – you slut!

So I drink. That I can do. If you start right away in the morning, a few gramos are enough for the whole day. Sometimes I get up in the middle of the night and then start again in the morning. It's made me slimmer around the waist – you whore!

"Madam ... Madam..." Who called me that last? Julda Serafin. My son's victim. "Madam," says a young girl to me from right up close to my face, "could you tell me where Miss Madda Serafinová lives?" Have you been sent from beyond the grave, little girl? "My name is Jana Rybářová." I don't care what your name is. Leave me alone. "I heard that there's a vacant spot in one of the flats and I'd like to move in..."

A vacant spot in one of the flats ... Roman made that spot vacant. With a dagger.

"Get out of here immediately! Do you hear me? Immediately!" I couldn't control myself in front of that little hyena who's biting into a corpse when it's still warm. I screamed at her. I must have looked hysterical. And my breath smelled of alcohol. "Under all circumstances you must preserve that which is imperfectly called taste," my father used to say to me, "always, even when – *quand même*." Dear Papa, how can I preserve that which is imperfectly called taste when my son, your grandson, has killed a tenant like some sort of animal? "The more, the worse..." You taught me that in two languages, and it has literally come to pass, "*cela va au pire...*" that was your bequest to our world, "*...quand même.*" *Merci, mon père.* It's really like that. For the thirty-five years I've been alive –

The days drift by. October arrives. The itinerant workers are leaving. I know them all already: Olda, Roman's victorious rival in love. Stěpa, who has these fits where he howls. The little criminal Valtříček, he stole one of our oil lamps from the basement. Dízlák, who when he sees me ostentatiously licks his lips. In fact, all four of them desire me. They're so vulgar. I'm looking at all four of these men when old Teo opens his former shop window right above me. Why does that old man keep staring at me like that? The workers have left. Peace once again. How much more of this peace can I bear? But they'll be back –

The days drift by. Roman's waiting for the trial. He'll get seven years. Maybe a little less, maybe a little more. On the other hand it's possible to get part of the sentence commuted. The leaves on the trees are changing colors. An October oak looks like an oak in May ... the yellows and solid reds of its young sprouts. Now the leaves are death heads. But the oak won't start shedding its leaves till early spring ...

In our apartment I can't avoid that water pipe, forgive me or condemn me, it just sits there and endures, should I have it torn out? Or should I hang myself from it – The upper part would hold me. I walk past its vertical trunk, a silenced telegraph pole.

The pipe shines in the darkness of the hallway. I fearfully place my hand upon it. The metal is cold. Silent. Dead. The days drift by.

Borek – I cannot tear out my ears in addition to my heart, you knocked on the pipe and I heard it, the day before yesterday, before that a week ago, but only as if you had simply brushed against it accidentally, then even harder the day before yesterday, and yesterday for the first time I once again heard that BANG with your pliers, you started – no, that's horrible, I saw that pipe the entire time and knew it was unremittingly here, that it's STILL HERE – and yesterday you started knocking again. It's four o'clock. You've been banging all this time and I've been standing here all this time – I should run away and jump in the river –

BANG! BANG! BANG! BANG!

It's you who's once again begun our telegraphing and only now can I confess that a week ago I ran in here with my telegraphing scissors, but I had enough strength to throw them down, the scissors burned, the pipe felt like ice. And now I'm standing here again with the scissors and I beg you to throw down your wrench, you up there, above my head, perhaps I'll hear the metal fall on my ceiling like the final period of an unfortunate chapter – already Dáša can look her former lover in the eye, why can't I?

BANG! BANG! BANG! BANG!

You bang away, Borek – I uttered your name only a moment ago and before that a thousand times, but I did not let it past my lips ... I still need a lot of pain. Evžen refuses to provide it. Punish me for still being alive. You'll do it, right? My archer. My Julien. My catastrophe. My deluge –

BANG! BANG! BANG! BANG!

I hold the scissors a centimeter from the pipe and hesitate one last terrible second, Borek's beating on me, the only boy I have left. Blows give things shape.

Clink!– Clink!– Clink!– Clink!–

My scissors bang on our mutual metal.

BANG! BANG! resounds fatefully throughout the building – BANG! BANG! I'm coming, my boy –

Borek Trojan stepped off bus No. 12 at its terminus and slowly descended the hill, crossed the asphalt road, waded through the fallen leaves in the yard, reached the villa in its large garden, unlocked the garden gate and then the blue door beneath the metal lantern.

Alone in four rooms. I practically live only here now. There ... in our building it's disgusting. Here I have lots of room. I sleep in a bedroom on a king-sized bed with night tables on either side. I still haven't looked to see what's in their drawers. And I won't. I work out on the terrace less and less. I'm always tired in the morning ... and could go back to sleep. On the other hand I've been sleeping worse and worse at night. I take the bus to the factory and back. Sit in the leather armchair in the room with the picture window, and past the tree trunks I can see part of the river. It's peaceful here.

Other times I sit in the study with the dark leather wall covering. It's completely silent in there. I don't like the yellow room with the window facing the highway: for one thing the traffic is really loud, even though only a few vehicles pass by each day. I also don't like that rustic furniture. So, the port has been taken. The fortress as well, but the garden bungalow is much more comfortable, of course. I wait for Zita. She's sure to come. She always comes at a regular hour.

I have lots of free time. I eat often, but always just a few mouthfuls. I open the refrigerator and think about what I'm hungry for: ham, Hungarian salami, Rhine salmon in oil, stuffed olives, apple concentrate, Mosel white, white Cinzano, champagne. Ronda, Soviet export Stolichnaya, Gold King whiskey. I drink more than I eat. And in the study there's Courvoisier VSOP in a stylized gun-carriage, a company gift for hard-working customers. Purple *Parfait Amour* and Nuncius, a liqueur that pleasantly facilitates digestion. Dutch cigarettes, H. Upmann Havana cigars in earthenware cigar cases, wrapped in palm fronds. How much do they charge for a joke like this? It no longer interests me. Probably a lot. I don't care. I smoke them only halfway down. Dr. Gráf's holiday smokes. I feel sorry for him. Not really. It's more like indifference. When we run into each other at work we greet each other without exchanging a word.

Zita arrives in the afternoon. We kiss for a long time and for a long time we don't exchange a word. We sit in the large room with the window looking out over garden and river. The leaves on the trees are turning yellow, they fall off, spin and quiver in the air, and softly fall to the ground. October is at its zenith.

We feel no need to leave the house. We like it here. Sometimes Zita gets up from her chair, a glass of cognac in her hand, and stands by the window. I know what she's thinking, and she knows what I'm thinking, and we both know the other knows. We love each other more and more, if that's possible. Love isn't sex, it's not even erotic. Love is being together. Its highest degree is being together without exchanging a word. In weariness. In death.

The heights of love – and its depths. Its depths are more spacious. We lie next to one another holding hands, not exchanging a word. Are we thinking of death? We are both thinking the same thing.

October comes to an end, November arrives. November moves toward winter. I've been living here a month – it seems like ten years. Some afternoons I drive into town. I've had three suits made for me, all gray. I've become fond of dark-gray woolen flannel. I have fourteen white shirts from Primus, two of them made of Dutch nylon with wide stripes, ha ha. Yveta gets a commission on this as well. I've turned a bit blue myself, I think. Now I have four pairs of shoes, two of which have never seen my feet. Cufflinks from Zita: sapphires in gray platinum. Sixteen delicate handkerchiefs from China. Zita's dressed me up like this. Don't I deserve it after so many years of poverty? I'm a debtor – better than a creditor holding uncollectible debts.

I don't like going into that building ... On our street – people stare. Mean stares that make me nervous. Besides, I don't have a very clean conscience. Leave me alone. You're pitiful and loathsome.

Alex lost Dáša. She was shocked by Julda's death and finally left him. She no longer comes to clean his room – they say she's once again helping to clean the church. She's boring.

I ran into Madda Serafinová. I don't understand how once I could have – she's dirty. She gave it to the itinerant workers, who now are gone, and now she gives it to whoever happens to be around, including her brother Alex – like a herd of swine wallowing in the mud.

And Madda lost more than just her Olda. As soon as the workers cleared out, there was a distasteful scene. Alex broke into Madda's room in the middle of the night, and the two fought like wild dogs. Alex being of course the stronger of the two, he finally dragged his nearly naked sister by the hair and kicked her down the stairs. It's repulsive. He threw her things down after her, and we're already moving in again! That ugly scene gave me a bellyache. Alex had to carry my suitcases himself (with Zita's vouchers I'd bought a new Samsonite suitcase made in the GDR, absolutely reliable and elegant: it looks like an aerodynamic safe) across the hall into our new room. Now Madda lives alone downstairs in the itinerants quarters.

Another move. How many more times? … Another new room. Acquired through murder and violence … monstrous. Will it never stop?

I don't care anymore. Finally we're living in the right place. After all, this was originally a men's one-room flat. At least Bogan Tušl's office workers won't bother us anymore. Our previous room, the one with the tracks, will remain empty and at the disposal of the factory administration.

The office workers no longer bug us, but other wet blankets do. Something's always coming up. Apparently there's a girl putting pressure on us, some Jana or Jarka Rybičková or something. But the factory administration stood up for us. Will there never be order in this building? And so the new girl lives in the itinerants quarters with Madda. What more could they want, they've got five cots, for crying out loud! I lived there two years and it was more than satisfactory. I wonder what else that brat will want! Apparently the girl's stubborn and pugnacious. It doesn't interest me. The ejected Madda soon recovered. She's already sleeping with Alex again. What a crazy building … I'm leaving for our villa on the river. It's wonderfully peaceful there, I'll wait for Zita.

Surprisingly, Bogan Tušl turned out to be a nice fellow. He offered me his old position, head of the planning department. Quite decent pay … I'm really a chemist, but managerial work has a lot of similar elements that … that can almost only be done in the office. Was I meant to run around damp buildings in dirty overalls issuing soap and toilet paper to old ladies till the day I die? I have a nice office in the White House, as the women jokingly call it. Not a very funny name, it's just an administrative building. By the window in my office on the second floor two philodendrons grow so thickly that I don't have to look at the factory.

Zita, my love. You've become for me the whole world, including the stars above. You've made a real person out of me. I'll never forget you – but we're not saying goodbye yet, are we? … We'll never say goodbye. Even if we have to die together.

A heavy mist lies on the river, and for a few days it stays through into the night and the next morning. The river's cold, and it's as if its cool water rose up and wet the grass in our garden. How quickly the summer flew by …

Zita and I walk through the wet grass and kiss in the cold rain. Our hands are cold. The trees are already bare. Only the oaks hold on to their leaves. Till spring. Will there be another spring? We run into our house and light a fire.

The days drift by. The trees disappear behind the gray curtains, completely blotting the river out. It gets dark early now. We sit in our armchairs warming glasses of cognac with our fingers and staring out the picture window at the garden. It keeps raining and we can barely see out. We watch the rain flow down the window.

(To be continued)

CONQUERORS

Even before the red plastic alarm clock rang on its sounding board (the round seat of the only chair in the itinerants quarters), Jana Rybářová was standing at the window gazing skyward so she could see the dome of the celestial hemisphere through the morning fog, and when it seemed to promise blue skies, she rejoiced: it's going to be a beautiful day! And because the cheap alarm clock went off today fourteen minutes early for a change (yesterday eleven minutes late, it cost sixty crowns, which is a lot of money for me), Jana stood at the window and in the chilly morning air pressed her folded arms to her body, dressed in her woolen nightshirt (which she'd inherited from her mother: even though it had been washed so often it was almost transparent and had shrunk by a quarter, it still reached well below her knees), stared at the sky, and rejoiced that it would be a beautiful day. For her roommate, Madda Serafinová, it was still midnight.

Jana threw off her bedding (that is, a coarse gray blanket with suspicious spots that had hardened, a laughably short sheet, stabbed through with bits of straw from the straw mattress, and a little pillow as if for a dog), to air it out, and on the empty bed next to hers (we live luxuriously here: five cots for two girls!) began her morning exercises by flexing her tummy muscles ("Girls, you're going to have tummies boys will die for–" the technical school exercise instructor laughed as she taught the blushing students from a stepladder), and after a rich composition of exercises working out a broad range of muscles, she finished with twenty push-ups, twenty good, honest push-ups, twenty times her rigid body descended so the tips of her breasts touched the floor, then she did three more, and with the last of her strength she jumped to her feet, breathing heavily, red in the face, covered in sweat, happy that she could already do twenty-three, how wonderful it is to be a young, healthy girl, Jana opened the faucet all the way and set her face, shoulders, and breasts against the briskly spurting cone of water (glad that Madda was still asleep, because Jana was ashamed of bathing in front of her companion naked) and gulped greedily until, her hunger somewhat abated, she got dressed, placed a tin cup of milk on the burner, and woke Madda.

"Leave me alone, damn it, fuck off–" Madda yelled furiously, her eyes glued shut with sleep, and she tried to roll over and face the wall, but Jana assiduously carried out her daily task (for which Madda soon will begin to thank me) by pinching her armpits especially painfully (after all, at home I used to wake five siblings up, this is child's play compared to that!) until Madda finally lowered her feet to the floor and sat up softly mewling – Jana turned away, she was bothered by nudity served up so shamelessly, and she tended to her milk. She drank it warm, at about 30°C, just like the goat's milk at home, which came straight from the udder – I wonder if I'll ever taste it again ... But she liked this store-bought cow's milk too, separated as if to increase its almond taste (I want to taste it, so it's there), and Jana drank it daintily in small, swift sips. Then make the bed, brush my shoes, wash my hands again, comb my hair –

"You're so capable in the morning..." Madda yawned, she was still sitting naked on the bed, rubbing one leg against the other and lethargically scratching her back. "...thanks for waking me."

Jana smiled at her companion and left, the dome of the sky really did seem to have become blue, and Jana quickly proceeded down the dusty street. In the morning mist, the blue-gray outline of the factory, tower, concourse, and warehouse, which seemed bigger than her entire hometown of Malešice, were emerging on the horizon like the silhouette of a fanciful city ... The things one could do here – and the things that are being done instead:

"...and then when I looked in the toilet, I was completely dismayed," the laboratory director, Comrade Engineer Helena Secká, was saying. "Can you believe, my urine was oily!"

"And you think it was because of that?" inquired the young and vivacious, but already thoroughly corrupt Evka.

"Hmph–" Kamilka contemptuously harrumphed. She was the practically inactive but untouchable daughter of a deputy director at neighboring Cosmopharma (Helena, the wife of Cottex's deputy; Olga, his former mistress; and Evka, his next, just as soon as her breasts finish growing – is this the product development lab or the Department of the Once and Future Harem?!) and Olga silently, although obviously intensely, was thinking about her butcher at the slaughterhouse.

From day one, all four women considered Jana Rybářová a country bumpkin and, completely disregarding industrial chemistry, assiduously attempted to initiate her into the most intimate workings of the female body in heat, complete with technically detailed descriptions – if this is what they call love, then they are pitiful compared to me, even though they've had hundreds of lovers (thus far Jana had not had a boyfriend) – I know more about real love than all four of them put together.

"So tell us already, Olga–" inquired the vivacious Evka, the indispensable audience for absolutely anything, "–how it was last night."

"You go first," yawned Olga.

"I didn't do anything yesterday, but today I will. I want to try out what you were talking about yesterday..."

"Definitely try it, it's amazing–" Olga suddenly livened up and took a long drag of her cigarette, as if she wanted to inhale the whole thing at a single go, "but first make sure you bring him to the edge, so then you can–"

"I'm going for some distillate!" shouted Jana, and she quickly slipped out of the lab.

Olga's instructions proceed in gruesome fashion – I've heard them twice already. When two people really love each other, they can probably do absolutely anything ... But if they don't love each other, they're pigs. And Olga doesn't love her butcher, she's just giving him permission. And what's more, to say these things, you have to be a really filthy pig. You can do these things with the deepest love, but only in the dark and only if you wipe them out immediately with a gentle kiss on the cheek ... and so I go for distillate ten times a day. There's not much work here, but the lab is amazingly well equipped. In time I'll think up something –

At noon the insulation installer Karel Pekař shows up, he's just returned from military service and got it into his head he'd go out with me: his hair's too long and his pants too short, it's hard to say anything about the rest of him, he's neither handsome nor ugly, and he likes flying motorized model airplanes on a string, they have contests on Sundays and Karel slaughters them every time – a cute pastime, but a little childish, isn't it? – and he always asks me for tetranitromethane, an explosive, and some kind of Japanese balm I've never heard of. Besides model airplanes, he doesn't know much of anything ...

"So where are we off to today?" Karel Pekař says to me.

"I can't today. I've got a lot of work."

"Oh come on, please, what kind of work could you possibly have?"

"I don't know which way to jump to first!"

"So jump with me..." Was that Ústí slang or a slip of the tongue?

"And where would you like to jump with me?"

"I didn't mean it literally..." A slip of the tongue, of course.

"He calls it *jumping!* Hihihihihi–" squeals Evka stupidly.

"Jumpers are the best…" says Olga ambiguously, like heck it's ambiguous, she's once again unambiguously heading for the only topic that interests her, and Karel guffaws like an idiot until he's covered in sweat, the poor guy.

"I'm going for some distillate!" I shout, and then I just go for a walk in the courtyard. Nobody minds and everybody does it. Below the director's window is a garden of fabulous white gladioluses. Already they're starting to wilt, someone should dig out the bulbs and store them over the winter, nobody's caring for them, when I first started working here they were blooming beautifully, that was when Mr. Julda Serafin was caring for them, a good person – murdered by young Master Gráf.

Two office rats in white coats are walking in the courtyard. They're issued new coats twice a year, whereas in the lab we only get them once … They carry themselves like swans but they're really silly geese, the office aristocracy … On the first day, when I tried to join them at their table in the cafeteria, they moved away as if they abhorred me – they think they can be haughty and silly, because their fathers work in the administration somewhere. To them I'm just a country bumpkin. My father's dead and I fend for myself – what will be left of you, you old cows, when yours die? Don't think they'll be here forever –

After returning from work, a well-rested Jana tidied up the itinerants quarters, which meant throwing Madda's things into the closet, then she rinsed her underwear (she has only two pair, the third, delicate and completely white, she hasn't worn yet), out of excess of energy practiced a set of Spartakiad exercises, and wiped herself off with a damp towel – meanwhile she could hear a silver murmur from above, on the second floor the Gráfs are showering, that's justice for you: who gets dirtier at work, a lab worker working with acids, lyes, and poisons and a worker in operations – or the director?! – and she irritably scanned the wretchedness of our woeful habitation, a ceiling that looks like it's been shot at, dirty walls and broken floor boards on which sit five cots, a broken table, a single chair, and on the wall a faucet – this is probably the way hardened criminals live in prison. While upstairs there's a completely empty room on the third floor, and technically it's even supposed to be a women's one-room flat – why don't the Gráfs, the Seckýs, and the Tušls fix it up and give it to us – but why would they go to the trouble, you silly goat, they all have apartments with at least three rooms, bathrooms, balconies, telephones, refrigerators, television sets, garages, and riverside villas, just be happy we let you into this building, you must always greet and thank us most kindly

– Loathsome creatures, is it really too much to ask for respectable accommodations?!

To calm herself, Jana ironed both her dresses, which she'd ironed just yesterday, and rearranged her things in her suitcase (her as yet unused set of underwear made of delicate white nylon, a Swedish textbook, *Ivanhoe* by Walter Scott, a Vikomt tennis racket, her savings passbook with a fifty-crown deposit from her first paycheck, for a total of 350 crowns, a spare tube of Pearl children's toothpaste, pink and sweet, a rabbit's foot from Father for good luck, and a little pair of still unworn slippers made of delicate white leather), all her possessions, how many more things *I would be capable of caring for   How much more underwear I could attend to For two adults   And children* – Jana sat down on the lone chair and with her hands on her temples buried herself in the knightly novel *Ivanhoe,* which she'd read many times before, the beautiful story of the stately, noble knight King Richard the Lion-Hearted and his battle against the treacherous, base, immoral Normans, they're the ancestors of today's French, *I would love to live in Sweden   In a white house on a granite cliff overlooking a blue bay   Clean deep forests of spruce   Barefoot on the cool sand by the sea   Kissing at high tide* … Jana learned twenty new Swedish words, and then with her nylon net bag wound around her wrist – I like to have my hands free – set out on foot to town.

Streets full of cars with stupefied faces behind the windshields, the back seats are always empty, I wonder how they see the world – definitely differently than we pedestrians see it – maybe there are two, completely separate worlds …

Streets full of men with gaping stares undressing me with their eyes, do they really think they're going to whisk me straight from the street into their bed?! – As a very pretty girl, Jana Rybářová looked upon men's interest in her with derision and contempt. What do you know about love, you long-hairs, you baldies, you big-bellied bigshots – *my man is slender as a greyhound, with hair of silk, dressed in scarlet and glittering, golden armor, like Cleopatra's Antony* …

Behind the glass of the Savoj Café sits Borek Trojan and Zita Gráfová from our building, that slut shows herself in public with her lover, her son's in prison for murder – I guess the director's wife can do anything she wants. How that old witch greeted me the first time in our building: "Leave immediately!" she screamed at me, and her breath smelled of rum, the bitch who has the only bathroom in the building all for her own filth – how could Engineer Trojan demean himself with her?

Jana Rybářová concluded her daily walk at the bridge across the Elbe, the pure, beautiful arch made of steel, rivets, and metal plates brings to mind knightly armor, and overlooking it a wooded medieval hill with villas set in golden October gardens *to have my own white house Surrounded with fir trees that are forever green And out back strawberries and currants A glass terrace with a view of the town Bright rooms Flowers in the windows Bedrooms with glass doors so we can see the trees when we awake And fall asleep to the wind whispering through the treetops A white bathroom with hot water Two bars of soap in net bags: a pink one for You and me to share Even when bathing we'll be together And a little bar of soap in the shape of an animal for our child's enjoyment* – across from the train station Jana bought a bottle of milk and three eggs, I still have a piece of bread left, and she rode the streetcar home, next time I'll walk ...

On her way down our street, she avoided the drifts of beige dust and glanced sternly at the scratched facade of building No. 2000, they didn't want me, but here I am – then she noticed that through a slightly opened window on the first floor, aged Teo was smiling at her from atop his pile of bedding, and she ran into the building.

Jana washed her hands, turned on the electric burner, and placed on the coil a saucepan with a tablespoon of vinegar on the bottom – you can get by without fat, you'll save your money and your health, fat is bad for you, and the Japanese for instance hardly use oil at all, and practically don't even know what butter is, and then she wolfed down three fried eggs with the piece of bread, carefully swept the bread crumbs into her palm and put them in her mouth. It was already getting dark outside, days are getting shorter and soon winter will be here ... it's going to be a sad Christmas this year ... but then the days will get longer again, at Christmastime the pagans used to celebrate the Day of the Invincible Sun, then January will arrive with its bright afternoons, February with its pink snow, March winds blowing across the puddles, swirling water, the earthy smell of April, then May, the month of stars and love –

Madda burst into the itinerants quarters wearing a crumpled minidress that might have once been white, and with a snort she lay down on a cot, obviously not hers. "I had another man today. He looked fairly decent in the car, but when we got down to it–" "You don't have to tell me everything–" Jana said with revulsion, and she was sorry she hadn't washed herself before her roommate arrived, I can't stand sleeping unwashed, it feels so good to be clean in bed – Jana felt disheartened, washed her feet, then put her shoes back on and took her shirt off, washed her neck, then put it back on again, and so on, washing one bared body part at a time –

Madda seized the sink simply by walking toward it naked, Jana quickly retreated upon first contact with Madda's already extremely womanly body, but at the same time it's really beautiful, some people are just born like that – Madda stuck her belly button under the faucet, turned the water on, squealed that it was cold – that's all she washes – then rubs her belly on the blanket of another cot – that's how she both dries off and exercises.

Jana lost the desire for any further purgation in the same sink her wild companion had just used, she lay down but couldn't keep from looking at that animal: Madda unwrapped a piece of moldy cold cuts from a newspaper and bit into it like an animal, then she wrapped the gnawed, spit-covered remainder of the meat back up in the newspaper and opened a bottle of beer, which she finished off in three gigantic gulps, during which her Adam's apple surged up and down like a piston, like a construction worker, but a construction worker with the throat of a beautiful woman, then she blew her nose into her palm and wiped it carelessly on the blanket, which she then used to wipe up the drops of beer she'd spilled on her breasts. With a piece of newspaper she stoppered the last swallow of beer in the bottle (in case she wakes up in the middle of the night: but she never wakes up in the middle of the night, and the last swallow of beer serves as her entire breakfast), still naked (she won't get dressed till she goes to work and she only wears underwear to the café in the afternoon) she rubbed her bare feet against one another (her calves are marked with black smudges from her soles) and then with a lit cigarette between her teeth sang in a strained voice some English pop song, indifferent to both rhythm and lyric, emitting soft, heart-breaking howls, rather than a waltz or a fox-trot, suddenly she broke out in tears, which coursed down her cheeks, and then absently wiped them across her body (due to her earlier ablutions a palpable, smudgy film arose), she slid along the wall to her cot, suddenly bent her legs at a prurient angle, and broke out in laughter, she laughed her heart out, then let her legs fall, and Madda fell asleep with an innocent, childlike smile on her face.

Jana sighed, and when she was sure her companion was fast asleep, she at last undressed completely and, as was her want, took a slow, Epicurean sponge bath – at home in the evening I used to go to our little wooden laundry room in the courtyard, which I had all to myself – and lay down to sleep.

Why can't I fall asleep after doing all day everything I'm supposed to do? I feel hotter under this blanket than I ever did at home beneath my comforter, probably that cold water warmed me up, Arabs always cool off with a warm bath – but didn't I bathe at home in cold water too? ... Jana rolled over and really wanted to go to sleep, but odd feelings confused her and kept her from sleeping. Dear stars, won't you soon bring me love ...

On the table of the ever idle lab worker Kamilka lay a wrinkled piece of paper, and over it the heads of chemists Kamilka, Evka, Olga, and Helena were intently bowed. "We've been waiting for you, Jana–"

"Playboy Survey" stood at the top of the sheet – the rest Kamilka was covering with an old piece of pink blotting paper – and then: "Fill out in private!" So the product development laboratory would of course complete it publicly and collectively.

"1) Do you conduct or listen to discussions about sex:

    a) uninhibitedly

    b) with some excitement

    c) with embarrassment

    d) with revulsion"

"Okay, let's go!" Kamilka orders, and she taps her golden pencil on the blotting paper where she already has the lettered columns H (Helena Secká), O (Olga), E (Evka), and J (me). Kamilka doesn't have a column, because she says she's already read it, and that would spoil the game. Is this a game or a survey? Apparently it's a research survey and everyone keeps yelling at me to stop slowing them down. Here's the main thing: most of all, they desire to research themselves – but it has to be *in front of everybody* – and to use me as an amusing supplement.

For 1 they all write a, "uninhibitedly," and I write, honestly, d, "with revulsion." They all laugh at me. Who's the pitiful one here?

"Okay, next question," Kamilka orders, and with her white hand (in which she'd hardly ever held anything heavier than a cigarette) with its large blue stone set on a massive golden ring (how many of my paychecks is it worth? If I were to save my fifty crowns a month ...) she pushed the blotting paper a paragraph lower:

"2) Is sex for you:

    a) a necessity

    b) a habit

    c) a dull matter"

Without thinking, Olga writes 2a, and everyone laughs, Helena 2c, and everyone laughs, Evka 2b, and everyone laughs. "Now Jana–". I write 2a, because that's the closest of the three alternatives – "You have to tell the truth!" yells Kamilka angrily, but the others are anxious to get to the rest of the questions – no, they're anxious to get to the rest of *their own answers in front of everybody*, and to me, the amusing supplement. I'm being paid for this too?

"3) At the instant of penetration–"

"I'm going for some distillate!" I shout, and I run out and walk around the courtyard, Mr. Julda Serafin's white gladioluses below the director's window are almost dead, when their time comes I'll dig up the bulbs and save them for spring ...

I walked around outside as long as I could, but even so I came back too early, for question number

"12) Do you sometimes long to have sexual intercourse:

    a) in a large group

    b) in front of one witness

    c) in front of a camera

    d) in front of a mirror

    e) without witnesses, a camera, or a mirror"

Kamilka writes as the others dictate their answers, H–12d, O–12a, E–12c, J–that's me.

"Twelve b," I say.

"And who might that witness be?" They laugh at me.

"Well, him, after all..."

"Who's him..."

"My husband, of course–"

Their laughter is long and loud, and they say I should have said 12e, but they don't understand that "with" means so much and "without" so pitifully little, they understand absolutely nothing about love.

"13) When you see a squirting–"

"I'm going for some distillate!" and I won't return until this abomination is over.

In the courtyard Karel Pekař grabbed me by the arm and I couldn't get away from him, he practically begged me to come with him for afternoon tea at Větruše – that's the restaurant with a tower like a castle high above the town and river – I said I would.

In the afternoon I was home alone and so I washed my entire body, it was beautiful, then I put on clean clothes, this always gives me a marvelous feeling – Karel was waiting out front with his motorcycle, we drove through town and went up the asphalt, tree-lined road, Větruše is really like a castle above the town, and the forest begins right behind it.

I love to dance – especially the mazurka, or jazz, cool and slow, and best of all the waltz, where you just float along – when both know how to dance. Karel Pekař doesn't.

He apologizes over cooling hot dogs and secretly has a rum at the counter to give him courage, a little red face beneath matted hair – Karel can't be the one.

"May I have this dance, Miss Rybářová? Excuse me, Mr. Pekař–" It's Deputy Engineer Secký, my boss's husband, he's been sitting up on the railing with some girl, but he hasn't danced with her at all.

From up close I can see Frank Secký's fabulously white shirt, so white that if it were any whiter it would be sky blue ... And he smells wonderful.

And dances splendidly. I surrender to his lead. The next piece is a waltz, my blue love – "Excuse me, Jana, I have something in my eye. Could you reach into my pocket and pull out my handkerchief – here, the left one–" Frank blinks his eye, I reach into his left pocket, it's empty, there's a hole at the bottom of it, inside he's got –

Jana stiffened and blanched. "You pig–" she said in a quivering voice, "you pig..." Then slowly, circumspectly, amply, and with good aim she spat into Frank Secký's face and fled from the dance floor – I scrubbed my hand for about a half an hour in the bathroom (and the next day at the lab I washed it repeatedly in hot lye until my skin began to crack and came off in whole sheets).

Karel had to take me home right away, the ride and the brisk wind in my face made me feel a little better, so I let Karel drive me around Střížovický Hill and we came home after dark.

Of course, on the steps Karel tried to embrace and kiss me, a guy's supposed to do that when he drives a girl home on a motorcycle, but his face – of course it's young, smooth, and warm – when it was pressed up against mine it seemed like I was pressing my face against my own elbow, his hands on my shoulders were simply heavy and his fingers were clumsy and then rude – he was trying to take me right then and there! – It's not for this moment on the stairs that I've remained pure for so long, Karel Pekař, you are not to be the witness ... You offer so little, I want – everything. And when it comes it must be great – Not like this.

Jana pushed the boy's face away with the palm of her hand. "Bye," she whispered, then she disappeared behind the door and locked it. Bye, Karel. You're not the one.

Then suddenly I wanted to cry, in a saucepan I mixed up some butter, cottage cheese, and milk, and my tears fell into the spread our father liked so well, I kept crying more and more and couldn't stop, what kind of life do I have, don't I try hard to do everything the way it's supposed to be done, I never do anything bad – and what do I get in return, the world is placing too much on my shoulders – or maybe what's left for me of our wonderful world is pitifully little, and the worst is, now I can't see anything ahead of me, what will come next – not even a spark in the darkness.

"Why are you crying," Madda said when she came home. "Don't cry, don't be a cow–" but I really was crying like a cow, it was just pouring out of me. "Stop crying or I'll kick you!" Madda warned me, but in a friendly way, and then she pinched me under my arm the way I do to wake her in the morning ... she pinched my arm to snap me out of it.

Madda's not cruel, she's just unhappy – even though she doesn't realize it, or maybe it's not unhappiness, she's just not clean – but what am I today? What will I be in a year, two years, five –

"Jesus Christ, stop crying! Look, I'm on my knees begging you – Are you going to stop, you stupid cow?" Madda was actually kneeling, and tickling the back of my knees, finally she scraped together some money, I gave her twenty-five crowns, and she said she was going to go buy "vitamins," meanwhile I prepared supper for two, Polish sardines in tomato sauce with onions, and from another box "Mexican canapés," sardines on bread, fry them a little, and to top it off I made some real mayonnaise, I blew my food supplies for the whole week, and besides that you're supposed to have real herring for the Mexican canapés and white rolls instead of bread, and real oil for the mayonnaise, and what's more, now my twenty-five-crown emergency money is gone – Madda returned with a whole half liter of Jägermeister, but we polished the whole thing off and it was tremendous, the last time I had a feast like this was at our graduation party.

When I confided in Madda about the horrible experience with Secký, she got so mad it took her nearly the rest of the bottle of Jägermeister to calm her down, but that was fine with me, I don't really like alcohol and need just a little, then long into the night Madda told me about her lovers, she's been through ghastly and unbelievable things, really horrible things, but what's strange is that she doesn't differentiate between her men, she puts them all together into *her one and only man*, and in her eyes he's a *real* man ... and maybe in my eyes too – no, it just seemed that way for a moment because I was a little drunk.

And Madda told me about her one true love, the young Roman Gráf, she called him "my bleu blues" – she really loved that guy and he must have been beautiful with his delicate white hands like a priest's, and when he took Madda to Karlovy Vary, where they spent days and nights in pavilions made of glass and blue metal, with cream-colored ornamentation, fountains that spurt out warm, healing water, and then they'd fall asleep like brother and sister holding hands – but then Madda started to torture him and maybe that's some kind of strange law of real, powerful love, that two lovers want to experience everything together, both good and evil, such a strange law, whereby each is displayed to the other in the harshest possible light, because to love someone is to come to know them and be together in absolutely everything –

Madda got drunk, laughed, cried, and told me about her *only man,* the most terrible things, things that weren't even in the *Playboy* survey, and I listened to it all and tried to inscribe it in my memory so one day I'd be able to provide my *only man* absolutely everything that makes up love between a man and a woman, and it was so much that it was ghastly and wonderful at the same time –

That night, for the first time in my life, I went to sleep unwashed, we pushed our cots together and fell asleep hand in hand like two sisters, there really isn't that much difference between Madda and me, it doesn't matter that she didn't have a good upbringing and has no good manners or habits, it's not her fault, but we have the main thing in common …

Madda fell asleep like a child and I caressed her face, I still couldn't fall asleep, I wanted to think about my previous boyfriends, Sebastien Winter from Louny, whom I loved but he never knew and died a terrible death, or the Prague medical student, Eda, the only one allowed to kiss me on the lips, but I never allowed him any more, and that night when we were supposed to be together for the first time, I was left all alone, just like at the graduation party, when I had permission to stay out till morning, but each time I was happy, the offering I keep bringing to the altar of love will one day blaze forth, my husband will have me pure … and whole. What will he be like? Not like Karel Pekař, or Sebastien Winter, he was weak, not like Eda, he didn't know how to be gentle, what will he look like … Older than I am, but not by much, definitely slender, tall, handsome, smart, strong, and gentle … Like for instance Borek Trojan, who also lives in our building … I wonder what his hands are like. White and delicate? … That's how he might look, but he'd have to leave that disgusting witch Gráfová immediately, he'd have to be totally … and completely …

Jana smiled into the darkness and recalled her graduation dance at a restaurant above the Ohře River, I was Queen of the evening – was that only four months ago? – *on the dance floor wearing a white dress And white shoes You may kiss me on the lips, and lower Our wedding gifts are waiting in the next room Our mothers are preparing our wedding bed Let's go dance again Just for a bit First thing tomorrow we're leaving for our honeymoon in Sweden We'll sit on the deck, laugh and drink orange juice through a straw You'll wait beneath my window in a wicker chair*

Beyond the railing and beyond the blue band of the silver, rippling sea
emerges Sweden   A white port and tall white clouds above it –

Suddenly shouting, an awful racket, a powerful pounding on the door,
from their fortress they heard the rattle of metal without, Jana sits up in
horror and then a dark silhouette smashes the half-open window and an
enormous man falls cursing to the floor, another crawls in through the
window after him and runs to the door, opens it, and more men stumble in,
the room is suddenly full of men and everyone's yelling and howling. "The
workers–" shouts Madda, who's finally woken up, and she jumps up out of
bed. "Hi guys – where's Olda – OLDA – –"

The men are acting as if they're in a conquered city, shamelessly
pillaging our poor household, the fat one eats the rest of the Mexican
canapés and starts rummaging through our wardrobe, a giant in overalls
finishes off our bottle of brandy. Madda doesn't hear anything, she's
hugging a sturdy-looking man with graying temples, hanging on to him,
swaying beneath him, a chalk-white guy sits down next to them on the
ground and begins kissing Madda's knees – shrieking with fear, Jana grabs
her clothes from the wad in the fat one's hands, pulls her dress on over her
head, puts on her shoes at the same time, and avoiding the men's grabs at
her runs several times around the room, finally jumps out the window into
the dusty street, and runs as fast as she can in the direction of the dull glow
above the rooftops ... halfway to town she runs out of breath and stops
running.

Beneath the stars Jana Rybářová proceeds toward town, swallowing
her tears, how many more times today will I start crying and where am I
supposed to go now, I'll go back to Malešice and stay with Mother, but
what will I live on, there's no work for me for miles around and Mother
doesn't have enough as it is for herself and three small children, and she's
a widow, oh dear stars, why are you so cruel to me when I try so hard and
so earnestly to be good, the streets begin to brighten and ahead the main
avenue glows and beyond that the square, display windows, locked and
lighted, full of beautiful things – the world of the lucky, inaccessible to me,
I'll just pass it by on the cement sidewalk, oh town, I dreamed about you
so much and felt so lucky I'd be able to live in you, and you keep showing
off nothing but how horrible you can be, I dreamed about a town that was
white and blue like a summer morning – Like an inviting port, the train
station shone into the darkness.

The fluttering hum of the fluorescent lights wafted down from the
ceiling like an entombing snow. In despair, Jana stood before the
DEPARTURES board and bit her lip, the train to Most and Malešice

doesn't leave till 5:16 and it's not even midnight yet, what am I going to do for five hours here alone –

Jana paced the station, through the hallways and up the steps to the platform, she slowly walked beside the shiny rails – jump beneath a train and I'll have peace forever ... NO – all the way to the amusement park of signal lights, a long coal train rumbled by on the neighboring track and from the steps of the last car a man was waving a red lantern. After a few minutes an engine drove by and then another coal train rumbled past in the opposite direction ... the trains run day and night, in the morning there won't be anything left that was here yesterday, things move on, continue, purify themselves like a spring river, they fly and rush along, disappear, and new ones take their place, ever newer, and the old are taken away into the darkness of forgetfulness, and out of commission, thousands of trains are leaving at this very moment and the wind from their wheels sings in my hair – how wonderful to be a young, healthy girl, and I won't even be twenty for a while yet! – and the engines shriek and rumble as inescapable victory approaches through the night.

I WANT TO LIVE HERE, SO I WILL – Jana returned to the hall and bought the cheapest ticket in the direction of Most for only 0.60 crowns, just to be able to sleep in the train station waiting room, this is something I know how to do, I'm a railroad girl who used to ride the train to school, tomorrow I'll go to the director and complain and he'll have to give me a decent place to live, this is what he's paid for, and pretty decently I'll bet, I'll say the factory's responsible for my living arrangements, it's also responsible for other things and it's going to have to start coughing it up, since being nice hasn't worked, and maybe it's good that all this happened today, maybe really good, at least now I'm no longer going to wait like a calf for whatever the nobility deigns to toss my way, in the morning everything will be different, in fact it's already better, and maybe it's not really so bad that those workers showed up, in the end all they did was laugh and didn't even touch a hair on my head, that giant bleated something about how I'd gotten into their room, so the room is yours? Since it is named after you, please be so kind as to keep your itinerants quarters, I'll get a new place to live. Those workers really weren't cruel, when they laughed – it's your thing, gentlemen, I, on the other hand, won't laugh tomorrow, I'll make a big deal of it and make them take it deadly seriously. If I have to, I'll take it to all the committees and even all the way to the president, I will not take this, Mr. Gráf! And then I'll laugh – best, because last – under very different circumstances ...

I decided to live here, SO I WILL – and if someone's decided other-wise, then let him be the one to change his mind. I've retreated enough already, to the very edge, an hour ago even from my very bed, and every athlete will tell you, Your Blue Highness, that with your back to the wall you can even win hopeless matches –

In the glassed-in waiting room there were barely ten people, men with their wives and children, Jana made herself comfortable in the corner, and hardly had I closed my eyes –

"Let's see your ticket, Miss!" A cop in a railway uniform.

"Here you are." I showed him my ticket.

"You're only going to Trmic? But you'll get there faster if you take the streetcar–"

"I decided to take the train."

"Or to sleep here after a night on the town. This isn't a hotel, Miss!"

"Do I have a valid ticket or not? I do! And if that's not good enough for you, you can take me to railway security and I'll explain it to them."

"Leave the girl alone," said the man sitting next to me, "if she's got a ticket…"

"I know your type, you'd turn this place into a hotel…" mumbled the cop, already retreating.

"We're telling you to leave her alone–" said another man, who held a sleeping child in his arms, "and leave us alone. This is a waiting room, and children are sleeping here. And if you wake up my baby, you clown, I'll–"

The cop disappeared, and the men smiled at me. Their wives went right back to sleep, only now perhaps they huddled a little closer to their husbands than before. They're safe with them …

With their protectors. Isn't that a husband's primary job? A woman gets so many rewards for it … hundreds more than in a hundred issues of *Playboy*.

I'm not even twenty, but I think I already need a husband. I deserve him. I have the right to him. I WANT HIM – and I will have him.

WHO'S WHO

Jana Rybářová (19)

When her father announced to young Jana that the Second World War had ended, the four-year-old girl asked him what the war was. When she learned that evil soldiers were going after good people and now were being thrashed, she watched with childish glee as the final German soldier (whose five companions had just been killed in the local candy store), smashed head and all, was trying in vain to escape the fathers chasing him with pitchforks and scythes across the Ohře River. Yes, the poor soldier was hurt, but then he shouldn't have been so mean, he should have left the good people in peace.

"Truth prevails," her father Alois Rybář, the village scribe, autodidact, and idiosyncratic thinker, used to say to his six children, and what Father said was law for the Rybářs. Before every meal the children crossed themselves, they'd gather any breadcrumbs that had fallen to the floor, kiss them, and toss them into the fire. How you treat bread crumbs is how you treat people – the bread knife must be sharp, and the cut even.

Jana spent her childhood in a poor but scrupulously clean little house with a small garden and a view of the endless wall of the sugar factory. She began work at the age of five, and loved it. When a wild tomcat began stalking the chickens entrusted to her, she asked her father for help. Father hammered together a trap, into which the malefactor fell. He was left there to die – not at all quietly, by the way, for it first went insane from hunger – and for some time its wails issued from a corner of the garden. Well, it shouldn't have killed our chickies.

The Rybářs responded to the Communist coup of 1948 with satisfaction, but without any great hopes, with all the children they had, they were poor both before and after the coup. In elementary school Jana Rybářová was the best student in her class and fell in love with the seventh-grader Sebastien Winter, the son of a nationalized textile wholesaler. Sebastien was as handsome as his patron saint, he spoke with a soft voice, and a sad smile always adorned his suffering face. Jana's youthful ecstasies, which, by the way, were never declared, did not last long (the Winters were exposed as hoarders and enemies of the people, on public display on the square were bolts of cloth, money, and marmalade which had been taken from their home and shop, all the Winters were locked up, and as for Sebastien, after several months of re-education, during which he was transferred to the cell block of homosexual criminals for bad work morale, he died of his own accord), but they marked Jana's conception of love. Jana believed in purity and in her reward therefor.

In school, Jana excelled especially in mathematics, physical education, and religion, which was later abolished, and she entered a technical school specializing in chemistry. In her new school she soon worked up to being one of the very best and came to love her technical subjects for their unambiguous clarity. Sports she loved both as play and as honorable struggle. At the recommendation of the district board of education and culture, the physical education teacher selected the sixteen-year-old Jana to become a model for a local sculptor who was preparing a sculptural decoration for a new school building. The sculptor was a white-haired, delicate old man with beautiful hands marked with tiny liver spots, he talked to Jana for a long time about art, but when he asked her to take her clothes off, the girl ran out of his workshop in terror. She never looked the sculptor in the eyes again and never answered his greetings.

The same year that Jana's father completed his thirty-fifth year of employment at the Malešice sugar factory (for this rare anniversary he received from the factory administration and the company board of directors a tricolor certificate and a hundred-crown note), he died tragically, and after a tearful night Jana conceived a mortal hatred for God. If He exists, then why did He let our good father die?

The last summer of her high school year, Jana met a Prague medical student named Eda on a hop-picking brigade at the local agricultural cooperative. Before supper they would walk together through the meadows along the Ohře River, and Jana allowed the young man to kiss her on the lips. The evening before Eda's departure, Jana promised that she'd come to him after supper, but then she stayed home and in the morning awoke with a feeling of having prevailed.

She had the same feeling during her graduation at a restaurant by the river (their parents had allowed them to come home after midnight), she danced all night with her classmates and sensed her own and their desire, but managed to overcome the growing temptation and walked home alone through the early morning meadows. From the Louny plains rose ancient, steep volcanoes, and Jana thought about her future husband. He must be strong and gentle … Only for such a man have I preserved my purity.

On the first of September Jana Rybářová signed on with the product development lab of national enterprise Cottex in Ústí, and on the very first day decided that here is where she would live.

(To be continued)

BESIEGED

Borek Trojan stepped off bus No. 12 at its terminus and slowly descended the hill, crossed the asphalt road, waded through the fallen leaves in the yard, reached the villa in its large garden, unlocked the garden gate and then the blue door beneath the metal lantern.

I walk through four rooms. Take a piece of ham from the refrigerator and throw away what I don't eat. A swig of vodka straight from the bottle, maybe it'll revive my appetite. I don't like the yellow room. Zita wants us to live in it. It's dark in the study almost all day long. We should have taken down the leather wall covering for the winter – is it winter already? Mostly I sit in the room with the picture window overlooking the garden and the river. With a glass of cognac. You can't see the river anymore. Is it still flowing? Have to add some logs to the fire.

November strips the trees and slinks through the wet grass of the meadows towards December and the end. A strange tree stands just outside the window. Its leaves are completely red and heart-shaped like a linden's. But it's not a linden. Maybe I just want it to be a strange tree. It's already completely bare – except that all the way up at the top the last red leaf is gleaming. It sways and trembles in the wind and rain – but it's in no hurry to fall and join its thousands of companions already long dead on the ground. It's shining all the way up at the top, as if it were shouting. As if that leaf were the tree's reason for being.

So how does it differ from the thousands of other, perfectly identical leaves? By what odd concatenation of biological and mechanical accidents? A leaf like any other, but its stem is stronger. Its cohesion to the tree has to do with the stem, after all. A miraculous stem – will nature allow it to hold on through the winter? Can nature possibly allow this – with its enormous waste and tremendous variability. If it could create the duck-billed platypus. The gigantic Californian sequoias that grow for four thousand years. The tree in Ceylon whose leaves change color with the wind. The chameleon. The Maledivan double-coconut that takes ten years to ripen. With all this, can't nature allow a single tree in Ústí nad Labem, northern Bohemia, ČSSR, Europe, to hold on to a single leaf? Is that within its capabilities and possibilities? Or the power of omnipotent gods? Or modern science? Isn't that miraculous stem a threat to the entire planet – if it holds on to the branch? What then can be counted on? And if it falls – how powerless and dull is nature in its tremendous variability! How powerless and without a shred of fantasy or esprit are all the omnipotent gods! How powerless and blind is modern science, which searches for lichens somewhere on Venus or Mars! Why so much about a leaf? Perhaps it's the story of our life. Or more likely its last chance ...

The sound of an engine, then silence. It's Zita. Now she no longer arrives at a regular hour. It's better like this. Lately Zita's been nervous, irritable ... and depressed. The worst are her fits of self-destruction. Because she's destroying me as well.

Zita walks into the room. I hear her breathing and I'm afraid to turn around. I'm afraid of the unfamiliar mood I sense from her breathing. Dear, must we torture ourselves?

"I'm here," says Zita, standing behind me. Her worst possible mood. "Come sit next to me..."

"You don't even get up to greet me–"

"Zita, please."

"If I'm bothering you, I can leave. I have a lot of work at home."

"Please. Zita."

"You're bored, aren't you!"

"I'm thinking about a leaf. See that last red one all the way up at the top–"

"Perhaps I should kneel before you so you'll finally deign to show me your face. Or do I disgust you so much that you're trying to shorten the time you have to look at me – only when getting dressed and eating?!"

I stand up, rage pounds in my temples. I pull my sweater off over my head – it happens to be from Zita – and throw it at her feet. My shirt flies after it, one of the ones made of Dutch nylon, with wide stripes. I unfasten my trousers. She's outfitted me completely ... like her jockey.

"Knock it off..." says Zita derisively. "You'll get cold again..."

Once I told her I was cold here. This is probably the fortieth time she's reminded me of it. I'm already naked. Even my underwear belongs to her. Even my socks. "Will you at least lend me a towel to wear around my waist? And your car – I'll somehow manage myself to run up those two flights of stairs..."

"You want to drive home in my car with just a towel around your waist? No, forgive me, Borek, my dear..." She kisses me, I turn my face away. She kisses my shoulders and sinks down on her knees before me, she's already lying on the floor and I feel her lips on my bare feet ... Like in that film based on Stendhal's novel. When Mme. de Rênal was kissing Julien's feet, the whole Revolution Theater in Ústí roared with laughter. I kneel down to Zita, my empress. We kiss. We make love like never before. Then Zita laughs like a little girl ...

"You don't like me anymore, do you!" she says without the least transition. Or was it perhaps because I pulled my arm out from under her, since it had fallen asleep? I embrace her again – she pushes me away.

"I guess flattery works better before lovemaking than after..." I try to assume a light tone.

"It's better to read the newspaper afterward, isn't it!"

About four days ago I actually did reach, unconsciously, for the newspaper – but I'm not reading the newspaper now!

"But I'm not reading the newspaper now! How many times are you going to bring that up? You're incredibly charming: maybe right now I actually am cold – try to understand, I'm naked, the fire's gone out, so I'm cold – but I'm afraid to tell you!"

"Afraid? But you just told me!"

"I just wanted – All you want to do is argue!"

"And all you want to do is read the newspaper again!"

"So you go and argue, and I'll read the newspaper!"

"And that's how I'll meet you halfway!"

"You won't just be meeting me halfway. I'll be meeting you, too!"

"Well, if it troubles both of us so much–"

"A few years ago the French company Hoffmann-La Roche developed a calming preparation, which we import. It's called Librium–"

"Get away from me. I'm leaving."

"Ditto." We get dressed as if it were a race. A sad race. And an angry one.

"You're repulsive."

"Ditto."

"I hate you!"

"Ditto."

"That's just what I needed to hear! That's why I came here!"

"Needed – or wanted? And so you provoked me! You admit it yourself – you arranged it all before you even got in the car – that's exactly why you came ... just like stopping off to pick up clothes from the cleaner's!"

"You said you hated me."

"All I said was: Ditto. I say that to whatever you say ... Zita, please..."

"You're staying here?"

"That doesn't exactly sound like an invitation."

"I'm going."

"Ditto. By bus."

She left. I stayed. How many of these scenes can love take? Should I leave all her things here ... must I really leave with just a towel around my waist? With a borrowed towel, at that. I can't take the bus in a towel. Besides, I have a lot more of her things at home, in my Samsonite suitcase. My aerodynamic safe: like a pilot's. When there's a problem with the plane, you throw it out with its own parachute. The shirts and underwear are saved. The pilot dies. On my strange tree, all the way up at the top, the last red leaf is gleaming. I wave to it: hang on! I leave.

For the first time in a long time, I once again sleep with Alex, in our new room on the third floor. On the bed where Madda slept with Alex. By the window where Zita's son stabbed Julda Serafin with a dagger.

This morning was the first time the director, Dr. Gráf, did not return my greeting. Painfully awkward. A meeting at eleven in the director's office. My new boss, Bogan Tušl, gave me the task of defending our proposal for the project. My first test. I have a bad feeling that the factory administrators don't listen to me. They look at me as if I were naked. The director mocks me outright: "Basically, our young comrade is asking us not to make any changes in our production so that he won't have to calculate the final quarter again ... shall we save him this half-hour of work? It'll cost us only about six hundred thousand." They all laugh. Tušl's abandoning me, casting me off. I want to explain, but the director cuts me off: "Read over what you wanted to read to us, young man, and the matter dismisses itself. Next." I feel as if I've been slapped.

"It's true the director has something against you, and that he's hard on you," my boss Bogan Tušl drills into my skull. "But I'm not surprised at how he's treating you ... Look, couldn't you just end this thing with Mrs. Gráfová once and for all? Do it tactfully, of course, but definitively. It's no longer acceptable, okay? What do you want? Advancement – or smooching with that pitiful woman? Don't you feel sorry for her? Look, it's got to end anyway – one way or another!"

I look into the boss's eyes and see the impossibility of talking with him about love. I ask him by way of conversation:

"What does that mean: one way or another?"

"It means that if you don't end it, the director's going to cause you such difficulties that ... that..."

"That you'll have to fire me yourself."

"Dump her already, she's just an old, slightly batty woman who drinks too much and has a boy in prison ... did you know that she didn't even go see him the last visiting day..." (that was Friday: Zita came to see me and we had a fight ...) "...and after all, there are so many beautiful women, and a lot younger. I've already grown used to you, Borek. I wouldn't like to lose…"

Professional cynic and right hand man to Gráf, Frank Secký came to my office "just to sit for a moment," as he put it. He sat down and didn't say a word for probably twenty minutes.

"Well," he finally said.

"Yes, Comrade Deputy?"

"You know what."

"Really, I don't…"

"Yes you do."

"Are you trying to tell me the director sent you here concerning a certain delicate matter?"

Frank Secký gave me a presumptuous smile and tapped his cigarette ash onto my philodendron. But then again, the plant belongs to the factory and hence is governed by the director and his deputies. I wonder what my last, red leaf is doing on that strange tree. Is it still hanging on? Frank Secký is once again giving me a presumptuous smile. He has all the time in the world. He's carrying out an assigned task.

"I see you're not very good at making calculations," he smiles at me with malicious glee.

"You mean right now or in general?"

"Right now. Well?"

"Well, nothing!"

"You're nervous, boy."

"It just seems that way."

"It's obvious. Well?"

"Since you obviously have nothing to tell me, you'll certainly excuse me if I step out … for about an hour." I hate myself for stuttering and blushing. A cold beast is sitting across from me.

"Just sit down. Well?"

"I'm going to take a shit, Mr. Secký!"

"I'll be brief. Leave Mrs. Gráfová. Or you're out. Out of the factory. Out of your building. With bad references. With a legal suit. There are plenty of chemical engineers – in Bohemia, in northern Moravia, even in eastern Slovakia. Piss on it all. Even if you have to piss blood. Then flush properly and don't forget to wash your hands."

After all, Tušl and Secký are paid to … to create a comfortable working atmosphere for all employees. Including the director. But Dáša Zíbrtová – or is Gráf going to send her to see me too? They play bridge together …

"Leave Zita, Borek, she's a broken woman..." Dáša says to me.

"Wouldn't that be cruel of me to simply leave her right now?"

"Will it be kinder to do it later?"

Dáša's turned to religion, and to her a thousand years is nothing. The shortest time period that she considers worth even mentioning is at the very least an eternity. Our Saint Europa Zíbrtová ... Alex brought her whole armloads of beautiful flowers, and if I know Alex, he didn't pay for them, and now he's jubilant that Dáša is speaking to him again and has accepted the flowers – as long as he doesn't know she took them to the Archdeacon Church. Of course, no one could ever get Alex to decorate a church.

Madda herself told me how morally depraved she is. She came to borrow some matches once, then a pack of cigarettes, then fifty crowns, and when I finally refused to loan her another hundred (naturally, she never returned the fifty, and any reminder of it she refers to as niggardliness, of course she formulates it more strongly), she told me I was a gigolo. Then when I thought about it, I wondered why I didn't hit her. Because I'm thankful someone will still talk to me? Or because I'm afraid of her now? Why *now* ... In the end, you've got to envy Madda. She'll brush it aside, stuff herself, go to sleep, all the time fit as a fiddle ... *to live like a savage somewhere deep in a primeval rain forest   In a round village of hovels made from banana leaves   To sleep on the well-packed clay   To live by hunting and always have an appetite   After dancing 'round the fire, to have all the women of the tribe   And at the same time none of them   To lie like an animal in the grass blinking at the sun* – oh, didn't I dream like this not so long ago ...

Among people I feel like a rat in a trap. Their grip is tightening. I sense a hatred in their eyes capable of anything ... It rings in my ears: it's probably Roman Gráf thinking about me right now, there in his cell. If they let him out this evening, there'd be another murder in my room tonight.

The atmosphere of an all-out manhunt: even that new girl in the building had the nerve to say something to me. Jarka or Jana Rybenská or Rytířová, something like that. She came to see me completely calm, knocked and asked me to come out into the hallway. Something about her living arrangement – some sort of confusion.

The girl speaks too loud for my taste. Badly dressed: blue skirt and red sweater. An impossible blouse. Shoes from probably 1905. A disastrous hairstyle, but her hair is thick and naturally curly. She'd actually be quite pretty ... Impudent eyes. And impudent breasts –

It's not my fault, girl. The problem is that the itinerant workers weren't notified that, due to recent events, they were going to stay in a hotel, so they went straight from the train station to the itinerants quarters. The telegram was sent late. It happens. Apparently, the girl had to sleep at the train station. Couldn't have been all that tragic. And she could even have slept in the reserved hotel room ... But of course nobody told her about that.

She asks whether I'd be willing to give up my flat to go sleep in a hotel so four guys could sleep in my place. You put it so demagogically, my little one. Besides, the itinerants quarters isn't any kind of place for anyone. After all, I also go and stay in Zita's house by the river. She asked if it was fine by me. Fine by me? And how long this provisional arrangement was for. Provisional arrangement ... For a year, two years, five. Who knows what will happen in a year, in two years, five ...

Jana will give me no peace. Her name is Jana Rybářová and she keeps coming back to press her case for a flat. She's nineteen years old – a fabulous age. My father and mother are also six years apart. How old is Zita, anyway? Jana's really pertinacious. And very pretty. Her breasts ... she must play some kind of sport. She wants me to intervene on her behalf and talk to Tušl. I need someone to intervene with him on my behalf. She says I wouldn't be able to stand living in the itinerants quarters either. I stood it for two years, Miss. She says it's a pity there's an empty room right across the hall. There's tracks on the floor in that room. She says the maintenance men could remove them. But we already borrow our maintenance men from Cosmopharma and there's always desperately few of them, Miss. She says they'd be able to do it in half an hour. They could come during working hours. And she would pay them a bonus herself, in advance. But, she says, the factory must have plenty of money since it returns hundreds of thousands of crowns from the wage fund to Prague – where do these people get it from? Just between us, we did in fact return to the Union almost 480,000, but that was a tactical-strategic move. We require certain services from people living in Prague. If we give away all the money, what are we here for? It's a question of revenue ... As well as wage reports ... And wage ceilings ... Regulations and correlations ... Jana laughs at me. It seems, she says, I'm talking nonsense. Well excuse me, Miss – and she says I didn't answer her at all – she's a sharp girl. We'll be hearing more from her. Am I still sharp myself ...

The conversation with Jana delayed me – when was the last time I enjoyed myself like that? – and I arrived a half hour late for our rendezvous on Slaughterhouse Street. Zita was already parked there with her lights off.

"Have you been waiting long, dear?"

"I don't know what came over me today, I arrived a half hour early." We immediately begin kissing. Zita drives through town like the devil. We no longer take detours or side streets – straight through the square. In the house we take off our clothes right after closing the door. A wonderful race. We're possessed. Zita's quicker than I am, and I make love to her in my socks. We don't waste a precious second –

After our scene, it's as if our love's grown stronger. A three-day separation has proved to us we cannot be without each other. We keep making love more and more – and keep torturing each other and ourselves as well:

"I'm a burden on you."

"No, you're not."

"I am!"

"You're not. I'm the burden on you."

"So you want to get rid of me!"

"I don't, for God's sake! Wouldn't I have done it long ago?"

"You've already thought about it, then?"

"No I haven't. I'm just showing you–"

"You think about it all the time. You find it cold with me. You're just waiting for the right opportunity!"

"You're cruel and mean!"

"I hate you!"

"I love you!"

"Forgive me..."

"No, you forgive me."

"My dear..."

"My love..."

She cries and I comfort her. We kiss and get mad. We talk about suicide for the first time. We bite each other. How delicious it is to give and receive pain ... The taste of blood. Don't lovers and murderers really have a lot in common? ... Then we lie there as if dead. Which of us is the executioner and which the victim, who wields the knife and who gets stabbed? The more I think about it, the less difference I can find ... We shall keep on murdering each other.

The beautiful girl, Jana Rybářová, came to tell me winter was approaching and the itinerants quarters has no heat. She's battling for her own flat with the tenacity of a crusader in the Holy Land. I'm the heathen dog. I no longer can look at her. I flee to the house by the river. I wait for Zita: I'm afraid of what kind of mood she'll be in today. Just in case, I prepare myself with alcohol. Two vodkas, two whiskeys, and a little cognac:

to weatherproof myself. Zita doesn't arrive till evening and doesn't even want to get out of the car. A formidable scene in the rain. Then we make love in our wet coats. For the first time Zita's driven me home. Together we climb the stairs. On the second floor we kiss.

In the night I'm awoken by scratching at the door. Like an animal's ... They're here already... I'm afraid to open my eyes. Alex gets up and goes to the door. It's Madda – they whisper something to each other. Alex comes back for something and goes out again into the hallway.

Suddenly I hear the sound of metal on metal and metal on wood. Pliers. And a crowbar. And that's probably a battering ram being used to seize the fortress ... And now I hear the voice of Jana Rybářová. I light a cigarette and look at my watch (a slim, gold Cortebert from Zita): midnight. Now I know what it is: Jana and Madda are breaking into the room across the hall. Like I did with Alex. Into the women's one-room flat.

Should I go help them? Going's bad, but so is not going. What should I do? I smoke another cigarette (Kent, Zita's favorite brand) and wait until they come and get me.

I smoke a third cigarette. The banging outside the door continues. I begin to understand. They're not going to come for me.

I'm alone already ... No I'm not! I leap out of bed, go to the water pipe, and make it ring. Not with pliers – Alex took those for the night assault – but with my golden fountain pen. Also a gift from Zita. Now it's not going to be my BANG! and Zita's Clink! now we both just Clink! I've converted to Zita's code. The blue code of a fallen empress –

Clink!–Clink!–Clink!–Clink!–

With that horrible racket in the hallway, will Zita be able to hear me? Will this raging building let our messages through? I press my ear to the metal pipe. Zita! My love! My life. My death.

Why when you're deeply in love is it impossible to sit calmly in your armchair? Why do you squirm like a wounded animal? Why do you wail, groan, and howl? After all, don't we express pain and pleasure just the same? Why is it when you're deeply in love you sweat, shout, and writhe?

"A few years ago the French company Hoffmann-La Roche developed a calming preparation, which we import. It's called Librium–" Borek said to me on Friday, on my imprisoned son's visiting day, the day I sacrificed ... to make sure I was capable of hating Borek? Then why did I kiss his feet? My Julien – how many boys do I actually have now? Why did I leave him? And why did I make love to him before that? And why did I offend him so before that? TO RECKLESSLY DESTROY BY WHATEVER

MEANS POSSIBLE THE MECHANISM THAT LEADS THROUGH
SATIATION TO INDIFFERENCE AND DEATH –

To rouse him with pain when he begins to nod with love. Of course I
hurt him on purpose. And of course with a lie. After all, I'm happy that I
can clothe Borek. I'm used to dressing a boy ... new clothes bored Roman.
Borek was jubilant about them. He was incredulous when he had to get
measured at the tailor's. I chose the material and the cut myself. After the
first measurements at the tailor's, he came home excited: "I'm going to have
three new suits!" he said as if he were saying: "I'm going to have
Versailles!"

When he brought them home, his gray flannel Versailles, he couldn't
get enough of walking through his new galleries, staircases, and parks – for
almost an hour he practically danced for me in front of the mirror. He made
various combinations of the three pairs of pants with the three jackets and
the three vests ... how much is three times three times three? He almost
cried with joy over the dozen white shirts I bought him. He said he adored
the feeling of nylon against his skin ... poor thing: I'll have to buy him a
dozen shirts made of real silk. He was intoxicated with the contrast of his
dark skin against the bright white (I'll get him some cream-colored) nylon.
His happiness made me sentimental, and this chord aroused me: we'd hardly
buttoned up the first shirt when we started undoing it again. I gave him my
father's sapphire cufflinks. The socks from Bond Street I put on him myself
... Now he dresses like a gentleman – dresses himself ... When Roman
returns, how happy he'll be to have new white shirts made of silk instead
of those prison rags on his body!

I really hurt Borek, and it was all lies. After all, I'm happy that I can
feed him! I'm used to nourishing a boy ... Roman hated food and wouldn't
eat meat at all. Borek was in ecstasy over the meat I served him. "We'll be
able to put it all away..." He trembled like a madman over the roast turkey,
our first supper in the country house. I ate a wing and a couple of pieces of
dark thigh meat – and Borek ate the rest of the three-kilo bird himself! He
tossed away his knife and fork, picked whole pieces up in his hands, broke
them and pulled them apart, snapped the bones, and the fat streamed down
his arms. He took off his clothes for this meat orgy and thrust his whole
face into the turkey's entrails, right up to his ears – I understood that this
was a spiritual matter – Borek gorged himself like a barbarian king. How
greedy he was and how insatiable ... and now he's sated. He drinks more
than he eats, more cold apple concentrate than warm meat, and after every
meal a glass of the digestive liqueur Nuncius ... When Roman returns, after
that prison fare, he'll have a tremendous appetite for meat!

Can one imagine a greater delight than introducing a boy to the ways of love? I'm so happy I can suckle Borek's longing. I'm used to tending to a boy ... Before he got to know Madda, Roman was ashamed in front of girls, he belittled them and never confided in me anything. Borek tells me everything, "You're like a high priestess of love..." he moaned to me, then shouted: "...like a goddess–" How greedy he was and how insatiable, now it's as if his fortified blood ... had become weary. How searing was his lovemaking ... now it's out of pity ... He's cold with me. And I with him. We're all the more depraved ... When Roman returns, what a hunger he'll have for women and how eager he'll be for my lessons, and how glad!

Can one imagine love without delight? After all, I'm happy if I can make Borek laugh. I'm used to pleasing a boy ... Roman was sad and kept getting increasingly bitter. Borek went wild with delight. He'd choke with laughter till tears ran down his cheeks. Now he's sinking into a nostalgic fog ... of course with me and beyond me, but I need to have him always up above, on the sun ... Sadness probably is to love as night is to day. The weariness is what's bad, that's the rust, the mold, the cancer ... it's indifference that kills in the end. When Roman returns, after all those years of prison cells and prison yards, how jubilant he'll be to go into town all by himself, drive anywhere, fly to Paris, or even just swim in the river!

It's indifference that kills in the end, and indifference begins with weariness and comes from satiety – TO ESCAPE FROM THAT FATAL STAIRCASE! Me and my boy. Is that perhaps a law of genuine, powerful love, that it brings with it torment and suffering? Isn't what has long been prescribed for the revival and improved circulation of torpid, satiated bodies – since the body is animal – the laceration of their souls?

So we torture one another assiduously. Bystanders willingly provide us with the whips, the burning sulfur, the glowing pliers.

One can even inflict pain with cold water. Evžen has grown hard and cold.

"Wouldn't you like to move to the riverside house permanently?" he asked me.

"Not yet, dear."

"I'd actually welcome it."

"Yes, dear."

"Until then, whenever you come back from the riverside house, could you please take a bath and scrub well. For purely hygienic reasons..."

Evžen retains a motionless mask, but his voice is a quarter tone higher. I've lived with him seventeen years: this is his way of showing cold rage. Evžen can never be hurt. Armed with infinite patience he lies in wait. And at the proper moment, calculated with a chess master's exactitude, he coldly liquidates. Most likely via someone else's hand. He knows how to command. I wonder what Borek has to go through at the factory ...

"Zita, darling," Evžen is attacking via Frank Secký, his favorite knight, "aren't you overdoing it just a tad? After all, you look completely run down."

"But I feel fabulous."

"So Zita, our dear beast of prey, you've taken up a new sport! It looks like it's worked wonders, your skin looks fabulous ... If I didn't hold you in such high esteem, I might give you a go myself ... Seriously, you do get me steamy. You have a certain sex appeal. But just between us girls, isn't it just a little ... monotonous, always the same drudgery on your back – I'm sorry, that just sort of slipped out. Originally, I intended to talk about art. You know, Helena and I have come up with something so wonderful ... you need four people. It's really fantastic for youngsters. Maybe you could come by and see us some afternoon."

"With Evžen?"

"For goodness' sake, not a word to him!"

I laughed at Frank. I understand, Evžen, that you can only play with the timber you have at hand – but with this rotten fence post? With no ivory at hand, Evžen moved another rotten fence post on the chessboard:

"I told myself I just had to come and see you again," jabbered Helena Secká, that cold, lecherous goat. After almost two years she just now decided to stop by for a visit.

"So who all was present at your saying this?"

"You're quick, you always have been, you've always been my exemplar, and so listen, dear heart, you must tell me how you *do* it, how do you keep that *marvelous* figure, look, you aren't even wearing a bra now, do you even have one? Well, you're just like a little girl, like a *gymnasium* student, how do you *do* it, you're so *sexy*, you've got to tell me your secret, after all, we've never kept any secrets from one another, you've got some *tricks*, don't you, some sort of *special* secret, you really *must* tell me–"

I saw in my mind's eye what poor Helena was probably seeing in her mind's eye, and if so, it was possible to describe to her in detail yesterday afternoon – Evžen deserves it for choosing such pitiful characters. But if he wants it, my dear goat, I'd be glad to share it with you: "Just between us girls – but, Helena, not a word to anybody!"

"Silent as the grave, like filleted fish!" She was literally sweating with excitement.

"With your Frank ... admit that it isn't worth a thing."

"Less than nothing, we have to arrange everything a half hour beforehand to do anything at all–"

"Shush! Do you want me to tell you or not?"

"I'm all ears, as the Germans say..." Already she was barely able to breathe.

"Find yourself a younger man, Helenka."

"And then what – –"

"That's it, my dear friend. The rest will come of itself."

"You just don't want to tell me anything..." She puckered her lips into the shape of a horseshoe. Like a thirty-year-old little girl.

"Tell Frank. And come see me after Christmas."

"But I'd never tell Frank that–"

"I mean tell Evžen via Frank. And now please excuse me, I have to take a bath. After your kind visit it's really urgent. So till Christmas, dear heart. Or better, till Easter."

Maybe I should kick her one of these times. But there are more and more of them, and their hatred is climbing up the wide staircase. Dáša Zíbrtová wanted to pray over me as if I were a corpse – later, dear. And I'm no longer going with you to the Skorotice Church, because of its Virgin Mother who's allowed to hold her Son on her lap. I'm only allowed to see mine every other Friday – and then I cry for the next fourteen days.

Roman wears a gray one-piece uniform and a dreadful shirt. He stands facing me and doesn't talk. "Yes, Mother." OW. "No, Mother." OW. He doesn't want anything, doesn't need anything. His silence is horrible. His eyes – OWWWWWW – but when I'm with him, I'm really thinking of you, my son, it's for you I buy the gray flannel and the white shirts, for you I pluck and roast the turkey, you I want to advise, you I want to drive around in my car and you I want to make laugh – Roman is silent. So you're tired of my maternal love?! You're not even capable of hating me, are you! But you cannot die, I must die – before you. Roman is silent.

It's his eyes that speak, and his silence is a terrible accusation. His eyes tell me I have only one boy. Him – my son.

And that's precisely why I chose to go see Borek on Friday, Roman's visiting day. To prove to myself I had to choose between my two boys. I went to Borek for the mercy of his hatred. Unbind me and leave me to my son – That's why I hurt Borek. That's why I kissed his feet. That's why I had my fill of him until I fainted. That's why I declared my hatred to him. That's why I left him.

I arrived home clean again. That's the end. Just a mother again. In fourteen days I'm going to see my son, and his eyes will know it even if I too am silent.

It was an evening of peace after long weeks of torment. I took a bath. I tried to sing in the bathtub. I prepared an exquisite dinner. Evžen's scrutinizing me. What will his next move be? Don't forgive me, but I've renounced my love only for Roman's sake. Your forgiveness would be cold as your anger. Let's forgive each other for what we did. What we did? Nothing's what we did. We've just grown used to one another ... Seventeen years. Another seventeen? Another two times seventeen? I watched television with Evžen. I fixed us two manhattans. I put on my new pajamas. Cold cream, skin lotion, toothpaste, mouthwash, douche, hairnet. Two tablets of Gastrogel. One tablet of Dormital. A tablet of Librium. A swallow of Ronda. The pain crept up on me at night, it roared in the darkness and its fangs scraped against my skull.

I held on for three days. Borek and I both held on for three days. Three times twenty-four times sixty times sixty stabs. So much love and so much hatred Borek and I managed to give each other that Friday afternoon, that we were full of both and we held on three times twenty-four times sixty times sixty indentations. But we didn't die.

Our three-day separation proved to us that we cannot be without each other. We make love as if possessed and then we torture one another as if possessed.

We make love on an executioner's block and in our confusion we cannot tell who is executing whom, the condemned kisses the hangman and the victim exposes himself to the murderer's blade. The prosecutors shriek with fury: but as long as they can't pull us apart, there will be no beheading.

His head cast down, Borek Trojan quickly walked through building No. 2000 and, on the second floor, scarcely a step from his door, he was assailed.

"Good afternoon, neighbor," Borek heard the mocking voice of Jana Rybářová, our new neighbor who moved in here during the night wrongfully, illicitly, and illegally. By force – as I once did. And without my help ... "–so I'm living here now," her voice contains unconcealed aggression, "despite all your rules and regulations–"

"Congratulations. Personally I'm glad that ... that..."

"But you're not glad at all. How are you going to explain it to your boss?"

"I'll look after my own affairs, if you don't mind. And now, if you'll please excuse me–"

"I won't excuse you a thing. When I came here to kindly ask for a place to stay, you acted like an office rat. Have you already forgotten what it's like to have a bad living situation? When you're living in a ten-room riverside villa it doesn't even occur to you, does it?

"Excuse me, Miss, but you're definitely beginning to annoy me!"

"I excuse you? You've got some nerve! Okay, I won't keep you any-more from your, ahem ... *work* – Just one more thing: You are repulsive!"

I closed the door behind me and felt sick to my stomach. A terrible thirst for alcohol – but not a drop to drink. Alex drank it all up. And the water doesn't flow up here to the third floor. What am I still looking for in this building? The neighbors have already written me off.

"Can't you maintain a little order in this building?!" I am berated by my boss, Bogan Tušl, who himself has obviously just been berated. "It's the law of the jungle. The administration wants to keep that room empty out of principle. You have to help me, Borek ... with everything. We're in the same boat."

"And where is this boat sailing?"

"The instructions come from the administration. Here's your task: think of some way to get those two girls down into the itinerants quarters as soon as the workers leave. That's an order. I'm not going to put it in writing – but its fulfillment will end up in writing."

"Aye aye, sir..." I say dejectedly, and my anger rises. Crests at hatred. And the wave ends in deep depression. I spent eighteen years in school in order to learn something and become someone, in order to start accom-plishing something. And how do I start: crushed by the director and his deputy, despised, hated, and abused by all, and now this disgraceful task, and if I don't complete it – just like when we presented that plan – he'll shamelessly abandon me in a second. Not even the super-efficient Tušl, and his furious bitch Jolana, could defend that room against me and Alex. Why should I be successful? A task for a chemical engineer: move two girls against their will out of a women's one-room flat into the temporary housing facility for itinerant workers. That is, punish someone for some-thing I myself got away with unpunished. A constable without any hope of success. Of course he doesn't order me to shoot the girls, just move them. What's the difference, actually? Like the difference between an executioner and an eater of his own excrement. Why did they suddenly find the nerve to ask me this? Why suddenly am I not so tough?

Borek lay on his stomach and like an enraged animal bit into the fringe of the bed cover while Zita gently caressed his back.

"My little boy…" I whisper, and I touch him cautiously – why do his shoulder muscles jerk so when I touch them? – "People are mean. That's why we won't even let them enter our thoughts…"

"We'd probably have to crawl into a coffin and nail the lid shut from inside!"

"Wouldn't that be better? …"

"Certainly. But after a moment we'd have to get up and go back among them."

"My little boy … My child with a scraped knee…"

Why does he keep pulling away from me? Why does he prefer my reproaches to my gentleness – I have inside me an underground lake of affection fed by an invigorating underground river. Why won't you let me care for you? "Please stop treating me like a little boy … I'm not sixteen anymore–"

Roman is sixteen. Borek probably didn't realize that when he spoke – or should I leave him again? Each time it will be harder and harder to return – for him, that is … I throw myself at him and embrace him, his entire body with my entire body – With rough movements, Borek pushes me away. I'm beginning to understand them, I'm beginning to fear them … Involuntary violent movements, the movements of a drowning person trying to get to the surface, the movements he assails his rescuer with … But I am not his rescuer, I am the water pulling him under.

Borek extricates himself, moves away, and then, as if guilty and full of apology, he gets up and crosses the room. My fear becomes tormentingly acute: Borek is here with me, in my room, but now he's going … alone … down a path I cannot take.

"Borek, dear. Come here, to me…" Have I succeeded in concealing my anxiety?

"Leave me alone. I have to think."

"About what?"

"You wouldn't understand."

Borek walks back and forth across my room, from the window to the door, back and forth, but somewhere his short route is being measured, and step by step he's leaving me behind … as if he were leaving our besieged fortress for somewhere else. When you smash this straitened circle asunder, will you come for me on a white horse? …

"Forgive me, Zita, but right now … I need to be alone."

"I understand. Scoot!"

He gets dressed. His underwear's from me, his British socks from me, his white shirt from me ... does the feel of nylon against his skin still delight him? You foolish woman, it's just clothing, after all. His clothing. I lie in bed and look at him. Should I jump up quickly and embrace him? – and once again feel his drowning swimmer's movements, those rough movements directed by the panic center, by self-preservation ... those movements directed at me.

"Take the car..." I say. As if I had grabbed his leg and was pulling him under ...

"Thanks. I'll walk."

"So, have you thought of anything yet?" asked Bogan Tušl, winking at his subordinate Borek Trojan.

I look at my boss and suddenly notice several details: a fine network of lines beneath his eyes, and bands of tired-looking skin. His temples are turning grayer day by day. And he's grown unappealingly fat!

I look at you, Bogan Tušl, and I'm astonished. You've aged ten years in the past six months! You work too much: for Deputy Abrt, who now wants to retire less and less every day. And then for me – I'm still not trained yet, and for strategic reasons you're not really in any hurry to train me. And finally for yourself ... how fresh you used to be when you were doing one-third as much work! And how sharp you were ... now you just beg your subordinate to do the dirty work you don't have strength for anymore. At first you were rewarded for it as if it were merited. Now it's simply a difficult duty. And how poorly rewarded: you got a raise of 181 crowns along with permission to move illegally into a new apartment, which could be taken from you at any time. The pay on your blue boat is miserable, Your Highness. So maybe I'll go on a little strike. I came aboard as a scared little cabin boy. I spoiled my debut. So let's try to fix whatever we can: the cabin boy has brought a dagger back from shore leave.

"Don't count on me anymore to do your dirty work, Bogan."

"Have you lost your mind?!"

"I was supposed to get a raise from the very first day. Where's that document?"

"Only when you work harder."

"You've worked yourself all the way to the top and even taken to welding tracks together – by the way, have they given you the papers for your apartment yet?"

"What's gotten into you? You were almost starting to be reasonable

... Well, do as you like. Get ready for another job change. Of course, you can't go back to operations anymore – your place has already been taken."

"It's kind of like we're playing chess, and I've lost a piece. Do you play chess? No? Too bad. You'd know that with the loss of a piece, the game itself gains. If there's no chance of a draw, all you have left is to exploit the mistakes of your opponent in order to win."

"You want to beat me? Well, then you might just as well clear out right away."

"So you've decided to throw me out into the street, Comrade Tušl, just because I refuse to move two girls illegally out of a women's one-room flat into the itinerants quarters? So the flat will be free for your schemes? With today's housing shortage, that's practically a crime. Or are you throwing me out because I have more education than you and you don't want the competition?"

"What are you talking about, Trojan! – This is simply rude!!"

"Why do you insist on believing that you have a monopoly on rudeness? And I'm not the only one in this factory who's vulnerable. Don't forget, Bogan, my friend, that you still don't have papers for your apartment. You seized it wrongfully, illicitly, and illegally. But Gráf and Secký knew about it? So much the worse for all three of you. For what services did they give it to you? By the way, why is it that you're the one cleaning up the schemes you reported on in the first place? Does it by chance have to do with your apartment?"

Tušl yelled at me for about ten minutes – the boss must preserve decorum – but he hasn't mentioned the women's flat to me again. He even seems to be more polite towards me: oh, my boss has started courting me ...

Keep on your toes: don't get complacent. Men are always best at attacking. I recall a piece of knowledge from my youth – but am I no longer young? twenty-five – that besides nitrogen and other inert rare gases in the air, there is also oxygen. I take a deep breath. Craving ozone ... we also learned in school that in nature there is ozone after a storm.

In the factory cafeteria, in the hallway, the courtyard, in front of and inside the building, Jana Rybářová keeps passing me without a word. What a beautiful girl ... Am I really so mangy?!

"Miss Rybářová – excuse me, just one moment. I just want to tell you that they won't be bothering you about the flat anymore. And if they do – don't give up!"

"You want to buy me off cheaply, don't you, Mr. Trojan. For what, exactly? You don't have anything. And I want nothing from you anymore. I find the thought of it abhorrent."

Why is she so spiteful, unfair, and mean to me ... I discretely asked Madda Serafinová about it when I met her on the square. She gave me a mocking grin: she simply can't understand that I'm only thinking of my place among people, simply of the most modest modus vivendi in the building and at the factory ... "You'd really like to get Jana, wouldn't you! She's got a hot little body, doesn't she, Mr. Trojan!"

I dragged Madda into the Svět Café and invested four Georgian cognacs in her. If only Madda bathed more often ... but even so, there's something really exciting about her. Or is it just because ... Why was I such a cretin not to make love to her that time – who knows how things would have developed ... We laughed a lot and had a good time together. Making love with Madda is probably a very natural thing ... and doubtlessly has a lot to recommend itself. I felt a certain jealousy when Madda suddenly spied her worker Olda and left me right in mid-sentence – but before that, she managed to tell me a couple of interesting things about Deputy Secký's personal life.

Professional cynic, Gráf's right-hand man, and cold swine, Frank Secký came to my office again "just to sit for a moment," as he put it.

"Well," he said, and he tipped his ashes into my philodendron. That plant is mine because I water it, and if I want, I'll throw it out the window this very afternoon.

"Well," says Deputy Secký after a longish pause.

"Do you want something, Comrade Deputy?"

"You know very well what. Well."

"Well," I repeat. Rather primitive. I can do it, too.

"It's already the second of December."

"Time's just flying by, isn't it."

"Well."

"You want to talk about a certain woman, is that it? And I would like to speak about two other girls. What were you doing on the afternoon of the twenty-fifth of October around six thirty in the Větruše restaurant? Two witnesses have notified me regarding this matter ... Have you gotten that hole in your pocket sewn up?"

Frank Secký simply stares at me. So I continue:

"What were you doing on the afternoon of June eleventh in your apartment in Klíše around seventeen hundred hours? Only one witness has notified me, but she's a very ... resolute witness. She intensely dislikes you. Pulverizingly, if you'll permit me to use demolition terminology. What is the term used in official medical reports – when it's done by three in wedding clothes? Do you think it would be difficult to arouse the interest of our coworkers in this ... ahem, deviation? And even beyond the walls of our factory?"

"Let's set this aside for the moment. I'm the one who came to see you. And you know why. Well?"

"I have a mutually advantageous proposition."

"At last. We'll come to an agreement, don't worry. Go ahead."

"A little black-market exchange. Your client Gráfová for two: Serafinová and Rybářová. Well?"

"You're really pulling out all stops to amuse me, aren't you ... Mr. Trojan. Now, it must be perfectly clear to you that you're on your way out. Imagine a pink slip already in your hand. I'll have it typed out for you before lunch. Along with some other documents. You'll receive a packet of them after lunch."

"What else can I do? Since I've already decided I'm supposed to – fold like a jackknife – isn't that the way you put it? I just want to make sure for later reference ... What do you think, does a jackknife fold *quietly*? I'll gather together the files regarding the affair of Bogan Tušl's apartment and have it ready before lunch. Interestingly enough, the file begins with a lot of documents written by a mystery person–"

"As you wish, Mr. Trojan. You have no one to blame for the consequences but yourself."

Secký left. Since then he hasn't come to see me again "just to sit for a moment." And I haven't received my pink slip, even though several lunches have gone by – that rascal of a deputy didn't say which lunch he had in mind. Instead of the promised package, he sent me a beautiful desk calendar. He sent one to Tušl too, but mine has a sheet for every week (52 in all), whereas Tušl's sheets are typed on both sides (only 26). The consequences are quite bearable. As if the air were enriched with oxygen. Now for some ozone –

I went across the hall to borrow a cigarette from the girls. Jana doesn't smoke. She stands in the doorway of her conquered women's one-room flat, and in her eyes there is no compassion. She has no cigarettes. I must become scarce. Jana's a very beautiful girl ... and clean. So shouldn't she be good as well? I haven't the strength to leave. Or is it the strength to persist? AFTER ALL, NOW I'M FIGHTING FOR MY PLACE IN THIS BUILDING WHERE I'M CONDEMNED TO LIVE –

"If you'd be so kind, Miss ... Perhaps you could find one of Madda's cigarettes..."

Jana goes inside and closes the door in my face. But she can't lock it. I go in. Jana's ironing. White girls' things ... She looks for Madda's cigarettes, but of course she doesn't find any. Madda doesn't keep a supply, out of principle. Jana walks along the tracks on the floor as if floating on air.

"Are you really still angry with me, Miss? Why exactly?"

"Do you think you're worth it? There aren't any cigarettes. Go to the store!"

"I will, and thank you … sorry for wasting your time…"

"Your time, you mean. You'll have to beg your … girlfriend's pardon."

"No, right now I have time … the whole afternoon, in fact…"

"She gave you the whole afternoon off?"

"Jana, don't be like that. I have enough cigarettes. I just came … to tell you that you matter to me…"

"I was afraid you wanted to go out with me."

"Why is that frightening?"

"Can you imagine, you and me…"

"Yes, I can. Quite easily."

"Everything's always quite easy for you, isn't it."

"No. Just the opposite."

"You said I mattered to you."

"That's true."

"Then stop … making a fool of yourself. It's really embarrassing! When I think that a man like you … it's repulsive. Leave already, or…"

"Okay, I'm going…" (and at the door:) "…now I'm going to imagine you … whenever I feel like it–"

She threw a tennis shoe at me. I laughed. When was the last time I laughed? Jana is very young. Why very? Suitably young. I go downstairs. At the second floor I'm still trying to preserve the smell of ironing, the smell of a woman's cleanliness and something like … home.

Sitting on the edge of the couch in the room with the picture window overlooking the garden, Zita has stopped looking at her watch.

At last, the squeaking of the garden gate. Today for the first time Borek's arrived later than I have. So what? Aren't I a woman receiving a man? I'm apathetic. I'm just waiting to see what will happen to me. Prepared for anything …

Borek looks good. Borek looks different. Where has he come from? He falls into an armchair. Orders a cognac. Laughs loudly. He's come to amuse himself. He looks at his watch. Time is money. His time. All I have is money.

I diligently pour the guest another glass. As if I get a commission on every sale. Borek pats me ... on the behind. Should I let out a squeal of delight? Sit on his lap? Or will the gentleman first be wanting a dance? The gentleman would like another cognac. He sits me on his lap. I feel like a whore in a brothel. This impression grows stronger. He takes me ruthlessly. He's come to take what's his. Am I good enough today, sir? Did you like your little Zita?

Borek is finished. He's already completely preoccupied. He gets up, washes his hands, and quickly gets dressed. What else is there left to do here? Stick a hundred crowns in my garter? No: he pours himself another cognac. And sticks a cigarette in his pocket for the road. Once a smart Greek who got rich twice in his life coined the maxim: with alcohol collect after consummation, with love before. So I missed my opportunity. Borek's leaving. He looks good. He looks different now. A young man who has sinned in all propriety. He'll sleep well back home after this.

Will you come again, sir, to see your little Zita? Next time will you want some sort of *spécialité*, Sir? Perhaps I could prepare a little whip out of nettles, for example, so that I can thrash my legs about even more. Were you really satisfied with me today, sir? Come visit your little Zita again!

"So, bye," says Borek at the door.

"Will you come again?"

"One afternoon. The day after tomorrow ... or the day after that..."

Whatever is convenient for you, sir. For working men, afternoon sessions at a reduced rate. Drinks on the house. So come visit your little Zita again! And recommend her to your acquaintances. At Zita's you'll have the time of your life!

Why am I giggling like an idiot? My husband's given me up for lost, my son's in the clink, my lover's cleared out. I'm sitting disheveled on the edge of the couch in nothing but stockings, in one hand a cigarette, in the other a bottle, I'm cold and I'm giggling like an idiot. Why do I keep on thinking I'm not a whore? Why am I giggling like an idiot when I should be shedding tears and tearing out my hair?

Borek watched with amusement as Alex lay in bed assiduously coughing, his attempt to create for Dáša Zíbrtová the impression of bronchitis. Alex laboriously sweated and breathed almost touchingly. During the lulls between his coughing fits he would recite Ovid. Alex is a sharp one, he went to a classical *gymnasium*. Now he's showing off his splendid, athletic chest, seemingly unintentionally.

But Dáša's like a rock, she shows her disdain and is already preparing to leave. Alex covers his chest and fluently recites the Gospel of St. Matthew:

"Ne iudicate ut non iudicemini–"

"That's something about judging, right?" asks Dáša, who still isn't leaving.

"Judge not, lest ye be judged," Alex whispers between coughs so Zita has to come right up to him, "and now I'll teach you something really beautiful..."

"But then I really must go!" says Dáša resolutely, but nevertheless she sits down on the edge of Alex's cot. Alex's eyes flash with joy. The joy of conquering ... What chance does the dead Julda have against him? I wonder if I'll ever conquer a girl ...

I go across the hall to borrow a cigarette from the girls. Jana's not home. I hang around in front of the building. Like I used to. Like I used to sit on the steps with my bare feet in the beige dust ... everything was somehow better then. Why is that? After all, I have Zita now ... Maybe it was better then because I still had everything before me. What do I have before me now –

I go to Zita to make love and Jana to talk – I'm like the American F111 fighter jet, with adjustable wings – Zita's perfect and wise, Jana on the other hand is simple, almost too simple – in Vietnam the F111s, hit with primitive weapons, fell to the ground like bricks.

Zita, my love. We make love like never before – how many times have I said that already? The summit was achieved long ago. The summit is not an endless blooming meadow. The summit is essentially a point. After the summit comes the descent. But I don't want to go down yet ... I never want to go down. I'm beginning to feel somewhat better – with Zita or rather against her? That's really very inhuman of me. As is the fact that I'm really a very young man.

That last red leaf on that strange tree outside the window – has fallen now. How could it be otherwise?

CONQUERORS

Over fresh ruins, across bloody rivers
we go forward like a current,
like a terrible torrent of revenge –

In her fresh, girlish voice, Jana Rybářová was singing that old Socialist Youth song from the fifties as she knelt and scrubbed the floor of her third-floor one-room flat. Then with a wet rag she wiped the tracks on the ground, washed her hands, and stretched, how wonderful it is to be a young, healthy girl – then she learned twenty new Swedish words and rewarded herself with a bit of *Ivanhoe*.

With her mind on Richard the Lion-Hearted she threw a blanket over the table, and then a sheet on top of that, and commenced ironing the new dress she'd sewn herself according to a pattern she'd found in the East German magazine *Praktische mode*, it was made of coarse white nylon at 18 crowns a meter, 80 cm. wide. Sunday afternoon was peacefully flowing by, it's the fifth of December: tonight they'll be celebrating St. Nicholas' Eve, with its angels and devils.

Jana's mother asked her to come home to Malešice on the evening train so she could sit and chat with her daughter in the kitchen – but by afternoon she was already getting ready to leave. She wanted to properly prepare for the coming night.

She adjusted the window pane to get the best reflection (Jana owned only a small rectangular pocket mirror), tried on her freshly ironed dress, turned around in front of the glass with the close attention of an expert, ran her hands up and down her body trying to smooth out that tiresome wrinkle on the upper left-hand side – suddenly she stiffened when she saw herself in the window with her hand upon her breast. She bit her lip, turned her back to the window, quickly got undressed, hung the dress on a hanger, put on her sweat pants, sweat shirt, and coat, and with a yank zipped it all the way up to her chin. In the absolute silence she could feel her pulse in her temples. It still wasn't dark enough yet.

Borek Trojan. What will that name mean for me? Will it mean any-thing at all? Could I really love him? He said I mattered to him. "I have enough cigarettes," he said, "I just came to tell you how much you matter to me" – no, that's not what he said, he said: "*that* you matter to me." The cigarettes were only a thin disguise ... What will he do next? He scarcely does a thing. Naturally, I threw a tennis shoe at him. But he just stood there in the doorway laughing. Before that he told me: "Now I'll imagine you whenever I feel like it–" I wonder what he imagines. That we're together … that he's allowed to kiss me … caress me …

But he already does that, so what else would he think about! He does it with that … slut Gráfová. That loathsome, repulsive, dirty old witch – why doesn't he get rid of her? I'll bet she reads *Playboy* and does everything with him according to those horrible surveys … She's destroying a boy who could probably make a girl happy … Borek's pale and harried, his face looks devastated, and all those cigarettes he smokes, and how sad his smile is … Like Sebastien back in Louny … who died a horrible death. Isn't it possible to prevent another death? And isn't it a human obligation, after all? Shouldn't people live in dignity? And properly? And honorably? And justly?!

Jana went to the window and sternly looked up at the sky. In half an hour it will be completely dark. She crossed herself: she didn't believe in God but wanted all the good powers on her side.

She abruptly tore the string on the package she'd brought from home. She carefully pulled out some red cellophane, a Christmas tree candle, and a pumpkin the size of a child's head.

BESIEGED

Zita Gráfová swallowed a Librium tablet and waited for it to take effect. Tomorrow's St. Nicholas' Eve, the evening we always prepare for Roman's – ow ow. Evžen and I agreed today that we wouldn't say a word about St. Nicholas'. But I still can't forget about the fifth of December, when Evžen and I would get up in the middle of the night and with a stuffed stocking and a plate of sweets steal barefoot toward our sleeping son's window –

Perhaps I should already be dead. I've had enough. Borek comes to the river more and more seldom. I walk by the water pipe: our telegraph of love has grown silent. I wonder what Borek does when he looks at the pipe that leads down here to me? Why doesn't he at least caress me – with his wrench. He obviously hopes that by ignoring our telegraph he'll succeed in going to the riverside house on a different day than me … but I'm there waiting for him every day.

This afternoon: a horrible day. From the moment I wake up, it's painful to live, but this afternoon … alone in the riverside house. Borek doesn't like the yellow room with the window overlooking the highway, so now, even when he's not here, I never go into that room even though I like it the best. I don't want Borek to catch me in there. But Borek hasn't come.

I brought some food and drinks, but they won't fit in the refrigerator. It'll all go bad. Borek's no longer hungry. I can't look out the picture window because in the armchair in front of me I keep seeing Borek's short, thick, bushy hair, warm like animal fur. Beneath the chair are Borek's shoes, one lies on its side, both are covered with a lacework of dried mud.

An insane idea: I went for a walk. In December … I couldn't stand it in the house anymore. The grass is wet and gray and rots like a drowning man's hair. Damp, black tree trunks. The first snowflakes dance above the yellow river. And dissolve immediately. Soon the river will freeze and layer upon layer of snow, hard as glass, will settle on the ice. Borek said he'd like to go to Sweden. But snow makes me anxious.

At our riverside house, in the summer, you can hear the roar of engines, shouting, children crying and laughing. In the evening I drove through the alleyways between the other riverside houses with their boarded-up windows and doors. The bases of the little fruit trees were already wrapped up in paper for the winter. It's winter already, after all. The children are sitting all snug at home and their eyes are sparkling with anticipation. Tonight St. Nicholas comes.

The Librium's starting to take effect. Finally. A wonderful medication. Two chemists have recommended it to me: Trojan and Dr. Gráf. But I still won't be able to fall asleep. I'm wed to watching television with Evžen. For seventeen years – no, we didn't have a television then. I'm not even forty and I'm already dying of old age and decrepitude. I mixed two manhattans. Cold cream, skin lotion, toothpaste, mouthwash, douche, hairnet. Two tablets of Gastrogel. One tablet of Dormital. A tablet of Librium. A swallow of Ronda. Gods, armies, rulers – I beg you to grant me the mercy of sleep–

They offer insanity instead: out of the black sky a white, dead man's face in the window with burning red eyes and the red hole of a toothless mouth gaping horribly – I scream in terrror … It's Roman come for his presents.

CONQUERORS

"That's pretty sorry looking," Madda laughed when Jana, who was leaning out the window, finally produced her children's toy: a hollowed-out pumpkin on a black thread wrapped in red cellophane, with a burning candle inside, "you'd be lucky to frighten a crumpled old paralytic with that..."

Madda was also laughing because Olda was tickling the back of her knee, and he only left off when Jana glared at him (but after a brief pause he continued the foregoing quite a bit higher up).

"If you really want to have some fun, I've got something better," said Olda during that brief pause. "Take a handkerchief, catch a female dog, then rub the handkerchief all over the dog, really well–"

"Yeah, I know that one," said Jana. "We did that back home, too."

"But the best one is to stick a needle into their window," said Madda. "You jab it into the putty around the window with the head against the glass and stretch the thread across the street, and when you yank on it – women pray and men shoot..."

"How could I stick a needle into the Gráfs' window?" asked Jana peevishly.

"You'll come up with something ... Alex – Alex could maybe get up on the roof and move their television antenna so their picture goes out of whack. Then when he goes to fix it, he can stick the needle in the window sill."

"Madda, please, I'm begging you with all my heart–" said Jana, her eyes shining, "could you please help me?"

"I'll go see Alex right now. Give me a long piece of black thread, enough to stretch across the road, and a needle with a glass head. – And what do I get out of this?"

"I'll go to the movies and come back really late," Jana promised eagerly.

"Not enough."

"Then I'll go to the train station and sleep in the waiting room until..."

"It's too cold for that. Why don't you just turn toward the wall ... We'll be quiet, won't we, Olda–"

"Yeah, we won't do much talking while we're doing it–" Olda grinned. "But if Jana has to go to the train station again, I'd rather not stay. My conscience would bother me."

"So no more fuss, okay, Jana!" Madda barked. "You want me to help you, right? So, there you have it."

Madda went to Alex's room, and Olda started taking his shoes off.

During the night Jana lay there all bundled up, sweating under two blankets that covered more of her head than her body, but when the sounds reached her from the next cot, a sweat-covered Jana clenched her teeth and rammed her fingers into her ears, how long must I endure this, I want my own husband. *To live with him in our room   I'm an adult already   In his embrace*

And hear his sighs   Make him sigh with happiness, like that man in Madda's embrace   I'll do everything he wants me to   As long as we can share it, it has to be GREAT –

And one day I'll remember this St. Nicholas' Eve, the way I remember all of them, I remember how my brothers and I would wake each other up so we could see St. Nicholas and the angel. The devil frightened us even though we knew it was Father, Father, I want you to know I'm always thinking of you and that I'm doing everything I'm supposed to, just like you taught me, truth prevails and evil is punished, just like that wicked cat will die, first it will go insane, the bad ones will get potatoes, coal, and beatings with a broom, the good ones will get gingerbread cookies, apples, and caresses, we'll have lots of children and reward them justly, and then you'll reward me and I'll reward you and together we'll sigh with happiness continually, each day again and again.

BESIEGED

Zita parked her car at the corner of Slaughterhouse Street, and as soon as she saw Borek's silhouette through the raindrops on the windshield, she closed her eyes with happiness and reached for the ignition key.

Borek couldn't refuse me: I called him, said I was waiting, and hung up. Here he comes, his hands in his pockets and his head lowered. Against the rain? Or like a prisoner approaching the car that will escort him to the interrogation? It doesn't matter anymore. We're underway. My boy is sitting next to me and I can see him in the mirror whenever I want.

We decided not to turn on the heat, to crawl right into bed. We don't have much time. We hardly say a word. We make love as if we were punishing one another. This can't go on. We dress beneath the covers and dash out to the wet car. It keeps raining. I drive Borek to the corner of our street and let him out. I'm looking at his back – and he suddenly spins around, runs back to me, and kisses me desperately. Then once again his back. Receding in the rain of our street. With a horrible clarity, I suddenly realize that without him I won't have the strength to live.

At home I sing. I don't care anymore. It's all been decided already. Evžen and I watch television again. The picture was a little fuzzy yesterday, but Alex fixed it for us again. Tonight I don't take any tablets. I want to experience everything. Nevertheless, I feel I'll be able to sleep tonight.

And I probably would have if I hadn't been fated to face another night of insanity. In the middle of the night the window begins rattling with a horrible mechanical sound. Something like a jet airplane starting up. The window rattles as if the darkness itself were tapping on the glass with thousands of fingers. I'm afraid to go and see what it is. Evžen opens the window: he says there's nothing there. But barely has he gotten back in bed when the room is once again filled with a high-pitched crashing and crumbling and the sound of disintegration. They're coming closer. They're only a few steps from the bed. Day and night, they come closer. This is only their preparatory cannonade. When the troops break in they'll find only a white-haired woman's corpse.

CONQUERORS

Jana stood in the street in black rain falling from a black sky, assiduously yanking on a black thread that vanished into the darkness. When the second-floor window opened, she ceased her yanking and stood there silently. It closed after a moment, and Jana recommenced her yanking. Will an hour be enough? Better two.

Out of the night Jana yanked at the thread and raised her glance to the light in the third-floor window. Why aren't you sleeping yet, Borek? Are you reading or just thinking? Are you thinking about me, too? Why don't you come to borrow cigarettes anymore – I've bought five packs of your brand, Slavia, at seven crowns apiece, I could have lived a week on those thirty-five crowns, but for you I'd gladly give up more, even four hundred and fifty crowns, all I have … Where are you for entire days at a time? I see you less and less. You leave the building just twice a day and twice you return, which makes four brief trips through the building, and it's been a long time since you've knocked on my door. But when we meet, what will I say? I don't know. How can you not see?

Suddenly the light in Borek's window went out, I'm glad you're going to bed, sleep well – Borek's window opened silently, and his face shone through the darkness, lit by the bright dot of a cigarette, you smoke too much, Borek, and it's not at all healthy before bed, some day instead of a cigarette you'll get a sweet kiss good night, after all, you men are just like children and need someone to keep you out of mischief – Jana looked up at Borek's window, which was already closed and dark, she whispered her love up to him and assiduously yanked on the thread leading to the window a floor below, until she'd filled the two allotted hours. Then numb with cold, Jana went upstairs, brushed her teeth, and immediately dropped off to sleep the sleep of the just.

The following morning, the product development lab was dark because the previous night's storm had knocked out the electricity. Mrs. Helena Secká, Olga, Kamilka, Evka, and Jana were sitting in the dim light of a gas burner talking at length about Christmas, then men again, and Evka claimed that she knew nineteen different ways of kissing.

Jana stared into the tall gas flame shooting up unthrottled half a meter high, sending its searing blaze up to the dark beams of the ceiling. Jana was thinking about Olga's butcher, about Engineer Frank Secký, about Evka's most recent, and about Kamilka's forty-year-old sculptor who wants to carve her in Carrara marble, all these men were undressed by their partners and gamboled before Jana in the gas flame, and Jana inscribed into her memory all of the peculiarities, sentimentalities, tricks, hardships, spoils, and capitulations of love. Then when the power came back on, she asked Evka, in a whisper, to come with her into the storeroom and show her some of those special ways of kissing.

Most of all Jana liked taking a man's earlobe between her lips and immediately she tried it out on Evka while she was titrating hydrochloric acid with sodium hydroxide, she practiced chewing her lips, then decided to buy some lard and have lunch in the factory cafeteria, she drank her free half-liter of milk and with her lips still white from the milk went to the guard house behind the factory where Mr. Buřič, a former janitor at the former Louny high school, kept his dogs. She borrowed a bitch named Molly, led her to the old sodium room, closed the door behind her, took out a cambric handkerchief she'd received from her father at her confirmation, and assiduously rubbed Molly with it in the appropriate places for a long time, sniffing it now and then to see if it smelled strong enough, and when she was satisfied rubbed it a while longer still.

Then carrying the handkerchief in a plastic bag, she waited a good hundred and forty minutes on the landing between the second and third floors, ready to stick the handkerchief on Mrs. Gráfová anywhere she could, even into the back of the car if worse came to worst. But fortune smiled on the girl, and as Gráfová was coming down the steps, Jana managed to pass by her close enough to put the handkerchief into her coat pocket completely unnoticed.

BESIEGED

Zita fled down the main avenue, dashing through knots of pedestrians, chased by a pack of angry dogs, I ran into the Svět Cafeteria, an enormous dog squeezed through the glass doors after me and at the counter started clawing at me furiously with his front paws, they threw us both out. I didn't shake them off until I reached the new construction site on Potter's Street, where a young man opened a door just enough so I could squeeze inside the building. Then he had to hold me so I wouldn't fall. But I found it all too appalling to actually faint. The young man had a gray umbrella and a small poodle. He listened to me and then sniffed out (the young man, that is) someone's white handkerchief in my pocket. Meanwhile, the poodle peed on my stocking.

I know who's harassing me. And why. In swift succession, Frank Secký, Helena Secká, and Dáša Zíbrtová told me – that is, all of my acquaintances. Evžen remains mum in his weariness. It's that new girl in the building. Her name is Jana Rybářová. That young hyena who was trying to get that room even before Julda Serafin's body had cooled off. So it was for her my son committed murder. Mathilde de la Mole has finally arrived. She's here. She's very much here.

A death's-head – her childish cruelty. A needle in the window – the influence of urban legends. And that white handkerchief – she's sent me her seal: the sign of a bitch in heat. Mathilde de la Mole à la Czech.

That's why she squeezed against me that time on the stairs. Of course we'll meet again … In her cold blue eyes there's absolutely no mercy for me.

She's frightfully young. Provocatively. Perniciously. Nothing more, nothing less. A young barbarian. Primitively cruel like a negress in a primeval rain forest. Or our forefathers who would gather for a public flogging on Old Town Square – at that time merely a village green with pools of water and flocks of geese. She's a thousand years younger than me.

With smooth, taut skin. Firm meat. Sharp, pointy breasts. The legs of a rider squeezing her horse between her thighs and pounding its sides with her naked heels. It's easy to imagine her as an archer. Like Šárka – and she's chosen Borek for her Ctirad. She'll make sadistic love to my darling Borek, the way Madda made love to my son, Roman, and while she's at it she'll rest her naked equestrian legs on our quiescent telegraph pipe. All of my boys end up the same way.

She'll devour Borek before he manages to devour me. Oh world, if you can't think of anything else, then go to hell. I'll get there first and wait for you. I have the feeling I won't have to wait very long.

CONQUERORS

Jana Rybářová stepped across the tracks on the floor of her room as if she were dancing, a victory song was rising in her soul: Borek's been sitting here with me for three hours!

I'm pretending to iron, just to have something to do, because there's only one chair in the room and then just the two cots. He's got a date today with that old witch, and so I'm keeping him here no matter what. How easy it is ... I wonder if he'll try to kiss me today ...

"...and best of all I liked inorganic, because it seemed to me so pure ... from hydrogen and helium through light, silvery lithium, natrium, potassium, beryllium to the heavy metals and transuranic elements produced by cyclotron bombardment..."

"Why do you say: I *liked*. Don't you anymore?"

"That was a long time ago..."

"Oh shush, you've only been out of school a few years!"

"A lot has happened since then."

"It's only the bad things that make a person weary and old. Seriously, Borek: when are you finally going to leave that old Mrs. Gráfová?"

He bowed his head. HE'S NO LONGER DEFENDING HER! – He's sad, and I feel terribly sorry for him, I want to lift up his beautiful head and kiss that thin, pale face, but he needs thumping more than mollycoddling:

"So you liked the light, silvery metals. What do you like now? The mama of an imprisoned murderer? The director's little missus? An old hag who drinks rum? How much younger are you? How does it feel to be a kept man? I understand that a man has certain needs ... and that prostitution isn't legal. But how long do you intend to drag this out with her? Another year? Two years? Five?"

"I'd better go..." he says. He can't leave yet.

"If you want. But first you have to look me in the eye. – Why don't you want to? Isn't your conscience clear? Love wouldn't hinder that, would it? After all, one could love even a hundred-year-old negress."

"My life ... hasn't turned out very well."

"If you say that nonsense one more time I'm going to stab you with these scissors."

"I'd like to start again from the very beginning ... and somewhere else ... where there's a sea and clean air..."

"I'd like to go to Sweden..."

"You're not serious!"

"I know it could never happen. But I'd like to..."

"That's marvelous–"

"Marvelous? That it will never happen?"

"Marvelous because for me Sweden is ... but you'd never understand."

"You'd never understand my Sweden either. I want to find it here, on the Elbe..."

Now he'll kiss me. He's already standing there facing me. When kissing, what does one do with a hot iron? What did Evka say: the main thing is not to bump noses.

Borek stood there exhausted, as if standing itself took all the strength he had. Jana stepped across the tracks, took hold of Borek's head, and softly turned his face to hers. Then she carefully squeezed his earlobe between her lips. Then in a sudden flash of inspiration she took it between her teeth and softly bit down. Then harder.

BESIEGED

Zita lit another Kent, blew the gray smoke toward the ceiling, and in a perfectly controlled voice asked Borek:

"Are you in love with her?"

Borek merely shrugged his shoulders. HE DOESN'T DENY IT. I must preserve that which is imperfectly called taste, yes, Papa, *quand même.* "She's very young. I like her."

"Leave her alone."

"Of course, I like you more. But I won't stand in your way. You're twenty-five … I can see you two as a pretty couple."

"— — —"

"Why not. It's better to have children when you're young. Old parents are always crabby. I had Roman at nineteen."

"— — —"

"I can see you as a nice young father. Then the factory will have to get you a flat."

"— — —!"

"Having children is beautiful. Of course you can't have everything."

"— — —"

"How do you get along with her? I'd be interested to know if she has a sense of humor."

"— — —"

"Of course, you can laugh at practically anything. There's a certain Swiss who divides women into frigid goats and hot-blooded cows.

"— — —"

"What exactly do you hope to get out of love?"

"— — —"

"There's a certain Frenchman who divides women into those with whom you can still have breakfast afterwards and those with whom it's undesirable."

"— — —"

"Remember that time after our night at the river when we went to the Svět Cafeteria for breakfast and had hot dogs with horseradish and carp in mayonnaise?"

"— — —!"

"Borek! Borek … my dear. My love—"

He's crying! I quickly kneel before him, we both cry and rub our wet faces against each other, he kneels in front of me. We both kneel before each other. What is on the floor between us?

I run into Jana Rybářová and in her cold blue eyes there is no mercy for me. Hatred gives them that metallic shine. "Miss Rybářová … you left your handkerchief in my pocket. You'll find it in the middle trashcan at the corner of Potter's Street—"

The girl's jaw drops and she goes pale. But she immediately slams her jaw back into place. It clicks. But then she forgets to keep her mouth shut and between the two strips of vile pink (oh!) lipstick her splendidly developed incisors and eyeteeth glisten. Or is she baring her teeth at me already?

"I will never speak with you!" Miss Rybářová finally made herself be heard.

"You prefer other methods of communication. That's why you stuck a glass-headed needle in my windowsill. Barely enough black thread for sewing on a button."

The girl could think of no response. But Borek, too, owes me so many responses from yesterday ... obviously the girl's influence.

"Are you going to be out frightening people again tonight, little girl?"

She goes stomping out like a cow. If she'd stayed home on the farm she'd be a celebrated tractor driver by now or a splendidly paid pig feeder. But for a few twenty-heller pieces all she does is dawdle around the laboratory, where she's not needed at all. Why would she converse with me? She chooses weapons she's mastered. And what chance does a light, flexible, decorative dagger of mental advantage have against a massive, half-meter gothic sword which – if it gets in the first strike – smashes the enemy's skull along with the helmet? Her weapon is not intended for fencing. She's a cruel, brutal assassin. This is what executioners' swords looked like before they were replaced by the more elegant Parisian guillotine and the modern German axe.

Mathilde de la Mole a thousand years before Stendhal. So she's arrived. I already know the rest of the story: now Julien will come and shoot me in the church. But he won't die for it. On the contrary. Stendhal's Mathilde, however, did not get to keep Julien ...

Is it absurd to continue to hope? Just as absurd as continuing to live.

(To be continued)

On the 23rd of December, just before noon, six hundred liters of an overheated ethyl acetate-acetone mixture exploded, the roof of the concourse rose several meters into the air, after which it didn't exactly return to its original place, nor did it preserve its skeletal structure. No one was harmed, but a section of Cottex's courtyard disappeared beneath the debris of splintered beams, boards, and bent fiberglass-reinforced plastics, as well as four hundred kilograms of a highly reactive mixture.

The plant's director, Comrade Gráf, immediately ordered the entire staff to assist in clearing away the debris. A police wagon arrived on the scene before the fire department, ambulance, and a bus to carry away the injured. Within four hours the courtyard of the plant could once again be crossed. Especially appreciated was the participation in the clean-up by residents of the adjacent street: Comrade A. Růžičková, who'd been fired from Cottex for wounding a coworker with a broken beer bottle, and the spouse of the factory director, Comrade Zita Gráfová.

CONQUERORS

Jana Rybářová was among the last to arrive at the women's washroom. In eight shower stalls fourteen female employees were showering, two to a stall, and in the last just old Gráfová.

I stand near the clothes rack and stare at her, at that embodiment of immodesty and filth, how she makes herself at home in our factory washroom, too lazy to take those few steps home to take a shower, and she even has her own car – in a flash of inspiration Jana quickly undressed and hung her soiled lab coat and clothes on a hanger, her muddy shoes right next to each other under the bench, with the toes pointed toward the wall, barefoot and naked – with red circles behind her eyelids – she crossed the wet tiles to the last stall, Gráfová looks up and is already turning her back to me, I stand right next to her and press my body up against hers, here I am, let's have it out once and for all. Jana thrust her firm, pointy breasts into the soft, white back of the old woman, and in the hot spray from the perforated plastic shower head she walked around her as if performing an outflanking maneuver, face to face, now we'll find out who's going to win, she pressed her hard, pink nipples against the flat, dark areolas of the old witch's sagging breasts and against the rest of this fat, retreating, depraved piece of white meat, until the old, cast-off woman shook and ran from the cone of hot water spraying from the shower head and from the stage lights above.

Jana took over Zita's stall, and standing alone between the walls of glistening Luxfer tiles she showered as if dancing an ancient ritual. She reared up on her firm, slender legs and raised her arms above her head, inclining, greedily reaching for the conquered light and profuse hot water with her entire body, from toes to drenched hair.

How wonderful it is to be a young, healthy girl – tomorrow's Christmas Eve and the distribution of presents, and the day after that is Christmas Day, a thousand years ago it was called the Day of the Invincible

Sun, MY SUN that is already rising, the day after that is another holiday, and after that the greatest holiday of my life begins, I WILL HAVE MY OWN HUSBAND, then January will come, bringing more light, then February with even more, then March with even more, and then April full of sun, then May with its cascades of sunlight, and then a lot more in June – all the THEN's are mine already, and all the ones to come, all the good powers are on my side, life is wonderful, how wonderful it is to be a young, healthy girl –

"You're faking!" Dáša Zíbrtová screamed when she saw Alex in bed trying to raise the temperature of the thermometer by rubbing it with the sheet.

"I just wanted to wipe it off a bit..." Alex wearily lied.

"You're still the same old good-for-nothing. I'm leaving." Dáša left the men's one-room flat and slammed the door behind her.

Suddenly a completely healthy Alex jumped out of bed, quickly pulled on his underwear, and grinned at Borek: "Go to the movies, buddy. When you come back – two hours'll be enough – the usual twenty-five crowns will be waiting for you on the table, from our lovely doctor–" and he dashed out into the hallway after Dáša.

Two minutes later, when Borek was going down the stairs, Alex was climbing back up with Dáša in his powerful arms, Dáša was kicking, scratching, and beating Alex with her fists, Alex was grinning and tossing around his shrieking Europa like a rag doll in his arms, and without further ado he took her straight to bed.

Of the five movies listed on the playbill, *Firemen's Ball, Capricious Summer, Jules and Jim, Private Whirlwind,* and *Wake Up and Kill,* Borek chose the last, and in the Svět Theater in the Svět Passage he drank in the Italian tale of an outlaw who opened a display case of jewels with a pickax and stuffed handfuls of precious stones into his pockets. It ended with a storm of submachine-gun fire, and Borek left the theater with sympathy and understanding for the hunted gangster and unconsciously twisted his shoulders, as if he were shooting a long barrage of machine-gun fire.

Two hours were indeed enough for Alex. With a cigarette in his fingers he sat over Dáša's motionless body, grinned at Borek, and pointed with his thumb to the corner of the table, where another of Dáša's twenty-fivers lay. "I think I should hunt down a girl myself," said Borek.

"Denken tun die Narren," yawned Alex, "kluge Leute wissen – fools think, the clever know," then he put his cigarette out against the wall, slid his hands beneath Dáša's shoulder blades and rump, lifted her up, and placed her under the bed, spread himself out comfortably on the bed, and immediately fell asleep.

Borek lit a Kent, but after a few drags he put in out against the wall, smoking before bed is stupid, and no more Kents, they're too expensive and taste insipid. After a moment's deliberation he rejected the blue silk pajamas from Zita, lay down naked on his bed, on his left side, after five minutes turned over onto his right, and was just on the verge of drifting off ... when suddenly he smiled, as if remembering something pleasant, he opened his elegant Samsonite suitcase (of course it's mine, I conquered it, and it's more than a meager purchase, a suitcase to the victor and woe to the defeated), took out his switchblade, and calmly fell asleep with the quickly warming haft in his palm.

Torn from sleep by a blaring alarm clock, a rigid erection, hunger and thirst, Borek threw off the blanket and, after a long period of time, once again indulged in a quick set of early morning exercises, the six-month hiatus in his daily gymnastics routine betrayed itself in an unbearable pain in his shoulder during his fourteenth push-up, but we'll soon get back up to our usual forty plus, committing a minor act of violence first thing in the morning, if only on yourself, wakes you immediately into jet performance, overcoming oneself to overcome the world, or Wake Up and Kill.

I'm already sleeping well again, and I wake eager for lovemaking, a consuming hunger eats at my stomach, that symptom of youth which is also a symptom of victory. Enough feeling and enough words already. Now I feel like some action.

The outline of the factory, tower, concourse, and warehouse shine out of the darkness of the January morning like a battleship at port. In a few weeks it'll already be light at this hour. In a few months no one will dare act towards me the way they are ... beginning not to act towards me. In a few years – Meanwhile, patience – meanwhile, live. And a new love –

INCONSPICUOUSLY OBSERVE – done: she's clean, beautiful, fresh, athletic, healthy. And wonderfully, or better: wonderfully *suitably* young. She's nineteen (I'm twenty-five, Mom and Dad were also six years apart), she's strong, bright ... perhaps a bit too limited? But she's curious, and isn't the desire to learn better than knowledge itself? I can put more into Jana Rybářová's ruled notebook than in the margins of a novel by Monsieur Stendhal.

FOLLOW – done: she lives in our building, works in our lab. She goes into town every day between five and six, and returns an hour later. Due to Madda's restlessness, she's often home alone.

CHASE – Borek carefully (Jana has expressly forbidden me to visit her at work) looked through the glass doors into the product development lab. Jana turned around as if she'd felt his eyes on her neck and sent Borek away with voluble gesticulations. He calls her every hour. Jana always hangs right up. The rules of the game, the rules of the hunt …

"Evka…" Borek pleaded to the girl as he offered her one of the Kents he'd already stopped smoking. "Please tell me where Jana's always hiding."

In Evka's eyes there was an obvious desire for something to happen: "She just went to the sodium room."

Borek hurried across the courtyard to the sodium room, rushed into the low building, slammed the heavy metal-plated door behind him, and leaned against it, breathing heavily.

"Borek – are you out of your mind? Get out of here!" Jana screamed.

"Just five minutes."

Jana stands there, holding a large, blackened knife used for cutting sodium. My girl cutting light, silvery metal – Borek grabbed her by the wrist and pulled her towards him, Jana stubbornly resisted, my sweet athlete, this is hunting, you know, and thanks to your resistance it will not become a slaughter, Borek pulled the struggling Jana toward him and grabbed her breasts, for a year I rode the bus for three stops only to cop a momentary caress of a girl's chest, and the old excitement has suddenly returned, Jana broke out of Borek's grasp and ran toward the window overlooking the courtyard, Borek intercepted her and grabbed her once again, this time more firmly, once a certain Madda Serafinová escaped through the window when I was holding the door, now I know to hold the body, not the exits, Jana defended herself wildly with her fingernails and knees, once a certain Slávka from the warehouse, an ugly, scabby girl, crippled me with the same method, but your knee's not so disarming, and Borek ran his free hand over the struggling girl's body, "Borek … let me go … at least for a minute, something broke behind me–" once a certain Yveta tricked me like that and like an ox I let her go, but I won't let you go, my wonderful antelope, "You're barbarous, do you hear me? Mr. Trojan, I'm not one of those easy lays you're used to!" once a certain Zita Gráfová offended me that way and I just wanted to hit her, you however I'll kiss first, and Borek pressed Jana's head back against the wall and battled his way to her lips, when she could no longer avoid his, she bared her teeth and Borek kissed them, suddenly a sharp pain, the little devil bites, and draws blood, Borek applied all his strength to hold her, and Jana finally started to weaken, instead of resisting it's as if her arms draped themselves around my shoulders, no, I didn't just imagine it, now she's softly pressing her body against mine, her knees no longer try to hurt me and then, as if hesitating for a moment, begin to do the opposite, her lips intertwine with mine, we kiss and our eyes suddenly betray ourselves to one another. Then Jana suddenly tears herself loose and runs to the door. I'll catch you … CHASE – I'll chase you.

Borek stood in the courtyard in his white coat, wiping his bloody lip with his sleeve and shuddering with an intense happiness, you can't feel the cold at all now, January's ending and February with its lighter snow is on its way, March will thaw the edges of the winter monolith, glittering April and its gushing springs, the May of meadows, birdsong, and blooming chestnut trees, then June with its long days of sunlight culminating in the solstice, and we still haven't flown in an airplane, haven't even swum in the banal Baltic, let alone the Caribbean Sea or the Indian Ocean, we haven't seen the peaks of the Alps or the Caucasus, let alone the Cordilleras, the Andes, or Himalayas, and I still haven't lived in my own flat, I want a wife, to live with her and have a child, what is relentlessly being offered us in place of all this? Dragging myself along to a pitiful end with the director's aging wife, who keeps stepping on my heels for it? This town is probably too small for romantic passion à la Stendhal – sbohem, Zita, goodbye – but it's long enough to serve as a runway to overcome the fatal pull of gravity. Because you can always still pull out of a hopeless siege. Have we lost the airport? Then there's nothing left but to try a vertical takeoff.

In his office Borek dialed Zita's number, 386 57, waited for her to answer, and then curtly said: "Zita, today at four at the corner of Slaughterhouse."

I walk around my telephone justifying it all to myself, again and of course superfluously, why even on the novelistic level: in the end there was nothing left for Julien Sorel to do – and that was *some* kind of love – but physically liquidate Madame de Rênal. Thanks, Monsieur Stendhal, for your practical shooting directions. You're absolutely right: the only genuine solution is a practical one.

Eng. Borek Trojan looked at his Cortabert watch, and at 15:59 went to Slaughterhouse Street, crossed the road, and got into Zita Gráfová's waiting blue car. "To the river," he softly said.

As he stepped out of the car he put on his gloves, if there's an investigation it's best not to leave your fingerprints on either the garden gate or on the key, and it would be great if Zita would open the door herself, with her bare hand. So it looks like she brought me here. I'll be leaving this house alone –

Lock the door behind Zita and leave the key in the lock so that, just in case, it can't be knocked out from the outside. Any interruption is absolutely unacceptable.

My muddy shoes mark my steps across the floor, leave as few as possible: no pacing back and forth, which could create the impression of running around and, therefore, conflict. Zita lowers herself into her armchair, I stand behind her, the expression on her face could unfavorably influence the act. Keep the gloves on just in case.

"Zita. It's over between us."

"I know."

"But this time for real."

"We've said that before already. We made it three days without each other. Borek, we know we can't live without one another."

"And even less together. It's over."

"You could have told me that over the telephone. But you're here."

"So I could do it properly. Zita. You're married. Go back to your husband."

"You're giving me advice?" Zita's shoulders begin to shake from crying.

"Zita. You're a mother. Your son needs you more than I do."

"Ow. Ow. Owwww–"

"I no longer need you at all. Rather the opposite. You're in my way – in everything."

Zita slid down from the chair onto her knees.

"Zita. We could never be together. Live together. Get married – imagine our wedding. Would you take your wedding dress out of your closet?"

Zita lies on the carpet emitting weak, gurgling sounds.

"Zita. I hate you. Because you're ruining my life. You're trying to destroy me. And also, Mrs. Gráfová, let's not overlook a certain difference in age. You're ten years older than me. Ten years. I have not the slightest desire for a misalliance. I want something better. I'm in love with a young girl and I'm going to marry her. In short: you are *too old*."

Zita lies on the carpet, silent and motionless.

No one can foresee what she'll do when she recovers. But if she does do something, the investigators will be able to determine the exact time of the event, so I better hurry. Unlock the door and close it behind me, naturally with my bare hand. The same with the garden gate, touch this in a few places reachable only from the inside. She brought me here, it went badly between us, and I left. When I was leaving, she was sitting in the chair – no. She chased me out, screaming. But no one heard the scream. So:

after a short conversation she ordered me from her cottage with an offensive gesture, and so I left.

By bus, I happen to remember the exact time because it left the stop later (or earlier, it depends on the facts) than it should have according to the schedule, and I checked the correct time with the driver. Departure according to the timetable behind glass: 16:40.

"Excuse me, sir, what's the exact time? Four forty-two? Thank you!"

Because the bus left the stop two minutes late, and I checked the correct time with the driver. So then: 16:00, departure from the corner of Slaughterhouse Street. 16:25, arrival at the riverside house and immediately a bitter dispute with the deceased. 16:35, she ordered me from her cottage with an offensive gesture, and so I left immediately. At 16:39, I reached the bus stop. Why did I look at my watch? To check when the bus was to arrive according to the timetable. It was supposed to leave at 16:40. It arrived at 16:42, and I took it home, where I proceeded to the flat of my girlfriend, Jana Rybářová.

Borek ran up the stairs of building No. 2000. He slowed down and was already moving very slowly when he reached the second floor, he stood on the landing, Zita's white door shone in the darkness and I can no longer take another step upstairs. Zita. ZITA!!–

I turned around and hopped back down the stairs, in forty minutes I can be back at the riverside house if I take the streetcar and bus, and maybe I can still rescue her, Zita, my love, my catastrophe, my fate, I cannot kill you ... I'm not big enough.

As Borek ran out of the building, a blue Škoda was just driving up, it stopped and Zita Gráfová stepped out onto the sidewalk.

"_ _ _"

"_ _ _"

"Good afternoon ... Mrs. Gráfová," said Borek after a long while.

"Good afternoon ... Mr. Trojan," she whispered. Of course, it's a lot quicker by car than by streetcar and bus.

And Borek turned around and walked away, his soul rose up, fell, and struck the ground like a wave on a sandy beach, quickly receding in the form of a thin film and depositing on the sand a small crab with broken legs, a pitiful, grotesque little creature, Borek slowly walked to the stairs, his step quickened as he approached the second floor, on the landing he broke into a run and, completely out of breath, without knocking, he burst through the unlocked door of the women's flat on the third floor, "Jana–"

"I didn't hear you knock, Borek," said Jana Rybářová, her eyes sparkling.

"Listen – do you hear that? That's my heart beating for you!"

"Oh. It seems like you actually flew up the stairs. You're all sweaty and pale. What did you want to tell me?"

"This–" said Borek, he abruptly grabbed Jana by both hands and with a jerk pulled her toward him. Jana resisted, Borek attacked ... on the tracks welded together in the shape of a cross, the two young people began to playfully scuffle and jostle one another.

BESIEGED

Everything has lost its purpose. Soap just feels cold. Armchairs once again burn. I'm a cigarette butt, a ring of cooled ash. A streetlight in a city with a bombed-out power plant. Spoiled dough. Rotten meat. The dregs of wine – but you're flattering yourself, *ma chère*. You're more like coffee grounds left over from a shameless little episode involving a small-town little missus. In short: over. I'm *too old* already, you know.

With her teeth Zita Gráfová opened another bottle of white Cuban Ronda and drank it as if from thirst. Julien Borek only came to shoot me. I killed him too: I nourished his love as well as his hatred. The gunman is dead and the victim alive ... but that's easy to fix. Now the only question is: how? Gas? Evžen's never owned a revolver, and I'd never be able to fire one. With the decrepitude of age, every hour adds another year, and I can't survive any more such hours.

And so I drink. Gramos after gramos, I already have a good kilo-gramos in me. Today is Friday, my imprisoned son's visiting day – my son's a murderer, something more to trouble me – and I no longer have the strength to come before his silent, unpardoning face. So I drink more. Soon I'll have killed myself.

Tout est perdu – sauf l'honneur. But I lost my honor before everything else.

Boom! Crack! Snap! Crash! They're thumping away again downstairs. The itinerant workers have arrived. You've broken me, you red rabble from below. I'd like to at least die loudly enough to drown out your noise for at least a second. That's a fabulous idea, *ma chère*! Since nothing matters anymore. Just before death a brief moment to stop being afraid. After thirty-five years, why can't I finally be a man – or a woman? – and allow myself the luxury of being absolutely open? Probably not even queens could dare to approach the mob. Let's say I have an urge to chat with someone on my final day.

Zita drank deeply from her glass of pale sailor's rum and went downstairs, exhilarated. Now I could probably even bear running into Miss Rybářová. That young hyena shrieking impatiently over the still twitching carcass. This building already belongs to her. She's inherited it from me. I'm just going to take inventory – how did my dear boy put it? You have the most unrestrained fun when all is lost. And I've lost absolutely everything.

Crude male voices could be heard behind the door of the itinerants quarters, Zita trembled, took a deep breath, and went in. Dízlák, Valtr, and Stěpa stared at her in alarm.

"All your carrying on is bothering me," said Zita in a faltering voice. "Can't a person even commit suicide in peace!"

"But such a pretty woman – why would you want to knock yourself off–" Dízlák guffawed and rushed over to her.

"Come in and sit with us, Ma'am, do stay a while–" crowed Valtr.

The handsome Stěpa's face turned pale, and this pallor quickly flowed to his neck, right to the edge of his red-striped sailor's shirt.

"D-d-do you … like me?" Zita stuttered to Dízlák.

"And how!!" and Dízlák was already sitting the swaying Zita on the bed beside him.

"And I'm n-n-not too old?" laughed the drunken Zita.

"Hell, no! Not at all! Not even a bit!"

"And could you poss-, poss-, possibly even m-m-marry me?"

"How 'bout right now!" Dízlák roared with laughter and took Zita by her shoulders. Valtr squealed with laughter, and Stěpa's face reddened from the roots of his hair.

"I s-s-still have my wedding dress in the c-c-closet, with a-a-an eight-meter train and a v-v-veil–" Zita stuttered, Dízlák laid her down on the bed, Valtr snapped his fingers at Stěpa, who ran to turn out the light, and out of the darkness came Zita's breaking, rending voice: "I'm not t-t-too old…"

The men didn't answer in words. *Thrown into a cavern   And one after the other, the men rose from the fire and went to her   Finally, naked, tied to an ass, and sent out into the night, she met Christ –*

Late that evening Zita slowly stumbled back upstairs, exhausted, holding on to the railing. I was a woman this evening. I had three men. More than I've had my whole life put together. And these were kind. They told me it was as if I were young. And kept repeating it as often as I needed to hear it. As if I were young.

It's over, *ma chère*. Now I'm deadly serious. After that, there's nothing left to do. So, gas? That takes too long. Good families don't keep revolvers at home. A razor in the tub – I don't think I could stand the sight of my own body. A knife through the heart – I no longer have a heart. Jump from the window? I'm too old for that. How do abandoned old ladies die? Like abandoned old dogs, my dear. Ruff! Ruff! They simply die.

Well, so long, dear apartment, goodbye. The things I used to like, from the dessert service with the nice grape motif to both my boys, have been taken from me. And you, my fifth apartment, haven't grown on me. Except for the water pipe, that is.

So long to you, mute telegraph of my love. I've no more messages for you – in a sudden flash of inspiration, Zita ran lumbering into her room, pulled out Borek's black leather belt from beneath her pile of underwear, and resolutely stepped up to the water pipe in the hallway.

After all, don't we express pain and pleasure just the same? My final telegram. Addressee: Borek. Text: 0. Signature: 58 kg. of dead weight.

Alexandre Dumas wrote that hanging is a sweet death. He's obviously referring to the agony ejaculation of the victim. What does a woman feel?

Zita pulled the end of the leather belt through the buckle, to fashion a noose, and tied the other end to the water pipe. Then she brought a chair from the kitchen, climbed onto its round seat, and slipped the noose around her neck. Now just kick the back of the chair and away I'll fly, my boys.

Zita Gráfová crossed herself, looked at the ceiling, and gave the back of the chair a good hard kick. Naturally, she didn't fly away. She stayed there, hanging by the neck.

CONQUERORS

The red plastic alarm clock finished ringing on its sounding board (the round seat of a chair), and Jana Rybářová quickly roused herself from sleep, an important day awaits, but are there actually unimportant ones? – and Jana began her vigorous early morning exercises by flexing her tummy muscles ("Girls, you're going to have tummies boys will die for–" the technical school exercise instructor laughed as she taught this exercise to the blushing students from a stepladder), and Jana blushed, when Borek sees the results of my exercising … When will that be? – and to dispel her body's sudden confusion, she quickly went into a set of push-ups, twenty-six altogether, one more than last time – then she carefully looked up to see if Madda was still asleep, and since she was, she inquisitively ran her rectangular pocket mirror along her body, the skin on the back of my thighs is still rough, the lotion didn't help, Jana rubbed the back of her thighs with a burning three-percent solution of salicylic acid (doctors prescribe two-percent, to protect the keratin), which she herself had mixed in the laboratory, maybe it will go away in time, and then she put pinches of petroleum jelly on the tips of her breasts to make them more pliant. When he kisses them – –

Jana dressed, sat on the chair right next to the door, and waited with baited breath till Borek left his room for work. Borek isn't doing very well right now, it's as if he were seriously ill, as if that old witch Gráfová had him spellbound even after her death, maybe even more than when she was alive, then at least Borek would come here and there was that time in the sodium room – – With the death of that old witch he suddenly changed, it's as if since that day he were from another planet, he's incredibly tired, spent, so pale ... and he avoids me, even with his eyes. He doesn't try to grab at me or kiss me anymore ... But I'll break the spell of that dead witch ... after all, all the good powers are on my side.

A sudden sound from across the hallway, Jana jumped up from her chair, accidentally waking her roommate, Madda, and she carefully and quietly followed Borek down the stairs and out the building, in the morning my sweetheart is mean and irritable, a couple of times I caught up with him and he didn't say a word all the way to the factory, even though I tried really hard and talked about the coming of spring (it's already the middle of February!), soccer (that's the only reason I buy the newspaper), alkaline metals (I studied them using Professor Votočka's textbook, which Borek surely used as well), conditions in Africa, yachting, swimming in the sea, and Madda's carrying on with Olda (which I modified significantly), but he doesn't react to anything ... Jana followed twenty steps behind Borek, as if tracking him or rather driving him in front of her to the factory. The tower, concourse, and warehouse loom in the pre-spring morning like a city on the horizon, conquer it, my prince, for yourself and for me, I shall reward you with all I have and with all I myself will conquer –

In the seclusion of the glass storeroom, lab technician Evka wrinkled her forehead and after long deliberation said indecisively: "So what about this–" and she stuck the tip of her tongue into Jana's nostril.

"But you've already shown me that one," said Jana, annoyed, as she wiped her nose with the back of her hand, "don't you know any others?"

"I think that's all..." said Evka hesitantly.

"But you said you knew nineteen, and you've shown me only sixteen altogether, and two of those were dubious. So where are the other three?"

"Well, of course, there's regular kissing!" Evka was suddenly jubilant.

"That still makes only seventeen!"

"Then what about this…" said Evka after a long moment of concentration, and she bit the underside of Jana's arm.

"Biting's already been counted. Which means that you don't know any others, so next time don't brag about having nineteen when you barely have seventeen, two of which are dubious and one is normal kissing!" said Jana condescendingly, and she went back to her lab table.

After taking the wind out of Evka's sails – Kamilka wouldn't speak with Jana at all, and Jana had no interest in the sexual experiences of Mrs. Secká – Jana spoke for a long time with Olga about love, with burning ears she listened to the woman's advice: "…and most importantly, don't be ashamed to show him that you like it, you have to *act* so he'll notice it even in the dark, and even if he doesn't notice it, men have to *hear your moans*, and then he'll go absolutely crazy, and you'll get yours maybe *after* giving him this catnip, understand, but you have to *act* from the very beginning, even if all you feel is itching, burning, and biting…"

With eyes and ears wide open, Jana was always indefatigably on her feet and on the lookout, she would walk lively through the factory courtyard, past the doctor's waiting room and the cafeteria, past the garage and the porter's lodge, and increasingly often she dared to enter the White House and walk down the hallway between the forty glass-paneled office doors, trying to guess which silhouette was Borek's, what does my chosen one do all day, is he sitting in his office or next door in Tušl's, or in Deputy Abrt's office, sometimes he has meetings in the director's office, the whole planning department goes to lunch together, Borek sits with them but hardly speaks and eats very poorly, just a few spoonfuls of soup, he didn't even touch yesterday's country pork soup, today he ate only a couple mouthfuls and left all the meat on his plate, the only thing he eats all of is dessert, and he drinks tea … what are you going to look like, my dear. If you keep on like this, you'll lose all your strength … If only I could have lunch with him and make him eat a little, maybe even spoon-feed him – but of course that's impossible. I can't even sit with him at the same table, if a boy and a girl ate together here, this scandal-mongering crowd would give them no rest.

At home in her women's one-room flat on the third floor, Jana cleaned up, rinsed a few pieces of clothing, ironed a little, learned twenty new Swedish words – with the door to the hallway slightly open: Borek comes home either before I do or late in the evening, after all kinds of meetings – is it really only meetings? ... But he doesn't have a woman, that I know for certain ... am I really a hundred-percent certain? ...

Then the door across the hall slammed shut and footsteps went down the stairs, Jana tossed aside her Swedish textbook, listened a moment at the door, and then vigilantly set out after Borek. What does he actually do in town? He's tired and apathetic, it's almost pointless to ride in the second tram car, he wouldn't notice me even if I stood right behind him ... He walks down the main avenue like a sleepwalker – shop windows, people, cars, nothing interests him – and he takes the shortest route to the Svět Café, where there are terrific curtains on the glass doors so you can see inside, Borek ordered a glass of red wine, he didn't have hardly any lunch and now wine on an empty stomach, that's a fine diet – and you smoke too much, my dear. Then he went to the Svět Cinema to see *The Joke*, if only he'd laugh at least (in the dim light of the reflected movie screen Jana often turned around to see Borek's face four rows back, which looked like plaster, a death mask with heavy black shadows), and from the Svět Cinema to the Svět Cafeteria, where at the counter he gnawed on two open-faced sandwiches for an interminably long time and ordered tea and two large rums (at the Svět they don't serve alcohol unless you order tea, as well), he drank the rum, left the tea, and took the streetcar home, where he closed the door behind him and didn't go out again ... just like last time. Why doesn't he go skating, for instance, or to a play, or somewhere for supper, what does he do all evening alone in his room ... that dead witch still has him in her power ... doesn't he like me even a bit anymore? ... I don't understand men at all ... how long can they be without women ... The last time he was with the witch was in January, that Thursday before the Friday when the witch flew off to hell on her broom, but that was six weeks ago, how long can he go without – And he doesn't do anything all evening, just sits there locked in his room, Evka said that some do it themselves and get so used to it they don't want anything else, but that would be horrible – Jana sat on her chair near the partially opened door to the hallway and played around with a pack of Slavia cigarettes, Borek's brand, a blue bird with a black head against a white background ... When will he come to borrow a cigarette again? If only I could come to you, take your beautiful head in my hands, and kiss your thin, pale face ...

From below, two sets of footsteps are coming up the stairs, that's Madda and Olda, and if they don't say goodbye to one another on the first floor they're certainly coming here, but I don't feel like going to the waiting room at the train station anymore, this is my room after all – but I can't stand all those bothersome negotiations with Madda … I can't even look at the two of them.

Jana jumped into bed and covered her head with the folded-over blanket, but still she could hear every word ("Pssst!" Olda whispers, "Don't worry, to her it's already midnight–" Madda lies), and what comes next is even more tormenting, Olda moans with happiness in Madda's embrace and the pillow in my embrace is burning, now Madda joins in and I bite my pillow so I don't join them too – moaning, but out of pain, which would sound just the same.

"Couldn't you at least try to be quiet?!" Jana angrily told Madda when Olda had gone to sleep downstairs in the itinerants quarters.

"What am I supposed to do, bite my pillow?" Madda answered curtly.

"Listen, Madda, you're doing it partly on purpose … because it works like catnip on Olda…"

"It's not like I think about it, Jana."

"But there still could be something to it, couldn't there? You know, like unconsciously…"

"You know, they find it really annoying when you lie there like a log."

See, what Olga said is true and holds like the general laws of chemistry, there's probably a lot in common between the two, just like the mutual desire of positive and negative ions to bond and enter into other agitating actions, like for example dissolving metal in acid and exo- and endothermic reactions, it's as if there were an engineering network underground on which they build beautiful white houses with enormous windows and balconies, with kitchens, bathrooms, bedrooms, and children's rooms, with flowers on the window sills and antennae reaching up into the sky …

Then the last day of this leap-year February arrived, a day that comes only once every four years, for the first time the sky was completely blue and the bare trees on Střížovický Hill thrust their naked arms toward the sun.

Another important day, and all the following days will be even more important – is that the way it will always go? – how wonderful! I crossed the hall and knocked on Borek's door – nothing, I knocked again – still nothing, I was afraid that something had happened to him so I pushed against the door – right behind it stood Borek, pale and with an expression of horror on his face.

"Borek … has something happened to you?"

"No … I was just alarmed … by that knocking."

"But why? I just wanted to … I just came to borrow some salt."

"It reminded me of something…"

"You really look frightened."

"No one's knocked on my door for such a long time ... But it's nothing, it's over."

He's smiling at me! We say nothing. And I notice that ... for the first time in a long time he's looking at me the way a man looks at a girl. I'm happy and afraid that it will stop, and so I quickly leave. But I'll come again! We both forgot about the salt (but I've got a kilo at home I've hardly used half of).

The following morning – it was already almost light! – I screwed up my courage and caught up with him on the way to work. I told him some funny stories – how at home we killed a piglet and his leg was still twitching ... and Borek laughed like a little boy. He needs joy, and I could provide it even if I had to sew red dresses with farmers' wives ... I'll cure him. I'll make a man of him again. A man for me, a man for us both.

Since then, we walk to work together every day. And that same day, Borek came to see me in the afternoon, I had the Slavia cigarettes ready, but he no longer needed any excuse, and we talked as if we'd already been going together for a year – but haven't we been going together four months already? That annoying hiatus is already long, long forgotten.

We felt so good together, our eyes were moist. Even Borek's ... he finally told me a strange, old story about a certain Mrs. Derenal and some guy named Julian who shot her in a church – it seemed somewhat strained to me and not very well thought out, in short, I didn't particularly like it – until I understood that Derenal was supposed to be the witch Gráfová, and Julian Borek. In the story they finally executed Julian.

"But you're still alive, aren't you?" I pointed out to him, not without a little maliciousness.

"For now. And that's enough–" and already he was getting up and putting his arms around my waist, and already we were bumping into the cross-shaped tracks on the floor of my room again, he kissed me on the cheek – I still haven't let him kiss me on the lips, for now. "When you come again–" I said with a grin. "I don't know if I'll be able to find the time–" he said with a grin. The next day, just after I got home from work, I put on a new, pointy bra that cost forty crowns, and I hadn't even fastened it in back when Borek walked in. Since then we've been together all the time.

We kiss ... where is poor Evka with her seventeen ways of kissing, two of which are dubious ... When two people are in love every kiss is a new, more beautiful way of kissing. We sit together on the bed and look out the window, all we see is sky, but that's more than enough ... now, every day is longer and brighter than the last.

"I often remember," whispered Borek, "how we talked that time about Sweden … Do you remember?"

"I remember everything we've ever talked about. I'd like to go to Sweden, too … every day I learn twenty new Swedish words."

"I'd like to find Sweden here, on the Elbe … with you." And once again our eyes are moist with emotion … but we're not going to cry together, are we? … but it's just from happiness. Since that day Borek is allowed to caress my entire body, and the following day, Saturday, I went home to Malešice to tell my mother I'd be getting married soon.

Oh, how I love the month of March, the month of wind blowing across the puddles, the swirling water, the air smells of spring, Borek comes straight home from work, he attacks, I dodge and then expose myself to danger again, it looks like a game or a hunt, that's what true love looks like, the best things are always the simplest, we laugh together, April flies by smelling of earth, and May descends, the month of stars and love –

Even before the red plastic alarm clock finished ringing on its sounding board (the round seat of the chair, I bought the same one as Jana), Borek was standing by the window looking up through the morning mist at the dome of the night hemisphere, and when it seemed to promise blue he rejoiced: it's going to be a beautiful day! Then fully dressed he sat in the chair right next to the door and waited with baited breath till Jana left her room for work.

Torn from sleep by a blaring alarm clock, an excruciating hunger, and a burning thirst, Jana ran (throwing off her cotton chemise on the way, no longer with any regard for her roommate, Madda) to the faucet on the wall and quickly (annoyed by the ferocity of her body's longings, which she felt before she had sensed her body itself) opened the faucet all the way, set her face, shoulders, and breasts against the briskly spurting cone of water and greedily gulped until her hunger had somewhat abated. She hopped around naked (I'll save my towel for my dowry) in the low, May morning sun and nearly choked on an insane, groundless joy, the sort of utter joy that invigorates the body and convulses the muscles.

We meet in the hallway as if guided by a secret signal, our doors open at almost the same moment – what a beautiful girlfriend I have! – what a beautiful boyfriend I have! – and in an instant we agree to go dancing at Větruše today, and then we both go back to our respective rooms to turn on the water, because there won't be any this afternoon, it takes us the same amount of time, and then we hold hands and hop down the stairs.

Right after work, back in his room on the third floor on the right, Borek took off his clothes and looked at himself in the mirror, his forty push-ups a day were adding muscle mass to his chest, he flexed his arm and tested the rigidity of his bicep, I'm already twenty-six, just twenty-six ... he knelt down beside his cot, ceremonially opened his Samsonite-suitcase vault, and placed on his bed, as on an altar, his white openwork undershirt, white nylon shirt, his exquisite London socks, his white briefs – he hesitated for a moment and then replaced them with the red boxers – a silver-gray tie and a pair of cufflinks: sapphires in gray platinum.

Right after work, back in her room on the third floor on the left, Jana took off her clothes and examined herself in her little rectangular mirror, the skin on the back of her thighs was already smoother and her tummy was marvelous, just as the exercise instructor had promised, I'm already approaching twenty, just twenty ... she knelt down beside her cot, ceremonially opened her little suitcase, and placed on her bed, as on an altar, her still unused set of underwear made of delicate white nylon – she hesitated for a moment and then replaced the bra from the set with the new pointy one she'd bought for forty crowns – new white stockings, and from the wardrobe she took out her still unworn white dress sewn from a pattern in *Praktische mode*.

Borek shaved twice, made abundant use of Alex's Barberina cologne and Barbus lotion, and looked at his watch, still an hour to go, and he walked over to the window, the pointed roofs thrust themselves into the sky and the sky grips Střížovický Hill between its thighs, the wind couples with beige dust, and the axis of it all is the enormous smokestack of the power plant, like a triumphant phallus spewing clouds of smoke, VICTORY! I'm seeing red again. – Still an hour to go ... if only it would last fifty years.

Jana sprayed herself with Madda's Barberina cologne and worked into the rough skin on her thighs Madda's Barbus lotion, just a touch of vaseline to keep my nipples pliant, and then she got dressed, still an hour to go, and she looked around the women's one-room flat, a narrow cot stuffed with straw, a suitcase beneath the bed, a faucet on the wall, and welded tracks on the floor, today for the last time I'm going out still untouched, Jana once again knelt before her suitcase, took out Father's rabbit's foot, and with it she made the sign of the cross on her chest, may all the good powers be on my side, why aren't I moved right now – instead of tears behind her eyelids she saw red circles – as if bewitched by the white sheet of her cot, upon which it will happen, and it has to be GREAT – Jana tossed the rabbit's foot into her suitcase, along with her old tennis shoes, and she placed her still untouched little slippers made of delicate white leather beneath the bed – still an hour to go ... will all hours to come be ever more beautiful? ...

We went by streetcar to the railroad bridge and then walked up to Větruše, it looks like a fortress overlooking the city, there's a wonderful view, we drank some white wine, danced, and then went for a walk in the woods. We still haven't kissed yet today ...

"I love you, Jana."

"Me too, Borek."

"I want to live with you."

"Yes."

Then suddenly all of last week's worth of kisses, and that was our kissiest week, then all at once it was dark and we were running down the silvery-black roadway tiger-striped with the shadows of tree trunks, running toward town, which was waiting for us like a birthday cake –

Then without a word home and up the stairs, our hands no longer part, and together we open the door of our first room.

The girl has grown into a woman for me   Made of milk, sunlight, grass, and currants   Like bread   Like meat, wine, and flowers   Now it all is just for me

My husband   My only one   My fate   I waited for You and You came   Now we're together   It is for this moment that I defended my purity   Take me as your sacrifice, your prey, your wife   For You alone   I give them gladly

With girls' legs lift the heavy man's body off into weightlessness

But we're together   Think of yourself as well   Your joy doubles mine and returns to You four times greater   My dear   But You're more fabulous than I'd even imagined

I feared this, but it is wonderful   But I prepared for it as well   Everything in Playboy, *and love as well   Together we'll think of a thousand joys   You are the witness of my vertigo and my lust*

Begin to instruct me immediately   As long as it's together, let it be great

Of course You may even bite   All is fair in love and war   I will bite You too, with pleasure   We're together in the jungle   My antelope   Ow! Ow! Ow!   My Swedish she-wolf

It hurts me too, but also gives me pleasure   I'm happy that You sob in my embrace   Ow! Ow! Ow!   But if this were torture we'd already have died from it   But we're more alive   Don't spare me at all   And I won't spare You

We won't start sparing one another for twenty years   Now I march into You as into a conquered city, and I plunder and pillage You entirely

And we shall burn everything down   I want to lap up the white-hot plasma

I need to liquefy   You too   We shall flow together into a burning amalgam   Wish for more   What else   More

I want You forever   I want to live with You   My wife   I want to give You a child   May I?

You may do anything   Give me a child   You are my husband already

(To be continued)

HUSBAND AND WIFE

(A brief overview of twenty years of married life)

Naked, standing in the sea up to their knees, their backs to the European continent, hand in hand, Borek and Jana looked north where, they suspected, beyond the resplendent, watery horizon lay Sweden ... then they turned around and stepped back onto the sandy beach of the *Nacktbadestrand*. The newlywed Trojans' vacation in the Baltic East German resort came to an end. We'll save all year, and next summer we'll definitely go to Sweden ...

Borek hurries home through the August evening one night (after a series of strenuous consultations following the discovery of glass shards beneath her bedsheet, Madda finally capitulated and moved in with her brother, Alex Serafin, from the women's to the men's flat, and Borek moved in with Jana, from the men's to the women's flat of building No. 2000), carefully carrying his briefcase, along with three white gladioluses taken from the flower bed beneath the director's window, flowers for my wife, Jana's washing in the stoppered sink on the wall with water she collected in the morning, she caresses herself with pink, oval-shaped soap, rinses the soap so it will be smooth and foamless, and hangs it to dry in the net tomato bag for Borek to use as soon as he returns from work; when he runs it along his body, may it be a go-between for my kisses.

We ate six fried eggs (fried in vinegar: fat is unhealthy, and the Japanese, for instance, practically don't know what butter is) in five minutes, along with lots of bread, you're still hungry but in the evening you should eat as little as possible, only dumb ninnies stuff their craws at night, and we have better plans this evening than going to sleep. Borek can't get enough of caressing Jana's firm, slender body, and he's even more bewitched by the arousing development of her lovemaking, how resourceful my wife is and what a quick learner –

– how strong and gentle my husband is, Jana rejoices in Borek's embrace, and she quickly discovers ever newer methods to imperceptibly entice Borek's caresses in the desired direction so that she too achieves her climax, in time our bodies will find a mutual language, my husband doesn't need any catnip during lovemaking nor any theater, may he just leave room for my hand at the helm of our love, but I'm in no hurry, after all, Borek, your whole life belongs to me – Borek fell asleep like a baby in mid-sentence, Jana put him to bed like a suckling and stared at him long into the night, she caressed his beautiful head and softly kissed his thin, tanned face, you are my sun, my house, my garden and my field, my god and my house pet, I look up to you, support you, water you, worship you, and I will nurse you, raise you, cultivate you, feed you, suckle you, shoe you, groom you, and you will feed and protect me, what a long time it's been since I went off to sleep at the train station ...

It was Thursday, a completely ordinary day at the end of September, except that the sun had been blazing since morning, as if it were summer's final salute ... From his office Borek called Jana at the lab: "It's such a wonderfully sunny day outside..." "Okay, by the water tank in half an hour–" Jana phoned back, she'd asked Eng. Secký for permission to go to the dentist, and Borek asked Tušl for permission to go to the technical library. We didn't dare ask to go home, we met by the water tank and discovered that all we had was 2.20 crowns, which wasn't even enough for two bus tickets, so we walked three hours to the quarry in the woods, where the water is deep and warm, we swam naked, lay in the sun, which we both love, we can't get enough of its rays, even at the end of summer, we gathered the last soft and wrinkled huckleberries, took bites of raw mushrooms and drank water from the quarry with its thousands of piney-green algae, we banished our hunger with lovemaking in the grass till dark, and then with our wet clothes in our hands we walked back to town along the asphalt, on the edge of the highway we put on our clothes, in the Old Post Office Pub, after lots of haggling, Borek gave in and spent 1.40 crowns on his beer and Jana was left with .60 crowns for her soda and left a twenty-heller tip for the tavern keeper with a gesture that would have made Princess Colloredo-Mannsfeld proud, and we tramped further down the road, Jana made me hide in the ditch and stopped a Saab, but as soon as I came out of hiding, the guy in the Saab lost interest, Jana spat on his radiator, and before he drove away she managed to crack his rear window with a piece of granite, my amazing girl, my fabulous boy, we almost died laughing when the Saab stopped about a hundred meters away and the driver got out to check the damage, he didn't dare do anything else and disappeared in a cloud of dust, and we walked on, the three hours on the road turned out to be a quite pleasant evening walk, and then with just a simple wave Jana finally got a truck to stop, some guys were taking calves to slaughter, and on the way we became such good friends that after the slaughterhouse we went to our local bar, the Corner Pub, Jana danced with everyone and ate three portions of goulash, I had four, and then the five of us played pool, as the place was closing we each took two bottles under our arms and continued at our place till six in the morning, the boys went to snooze in the cab of the truck, and Jana and I went straight to work, this time we took all twenty-five crowns of ours and went straight from work back to the quarry, Jana's wonderfully indestructible, only when we got back home did her eyes begin to close, and on the front steps I picked her up and placed her already asleep on her bed, I was too happy to fall asleep myself, I caressed Jana's brown, sun-bleached hair and carefully kissed her closed eyelids, she softly purred, grabbed my ankle, and held on firmly, probably thinking it was a hand, my little lamb, and I didn't dare move and wake her, my heavenly girl, how many of her twenty years has she been alone among strangers – now she'll be with me forever.

I get up before Borek and put breakfast on the table while he's still exercising, I no longer have time for exercise ... but Borek doesn't do too many push-ups and even cheats on them, my hubby, he doesn't go all the way down, but now he has more important things to worry about, Deputy Abrt has died, Tušl was named as his replacement and Borek as his assistant, he has lots to do and goes to work earlier to be the first one in the office, and comes home later, too ... so sometimes I'm home alone, but there's always something to do since I'm looking after both of us, I've stopped learning new Swedish words, after all, I know about a thousand already – but I keep forgetting them ... Above all, to learn is to repeat.

On All Saints' Day we went to see Jana's mother in Malešice, we arrived on a clattering, jolting little train the likes of which are no longer in service anywhere else, we got there in the afternoon but it was already getting dark, we stood at the grave of Jana's father, Jana knelt and lit the round candle we'd brought with us, shaped like a double rose, her mother knelt beside her and both began to weep, I stood above them facing the grave, deeply moved, finally after many years they once again have a man in the family, and it was as if out of the darkness of the country graveyard a magnificent patriarchal cloak of fur had descended onto my shoulders.

For the first time we slept together in my parents' bedroom, in the bed on which I'd been conceived and where my father died, instead of a dead body there was now the young body of my husband next to me, and a feeling of something eternal and fateful strongly moved me, it subdued me and then made me glow, with a reverent eagerness I kissed my master and that night a passionate longing for servitude brought me for the first time to the climax of my love with my husband, who gives me all of himself and all that is mine.

Jana got so angry that she turned pale and started gasping for air when I inadvertently told her that my cufflinks (sapphires in gray platinum – worth more than all our other belongings put together) were from Zita. Jana picked them up squeamishly, wrapped them in a piece of newspaper, and hid them at the bottom of her suitcase, beneath her dirty underwear. I'll never be able to tell her that my sixty Chinese handkerchiefs are from the same source ... as well as my underwear, suits, and Samsonite suitcase under the bed.

Soon I learned to cook for Borek, after all, ever since I was little I've learned to understand all that the field, garden, and yard provide. On the cutting board I break eggs into a depression of flour, add salt, and knead the dough with the hands I use to caress my husband, I place food in his hands, happy to see his appetite and his sating it, I watch the food in his mouth, between his teeth, how it slides down his throat when he swallows.

Jana's already carrying our child beneath her heart, and I want to protect her ever so gently, my wifey is afraid (but she'd never admit it for anything on earth!) of this long hiatus in our lovemaking, she worries about me (sweetly but unnecessarily) and tries to postpone it just one more night and then another, so I pretend to fall asleep as soon as I lie down and confront her searching looks with closed eyelids ... I'll wait for you, these few weeks won't kill me and if worse comes to worst – Jana noticed it when she was making the bed in the morning, and I was terribly ashamed, "Why didn't you wake me up?" she asked like a teacher interrogating a pupil. "But you were sleeping so beautifully..." I truthfully replied, and Jana responded: "Next time wake me up! Do you understand – I want you to!" Even my shame and my disgrace belong to her now, it's sweet to realize that, her loving care seizes absolutely everything, as if we've already dissolved in one another.

Now nothing belongs exclusively to either one of us alone, everything belongs to the other, how deep is the slave's joy to be absolutely possessed – and the joy of the slaveholder to possess absolutely. To know that the joy the slaveholder gets from his unlimited power is further increased by the evident joy the slave gets from his subordination ... to know absolutely everything about each other.

We walk toward each other along the tracks on the floor, they're still here, at first the factory administration didn't want to have them removed because they say our cohabitation in the former (it's our flat now!) women's flat is wrongful, illicit, and illegal, after Borek was appointed Tušl's deputy and in view of his ever more powerful position in the factory, it should be easy to arrange in a single afternoon, we're expecting a child, after all, and need an apartment, the tracks on our floor help make a good argument, WE WANT AN APARTMENT – and we keep running up against the icy indifference of the administration. "Two types of people inhabit this planet," says Jana, "those with an apartment and those without. And between them a barbed-wire fence ... Ow, when I think that soon there will be three of us in this room–" It's simply a provocation when one person has everything and another nothing, why does an old widower like Gráf who now just has a son (locked up, of course, seven years for murder) need a three-room apartment on the second floor, and a four-room riverside villa (with a glassed-in veranda) on top of that? Jana needs to wash clothes and when she turns on the faucet above the sink on the wall: a few rusty drops, rattling, and that's it. "Old Gráf is showering again, when is he going to kick the bucket? – my wife naturally seethes, I grab a poker and stand beside the water pipe, one arm raised – I freeze, I once used this water pipe to telegraph – – "I'm going to have to bathe the baby in the basement–" my wife cries out, and I'm already laying into the pipe blow after blow, metal on metal, let his lordship in the shower take notice of our poverty, Borek delivers stroke after stroke to the pipe, until his arm weakens and slackens.

They finally put us on the waiting list for housing, but only after innumerable reminders and the birth of our child (*1st year of marriage*). It's a girl – 4.25 kilograms of live weight, Borek had his way and we named her Yveta.

Jana won't go to work for two more months, and it suits her wonderfully. She gets plenty of sleep and plays all day with the baby, now she cooks fabulously and everything in butter (I got another raise) because I've fallen in love with the sweet smell of its disintegration as well as with its taste. "Fat is bad for you," my wife warns, shaking her finger at me jokingly. "The Japanese, for instance, practically don't know what butter is," I comically complete her beloved slogan, and we sink our German silver spoons (12 pieces for 360 crowns) into the omelets resting on delicate brand-name porcelain plates decorated with a sweet bird motif, from Jana's dowry (inherited from her grandfather, who won a hundred and twenty-five thousand crowns in the national lottery), then chocolate cake with whipped cream and a bottle of Green Valtellina wine.

I managed to find some large Bulgarian grapes with oval-shaped pits and hurried home, it's a beautiful late September day (like the day last year when we skipped out of work and walked to the quarry in the woods ...), making love in a bed is better than in the grass, put Yvetka to sleep, and already I'm opening the door impatiently, like a lover – the wife is sitting at the table wrinkling her brow over dozens of envelopes with money in them: there's a bill from the Insurance Office ... It's not that we don't have it – altogether in the envelopes we have well over two thousand – but here every crown has its firmly assigned place, for two hours we take hundreds and fifties from the envelopes "Sweden" and "Carpet" and put them in the "Television" and "Other" envelopes so those ninety crowns would some-how be available ... Finally we had to take them out of the "Sweden" envelope, we didn't make it there this year anyway, but spent a beautiful fourteen days at Lake Svět near Třeboň for only eleven hundred crowns.

I had to let my hair grow long, and now Jana's holding my head in the sink with soap bubbles, washing me like a dog, I feel her warm, wet hands and snap my teeth at them. Borek finally let his hair grow out properly instead of just that coarse fur on his head, after all he's not a little boy anymore, I washed it with shampoo and now can't stop caressing it, his hair is so soft, smooth as silk.

I run home from work through the snowstorm, for 380 crowns we bought a Club 1 electric heater with a fire-brick lining, in the basement we have thirty meters of first-category gray brick from the Columbus Pit, the room's as warm as a hot spring and I immediately take off my shirt, you need science and art to heat effectively with bricks. Borek shovels out the ashes, then opens the upper feeder door and with the poker and shovel he gathers the individual chips that haven't fallen through the grate, he makes a horrible mess, but I look forward to seeing my husband bent over the fire, how it illuminates his bare chest with red flashes of fire.

Little Yvetka is already more than a year old (*2nd year of marriage*) and is already sitting up in her crib and can unfailingly tell the difference between Mama and Papa. I'm sorry I can't nurse her anymore, yes, her teeth really hurt, but when I remember her little fingers on my breasts ... I'm already back at work, I don't know what to do first, and now Swedish is out of the picture for good, we also figured out that we wouldn't be be able to afford Sweden this year either, moreover we started a new money envelope, "A" (automobile) with an initial deposit of 20 crowns. Our vacation at Lake Svět in Třeboň was wonderful, the swimming was definitely better than in the North Sea, the water here's so warm ... and the magical walks in the evening along the embankment lined with ancient oaks, I fell in love with the white tomb of the Sternberg princes, and every day Borek put away three portions of fried carp.

Borek walks to work in the morning and with every step glances at his shoes made of perforated imitation chamois for 59 crowns, its rubber soles are invaluable, the shoes have lasted two whole years and the longer I wear them, the longer my new, still unworn black calfskin moccasins will stay at home in the closet. An anti-Gráf contingent has formed among the factory technicians – Mr. Gráf has quite a few difficulties right now – and I've earned myself a solid position among them.

On January 1st, Jana started her new position in the pricing department, after Jolana Tušlová was promoted to Director of Invoicing. I was glad to leave the dilly-dallying of the laboratory, I'd never make director, and besides the scientists in the laboratory, there's room only for assistants – in the elegant office on the second floor of our White House I got a beautiful desk with eight drawers all to myself – in the bottom one I put the rabbit's foot Papa gave me. There's plenty of work here, but I like it, on the very first day our company lawyer and dandy Dr. Smetana came and introduced himself, you should see his sideburns – but he's handsome and he's going out with Evka, who's getting a divorce because of him and who's sleeping at his place. I'll be working with Dr. Smetana.

Jana likes making love best on Sunday mornings, it's her form of exercise, sweet as cocoa with whipped cream for breakfast, it suits her tremendously, I let her frolic all over me, she's already caught up with me in everything and in some things is way ahead, I'd go back to sleep afterwards, but Yvetka's already waking up, my sweet little girl, she wants her papa, and I teach her to walk, doctors recommend you don't hold the child by the hand, but only reach it out to her so she can hold on to it herself, an emotional relationship is thereby formed, Yvetka holds me firmly by the hand and bravely takes her steps between the tracks.

She's growing like a weed (*3rd year of marriage*) and we decide to pierce her ears. Jana sterilizes the needle and thread in boiling water, I keep it boiling, and Borek looks terrified, I tell him to place Yvetka on the table and hold her firmly, I take out the needle and thread and approach Yveta's earlobe, the girl screams as if she's been murdered, Father is just as afraid and can't hold her down, come on, you're a man, aren't you? I look at Jana and feel kind of woozy because it's like when you kill a carp, Jana approaches with the needle, pierces her ear, and the blood flows, Yvetka writhes and screams in terror, after all, we're standing over her like murderers – we're doing it out of love for you, our little daughter. So we won't have to buy earrings (for health reasons only expensive metals can be put in children's ears – silver at the least, better gold, and the best, of course, is platinum), we've had my old cufflinks remade into earrings (sapphires in gray platinum), I'd rather not mention to Jana the remaining bit of platinum, so I hide it in a secret box with some strands of Zita's hair.

We already have 2,300 crowns in envelope "A", and so we open another bank account with it, someday we'll go to Sweden, first class – the Bulgarian sea is warmer and on the very first day we got sunburned, which had never happened to us before, we carefully trudged back, naked, up to the 7th floor of the prefab Hotel Glarus (with a view of a bare hillside: a 150-crown discount per person), rubbed each other with cold cream, and hissed with pain. On the last day we took a ride on a hydrofoil, *The Comet*, which travels at 62 km an hour above the water, we'd been looking forward to this ride our whole vacation, but to tell the truth, after an hour it's no longer much fun and Jana threw up on the rear deck.

Jana is more and more nervous every day and is beginning to show a tendency toward hysteria, of course she's up to her ears in work and all they do is keep promising us an apartment (*4th year of marriage*), but it's not my fault, is it, another of Jana's hysterical scenes, and so I slam the door loudly and stay in town until around midnight.

Borek came home drunk at two-thirty, it wasn't the first time I was home alone, but it was the first time I'd been abandoned, I felt like doing something with Evka, but I couldn't leave Yvetka alone and I didn't want to sleep, so I drank a bottle of wagtail that we'd brought back from Bulgaria, in the morning, at work, Evka felt sorry for me and told me in detail what a wonderful lover Dr. Smetana was.

I bought Jana ten red roses and we promised each other it wouldn't happen again, but love without anger isn't loving. Then I went to buy some wine, in the Corner Pub all they had was cheap vinegar, and so I went to town and bought three bottles of Gewurztraminer, a delicious and refined wine, and our lovemaking blazed up like a forgotten jewel, Jana got me to agree to one of her positions, which she begged for and which is the only one that completely satisfies her.

Only in bed did Borek and I become completely reconciled, which they say is a tried and true method, but isn't it a little inadequate? – I'll have a scar from this forever, how can a man leave his wife and child over such a little thing?! – Even for just one night. Borek tried everything to make it up, I was touched – roses, wine, kisses, and then at night … we react to each other's slightest movement, sigh, or whisper, our lovemaking has taken on the taste of bread, it's perfect, simple, and completely satiating – but it's not the man's ability or even the woman's, it's a mutual, thankful obligation.

Praises be! We got an apartment ... finally. Lately we'd come to doubt so strongly that we'd ever get one, we showed up at the new building at five in the morning, four hours before the building inspectors (just after we got there, more future tenants began to trickle in, and we counted with horror to see if there were more than thirty-six and wondered if we should take the apartment by force), the housing inspection committee issued everyone keys, and when they came to our apartment to ask us to return them because they said they wanted to replace the tiles that were bulging – we know these tricks of theirs – Borek held on to the keys until his knuckles turned white, we conducted the committee out the door and locked it behind them. We have two rooms, a kitchen, bathroom, balcony ... we moved in that very day and the first night we slept on borrowed air mattresses.

Jana's been sitting in the tub for two hours now, this is the first time in my life I've ever had my own bathroom, at home I always had to go to the laundry room in the yard and bathe in cold water, this is a different kettle of fish, but Borek ruined my soap, he pierced it with a magnetic spike so it would stay on its metal holder, but now the lather isn't very good, and no sooner did I buy Yveta a little soap bunny than she bit off his ears and tail and started throwing up soap bubbles.

Borek took over half the room for his "study," and it wasn't a week before it all turned into a nightmare, on the other side of the thin wall the neighbors installed a television, and now opera programs and advice to farmers blare into Borek's English lessons, the doors won't close, the toilet seat is broken, and the tiles are bulging like waves in a stormy sea – those workmen are a bunch of beasts, instead of working they lounge around with bottles of beer, a horse-whipping's what they deserve, and on top of everything you have to give them money – who gives us money?! – and we do more and get less than these geldings! – we have to be nice to them and fear them at the same time.

We can't keep the baby all to ourselves anymore, she has a new friend, Blanka, and she's always dragging her over to our place, the sweet little girls pull their pants down, whisper words to each other such as "doo-doo" and "butt" and laugh naughtily, Yveta's stubborn, hard-headed, and full of fury, and we have less and less time for her (*5th year of marriage*), fortunately we have Grandma, but she just spoils the child ... in our new apartment we have less space than in our old, and we trip over each other and get on one another's nerves, a regular zoo.

I'm waiting on the square for Jana, we're going to buy carpeting and a bathroom rug, it's going to be great shoving the carpet into the streetcar and then moving all the furniture to put the carpet down, a wonderful program for the afternoon ... and then on top of everything it seems the streetcars have stopped running – how long am I going to have to hang around here?! It's March and there's something in the air, and there's something in the gait of the women ... perhaps the streetcar will never come. Maybe they're not running because of an accident, with a bus perhaps, three victims and among them ... J. Trojanová. That would be ... horrible, of course, what about Yvetka ... she could live with Grandma in Malešice, the apartment ... only if you weren't tied to this stupid town and that stupid factory, I'm not even thirty yet ... The streetcars have started running again and Jana arrived on number sixteen, apparently she had to redo something at work, but I have more work than you "and I left it behind since we agreed..." "But it was only twenty minutes–" "Twenty minutes? I've been hanging around here for an hour!" ... It took us all evening to put down the new carpet, Jana vindictively cleaned out the corners of the room, which we usually don't even notice, just so I had to stand there waiting for her like an ox.

We celebrated the end of the quarter and then Evka dragged the whole department out to a wine cellar, Borek was in Prague again, he might as well move there, and so I called Grandma and asked her to watch the baby, I said I'd come home around nine (Borek will get home at nine-thirty), I borrowed two hundred crowns from the "Sweden" envelope and showed off a bit, Dr. Smetana was wonderful, he taught me to dance the letkis, and after each dance he kissed my hand, and then even during the dance – oh God, when's the last time I laughed so much? ...

They call her Niky, she's nineteen and works in the export department of the Prague headquarters, we met in the elevator, which stopped between the fourth and fifth floors with us and the general director in it, the director got upset and his bald head turned red, Niky made donkey's ears over his shiny, red bald spot and we both died laughing later when we talked about it at the Piarist wine cellar, Niky dances the waltz wonderfully, she took me to the Golden Jug, where we drank fantastic iced Mikulov sauvignon, with her long nails Niky brushes her hair from her forehead and closes her eyes when kissing, she has a tiny, perfect studio flat in an experimental building in Líbeň, a mirror above her bed and a panther made of black plastic, she kicks off her shoes at the door and approaches me naked but for a smile and tall boots made of soft black leather.

So I guess it's divorce, it's high time to admit I was wrong about Borek, after all, he left me and Yvetka two years ago – how can a man leave his wife and child?! – and that time I let myself be hoodwinked by his lies. I would forgive Borek anything, but not unfaithfulness. I asked Dr. Smetana to write me up an application for divorce, at home I packed Borek's things in a suitcase and left it in the hallway, outside the locked door.

Jana packed my suitcase herself, I found it in the hallway, at least there won't be any distasteful scenes, I look at the locked (Jana left the key in the lock, on the inside) door of our apartment and feel bitter that after six years (*6th year of marriage*) I haven't earned anything more than some underwear and socks, Zita Gráfová was more generous ... what kind of love is it that can't forgive ... it was too easy for Jana to throw me out of the apartment, an apartment I got for her, that's all right, I've managed to get several places and I'll get more, it's never too late to start all over ... and thirty-one's just the right time. Freedom! Thank you, Niky, for showing me how petty and pitiful my wife is, if I hadn't met you, Niky, I would have lived the rest of my life in self-delusion. With her long nails Niky brushes her hair from her forehead and closes her eyes when kissing, she says I can live with her, and she takes me insatiably – her predatory nails on my neck – until it takes my breath away – how sweet it is to be destroyed – then she turns her back to me and falls right to asleep. Completely empty, as if eaten up and sucked dry, I stand naked by the window, I shiver from the cold and look out at the unfamiliar street of an unfamiliar city, suddenly I feel terribly alone in an unfathomable stone sea of buildings, from our window at home you can see the green Střížovický Hill, and right at the end of the street there's a line of trees, right before Christmas Eve supper I take Yvetka to the first tree, she puts her arms around it and calls in her sweet, hoarse little voice: "Come, Santa Claus, come to our house tonight..." what will Christmas be like in this tiny prefab cage, once again to live in a single room and start all over as a chem. lab technician, something I thankfully left long ago, to make love with Niky and live with her, those are two very different things – won't it be the same with Niky in six years, or even a lot worse and a lot sooner than six years? – moving from one cage to another, I saw freedom for just ninety minutes out the window of the afternoon train from Ústí Main Station to Prague Main Station, to leave is easy, harder is to hold on to what you've conquered, but maybe it's worth it, of course it's worth it, after all, I loved Jana a hundred times more than I love Niky, and what's left of it all ... and what's left of me? There's still something and there's still a great deal of Jana! ... but after all, I betrayed her! –

I dragged myself and my suitcase through the concrete plains of this dirty, empty, unfamiliar city with a million cracked facades and lousy public transportation, and then I waited for the night mail-train on a bench in the train station with some horrible individuals ... as horrible as I am: the cast out. I made it back to Ústí at four-thirty in the morning, and since five I've been waiting on the landing in front of a white door with my name on it ... I'll never forget that hour beneath the white gate of my family's fortress, which had fallen out of sight.

The chain scraped and the white gate moved – I remember with horror how I lived through those moments in front of Zita's door, on the very first day I put a chain lock on the door of our new apartment – the door opened a little and a dark crack widened between the door and the white wood of the door jamb.

"What else do you want?" whispered Jana.

"I want you to forgive me."

Jana slammed the door, and I could hear her walking back and forth inside, then someone talking, she's saying something to Grandma, and then Yveta's rejoicing: "Daddy's here!" And after a long time the white gate stirred once again and opened, Jana walked past me silently, and I said: "Jana! Please..." Jana left without a word and I stole inside like a murderer. It's never too late to start over again –

So my husband's returned. I took a long detour to work today, Dr. Smetana was already waiting for me at the office with a closely typed sheet of paper – the application for my divorce from Eng. B. Trojan, and I read about my marriage to the aforesaid and saw the list of horrors I lived through those six years, but what we lived though wasn't all horrible ... Dr. Smetana explained to me in detail how to answer the questions of an intimate nature, as I kept giving him more and more details he gradually got excited and insisted on hearing more, so that by afternoon he was explaining more to me in his apartment ... "You sure are dumb..." Evka said to me when she found out I burned Dr. Smetana's sheet of paper in the ashtray right before his eyes. It's as if they were feeding off the laying bare of our life ... I don't speak at all with Borek because I know that hurts him the most, first he begged, then he fawned, later he got angry and went into a rage, now he just groans – I want to punish him firmly, and so I remain silent and sense how my persistent, icy silence tortures him more than if I were to pierce him with burning nails, I'll wait until the one who betrayed me bleeds to death and dies in pain, and then in his place my husband will return. It's never too late to start over again –

We live next to one another cautiously and anxiously, as if we were made of the thinnest, most breakable glass, we're starting to speak to one another in the shortest possible sentences, on the most unavoidable occasions, and only on the most ordinary topics, every potential possibility for disagreement we avoid by a nautical mile before it can ever come to pass, and often it's funny how out of consideration each of us crawls back into his shell like a snail afraid it might bother the other snail with something. Fortunately we have the child, Yvetka's delightful, and Grandma conscientiously cares for her, and then we have a lot of practical matters to attend to, we've definitely decided to transfer the contents of the "Sweden" envelope to the "A" envelope, we already have over twelve thousand crowns saved for our car, thanks to Grandma we spend our evenings peacefully, each in his own room, Borek's already mastered English and has started learning French, I learned English in less than a year (*7th year of marriage*) studying evenings and taking an evening course at the factory, and I also want to learn French, it's such a wonderful language, how many letters it takes to make the simplest of sounds, and I'd love someday to read in the original language – now, when the amount of my work has begun to lessen – the authors I've discovered: Stendhal, Maupassant, France, Colette. Jana cooks wonderfully, better and better and more and more, before supper an aperitif is now essential to whet the appetite, we indulge in heavy fatty meats and spend more on wine than we used to spend on our entire livelihood (each of us got a raise), for breakfast I have buttered rolls, which I cover in even more butter before I eat them, those poor Japanese don't know what they're missing, after all it's quite pleasant and appropriate to destroy oneself.

On the first free Saturday of August we were home alone, the sun was beating down so fiercely we stayed inside and pulled down the shutters, Borek was in his room dozing over a French novel with a yellow cover, I took a three-hour bath and then just walked around the apartment, the heat outside was getting worse and so I walked around naked, the heat set my nerves on edge and finally I went into Borek's room. I look over the open book at the white skin of my wife, why did you come in here, dear, and I take my time getting up and going over to her, we'll let her walk around barefoot till she gets tired of it, like an animal that's fallen into our trap, I'll tear you apart, when I feel like it, when you beg me to, and then I make love to my wife cruelly and mercilessly as if I wanted to stab her to death, and I don't let up until her hoarse moaning ceases. Then we took a short nap, Jana cut Borek's toenails, Borek took the laundry out to the drying room for Jana, we wolfed down four bacon omelets, raised hell till morning in the Svět Pub and got wonderfully drunk, then we slept through a monotonously sunny Sunday (we agreed that we were already looking forward to winter) with aspirin and closed shutters. Now and then you have to destroy yourself a little.

Seven – is she already that old? – Yvetka's a bright little child and we're really glad she can amuse herself now (*8th year of marriage*). I ran into Niky in Prague: in two years she's managed to get married and divorced and smells like a brewery. Television has started to bore us, we buy lots of books, we got season tickets to the opera and set up a stereo system in the apartment, before bed we always listen to some hot jazz and drink a glass of whiskey on the rocks.

At the factory Borek's aiming for the top (*9th year of marriage*). An interesting game is unfolding: Jan Hurník, Gráf's deputy, has been transferred to the Prague headquarters and is taking his deputy, Bogan Tušl, with him. After all these years together, Bogan and I have become very close – a valuable position in the Prague headquarters. The new director, Landa, is wonderful: he suggested right off we use the familiar form of address. Caha became the economic deputy in accordance with his position on the ladder of succession: weak and lukewarm, like dishwater. Now I go to Prague regularly. I'm systematically strengthening my relationship with Tušl, and it seems to be working. I talked Jana into allowing herself to be elected to the factory administration. I find my wife a capable coworker (*10th year of marriage*), she organized a women's corner at the factory, which got her some decent publicity, and she managed to get on the local departmental administration. In opposition to Caha, I pushed through my idea of continuous large-capacity driers. Caha tried to go over my head. I brought all the documentation to Prague and won Tušl over to my side. Caha's been transferred to Jihlava. I've become the youngest deputy director in the northern Bohemia region.

My husband lives only for the company now (*11th year of marriage*). I took an unpaid vacation: my nerves have been giving me some trouble lately. Grandma died. Yveta's transferred her affections elsewhere. In some matters it's difficult to understand her. Today's schools seem pretty repulsive to me. At the spa I met a professor of literature who thought Alphonse Daudet was a swimming champion. What do we pay these people for? I feel weary. Best of all I like to be alone. I read … now I'm reading Virginia Woolf. At the spa I spent a whole day reading a poem by Paul Claudel. I've come to adore walks in the rain.

I asked Jana to take pork off our menu for good and to replace butter with oil (the Japanese, for instance, practically don't know what butter is).

I ignore my wife's mocking looks and try to eat as little as possible at supper. After starchy foods and after white wine I have to take a tablet of Gastrogel (*12th year of marriage*). The ideal supper is a glass of good cognac. Jana's become neurotic. Yveta's too much for her. Sometimes I take Yveta for a walk, the girl confides in me ... I'd almost say she worships me – unfortunately I have less and less time for her. We bought a car, a Škoda 1000-MB (a thousand small pains for forty thousand crowns). Now there's really nothing else to save for ... in Sweden it'll probably be freezing and the water cold. Now we both long only for the south ...

Our connubial love has become plump and mature: sexual camaraderie (*13th year of marriage*). A conspiratorial alliance against external enemies (former allies: that's how we met, after all). Lovemaking: cheerful, economical, appreciative, grateful, rational, comfortable, healthy, apologetic, thoughtful – TO WALLOW IN A THICKET OF THORNS – and its fruit like an apple from a well-tended tree, hoed, manured, watered, and pruned, protected against insects by a lime coating and against rodents by wire netting, its fruit large, plump, a rich color, smooth, shiny, sweet, satisfying, perfect ... unlike what occurs in nature. In California they say the apples are packed right on the tree ... The reason the Czech apple has conquered the Swiss market against a thousand famous and perfect varieties is a curious one: they sometimes find worms in them ... living proof of their non-industrial origin. Conjugal sex after so many years ... familiar: it no longer plays a very big role. There are other more aesthetic and ... cleaner things. Culture for instance. It's best for each to go to bed at a different time and thereby avoid the enervating irritation and expenditure of energy ... for the sake of our health. And when it does happen – then destroy oneself in an orderly fashion.

An interesting situation has come up: Landa, the director in Prague, is fading away. The men at headquarters are writing him off. I spent a happy three hours with the headquarters' librarian ... a slender, tanned blonde (*14th year of marriage*), sexy in an athletic sort of way ... she sat facing me on the table top. Then Tušl was pissed that he had to hunt me down over the loudspeaker. It was about something fairly important: the ministry wants to invade our jurisdiction via the National Committee. I assured the people at headquarters that I'd hold on to Cottex. Apparently Landa was at the Minister's and is writing up a memorandum for the Presidium. Landa never did excel at assessing situations.

Our fifteenth wedding anniversary: Borek was very solicitous (roses, champagne, jewelry, etc.) and then right after dinner he had to rush off to Prague. I was left alone with a barely eaten cake (Borek had only a thin slice and then three tablets of Gastrogel). I drank up the bottle of champagne almost out of a sense of duty, it was a bit too sweet for my taste, but I fixed that with some cognac. I played Debussy on the record player: "Reflections in the Water." I'm thirty-five years old. Borek's forty. Do we still love each other? It doesn't matter anymore. Yveta's fourteen: her breasts are already showing. I'm afraid they've already felt the touch of a boy's hand. Of course she doesn't breathe a word of it to me, there was just a hint of it in something she said to Borek ... daughters always gravitate toward their fathers. Borek reproaches me for not raising her at all. It drives me crazy. And besides, Borek tolerates everything she does. A really simple way of raising her. And lazy (*15th year of marriage*).

Director Landa's fallen off his pedestal, and cracked a couple of vertebrae: he'll be working as a technician in Bruntál for barely two thousand a month ... no tree grows to the sky. The provisional running of the factory has been entrusted to Drtílek, but this is only temporary. Duda, that is, Eng. Paroubek, is supposed to arrive and assume the post of director. Of course Duda is no specialist, I found out he didn't even graduate from a technical college ... Apparently Paroubek had some sort of screw-up in Kralupy. I inconspicuously sent Střelák, my man, to see him. Střelák brought back some interesting information. I informed Tušl. I succeeded in burying Duda's project of continuous large-capacity driers. Duda was furious, he thought poor old Drtílek had done it and reduced his bonus ... but that was a *faux pas* that is simply not done in our circles ... All this amuses the men at headquarters. I've become friends with Duda. Duda's made a fool of himself once and for all. Paroubek's been caught with his hand in the director's fund – that penny-pincher was buying American cigarettes on his expense account and his son was selling them to a waiter! Dr. Sekanina will be the new director – but can a bankrupt lawyer really run our firm? I make the rounds of the Ústí city, district, and local committees. It turns out that Sekanina is Tušl's man. But the new general director, Blumenfeld, has brought with him a new first secretary, Tušl's now just an ordinary deputy ... The men at headquarters are looking at me with interest (*16th year of marriage*). Tušl's launched a grandiose operation through the deputy chairman. General Director Blumenfeld has been named ambassador to Malaysia, and our everlasting (because he hasn't done anything for years) Jan Hurník has returned to us and occupied the vacated throne. Tušl has once again become First Deputy and de facto head of the concern. He'll want to staff Cottex with his own men and will select Sekanina without hesitation. There are those at headquarters who would prefer me. I decide to undertake a dramatic step: I arrive in Prague in the middle of the night and ring at Tušl's villa. From the window I hear Tušl's exasperated voice ... he comes to open the door extremely pissed. An insane moment: I suddenly realize that in the next hour I can destroy myself for good ... and it suddenly seems attractive: to rid myself of all this crap ... I find it hard to control myself and I follow Tušl up the stairs. The dice are cast ... Sixes.

Borek's become the director of Cottex. Now he works well into the night. We both take Librium (*17th year of marriage*). It's not appropriate for the director's wife to work for her husband's company. In two months I'll replace the wife of Armokov's director on the local Czechoslovak-Soviet Friendship Committee. I'll have a car at my disposal – the third one in our family. Two months at home ... I lie around and stare out the window. I've already read all our books ... well, not all of them. Some I'll never read ... I look at their spines behind the glass: we already know everything about each other. I have well-founded suspicions Yveta lost her innocence even before her first dancing lesson. Borek bought her a platinum ring with a sapphire (to go with her earrings), and he bought me a stole made of silver fox. I'm sitting in the first row of the orchestra and sense unfriendly eyes upon me. Naturally they envy us ... but their hatred is so strong. – We're going to move into the director's apartment, these two rooms haven't been enough for us for a long time now.

Jana's modernizing our apartment on the second floor, and I've renovated the entire building No. 2000: central heating, bathrooms, gas, parquet floors in all the rooms. In every one-room flat the same standard furniture, a rug, curtains, radio, a vase made of stained glass, and a reproduction of Renoir's *Déjeuner sur l'herbe* (*18th year of marriage*). Vigorous reforms at the factory. People are looking at me distrustfully. I'm totally alone ... the main thing is not to look frightened. – Technology Deputy Ruml has been going to Prague suspiciously often. My dependable Střelák has been rendering me invaluable services. Ruml has secretly met with Tušl. In the reorganization of Cottex I abolish the positions of technology deputy and economic deputy and replace them with my single deputy, Střelák. Yveta's not living a good life. It's as if we neglected her upbringing ... but now it's too late. The stress is continually growing. I've bought a small sailboat, some sports ... essential relaxation.

Borek and I went to look at our new house on the river. With our new boat, it became essential. Our good Frantík Střelák obligingly arranged the purchase for us. Former director Gráf used to live here, completely alone ... in the last few years they say he almost never went out. When he was signing the paperwork in our apartment, Evžen Gráf softly chuckled: apparently the painting *Rhythmic Progression* (a relentless geometric figure of vertical lines with a small black square in the lower right-hand corner) belongs to him. It was here when we arrived and of course we'd be glad to return it to Dr. Gráf ... the old gentleman decorously refuses. Borek offers him a tour of the factory Dr. Gráf directed twenty years ago ... the old man decorously refuses, he even refuses a glass of cognac and in a soft voice asks for a straight glass of water. He barely wet his lips with it. He even refused to let us give him a ride home ... he left on foot, limping along on a cane. The old gentleman ... died not long after in Prague: at a ripe old age and completely exhausted. Exhausted and disgusted with the world –

We celebrated Yveta's becoming an adult (a cake with eighteen candles, white roses, champagne, jewelry, etc.) and she was overjoyed when Borek arranged for her a holiday trip to Sweden ... she returned disappointed (*19th year of marriage*). We spent ten days driving through the south of France: Avignon, Menton, Monte Carlo, Cap d'Antibes ... nice but rather exhausting. And then a week in Tunis ... we saw people practically naked, living on literally nothing. They were begging, but there was something in their eyes, something atavistic, wild ... arousing in a startlingly way ... even though we were warned against it, Borek gave a franc to a small girl, and suddenly we were surrounded by a hoard that almost tore us apart –

The most beautiful month of the year is October. We're alone together for a whole day in the Krušné Mountains. The mountain meadows ... we both love them. The sun rises out of the grass. The grass is almost like metal, red at the tips as if burned by a bloody wind. We leave the car and walk for a good hour. Exhausted and intoxicated by the late-afternoon sun ... In the scenic Mosquito Tower restaurant we had iced juice and pineapple. And as soon as we got home, even before showering, tall glasses of gin. While drinking them we ate the entire contents of our pantry – tomorrow morning we'll feel awful. It's just to stifle the sadness ... but the sadness cries out louder and louder. Strangle it ... it strangles us. A stack of frenzied music on the record player. After an eternally long time we once again want to be together ... Is it out of love, need, or desperation? We approach each other: two craven heavyweight fighters stepping into the ring once again. But there's nothing to fight about. The result is agreed upon beforehand: we both will lose. And tomorrow we'll lie around all day as if slain (*20th year of marriage*). The final thrill: to thoroughly destroy oneself.

LET'S MAKE LOVE NOT WAR

A blue Renault with a plush tiger in the rear window slammed on the brakes in the Cottex courtyard. Borek and Jana Trojan have come with their daughter Yveta and their neighbor in building No. 2000 Miss Broňa Berková to an evening celebration in the factory dining room. The car doors slammed in animated conversation and the four approached the festooned, illuminated entrance. The plush tiger in the locked car looked on sleepily.

The hall was filled with festively dressed people, clean-shaven men in fresh white shirts, women with shining eyes – laughter and joy, and flowers everywhere: in the little vases on each table, in the two rows of flower pots around the orchestra, in the women's hair ... The electrician Alex Serafin tried several times in vain to kick up his usual rumpus, but was finally shoved into a remote corner, where he proceeded to get drunk straight from the bottle and fall asleep on the floor.

A young engineer by the name of Dominik Neuman respectfully bowed to Borek, his director, and Jana, and asked their daughter Yveta to dance, receiving three smiles in return, Yveta impatiently jumped up from the table and the beautiful young couple sailed onto the floor.

"Who's that?" Jana asked her husband.

"Our new cyberneticist. Nice couple, eh?"

"They look good together ... very good..." And Borek and Jana watched their daughter dance with the nice young man.

Dominik gently held Yveta by the fingers and around the waist and, thrilling all over, he looked at her golden hair and pale skin and the blue veins that showed through it, he inhaled her scent and as he spun around he returned the smiles of her kindhearted parents, he led his princess in circles around the floor further and further, all the way up to the music ... A handsome boy and very nice, Yveta was jubilant in his soft embrace, and if he keeps being so nice we'll make love and it will be beautiful ...

In Teo's room on the first floor of building No. 2000, Teo and Iša, his thirty-three-year-old son, stood silently facing one another. Avoiding his father's fixed gaze, Iša ran his eyes over the white walls and cloudy mass of bedding piled up to the window and shuddered at the sight of the long whip made of hippopotamus skin with its handle of hardened wicker, which hung on the sill of the enormous eight-paned window, and when his eyes came to rest on the metal pole two meters long, standing ready by the window frame, an agonized moan escaped from his lips. Teo put a hand on his son's shoulder, Iša bowed his head and walked from the room into the street of beige drifts of desert dust.

To the delight of everyone in the hall, ladies' choice was announced. Dominik came to ask Yveta's mother, Jana, onto the floor, Borek smiled and bid them a nice dance, then Broňa Berková emerged from the crowd and cheerfully asked Borek. The orchestra launched into a polka and Broňa placed her arm lightly around Borek's neck.

The newlyweds Břetislav and Jitka Trakl glanced at each other and hand in hand ran from the hall, hurried across the courtyard and down the evening street to building No. 2000, then ran up the stairs to the third floor. They were already kissing when they locked the door of the women's one-room flat behind them, they turned on the light for just a second and immediately switched it off again, and their joyful laughter and ardent caresses resounded into the darkness.

A wave of excitement went through the hall when Iša, Teo's son, entered accompanied by Madda Serafinová. A successful and well-known first-class prostitute in Ústí, Madda looked fabulous at forty, thanks to the best cosmeticians, masseuses, and dressmakers in town as well as tennis, badminton, yachting, and frequent trips to her beloved Karlovy Vary and to the sea with her rich lovers – all this she had suddenly and sensationally renounced for Iša, her final and purely platonic great love ... Iša's entrance aroused tension, excitement, and fear, because the town had never had a prophet within its walls and at this critical time – THINK NOT THAT I AM COME TO DESTROY THE LAW, said Iša, BUT TO FULFIL.

And with moist eyes Dáša Zíbrtová looked past her sleeping Alex, toward Iša, and suddenly recalled her former love for Julda Serafin – those bright, long lost days when I felt so pure and so happy, when I was capable of finding joy in something as simple as the morning sunlight on the blinds or simply in the fact that it was morning, in the dusty leaves of acacias, in the meowing of a cat, in the rusty wire fence, in the smell of asphalt, and even in the dust itself upon the road, and at the same time I loved not only the children at the old rectory but their impossible parents as well, and my angry Nurse Jandová and my butcher patients at the slaughterhouse, and even those malingerers who care only about building their country houses on the Elbe while collecting sick pay ... I actually *loved* all of them ... and maybe that's why I was so happy then ... And Dáša Zíbrtová looked up at Iša hoping that perhaps he could help her renew that *miracle* ...

The anniversary celebration came off beautifully. The factory dining room was filled with music, and it was as if everyone had forgotten their quarrels and contentions, they laughed together, danced and embraced, and the hall resounded with crescendoing song ... now Dominik danced only with Yveta, in an ethereal embrace, and they kissed each other with their eyes, Borek danced with Jana and then again with Broňa ... Smiling, Jana passed them on the dance floor, delighting in the sight of her husband, her daughter, and her daughter's gentle suitor ... And emotion rose in Borek's throat as he listened to Broňa's laughter against his cheek, bewitched he circled the smooth dance floor in amazement, how much joy there is in people, and he was happy with them all ... like a very young boy.

Then when night descended, everyone exited the hall and dispersed through the dark courtyard to their homes. The group approached the parked blue Renault laughing, Jana and Borek got in the front seat and Yveta in the back, and a merry argument broke out whether to give Dominik or Broňa Berková a ride – with a sudden feeling of intense happiness, an exhilarated Broňa was inhaling the fresh night air with her face upturned toward the stars, how wonderful it is to live on this earth of ours ... enthusing just like a young girl. Then through the darkness an awakened Alex Serafin suddenly stormed up to the car, gave Broňa's thigh a fleshy pinch, and shoved his way into the car. The engine blared to life, Broňa and Dominik remained standing on the pavement, and from the rear window of the car the plush tiger bared its teeth at them – then with the car's sudden jolt it started rocking as if preparing to pounce.

CONQUERORS

Bright red, brightly polished fingernails clenching the pillow, and above the edge of the covers green eyes peeping out behind long, arched brows, Broňa Berková followed every movement of her hated – and hating – roommate (in the women's one-room flat on the third floor of building No. 2000) Jitka Traklová. Every day begins with a fight for the bathroom, the stove, the dishes, and for room ... the entire room: to acquire it, Jitka married Pharm. Břetislav Trakl (from the men's one-room flat across the hall), who was just as young as her, for this flat she disposed of our former roommate Madda Serafinová and now she and her husband are trying to dispose of me and get the whole flat for themselves – but am I supposed to jump out the window just because that bitch managed to get married?

Jitka suddenly threw back her covers and in the same instant her heels hit the carpet; Broňa, however, was quicker, darting off a second before and already she was running headlong into the bathroom – I know, I could simply get up fifteen minutes earlier, but why should I not get a decent night's sleep just because of that pig? Besides, she'd end up getting up an hour earlier, which she's already done. – Broňa ran into the bathroom, slammed the door as loudly as possible behind her, and locked it: now I'll stay in here a good hour, and our poor little Jitunka won't get to bathe again today; this month I'm in the lead 14-8.

Broňa turned the cold and hot water on full – on the third floor we have water only early in the morning, as long as His Lordship on the second floor hasn't taken it all – and stretched in front of the mirror without the slightest embarrassment (in fact, the opposite), with an expert's eye and from various angles and in various positions she examined her proportions – her shoulders, arms, calves, and thighs – and then she stepped away from the mirror all the way to the opposite wall to see herself entirely, and then she walked right up to the mirror and studied particular details – altogether O.K. How wonderful it is to be a young, healthy girl –

From the other side of the thin door, she could hear Jitka's furious stomping, and so Broňa delightfully submerged herself in the warm water, now Jitka starts pounding on the door and the usual dialogue begins ("We'll settle this another place and another way!" "You know what you can do, you dumb goat!" "And what are you? A common slut–"), today I conquered the bathroom, these are just pot-shots, through the door I can hear Jitka cursing like a sailor as she washes in the sink (she doesn't even have a mirror – heh-heh-heh!), she pounds again and finally goes off to work, SLAM – on top of everything she broke the door.

To get me back for the bathroom, that slut took her revenge in the low and despicable manner of a scullery-maid: she scalded the milk in our saucepan (because of me that dumb cow drinks only scalded milk!), she ate up my Orange cookies (90 hellers a package – but I still have eight of them hidden behind the stove, heh-heh-heh), she turned off the gas, unscrewed the control valve from the main gas connection, and apparently took it with her to work ...

Broňa proudly curled her lip, turned on the gas by placing a long fingernail in the groove of the cap, took out from the end of her black shoe a plastic bag of cheap Chinese tea, sniffed it (to see if that cow Jitka put something in it), and before she made the tea looked over the room reprovingly (two red daybeds, beneath each of them a suitcase and between them a deep-red rug, two small cabinets for bedding, their flat surfaces serving as night tables, a shared light-colored wardrobe with doors covered in synthetic white leather, two red chairs at a small glass-topped table, a vase of stained glass, and on the wall a reproduction of Renoir's *Dejéuner sur l'herbe*), thinking of a way to retaliate, in sudden inspiration she walked up to the wardrobe, took Jitka's skirt off its hanger, and with her bright-red nail ripped the zipper from the material such that it would fall off the first time she tried to zip it up, she drank her tea and wolfed down a package of Orange cookies, she chewed up the cellophane wrapper with her shiny teeth and shoved the sticky ball all the way into the toe of the left shoe of Jitka's dress shoes, performed several perfect somersaults on the carpet, and to the music on the radio, still naked, she did a little dance, choking in the low, early morning, red sunlight, with a groundless, total, insane happiness that takes the breath away and convulses the muscles.

The blue-gray outline of the factory, tower, concourse, and warehouse, resembling in the morning mist a dusky prison ship with a thousand closely packed cabins, which will never take us *to the white port of the land of a thousand lakes* ... happy, however, that we're at least sitting by the door of the admiral himself.

Broňa climbed up to the second floor of the administration building (the White House), her metal-tipped high heels resounded through the entire dark hallway of forty office doors until they stood before the last one, the one with the blue-and-gold sign ADMINISTRATION. On the other side of the door a narrow anteroom with a window overlooking the courtyard, a desk, a small table with a typewriter, a telex machine, two chairs, two philodendrons, and two doors: on the left DEPUTY DIRECTOR, on the right FACTORY DIRECTOR.

Broňa unlocked her desk, removed the typewriter cover, watered the philodendrons, and opened the window – for a miserable thousand crowns a month that should suffice for today. The rest of the day is mine ... how to kill so much time so I'm not bored? For fun I started taking aim at Comrade Director Eng. Borek Trojan.

He's so ... decadent, like those long, melancholy songs about nothing. Always tired, always listless ... he'll stand maybe fifteen minutes looking at the flowers I have to put in the vase for him. I'd say he's terribly bored, he's arranged it so his deputy, František Střelák, arranges everything for him and then he just blesses it like the Pope from his balcony. He signs his name forty times a day and then, exhausted, has himself taken home by car. He is an extremely sad and weary old man.

But he's also quite handsome: always in gray (but he has plenty of those gray vestments and always stitched together from the best material, he has them made in Prague), splendid white shirts and fantastic socks, his specialty, they have to be imported from some thoroughly imperialist country, wonderfully light and beautifully rigged out Italian shoes, even his hands are beautiful, like hands that haven't done anything for a long time ... a thin, pale face, already rather worn, wrinkles and such, but at the same time interesting with those silver temples, sad old eyes, and instead of a smile he grins, tall and slender, but already he's beginning to get a belly ... he's breathless after climbing one flight of stairs.

I caught his eye as soon as he caught sight of me at the anniversary celebration in the factory dining room. That was when I was still working in payroll, worn out and incredibly fed up ... In his wide-open eyes the very first time I danced with him, I could see myself completely naked – but after that I didn't run into him very often, he always got in the car right away to go home or sat up high above the crowd on a dais beneath a red banner ...

But there's justice in the world after all, and so beginning the 1st of March he made me his secretary, that is, his sexretary, you know those old tricks, we see them in every other movie, and that's just how it went: first the little chats, then he comes up behind you when you're tapping away on the typewriter, then he's showing you something in a document and caressing you with his other hand, he's sniffing at the back of your neck and then he tries to kiss you behind the ear ... And then he let his hair down in a quite surprising way: every day at noon I take from his desk a notepad on which he's scribbled the things I'm to see to in the afternoon, but he doesn't scribble much and I don't have much to see to, so I noticed it right away: "Kissing is cultivated biting," he wrote, "consequently you are to report to me and bite me at 15:00," and attached to it his big director's signature.

15:00 is three in the afternoon (our director likes to play soldier and on principle does nothing from 14:00 to 15:00), and during this hour I'm nervous because behind his door I can hear his every step, and the whole hour he walks back and forth like a prisoner pacing his cell ... as if he were getting ready to kill me rather than just make love to me.

At 15:00 I knocked and entered. Borek Trojan sat at his enormous desk with his head bowed, he didn't even look up at me, didn't even move as I approached him – more and more loudly because it seemed he was sleeping – he bowed his head lower and lower, and when I reached his desk – I was almost stomping by then! – and went right up next to him, his forehead was touching the desk. So I looked at my boss's neck – does he want me to kiss him or seriously bite him? ... Kiss a man on his spine – well, to each his own – but no one's going to go to sleep on me, and so I did in fact gnaw on him a little. He just shook his shoulders a little and that was it, so I got angry, walked out, and slammed the door behind me.

The next day Eng. Trojan showed up shockingly early, instead of 07:30 (as usual) he came in at 07:06, wearing a gray borsalino and gray calfskin gloves, and carrying a gray umbrella under his arm, and he walked straight up to my desk. I smiled at him, but he was once again like ice – only an amused grin, like when he's sitting high above the crowd on his dais beneath the red banner.

"Open all of them–" he muttered through clenched teeth, and he jabbed his umbrella into my desk drawer, so I opened all three, but with the curved handle of his umbrella he pulled out the drawer so far, it would have fallen on the floor if I hadn't grabbed it quickly and set it on top of the desk. He fumbled around until he found the notepad (it was in the last drawer), then he fastidiously picked it up with his gloved hand and took it into his office. Deputy Střelák called me after lunch and told me that from 1 May I would be working in the invoicing department, where I'd receive a hundred crowns more a month. I told him no, that I'd rather leave Cottex.

But go where, *where,* WHERE?! – Broňa slammed herself down on her daybed in her one-room flat and in a fit of rage bit into the red mattress, beat her fists on it, and gave it a kick, where can a poor girl go who has only a few rags and some junk, a toothbrush, comb, and lipstick, everything would fit into a single small cardboard suitcase, and the rest is just fucking shit, a monkey in a cage has more than I do, even this bed, this wardrobe, and these shitty chairs belong to Cottex, that is, to the administrative nobility, and it's for them I graduated from college, did my multiplication tables, do my typing, and will give all the years of my life until I dry up like an old lady, they're here to give orders and I'm here to obey them, to make them tea, water their flowers, bring them cigarettes, and wait till one of them wants me, and all for miserable pay, and I have to constantly thank and applaud the ones who fucked up the world for us, for us poor people, and then seasoned it with a view of the rich, why doesn't Yveta Trojanová, the daughter of that pig, who's the same age as me, why doesn't she have to work like I do, why does she get whatever she points her finger at, a finger with a platinum ring with a sapphire that cost five grand – she drives her ass around in a car and flies every year to the sea, is the hole in her butt any different from mine? –

"Bronička, would you be so kind as to, ummm, you know–" says Jitka Traklová in a voice that sounds like cutting glass, she's already standing at the door, with her hubby behind her, Pharm. Břetislav Trakl, they came to do it on my bed, which isn't even mine.

"I have a headache!" Broňa interrupts her.

"But a little walk will do you worlds of good–" says Jitka Traklová in a voice that sounds like slag being crushed, and behind her her grinning red-eared half-wit, impatient to be let in.

"I'm not moving! I live here, don't I?!" Broňa screeches.

"You must certainly recall our little agreement…" says Jitka in a voice that sounds like glass shards smashing against a wall, and that saphead Břetislav is already impatiently clenching his eternally damp paws.

"Kiss my a--!!" squawks Broňa, but there were two of them, that is, one more than Broňa, Břetislav and Jitka entered and each headed for a different end of the daybed, they tipped it over and emptied Broňa onto the floor, Broňa wrapped herself up in the rug, but this wasn't a good idea, Břetislav and Jitka grabbed the swaying bundle and, protected from Broňa's claws by the thick bouclé fabric, carried her out into the hallway and merrily dumped her onto the steps.

Down the main avenue toward the square, the bridge, the port, the train station, and on the main avenue two ice creams at seventy hellers apiece, in the Svět Cafeteria tepid sausages at a bespattered counter, a small beer at The Five Arches, a beer at Střekov on the Elbe and another at The Lookout, and a beer for eighty-five hellers at the train station buffet and another at The Linden Tree, streams of people in the streets who have their own beds and their own wardrobes all to themselves, crammed with their own clothes, and they have little wardrobes just for shoes, which are filled with just their own shoes, the girls have fathers and the women husbands whom they chose themselves and who they don't only have to listen to and who for that get driven around in a car and bought ice cream, roses, and sapphires in platinum IF ONLY A BOMB WOULD FALL ALREADY and we'll all crawl around naked on all fours, the punishment for wearing real gems should be a shot in the belly, and that for riding in a car hanging by the feet above an anthill, what are all these display windows for when in my purse all I have is a payslip for the rent, rip out the paving stones, knock down the lampposts, overturn the cars and tear down the electric wires, light up the gas pumps with matches, and on the main avenue and on the square organize a Great Ball, instead of confetti, shards of glass from the display windows …

Not till early morning did Broňa drag herself home, but what kind of home is this doubly someone else's room: the administration's and the Trakls', those little puppies who crawl all over each other and suck up to anyone, so in five years they can get an apartment, in ten years they'll buy a refrigerator for it and a television, and if they suck up for another twenty they'll have saved enough for a jalopy and a third-category taxable pension, bowing and scraping till they die, and crawling through this shitty town where day and night the deadly dust of the power plant's smokestacks falls and where all the children have a cough from birth, I want to go *to the land of a thousand lakes With fragrant pine trees on sandy shores*

Eat mouthfuls of cranberries from the pure earth Cool water clear as the air on a high cliff Where the salmon dance On a white boat beneath a white sail heading toward the white port of the blue North One day I shall lie on the deck of our sailboat "What are you laughing about?" Erik will say

Erik is my husband With blue eyes and hair like platinum With his white, delicate hands he caresses me reverently, like a priest "So what are you laughing about?" Erik smiles "I'm thinking about the time I was having these funny problems with this factory director in Ústí nad Labem. Where I'm still living. Haven't I had enough of it already?!"

With eyes burning from lack of sleep I look at Comrade Director: a gray borsalino, gray duds made of authentic Turkish kamgarn, at least 450 crowns per meter, but probably bought with Tuzex vouchers, a shirt as white as a seagull and a narrow tie (wine-colored like his handkerchief and openwork socks) interwoven with golden worsted yarn, and that gray umbrella, I won't forget it as long as I live – what will he do with it today? He acted sovereignly – he hung it on the hook – he didn't do anything. But *I* can't afford to do nothing, for *me* it's a question of my daily butterless bread, Your Excellency, and now down to business: how to take this gentleman down a peg or two, break and tame him and make him eat from my hand so he'll give milk, butter, and whipped cream?

First of all, OBSERVE how this tall, wild animal lives:

07:30 (till then he's completely unapproachable, locked in his apartment on the second floor, bolted and chained, he rushes down the stairs to his car, rushes to work, from the car to the second floor of the White House) - he comes in and immediately disappears behind the door to his office. He may not be disturbed because he's reading: one foreign daily, four from the central office, two local ones, one regional. Of the weekly journals he reads two political ones, sixteen technical in four languages, two Czech cultural, one puzzle magazine, one chess magazine, one sports magazine, and a humor magazine called *Porcupine*. He *really* only reads the last one, I tested it, a few times I hid his daily and weekly periodicals, his foreign ones, his technical, political, and cultural ones, and he didn't miss them at all ... but as soon as I held back *Porcupine* for just a single day, he stormed all over the factory, from the poor porter, Archleb, all the way to Deputy Střelák. Pretty good, huh?

08:15 - I take him some weak Indian tea without sugar and without anything, just warm water, fresh flowers for the vase, and I water his palm. The first appropriate moment – but it's so early that he's still not all there. No luck.

08:25 - conversation with Deputy Střelák. Střelák talks, Trojan feebly nods, could be he's basically finished with the running of Cottex.

08:40 - a walk around the factory, which he calls the "grand rounds." As a rule, our sovereign takes the same route every day, his head held high and a severe look on his face – so nobody dares bother him. And the whole walk is just so he can have a decent bowel movement. Twice I remember it didn't work – and all of Cottex felt it, from Střelák all the way to poor Archleb. So:

09:20 - WC, where I probably shouldn't follow him. But that's a better place than for instance the glass works or the slaughterhouse, starting all over again from the bottom –

09:35 - he attends to the mail, that is: on every letter, order, set of instructions, invoice, form, reminder, without undo thought – because it must be done at a rate of 10 pieces per minute – in the upper right-hand corner he scribbles a letter, and his alphabet has awfully few letters: "R" means: reject, toss out, kick out ... in short, to hell with it. "!" means the opposite: comply, fulfill, arrange, send, pay, thank ... and do it immediately, actually this symbol is reserved for correspondence from General Director Tušl and the regional, district, and city committees (with the ministry and the government, on the other hand, we're at war, so we write "R"). "?" means: into the drawer until they write again. "BA" means send it to business administration, "T" to the technical department. "TG" to the technology department (that's all we have), toss it around their neck and let them worry about it. And finally "FS," the initials of Deputy František Střelák, means: "Frantík, take care of it!" On about a third of the letters His Excellency writes "R" and on more than half of them "FS." Actually besides "BA," "T," and "TG," everything is "FS," and the "BA," "T," and "TG" are taken care of by "FS" as well, so basically all of the mail and all of Cottex is "FS."

10:00 - an administration meeting. Střelák proposes, the leadership are doodlingly frightened (only the chief technician Neustupa grumbles now and then), Trojan blesses.

11:30 - visitors and telephone calls (on four lines) in the presence of Střelák.

12:30 - lunch. In January His Excellency introduced into the dining room white tablecloths, lace curtains, three fans at 360 crowns apiece, and three reproductions of the local, hideous countryside at 60 crowns apiece, as well as knives and forks (before there were only spoons). During the quarterly inventory (physical status up to 3/31) the following were discovered missing: "Tablecloth, white" 3 pc., "Lace curtains, carton" 1 pc., "Fan, elec." 3 pc., "Utensil, fork" 16 pc., "Utensil, knife" 58 pc. Only the reproductions held their ground, the employees showed the greatest interest in the item "Fan, elec.," where the decrease amounted to 100% of inventory. Exciting, isn't it. In school we calculated with billions and changed U.S. dollars into rubles – and how ungrateful this lousy bunch is. Disgusted after the failure of his magnanimous act, His Excellency came to hate the factory dining room (all their requests got an "R") and now he has the office messenger, A. Vajtingrová, bring him low-calorie lunches from the Corner Pub. Impossible during lunch – His Excellency eats slowly as if he had tonsillitis and then sits there exhausted, wheezing in his armchair.

13:00 - more visitors, if there are any, and telephone calls, but preferably not, and only very rarely, top-secret visits from Prague or from the committees – out of the presence of Střelák! – during which all of Cottex trembles in dread that this month, for the second time already, they're considering its shutdown, transfer, takeover, uncoupling, et cetera.

13:58 - telephone conversation with Madame Jana von Trojan, that is, his spouse or old lady, that old, snorting cow who goes around in one of three fur coats (short, mid, and seven-eighths) and appears exclusively in one of the following automobiles: a blue Renault (the family car), a black or Gray Tatra 603 (the Cottex director's company car), a silver Tatra 603 (the company car of the welcome office's regional director – how could a girl like me become the director of the regional welcome office, I ask you? – and the representative to the regional national committee), old lady Trojanová, with whom old man Trojan has nothing to say (I have no problem eavesdropping on their telephone conversations):

"Comrade Trojanová, please ... Jana? It's Borek."

"So how's it going?"

"Oh, you know. How about you?"

"Nothing special. I've got the Belgians here."

"You'll be home late."

"You're going to Prague tomorrow."

"How's Yveta?"

"I haven't seen her."

"Don't forget to buy some mineral water."

"Okay, bye."

After a conversation like that with a wife like that – probably even a hundred-year-old Chinese woman could make the poor man come.

14:00 - the director disconnects three of his four telephone lines, and an hour of silence ensues. Nobody knows what our sovereign actually does during this time ... but I'm beginning to suspect: nothing. He dozes or stares off into space –

15:00 - Deputy Střelák arrives, and after him the chairmen of the party and the Cottex factory committees – goodwill or fuck off (with respect to money).

16:00 - Deputy Střelák arrives.

16:10 - the director leaves, "Goodbye, Miss Berková," before the note-pad affair "Ciao, Boni," after the affair only "S'long," as inconspicuously as possible, as if a half-drunken German were saying it.

And rush down the stairs to the car, rush home, and from the car rush to the second floor of our building, bolt and chain-lock the white door.

Nobody knows what our sovereign actually does at home... but I'm beginning to suspect: nothing. He dozes or stares off into space –

Because you can hear something through the floor, especially when you throw back the rug and listen through a wine glass. From the Trojans' on the second floor all you can hear is the opening and closing of doors now and then, dialogues like in those film festival movies for most particular audiences: rare, brief, and deadly dull, the only thing you can hear almost always is the sound of the shower in the bathroom – as they take all our water and send it off into the sewers.

Only on summer weekends does the second-floor nobility drive out in their blue Renault to their house on the river, they have their sailboat there, the *Yvette*, and nothing less that *their own dock* for it ...

I followed Trojan there and spent a whole Saturday afternoon watching from the bushes on the opposite bank. He didn't sail much on his *Yvette*, he mostly just sat around or wandered around his dock, lazily looked around, smoked, and all in all: nothing. He dozes or stares off into space.

A very sad and bored old man ... but how sad and bored can someone be who makes five thousand a month? ... And his pay is only a portion of his total income, our boys from research and development assiduously add their sovereign as co-author to their patents so that, for instance, the New Trojan Method (Páral's methanol isolation of cholesterol from lanolin) brought him 57,352.25 crowns last year, and he'll get the same amount for the next three years ... for doing what, actually? For his "Big Director's Signature," 1 pc. (on the original; the copies he just initials). He's decadent

– he didn't even want to see the packet of money, he couldn't even be bothered with it … he just had it transferred to his bank account, and the interest alone from this bank account (the bank sends him a "Daily Account Notice" in an unsealed envelope, heh-heh-heh) is just cause for disemboweling those sharks with a dull and rusty sickle, what are you supposed to think when you read that someone has a "Previous Balance of Unused Capital … 131,718.32 + New Balance of Unused Capital … 199,070.58 +," or when you read in the Interest column, "To receive" – that is, the bank is to give the Trojans – "37,888.73," you understand, he just scrawls 37,888.73 on some red form, attaches his signature, sends the red form in an unsealed envelope to the bank with a .20 crown stamp – and the bank plonks down 37,888.73 crowns cash, sends it to his home or wherever he pleases, thirty-seven-thousand-eight-hundred-and-eighty-eight-crowns-and-seventy-three hellers – just like that, just for being so kind as to personally write "Borek Trojan."

When I wanted to borrow a blanket 'cause I was cold in my room, I had to obtain two letters of recommendation, get three approval stamps, thank five different people, show my ID, and write an affidavit … for one dirty, lice-ridden blanket with cigarette burns … and on top of everything, whenever they take an inventory of the one-room flats, I have to show it to the committee so they know I didn't steal it …

But why do I just keep tearing at my hair? When we get right down to it – girls, ladies, grannys, you'll certainly approve – this is worth causing a little trouble over. And you, comrades, after all, you're the ones who beat it into our heads all those years in school that in this country we're all revolutionaries and fighters for justice – or is that no longer the case with you? … Well, for me it is, heh-heh-heh –

So now once again I'm on speaking terms with Comrade Director… How could it be otherwise? We know how to go about it … we've had experiences with this sort. The main thing when you're working with bigwigs: you can't just bow down to them all the time, everyone does that, they need it just like old Archleb needs his booze, but what really gets them going is when you stick your little fist between their eyes, that's how they get their thrills. And we girls supplement this by wearing miniskirts and cleverly chosen bras … meat that's initially only meant for looking at. Altogether nothing out of the ordinary, I know … but it puts you in the driver's seat.

And then it whizzes along just like in the movies: again the chats, again he walks around behind you when you're tapping away on the type-writer, again he points to something on a document while his other hand rubs your back, again he blows on your neck, and again he tries to kiss you behind the ear ... only now we're in the second round of our match ... only now I'm taking control. Boys ... boys are simply covered with buttons, and when you press them just a little bit, it's like out of a vending machine: a roll of caramels or a pack of cigarettes, a condom, a sapphire in a platinum ring, a sailboat.

And then one hot July (it isn't any accident that the revolutions in France and America took place in July) afternoon I set to it and burst into his office at 14:20, that is, during the hour our most senior animal hides most deeply in his game preserve – Trojan gazed at me: not even the all-powerful Frantík Střelák would have dared to do this ... I approached him on the carpet, and he looked at me without uttering a word – let me tell you, girls, it was infernally exciting – he didn't try to do anything at all, and when I was standing right there over him, it was as if he'd bowed his head, and I thought he was going to put his head down on the desk again and refer me to his vertebrae ...

I took his head firmly in my hands, no resistance whatsoever, and started kissing him, using one technique after another, until when I bit him – I'm sure that will be to his taste! – on the ear, he finally became animated and stood up, which was great because he really knows how to kiss, I kept my eye on the clock above his head, 14:32, Střelák will be here in 28 minutes, at 14:40 I placed his hand as if on my heart, he started going crazy, at 14:46 I let him unclip my bra in the back, now he was completely insane and I looked down from above at his trembling head, this time I was high on the dais beneath the red banner looking down with an amused expression on my face ...

14:55 - the end of the parley, in the second round I racked up a lot of points, I pushed him away like a calf from a feeding trough and went back to my desk, it was already 14:57, and at 14:59 in burst Střelák.

I felt great ... I walked around town, drank two glasses of white wine in the Svět Café and bought a pack of American Kent cigarettes for twenty crowns, once again I pictured Borek's eyes as I drew near him ... and his head on my breast as I looked at him from above as if from a balcony.

What will Borek do tomorrow? He'll be his regular stiff self, but that's all right, I'll fan his flame again ... I climb the stairs of our building and in the gloom catch sight of the white door of Borek's second-floor apartment, like the white gate of a castle we'll soon invade –

In our one-room flat that slut Jitka was already snoring, I was happy, the whole day came off beautifully for me, I quietly took off my clothes and looked at myself in the bathroom mirror, how wonderful it is to be a young, healthy girl, Borek's twenty-five years older than me and so he'll appreciate me all the more, of course he doesn't look all that bad, his legs are still nice, as are his shoulders and back, I gave him a good looking over from the bushes across the river when he was in his bathing suit, the man who's going to take me up and away must separate himself from his family, I'll replace them and be a hundred times better than those two carcasses, and we'll tear ourselves away from this stupid town, I want to go to Prague and farther, *to travel around in limousines, sleeping cars, and airplanes   To distant cities and ports   To sleep in enormous bedrooms in palatial hotels Straight from bed to a pool through whose glass bottom you can see into the bar   To drink orange juice through a straw for breakfast on a terrace beneath a sunshade   To feel his priestly hands on my body, a body tended by Parisian masseurs   To drink his adoration like champagne   To gain freedom ... from him as well   He will grow old and die   I will be beautiful another twenty-five years*

I'll have a hundred husbands   The last will be my Erik

Broňa lay down on her cot and suddenly shot up in horrible pain, a thousand knives went through her body – shrieking like a madwoman she ran to the light switch and in the piercing light she saw drops of blood on her skin ...

As she pulled back the sheet from the daybed she heard shards of glass crunching ... Broňa picked up the sharp, fragile shard with the white letter W on it – a crushed lightbulb in my bed. The slut Jitka was choking with laughter beneath her covers.

With eyes burning from tears and lack of sleep, my throat parched with anger and hatred for the entire world, I gaze at Borek Trojan: a gray vestment of natural silk, a shirt white as sea foam and a narrow tie (just as blue as his handkerchief and his openwork socks) interwoven with silver yarn, what will he do today?

"Morn'," he said like a surly German, and he disappeared behind the door to his chamber.

But *I* don't have any chamber to disappear into and not even a bed anymore, I can't afford to keep replaying only the beginning of the role of sexretary in an addle-headed film comedy, I have to take things firmly in hand, HUNT A MAN DOWN, POUNCE and SIEZE him firmly, like when a man rapes a woman ... aren't I the man in this relationship rather than that decadent? ...

Let's go for it all, and so quickly *drive* into the third round of our match, which must be the last, he gets a T.K.O. and I get a silver vase, let's go, I hop down the stairs of our building and gaze at the white door on the second floor, *drive*, I gaze so hard at it that my sight will penetrate the white wood and stab his body like the shards of a broken lightbulb, let's go, 08:15 - Indian tea and an imported superstare for impotents, *drive*, did he even notice I'm not wearing a bra, let's go, bring him a bouquet for his vase as if I were bringing him my very self, *drive*, while watering the palm show him my butt, let's go, in the morning he's still not awake, *drive*, but days don't end with mornings, let's go, 08:40 - he leaves for his rounds, *drive*, hand on heart and a stare like from an anti-tank weapon, let's go, 09:20 - I happen to be hanging around outside the WC, *drive*, and I'm still hanging around at 09:35, let's go, I place the mail on his desk and practically myself as well, *drive*, a meeting with the administration, instead of eight cups of coffee I bring in my breasts on the tray, let's go, 12:29 - I take his lunch tray from old lady Vajtingrová and serve him by hand, which he liked so much yesterday, *drive*, 13:57 - I once again inquire if he has any more special requests, let's go, his conversation with the old lady is shorter than usual, *drive*, 14:00 to 15:00 - we sit divided from each other by just his door, let's go, we doze and now he's staring off into space, or he's awake and in that space he's already starting to see me, *drive*, 15:02 - look in past Střelák's back, chirrup "Goodbye..." and display my much desired teeth, let's go ... I have to go home already, overtime is no longer tolerated, but now I'm on military alert status day and night, *drive*, I hop up the stairs of our building and gaze intensely at the white door on the second floor, let's go, did I just imagine it or did the white door actually shudder beneath my gaze, *drive*, on the third floor, home – this is supposed to be my home? Let's go!! – lengthen the rear slit of my red minidress all the way to my coccyx, *drive*, tomorrow I won't even wear panties beneath it, let's go, it's July, after all, the month of heat and revolutions, *drive*, I hop down the stairs of our building and gaze at the white door on the second floor so intensely that his bed must have glowed and burst into flames, let's go, 07:30 - "Good morning, Comrade Director" – in the voice of a woman to whom her man has just returned after two years of military service without a single weekend pass, *drive*, 08:15 - make Indian tea with the water I used yesterday to boil a kilo of celery root, stick the flowers in the vase as if I were sticking that into that, *drive* – how long can anyone keep this up? I could for maybe a year, so let's go, bare my desirable teeth at the corpse-to-be, *drive* –

After eleven days he's literally glowing ... the only thing left is to DO THE DEED.

In the hot air of the anteroom Broňa impatiently waved her hands so the fresh red paint on her freshly painted nails would dry more quickly, and she looked at the electric clock. 14:02 - the light on her telephone panel went out – Trojan's disconnected three of his four lines. Let's go – with icy calm Broňa took a notepad out from the bottom drawer of her desk, sat down at the telephone, lifted the receiver, and carefully crossing out number after number on the pad called everyone and told them dryly that the director was busy this afternoon, was canceling, postponing ... last of all Deputy Střelák.

The Perfect Crime ... just like in the movies. As if in the next few minutes I weren't going to premeditatedly make love to Borek Trojan but premeditatedly murder him ...

Broňa slowly returned the receiver to its cradle, turned off the entire apparatus, and rose with a glance at the electric clock – 14:14 - DRIVE –

"You know, it was fourteen fourteen, Erik, I did it entirely in military fashion, fourteen fourteen ... and since then every time I see the number fourteen..." "But that was a long time ago." Erik smiles and takes the tip of my nose gently between his long, white, beautiful fingers, "...that was in the distant past, as if a hundred years ago..."

14:15 - POUNCE –

"Lately–" Director Borek Trojan smiled at his secretary, B. Berková, when she entered his office at an unusual hour and locked the door behind her. "–you've made a habit, Miss–"

"Borek ... Oh, forgive me, Comrade Director, but I have to tell you something..."

"Is it really so important?"

"I can't take it any longer..."

"It is too hot ... ahem, this afternoon. Wouldn't you rather..."

"You know that I'm in love with you."

"But Miss Berková..."

"And yearn for you."

"I'm afraid that's ... Wouldn't you prefer..."

"And want you..."

"I ... rhmhhrpf. Look, Miss, at the very least this is certainly in bad taste–"

"I want you – I WANT YOU–"

"Broňa, I – – – Be reasonable, Broňa! Someone could walk in here at any moment..."

"No one will come in."

"At three the chairman of the factory council will be here–"

"I called him and postponed till tomorrow."

"At fifteen-twenty that pensioner who I–"

"I canceled it."

"And at fifteen forty–"

"I canceled everything for today. No one will walk in."

"Střelák…"

"I called him too."

"So that's why, on the telephone, he was so surprised…"

"So you knew already … didn't you? Before I came in–"

"Broňa … Be reasonable … Please…"

"Reason is useless. It's cold. You know that … Come to me … come. I want you–"

I'll never forget the expression in Borek's eyes – as if grateful for being hunted down … SEIZE –

"What wonderful claws you have…" he whispered hoarsely when I ran my hand beneath his shirt.

15:10 - we canceled the driver to take Borek home, I went out first and, as agreed, waited for Borek at 16:00 at the corner of Slaughterhouse Street. As I was climbing into his blue Renault I saw something like fear in his eyes – He drove the car and thereby he was the one who spirited me off – heh-heh-heh. I gave myself up to the cushioned seat and played with the image that I was carrying him off in my teeth.

We were together at the riverside house… and many times since. Knockout after knockout. In my embrace Borek turns red, loses his breath until he starts to wheeze – is he helping himself to too much … but he *wants* it to be brutal – as if he were dying with me rather than getting pleasure from it … after lovemaking he lies there as if he's been murdered.

WHO'S WHO

Broňa Berková (19)

A barefoot, dark-haired little girl in a frock, without panties, sitting on the edge of a path leading to the forbidden garden of a deluxe mansion, uses her hands to shovel sand over her legs, leans back and shovels more of it further up her little body, all the way up to her chin (like children in Ostend, Biarritz, Yalta, St. Tropez, and Miami on the beach beneath their parents' loving gaze).

"But you can't go around begging from strangers…" said Broňa's father, the porter of the Ústí government mansion for special occasions, when Broňa brought home candy and foreign coins – the girl loved them and quickly learned to recognize them all – from the guests: Polish generals, Belgian trade-unionists, Italian industrialists, and parliamentary members from the Estonian Soviet Republic. When the Finnish ambassador bestowed upon Broňa a full-color publication from his marvelous *land of a thousand lakes*, her father wanted to return the gift immediately, but the girl pressed her take to her flat chest and surrendered only after a protracted skirmish had left the book scratched and torn to shreds from Broňa's nails.

After a difficult life of poverty and renunciation, Broňa's mother spent her last years ill, tied to a wheelchair. Broňa would wheel her around among the luxurious, silver government limousines and select the car in which she would one day drive.

Broňa's father was a decent, conscientious man without much cunning, and a quarterly drunk. After weeks of anxious attendance upon government guests, he'd drink himself into a stupor on local rum, sit in the small kitchen of the garden house cursing and lamenting his fate, and behind closed curtains shake his fist at the mansion's powerful guests.

When in the middle of their Christmas Eve supper one of the delegations suddenly cut its vacation short to return to their country, where a revolution had erupted, Father woke his young Broňa, who was slumbering after the meager Christmas supper of a porter's family (fried fish fillets, apples, and nuts – Broňa got an orange and a plastic car from Santa) and brought her in his arms to the vacated and wonderfully lit dining hall on the second floor of the mansion. "Long live the revolution!" her father shouted, toasting to the second course of the holiday meal with a glass of eighty-year-old cognac (turkey with chestnut stuffing, chicken breast in aspic, anchovies, and pike in wine) then, elated, he turned to his daughter: "Santa's wonderful, isn't he!" "I'd like to lock him in the closet so he'd have to give us presents every day–" said the girl as her teeth tore into a piece of dark, fatty thigh meat.

Broňa had gone to three different schools, all of them select, and she'd left them all uncompleted (an engineering program, a sailing school, and an economics intermediate school). As the prettiest girl in her class and in her grade (red nails, the longest in the entire school), she hardly studied at all – numbers came easy to her but the rest didn't interest her. At her premature departure from each school, her teachers shook their heads as if to say that her lack of discipline was ruining her life. The next prominent guest of the government mansion, however, was always happy to get the charming porter's daughter into a school – isn't she a daughter of the working class, after all?! – of her choice. The postal minister kissed the best.

At her defloration by a handsome young married intern, Broňa felt only pain and fear of pregnancy. The intern immediately provided her with professional assistance and wrote her a prescription for a certain medication. Broňa went into town, and when it began to rain she sat in the Svět Café, on the second floor, overlooking the square, drank a glass of white wine and smoked two cigarettes, the rain flowed gently down the large windows and Broňa recalled again and again with relish the terror in the intern's eyes and his anxious pleading as he knelt before her ... and felt cheated that everything was over so quickly. In fact the intern soon made it clear he didn't want to see her again. The forsaken girl felt anger and vengefulness toward the whole male race, and when a year later the intern divorced his wife for Broňa's classmate, who was ugly yet obviously smarter, Broňa swore that at the next opportunity she wouldn't surrender without a fight.

After leaving the economics school (she didn't manage to pass the final exams), Broňa began working in the accounting department of national enterprise Cottex, because she liked to count money. Here, however, instead of financial excitement, the greedy girl of the world was greeted by the laborious recounting of hellers on wage sheets, and the hideous, old-maidish directress of the accounting department followed every move of her new, attractive (and none too conscientious) subordinate.

Her mother's death and her father's dismissal from the household for his increasing alcoholism caused the irretrievable breakdown of the Berkov family, and Broňa moved into the factory's one-room flat. Because her pay was so low, with no practical prospects for advancement, and because she wasn't used to managing her own money and, at the same time, was used to dressing well, Broňa often went hungry. However, she proudly rejected numerous offers from men, which were often connected with material advantages. Only when she succeeded in arousing the interest of the elegant, handsome, and virile director, who made her his secretary, did Broňa appreciate her opportunity, and she hurled herself into it body and soul.

With her first bonus, Broňa paid for a four-day trip to East Berlin. She spent the first three precious days looking at tiresome museums, but the last day in Potsdam made up for everything. She walked, enchanted, through the grounds of the emperor's estate, Sans Souci, with its ponds and pavilions. The Neuer Palais astounded her with the luxurious, icily refulgent magnificence of its halls, behind the back of the tourguide she crossed the red rope separating visitors from the emperors' furniture and, fascinated, ran her long, deep-red nails along the expansive carving of the old silver wood.

Ready for the pounce, Jitka Traklová followed every movement of her hated – and hating – roommate, that monster Broňa Berková, and as soon as it seemed Broňa had opened her eyes, Jitka sprang out of bed – but the vulgar Broňa naturally dashed to the door before her to monopolize the bathroom … Living like this is simply wretched –

Jitka paced back and forth before the door of the locked bathroom, beating on it now and then with her fist or a shoe, and she prepared her breakfast: powdered milk (Břetislav calculated that it's cheaper than real milk since, after all, we don't pay for the water) and six (one each for breakfast and two each to take to work) slices of bread with potato spread (a half kilo of potatoes, 1 egg, 1 block of processed cheese, 5 decagrams of yeast, a teaspoon of mustard, a teaspoon of peanut oil, and salt – so it has carbohydrates, protein, fat, and even vitamins, and it's relatively inexpensive, Břetislav figured it out and concocted it according to his charts), she poured the hot milk into two mugs (she left what little remained of the milk in the pan on the stove so it would be scalded for that slut Broňa), and carried breakfast across the third-floor hall to the men's one-room flat.

In his black boxers Pharm. Břetislav Trakl kissed his wife on the forehead and took the tray from her as carefully as possible, so as not to spill even a drop of milk.

"Why is it you're still wearing those boxers," said Jitka. "It's Saturday already–"

"I thought since they're black I could wear them longer–"

"And who's going to wash them?! – Take them off, right now!"

"You and your washing … this underwear won't last even a year…"

"They won't last if I have to scrub them with a brush on the washboard – take them off, now!"

"Well, at least until after I bathe this afternoon…"

To disagreeable grumbling, Břetislav backed into his room holding the tray (two red daybeds, beneath each of them a suitcase and between them a deep-red rug, two small cabinets for bedding, their flat surfaces serving as night tables, a shared wardrobe with doors covered in synthetic white leather, two red chairs at a small glass-topped table, a vase of stained glass, and on the wall a reproduction of Renoir's *Dejéuner sur l'herbe*). Jitka was right behind him. On one of the daybeds Alex Serafin was sleeping with Dáša Zíbrtová. They'd kicked off their blanket in the heat so that one could see the tight embrace of his hairy, gorilla limbs around her withered body.

"Take them off already–" hissed Jitka, and Břetislav unwillingly removed his underwear, Jitka searchingly looked her husbands' naked body over and ran her hand along it, then she took out his blue (almost white from all the washings) jockey shorts from the wardrobe and selected one of her husband's clean shirts.

"No, not a shirt!" said Břetislav resolutely. "Look at that worn collar … after eleven washings! And do you know how much it cost? Forty-five!"

"If you'd buy the ones for sixty, they'd hold up through many more washings!"

"A shirt for sixty crowns!" Břetislav voiced his shock so loudly, he woke Dáša Zíbrtová.

Jitka returned to her room, turned off the gas beneath the charred remainder of the milk, unscrewed the control valve from the main gas connection, and placed it in her purse as well as, in a plastic bag, the two slices of bread stuck together with potato spread and a package of Broňa's Orange cookies – I simply adore sweets – and this is pitiful compensation for the gas that slut Broňa burns up for nothing and we have to pay half of … in that single column alone we lose 4.50 crowns a month, Břetislav figured it out. Jitka pounded on the still locked bathroom door a couple more times and stormed out into the hallway, slamming behind her the door behind which Břetislav was impatiently waiting.

Through the drifts of beige dust the Trakls hurried toward the factory (the outline of which, the tower, station, and concourse, in the morning mist could perhaps remind one of a boat) discussing their plans for the next day as if it were another battle in their just war for decent living quarters …

"Today go see Alda, Bindr, and Coufal," Jitka was saying emphatically.

"And you should have another talk with Drtílek, Ebrt, Fiala, and Gan," Břetislav was saying as he counted on his fingers the individual assaults.

"I've complained to all of them at least ten times…"

"We have to do it eleven, twelve, thirteen times–"

"They already have an apartment, that's it … so they just blow us off."

"But we'll have an apartment too!"

"Two kinds of people inhabit this planet: those with an apartment and those without. And between them a barbed-wire fence…"

"So let's cut through it and shove it up their asses!"

"If only we had a child…"

From outside in the courtyard through the window of the planning department on the second floor (of the White House) all one could see was a green thicket of two philodendrons. From her chair behind them, right up next to the window, Jitka Traklová could see the whole courtyard through the leaves, from the gate to the boiler room and the garage ... our entire workaday world.

Jitka whizzed along on her electric calculator, traversing decade after decade, then she set right to work on the wage recalculations for Břetislav (he worked on the same hallway, in the payroll department, he'd abandoned his pharmacy job for a while because he made 46.70 crowns a month more here and also could see who made how much at Cottex – which might come in handy ... And Břetislav in turn helped Jitka with her operational lists, they were both tremendously efficient), through the leaves she suddenly caught sight of Alda (chairman of the housing commission) in a conversation with Gan (head of the works committee) and immediately ran out into the hallway, knocked on the glass of Břetislav's door (the office across the hall and thus without a view of the courtyard) the agreed-upon code, and as she was running down the stairs Břetislav caught up with her, and the Trakls threw themselves upon the frightened pair in the courtyard, pulled Alda away from Gan, and dragged each away to a different corner.

Břetislav and Jitka went back to their offices and every now and then the indefatigable couple would rush from their lairs out on new raids, they swam through the dark hallway of forty office doors like two barracudas in a warm, slumberous sea, they could guess the possible prey from the silhouettes behind the glass doors and pounced on them like lightning.

When the siren announced the end of the workday, Jitka walked over to Břetislav's office, beneath her gaze he had to remove his clothes and put borrowed overalls on his naked body.

"Why do you need underwear beneath your overalls? And clean ones at that!!" Jitka yelled at Břetislav, who then went out on a paid work brigade to clean bricks from the demolished sodium room. Jitka had already labored an hour before work in the packaging warehouse, for a 25% bonus.

"Europa, you really are an imbecile!" Alex Serafin berated his inseparable companion Dáša Zíbrtová when the poor, befuddled old thing put sugar in his beer instead of salt. Alex, wearing nothing but his impressive black fur (without a single gray hair), was rolling around on the red daybed – he couldn't stand sheets, which apparently irritated his skin – and Dáša, whom he called Europa on principle, assiduously bustled about the room in joyful, devoted servility ... her enslavement had already reached an extremely unsavory level: Alex would take all of Europa's money, order her around, laugh at her, and beat her – she worshiped him for this, as if it were exactly what she required to be happy ...

What was worse was that Dáša practically lived in the the men's one-room flat with Alex, and her negligible sense of order and system alternately irritated Břetislav and filled him with contempt. Coming home from work, Břetislav stepped over Dáša cleaning Alex's shoes, threw her net bag on the ground (she'd tossed it on the daybed), sat down, and took out of his suitcase some well-thumbed sheets of paper with the inscription *Our Household.*

When Břetislav was still Jitka's fiancé, he purchased in a stationery store, for 1.40 crowns, a notebook with the pre-printed columns, "Rent," "Footwear," "Milk, cheese, butter," "Transportation," "Recreation," and several others, which would "structure," as Břetislav enthusiastically explained to his eager fiancée, their household expenditures into a "prescriptive norm." This notebook, whose columns Břetislav filled out daily with indefatigable care, soon became his dearest (and gradually only) book. The left- and right-hand pages of *Our Household* always had pre-printed corresponding columns. In the left one, entitled "Estimated," items of planned expenditure were entered, while on the right, entitled "Actual," were items of actual expenditure. So, for example, for the month of July you could enter in the column "Milk, butter, cheese" an amount of 63.10 crowns – estimated from the average consumption calculated according to quarterly and yearly averages – and, with the substitution of powdered milk for real, achieve a savings of 3.74 crowns, which is then entered into the balance column in blue (or in red if the expenditure is greater than the estimate) on the final page, which favorably influences the monthly economic results of *Our Household.* The pre-printed grid system of rows and columns facilitated a quick daily overview, the observation of the growth of individual columns, a comparison of the expenditure for shoe repairs during the summer as compared to winter, the caloric intake of carbohydrates consumed over a week, month, and year, the drop in the price of oxtail in the column "Culture," and an overview of individual consumption trends – operational tracking that forms the basis for management, regulation, and control.

Easily and gladly the young M.Pharm. Břetislav Trakl forgot his erstwhile pharmacy training, the abundantly interlarded Latin phrases, and with numerous intrigues he pushed through his transfer from the laboratory to the payroll department, so that he could enter entirely into the realm of exciting monetary levers – or rather axles, around which everything on this planet revolves.

Dáša Zíbrtová was preparing her Alex's daily banquet, she was cooling beer in the sink and wafting through the room was the aroma of cured meat, Břetislav was immersed in his calculations of the savings that could be derived from exchanging the more expensive hard curd cheese for the cheaper soft one, which he would then finish drying at home – suddenly

Jitka barged into the men's flat, "Leave that for now, Břetislav, and come help do the wash!"

"But it's not even six o'clock, and Broňa…"

"You're afraid of that slut? And you call yourself a man?"

Broňa was sitting on her daybed filing her nails. "Hey, get out!" she shouted as soon as she caught sight of Břetislav entering. "It's not six yet!"

After a protracted battle, it had been agreed that Broňa would leave the flat every day at six and stay out till nine. For that, Břetislav would not come into the women's flat at any other time. But can one really acquiesce in the rigid dogmatism of agreements that preserve an unmaintainable status quo? If so, then the U.S. would still be a British colony and the Czar would reign in the Kremlin.

"We'll just be in the bathroom," said Břetislav politely, "we're washing clothes today…"

"And what if I just happen to want to take a bath right now!" Broňa shouted; meanwhile, however, Jitka had locked the bathroom door and come into the room demonstratively holding the key between her teeth.

"We'll be finished in an hour." Břetislav combined his own diplomacy with Jitka's force. "And then…"

"You have no business here till six o'clock, Trakl!" Broňa shouted. "So scram – now!"

"And what if we asked you nicely…" Jitka snarled through her teeth, which were still firmly clenching the bathroom key, "that for once you be so kind as…"

"Out!" Broňa shrieked. "And hand over the key – I'm going to take a bath!"

"I told you," Jitka was saying to Břetislav, "niceness won't get you anywhere with this bitch–"

Broňa pounced on Jitka, and Jitka stuck out her leg. As she fell, Broňa pulled Jitka down with her, and they both tumbled onto the carpet, where a free-for-all began, in which the more combat-ready Broňa quickly gained the upper hand. "You're going to let her cripple me?!" Jitka shrieked at Břetislav when Broňa was kneeling on her stomach, Břetislav sighed, took a deep breath, grabbed Broňa by the hair, and patiently, but with all his strength, dragged her off to a corner of the room, Broňa let herself be dragged to the window, where she suddenly shot up, rammed her knee into Břetislav's groin, and ran her claws across his face until the bloodied pharmacist hobbled away groaning. Then when Broňa, furious with rage, fixed her predatory gaze on Jitka, the abandoned newlywed tossed the bathroom key on the carpet and fled into the WC, where she locked herself in.

Jitka was seated on the toilet seat carefully applying saliva to her scratched face and lovingly thinking of Břetislav, how he stood up for her ... Břetislav's a wonderful fellow ... Jitka's gaze fell on the roll of toilet paper, and an idea flashed through her mind: beginning tomorrow I'll wrap our sandwiches in this paper before I place them in the plastic bag ... Jitka laughed to herself, gently rotated her engagement ring around her finger, and began to sing softly to herself.

The smell of cured meat filled the men's one-room flat, with his bare hands Alex was tearing the meat apart on the black lid of the pot covered with drops of condensed steam, while drinking beer richly spiced with Jägermeister – his face covered with iodine and still hissing with pain, Břetislav was mapping out in the pages of *Our Household* the distribution of crowns and hellers in the various "Estimated" columns for the coming month. Extremely irritated by the odor of meat and alcohol in his nostrils, he angrily lowered the item "Meat" by 4.36 crowns – to maintain the progress of our monthly savings by 20 crowns – and he took a deep breath.

"Europa, give that guy a shot of Jägermeister–" Alex roared good-naturedly as he raised the bottle.

"Thank you, Mr. Serafin," said Břetislav dryly, "but I don't drink, on principle–" and he resolutely lowered "Culture" by 2.44 crowns, to a round 15 crowns (a subscription to the newspaper *Rudé pravo* and one movie in rows 5-9).

"Come on, have a drink with me – it's free!" Alex shouted.

"Thank you, that's very kind, but I really..."

"Or I'll take offense – Trakl! You know that I can get offended!" Břetislav painfully recalled how the "offended" Alex (when he brought seven friends home from the Corner Pub at three in the morning, he was offended that he'd "flustered" Břetislav, as Břetislav had diplomatically formulated it) battered his head with a table leg, and with a forced smile Břetislav went over to drink with his roommate.

"Hands behind your back!" Alex cried delightedly, and he rammed the bottle of Jägermeister into Břetislav's throat the way one injects a horse. "Well – good, isn't it–" Alex guffawed like a callous veterinarian. "Very good and smooth," said Břetislav, and so he received another injection. "You're a bastard," said Alex to motivate himself, "but you're so boring it makes me want to faint. Hey, pitiful Europa – what happens when these people grow up?"

Břetislav reduced another column of *Our Household* with an austerity that increased the progress of their savings by 35 crowns ... of course it comes with the price that in the column "Entertainment" we have to write

"0" (last month we spent 3.20 crowns in this column: two sodas at an afternoon dance given by the gardeners' club, where there was no cover charge and the average age of the participants was 65 ... aren't even these 3.20 crowns a waste for that kind of "entertainment"). Břetislav suddenly stiffened over the white square condemned to the grievous entry "0" – and in an unfathomable groundswell of thought he suddenly tossed aside the black pencil, picked up the red one, and inscribed in the square – holding his breath, blood pounding in his temples – the stupifying number *10,000.00* ...

"Where have you been?" yelled Jitka – her scratched face covered in iodine like warpaint – from the doorway of the men's flat. "It's six-thirty already–"

"I'm on my way–" Břetislav shouted as he quickly came to his senses and hurriedly erased the red madness ... he erased tenaciously and persistently until the smooth surface of the paper had eroded, the red from the graphite pencil had long ago been safely erased, but a deep relief of the inscription *10,000.00* was still visible as if it had been ingrained in the cellulose of *Our Household*.

Out of spite, that beast Broňa had vacated the flat a half hour late and the Trakls immediately set to work, first they rinsed their plastic lunch bags in warm water and hung them inside out to dry on the frame of Renoir's *Déjeuner sur l'herbe*, and with a thorough inspection of each individual piece of clothing they washed their laundry in the tub, after which Břetislav stripped naked and Jitka soaped him thoroughly up.

When she turned on the chrome faucet above the tub: a few rusty drops, rattling, and that's it. The Trakls looked at one another with glaring eyes. From below, they could hear the silver timbrel like a fountain behind the bars of a prince's grounds. The Trojans are showering down on the second floor.

"So, now you can wipe off the soap with newspaper!" Jitka shrieked.

"Well, I'll be ------!" Břetislav screamed.

"Those damned idiots are sending our water down into the sewer ... all day every day. What do they care about us – and we want Trojan to give us an apartment ... HE-ALREADY-HAS-ONE – three rooms for three people, along with a garage, a riverside house with ten rooms, and his own dock for his own boat ... What are we to him? At most an annoying bedbug!" and Jitka started beating her fists furiously against the water pipe.

"Wait, not like that–" shouted a belathered Břetislav, and he began beating his shoe against the pipe.

"I'll probably have to go bathe the baby in the basement!!"

"Out of the way!" yelled Břetislav, and blacksmith-like, with a heavy wrench, he showered the pipe with well-aimed blows, stubbornly pounding metal against metal, until his arm finally gave out.

Then, after he'd wiped the soap from his body with Broňa's towel, he brought over *Our Household* and Jitka brought out her "Journal of Expenditures."

"How can this be eight crowns thirty?" said Břetislav. "There's still one crown fifty missing–"

"I…" Jitka confessed, "I bought a Tatranka. You know how I like sweets."

"But we'll never get anywhere at this rate! You like sweets – well, I like beer and maybe even some smoked meat every now and then. But we simply can't afford it … if we ever want to have anything. And a Tatranka for one-and-a-half crowns. You might as well have gone ahead and bought a more expensive Miňonka for a crown ninety, you simply have no sense! For one crown ten you could get those nougat things, and for ninety hellers you could get Vafles, those would serve the same purpose, wouldn't they–"

"But there weren't any nougats or Vafles at the canteen…"

"Canteen! How many times have I told you that you have to buy sufficient amounts of what we agree upon in the supermarket beforehand! If you had ten Vafles at home you wouldn't have to rely on the canteen!"

"Oh please, how am I supposed to buy ten Vafles out of my daily allowance…"

"Look, just let me know and I can take it out of the next decade!"

"Right, I'll buy ten Vafles and Broňa will eat them all – that fucking cow. Look how she scratched me up again … Břetislav, we have to get her out of here as soon as possible or I'm simply going to collapse…"

"But how? With Madda Serafinová it was easy … remember?"

"But that was just a dumb little animal, and in the end she was glad to go … But Broňa? She's a crafty, vindictive, bloodthirsty beast…"

"We have to do the same thing we did to Madda. Little annoying things, then work the public so that no one says a word when we toss her out on her ear…"

"Broňa's in a different class … And now she's seeing the director. When she tames him – and Broňa can do that like no one else – she'll just crook her little finger and we're the ones who'll be out on our ears…"

"That's bad … or maybe that's a good thing!"

"It's tragic."

"But tragic for whom? Can the director of Cottex be allowed such licentiousness with his own secretary? Why do you think Blum, Ježek, and Rumltanc left?"

"You think ... But then we'd have to ... in a very big way..."

"A series of letters. Witnesses. Photographs ... and that could bring down the director himself..."

"Fantastic..." gasped Jitka, and her eyes flashed. "Fantastic ... for us that could mean ... everything."

"Or we could lose everything, our hope for an apartment, this room, both our jobs..."

"To win everything! What else are you expecting from Trojan, happiness – hope for an apartment? What? This one-room flat? He hasn't even promised it to us yet. And our jobs ... when's the last time either of us received a bonus? But if new people came in..."

"Bring down the director? The two of us? That's insane..."

"Of course not just us, but do you remember what Gan was saying about Neustupa ... and the secret meeting of the technicians in the laundry room ... and the clique of Alda-Bindr-Coufal-Drtílek-Ebrt-Fiala-Gan ... they've already brought down a couple of directors ... and Trojan's already washed-up anyway. And they say Střelák himself has indicated the same thing ... and lately he's been cultivating General Director Tušl in Prague ... remember when Trojan was in Paris and Střelák kept going to Pardubice when Tušl was speaking there..."

"Yeah, I've taken note of that as well ... It's seriously starting to come together..."

"And when Trojan falls, Střelák will become Director. Střelák will make Plavec his deputy – that's clear. Plavec hates Trojan and is in with Střelák. After Plavec, Ruprt will become head of the planning department – and I could be his assistant..."

"Jituš ... you're amazing..." Břetislav whispered excitedly as he placed a hand on Jikta's lean, bare thigh.

"Turn out the light ... and throw me that handkerchief. Give me a child, today, now ... and the new people will give us an apartment–"

Darn the heel of your left sock, the tip of the right one, and the whole pair is just like new   Always buy shirts with replaceable collars   I know we have to save, my dear   But I want you straight from the box

Pickled herring is enough for both of us for supper   It contains protein, fat, and iodine   How many geniuses ate nothing but fish their en-

*tire lives   I like to care for you, to be sure you're healthy   My amazing girl
My splendid wife*

We'll live here together   The entire room to ourselves

*Our soaps will kiss in the bathroom   We'll push the daybeds together
Go to bed together   Sleep together   And wake up together*

*One day we'll travel to the sea together   And sail a ship upon it   On
the deck we'll drink orange juice through a straw   And sleep together in a
cabin just for the two of us   We'll get an apartment*

*A beautiful apartment on the second floor   Two rooms, a bathroom,
and a kitchen   A small balcony would be enough, a half-meter square
You'll sit out on it and read the newspaper   I'll stand on it and call our
daughter out of the sandbox for supper. I'm happy when I can sate your
appetite*

*I will never be sated with you   Through a snowstorm I will run home
to our warm little nest   I'm happy when you're happy*

*Together we shall elbow our way to the top   When we're together we
can master the entire world   We're young*

*We are clever and strong   We are hungry   And we know how to
calculate*

We shall get what we want   We shall win

```
begin integer i, j, count:
integer array T3B (1:14), T3A (1:90), T2A (1:1260);
switch SSS: = L3, L5;
TAPECODE (1, 2, 0, 0);
for i: = 1 step 1 until 14 do read (T3B, i, 1);
for i: = 1 step 1 until 90 do read (T3A, i, 1);
for i: = 1 step 1 until 1260 do read (T2A, i, 1);
```

the electronic SAAB computer began to spout with mind-numbing
speed, the operator N. Nová sat in her chair at the control panel, and
behind her the young (25) master of the machine (a programmer from
national enterprise Cottex) Dominik Neuman paced back and forth, waiting
calmly for the machine to run his program in half an hour, Dominik had
worked on, analyzed, and fine-tuned it for six months. Dominik paced back
and forth along the specially insulated floor, between the specially insulated
walls, beneath the specially insulated ceiling, in the illumination of lights
that were of a constant brightness, through the air that was kept at a constant temperature and humidity, he silently walked back and forth in his
crepe-soled sandals wearing simple gray pants and a gray work jacket
directly on top of his dark, bare skin, he felt hungry but did not rush off to

still his hunger, one thinks best on an empty stomach, and with a full stomach the only thing you can do is hit the hay. Dominik stepped up to the printer and read the gradually emerging answer to his question,
J: = 1;
if stack (count) = 9999 then goto L10 else
if stack (count) = 999 then begin printtext

answered the computer, a wonderful Swedish SAAB cybernetic machine, in *algol 60* (English was its default language; it could also answer in its mother tongue, Swedish, Russian, or even Swahili or Urdu ... but we outgrew that already), Dominik ran the tip of his tongue over his dry lips, everything is O.K. (or good, kharasho, gut, bene, or however you want), and quietly walked over to the control panel, stood for a moment behind his operator, N. Nová was reliable and almost as precise as the machine itself, beneath her transluscent blouse you could see the contours of her dark athletic shoulders and, from above, the mild curves and dark valleys of her breasts, Dominik ran the tip of his tongue over his dry lips, this is a woman, and he allowed himself a moment of excitement and its sweet tingling, he lightly pressed his body against the back of the operator's chair and, frightened by the sudden burning of his abruptly growing desire, quickly walked back to the printer,
L5: count: = count + 1;
stack (count): = stack (COUNT + 1);

good, hang on, SAAB, I'll be right back, Dominik quickly crossed his specially insulated, soundproofed, and climate-controlled room beneath lights specially supplied by a specialized Austrian company, which gave off sterile, colorless light, through padded metal doors, and down a short, narrow hallway, onto dark, damp, dirty, and horribly banged-up stairs – those idiots in their stupid, swanky offices on the second floor, with their shag carpets and palm plants like in a butcher's shop window threw me along with my machine down into the basement among the rats! – and through other, undefined rooms – a cracked cement floor, smashed boxes and barrels, scraps of paper, and the pervasive odor of feces – he walked out through the courtyard gates, blinded by the bright light of the summer afternoon, squinting, and with delight felt the sunshine on his skin –

Suddenly "Jeen! Jeen! Boomtarataa!" The factory band, crowds thronging the courtyard, and right on the other side of the gates the fat, sweaty old fogies, the local bigwigs, holding the texts of their bungled speeches ... they're celebrating the new warehouse the bigwigs fought three years tooth and nail to prevent.

Dominik once again squinted and faced the final caress of the sun's rays, then he went back downstairs to the rats in his basement, he glanced at his watch, quickly swallowed two cubes of glucose along with some milk, it will take effect in ten minutes, there won't be time to eat.

```
J:=2;
goto L3 end
L9: count: = count+1;
goto L2;
L10: end program;
```

Leaning against the wall of the workshop, off to the side of the celebrating crowd, itinerant foreman Stěpa looked indifferently at the construction of the enormous warehouse he'd just finished, "...so that once again, learning from the mistakes of the past and the development of modern technology, we can master the most demanding tasks in the service of our ultimate goal, the liberation of man..." a pale fellow prattled into the microphone, that's probably the local director, Trojan or whatever his name is, bundled away somewhere all this time and only now coming out to lick his whipped cream. Stěpa spat between his teeth and hatefully looked over the crowd thronging around the dais, these fattened office rats walk around here in their white coats like pharmacists, paper buffoons, all day they wallow around in their offices where they've had air-conditioners installed, guzzle coffee and iced cola, and have those whores of theirs just out of school skip around them, after work they screw them on their desks and pay them overtime – Stěpa's face turned white, as if all his blood were flowing out of his face and, shoulders down into his body, he looked at the little group of laughing girls wearing white coats and tried to guess which of them was wearing nothing but a bra beneath them.

Lounging on a cracked barrel, from which asphalt had oozed out, itinerant worker Valtr squinted and voluptuously scratched at his round paunch, in a couple of days we'll polish off this here Ústí and head off to Jablonec, then Brno and Ostrava, Ústí's not all that bad, but it's not as much fun as it used to be, nothing on this fucking planet is as fun as it used to be – Valtr was over sixty now and went on working crews just for fun (like Graham Greene to literary congresses) – but if you want to, you can always find a bit of fun ... Valtr suddenly spotted a girl in a white coat offering the notables around the microphone a tray with glasses of something on it, and when nobody wanted any, she set the tray down on a box and disappeared, Valtr deftly slid down from his barrel and stole toward the tray.

After the end of the celebration, the young itinerant worker Limon stayed behind, up on the frame of the warehouse where that morning he'd climbed up to plant the maypole. He took off his shirt, lay down half-naked on a girder that was just as wide as his narrow, boyish body, and exposed it to the sun. The minute, red chancres breaking out all over his body were causing him serious concern, according to the guys this was because Limon was lacking "frequent and abundant sexual intercourse," which Limon was not able to secure, but he believed the sun would cleanse his skin, he wanted to be pure and beautiful for the girl he longed for ... Her name is Yveta, she's pure and beautiful with golden hair and pale, delicate skin with blue, luminous veins... Limon leaned his head against a vertical girder and began to play softly on his small, scratched-up harmonica, in the frame created by the girders covered with bright-red, anti-corrosive paint and his shiny, sweaty body with its two points of stiffened nipples, the green side of Střížovický Hill shone like hot, green fur beneath the burning sky, Limon pulled out his half-drunk bottle of milk and quickly finished it off – it looked as if the large Adam's apple in his skinny neck were climbing from the foot of the hill up into the sky.

At the screaming of the siren, the men's shower room in the basement quickly filled, in the dull light of the wire-encased lamps and the white whisps of steam, din and laughter resounded, naked men ran across the wet tiles and crowded into the shower stalls, dozens of arms vied for each shower head and streams of water danced on the jostling, muscular shoulders and flattened into a shiny film as it coursed down backs and chests and glistened on thighs and sex organs, Štěpa stood stiff as a rail and the water trickled down the wet hair plastered to his head, Valtr was slowly spinning, grunting with pleasure, and Limon danced on his restless legs, Dominik battled his way to the water valves, blocked them with his body, and rotated them forcefully, above the crowd in the shower stall the plastic shower heads groaned, rattled, then began to spout ice-cold water, the men cursed and ran to other stalls, and Dominik showered luxuriously alone ... until they discovered his trick, but by then he was toweling himself off.

The beige dust of our street, burning from the brutal July sun, looked like sand dunes in an Asian desert, we've got to have a storm, a real storm with lightning, thunder, and torrential rains – in his ground-floor room in building No. 2000 (the "guest room" or "itinerants quarters" for the temporary housing of itinerant workers, where we've already been waiting two years now for something to open up upstairs) Dominik sat on his red daybed, there were five of them here and besides those five small cabinets for bedding, their flat surfaces serving as night tables, a shared light-colored wardrobe with doors covered in synthetic white leather, one red chair at a small glass-topped table, a vase of stained glass, on the wall a water pipe with a sink and a reproduction of Renoir's *Déjeuner sur l'herbe*.

The burning sun beats against the window. Hot air quivers above the metal windowsill and through the open window wafts swirling beige dust from passing trucks and the sweet, tar-tinged fragrance of melting roofs – in the room it was nearly 30°C – Dominik undressed and with a sigh splashed himself as much as he could with water from the faucet. When he turned off the faucet he heard a light, silvery fluttering in the heat of the room, like rain falling somewhere inaccessible up above ... The Trojans on the second floor are taking a shower. And Director Trojan told us a bathroom simply wouldn't fit down here –

From his half-empty cardboard suitcase containing all Dominik's belongings (eight shirts, four of them nylon, a few socks that didn't always have a match, ten books, and his most valued possession, acquired for half of his traveling expenses on a study trip to a computer manufacturer in Sweden: a silver-handled Chinese dagger), he took out a grubby copy of the Kinsey Report, about women's sexual habits, and buried himself in the arguments for premarital amatory games leading to orgasm: statistics show that their execution increases the percentage of sexually satisfied couples.

Outside the door he could already hear a din and clamor, the workers had come home via the Corner Pub, exhilarated and sweaty they threw off their clothing (Limon his first-class suit and a shirt made of Dutch nylon, with wide stripes, Stěpa and Valtr their rarely changed overalls), they clamor and bluster – in the room it's 30°C – and they're already collecting for beer, the youngest, Limon, takes the "jug" (that's what we call the twenty-liter tin can) and runs out in only his underwear to the pub, cold beer by the liter straight from the can passed from hand to hand and hot, cured meat to go with it, served straight from the pan, singing and glistening fat overflowing onto naked chests and elbows, Valtr roars with satisfaction and furtively pulls from Limon's pocket an eloxal-coated lighter, ruddy Stěpa's stomping in time and with his thumb he connects the drops of sweat into a stream in the middle of his chest, which is now the color of raw meat, and the young Limon is playing his harmonica more and more wildly, during the breaks they talk about women until the air thickens – in the room it's well over 30°C – Dominik looks at his watch and gets up.

"You're going out with Yveta–" whispers Limon eagerly.

Dressed in his best nylon shirt (just the left tip of the collar was starting to fray), a red tie beneath his throat, his suit expeditiously cleaned and his boots attended to in military fashion so that they had more polish than actual leather, the shine would last for about an hour – on the terrace of Větruše Restaurant Dominik Neuman pulled out his cuff with a black cufflink (for 9 Tuzex vouchers), sipped his red wine, and smiled cheerfully at his companion sitting opposite: Yveta (the daughter of the director, Trojan), a girl out of a magazine and as stimulating as if out of a *dream* –

"...so we've been all over Europe. But the south was the real thrill, you know, we went to Turkey on a Čedok tour and drove through Istanbul on a bus, there were so many beggars crowding together on one small square that it was absolutely impossible for each one of them to get maybe even a heller..." Yveta prattled on unaffectedly, and from the sapphire in her platinum ring (worth three of Dominik's monthly paychecks) a reflected ray of sunlight shot out in a blue, luminous shaft.

"Looking at beggars from a Mercedes tour bus with a radio, refrigerator, and air-conditioning? – It's true, I traveled across Europe hitchhiking, but I didn't find anything that exhilarated me much either," said Dominik, and his voice suddenly came to life: "For me Canada would be a real thrill..."

"I'd much rather hitchhike than ride around in our car with Mom and Dad ... they're so annoying. I'd like to just go ... the way young people travel around Europe today..."

"The ones who have a rich papa and an open bank account in some big bank with lots of branches all over Europe ... It's true, your father's rich – but for that kind of trip he'd have to be rich in convertible currency."

"I'd live on nothing but fruit and milk ... I'd go around barefoot in jeans..."

"And in the winter?"

"I'd always follow the sun ... from Holland to France, then Italy or Spain and then Africa ... with a group of young people who are fun to be with..."

"It'd be great to go from one bash to another, and if there wasn't any you'd organize one: smashing display windows in Berlin, pulling up paving stones and building barricades in Paris, tipping over streetcars and setting cars on fire in the streets of Rome–"

"I was thinking more of doing nice things ... like sitting in the sun, playing, and making love..."

"But we can do that here in Ústí..."

"Let's go dance."

(Dance: the conventional silent-block between eating and fornicating.) "Are you here with me on the dance floor or in a boxing ring?" Yveta laughed in Dominik's stiff embrace.

"I'm simply here with you."

"It's making me hot."

"I already was this morning in bed when I was thinking about you."

"So let's see, you got up, worked out, went to work, shaved, ate and drank here, and now you're dancing with me ... and you keep looking at your watch behind my back and thinking about all you have to get done today..."

"You're right. It's a waste of an afternoon, all this stupid prancing around on the floor..."

"So now you're going to suggest a walk, you'll kiss me behind the first tree we come to and then at the second one–"

"A little further on I've got a nice little place picked out..."

"Picked out ... Well, come on then, it makes me nervous to feel I'm so obviously taking up your valuable time."

Beyond the asphalt road roared a dark forest in which lay a warm pit for the body of the blue princess.

"My beautiful antelope..."

"My furious wolf ... Ow! That hurt!"

"I'm madly in love with you–"

"I hear ... a lot of hunger... and very little love..."

"Words, words – who said that? It doesn't matter. Come on."

"Dominik ... you know I want to make love to you. But why are you getting in the way? In your own way. Your nose is cold, wolf, only your belly is warm. I want to make love – not butchery, for God's sake!"

"Words, words, words – Shakespeare. He was a poet, right? Come on."

"We haven't even laughed once today ... and love is supposed to be a happy thing, right? ..."

"So next time we'll go see a comedy. Come on."

"You don't have to pretend so hard you're not looking at your watch. Look at mine ... it's not even midnight ... Oh, you have to get up tomorrow for work, don't you ... When?"

"Five."

"I'll probably get up at noon."

"Why tell me about it? I already know."

"Perhaps to make you a little mad..."

"Well, you succeeded. Thoroughly."

"Or perhaps to do a little harm to your male arrogance..."

"That you'll never do. Never."

"Or maybe so we'll finally have at least one laugh ... I'm sorry. And so since today you've already gotten up, gone to work, shaved, eaten and drank, danced – come on. Just one final tiny wish before we do it: make some kind, any kind, of joke..."

Dominik looked at Yveta's face, which was turned toward him, and pressed her to him with his hands, body, and legs, but this strange girl is somewhere a thousand kilometers away – how did your blood get so blue, Yvette, who has to joke before the flames, isn't ardor the summit of poetry ... I've had lots of girls and I'll have lots more, from the last bunch of girls I barely remember a single one, and the things we did! ... From you I'll remember – and I'll never forget it – that I'm able to conquer anything.

"Okay," laughed Dominik, but it sounded like he was clearing his throat, "a joke for Yvetka: once upon a time there was a young man who as soon as he woke up thought about a certain young girl, after he got up he went to work, shaved, ate and drank, then danced with and kissed her – and when he'd placed her on the ground, he began to feel sorry for her because she was so dainty, so he called her a taxi and sent her home to Daddy. So let's go – no, not that ... Let's go call a taxi!"

"But I don't want a taxi – not yet. Right now I want to be with you."

"But I don't anymore. Maybe some other time ... if I feel like it."

In the coatroom of the restaurant Dominik ordered a taxi from town, and when it arrived he opened the door for Yveta with facetious gallantry and shouted our address to the driver, "You're walking?..." Yveta asked softly. "So I don't have to pay." Dominik grinned at her. "I'm not as wealthy as Daddy–" and he slammed the door like the lid of a coffin.

And now a little compensatory exercise before bed – a guy's got to get tired somehow – Dominik raised his fists to his chest and set off running down to the city with a long loping stride along the silvery-black, tiger-striped asphalt, hello, little stars above, hello, little lights below, you up above are certainly pretty but you're a little out of reach, *understood*, so I'll have to content myself with the ones down below, undoubtedly I'll live to see weekend trips to the moon, but till then I don't intend to sit here on my hands, there's still plenty to do here on this old, cooling star that is still worth burning down completely and building everything over properly from scratch, *cities of glass and aluminum Along blue rivers of drinkable water Everyone gets a house with a veranda facing the sun Electronic highways that supply cars with power Before supper perhaps a rocketship to the sea for some exercise Bathing suits prohibited And more coeds studying sex than philosophy* – Dominik proceeded toward the city along asphalt, concrete, and paving stone.

The streetcars don't run after midnight, so it's still another hour on foot – suddenly exhausted, Dominik dragged himself further through the night, weaving with fatigue.

"Young man..." said an elegant fellow standing over the open hood of a car, "could you give me a little push?"

"Sure, but then could you give me a lift home? ... you're going my way, and it's only about five minutes..." said Dominik.

"Of course, I'd be glad to! Okay, I'll release the brake, and if you'd be so kind as–"

The fellow hopped into the car, and Dominik began to push from behind, for a long time the engine wouldn't catch and a sweat-soaked Dominik toiled away like a galley slave behind, he was already pushing at a run, and suddenly brrpbrpbrp-bruuum bruuuum, the car farted a cloud of exhaust in Dominik's face and was already speeding away ... and it kept on going.

I think this twenty-hour day's been too long and full of too many disappointments, or maybe my battery of patience has been drained or all my accumulated anger's been dissipated by a little spark that set off an explosion, and its lava is consuming the river bed of the Earth – Dominik ran through the night and would have roared if he'd had any breath left, but all he did was wheeze like the surf breaking on pebbles flowing in the opposite direction, like a wild animal raging in the iron net of its ruthlessly mathematical intellect and with every lashing out of its paw, the cruel, razor-sharp edges of its tensed steel wires bizarrely swell – "...so seriously, you've broken up with Yveta Trojanová?" Limon kept on asking after he'd woken up, his moist eyes shone in the darkness.

"Absolutely seriously, and now I'm transfering her to you, along with her papers. With her it's simply: roll around with her somewhere by the pool on a blanket, tell thirty jokes, play for her on your harmonica, and she'll spread her legs for you. And spend all your money on her, but don't worry, she won't ask for alimony." Until morning Limon kept asking for technical details, his big Adam's apple pulsing like a piston in his skinny neck.

That whore's history, but it doesn't matter, I was just blowing my nose, that's all, now to expand the range of the integral to an interval of zero to infinity – stupefied by sleep, Dominik battled his way through the warm, naked, male bodies to the sink on the wall and quickly (unnerved by the frightening intensity of his desire and a wild vengefulness) opened the faucet all the way, set his face, shoulders, and chest against the briskly spurting cone of water, and gulped greedily until his hunger had somewhat abated, and then when Dominik looked out the window – today will be a beautiful day! – he nearly choked on an insane, groundless joy, the sort of utter joy that invigorates the body and convulses the muscles.

The blue-gray outline of the factory, tower, concourse, and warehouse resembling in the morning mist a tethered aircraft carrier captured by mercantile town council members; below, however, beneath the draft line, among the rats, I immediately set my machine shop in motion, which is fatally important for the next sailing, if you haven't figured that out by now, Your Lordships driving around in cars with your own personal bank accounts, you overfed nobility on the first-class and deluxe-class decks, grab your hats, we're sailing down the hill – "Good morning." Operator N. Nová smiled. "Good morning." Dominik smiled and immediately switched on the machine:

BEGIN COMPARE GENERALIZED GOOD TRANSLATION; INTEGER ARRAY A (1:7); TAPECODE (2, 2, 0, 0); READ (A1, 7);
BEGIN INTEGER D, J, K, M, N, MINT, MANT, GOAL, MAX, MIN, ILENGTH, OLENGTH;

Eng. Neustupa, Ph.D. stomped down the basement steps and came through the metal door (Cottex's chief technologist, the best agno- and lanosterol specialist in Central Europe, who because of his abilities has fallen into disfavor with Director Trojan – to whom, of course, Neustupa has decided not to capitulate at all, quite the opposite, in fact – and now is the head of the anti-Trojan revolution), "Hi," said Neustupa, "well, are you going to make this thing for us?"

"I just turned it on." Dominik beamed.

"Great. And what if someone from the administration wants to know what program you're running?"

"Impossible. Not a single one of those fogies understands a thing."

"Great. When you have it, call me. Let's meet again at three-thirty in the laundry room."

"Why not here? As long as I've been here, none of the nobility has dared stick his head in ... They're afraid of rats."

"Great. Everything's already in motion. Now Trojan is entirely alone – we might have a new director inside a year. Okay, three-thirty, here–" and the two technicians firmly squeezed hands.

NEW DATA: READ (MAX, 1); READ (MIN, 1);
BEGIN INTEGER ARRAY SUP, DIST, RULE, INIT, FINAL (1: MAX);

the machine ineluctably spouted the purest, most absolute exactitude, it's only able to count and compare, its mind knows only two numerals: 0 and 1 – but with these it will master projects such as computing the enormous cascades of a hydroelectric plant, it will find the mistakes of a sleepy accountant in payroll, it will prove the sterility of Trojan's administration of Cottex or calculate any number of variants in a thermonuclear conflict, during which it will take into consideration such things as the change in weather over southern Labrador, the condition of granaries in India, the number and weaponry of Argentinian jet fighters, the depletion of strategic cobalt reserves in Canada, the capacity of the Brno munitions factory, and the speed of convoys in the Caribbean, all this with just two numerals, 0 and 1, actually two states: current on–current off, state of calm and state of excitement of the electronic cell, like the biologic cell in a lily, in rotting fecal matter, in a snail's antennae, a bull's testicle, the tip of an elephant's trunk, or a neuron in a human's brain, the ancient and eternal pulsation between the pole of life and the pole of death, good and evil, love and hate, pain and pleasure, devil and angel – between the pole of darkness and the pole of light,

PRINTEROPEN (0); PRINTTEXT (12)

PRINTTEXT (6) SP LEVEL 5SP SUP 3SP DIST 3SP RULE 3SP INIT 2SP FINAL

the supreme discovery of the human mind: refining the human mind to any desired precision, today, with a strong enough battery, it would be a mere technical trifle to overthrow all the emperors, kings, presidents, prime ministers, dictators, chairs, leaders, and shamans and read to them a printout with absolutely precise directions on how to make all of their subjects, everyone on the planet, finally prosper in consonance and harmony, how to ensure forever a market for Brazilian wrought silver, American wheat, Soviet natural gas, Ghanian cocoa, German coal, Tahitian conch shells, why, even Czechoslovak shoes, and to shod the barefoot in the Bengal lowlands, clothe the naked in Paraguay, and feed the starving two-thirds of the planet, which only feeds the third thirds now. And more –

moreover, a smaller machine somewhere in the corner could calculate, at no cost, the way to transport all this by land, sea, and air without a single delay at Kennedy Airport in New York, or Adler near Sochi, or on the grass-covered runway on the bank of the La Plata River, without a single empty freight-car departing Cherbourg to Vladivostok, the Atlantic Ocean to the Pacific Ocean, or the Ústí West Train Station to the Ústí Main Station, and with cargo in all ships, the oil giant *Magdala*, Shell's 213,000-ton oil freighter, a Hong Kong family cutter, a Japanese one-million-BRT tanker, or a river boat from Ústí nad Labem to Magdeburg (GDR) to Hamburg (FRG), in both directions –

and another smaller machine in another corner would figure out, at no cost, how to pay for it and how it would all tremendously pay off –

only there's no denying the emperors, kings, presidents, prime ministers, dictators, chairs, leaders, and shamans fall short of, provided there are
several of them together, the ingenuity of the average upper-school student,
and that's been the case for the last few thousand years – to which over
14,000 wars during this period bear witness – thus after these last few
thousand years it's high time to carefully ask ourselves how many thousands
of years we have left – through how many more wars, a single one of which
could absolutely be the last, do we have to wait patiently beneath the stairs
of palaces or platforms, in front of television screens, to watch how once
again those blunderers blunder and fuck things up ... isn't it almost about
time, after these thousands of fucked-up years, to pull ourselves together
and say something? ... Or even have a whack at it? –
L:END
TYPETEXT END OF TRANSLATION – BEGINNING OF SYNTHESIS

*cities of glass and aluminum   Along blue rivers of drinkable water
Each his own room and every family an apartment   Even at the price of
someone having to wait a year to build a garage   Each with clothes and
shoes because even in sunny India it sometimes rains and gets cold*

*Even at the price of Paris's Dior having a little less golden satin for the
ball season   Each doctor in Nicaragua a car   Even at the price of
someone's second car   Each with enough money so that the loss of a
package containing someone's weekly salary would not be a family tragedy
Even at the price of a worse summer season in Cannes and the Canary
Islands   All this for three billion   Even at the price of a few thousand
deaths*

Some of them hideous
END;
CLOSE PRINTER
IF SUCC = -2 THE BEG STOP
GOT NEW DATA END
ELS GOT L9
END;

Down the basement stairs, shuffling and panting – what sort of old
man is coming to see me – through the metal door came old Trojan, for the
time being still the factory director. Exhausted from the descent, he pants
and wipes the sweat from his brow ...

"Well, well," my director for the time being said spiritedly, "I was
passing by and thought I'd come have a look in here."

"It's definitely worth it." Dominik beamed.

"Well, well ... this is the toy that cost four million."

"The best investment you ever made."

"Nice little machine, isn't it. From Sweden ... You know the wife and I ... our whole lives we've wanted to go to Sweden..."

"But that's not a problem. I've been there twice, and the year after next I'm going again."

"...but it's never worked out. Why exactly? It doesn't matter. What did I want here ... ah, I know. I asked you a while ago to calculate ... do you remember? That project of mine to reorganize the firm. It's not really all that important ... I just wanted to ... just for my own information ... nothing official ... to find out before I actually do anything..."

"The deadline is Thursday–"

"Oh, don't be so businesslike ... I just wanted to ask in a neighborly sort of way..."

"–and on Thursday at ten hundred hours it will be on your desk. That is ... on the desk of your secretary, Berková. She will give it to you from me."

"Okay, okay, my boy ... Fine. I'm in no hurry, after all ... I was just passing by ... Do you think the project looks workable?"

"I never think anything. I'm just paid to run the computer."

"Why is it you young people are so snippy? ... I'm just interested in your opinion of my project."

"Your ... project ... if you can call it that ... I'll deliver it to you on Thursday, as you wished, in quadruplicate."

"It won't work..."

"Not in the least."

"I ... suspected as much. I was ... a little romantic ... in my estimation. Like when I was a student..."

"That's ... a quarter of a century? Since then some things ... a lot of things ... almost everything has changed."

"I know, of course, I know ... Technology ... flies. All right. Let's not talk about it."

"On Thursday at ten hundred hours you'll have it on your desk in quadruplicate."

"That no longer interests me. Listen, Neuman ... Dominik, can I call you that? Okay then, Neuman. I've heard that you and my daughter ... Yveta..."

"That hasn't been true for a long time."

"But? Just yesterday afternoon it was, wasn't it?"

"Yesterday afternoon ... might as well be a thousand years ago. Do you have any further requests?"

Two men facing one another over a computer, an affluent, refined, elegant forty-five-year-old with gray temples and a belly, and a thin young man in a gray lab coat over his bare, tanned body, Dominik beamed – or was he baring his teeth? – you old, rotting whore, for those five thousand a month (which is grotesquely little for the director of such a large enterprise) you're ready to push aside, bury, trample, suffocate, strangle everything, why don't you just drag yourself to a grove of urns, you cadaver, we'll cremate you on the way because it's a waste of time to make any fuss, now it's our turn, yours is already past, you cretinous pig, you want to turn this wonderful adventure for boys, this chemical factory, you want to make it into a step-ladder to a warm sinecure in an office with gilt frames and a thick carpet like in a *chambre séparé* in a Parisian whorehouse, you stone-cold swine, all you can manage is to waylay your own sexretaries, and that with only a considerable amount of help from them, go crawl away and die somewhere, you're finished, now you just reek –

"Okay, see you later." Director Trojan grinned and went back up the basement stairs.
STOP (BEGINNING OF ANALYSIS);
STBRL ANALYSIS; TAPECODE (2, 2, 0, 0); WELL TRANSLATE;
STOP (READ NEW DATA); GOT NEW DATA
END END END

(To be continued)

BESIEGED

Into the night street, where drifts of dust gleamed deathly beneath the black bulwark of the building, Yveta Trojanová stepped out of the taxi and dragged herself up the stairs, stood for a moment on the steps before her second-floor landing, we could have sat right here together kissing each other good night ...

She walked lethargically through the white door, kicked off her shoes at the threshold, and walked down the hallway without any apparent aim in mind, through the kitchen and the dining room, bottles gleamed behind the glass of the sideboard, with her teeth Yveta uncorked Daddy's Courvoisier and took a big gulp, just so I'll feel like a cigarette, and she lit one of Daddy's Kents, the first one of the evening because Dominik doesn't like girls who smoke. Dominik has a cold mouth and cruel, accusatory eyes, why does he insist on seeing everything all the way down to the bowels, those kinds of people simply don't know how to enjoy themselves, they take joy only in their own cruelty ... Dominik's looking for a girl the way you probably buy a horse, he sticks his fingers in their mouths, feels the thighs to see whether it'll be a good work horse, then he harnesses it to his cart and the horses drool side by side on the bit, sweat on the shaft, and pull and pull until they fall and die of exhaustion –

Yveta walked into the kitchen, opened the refrigerator, and sprayed soda water right into her mouth from the pressurized bottle, making a hideous combination with the cognac, with her fingernail she opened a carton of frozen strawberries and from the icy mess dug out several fat ones, she once again drank some soda water from the bottle – it's horribly quiet here ... ran into the bathroom and impatiently turned on the shower until ropes of water thrummed on the white enamel and shattered the deathly silence of the building.

With drops of water on her body she stood before the mirror and with Mom's lipstick drew a little heart below her collarbone, she threw the lipstick into the sink, and when she laughed her breasts shook, Yveta gave them a little fillip, so what about it, poor girl, and straggled along further, not even at night does the heat desist, it's because we're so shut in, Yveta ran from window to window, pulled up the eternally closed shutters, and opened one window after another to the night breeze, hello dear stars, hello girls, I'm here and I'm sad ...

Okay, another little swig and then I'm hitting the hay, Yveta stretched herself out uncovered on her bed in her room and strained her hearing as if expecting to hear a liberating slogan in the distant roar ... but that's just the drone of their stupid power plant or whatever, nothing else is going to happen today, a wasted day and a wasted night like in a morgue, Yveta tossed and turned, pressed her folded-over pillow first to her face then below her belly, she dozed off then woke up, what was I just thinking about, I was dreaming, it was a movie or a book, *the boat hoisted anchor and the bound female captives began to sing beneath the mast*, Yveta lowered her eyelids and her hot palm burned her hip, *he gave the order to raise the sails and went to her below deck "I hate you, John Huston–" she hissed and spat in his face, and with a laugh he lay down beside her on a tarp, and the coils of rope reeked of salt and tar and rats' feet on the wooden ceiling and the rock of the ship as wave chased wave*

She woke up covered with sweat, lying in the sun, but it's just the sun shining into my bed through the open window, great, Yveta went into the kitchen, it was almost ten o'clock, opened another carton of strawberries with her fingernail, took out several fat ones, drank soda water from the pressurized bottle, and went back to lie on her bed in the sun, then the golden trapezoids abandoned the bed and wandered up the walls, Yveta transferred to her parents' bedroom, vigorously raised the blinds, opened the window wide, stood on her tiptoes, and leaned out the window to inspect the sun's path, then she grabbed her father's bed, dragged it right up to the window by its headboard, and turned it so the sun shone directly on it and for as long as possible – in so doing she had to move the night table and both chairs, rearrange the room significantly – on the bed she piled the blankets and covers from both her parents' beds and made a wonderful chaise longue, Yveta found some music on the radio, lay down, closed her eyes, and sunned herself, languid from the heat she dozed off and woke up … down on the street a harmonica warbled.

It must be afternoon already, the harmonica played on, that's Limon playing for me, the guy from downstairs who loves me but is shy – he lives directly below us in the itinerants quarters and plays for me as soon as he gets home from work, here everyone goes off to work somewhere so they have to go to bed early, that's why the place lives for only a moment in the afternoon … but when there's something going on downstairs, it's nice to hear it up here, there's a bunch of them living down there and they know how to have fun … "You still sleeping?" says Daddy in the doorway.

"I'm not sure."

"Why don't you get up?"

"What for?"

Mom and Dad have come home from work, they immediately close the windows and pull down the shutters.

Our family:

Daddy sits dead tired in his armchair with a copy of *Chemical Engineering News* on his lap with a picture of some kind of tower on the cover – he's had the same copy with the tower on it for a month now. He surely knows it by heart … but it's obvious he doesn't read it at all. He just keeps it in his hands, like a fence, so no one will speak to him.

Mom: she'd like nothing better than not to have to talk to Daddy. And just in case he might want to, she reads a novel, *Meeting in Bruges*.

When's the last time these two encountered one another? … Do they still sleep together … hardly. It must be horrible sleeping next to one another and … nothing. Like prisoners who aren't even fags.

Daddy. He slaved away his whole life to become director of that horribly boring and horribly dirty factory. He succeeded – and now what? Why isn't he celebrating? Because he's worn out. Frantic tedium. Normally Dad is so annoyed that it's a pain for him even to speak. Because he doesn't have the strength to commit suicide, he's started going with his own secretary. The girl's using him. He's so desperate, he's even grateful to her for it. What's there left for him if he's already forgotten how to live? Outside, Limon is playing his harmonica for me.

Mom. She couldn't care less, but feels she can't let anyone know how horribly little she cares. That's simply not done in better society ... And so Mom preserves some decorum, pretending it bothers her, but she lets it bother her in a comfortable sort of way. This bother takes up less time and attention than, for instance, a manicure. She pretends to be offended and reads *Meeting in Bruges*. Daddy avoids her – great! At least she has peace and quiet to read. Maybe she's almost even happy ...

And Daddy probably knows it doesn't really exasperate Mom, he probably even knows she's almost happy knowing that Daddy knows even this about her – rotten, isn't it? Outside, Limon is playing his harmonica for me, he wants to make love to me.

Mom. Above all Mom is tired. Horribly. And she keeps getting more tired. She's also in charge of some stupid office that constantly makes coffee and serves sandwiches ordered from the cafeteria. Between cooking and washing, Mom laboriously taught herself a few foreign words – as if years ago she suspected we'd have a maid and she wouldn't have any work to do – but she can't really speak, mostly just a few phrases like: "Would you like some more sugar?" "Do you smoke cigarettes, cigars, or a pipe?" "From here there's a wonderful view!" and "This castle is from the fourteenth century." And now she sits in her stupid office arranged for all these Belgians, Poles, and Mongols who have business at Prague Headquarters and just come here on an excursion so they don't have to return their traveling expenses, but everyone pretends it's all terribly important, and Mom makes them coffee, sends to the cafeteria for sandwiches, and makes conversation with them: "Would you like some more sugar?" and "Do you smoke cigarettes, cigars, or a pipe?" after which she bundles them into a car and takes them – always by the same route – up to Střekov, "From here there's a wonderful view!" and then to Střekov Castle, "This castle is from the fourteenth century." Why does Mom do this when we've got enough money? When she herself says what a pain it is and how it makes her so tired and worn out? Why does she drive these people like harnessed horses till they practically drop from exhaustion? Outside, Limon is playing his harmonica for me, he wants to kiss me and make love to me.

Our family suppers:

A tablecloth on the table (beneath which is another one: the table is made of beautiful wood, but all you can see is the lower part of its legs), a small plate with five slices of bread (four and a half of which will be left over and thrown out), a pitcher of ice water (I can't remember the last time anyone drank any of it), a porcelain thingy-bob with salt, paprika, pepper, mustard, vinegar, and oil (except for the salt, they sit there for show), and for each a napkin (which no one's ever touched, so they won't have to be washed).

This is how our scrupulous mother spent the evening. She:

1. Washed the dishes.
2. Prepared omelets.
3. Prepared spinach.
4. Fried fish fillets.
5. Cooked the omelets.
6. Put the fish fillets inside the omelets.
7. Fried the rolled omelets like cutlets.
8. Meanwhile made soup and tea.
9. Carefully laid everything out on the table.

This took her two hours. We ate it up in ten minutes. I'm the only one who ate everything on my plate. Mom left a quarter of it, Dad half. Now we sit for a moment, for the sake of propriety, and another day is gone – but do you know, you two pitiful things who must have loved each other once, how good warm milk tastes in the morning in the cafeteria when the street is wet and you can smell the asphalt? What a delight it is to eat hot potato pancakes on a bench in the park? Or a sausage at night on the square? We sit here like three mummies – do you know all the things we could be experiencing at this moment? ...

I probably don't know what I want ... BUT DEFINITELY NOT THIS. I wish vacation would be over and I could go back to Prague. I'll go to classes or maybe even wash dishes in a dining car, but I'll live among people who are still alive – outside, Limon is playing his harmonica for me, he's young like I am and wants me.

"Where are you going?" asks Mom.

"Out."

"Now, at night?"

"What would I do here?"

Mom and Dad are silent. I change clothes in my room, just a dress over my bare body, and I'd really like to go barefoot ... I feel like having something spicy. I'll go see Limon, the guy from the itinerants quarters beneath our carpet. He'll eat me without bread, without ice water, without salt, paprika, pepper, mustard, vinegar, oil, without a tablecloth and without a napkin – in front of the building he greets me with his harmonica.

"Seeing you reminds me of this joke," says Limon, and he's a really handsome guy, or at least young, and all young people are great, they're not dead yet, "have you heard the one about the sailor stranded on a desert island?"

I've heard it, but I want us to laugh, Limon's told me loads of jokes, he has them written down in this little notebook, and because he's got such large handwriting he's read me the whole notebook, and during the last joke we crawled through a hole in the fence into the slaughterhouse – a little way from our building, but it's deserted enough for a murder ... or for making love. But right on the other side of the fence Limon jumped me.

"Wait ... Play a little more..."

Limon doesn't want to play anymore, his Adam's apple is bobbing up and down in his skinny neck, as if he were already swallowing, and his eyes are shining, he's insanely impatient, don't worry, you'll get what you want, but let's play a little more, after all, the best is beforehand – but Limon also has to get up early in the morning and I'm afraid to say it because I'll offend him, those boys from downstairs are all so terribly proud and also terribly impatient and mean, I suddenly seem to be a stranger here, it's frightening, Limon's fingers feel like they're made of sheet-metal and they're somehow angular, it hurts and he's wild and angry, as if he wanted to strangle me rather than make love to me, but I'll gladly give myself to you if only it will be nice together in this sad world, where everyone's alone and therefore sad, and where it's so great and beautiful to be together, so let's go, we're going to MAKE LOVE NOT WAR – *we'll run away from here together   And you can even take your friends along*

And your friends can bring their girlfriends and their guitars   We'll go from town to town   Always following the sun to the south   We can all live in a single room   After all we're young, and why should we be ashamed   Whoever wants to can go to work in the morning   And bring back milk, cigarettes, and oranges for everyone   And flowers

WHO'S WHO
Yveta Trojanová (19)

A barefoot, blond little girl in a frock, without panties, beneath a sunshade, where the wind has created smooth, even drifts of beige beach sand, uses her hands to shovel the sand over her legs, leans back and shovels more of it further up her little body, all the way up to her chin (like children in the dust in front of our building) on the beaches of Varna and Nesebur in Bulgaria, Yalta in the Soviet Union, and Mamaia in Romania.

"First work, then play–" Yveta's very busy father, the director of an Ústí industrial factory, hammered into her when she wanted to play with him. But her mother and father always work so long they're too tired to play with the little girl – when's the play going to come after the work?

Always clean as a whistle and wearing a beautiful frock from her crammed closet, Yveta would stare enviously out the window, where children were rolling around, pushing, and fighting in the dust. Yvetka passionately wanted to gain their friendship, so she'd give them chocolates, foreign chewing gum in the shape of cigarettes, and high-calorie snacks, which she didn't eat herself. Mother, who grew up in the country, prepared meals so that the family actually ate once a day: all day from morning till night. When Yvetka brought a flock of children home for the third time and asked Mother to butter a slice of bread for each, Mother gave the children just a handful of cheap sour candies and spoke with a tearful Yvetka long into the evening, trying to convince her she couldn't simply "feed the whole street." The leftover bread – and often that was half a loaf a day – the Trojans collected in a bag in the bathroom, and when the bag was full, Yvetka's grandmother would take it for the rabbits.

In the evenings Father would sit over his official papers, Mother over a book, and Yvetka, left alone in front of the television or over a French textbook with pictures – it's easiest to learn a foreign language at a tender age – with a cold cutlet or piece of cake, so she wouldn't make any noise, would dream up long, strange adventures she'd continue every evening. Once, in the evening silence of the quiet house, she took off her clothes and in a vague state of arousal crawled beneath the table. Upbraided by her mother and warned of horrible dangers, the lonely fourteen-year-old girl began to play with her body out of boredom.

As the daughter of a deputy and later director of the company, Yveta found herself in the society of children of deputies, directors, and chairmen, who organized frequent parties in the large apartments and villas of their invariably absent parents. Yveta soon learned to drink straight Scotch whiskey without the slightest consequences, because quality alcohol does not cause hangovers. Once, in the villa of Robert's parents, everyone took a pinch of bitter white powder that was supposed to be the famous LSD. The drug had absolutely no effect on Yveta, but when everyone else was shouting that they saw various peculiar things, Yveta began to scream that hosts of swarthy hands were reaching out for her and thereby reaped considerable success.

During her defloration by a young, handsome Ústí writer of morally seditious books, Yveta felt only pain and fear of pregnancy. Immediately after the act, the writer secretly wrote her something on a stiff white card that he sealed in a white envelope, and he asked her to go home and read it immediately because the girl's crying was getting on his nerves. Burning with curiosity, Yveta went outside and opened the envelope immediately; on the card was a drawing of a little flower. Meditating over this message, Yveta sat down on a bench in the Stalin Gardens, where the jasmine had just bloomed, smoked several American Kent cigarettes (Daddy's brand), and felt completely happy.

Yveta spent three semesters at three different post-secondary schools, all of them very *au courant* and all of them unfinished (medicine, film, journalism), because her initial interest kept evaporating. Daddy was always a little angry because it cost him considerable effort to get Yveta into these schools, whose number of applicants was always several times greater than the number of acceptances. When she was studying in Prague, Yveta lived with the widow of a certain director in a large, beautiful room with a separate entrance, a piano, balcony, telephone, and a silver basket for calling cards in the foyer, for 400 crowns a month without breakfast.

Well supplied with money from her mother, and especially from her father, Yveta lived in elegant, bohemian style. She sometimes lunched in the Ambassador Hotel and sometimes at the Koruna Cafeteria in the arcade of the same name on the main square of the capital, she went to premieres of avant-garde plays and met Josef Somr, she had parties in her room, at which everyone sat on the floor, she walked along National Avenue barefoot, dined at the Writers' Club, kissed Allen Ginsberg during a visit to Prague, and he played for her on his miniature golden cymbals, she got John Steinbeck's autograph, at an adult ed lecture at the city library she discussed sex with Vladimír Páral, on Charles Bridge with colored chalk she mistreated four meters of stone railing, in Chotkov Gardens she and a friend were raped by Syrian students, in a demonstration against the Vietnam War she broke a window of the American Embassy, and sitting on ice-cold paving stones she listened to a cycle of sacred music concerts in the Church of St. Jakub.

After several fleeting love affairs, Yveta became the lover of a student named Hannsheiner, the son of an enormously wealthy Hamburg ship-owner. In soft, phonetic English, Hannsheiner initiated her into Zen Buddhism, whose foundation he enthusiastically explained to Yveta thus: "The old master promised to explain to his students what Zen was. He stepped before them holding a flower in his hand, bowed, and left." Yveta was wild about Zen, and over elegant dinners in exclusive restaurants Hannsheiner described to her the horrific poverty in the ports of Alexandria, Bombay, and Djibouti (where his family's company had offices), and clinking the ice in his glass of Campari he spoke of his decision to study sociology (in fact, he was studying mechanical engineering) and dedicate his life to serving the poor, among whom he also would divide his enormous family wealth created through the exploitation of the proletariat.

When in October her mother went away to treat her nerves at a sana-torium in Gráfenberg, for the first time her father took Yveta with him on a business trip, to Munich. Immediately upon exiting the train, the nume-rous families of Greek, Spanish, Portuguese, and Turkish *Gastarbeiters* sitting on their bundles in the ultramodern, glassed-in hall of the Munich train station excited Yveta. After her father's successful business meeting, Yveta ate a Riesenkalbshaxe, an enormous joint of veal weighing over a kilogram, cooked on an infra-grill, for eleven marks, on an evening walk with Father she saw groups of young people from all over Europe with long hair, guitars, most of them barefoot, sunning themselves on the steps of the old royal residence, and as the sun was sinking in the west and darkness rising, the young people would sit higher and higher on the steps, like birds. "Bye, Daddy," said Yveta, she climbed up to the highest step, took off her shoes, sat down on the stone, and inclined her face to the last rays of sunlight.

The big black company limousine of the factory director of national enter-prise Cottex whizzed along toward the capital at 80 kilometers an hour, 140 on the straightaways, the uniformed driver passed dozens of vehicles, on the back seat in rapt conversation about copies of highly confidential bundles of documents, sat Deputy Director František Střelák and the Direc-tor himself, the limousine drove through the metropolis to the admonitory blare of its horn and with a lurch halted in the cement courtyard of general headquarters, the doorman saluted, the chauffeur opened the door, and both executive functionaries climbed to the second floor. "Exactly seventeen hundred oh oh hours–" said the factory director sternly to his favorite, his deputy, and he halted.

As soon as Střelák's back disappeared into the door of the secretariat, Borek Trojan turned on his heel and hopped back down the side stairway to the first floor, he executed a couple of dance moves on the landing between the floors, and with a quiet laugh, snapping his fingers to a letkis rhythm, went downstairs. In the darkness of the hallway were hundreds of packages of something piled up to the ceiling, Borek ripped open the covering of one and pulled out a large white card with double perforated edges, aha, here they've just started on perforated punchcards, in Ústí we're much further along, we started right off with cybernetics, managerial tomfoolery, and how desperately dull it will be to rule according to orders from machines, stick it somewhere, Borek rolled the card into a little cone and stuck it into the package like a flower, so long, colleagues, I'm playing hooky today – and he slipped out the back entrance from this uninteresting hole in the wall.

Below the Žižkov bridge, eating Italian ice cream from a cone, Borek licked the ice cream and at the window of the Central Committee of the Revolutionary Trade-Union Organization smiled at two very sexy secretaries wearing sheer nylon blouses, hi, girls, too bad you have to work, and he took a streetcar – when's the last time I took a streetcar! – at random toward the city, absorbed by a billboard "Know-How and How to Achieve It," he got off near a movie theater and saw a matinee of a sophisticated British slapstick comedy, he sat in the theater practically alone and loudly laughed when the London louts dragged an iron bed through the streets, he left the theater and sat in the public gardens delighting in the flaming tones of the October leaves, and as he was walking among the trees to secure different views of the treetops and new stimulating contrasts, the inscription on the white facade of a cathedral shouted out at him AVE CRUX SPES UNICA, the cross is the only hope, it's best to live without either, Borek shrugged, boarded another streetcar, amused, headed somewhere else – who knows where – and alighted when he was attracted by a blue neon sign in the shape of a fish glowing in the darkness of a passageway, just a symbol, today, but a little fish would taste good about now, Borek looked through a half-covered window into the 1st-category fish restaurant, Grill, and bored by the tables with their excessive silverware and their ostentatious, over-starched white tablecloths, walked deeper into the passageway until the smell of fish struck his nostrils, behind the swinging glass doors odd characters stood at the counter over beers, and from the kitchen, plates, and bowls came the smell of fried, baked, and marinating fish, Borek got some fried sturgeon and baked trout, with a side of *pommes frites* like a poem, pay first, this is fun and it was ridiculously cheap, Borek went from counter to counter and stuffed himself with fish prepared nine different ways, tomorrow I'll feel horrible, you have to destroy yourself a little now and then, so I'll burst, Borek stood in line in front of the tap for probably the fifth time, and after his sixth beer he met an enormous fellow who led him across the square to a chess café, with a little alcohol chess is fantastically amusing, so two Cinzanos and I'll pay, we play for money, five crowns a game, of course Borek won the first game, and of course the other fellow won the rest, those five crowns were important to him, I'd give you twice as much for such a good time, but you're starting to bore me with that toilsome pondering of yours, he answers the breathtaking sacrifice of my queen with the boring move of a pawn, Borek scornfully tossed his opponent's five crowns onto the table, lifted the cloth chessboard by the corners, and poured the chess pieces into his opponent's lap, he crossed the square and entered a museum for a moment, stood before imitations of the world's largest diamonds, caressed an excision from a thousand-year-old sequoia, and in the youth café Luxor, to light music, ate Parisian bananas almondine covered in chocolate sauce while watching a pair of sixteen-year-old breasts.

His watch shouted 17:00 at him, and Borek quickly paid, hopped into a taxi, ran through the rear entrance into general headquarters, crossed the ground floor, the porter's lodge received a message that his car was already waiting, with a severe expression he went out into the courtyard, the chauffeur opened the door of the large black company limousine, in the back seat was Deputy Střelák with bundles of new highly confidential documents, the doorman saluted, the limousine drove through the metropolis to the honking of its horn and whizzed along home at 80 kilometers an hour, 140 on the straightaways, the uniformed driver passed dozens of vehicles, Deputy Střelák was reporting on new, dangerous, and powerful groups that had formed in the company, that we're missing sixteen million, and that Neustupa has been to see Tušl once again, with a lurch the car stopped in front of building No. 2000, which already needs a new facade again, and there are no facade-repairers around, the chauffeur opened the door. "Till tomorrow–" the company director said sternly, and he climbed the stairs, his heart was pounding in his throat and his stomach pain was becoming unbearable, his wife was arguing with his daughter about a hundred and fifty crowns, take them and now be quiet, Yveta takes them contemptuously, Yveta's contempt grows along with Jana's anger that this is no way to raise a daughter, to ensure a good upbringing we'd have to argue all night long, for supper repulsive dietary curd-cheese pancakes and enough tea to make you vomit, outraged, Yveta locks herself in the bathroom, from up above BANG! BANG! BANG! BANG! from the pipes, that's the Trakls again beating a wrench on the pipe, telling us they want an apartment, then above the bedroom Alex begins stomping, along with his old whore, and the roar from the itinerants quarters down below goes on long into the night, I'm surprised they haven't murdered me yet, but they're doing it slowly, which is a much more reliable method –

Hardly have I finally fallen asleep than the alarm clock blares, Jana looks horrible in the morning, I cut myself shaving, blood flows out of me, a gulp of much too hot coffee, the chauffeur opens the car door, the limousine dashes through the desert dust of futility, why don't I walk to work, it'd be healthier, the chauffeur opens the door, but I'm already sitting here – aha, get out, the new warehouse still doesn't have a gate, but why is that, after all I was told – careful, there's Trakl, and he's already running toward me to talk about the apartment he wants, of course they want an apartment, that's normal, and they're normal, they're so normal they're almost perverted, and the courtyard is full of foam, a pipe has broken somewhere, yellow-green bubbles, it'd be highly unpleasant to step in it, "Sprinkle it with sodium carbonate!" and right up to the second floor, the door DIRECTOR, that's me –

"My dear–" whispers Broňa, my final happiness, her eyes flash, a wild kiss and a desperate embrace –

Footsteps outside the door, they quickly pass: behind the fortress of a padded door. I had it restuffed myself. And established a morning routine that from now till 08:15 provides me with 45 minutes of protection.

A pile of newspapers. What's the world doing today? IN SAIGON THE HIGHEST STATE OF READINESS   GENERAL MOBILIZATION IN THE SOUTH   FAMINE TAKING HEAVY TOLL IN BIAFRA INTERROGATION OF ASSASSIN

FIRM POSITION OF EEC TOWARD FRANCE'S DIFFICULTIES SAIGON ANTICIPATING ATTACK   EVACUATION OF "RESUR-RECTION CITY"   CAMPAIGN OF THE POOR IN THE U. S. ABOUT TO COME TO A HEAD   DEATH IN THE SIFAR AFFAIR   WHAT ABOUT POLITICAL PRISONERS?   PUBLIC EXECUTION IN NIGERIA

08:13 - Broňa will come in two minutes. Dear, come here and do something for me – LICENSING THE PENITENT'S CRAFT writes Zikmund + Hanzelka from Ceylon:

"A little farther on, they were stabbing someone. Around his neck was a rosary with a hundred and eight beads, around his neck a red hand-kerchief, his hands bound in front of his face. Two very focused men were stabbing a half-meter silver needle into the skin beneath his arm, a third was holding him by the elbow and sprinkling ashes, a fourth pulled his hands apart to place an iron frame over his head: metal suspenders connected by a transverse band beneath his neck and on his shoulders, with openings for his hands. Assistants pushed the needles through the arms, bent the frame to the waist. Only then, when he raised his hands above his head, could they look into his eyes. Icily calm, the eyes look absently toward the horizon.

"Then he slowly turned around. On his back, beneath his shoulder-blades, two pairs of hooks attached to ropes, someone had harnessed a barrow with a red roof of palm leaves. The assistants stepped back, shouted haroohera in unison, the human porcupine with silver spines stepped forward, all around them wooden carts creaking by.

"The crowd stepped back to open for the penitent a path to repentance.

"WILL MY HOROSCOPE CHANGE?

"Afternoon clouds gathered above the jungle, and in a moment it was pouring. The thin saris stick to the women's bodies, the pilgrims wade through dirty puddles."

Broňa enters with a tea tray, and her thin red dress clings marvelously to her body, which I know ...

"You look tired, Borek."

"I am tired, dear."

"I could cheer you up–"

"Not here."

"Well then, let's go somewhere–"

"Right now?"

"Yes!"

We laugh. Why not? Because in a couple of minutes Střelák will be here. But who's in charge of whom? Yesterday it was wonderful playing hooky ... We kiss until 08:24, and Broňa runs into Střelák on the way out.

Střelák tells me I must berate the technicians and praise the technology department, maybe I should do it the other way around, but it took me an hour to work through it, meanwhile Střelák had me increase the bonuses of Alda, Bindr, and Coufal, and reduce Kroupa's, whose existence, let alone his slip-up, I'm just now hearing about, and in the meantime Střelák ordered me to approve the payment of something to someone and another twenty-four things, he's right, maybe not, the main thing is he's already leaving, and with a relief that alarms me I set out on my rounds of the factory, people greet me and I feel their glances on my back, no longer the tiniest bit friendly, a new warehouse without a gate gapes the black maw of its entrance at me, two years ago I'd have turned on my heels, burst into the technology department with a bundle of thunderbolts, and in twenty-four hours there would've been a gate, so why don't I do it now, after all, I'm not afraid of these people, or am I? ...

I walk further down the concrete walk, I feel my old, tired heart and carefully avoid the yellow-green hissing foam that the sodium carbonate has not yet smothered, and even when it does disappear, a pipe could burst at any minute, or worse, I steal along anxiously, hoping no one will pounce on me with some request whose approval or rejection, if even for them important or even fateful, I don't care one way or another about, but it still scares me to death ... Why? Shouldn't the petitioners be more frightened than me? It's strange, but it's exactly the reverse ... And then relieved I haven't suffered another slashing, I lock myself in the bathroom, where you can't even read a newspaper – my one and only absolutely safe place in the entire factory. And most peaceful – and isn't peace happiness?

On my desk another pile of attacks on me, letters, orders, directives, invoices, requests, reminders, three hours of total concentration and I'd be able to repulse this daily bombardment, but it's already 09:35 in the morning and I feel exhausted and incapable of concentration, moreover, in twenty-five minutes the factory administration will gather here for a meeting, so without thinking I write in the upper right-hand corner the symbol "FS" and realize that each time I write this symbol, some of my vital energy drains away – here they come, it's already 10:00.

"FS" sits down beside me to prolong our regimen another day, across from him the chief technician, Neustupa, to plant a few more mines and from time to time fire an underwater torpedo, the other five chairs are occupied by supplementary members of the administration, like spectators at a daily corrida, and Broňa brings everyone coffee to quicken their senses, so that every sword thrust into my bull's flesh and every jostle of horns (but this doesn't happen much anymore) is duly evaluated, and according to the score of delivered and received blows, the degree of instability of my stability is established for another twenty-four hours.

"It's fascinating that the factory administration has thus far been unable to take a position..." the torero Neustupa ambles forward with a red cloak for the first round, and I'm feverishly thinking what position to take the minute before he finishes, "...and inasmuch as the trend toward continualization is perhaps more than obvious..." Neustupa continues logically, and I see with joy that I suddenly understand the issue perfectly, and that what is being said is absolutely correct, I'm already opening my mouth to ratify, as is my right: "Approved. Next."

–but at the last fraction of a second I realize I'm a bull that cannot fall into the arms of the torero, the spectators would throw their cushions into the arena and the bull would be ignominiously destroyed by the assistants, an icy fear completely paralyzes me, I disguise my open mouth by swallowing a tablet of Librium, and in the moments thereby gained I notice Střelák's raised eyebrows, the secret code of our duumvirate, I take the floor and with a strenuous attempt at a decisive tone manage to get out: "We've already heard ... enough about these matters. I don't see ... anything productive coming from further debate. Next ... please."

I notice Neustupa's mocking grimace, he leans over to his assistant and both impudently guffaw, but Střelák's clanging voice has covered my retreat, and the jousting continues a little further on down the sand, snatches of sentences fly across the table: "...if the Japanese hadn't blocked all the sulfoxazo- and sulfisoxazoderivatives..." "...the State Bank has categorically refused..." "...or, fourthly, to compensate those sixteen million with a promise of further..." "...in a situation when the district is not fulfilling its milk purchase..." "...ordinary white shirts and ties should be enough for the musicians because, comrades, I think a workmen's band wearing blue smoking jackets would not properly fulfill the..." I preside expertly, I call upon people to speak and I file away what accrues from the discussion, suddenly an urge grows in me for my own intervention and a declaration of my power – for power not employed withers along with its bearer – the urge becomes a need and more, it is my existential necessity. So I say:

"And when will the new warehouse have a gate?"

Everyone looks at me, astonished, Neustupa splutters with laughter, Střelák is agitated and leans toward me whispering something I don't understand, "...after all, since the workshop has ... as per the agreement between Klouzek and Dymšic..." because I'm not listening to him, I feel sweat oozing from every pore, until I vaguely recall that I did something like this before, and that it's not a matter of the gate anymore ... It's a matter of my making a horrible fool of myself, but neither directors nor bulls are to be ridiculed, on the contrary, they must remain reserved to inspire respect and fear, now there's nothing left to do but toss the shroud over the frightened bull that collapsed by goring his own leg. I get up, go to my desk, dial a random number, and whisper inaudibly into the receiver until I hear the conversation at the table has turned elsewhere, fortunately it's 11:28, so I return to my chair to close the meeting at the appropriate moment: "So, everything's clear. If nobody has anything else–"

"And when will the new warehouse have a gate?"

Neustupa. Everyone stiffens. This has never happened before. This is outright rebellion.

I look at the people before me. Am I really just here to be laughed at? I've done more for this factory than this whole lousy group put together. I've given it all my strength. And every single person in this group has something to thank me for. I made them. Why aren't they rushing to help me? I'm having more and more of these memory lapses ... because I've worked too much. Well, then I no longer will. Now I'm just going to have some fun. I've grown tired of being your bull, you scum. Now I'll sit in the president's box.

"Neustupa, what am I paying you for?"

"Excuse me, Director, I don't understand..."

"Neustupa, I remember when you came here eight years ago. Do you remember how you fled in fear from the infuriated night shift? How you were absolutely worthless as an operations technician. You've changed since then – so have I. It's only human, right? But words such as fair play or gentleman have never been in your vocabulary. I refuse to cultivate you anymore. You bore me. I could have thrown you out a hundred times. But instead I made you the third man in the company. Right now I'm going to think over what to do with you ... when I feel like it. Until then you are excluded from all meetings of the administration. Your breath smells. I've grown weary of you. Out!"

They go out like whipped dogs. I despise them. Every one of them is my creation. My lackeys and my knaves. You disgust me.

"Yes, you were right to show a firm hand," prattles a dismayed Střelák, my #1 knave, "however, it's surely going to be problematic..."

"Střelák. I want a car to Prague. Immediately."

"But the secretary of the city council will be here in a minute and after him the chairmen–"

"Take care of it. It doesn't interest me. Go get my car."

"When will you be back?"

"When I feel like it."

"But–"

"Go!"

Quiet. I'll go to Prague with Broňa. My final joy. I call her in and kiss her.

"Broňa, dear, I've taken the next two or three days off. Would you like to spend them with me?"

"Three days isn't very long – I want to be with you for thirty years!"

"In Prague."

"Or Hong Kong or Rožnov pod Radhošt!"

"Then call Prague and reserve a studio apartment in the staff quarters ... for a long time. I'll go by car. You take the afternoon express train at fourteen-ten. Can you make it?"

"I'd make it if the train left in half an hour. What should I take with me?"

"Your lips. Hair and shoulders. Breasts, belly, hips, and thighs. Teeth and claws."

"Okay, I'm already out the door–"

For the first time I sit in the front seat next to the driver. A pleasant trip. Along the river ... against the current. In an instant we're in Prague. To avoid superfluous explanations I send the chauffeur for the key. He returns in a second, holding two keys on a chain. Broňa will get the second one.

The staff quarters of the general headquarters is six one-room flats taking up one half of the tenth floor of a pre-fab high-rise. From the window I can see the hideous industrial quarter far below. I have an entrance hall and closet, a shower nook, and a small room: two red daybeds, a rug between them on the floor, two red chairs at a small glass-topped table, on which sits a vase made of stained glass, and on the wall a reproduction of Modigliani's naked orange girl ... she looks just like Broňa.

I doze a bit, take a shower, swallow two fortifying tablets: I feel superb. I could even bear my own execution. In two hours Broňa will arrive. She'll come through that door. Sit in that chair. Her hairpins in her wonderful teeth, she'll comb her hair before this mirror. The bright red of her nails will flash   *she'll have me on that red duvet cover   Her lips open with an insatiable hunger   The glitter of her teeth in the damp darkness   Her nails dig into my shoulders   The red she-devil from the roaring ghetto   Penetrate my blue port   And together we'll fire on our white mansion*

We burn down my admiralty   Let the whole shore go up in flames Plunder me   Eat and drink me like cherries   Crush even my seed and eat my fatty pith   Spit out my shells   Finish me off and kill me   My love   My catastrophe   My deluge

What did I used to dream about? ... Now the only thing that's of any account is this. Let nothing human be foreign to us –

Broňa arrived less than two hours later. Like a hurricane, like a tornado. She comes in through that door. She can't stay seated in the chair very long. We look at each other in the mirror. The last snapshot of me alive ... and already, without delay, she's starting to marvelously murder me.

Her body is her only weapon. The poor girl – it's all she has in the world. But her only property is worth a lot. A wonderful jaguar: warm slender firm muscles from neck to feet, hands, elbows, arms, shoulders, thighs, calves, her whole body is firm, hot, taut, nimble, agile and responsive, like a single perfectly functioning supermuscle controlled by ravenous instinct, lightning quick perception, the agile supermuscle contracts like a carnivorous plant, sucking with every pore – what a grip! How can I not fall with delight into such a splendidly equipped abyss? Her nerves must lead from the center of her brain directly to her razor sharp teeth and nails. All in all: a wonderful assassin.

We don't have much time, just a day or two now, all in all a year or two, we breach the border between day and night, we go out toward morning for hot cured meat and bring home milk and wine, during the day we sleep, and each new evening there awakes a more ferocious madness ... what a delight it is destroy oneself so adeptly.

"And we'll buy a small, fast car, a two-seater convertible–" Broňa whispers eagerly as she presses against me, "and we'll go to Finland together..." I feel marvelously dead and agree to everything. My jaguar wants from me a trifle: the whole world.

October is at its peak, a regal month. This city knows nothing about it. It wakes up like an alcoholic in a thick, cold fog. After our day and two nights of insanity Broňa hurries to the morning train, back to Ústí thrilled with her new key and senselessly fresh, as if after a bath – I remain lying on the couch as on a bier.

I sit up to take some tablets and give myself an injection. It's two hours before I'm able to get up. Completely empty, devoured, sucked dry, I stand barefoot by the window, I shiver from the cold and look out at the foreign street and foreign city, at the endless stone sea of buildings ... Once I stood like this in a similar pre-fab cage. Fifteen years ago ...with Niky. That time I returned. For little Yvetka, to lead her to the tree on Christmas Eve and call with her: "Come, Santa Claus, come see us tonight..." The adult Yveta no longer needs me. She despises me and probably doesn't even hate me anymore. That time I returned for Jana, home to my factory, to my town ... that time I still wanted and needed to live. Which is no longer the case. Rather the opposite.

I'm empty. I lie down again and look at the ceiling. What's next? I really don't care. I'll stay here. With Broňa, with my absinthe, by which I'll die. How long will they let us live here? As long as Tušl is general director. Probably two or three years. I'll have taken care of everything by then. Two hundred days and two hundred nights, like these last few days and nights

... and at most the same again, and my teeth will no longer hurt. Heh-heh-heh, as Broňa would say.

The tablets and injection are starting to take effect. I feel better. Except my heart skips a beat every now and then. In a moment it'll be better. I think about the coming days and months. I imagine it in color: in the afternoon in town I meet Broňa. We go to the river. An exquisite supper with wine. Dancing. At night lovemaking ... as long as my strength holds out. Preserve the level of efficiency with reckless medication. Fortunately I have connections at the best pharmacies. I'll preserve myself during the day. No agitation. No more work. No Neustupa, Střelák, riff-raff, missing gate, or banging on pipes. No despising daughter or neurotic wife. I'll go watch how others play chess. Concentrate only on myself. An elegant death in the style of Petronius: bleeding to death in warm water with a young girl ... How many people on this lice-ridden continent can afford such a princely end?

I lie on my back and softly laugh to myself. I'd laugh out loud, but my sick heart won't allow it. Why should I guffaw? I can hear it either way.

Somebody's ringing. Already I feel good enough to get up and open the door. It's Tušl's chauffeur – I'm to go immediately to the general director's office. "Wait downstairs and in the meantime go have some goulash ... I'll be down in half an hour."

I lie down for a while longer. I think about the trees in the park. About the castles and fortresses along the Vltava. About music ...

I don't get up until I'm fit as a fiddle. I scrupulously dress. Cologne, cream, powder. A little manicure and wash my hands once more. I'll never get them dirty again. I stare out the window for a moment. I feel so light ... I see the world as from a balloon.

"Are you out of your mind?!" shouts Bogan Tušl, the general director. A dust-covered palm plant juts up behind him. What do you have a secretary for, my poor friend?

"On the contrary."

"What's that supposed to mean?!"

"Transfer me here to Prague. Please."

"I don't have anything here for you! I need you in Ústí!"

"I don't want to be there anymore. I can't, do you understand? I need to slow down. I'm not healthy anymore. I need something less strenuous."

"But you're ten years younger than I am! You weakling! You – –" Tušl wheezes with laughter until he starts to cough, and he coughs until he turns red. Overworked, exhausted, on the verge of a heart attack. A pile of papers on his enormous desk. An overflowing ashtray. Unfinished coffee. A tube of tablets. At the end of our millennium, ruling is getting more and more poisonous. Kings used to arrange their affairs between deer hunting and a rendezvous at the China Tea House by a pond in the grounds of Sans Souci. Now they write boring speeches well into the night, sweat before television cameras, answer impudent questions from journalists, and at three in the morning are woken up by an insurrection of the natives.

"I'm ten years younger, but compared to me you're still a boy," I say fawningly, because this is my future and final job, "how do you stay so fantas-tic-ally fresh?"

"Ha! Ha! What you need is regimen and system. As soon as I get up in the morning..."

Tušl gabbles on for about fifteen minutes. Incredibly boring – but these fifteen minutes of boredom are a hundred times better than hours of neuroticizing toil at Cottex. I listen to the general director and am obligingly amazed. It's easy –

"I'm very much looking forward to working under your personal direction..."

"So you really mean it?"

"Absolutely. Please..."

"I'll think it over. Right now, I could use a dependable man ... But you realize that it would be a second-class position. Why don't you think it over. In principle, I have nothing against it ... Let me know in a week. Definitively."

I ran out into the hallway and pressed my forehead against a window pane. Hallelujah! The governor will forgive a portion of my sentence on Devil's Island! Of course I'll be dependable. And I'll never do anything else ever again. For three-and-a-half thousand a month – that's not a bad bargain. For that, I'll be dependable every day (except Sundays, national holidays, and Saturdays off) from eight-thirty till lunch, and after lunch I'll disappear. I know exactly what awaits me. As a dependable man I'll go on visits every now and then as a member or numerical filler on delegations to Budapest (chestnut purée with whipped cream and fabulous poppyseed strudel), East Berlin (Kalbshaxe and an excursion to Potsdam and Sans Souci, which means "without a care in the world") and Moscow (caviar, Dagestan cognac, and the Tretiakovsky Gallery), Paris now and then (Caravelle, lobster, champagne from Champagne, and a tour of Versailles), and this year we have several invitations to a congress on applied chemistry in Oceanside, California, Pacific beaches – oh, I'll be dependable, all right!!

I'll plunge into that second-class but eternal set of professional dependable men, which no ruler can do without. Something like courtiers used to be. Every day someone flies into Prague who has to be greeted. An hour in the car to the airport, toasts in the airport lounge, and an hour return, that's three hours in all, at departure another three, someone's got to do it. And official dinners, a tour of the city, Zbraslav Castle, the factory, and Karlstejn Castle. Then in the evening take the guests to the National Theater and a cabaret at St. Thomas'. Then at night Broňa ... what a way to die! ...

I ordered a car to Ústí and before it arrived smoked a cigarette in the courtyard. Suddenly three cars drove up and some dusky-skinned gentlemen climbed out, two wearing silk turbans – after them my local accomplice Otík.

"Nazdar, Otík!"

"Nazdar, Borek. I've got some Indians here. Want to come to lunch with us at the International?"

"Next week. How's it going?"

"You know how it is. I'm just coming from the airport..."

"Are you going to the National Theater this evening?"

"Yep. And then to St. Thomas'; if you had some time maybe..."

"Next week. I mean it."

My car arrived. I finished my cigarette and felt like laughing. That is, I felt marvelous. I've gotten everything taken care of. First I drove to the Bellevue Café on Letná Hill (creamy roquefort, a buttered roll, and a glass of white burgundy) and then homeward at a merry one hundred to a hundred and fifty along the river, with the current.

The family is surprised at my happiness. I refuse the dietary steamed fish fillet – fried sturgeon and baked trout await me beneath the blue neon sign – and for the first time in a long time I open a bottle of wine at home. Then another, and then a third. My heart races at a frightening gallop. You poor trotter ... but it's running that'll get you there, in the end. I already know the goal of your steeplechase. You'll fall mid-stride – I've chosen for you the most beautiful death.

"You're great today, Daddy..." Yveta sits on my lap the way she used to long ago. Delightful. But I can't breathe.

BANG! BANG! blows on the pipes resound from up above and there's a roar downstairs in the itinerants quarters, BANG! BANG!

"Yveta, you're a smart girl. Advise me."

"Me advise you? Boy, this has never happened before."

"If you were in my place ... and were offered the opportunity to leave all this stuff here, would you go?"

"Absolutely. I'm going to myself."

"What would you take with you?"

"The less junk the better. My tennis shoes, a sweater, my cowboy boots ... in my pocket a highway map, cigarettes, and an orange."

Laughing, I turn my face to the ceiling. She has no interest in what I'll leave her in my will. Our furniture, our glass, our carpet, our chandeliers and curtains, our apartment – our whole life has come down to this accumulation – and my daughter spits on it. It's junk. She despises it. She hates it. She's right. I look at the picture from my ancient predecessor (kings left their portraits behind) Evžen Gráf: *Rhythmic Progression*. A relentless geometric figure of red, yellow, and blue vertical lines. What does that small black square in the lower right-hand corner mean? BANG! A period? At the end of what? BANG! BANG! BANG!

"Yveta. I'm going to be in Prague from now on."

"For good?"

"Until the very end."

"How great that's going to be! Daddy! You're marvelous!" We kiss. We like each other again. In parting we have found each other.

Yveta alternates with Jana in the bathroom. Jana walks up to me. My queen. She's still pretty. She's forty years old. We've tried everything possible together. Everything.

"Jana. I'm tired."

"I know."

"I need to rest."

"So do I."

"I know."

"So then..."

"I'm going to be in Prague. I'll send you a thousand crowns a month. To start with, I'll give you thirty thousand from the bank. I'll leave you the car. Is that enough?

"More than enough. Thanks."

"We won't divorce, okay. I still love you. But in a different way. I'm simply tired. I can't go on like this."

"I'm tired, too. It'll be better like this. Will we see each other often?"

"Certainly. Why not? Whenever you like ... Whenever you need to ... write, call, come for a visit."

"You too. Whenever you miss me ... write, call, come for a visit. And next summer ... we wanted to go to Egypt together. To the Red Sea–"

"Of course, we'll go! I'll take care of it. As long as they're not shooting there..."

"They say there are enormous shells lying right there in the shallows. Anyone can pick them up. I'm looking forward to it. I'll count the days again ... like I used to. When it was still nice..."

"It'll be nice again. But it wasn't that nice, was it. It'll be much better."

"I know. That's how it is."

"I know."

We know that this is dying ... But can't we arrange even this tastefully, with tact and a certain elegance? When there's money ... it's easy. We experienced twenty years of weakening love. Are we supposed to experience our remaining twenty years in strengthening hatred? We won't divorce. We just won't live together. I envy aristocrats, our national writer and deep connoisseur of love sighs that they don't have to live together the entire year ... That's how it is. Like a king going out to battle in the summer and returning in the winter BANG! to his loyal BANG! guarded castle BANG! BANG!

They're making themselves heard again. Above and below. They're approaching. Please, let us sleep ... BANG! BANG! BANG! BANG! BANG! BANG! BANG!

They don't have any water. They claim that nothing's been done in this building. But didn't I put down parquetry on top of the wooden floors I lived on myself – and with tracks on top! – and then didn't I add rugs? And what about the kitchen corners, bathrooms, red daybeds and chairs, glass-topped tables, stained-glass vases, and reproductions of Renoir's *Déjeuner sur l'herbe*? I did it all. They claim it was nothing. Two divergent accounts of the same thing. Who's right? What good are the bathroom and kitchen corner without water? But if the water pressure is always low? ... You'd probably like a water pump on the roof. Give me some peace. I want to sleep.

In the morning I get up when I feel like it. I'll be late for work, heh-heh-heh. I look out the window. Why do we have to live in the hideous industrial quarter? ... I send the chauffeur away. For the first time in years I walk through the drifts of fallen beige dust. The blue-gray outline of the factory, tower, concourse, and warehouse in the morning mist ... I've taken this route so many times ... I used to ... I walk through the desert dust of futility. Sand is the end of stone. I arrive late. I'll leave just as early. A fanfare!

The new warehouse yawns its gateless entrance at me. What if I had them put a wire-encased lamp up there? And above it a sign reading ABANDON ALL HOPE YE WHO ENTER HERE or ARBEIT MACHT

FREI? What percentage of industrial employees find satisfaction in their work? Probably very few. That's why they keep building new factories.

Broňa flings herself at me through the leaves of the philodendron and presses me to her. Her hot firm body in tropical leaves. My jaguar ... may I be the antelope? Heh-heh-heh. What a death!

A pile of newspapers. In the last two days has the world relaxed as much as I have? A FRIGHTENED AMERICA ASKS: WHAT'S HAPPENING? A STORMY ROMAN TUESDAY IMPERIALISM: MURDER IN THE COURSE OF ROBBERY "PREVENTATIVE TORTURE OPERATION" PERSONAL CONTACTS ARE VERY USEFUL ANOTHER VICTIM OF HEART TRANSPLANT ATTACK ON CARDINAL ŠEPERA BALLOON CREW PERISHES THERE WHERE MURDER TRIUMPHS PREPARING FOR THE FIRST HEART TRANSPLANT IN CZECHOSLOVAKIA

A delightful morning, isn't it? SERIOUS INCIDENT ON THE JORDAN BORDER. Oh, go jump in a lake. EIGHTEENTH NUCLEAR EXPLOSION THIS YEAR, but this isn't nice at all: "The route of Icarus, which is quite well known, has caused people to fear the end of the world. In its extended elliptical orbit, Icarus will first appear far beyond Mars, near the Sun." That's already been established. "Its temperature will fall to below freezing. The Sun will then heat it to 600°C." Isn't that wonderful? "Panic has arisen because according to initial calculations, Icarus was supposed to collide with Earth. We know this has not yet occurred. Thus once again, another deadline for the end of the world has passed." Next time it's completely certain to come off, either due to Icarus, the bomb, or our own doing.

08:15 - Broňa enters with Indian tea. As precise as ... time itself.

"Girl, I really like you!"

"I like you too, my gray-haired little boy!"

"Would you like to live in Prague with me?"

"Would I!"

"Then start packing your bags."

"This afternoon!"

"Hold on a minute ... Let me think about this a while ... I'll let you know..."

"You just try and change your mind!"

"You wouldn't let me anyway, would you."

"You better believe it!"

She's beautiful. She's decisive. No inhibitions. She cannot but win. And isn't it a good idea to always cling to the victor? Yes, I know.

I go have another look around the factory. These walks – between you and me – have been only constitutional these last few years. I walk through my towers, concourses, and warehouses ... I prefer to look at the ground. Suddenly I'm afraid: in front of me on the cement floor some sort of fantastic animal is stirring, a fabulous scaly monster glistening with blue, green, and gold ... I take two more steps ... forty flies with shiny backsides rise up into the air and a piece of shit is left on the cement floor. So I go sit in the WC.

It's 10:00, they're already coming. "FS" sits to my right: my prompter. Then the supplementary members of the administration. Where's Neustupa, my torero?

"Where's Neustupa?"

"You barred him from meetings of the administration, Comrade Director."

"I did? And it's a good thing I did! But without him it'll be boring. Call him ... and before he comes: last time you disappointed me horrendously, señors. Today I expect you to express your loyalty. Or are you against me?!"

"But Comrade Director–" "It was difficult, but today–" "But Borek, I just–" "Neustupa is acting as if he already–" "I'm glad that finally–"

"Bon. I'll listen to you with interest. Call Broňa. I'll have her take it down for the record. I'll take it with me to Prague. There will be serious consequences. I'm preparing some changes."

Broňa sits facing me, at the end of the table, with a notepad on her knee, on my left is the rebel Neustupa, wearing an intractable expression. Where are the times when rebels were hanged by their ribs on a hook ... after a prolonged whipping? The degeneracy of power is absolute.

"Neustupa. I banned you from meetings of the administration. Today I had you summoned simply so you could respond to the following points. So, here we go!"

I clap my hands and we're off. "I have here before me the layout of our comrade Neustupa's development section and I'm looking in vain for–" the chief lackey Střelák begins carrying out the punishment by placing Neustupa on the stand. "If the technicians think–" my knave administers the first blow from behind. "How could you break so much laboratory glass? Who permitted you to write off this boiler? Where did six platinum crucibles disappear to?" the experienced flogger, my chief accountant, whips the rebel, and already the insubordinate bumpkin writhes beneath the blows, the lashes whiz through the air, and my blood scribe Broňa eagerly takes notes ... blessed are the powerful who still can summon their rebels to interrogation. But when the rabble themselves force their way through the broken gates into the ruler's court ... Well, that won't happen for a while.

My lackeys are plugging away. It's a question of my favor and their bonuses. My knaves. My royal council. My professional dependables for two-and-a-half thousand a month. That is, a thousand less and a class lower than I'm descending to. For them there won't be any Budapest, East Berlin, Moscow, or even Paris, no chestnut purée, Kalbshaxe, Dagestan cognac, or even lobsters, no Sans Souci, no Versailles, and no Broňa, at most they'll get to Plzeň or Pardubice, have expense-account cutlets, beer, and cake made with margarine, and at the most lay some sleazy girl somewhere out back on a pile of sacks.

They mean nothing. And neither will I. I already mean nothing ... My successes, my new warehouse, my cybernetic machine, my four Red Banners and my Order of Work, my patents, and my citations in the German *Chemisches Zentralblatt*, in the Soviet *Abstracts Journal*, and in the American *Chemical Abstracts* ... are nothing. Ancient laurels ... laurels for the grave.

Already everything is different and somewhere else and for other people. Science marches, engineering runs, and technology flies. Twenty years I battled my way to power and for a few years I gathered my honors ... and during this time the world has changed to my disadvantage. My engineering diploma, a quarter of a century old, is now just a family heirloom. But I don't want to sit on a school bench again. The king lays aside his armor and leaves dressed in silk through the grounds of Sans Souci to the China Tea House above the pond, where his village beauty awaits him...

My lackeys are plugging away, but Neustupa is beginning to get the upper hand. A persistent fellow. The rebels always win in the end. This crazy masquerade since time immemorial ... no longer amuses me.

Neustupa goes on the attack. In a few years he'll probably be the director. I do not envy him these few years. It'll be worse for him than it was for me – power keeps degenerating. These people will wear out even more than me. And get less enjoyment and fewer honors. All the same ... a hundred hounds for every stag. When Neustupa takes my place in this chair, another rebel will sit in Neustupa's hard rebel chair, perhaps Dominik Neuman or someone else will begin to gnaw away at his leg. Nowadays people do not lie piously in the dust before the Great Mogul's golden carriage. Today people think up political tricks, throw rotten eggs at rulers' cars, and shoot presidents like dogs. Colombian guerillas kidnapped an archbishop.

Neustupa batters my knaves over the head. One day he'll be the director. He'll walk through the courtyard, attend to correspondence, fear everyone from the drunken porter to the Minister of Industry, and die of a heart attack. Yveta's right: it's stupid and painful and all for naught. A prisoner of the mob. Who really rules? The inconspicuous little men in tweed jackets and polyester trousers with briefcases beneath their arms, Alda-Bindr-Coufal-Drtílek-Ebrt-Fiala-Gan – it's their world. And they get the least out of it.

"But since it's common knowledge why it wasn't done long ago!" shouts Neustupa, on the attack, now directly at me.

"Should I put that in the minutes?" asks Broňa, sitting over her notebook.

"Especially that!" I smile politely at them both. It's already in the minutes! It's all been written down: the necessity to redistribute food, rescind the death penalty, introduce birth control here and rescind it elsewhere, the human rights charter – the creation of general affluence could be begun without delay, the appropriate measures promulgated this very week … Surprisingly it's not occurring. The charm of meandering … The weariest river … Who wrote that? It doesn't matter.

"There must be order!" roars Neustupa, red as a turkey.

"Should I write that down?" asks Broňa.

"In block letters!" I laugh at them both.

My estemed red darlings. Don't expect that by shouting your slogans you'll become lords of the factory, of television, of airplanes and tanks. Owning all this makes you turn blue. Therefore, thank our antagonism for your beautiful, healthy red color. But you too will turn blue one day.

"Does the director know the state of operations at all? I will prove he does not!" Neustupa fires off.

"In the minutes?" asks Broňa.

"No. He's starting to annoy me now. Just write: Comrade Neustupa was ordered from the room for making unfounded personal attacks. In view of his unsatisfactory work and unreliability, it was suggested that Comrade Neustupa be immediately removed from the position of chief technician. The director agreed."

The shooter will finally be victorious. Until then, of course, he'll be shot at. He should be thankful. Otherwise he'd merely be a member of the execution squad.

Neustupa stands up and delivers a kick to his chair. Now you're going to have great troubles, dear heart. In parting I'll make it difficult for you from the basement to the attic. In the doorway he gets comically entangled and runs into the flower pot.

"Neustupa, I hope you're not planning to take that palm with you. It's mine!" Neustupa disappears. We sit there and laugh.

"Broňa, take down the following: Comrade Neustupa agreed to his removal. Prepare thirty copies. Everyone will sign all of them! There is no need to record his attempt to steal the palm."

We sit at the ruling table and merrily laugh. I've already seen too many oceans. How viciously the waves rush to shore! And how many of them there are, how threateningly inflated they are on the open sea, and how promisingly they swell, and how weakened they are, when they strike the beach, by the sand flowing in the opposite direction, becoming nothing but ridiculous flaccid slaps ...

There are so many waves. But never mind, I put another rebel to death. He was totally right. He's extremely capable. The factory will suffer without him. The irony of the human *curriculum*: first light the fire, then warm yourself by it, then cook the sausages, and then extinguish it ...

But never mind, well before lunch I did in another rebel just because I felt like it. I'm full now. I've already forgotten what hunger is ... and my strength departed therewith. To enter once again among the hungry ... I could do that: take part in the battle against world hunger. For cosmetic reasons: to remain eternally young. Even a well-fed notable swollen from affluence, who reigns over industry ... and perhaps even a lot more effectively than a bearded fellow with a submachine gun in the jungle. But proclaiming it would be a faux pas and carrying it out extremely tiresome.

How shall I fill the time till lunch? I'll summon my physician. "Call Doctor Zíbrtová for me ... her consulting room is full? Those people can wait a little!"

Dáša Zíbrtová looks pleased to see me. She doesn't want to take a seat. Apparently she's once again left Alex Serafin. I wonder how long she'll survive without him.

"Dáša. I had you examine me, and you still haven't told me how I'm doing."

"_ _ _"

"That bad?"

"Very bad. If you want to live another ... twenty years, leave Broňa immediately."

"And if I don't?"

"Then you should think about a will."

"I've already thought about it, but no one's interested."

"Then think about your tombstone inscription."

"I have one: I lived the way I liked. Why I died, I don't know."

"You know why. And you didn't live the way you liked."

"Exactly! So I'll start right now–"

"Is it worth it with such a short time left?"

"What will I die of?"

"Heart failure as a result of total exhaustion."

"Thanks for the good news. Now I feel like returning one of your twenty-five-crown notes–"

She'd her say and was off. Heart failure as a result of total exhaustion ... heh-heh-heh. Isn't it better to die from too much lovemaking than hardening of the arteries ... or a bomb? Heh-heh-heh. Two years of love for twenty years of neurosis – now that's a bargain! The dying man is restored to life only when killing himself. That's actually an improvement, relatively speaking ... To love or stab oneself to death ... Don't we express pleasure and pain just the same way. Zita, my love! And love the same as death? Aren't both together a thousand times better than the tepid absence of both? I will gladly die ... I will even do my best to. The sarcasm of the human *curriculum*: first light the fire, then warm yourself by it, then extinguish it – and in so doing burn up in it.

The king lays aside his armor and with a rose in hand leaves through the grounds of Sans Souci to the China Tea House above the pond for a rendezvous with a young noblewoman before the great soirée in the Mirrored Hall and an intimate *souper* in the Pink Boudoir –

"Borek! What are you doing, my little gray-haired boy!"

Broňa bursts in on me like the impatient daughter of a stable hand. "Leave me alone for a moment ... Please. Just for a moment."

My heart hurts. And my stomach. The end of my story suddenly feels cold. With my own secretary ... my fate had a feeble fabulation. So now at least once more with a young beautiful girl YOU WILL DIE LIKE A DOG.

Well, I've had a good time. I've traveled through Europe. Loved three women. Given birth to a beautiful daughter. Become the boss. The art of leaving at the appropriate time is a manifestation of self-respect and taste and tact OR FEAR AND FAILURE? HEH-HEH-HEH!

I simply feel like a little rest, flowers, wine, love, and music ... I will die in warm bloody water with a young girl, elegantly, like Petronius. OR LIKE A RAT SQUEEZED AGAINST A SEWER GRATE? HEH-HEH-HEH!

Well, well, well. To destroy oneself completely ... won't it at least be fun? PROBABLY LIKE THE DEATH OF A KICKED AND BEATEN DOG.

WHO'S WHO
Borek Trojan (45)

Hardly had the young boy gotten into his little head that we lived in a free republic and had Uncle Beneš as our president, when it wasn't true anymore, inasmuch as the Protectorate of Bohemia and Moravia had been proclaimed, and motorized units of the occupying German army were moving into his birthplace of Brno. His father, a former allied soldier in the First World War, tailor, and fervid patriot, instilled in the five-year-old child a hatred of the occupiers, which the sight of Brno German women with net bags full of Italian oranges meant only for German children was sufficient to foster. Then, when the eight-year-old boy weakened in his dislike of the Germans, having flared up with wonder at a beautiful German Focke-Wulf 190 jet fighter, into which a kind lieutenant of the Luftwaffe had allowed him to climb at an exhibition, he was reminded of his obligatory hatred by the execution of his father.

"But you can't steal that..." Borek's mother berated him when the Red Army had occupied Brno and her son had broken into the office of the firm of W. Pawlitschek (a plumbing factory) and stolen some knives and blotting paper. The boy was compelled to return his meager booty. While so doing, he ran into Mr. V. Petříček (of the plumbers workshop), who with his wife was carrying out four typewriters and one electric adding machine in a washtub. Then when the virtuous youth saw members of the numerous Petříček family riding around in the repainted Mercedes of Dipl. Eng. Wenzel Pawlitschek (killed by angry patriots, all of them members of the numerous Petříček family), he became bitter and made up his mind that he wouldn't be so stupid as to let the next takeover slip by.

The shaggy, scabby, and undernourished fifth-grader Borek was convinced by his mother and the majority of his teachers to believe in democratic, humanistic ideals whose lofty abstractions did not superabound with amusements, thus burly Uncle Petr rather easily won the eternally hungry and poorly clad sixth-grader over to the class struggle with practical slogans such as: "Have you seen that swinish lawyer Vaněk, how he drives his ass around in a big fancy car? Do you have a fancy car? So, there you have the beginning of the class struggle."

Borek nourished his implacable class antagonism from morning, in school, where during the break he would eat his snack of bread and turnip marmalade, while the little boys of directors, building contractors, and surgeons would stuff their craws even during class, beneath the benches, with rolls covered in meat drippings from the black market or imported peanut butter from the UNRRA charity organization (which the U.S. probably wanted to give to starving people), till evening, when he would stand before the neon sign of the famous Brno bar Bolero, eagerly examining the photographs of half-dressed dancers behind the glass and selling American cigarettes to the exiting guests, with a mark-up that would rise with the level of the customer's intoxication, from fifty percent to the confiscation of the entire wallet of the tottering débauché – but is it really fair that one carouses in a bar while my invalid mother and I have barely enough to pay for our food-ration coupons?!

Soon the class struggle was victorious throughout the entire country; however, seventh-grader Borek did not celebrate for long because his mother, due to some bourgeois administrative oversight, disappeared for a year into clinical diagnostic confinement, and shortly after her return, in view of her grotesquely small pension, she died. The fourteen-year-old boy swore revenge on the entire world, and since the irreconcilability attached to this Central European fate had already become his own, he concentrated his antagonism on the irreconcilable battle between two classes: the exploited (me) versus the exploiters (everybody else). It's surprising how many fellow-believers he met up with on his life's path ...

In later years Josef Stalin was elevated and later repudiated; however, these ideological discriminations only marginally interested the boy, who practically supported himself through various but always humbling wages during the school year and during vacations, and then on the honorabe but practically unpaid obligatory work brigades in brickyards, ironworks, gasworks, and the transporting of fecal sewage. While his luckier (because according to their papers more proletarian, but at the same time incomparably richer) classmates comfortably studied in universities and cuddled in their enormous bourgeois, centrally-heated apartments to the sound of illegal jazz from imperialist radio stations, the bourgeois orphan (son of a private shoemaker) shared an ice-cold basement flat with rats, worked as a lab assistant for miserable pay, and evenings took engineering correspondence courses, which altogether took an entire six years of his life.

At his new workplace in Ústí nad Labem he fell into a scandalous, but fortunately brief, relationship with Zita Gráfová, the spouse of the factory director and the neurotic mother of a psychopathic murderer, and the happy marriage of the young engineer with the lab assistant Jana Rybářová was soon blessed with a daughter, Yveta.

Engineer B. Trojan devoted all his strength to national enterprise Cottex, which under his administration far and away exceeded its targets, and four times he was awarded the Red Banner of the ministry and the union, as well as the Order of Work. Due to the efforts of Comrade Director Eng. Trojan, for example, a new chlorating warehouse was built, as well as a computer center, which serviced a number of other companies and institutions in the region, as well.

Moreover, the outstanding organizer Com. Dir. Eng. Trojan found time for his own scientific work and cooperated on several Czechoslovak patents, one of which, for example, the methanol isolation of cholesterol from lanolin (or wool fat, *ed. note*), is the pride of Czechoslovak steroidal chemistry. Its industrial application has afforded Cottex several million crowns in savings, and the sale of its license abroad has made a significant foreign currency contribution to our economy. Finding favorable attitudes among his coworkers, the factory director also devoted tireless effort to the social modification of the factory. For example, he modernized the factory's housing facilities and afforded the young employees civilized quarters that can justifiably be envied.

Here we cannot overlook the enterprising activities of the director's wife, Comrade J. Trojanová, by whose efforts the factory women's corner was organized, or her devoted work in the regional Czechoslovak-Soviet Friendship Committee as well as the regional information office. The couple's exemplary life found its natural continuation in the social aware-ness of their daughter, Com. Y. Trojanová, who actively participates in cultural and political undertakings of the national enterprise, for example, in the May Day decoration of the factory dining room, for which she enlisted the help of her father. Upon the completion of her studies she will undoubtedly take her place in the front rows of our new socialist intelligentsia.

In an attempt to assist by employing his unsurpassable experience in applying the results of the scientific revolution to new circumstances, Com. Eng. Trojan transferred to Prague General Headquarters, where he played a major part in working out a new model of management procedures.

His ceaseless activity, in which he never spared himself and to which he finally sacrificed even his family life, continued in his new commission with renewed energy, but unfortunately only briefly, for it was painfully cut short by premature death by heart failure as a result of total exhaustion.

A warrior has fallen, one who sacrificed his life for the sake of a better life for us all.

(Miss Broňa Berková did not take part in the funeral because on that same day she flew from Prague's Ruzyně Airport with her fiancé, Donald F. Symington, to be introduced to his mother and father, and to Symington Industries and Symco Enterprises in Oceanside, Cal., U.S.A.)

"A woman like you would still be too young even for the young Balzac..." says the count softly.

Jana Trojanová looked up and smiled at the white-and-gold disc of the clock above his head. Eleven fifteen. Only now am I starting to get over it a little. Our last family weekend ... I don't think I'd survive many more of them.

We were at our house on the river. Yveta was paddling on her air mattress across the chilly water to the other shore and was demonstratively bored. Borek was lying in a deck chair on his dock. Like a corpse already. I sat in a chair in the room with the picture window and tried not to see anything. But I saw that beast coming toward our house. That hungry wildcat with deep-red claws. Miss Broňa Berková, my husband's secretary. Like something out of a bad comedy ... but it looked more like an American jungle adventure, in which she plays Tarzan.

She made her way through the bushes and climbed through a hole in the fence. She approached Borek from behind, shot out from behind a tree and seized Borek with her arms and legs, with her entire body ... She threw him on the grass ten meters from our window. I looked on and didn't stir ... out of lethargy rather than anger. Then they hopped into the sailboat, and that beast spirited him away. Borek's sailboat ... his little boy's dream. It cost more than our car. Did he procure it for his own kidnapping? I couldn't care less anymore. It hurt my stomach rather than my heart. And my head, it still hurt on Monday morning. It's already Tuesday, eleven fifteen. Outside it's a beautiful October day, I'm drinking age-old Courvoisier and being courted by a count.

"In you consort the races from all of Europe..." says Count Guy de Roitelet, chief Central European representative of the British-Swiss-French concern IFI (Tirana and Bucharest likewise fall under his jurisdiction), who came here for an excursion before signing a contract in Prague. Yesterday we went together to the medieval castle. And stayed there well into the night. We became close. It was nice. Guy's leaving soon, tonight he flies to Paris.

"I'd like to go with you..."

Guy makes a beautiful gesture as if to say, Well, why not? Of course it's impossible. But why, actually? My visa's good till spring ... and I've got enough francs left from last time. I've also collected a pile of marks and dollars. And it's easy to buy more on the black market – and I have more crowns than is decent. So it's just a trifle – right. I'll wait a few more days until we've arranged everything definitively. Then I'll take a long vacation. Then I'll start to live a little.

"I'll come, definitely. In a week perhaps."

Guy kisses me on the cheek, we say goodbye, he leaves. I accompany him to his car on the square and return merely to lock up my office on the second floor. No one will come today, nor tomorrow. Long live my information office! Here I alternate relaxation with peaceful boredom and amusement. I'm afraid that the overwhelming majority of working women have it worse. I sit a while longer in my chair. I have plenty of time. I turn on some music, pour myself another two fingers of cognac. An Aramis cigarette. I squint my eyes against the blue smoke ... and suddenly I spy a fly on the chandelier. Newspaper in hand, I jump toward the ceiling and pursue it around the office. It flies out the open window. That got my blood going, I jump around a while longer till my fingers touch the ceiling. A little exercise. I'm in fabulous shape. A sweet, primitive desire to live washes over me – and brings tears to my eyes.

It's only eleven-thirty. I lock the office and go to the park in front of the hospital. A beautiful autumn day in mid-October ... I love the trees. The colorful harmony of their leaves reaches a climax only during these few special days. Then the leaves swiftly fall. I sit on a bench and dig a furrow in the sand with the tip of my shoe. A young soldier at a kiosk is charming a young nurse wearing a white-and-blue striped blouse and a white cap. She obviously just came from the hospital. Her patients – but they can wait. Suddenly I feel free ... I feel good. I feel calm. And maybe even happy ...

I dig a furrow in the sand, then wreck it. The golden maple is bathed in a soft mist. I think about the trees. And, of course, about Paris. I like that city. Today is Tuesday. Everything here will be arranged by Sunday. Meantime I'll put in for vacation and reserve a plane ticket. So, Wednesday? I could easily do it Tuesday. It calms me to not really care. Let it go? Paris won't run away. But these special days at the peak of October ... a princely month.

First thing in the morning climb up to the mountain ridge.

When it's still misty. The branches drift out like the gray wings of enormous birds. The colors are subdued, soft pastels. The sun penetrates the mists and the warm rays delve into the coarse bark. The swaying spots of light grope their way through the crowns. I lie down in the mountain meadow above Nakléřov Pass. Below it, Napoleon was defeated, he drank the same brand of cognac as me. I laugh to myself. An old lady in the park looking forward to a trip. Why not? Why not? Old ladies live in calm and peace. And we'll go to Paris only when the tourist season is in full swing. Now I'm probably laughing out loud. I feel good. Tonight I'll sleep so well. And I love to sleep. And really need to.

The soldier and the nurse have made a date, and each goes his separate way. He must learn to kill and she to heal. Then they'll come together and create a new person. There will always be someone to kill and someone to heal. I rise. Already it's five to twelve.

"A package came for you," Yveta informs me at home. Barefoot, disheveled, unwashed – but I've decided to no longer let it bother me. You're already grown up, Miss. Do what you know how to do.

"There's something clumping around in it..." the young girl adds, a dumb look on her face.

I cut the twine, tear off the wrapping, inside is a shoebox – and as soon as I took off the lid, a black cloud of birds burst forth and wildly beating their wings flew around the room in an insane whirl, smashing into the chandelier, slamming against the window panes, falling on the floor and madly taking off again, colliding with the walls and leaving black smudges, and black dust keeps falling from them ... in only a minute they'd made a terrific mess of the room, and they flew on desperately squawking until – shaking in fear and disgust – we caught them with our hands and flung them out the window.

Sparrows covered in soot. Someone's played a very primitive joke. Who could it be? Well ... practically anyone in this building, factory, and city –

"Mom, don't cry..." Yveta whimpers.

I cry even more. I don't think I've ever bawled like this before. A heavy slab of bitterness rises within me – and sinks back down. My tears fall on my hands, and my daughter wipes my wrinkled skin. "Mom, please, stop crying..." She herself is starting to turn on the waterworks.

"What's going on here?" Borek says with alarm in the doorway, and he suddenly gets angry. "Who would do this to us?!"

"You know very well."

"Who? Tell me and I'll take care of it right away–"

"Practically anyone in this building, factory, and city. You know as well as I do. Borek ... I'm afraid. When I'll be alone ... I'm afraid. It's what's in store for you as well."

"I know..." I hear Borek's desperate voice. "I know–"

All three of us cry. The entire family. Are we really still a family? But that can never be destroyed, can it? ...

"Borek. Don't go ... What's done is done. Both of us are tired. Let's rest together. We can still have another peaceful twenty years, can't we? ... There's still time–"

"Yes ... We could..." My husband swallows his tears. My god and my house pet ...

"Borek, let's get rid of the riverside house. It's never brought us anything good. Has it ever given you any happiness ...?"

"... No. No! Not even a little. Maybe at first ... no. On the contrary. Everything else – but happiness."

"Promise me you'll never go there again..."

"I don't even want to. I'm afraid of it–"

"This is your home. And when we're together–"

My husband eagerly agrees, he kisses my hands and I run my fingers through his hair. Already it's going gray, but it's warm and thick like it used to be ... And so short.

CHRIST IN BUILDING NO. 2000

> *And the word was made flesh*
> *and dwelt among us.*
> –John 1:14

Building No. 2000 slowly got used to the idea that Iša, Teo's son, might in fact be God, even though it isn't possible – in any case, however, the rumors circulating about his strange deeds, some of which one could, with a maximum of good will, even call miracles, awoke the desire to make the most of this practically new tenant on the first floor.

One of the first meetings transpired in the women's one-room flat on the third floor. At the glass-topped table, M.Pharm. Břetislav Trakl settled down in one red chair, his wife Jitka in the other, Broňa sat listening on the red daybed beneath Renoir's *Déjeuner sur l'herbe*. As if sitting before a television whose program we're not sure will be engaging – and who's got time for just talking? – Břetislav spread out on his lap his everpresent *Our Household* and Jitka's "Journal of Expenditures." He worriedly ascertained that on the left side of "Estimated" in the column "Milk, butter, cheese," the permitted number of crowns, 63.10, had already been exceeded by 8.15 crowns in the corresponding column on the right side, "Actual," and with a heavy heart he entered this deficit in cautionary red pencil. Jitka was sewing the worn edge of Břetislav's boxer shorts and considering how to usurp the bathroom for today's laundry, all the while thinking about the child beneath her heart, fearing it would be twins. Broňa was filing the nail of her pinkie and planning immediately after the meeting to rush into the bathroom ahead of Jitka, since she had an important date with Borek Trojan at the riverside house –

"*Come to me*," said Iša.

We stiffened. But that isn't possible –

"We all have jobs," Břetislav explained when the first stupefaction had passed, "and we have to work because we need money…"

"*You cannot serve both God and Mammon*," said Iša.

"But we're not talking about Mammon," answered Jitka nervously, "just about having money for food…"

"*Isn't life more than food?*" said Iša.

"…and for clothes…" added Broňa.

"*And the body more than clothes?*" said Iša. "*Look at the birds in the sky … Your heavenly Father feeds them. Do you stand above them?*"

We were astonished. Iša *didn't speak like a mere preacher, but as if he wielded power … AS IF IT WERE ACTUALLY POSSIBLE* –

Broňa rotated her nail file in her hand, as if she were seeing it for the first time in her life. So Borek will like me … that sick old boy who in a couple of months will die, besoiled, with a groan … Of course I'll find another. *I'll have a hundred husbands* What will become of me after them? *The last will be my Erik* By then I'll be an old, wornout whore, just a mattress, and I won't care anymore. *His white delicate hands, like a priest's The hands of Iša Follow him to the land of silver*

For love that's neverending

M.Pharm. Břetislav Trakl gazed at his preprinted system of rows and columns on the "Estimated" and "Actual" pages of *Our Household* with the horrible feeling of a sliding and rattling of the edifice, whose construction requires the best of my strength, a deficit of 8.15 crowns causes me worry, it's not a lot of money, but it demolishes the entire system, what will become of the system when prices rise again and the purchasing power of the crown decreases, and what if I don't get my bonus, something I practically have no influence over, or if we fall ill, or if we have twins – What was Iša saying? … *shall be likened unto a foolish man, which built his house upon the sand* And isn't it terrible, for example, to have a child because of an apartment, and at the same time tremble in fear of disproportionately costly twins? Jitka's hands, which were holding the worn and contemptible shorts, dropped when she saw in the eyes of her husband a reflection of her satori, or rather anti-satori, since it was icy and grim … My God, how we're living –

And you certainly know the depressing feeling when the pneumatic doors of a departing, illuminated bus are closing, a bus that would have transported you to happiness – but nevertheless you stand there as if paralyzed.

"Well, if you're Jesus Christ," said Valtr sprawled out on his red daybed, "then show us one of them miracles."

"*He that hath ears to hear, let him hear,*" said Iša.

"We don't need any miracles," Štěpa broke in angrily, he was standing by the window with his back to the itinerants quarters, "just a little bit of completely ordinary justice. And what do we get in the meantime? Nothing but toil and filth – for somebody else. Somebody else gets all the rest. We drag ourselves to death for them…"

"You shouldn't let them do it," Dominik objected.

"You really know how to talk nonsense, you've been to school, you're a gentleman," Valtr wheezed. "But what about us? We drag ourselves from town to town like rag-and-bone men…"

"I'm no rag-and-bone man," protested Limon (wearing a chic sweater of Australian wool over first-class overalls), "and you don't have to be one either, Mr. Valtr. After all, Mr. Valtr, you've been retired a long while now, and you drag yourself around with us because you're greedy for crowns, isn't that right?"

"What would you do if you could retire tomorrow?" Yveta, Limon's girlfriend, said with a laugh.

"Me? I'd … my God! Right away, first thing in the morning, I'd lie on my back somewhere in a meadow and … and maybe play my harmonica."

"Well, are we going to have a miracle or not?" Valtr snarled. "If not, I'll go have a beer."

"I'm already afraid of retirement," said Dominik. "It must be horrible … to be written off. I hope by then they'll have developed something to extend one's effectiveness as long as desired…"

"Why do you want to be effective for so long?" Limon grinned.

"So I'll be in shape when … functioning harmony begins…"

"And when is that supposed to break loose?" Limon chuckles.

"When hunger disappears. And rivers flow with drinkable water…"

"Whoever's not afraid to work doesn't have to be hungry," Limon proposed, "and in Šumava I can show you a river you can drink from, and what water! So there must be rivers everywhere with drinkable water, right? So what else? We already have all that."

"When all the grocery stores overflow with inexpensive, first-class goods ... A bar of chocolate or a nylon bag for a few hellers. And for everyone a car. And a highway from sea to sea..."

"They already have all that in the West," Yveta suggested, "and all the young people are tired of it and run away from it all ... That's not the fundamental thing."

"No, but first you have to have all of it," Dominik barked, irritated with the director's daughter, "and only then can we start with the fundamentals!"

"Why not the other way around?" A logical objection.

"The other way around?"

"*But rather seek ye the kingdom of God; and all these things shall be added unto you,*" said Iša.

"Because people want to live right now," said Madda Serafinová, "and not in thirty-nine eighty-nine."

"*Take therefore no thought for the morrow,*" said Iša.

BUT WE COULD SIMPLY DECIDE TO DO IT RIGHT NOW – everyone falls silent, confused.

"I see you're pretty weak on miracles," Valtr finally said, "and so I'm going for a beer. Who's with me?"

Perhaps something happened that afternoon in the itinerants quarters, because the next morning the young programmer of national enterprise Cottex, Eng. Dominik Neuman, came to his basement SAAB computer looking as if he'd had a *revelation* ...

"Good morning," his operator, N. Novák, said with a smile. "Shall we work on the gasworks or the slaughterhouse first?"

And even though that day she wore an especially alluring bra, Dominik didn't even reply to her greeting. The notion of THE OTHER WAY AROUND is always a delectable morsel for the mathematical mind ... the young engineer gazed with unseeing eyes at his wonderful Swedish machine, and as if suddenly repelled by the numerical solution of graphs of natural gas consumption or employees' wages, he dreamt of a fantastic universal project, General Love GL-1, as an enormous arch of integrals from zero to infinity ...

We too integrate, but always pitifully low, from zero to mere millions; perhaps many years from now people will advance to billions, and trillions

– from a trillion to infinity, however, is the entire universe … and then, we won't be here anymore. But don't we at least have an obligation to future generations – even so, in their eyes we'll just be ridiculous. And repulsive … *Take therefore no thought for the morrow: for the morrow shall take thought for the things of itself*, said Iša. *Sufficient unto the day is the evil thereof.* As the old men in power, who should be shot, are repulsive to us. *Judge not, that ye be not judged*, said Iša. Will we also be buried alive by those who come after us? … *With what measure ye mete, it shall be measured to you again*, said Iša.

This is understood even by the SAAB, which like a cow chews up only what you stick into its input-trough – but compare and calculate it can. And all at once the young engineer wanted to cry.

Enter ye in at the strait gate: for wide is the gate, and broad is the way, that leadeth to destruction, and many there be which go in thereat, said Iša. *Because strait is the gate, and narrow is the way, which leadeth unto life, and few there be that find it.*

Borek and Jana Trojan stood unmoving behind the curtain pulled across the open window of their apartment and silently listened to the words from below. Iša did not go up to them on the second floor, but spoke downstairs to the people on the street.

Take my yoke upon you, and learn of me; for I am meek and lowly in heart: and ye shall find rest unto your souls, said Iša. *For my yoke is easy, and my burden is light*

Our yoke, of course, is hard, and our burden unbearable, but we're tied to it, or rather we've been fitted to it, to our living, historical, geological, social, satisfying, and completely natural biological bicycle, on which we pedal and pedal until we fall off, dead.

GET OFF OF IT, Iša would say. *And come and follow me.*

BUT THEN WE WOULD HAVE TO PERFORM A MIRACLE OURSELVES –

IT IS WITHIN YOUR POWERS, Iša would say. IT IS LOVE.

An existence of luminous possibilities, upon which, for some reason, we will never embark, in fact, it makes us neurotic and angry rather than delighted …

So one Friday we summoned Iša before our building No. 2000, locked the front door so he couldn't escape, and right in front of the door we began to give Iša what for. Surprisingly, Teo did not rush to aid his son – he could have gone and unlocked the door from the inside or at least pulled down the metal shutter on his former shop window and protected his son. But Teo silently looked on from his eight-paned window, and then when the infamous whip of hippopotamus skin with its hard wicker handle appeared in his hand, we ripped it from him and whipped Iša with it until blood began to flow. Then, for even more fun, someone smashed a rusty, leaky pot over his head.

Teo silently looked on and then from the lower window pane he began to extend his two-meter metal pole – it looked like he was handing us another instrument for disposing of his son rather than trying to defend him … We ripped the pole from Teo's ancient hands, someone – it could have been any of us – grabbed it like a spear and with all his force thrust it into Iša's body and nailed him to the wood of the building's door.

"My God, my God, why hast thou forsaken me?" screamed Iša, fixed to the door. We were making an outright fool of him. Iša writhed in agony for about three hours until with the words, "It is finished," he died before our very eyes.

On Sunday morning, Madda Serafinová, Iša's adorer, came to see Dr. Dáša Zíbrtová and fanatically claimed that Iša had risen from his grave and spoken with her. Europa Zíbrtová was at that moment cuddling in bed with her companion, Alex Serafin, and reacted to these fantastic tidings with giggling and squealing, which may be attributed to either joy at the babble of Madda, the former whore, or to Alex's voluptuous groping beneath the covers.

And thus Iša's story, highly unbelievable after all, fell into oblivion around the factory, building, and city, in which, that Sunday, a film festival began, and races in the wonderful new cycling stadium, which the citizens themselves built on voluntary work brigades on Sundays and holidays.

LET'S MAKE WAR AND LOVE

Barefoot, a white dress over her bare body and flowers in her hair, Yveta Trojanová was greeting her party guests on the second floor of building No. 2000. Her boyfriend, Limon, was already sitting at the large oval table in the dining room leering at the plates piled high with pyramids of open-faced sandwiches. With a smile, Jana Trojanová was loading up the boy's overflowing plate and then she politely sat Břetislav and Jitka Trakl at her table. Only young people – we're going to have a good time! Yveta was enchanted with her idea of having this party. We all live here together, after all – why shouldn't we get along with one another? Dáša Zíbrtová enters, followed by her – after several incidents now obviously her permanent – lover, Alex Serafin, limping on his left leg.

"I prefer meat–" said Alex when Jana offered him a plate of pineapple slices with whipped cream, and he immediately pounced on some cold roast beef, sprinkling it generously with Paul Robert red wine. Dáša was selecting the best pieces of meat from the bowl and with laughter was sharing some of them with Alex.

"And I like sweets sinfully much..." laughed Jitka Traklová, her mouth full as she served herself a third slice of walnut cake.

"Then have some more," urged her thoughtful husband, Břetislav. "Look how skinny she is–" he said apologetically to Jana, the hostess, and at the same time imperceptibly pushed over to his wife Alex's plate of pineapples and whipped cream.

"I've never seen such a beautiful apartment before," Jitka conversed as she shot her eyes around the room. "And so enormous–"

Yveta and Limon sat close to one another, with one hand the boy embraced the girl's shoulder and with the other he reached for his sixth sandwich.

"So we can begin, can't we?" Alex exclaimed, gazing eagerly at the Courvoisier VSOP in front of the hostess, Jana. "Who else are we waiting for?"

"I think we're all here," said Jana. "But Father's still–"

"Mom!" said Yveta. "Come into the kitchen. I have to tell you something–"

"So out with it!" an exhilarated Jana said to her daughter in the kitchen. "Our guests are waiting–"

"Dad's not coming," said Yveta, looking past her mother's face.

"But this morning he said he'd come and help..."

"Dad went to the river ... with his suitcase. He's not coming back."

Jana blanched and reeled. A horrible silence filled the kitchen – from downstairs in the itinerants quarters came merry voices and a growing roar.

"Mom. Dear Mother..." whispered Yveta, holding her mother's elbow.

"I feel ... bad," Jana gasped, and she sat down heavily on the old kitchen chair.

"Dear Mother..." said Yveta, "don't think about it. This is why I thought of having the party ... so we wouldn't be alone. Come on ... We'll enjoy ourselves."

"You go. I'll ... be there in a minute."

"No. I won't leave you here alone. Not even for a second! I'll sit here with you until ... until you feel better again."

"Oh, you're afraid that I'd ... no. I really wouldn't."

"Then come with me. Our guests are waiting–"

"You go. I'm just going to–" Jana opened the refrigerator, pulled out a bottle of imported Stolichnaya vodka, and thirstily drank a third of it.

"My husband departed just in time." A moment later she was grinning and sitting at the head of the table. "And so you'll have to make do with me and my daughter–"

"We'll make do with you, all right!" said Alex in his powerful voice, and the party quickly got off to a vigorous start.

Jitka Traklová, that skinny little woman whose love for sweets was sinful, her mouth still smeared with whipped cream, was finishing off the last butter cakes and receiving from the hostess some chocolates from the glass sideboard.

"Have you noticed the silver spoons..." she whispered to her husband.

"Worth at least nine hundred," Břetislav calculated, he was rapidly calculating the individual types of open-faced sandwiches according to their raw-material cost: 1. caviar and egg, 2. Hungarian salami, 3. ham, and 4. the cheapest, cheese, and he went off hunting for them strictly in the order of their value.

As always Dáša made sure to get drunk as soon as possible – Alex was pouring her drink after drink – and she was the first to start shouting. Limon was dancing with an ebullient Yveta, he pulled her to him with both arms around her neck and ardently kissed her, Jana kept bringing more and more bottles from the pantry and the refrigerator.

"Long live us!" roared Alex, he drank his glassful, and in the Russian fashion smashed it against the wall behind him. "So nobody can drink from it again!"

As the glass tinkled to the floor, everyone fell silent, and in that moment of silence they could hear the roar from the itinerants quarters below, as if someone down there were beating something against the ceiling, and hence against this floor –

"We should invite those poor fellows up!" Alex exclaimed. "We're having a good time up here, and they can't sleep because of it! We've got enough food and drink!"

"But that's ridiculous!" yelled Limon. "It could get ugly–"

"Let's go get them!" the hostess Jana decided, her eyes were sparkling like glass. "Let them come ... we're all neighbors, right? At least it'll finally give me a chance to ask them not to break their parquet floor."

The three men that mother and daughter brought up from down below, Dominik, Štěpa, and Valtr, stood before the exhilarated crowd.

"Hey there!" yelled Alex. "It was my idea to bring you fellows up here!"

The party went into high gear and there was no dearth of fun, something for everyone, Jana danced with Dominik "cheek to cheek," and the former began to sing a song from her 50s childhood, "Over fresh ruins, across bloody rivers we go forward like a current, like a terrible torrent of revenge–" Dominik pulled Yveta up for a dance at the same time as Limon did, Limon pushed Dominik away with his knee, and Dominik flattened Limon with a judo move, and a nice match developed down on the carpet, Alex played the exuberant referee, a drunken Dáša Zíbrtová hopped around him, drooling and kissing her sweetheart, Yveta was laughing like crazy, and Stěpa, who'd interpreted Yveta's invitation personally and was still firmly holding on to Yveta's elbow, now embraced the girl with both arms and gripped her rear so tightly with his fingers they turned white, and the whiteness spread from his face to the shoulder blade sticking up out of his striped T-shirt, as if dancing Stěpa twirled several times with Yveta around the dance floor and was already pushing her from the room ahead of him. In helpless anger, Limon threw after him a greasy plate with a design of two gently kissing bluebirds. From my grandfather, recalled Jana, the one who won a hundred and twenty-five thousand in the state lottery on the number eight, and she sighed when another bird plate flew after the first. But aren't birds supposed to fly?

"What are you doing here sitting like cadavers?!" Alex yelled at the Trakls, who were still doing nothing but eating, and with a flick of his wrist he pulled Jitka up to dance and after the third twirl began unbuttoning the front of her blouse, emboldened by hazardous amounts of alcohol, for the second time in his life Břetislav tried to stand up to his bullying roommate, Alex of course would not give up, and another nice match broke loose down on the carpet.

"May I have a closer look at those pretty little glasses?" Valtr inquired of Jana, tapping with his horribly chewed-up index finger on the glass of the sideboard, and Jana gladly unlocked the glass door and took out the golden lorgnette with its handle studded with tiny gems (a few years ago she'd bought it from her former roommate and best friend Madda Serafinová when the latter was once again out of money), and Valtr went to "examine it by the window," as he expressed it. Of course, it was pitch-dark outside, and a little while later Jana saw Valtr sticking the "pretty little glasses," obviously absentmindedly, into his pocket, but she didn't care anymore.

Alex worked over M.Pharm. Břetislav Trakl but then magnanimously helped him to his feet, and as he was shoving him over to his wife, Jitka, he overturned the little flower table, and as all the flower pots were smashing against the floor, the Trakls took each other's hand and rushed from the room "to have a look at the kitchen," as Jitka chirruped, already Břetislav was pulling a five-liter plastic bag from his pocket, and in the kitchen the couple began first to plunder the refrigerator – Břetislav opened the bag and Jitka tossed in cans of liver paste (3.00 crowns apiece), then when they discovered sardines at the bottom of the pantry (7.60 crowns apiece), they emptied the liver paste onto the floor and loaded up the bag with sardines, the bag was already breaking when Břetislav spotted canned goose breasts and thighs on the top shelf of the pantry (18.00 crowns apiece), and the sardines flowed out onto the linoleum.

Meanwhile, Stěpa and Yveta had returned to the room, Stěpa fell to his knees before Jana, clapping his hands, and began to court her in his own irresistible way. Yveta was guffawing, but her unbuttoned blouse angered Limon, who slapped the faithless woman's face, not even the girl's claim that "nothing happened, he just wanted to smooch" would satisfy Limon, so to make amends Yveta announced that with this they were engaged, and as proof unfastened and handed the boy one of her sapphire earrings in gray platinum.

"Who's afraid of Franz Kafka!" Dominik was shouting drunkenly (he was not in fact drunk, but was firmly and systematically attacking Jana Trojanová), and the company accepted with jubilation his suggestion to play "some sort of nice social games," first, to warm up, let's play "Hoppity Hop on the Hostess," and Dominik jokingly knocked Jana, the hostess, down on the couch, Europa Zíbrtová shrieked with laughter and went to lend Jana a hand, Stěpa, however, wouldn't let go of Jana's legs, Alex burnt the tablecloth a little, and one of the last bluebird plates finally smashed into the swaying chandelier, in the corner Yveta was groaning beneath Limon, and into the darkness of the room came Břetislav's voice from the kitchen: "Pour out everything, they've got Hungarian salami," which was interrupted by the sound of breaking glass, which was Valtr opening the locked sideboard, and all sorts of things could be heard, only no one was listening any longer.

ALL-OUT SATIATION

(A Complete History in 360°, Garishly-Colored Roman-Circorama Panavision)

The fresh red blood from the interior and the mountains always ends up invading the blue cities in the lowlands and the rich ports   Because of them, dozing history will once again stir   Like when a locomotive slams into sleeping or dining cars   Like when a man conquers a woman, sexually

    The Romans lived like pigs in clover   A patrician lady on a fur rug admits a handsome young slave-boy that her husband, a senator, forgot to have castrated   When the senator learns of it, he'll swiftly correct his oversight   After lunch a landowner chases a young slave-girl across the grass into the shade of a fig tree   Before their orgy, a merry company feasts, lying on reclining chairs beneath a shower of rose petals   Mountains of roast meat

    Peacocks raised only on walnuts and almonds from the island of Chios Murenas fed on the meat of slaves   When the diner can eat no more, he dips a peacock feather in oil, and having thrown up he sits back down with renewed appetite   This is an era of the full flourishing of science and art And if someone complains, he is crucified, like those six on the Appian Way or that Jewish demagogue in Jerusalem, after much whipping and with a thorn of crowns on his head   As long as it keeps going like this, it's great But it keeps getting worse

    Until it's no surprise that the red people from upper Europe finally get terribly angry and invade the Po River lowlands   And burn the white port They ride horses into the atria of the mansions   A gentle girl plunking on a lyre is raped by soldiers   A young poet is killed on the steps of the temple And poor old Archimedes is stabbed over his geometry on the sand   Heh-heh-heh

    When the warriors have stuffed their craws and sated themselves, they themselves will turn blue   Instead of new handles for their swords, they'll think up new patterns for their ceremonial cloth

    The daughters of the barbarians will cut their nails and plunk on something

    Of course, in that case they need servants   Gothic is not particularly comfortable to live in   They'll figure out that the Romans were the best builders, and once again in Rome orgies in the classical style will flourish At the court in Rožmberk, four kilos of meat per person are consumed daily, not including fish and poultry   But not very much gold will fit into a renaissance hall, so baroque arrives   Then the even more golden rococo Descendants of the German invaders breakfast on a pair of doves, a half dozen quails, and eight thrushes, and they drink wine from liter goblets.

In England the meat from a baby cow is called "veal," whereas the animal itself is called a "calf," and meat that comes from a "pig" is called "pork"   This is because there are those who only raise the pigs and calves in sheds and others who only eat the pork and veal in palatial dining rooms   The hungry have a different language than the rich

"The people don't have enough bread?" asks Queen Marie Antoinette, shocked. "Let them eat cake!"   This is an era of the full flourishing of science and art   And if someone complains, like the one who tried to assassinate King Louis, they pour molten lead down his gullet, then draw and quarter him   As long as it keeps going like this, it's great   But it keeps getting worse

Perdidistis utilitatem calamitatis: YOU'VE LOST THE BENEFIT OF CALAMITY

Until it comes as no surprise that the red people from the Parisian ghettos finally get terribly angry and invade the palaces   They cut off the heads of King Louis and the beautiful Marie Antoinette

A gentle girl plunking on a harpsichord is raped by revolutionaries

A young aesthete is executed on the square   And the aristocrats belong on street lamps   Heh-heh-heh

When the revolutionaries have had their fill of revolution and have in general sated themselves, they themselves will turn blue   Instead of thinking up allegorical tableaus, they'll perfect their looms

The daughters of the barricaders will plunk on a piano   Of course, in that case, they need servants   Descendants of the revolutionaries founded famous Parisian restaurants   The specialty is duck à la Rouen: a young duckling stewed in champagne and its own blood   And a bit of caviar would be tasty   In Russia under the Tsars they eat well   But not everyone, because there are a lot of Russians   The district marshal of the nobility will drop by his estate after breakfast, he'll have killed, on the spot, a select calf, and will tear out the hot cutlets with his hands (let us not have any illusions about the consumption of veal in peasant families), and in the afternoon, out of sheer exuberance, he'll break a mirror with his forehead.

The great orchestrator of great orgies, the lover of Czarinas, Rasputin dances naked on a table in the Arkadiya Restaurant and then at four in the morning conquers his neighbor in his home, sexually   This is an era of the full flourishing of science and art   And if someone complains, before sending him to Siberia he'll get four thousand blows to his body and, as the law stipulates, even in the case of death the specified number of blows must be administered to the dead body   As long as it keeps going like this, it's great   But it keeps getting worse

Perdidistis utilitatem calamitatis: YOU'VE LOST THE BENEFIT OF CALAMITY

Until it comes as no surprise that the red people from the Petrograd ghettos and the Russian interior, who've never had enough to eat, finally get terribly angry and invade the Czar's Winter Palace and the noble country estates in the remote Mikhaylov province   The Czar's family is shot, including the pubescent princesses and children   The poet Osip Mandelshtam is beaten by his fellow prisoners for stealing, out of hunger, and escapes through the wires to die in the snow   And countesses are sat on their bare bottoms on burning stoves   Heh-heh-heh

Now we've won everything   For ever and ever, amen

Our students are penetrating the secrets of the atom   Our girls are plunking on electric guitars   Of course, in that case it would come in handy for a woman from a socially lower class of the population to earn some extra money by helping out with tidying up the household of a worker in a position of responsibility   We're living like pigs in clover   In the U.S.A 92 kilograms of meat are consumed per person   Frankfurt am Main has one of the most modern theaters in Europe, with an ingeniously decorated foyer that could hold hectares of gold   When visiting Paris, we recommend the national specialty: duck à la Rouen

Instead of old-fashioned orgies in the classical style, one can privately attend a more piquant show in Paris: the copulation of a woman and donkey on an obstetric table   One of the first *happenings* was a slalom of yellow cars between hanging sides of bloody beef   The specialty of strip-tease cabarets at Reeperbahn is the *Verwaltigungsschau*, that is, the "Rape Show," and the *Henkerschau* – a stylized spectacle of a hangman torturing a naked girl   The minimum required consumption during the *Henkerschau* is a cola with rum, but the guests drink mostly champagne   The first striptease show in the socialist lands opened in the Prague Café in Jablonec nad Nisa   Many young women applied for the jobs   In the Czech countryside, the rabbits and pigs are fed leftover bread, in the cities it's tossed in the garbage   They're arranging another striptease show in Děčín,

not far from Ústí   This is an era of the full flourishing of science and art
An American employee of the oil company Armaco in Riyadh accused his
house servant of stealing a fountain pen, but by the time he discovered it
was a matter of his own absentmindedness, the servant's hand had already
been amputated   As long as it keeps going like this, it's great   But it keeps
getting worse

ARE WE LOSING THE BENEFIT OF CALAMITIES?

Until it comes as no surprise that the red people from the Asian interior,
who have never had enough to eat in their lives, finally get terribly angry
and invade
 STOP! This is civilization, after all, progress and technology and
 And there's the bomb, after all, heh-heh-heh   Not the hydrogen
straightaway, we fear that more than the designated victims   But just a
little bomblet in a little local war, a little toy with three thousand metal
bullets hurled just as an experiment from B-52 and B-57 bombers (other
types are standing by in their hangars)   The technology of forcing metal
into bodies advances the swiftest   And only then will it have consequences
elsewhere   More metal into more bodies   And only after these ideas
subside will a jet eventually be designed to take three hundred passengers
across the Atlantic or to Vladivostok in two hours (more effective and faster
battle versions, of course, have long been airborne)   Force metal into bodies
more rapidly   And in preparation for the *overkill* (at the time of this
manuscript's preparation, this value is approximately 8, which means that
there are means available to kill each person eight times over; of course, the
overkill increases every day), the old-fashioned (because they don't kill that
many people) atomic bombs can be employed to desalt seawater for those
poor folk in deserts, force metal into bodies more rapidly, and it will have
consequences even for civilization, for example, they'll build WCs with pink
balls of deodorant for those poor folk, so we don't have to smell their piss
when we welcome them, and a network of insemination stations for their
cattle to lower the price of their meat and pelts, and then a birth-control
center for the people so they don't multiply dangerously, because this is an
era of the full flourishing of science and art, heh-heh-heh, and because it
comes as no surprise that the red people from the interior, who have never
had enough to eat in their lives, finally get terribly angry and invade

STOP! After all, the world is hastening toward peace, understanding, and love

By forcing metal into bodies Don't we express pleasure and pain just the same? Like when a man conquers a woman, sexually More metal into bodies Isn't the summit of love forcing something hard into a body? Heh-heh-heh The hungry have always been victorious over the sated

Why should it be any different now? Heh-heh-heh

PERDIDISTIS UTILITATEM CALAMITATIS

Suitcase in hand, Borek Trojan stepped off bus No. 12 at its terminus and slowly descended the hill, crossed the asphalt road, waded through the fallen leaves in the yard, reached the villa in its large garden overlooking the river, unlocked the garden gate and then the painted blue door beneath the metal lantern.

CONQUERORS

Bright red, brightly polished nails impatiently tap the crystal of her watch, at 20:00 exactly Broňa Berková gets up from her red chair, coldly surveys the women's one-room flat on the third floor one last time, and suitcase in hand runs down the stairs, darting a mocking glance at the white door on the second floor, from which she could hear drunken singing, and already she's proceeding through the beige desert dust to the bus stop on the corner of Slaughterhouse Street. "All the way to the end–" she tells the bus driver.

BESIEGED

With a glass of cognac in his slender white fingers Borek Trojan stood at the picture window of his riverside house and grinned into the darkness. Somewhere out there is my special tree. All its leaves are red and heart-shaped like a linden's. But it's not a linden. Or perhaps I just want to make it a special tree ... The ridiculous arrogance of a small landowner. Already its leaves are beginning to fall ... all of them will fall, eventually. Put simply, this tree is no evergreen.

In the dull glow at the last bus stop, a female silhouette. Broňa's coming. Absolutely precise ... like time itself. How she hurries ... like time itself. And also: *I'm already very old* ... Slightly stooped, as if she were being surreptitious, she swiftly advances through the darkness. Lost from sight for a moment ... she's advancing through the darkness. And already running into the light of my lantern. The last time I opened that garden gate I rolled up my sleeves ... before I shot Zita de Rênal. My executioner is arriving a little late. Sleeveless, of course: with a bare, unsheathed sword of claws.

I go to meet her ... Right at the door she throws herself on me and takes hold of me. Behind me I hear a soft, guttural laugh. She drags me to the bed, lays me down, and turns me to make it easier for her. She attaches herself to me like a leech so that I can't even kiss her, but can only emit weak, gurgling sounds. Her teeth run eagerly over my face, and she digs her red claws into my shoulders.

(To be continued)

Ústí nad Labem, Brno, Dobříš Castle, High Tatras,
Karlovy Vary, Zlaté písky, Hamburg, Gagra
18 August 1966 – 13 August 1968

This book was set in the Adobe Sabon typeface and printed by Data Reproductions Corp. in Auburn Hills, Michigan. The jacket was printed by Strine Printing in York, Pennsylvania. The book and jacket were designed by Robert Wechsler.

Lovers & Murderers is the fifteenth volume of Czech literature in translation to be published by Catbird Press since its founding in 1987, including works by Karel Čapek, Jaroslav Seifert, Alexandr Kliment, Karel Poláček, Daniela Fischerová, and Jáchym Topol. The Garrigue Books imprint for our Czech literature in translation was named in honor of Charlotte Garrigue Masaryk, the Brooklyn native who was Czechoslovakia's first first lady in 1918, the American who has had the greatest influence on Czech history and culture.

For more information about our Czech literature, as well as our American and British literature and our sophisticated humor, please visit our website, www.catbirdpress.com, or request a catalog from catbird@pipeline.com, 800-360-2391, or Catbird Press, 16 Windsor Road, North Haven, CT 06473.